Karl Joseph von Hefele

The Life of Cardinal Ximenez

I0592465

Karl Joseph von Hefele

The Life of Cardinal Ximenez

ISBN/EAN: 9783743313675

Manufactured in Europe, USA, Canada, Australia, Japa

Cover: Foto ©Raphael Reischuk / pixelio.de

Manufactured and distributed by brebook publishing software
(www.brebook.com)

Karl Joseph von Hefele

The Life of Cardinal Ximenez

THE LIFE

OF

CARDINAL XIMENEZ.

BY

THE REV. DR. VON HEFELE,

OF TÜBINGEN.

Translated from the German

BY

THE REV. CANON DALTON.

LONDON:

Catholic Publishing & Bookselling Company, Limited,

CHARLES DOLMAN, MANAGER,

61, NEW BOND STREET, AND 21, PATERNOSTER ROW.

1860.

LONDON:
COX AND WYMAN, PRINTERS, GREAT QUEEN STREET,
LINCOLN'S-INN FIELDS.

HIS EMINENCE CARDINAL WISEMAN,

Archbishop of Westminster, &c.

———◦◦◦———

MY LORD CARDINAL,

AMONGST all the great prelates who lived in Spain in the sixteenth century, none claims more admiration than the illustrious Cardinal Ximenez, the honour and glory of his country. Hence I know no one to whom this translation of his life can be dedicated with more propriety, than to your Eminence, who not only was born in that great Catholic country, but has also ever taken the most lively interest in its welfare, and been ready to defend it from false and unjust attacks.

Cardinal Ximenez was evidently raised up by God to do a great work in his day, for the attainment of which he courageously encountered and surmounted innumerable difficulties. And so do all Catholics recognize in your Eminence a "great priest," chosen by Providence to build up the walls of Jerusalem, in our own dear country of England, where your Eminence has surmounted difficulties of no ordinary character, that would have daunted less courageous hearts.

Cardinal Ximenez was likewise an illustrious patron of learning, and the first who had the honour of publishing a Polyglot Bible. And so do we recognize in your Eminence, one who diligently treads in his footsteps, by the constant exhortations and endeavours of your Eminence to aid and promote the advance of knowledge amongst all classes, Catholic as well as those who are separated from us. But especially do we admire, in the biblical learning.of your Eminence, a counterpart of that zeal for the purity of God's Word, and a critical knowledge of the Sacred Scriptures, which added so much splendour to the abilities of Cardinal Ximenez, and thus enabled him, as your Eminence has already done, to confer so many benefits on the Church.

May God grant your Eminence length of days, for the welfare of our holy religion.

Thanking you for the kind permission granted to me, of dedicating this translation to your Emihence,

I am,

My Lord Cardinal,

Your Eminence's most respectful Servant,

JOHN CANON DALTON.

CONTENTS.

CHAPTER VII.

CHAPTER XVI.

CHAPTER XVII.

CHAPTER XVIII.

CHAPTER XIX.

CHAPTER XX.

CHAPTER XXI.

CHAPTER XXII.

CHAPTER XXIII.

CHAPTER XXIV.

CHAPTER XXV.

CHAPTER XXVI.

CHAPTER XXVII.

✠

PREFACE.

—◦◦◦—

Europe contains no nation whose history is so interesting as that of Spain. The country itself is perfectly *unique*, both in its physical character, in its scenery, in the manners and dispositions of its inhabitants, as well as in its religious and political condition. It is a nation, however, difficult to be understood, except by those who have been in the country for some length of time. Every part of the continent but Spain has been trodden again and again by English travellers. Hitherto, the want of sufficient internal communication, united with civil wars, and an ungenerous prejudice in the English mind against Spain, may have deterred the great mass of our tourists from visiting a country whose historical recollections are so grand and so instructive.

But have Spaniards any cause to regret this circumstance? Certainly not; for those who *have* visited the country, either for pleasure or information, have all (with a few honourable exceptions) indulged in such misrepresentations and calumnies against the Spanish nation and her religion, as to make the name of an Englishman synonymous with everything that is dishonourable, arrogant, and abusive. Ford's "Hand-book for Spain,"* and Borrow's "Bible in Spain,"† are in a special manner samples of Protestant prejudice and base pandering to English bigotry. And then,

---

* With regard to Mr. Ford, who died last year, it is but just to add, that he exceedingly regretted having said so many *untrue* and *unkind* things about Spain in his "Hand-book," which, in other respects, contains such a mass of useful and interesting information.

† Borrow's infamous work received a severe castigation in the "Dublin Review" (No. XXVIII., May 1843).

what little confidence can be placed in the letters or reports of newspapers' "Own Correspondents" connected with Spain, Italy, or Austria. The Pope, the Queen of Spain, the Emperor of Austria, and the King of Naples, are the objects of unceasing, base, and calumnious attacks from the English press, with a few exceptions.

But with regard to Spain, though she is now fallen from what she once was, yet she is still a noble nation, great in the recollections of the past; while the historical names, that throw such lustre around her, can never perish or be forgotten in the annals of Europe. Hence, whatever her faults may now be, travellers should respect her for the many good qualities of her people; but especially when they favour us with the history of their " wanderings " in the Peninsula, they should above all things learn to speak the truth. It is far, however, from my intention to condemn *all* the works that have been written on Spain. In the vast domains of literature and of art England,* France, Germany, and America have contributed, each in its own peculiar way, to illustrate and make known all that can interest and delight us. Indeed, many of the writers belonging to those countries appear to have taken more interest in Spanish history and literature than even the Spaniards themselves.† This is much to be lamented, as most of the authors alluded to are anti-Catholic. Hence, in whatever directly concerns the Catholic religion, or the history of Spain's illustrious saints, kings, statesmen, or prelates, little confidence can be placed in the statements of Protestants; for either they do not take the trouble, like Robertson, to consult *original* authorities; or if they do, as Mr. Stirling, Prescott, and Washington Irving appear to have done, their prejudices against everything Catholic destroy half the value and interest of their works. Fortunately,

---

* For instance, Mr. Stirling's "Annals of the Artists of Spain" (3 vols. 8vo.; Ollivier, London, 1848) are a most valuable contribution to our knowledge of Spanish painters. He is now engaged on a life of Murillo.

† In the last century, there was a great revival of literature in Spain, though now it appears to be *dead*.

there appeared a few years ago (1844—the second edition in
1851) a work in German, connected with the life of the
illustrious Cardinal Ximenez,* written by Dr. Hefele,† in a
truly Catholic spirit. This is the Biography a translation
of which is now presented to English readers. A French
translation was published by Messrs. l'Abbé Sisson et
l'Abbé Crampon (Paris, 1856). Dr. Hefele's work is
remarkable for depth of research, clearness of method, and
elegance of style, He is enthusiastically devoted to his subject, and not without solid grounds. Hence, the public and
private life of Ximenez is described with admirable skill and
judgment, both as a religious, a prelate, and a statesman.
Not only has the author made use of the labours of preceding
biographers, but he has also drawn abundant materials from
the valuable letters of Peter Martyr; from the historians
Mariana, Pulgar, Ferreras, Zurita, Wadding, Brancas, Prescott, Florez, Marineo Siculo, &c. The transactions of the
Royal Academy of History, embracing the valuable communications of Muñoz and Clemencin,‡ have also furnished
their share. The history of the foundation of the university
of Alcalá, of the complutensian Polyglot, and the conquest
of Oran, forms brilliant episodes in the life of the Cardinal;
while the historical notice on the Inquisition, though considered as *incorrect* in many respects by the Spaniards themselves, is nevertheless worthy of the highest praise, on account
of the satisfactory manner in which he exposes the lies and
inaccuracies of Llorente.§

The biography of such a man as Cardinal Ximenez has
long been a *desideratum* in history. Sketches of his life

* This is the proper way to spell the name of Ximenez, though, according
to modern orthography, many now write it Jimenez.

† Dr. Hefele is still Professor of Theology in the University of Tübingen,
and is highly respected for his virtue and learning. He is a disciple of the
illustrious Möhler, and is the author of several other works. He was born in
1809.

‡ See the valuable work in Spanish entitled "Memorias de la Real
Academia de la Historia". (Madrid, 1821). It consists of several volumes.

§ A notice of the German edition appeared in the "Dublin Review"
(No. LXV., 1852).

b 2

have appeared now and then, but never a complete life in English, drawn from authentic sources. Two or three lives have been published in French,—one by Fléchier, another by Marsollier, and the third by Baudier.* These writers have taken their materials principally from Gomez, who wrote a valuable life of Ximenez in Latin, which was published in one folio volume at Alcalá (Complutum) in the year 1569.† It was for a long time the *sole* authority that was referred to; indeed, it will always form the basis of every biography connected with the illustrious Cardinal, inasmuch as Gomez had access to documents many of which are now lost, or very difficult to be met with. The university of Alcalá commissioned him to write the life of its noble founder, and well did he execute the task, though a few mistakes are to be found here and there, especially in the chronology.

After Gomez there appeared another life of Ximenez— or, rather, compendium—by Eugenio de Robles, entitled "Compendio de la Vida y Hazañas del Cardenal Don Fray Francisco Ximenez de Cisneros" (Toledo, 1604). This work is especially valuable for the interesting and curious account it gives of the ancient Mozarabic rite and office, re-established by Ximenez in the cathedral of Toledo, and continued to the present day.‡

This work was followed by another "Compendio de la

* Marsollier's life was published in Paris, 1693; that by Fléchier, which is far superior to the former, appeared in 1700. Baudier's "Histoire de l'Administration du Card. Ximénes," 4to., was published in 1635.

† Another edition appeared at Frankfort in 1581; and it was again republished in 1603, amongst the "Scriptores Hispaniæ Illustratæ." The edition of Alcalá is now very scarce, even in Spain; it bears the following title—"De Rebus Gestis a Francisco Ximenio, Cisnerio, Archiepiscopo Toletano, Libri Octo, Alvaro Gomecio Authore; Compluti, 1569." Nicolas Antonio gives a short biography of Gomez in his "Bibliotheca Hispana Nova" (tom. iii.; Matriti, 1783).

‡ El Señor Don Remigio Garcia, canon of the metropolitan cathedral of Valladolid, and formerly professor in the university of Toledo, has assured me, that the Mozarabic Mass is still celebrated every day in the cathedral of Toledo with great solemnity. The funds left for this purpose by Ximenez have fortunately been preserved to a considerable amount. There are several chaplains, who keep choir.

Vida Portentosa del Cardenal Cisneros, por Fray Nicolas Aniceto Alcoléa" (Madrid, 1777). Though short, it is exceedingly interesting, besides containing historical notices of some of the most illustrious men who were educated in the university of Alcalá.

After Gomez, the life of Ximenez by Padre Quintanilla, is the most known and interesting. It is entitled, "Archetypo de Virtudes, Espejo de Prelados, el Venerable Padre y Siervo de Dios, Fray Francisco Ximenez de Cisneros" (Palermo, 1633). The author, who was a Franciscan himself, spent nearly all his life in endeavouring to promote the canonization of Ximenez, to whom he was enthusiastically devoted. He considered him a saint in the strictest sense of the word : but his devotion often carries him beyond the due bounds of sober criticism. He is too credulous, for many of the miracles recorded of Ximenez cannot stand the test of that rigid investigation, which the Holy See always requires before a saint can be canonized. Still, as a whole, the life is very interesting and valuable, since many facts are recorded by him which are not mentioned by Gomez; he also seems to have examined with care the curious "Papers and Documents" which are still preserved in the library of the university of Madrid, connected with the beatification of Ximenez. (See the "Appendix," in Quintanilla.)

Gonzalez Fernandez de Oviedo y Valdés, in his work entitled "Quincuagenas," also makes honourable mention of Ximenez, in one of the dialogues which compose this curious manuscript. It is much to be regretted that a selection has never yet been made from the mass of information which the manuscript contains, respecting so many illustrious personages who were known to Oviedo. Two or three copies are preserved in Madrid, besides other "manuscripts" in the Royal Library, and that of the "Universidad Central," connected with Ximenez. It is wonderful that a good life of the Cardinal has never been published by any

of the Spanish academicians, although such abundant materials still exist. Don Modesto la Fuente, in his "Historia
General de España" (Madrid, 1850, tom. x. lib. iv. &c.), gives
merely a sketch; and this, too, is not written in a Catholic
spirit, but with many of those false and "liberal" views
which unfortunately prevail amongst several Spanish writers
of the present day.

For the sake of brevity, I omit other Spanish works, in
order to say a few words respecting Mr. Prescott, the celebrated American author, whose "History of the Reign of
Ferdinand and Isabella"* is most valuable and interesting.
Mr. Prescott has, it seems, been the first writer who gave
the English public an idea of the exalted character of
Ximenez—a sketch of whose life naturally appears in his
"History." Though the author has fallen into a few
mistakes, which have been corrected by Dr. Hefele; yet, on
the whole, he has evidently taken considerable pains to
consult all the original authorities connected with Ximenez.
Hence, short as the sketch is, it will always be read with
pleasure and profit. The judgment he has pronounced on
the character of Ximenez is, for the most part, exceedingly
favourable, though he does not admire his "political life,"
which he considers to have been arbitrary, and in direct
opposition to the constitution, as well as the rights and
privileges of the people.† Without discussing this point, I
will merely remark that, with all Mr. Prescott's learning and
undoubted ability, one thing alone seems wanting. He is too
much inclined to employ the words "bigotry," "intolerance,"
"superstition," "ignorance," &c., when speaking of the
Catholic religion or her ministers, and especially where he
treats of the Inquisition. For example, as Catholics, we

---

* The "History of Ferdinand and Isabella" was translated a few years
ago into Spanish, by Señor Sabau y Larroya, with several corrections and
additions.

† M. Léonce de Lavergne, a French writer in the "Revue des Deux
Mondes" (tom. xxvi. Mai 1841), passes a severe and very unjust judgment on
nearly all the actions of Ximenez, especially during the period of his regency.

cannot approve of such expressions as these: " Ximenez had
a full measure of the religious *bigotry* which belonged to the
age; and he had a melancholy scope for displaying it, as
chief of that dread tribunal over which he presided," &c.
(vol. ii. p. 329, &c. fifth edition; London, 1849). Again :
" He distinguished his noviciate by practising every ingenious
variety of mortification with which *superstition* has con-
trived to swell the inevitable catalogue of human suffering "
(p. 337, vol. ii.). Several most objectionable passages
likewise occur, in his remarks on the part Ximenez took in
the conversion of the Moors of Granada; but, as they have
been refuted by Dr. Hefele, it is unnecessary to dwell any
longer on the subject. Mr. Prescott should remember that
the offensive terms which he makes use of should *not* be
employed without good and solid reasons; for many facts
recorded of Ximenez may, in the eyes of a Protestant, savour
of "intolerance," "bigotry," "superstition," &c., and yet
may have no foundation in reality.

Hence it must be evident, that no one but a Catholic can
properly appreciate such a character as Ximenez. I do not,
however, mean that a Catholic writer is bound to defend *all*
the actions of the illustrious Cardinal; but that, being of the
same religion, he can more easily understand what were the
motives and springs of those actions which, in the eyes of
Protestants, so often seem to be either unaccountable, or to
have been the necessary consequence of what *he* would call
" bigotry and superstition." *

In the year 1813 (London: J. Booker, 61, New Bond
Street) the first English life of Ximenez was published by
the Rev. B. Barrett, who seems to have been a Catholic
priest. Though interesting to the general reader, it has
nothing original about it, consisting merely of a compilation

---

* What an immense difference there is between a Protestant's and a Catholic's
treatment of Ximenez, may be seen by comparing Prescott with Wadding, in
his "Annales Minorum" (see tom. xv.; ed. Rome, 1736).

from Fléchier and Marsollier, together with a few facts
taken from Dr. Robertson's "Life of Charles V."

The present life will, I hope, be more useful and acceptable
to the public. Dr. Hefele has taken great pains and diligence
in examining all the original authorities connected with
Ximenez; though the learned author would have acquired
more valuable particulars had he been at liberty to visit and
examine the libraries in Spain, and especially those of
Madrid. The first chapter of his work (German edition) is
devoted to a condensed account of the political state of
Spain previous to the reign of Ferdinand and Isabella. As,
however, it seems more properly to belong to an introduction,
I have embodied the *substance* of it in the following pages,
together with a few additional remarks of my own. "The
Visigoths," says Dr. Hefele, "overthrew, in the fifth century, the power of Rome in Spain; but scarcely had three
centuries passed away before their own throne—apparently
so powerful—fell beneath the attacks of Muza and Taric, in
the battle of Xerez de la Frontera (July 26th, 711). In the
north only, amongst the mountains of the Asturias and of
Biscay, to which Pelayo, a descendant of the ancient kings,
and a few followers had fled, was a weak but Christian and
independent kingdom preserved and continued. In the
Basque provinces the inhabitants were enabled to maintain
against the Moors the liberty of which the Visigoths themselves could not deprive them. The rest of Spain, having
quickly fallen under the Moorish dominion, was incorporated
with that power, under the rule of a caliph. In 756 the
independent throne of Cordova was established under
Abdalraham, a city that became the seat of the arts
and sciences, as well as the abode of luxury and every
kind of sensuality." (Chap. i. German edition, p. 1;
Tübingen, 1851.)

Dr. Hefele, in these few remarks, seems to suppose that all
his readers are acquainted with the early history of Spain,
and of its conquest by the Moors. If they are not, the best

account of the Moorish invasion occurs in Gibbon* (vol. vi. p. 87, &c. ed. Bohn; London, 1855). Mariana, and some other Spanish historians, place the *first* invasion under Muza in the year 713, and the battle of Xerez de la Frontera† in 714. But modern Spanish critics have detected—such as Lafuente and Ferreras—several mistakes in Mariana, especially in his "Chronology." The correct date for the first invasion, given by Gibbon, is 710; the battle of Xerez took place in 711, as Dr. Hefele mentions. The popular story of Count Julian's daughter Florinda—commonly called Cava—having been seduced by King Roderic, and the crime assigned as the *real* cause why the Moors were invited into Spain by Julian, is now considered a mere legend. Condé ("Dominacion de los Arabes in España," cap. viii. p. 13; edition Paris, 1840) expressly mentions, in a note, "that the whole account is a Moorish fiction."

The celebrated Don Pelayo is generally supposed to have fought at the battle of Xerez, and on his escape to the mountains of the Asturias, to have been elected king by his followers. The cave of Covadonga,‡ where he lay in ambush, and with only two hundred men defeated a large Moorish force, is still to be seen, having from time immemorial been considered by all true Spaniards as a "holy and venerable place." From Covadonga, Pelayo and his successors gradually extended their conquests to Leon. (See "Curso Elemental de Historia General de España, por Don Saturnino Gomez." Quinta edicion; Madrid, 1856.)

Dr. Hefele proceeds: "In the middle of the eleventh century a new and more important era commenced, by the

---

* In Spanish, the best account will be found in Conde's "Dominacion de los Arabes en España" (cap. x.).

† Xerez is about two leagues from Cadiz. (See Ford's "Hand-book for Spain," vol. ii.)

‡ It is situated south-east of Oviedo. The cave has always been sacred, on account of the associations connected with it. In the summer of the year 1858, the Queen of Spain visited the sanctuary, with the Infanta and the Prince of the Asturias, when they were both solemnly confirmed. The place is to be restored and embellished at the queen's expense.

formation of the different states of Spain. In 1028 Castile passed by inheritance into the hands of Sancho III., king of Navarre. In 1035 it was assigned to his son Ferdinand; and as this prince inherited, three years afterwards, the kingdom of Leon and Galicia, these three states — whose union, though sometimes interrupted, was finally sanctioned by law, under Ferdinand III., in 1230—soon formed the most extensive Christian kingdom of Spain, which was destined to free the Peninsula for ever from the Moorish dominion. Toledo, the ancient residence of the Gothic kings, having been retaken by the Christians in 1084, became the capital of Castile.

" This state fortunately adjoined the kingdom of Aragon, which, though weak in its origin, rapidly became powerful and extensive. Navarre, of which it was a part at first, formed, like Castile, a separate kingdom, under Ramirez, son of Sancho. Conquest and inheritance gradually added to the power and influence of Aragon; and when, in 1137, Barcelona was added to it, Aragon then became the second Christian state in Spain, while Navarre ranked as *third*. But various changes and inheritances between sons and daughters tended to weaken and dismember the Spanish states, until at length Ferdinand III. (1230), by a definitive law, effected the perpetual union of Castile, Leon, and Galicia. A like union took place, in 1319, between Aragon, Barcelona, and Catalonia.

" These Christian states, however, were numerous, and often waged fierce civil wars with each other. Hence the Moors had then but little to fear, even from the heroism and enthusiasm of the Spanish cavaliers. But about three hundred years after the Moors conquered Spain, dissensions began to creep in amongst the Saracens themselves; they were even obliged oftentimes to implore the assistance of the Christians. Moreover, exactly about the period that Castile and Aragon had recovered their grandeur and independence, the dynasty of the Ommiades was extinguished at Cordova under Hescham III. The power of the caliph then became divided and subdivided into several small states, just as the empire of Alexander was portioned after his death. In the year 1099, thanks to the bravery and exploits of the 'Cid Campeador,'* the Christians had reconquered half of the Peninsula, as far as the Tagus. The Moors soon began to experience a series of defeats. In 1212 Cordova itself, their proud capital, fell beneath the attacks of the Castilians at the great battle of Navas de Tolosa."

These few observations of Dr. Hefele comprise the substance of many volumes. A history, in detail, of the gradual formation and extension of the Spanish kingdoms, would be out of place in an introduction like the present. The general reader will find abundant matter in Prescott's introduction to the "History of Ferdinand and Isabella;" in Dr. Dunham's "History of Spain and Portugal" ("Cabinet Cyclopædia"), and also in the "History of Spain" (2 vols.; London, J. Goodwin, 1814). In French there is a short history, entitled "Histoire d'Espagne, depuis les Temps les plus reculés jusqu'à nos Jours, par l'Auteur de l'Histoire de Russie" (Lille, 1845), which may be read with profit. In German, Dr. Haveman, of Göttingen has published a valuable work on Spanish history, entitled, "Darstellungen aus der innern Geschichte Spaniens," &c. (ed. Gött. 1850). For a history of the Spanish Arabs, the reader may consult Mr. Southey's "Introduction" to his translation of the "Chronicle of the Cid;" Cardonne, "Histoire d'Afrique et de l'Espagne sous la Domination des Arabes;" and Conde's, "Dominacion de los Arabes,"† &c.

With regard to the old Spanish chronicles, most of them, however interesting, are to be read with caution, inasmuch

---

* His Spanish name is Rodrigo Diaz de Bivar. Bivar is a small place, two leagues north of Burgos, in the cathedral of which some curious memorials of the renowned warrior are still preserved.—*Trans.*

† See also the "Mahommedan Dynasties in Spain," by the learned Don Pascual de Gayangos. The English translation appeared a few years ago, in London.

as they relate many legends which have no foundation whatever in history. It was not till about the time of Charles V. that national chroniclers were appointed by the sovereign, though something of the kind seems to have existed under Alfonso the Wise. The " Chronica General de España, por Florian de Ocampo" (Alcalá, 1587; Madrid, 1791), is frequently quoted, and yet it is sadly disappointing; for everything is exaggerated, and so few authorities are quoted, that the author seems to be writing a novel rather than sober history. This work was continued by Ambrosio de Morales, who was appointed chronicler for the Castilian provinces by Philip II. In elegance of style it is far superior to Ocampo, besides being more trustworthy, as far as it goes. Still, great allowance is to be made for these writers, since they were under certain restraints, and could, therefore, not write with that freedom and boldness which later authors adopted. Zurita, Blancas, Garibay, Ferreras, Mariana, Pulgar, Salazar de Mendoza, Carbajal,* and others, whom it is unnecessary to mention, are writers more or less deserving of credit, though Mariana—the most known, perhaps, to English scholars—has fallen into many mistakes: these have been corrected by the learned annotations of the Marqués de Mondéjar, which are to be found in the edition of Mariana's " Historia de España" (Valencia, 1783†). This history has been continued by Miniana, with annotations by El Ilmo. Señor Sabau y Blanco, bishop of Osma (ed. Madrid, 1817). Masdeu has done much by his critical investigations to correct the mistakes of preceding writers, though, unfortunately, he had not time to complete his labours. (See " Historia Critica de España, y de la Cultura Española;" Madrid, 1783—1805.) The learned Florez,‡ in

---

* Carbajal is in manuscript.

† To this edition is prefixed an interesting life of the holy and learned Jesuit Father.

‡ Padre Maestro Fray Henrique Florez lived in the eighteenth century, under Carlos III. of Spain. He was an Augustin, and Professor of Theology in the university of Alcalá. Padre Antolin Merino and Fray Francisco

his "España Sagrada," which has been continued by Risco, Fray José de la Canal y Merino, should not be omitted by any one who wishes to become acquainted with the history and antiquities of Catholic Spain. His "Clave Historial,"* is exceedingly useful for those who wish to have a short summary of Spanish history, as well as of that of other nations. For the ecclesiastical history of Spain, I strongly recommend another work also, entitled, "Historia Eclesiástica de España, por D. Vicente de la Fuente" (3 vols.; Barcelona, 1855). It contains many important additions to the "History of the Church," published in Germany, by Alzog. The work is, moreover, written in a spirit eminently Catholic, and respectful to the Holy See, while the research which it displays reflects great credit on the author.

The preceding short and imperfect notice of some of the principal works connected with the history of Spain, will, I trust, be useful to the reader. To understand the difficulties that Ferdinand and Isabella had to surmount (before they ascended the throne), it is necessary to be well acquainted with the state of Spain previous to the fifteenth century. With their great and glorious conquest of Granada in 1492 every diligent reader of Spanish history must be familiar, by having perused the works of Washington Irving and Prescott. Justly does Dr. Hefele remark: "That never did Granada appear more secure than towards the middle of the fifteenth century. The city was strong in its position, and still stronger by the courage of its inhabitants. . . . This was the period, too, when the situation of the Spanish states was such as to raise the hopes of the Moors, and depress those of the Christians. *Then* it would indeed have been difficult, humanly speaking, to have foreseen the days of

Mendez have left us an interesting account of his life and writings. Besides his " España Sagrada," which was commenced in 1746, he is the author of several other valuable works. (See "Prológo por P. Fray Antolin Merino, tomo xliii. de España Sagrada ;" ed. Madrid, 1819.)

* The best edition of this popular work is that published, with corrections and additions, by José de la Canal (Madrid, 1851).

glory and splendour that were in store for Spain. Portugal had ceased to fight against the Moors, in order to direct all her energies to the extension of her commerce. In Spain, disorder and civil war reigned in almost every state. The possession of Navarre was disputed by John II., regent of Aragon, in favour of his virtuous son, Don Carlos, Prince of Viana, to whom Navarre belonged by right of inheritance from his mother Blanche. A cruel war was the consequence, which was terminated only by the death of Don Carlos, in the flower of his age, in 1461. This struggle for the possession of Navarre divided and crippled the power of Aragon; hence the religious war against the Moors was obliged to be suspended.

"The fiery inhabitants of Castile were also unable, like those of Aragon, to develop their energies. John II.[*] of Castile had nothing in common with John of Aragon but the name. Though possessed of many estimable qualities, yet during his long reign he brought more calamities upon Castile than any sovereign amongst his most depraved ancestors. He had no capacity for business, but was excessively fond of music and of poetry.[†] . . . But amidst songs and brilliant festivals, the nation was verging towards its ruin. All the cares of state were left to his favourite, Alvaro de Luna,[‡] an illegitimate descendant of a noble house in Aragon. This remarkable personage could ride, fence, dance, and sing better than any cavalier in the court. His influence over the king was unbounded. But gradually he began to lose the esteem and love of his royal master, till at length an occurrence completely alienated the affections of the king from him. John II., on the death of his first wife, Mary of

---

[*] The father of Isabella the Catholic. (See Prescott's "History of Ferdinand and Isabella," vol. i. p. 93, &c.; ed. London, 1349.)

[†] The age of John II. (1407—1454) was, according to Bouterwek, more distinguished for a revival of ancient poetry than as a new epoch. His chapter of the "Poetical Court of John II." is exceedingly interesting. ("History of Spanish Literature ;" ed. Bogue, London, 1847.)

[‡] See "Crónica de D. Alvaro de Luna" (Madrid, 1784).

Aragon, had formed the design of marrying a daughter of Charles VII., king of France. But Alvaro de Luna, in the mean time, without having mentioned the matter to the king, privately entered into negotiations for his marriage with Isabella of Portugal. The monarch, strangely enough, afterwards acquiesced in the arrangement, and the marriage accordingly took place in 1447. But the new queen, instead of being attached to Alvaro, or grateful for his services, conceived a great dislike for him, and endeavoured to wean the mind of her husband also from paying him that deference which he was accustomed to do. A plot was formed, when the unfortunate minister fancied himself at the height of his power. He was suddenly committed to prison, condemned to death without any legal form, and beheaded in Valladolid" (1453). So far Dr. Hefele.

As it is unnecessary to enter into fuller details, it will be sufficient to observe that king John II. died the following year, leaving the throne to his son Henry, who assumed the name of Henry IV. of Castile. His father, by his second wife (Henry IV. was the only child by his first wife), had two children, viz. Alfonso and Isabella, who afterwards became the great, good, and illustrious queen of Castile, which was united with Aragon by her marriage with Ferdinand. She had only attained her fourth year at the time of her father's death, having been born on the 22nd of April, 1451, at Madrigal.†

The accession of Henry IV. was welcomed with enthusiasm by the people; but their hopes were soon doomed to be disappointed. The public discontent increased every day. His expenditure was enormous: his crusade against the Moors ended in a mere border foray; his subjects were unheeded when they remonstrated; and the coin was adulterated to such a deplorable extent, that the price of the most common articles of food increased five or six fold; but above

---

* Madrigal is a few leagues south of Medina del Campo.

all, the immoralities and debauchery of the king were so
great, that his subjects could not longer restrain themselves.
A party accordingly rose up against him, burnt his effigy
under the walls of Avila, and proclaimed his brother Alfonso,
then only eleven years of age, as his successor. But another
party still adhered to Henry; for though they despised the
person of the king, they were not disposed to allow the royal
authority to be publicly degraded. Henry summoned all his
faithful subjects to rally round his standard; for he was resolved to settle the question by an appeal to arms. The
battle of Olmedo, however, was attended with no result.
Both parties claimed the victory. The consequence was,
that the whole country became a scene of anarchy and
bloodshed, which was put a stop to by the sudden death of
Alfonso in 1468. No alternative now remained but for the
subjects of Henry, who had opposed him, to negotiate terms
with him in the best manner possible. This was soon effected,
and a general amnesty was proclaimed by the king.* Isabella,
his sister, was also proclaimed heir to the throne, to the
exclusion of his daughter, Joanna Beltraneja. Henry afterwards endeavoured, in vain, to set aside this treaty. In the
mean time Isabella was publicly married to Ferdinand of
Aragon, in Valladolid, October 19th, 1469. By the death
of Henry IV., in December, 1474, Isabella ascended the
throne, under whom, and her spouse Ferdinand, Spain quickly
rose to a height of power and of glory never before or since
surpassed.† The illustrious prelate, who by his talents and
his virtues contributed so much to the glories of such a

---

* See the whole account in Prescott's "History," vol. i. chap. iii. p. 145.
&c.

† In the sixth tome of the "Memorias de la Real Academia de la Historia"
(Madrid, 1821), the learned secretary of the academy, Don Diego Clemencin,
has written most interesting and valuable "Illustrations," as they are termed,
of Isabella's character and policy. In the year 1858 I had the great pleasure
of examining Isabella's will, which is still carefully preserved amongst the
archives of Simancas. Her signature is scarcely legible. The will is dated
from Medina del Campo (now a most wretched place), where she died,
Nov. 26, 1504, aged 54.

reign, was Cardinal Ximenez, whose life I trust will prove interesting to every reader. Isabella and Ximenez are two names dear to every true Spaniard ; but while Isabella the "Catholic" has now become familiar to Englishmen, the noble actions and distinguished character of Ximenez are not so well known, nor appreciated as they justly deserve to be.

I have been unable to discover in what year Ximenez was sent to study at Alcalá de Henares, or how long he remained in the university of Salamanca. Dr. Hefele mentions that Ximenez passed "*six* years" there. But the present rector of the University has informed me, that all the "documents" connected with the residence of Ximenez in Salamanca having been lost or destroyed, it is impossible to ascertain in what particular year he arrived there, or how long he remained. Though Alvarez Gomez,* and Robles,† mention the fact that Ximenez studied at Alcalá and Salamanca, yet *no* dates are given. It seems that before he went to Rome he taught canon law at home, and that from the money which he received from his scholars, he was enabled to support his parents. (Robles, cap. xi. p. 37.)

Neither Gomez nor Robles mention how long Ximenez remained in Rome, though Dr. Hefele states that he resided there "six" years; but for this assertion no authority is given.

Cisneros, from which the family of Ximenez originally came, is not near Medina del Campo (as Dr. Hefele supposes), but about six leagues north-west of Palencia, in the ancient kingdom of Leon. The vast open plains in this part of Spain are called "Tierra de Campos" by Robles, which expression seems to have misled the learned author.

---

* "Hinc Salmanticam florentissiman omnium doctrinarum academiam veniens, civilis pontificiique juris studiis operam non inutilem neque infelicem dedit." (Gomez "De Rebus Gestis," lib. i. ; ed. Compluti, 1569.)

† "Le embiaron á estudiar la gramática á Alcalá, adonde se enseñaba con mucho cuydado y curiosidad en aquel tiempo ; y de allí fué á Salamanca donde estudió derechos, y salió consumadissimo jurista," &c. (Robles, ut supra.)

Dr. Hefele also makes a slight mistake in calling the mother of Ximenez Maria; — her real name was Doña *Marina* Ximenez de la Torre. She was a native of Tordelaguna,* where Ximenez was born. There were also two other sons; viz., Juan Ximenez de Cisneros and Bernardino. The former married, and perpetuated the family; the latter became a Franciscan, in the same order as his brother, the illustrious Cardinal. (See Robles, cap. ii. p. 5.)

Tordelaguna (now generally called Torrelaguna) is a few leagues from Madrid, in the diocese of Toledo. The Franciscan monastery founded there by Ximenez is fast going to ruin, and so also is the aqueduct which he erected to supply the place with water. A few foundations of houses in ruins are pointed out, as having belonged to the parents of Ximenez.

Uzeda (or Uceda), where Ximenez was confined by Alonso Carrillo,† archbishop of Toledo, is about a league from Torrelaguna. The castle must at one time have been very strong; but it is now a complete ruin. Ponz visited it in the last century. Few of the inhabitants now seem to know that the fortress had any connection with Ximenez. It was in this prison, according to Robles (from whom Dr. Hefele has taken the account), that a priest who was confined there with Ximenez announced to him his future greatness.

Dr. Hefele's parallel between Isabella of Spain and Elizabeth of England to some may appear unnecessary, inasmuch as Prescott himself admits "that their characters afford scarcely a point of contact." Dr. Hefele himself, too, must acknowledge that the more the history of Elizabeth‡ comes to be examined, the more is her character lowered; whereas

---

* So called by Robles ; Dr. Hefele spells it Torrelaguna, and so also does Ponz, in his "Viage de España," who gives a description of the parish church which Ximenez erected there. It is a Gothic building, and has three naves. (See Carta iii. tom. x. p. 33 ; ed. Madrid, 1781.)

† See a short notice of Don Alonso Carrillo in Pulgar's "Claros Varones de Castilla" (cap. xx. p. 117; ed. Madrid, 1789).

‡ Isabel in Spanish corresponds with Elizabeth in English.

the deeper we study the life of Isabella the Catholic, the more do we love, admire, and venerate her.

Still, as so many Protestants now admire Elizabeth, Dr. Hefele shows, by facts and proofs, that she cannot stand a comparison with Isabella of Spain.

But however much most anti-Catholic writers love and even venerate the name of Isabella—however enthusiastically they may exalt the character of Ximenez also—there is one side of the picture which always appears to *their* eyes dark and desolate. Who has not heard of the "Inquisition" that was re-established by Isabella, and supported by Ximenez, her faithful minister? What Protestant does not devoutly deplore the banishment and exile of the Jews, and consider that both Isabella and Ximenez were guilty of the "*greatest injustice*" towards these unfortunate people; while the establishment of the Inquisition by Isabella is proclaimed to be a blemish of the deepest dye on her administration? Mr. Prescott, with all his boasted fairness, nowhere shows himself more *unfair*, more unjust in his invectives, and more reckless in his accusations, than in his chapter on the "Establishment of the Modern Inquisition." ("History of the Reign of Ferdinand and Isabella," vol. i. p. 291; ed. London, 1849.)

Of all the institutions connected with the Catholic Church, the Society of Jesus and the Inquisition are *the* two, which in a special manner Protestants and infidels agree together in hating, denouncing, abusing, and calumniating, in the most shameful manner. Even the very words Jesuit and Inquisition have actually passed into the English language as having a meaning of their own, independently of that which belongs to them historically. Thus, when a Protestant hears the word "Inquisition" pronounced, his hair stands on end; and there immediately occurs to his mind all that he has ever heard or read connected with a secret, dark, and bloody tribunal, whose head-quarters are in Rome, under the guidance and direction of the Pope, the Cardinals,

and the Jesuits, but whose ramifications have extended to
every quarter of the globe, and especially to poor benighted
Spain; thus throwing a gloom of fanaticism, cruelty, and
bigotry over that once lovely and chivalrous land. Then
come before him, in terrible array, the dungeons, the
horrors, the tortures, the groans and shrieks of the victims,
mingled with the jeers and laughter of the inquisitors, who
take a most diabolical pleasure in witnessing the infernal
scene. He fancies that he beholds the "cruel" Dominic,
the "blood-thirsty" Torquemada, the "bigoted" Ximenez,
and even the "deluded" Isabella, together with the "stern,
gloomy, and savage" Philip II., surrounded with bishops,
priests, monks, ladies, and cavaliers,—all hastening—some
in one century and others in another—to witness an "auto-
da-fé," in Toulouse, Seville, Toledo, or Valladolid. But
should his imagination not carry him so far, our good Protestant is content to hear a lecture in Exeter Hall from
Gavazzi, Achilli, or the Madiai; and, as a matter of course,
believes what they tell him as firmly and sincerely as if the
God of Truth himself had been speaking!

Thus is the great "Protestant tradition"* of lies and
calumnies against everything Catholic perpetuated from
father to son, from one generation to another; and thus, in
a special manner, is given a kind of dramatic interest to the
subject of the Inquisition, which is invested with all the
characteristics of real life.

It is with shame and grief I am forced to admit, that a
few unprincipled Spanish writers (besides an American
one—Mr. Prescott†) have done more to spread erroneous
notions on the subject of the Inquisition, and thus pander to
English bigotry and prejudice, than any other authors with
whom I am acquainted. I allude to Puigblanch, under his
assumed name of Natanaël Jomtob; to Lorenzo Villanueva;
Adolpho de Castro; and Llorente. With regard to the first

---

* See Dr. Newman's "Lectures on Catholicism in England."
† Mr. Prescott died on the 28th of January, 1859, aged 63.

writer, who died some years ago in London, and published a work entitled "La Inquisicion sin Mascura"* (1811), the following are the reasons he gives for assuming the name of Natanaël Jomtob: "These Hebrew words are two proper names, which form the inscription, *Dedit Deus diem bonum.* I wish thus to express the happiness of being able to speak and write freely against the tribunal of the Inquisition, and the joy I feel in seeing it abolished." (Prólogo, p. cxv.) If the reader wish to know either the character of the man, or of his work, he will find the best authority in one of the "notes" inserted by Balmes in the appendix to his "Protestantism and Catholicity compared" (English translation, p. 400). To the same source we are indebted for most useful observations on Villanueva and Llorente, which show us at once how little dependence is to be placed on the statements of such men with regard to the Inquisition.† Dr. Hefele has also given us an insight into the character of Llorente, by the analysis of a short biography, which originally appeared in the "Revue Encyclopédique" (Avril, 1823), inserted in his chapter on the Inquisition.‡ Here in Spain his character is also well understood; but, independently of this point, one fact alone tells volumes against him as a writer undeserving of credit. Llorente himself acknowledges "that he burnt nearly all the 'official reports' connected with the Inquisition, with the exception of those that related to the history of some of the most remarkable persons," &c. ("Histoire Critique de l'Inquisition d'Espagne;" ed. 1818, p. 145.) Now, as Balmes justly remarks, ask every impartial man whether there be not room for great mistrust with respect to an historian who claims to be a *sole* authority,

---

* "The Inquisition Unmasked." It has been translated into French and English.

† With regard to the work of Adolpho Castro, entitled "Religious Intolerance in Spain" (Parker, London, 1853), I refer the reader to an account of it in the "Rambler," part ix. September, 1854.

‡ See also D. José Clemente Carnicero, "Impugnacion de la Obra de D. Juan Antonio Llorente" (Madrid, 1816).

because he had the opportunity of consulting the original authorities whereon he founds his history, and who, nevertheless, burns and destroys these same documents? Assuredly we may draw the conclusion that Llorente was apprehensive lest those documents should afterwards be examined.

I. Let us now come to the Inquisition. As it is a subject on which Catholics as well as Protestants are divided, I cannot flatter myself that I shall be able to satisfy every one. Dr. Hefele himself has taken a view of the matter different from that entertained by many literary men in Spain, and I believe in France also.* He seems to consider the "Spanish Inquisition" to have been purely a "political institution," preserved and encouraged by kings and queens for no other object than to advance the interests of the State. To support his view, he quotes the authority of Ranke, Leo, Guizot, M. Lenormant, and the count de Maistre, &c.† But, with all due deference to Dr. Hefele and the great names he mentions, I consider that the Inquisition was originally established by Isabella solely and entirely on *religious* grounds; and that afterwards it was of a mixed character, combining in its government the "political and ecclesiastical element." What was the state of Spain when the Catholic sovereigns ascended the throne? Difficulties of every kind surrounded them; but none gave them so much trouble and uneasiness as the Jews and the Moors. The former were then exceedingly powerful in the kingdom, both on account of their riches and their alliances with the most influential families. But for generations the Jews had been objects of fear and distrust, throughout the whole of the Peninsula. This was the case not only with regard to the unconverted Jews, but also with respect to those who embraced Christianity. Their sincerity was

---

* When the French translation of Dr. Hefele's work appeared in Paris (1856), the chapter on the Inquisition was severely criticised by *L'Univers;* and so also in the Spanish *Esperanza.*

† See the quotations in the German edition (chap. xviii.). They have been omitted in the translation, as well as a few other paragraphs.

generally distrusted, inasmuch as they were considered by the body of the nation as still identified in interests, in sympathies, and probably in belief also, with the rest of their brethren, whose creed they had outwardly abandoned. For proof of these remarks, the reader has only to consult the pages of Hefele and Balmes.*

Ferdinand and Isabella were informed of this state of things; and they knew also that a vast system of proselytism had been organized, to overthrow both the throne and the Catholic faith.† What was the expedient which they adopted to prevent the threatened danger, which was in reality so imminent? Animated with a desire to comply with the earnest entreaties both of the people and the clergy, and influenced also with a pure desire of preserving intact the Catholic religion, Ferdinand and Isabella solicited from Pope Sixtus IV. permission to revive the functions of the Inquisition in Castile, which for some time had gone into abeyance. Their request was complied with by his Holiness expediting a bull, dated November 1st, 1478,‡ authorizing them to appoint two or three ecclesiastical inquisitors, of irreproachable manners, who were to be bachelors in divinity or doctors in canon law. Hence, the Inquisition originated not so much in political, as in *religious* motives. No contemporary authority, as far I know, asserts the contrary; while Balmes, the best modern authority in Spain on the subject of the Inquisition, positively asserts "that it would be wrong in this affair to attribute all to the policy of royalty" (English ed. chap. xxxvi. p. 164). Lafuente, in his " Historia General

---

* Not to mention Zurita, Mariana, Zuñiga, &c. See also "Estudios sobre los Judios de España, por Amador de los Rios."

† When the Catholic sovereigns were requested to revive the Inquisition, they were simply told " that, as Catholic princes, they were bound in conscience to chastise such detestable error ; because, if they did not, the Catholic faith would receive great injury," &c. (Pulgar, " Crónica de los Reyes Católicos," cap. 77 ; ed. Valencia, 1780.)

‡ Considerable discrepancy exists among contemporary writers respecting the date of the establishment of the Inquisition. Amongst modern writers Prescott, Dr. Hefele, Llorente, and Carnicero, place it in 1478.

de España," expresses the same opinion : "Neither can I
find," he says, " in any contemporary author any indica-
tion which induces me to believe what certain modern
historians assert; viz., that the Catholic sovereigns in re-
establishing the Inquisition were influenced by *political*
considerations, and that they intended to harmonize religious
unity with political unity."* (Tom. ix. parte 2, lib. iv. nota
p. 232-3.)   Don Vicente de la Fuente, another writer of
the same name, and author of "Historia Eclesiástica de
España" (tom. ii. p. 478), gives the same judgment.   I certainly prefer the opinion of these Spanish writers, rather than
follow those mentioned by Dr. Hefele.

II. That the Spanish Inquisition was not merely a "political" institution, but ecclesiastical also, seems to be the
general opinion of most Spanish writers.   Catholic contro-
versialists, by endeavouring to prove that the Inquisition was
entirely political, hope by this line of argument to disconnect
the Church from the odium which is popularly directed
against that tribunal.†   But independently of the early
writers, such as Zurita, Zuñiga, Brancos, Paramo,‡ Pulgar,
&c., never making any such distinction in their works, it
must be evident, from a careful study of the Inquisition, that
the Church *had* a great deal to do with its organization and
proceedings.   Was it not established in virtue of a papal
bull, and did it not proceed, from its very commencement,
with the papal sanction?   Did not Sixtus IV. appoint Fray
Tomas de Torquemada, prior of the Dominican convent in
Segovia, to be the inquisitor-general for Castile, and afterwards

---

* "Tampoco hallamos de ningun autor contemporáneo una indicacion que
nos induzca á creer lo que despues nos han dicho muchos escritores de los
siglos modernos ; á saber, que al fundar la nueva Inquisicion, obraron los
Reyes Católicas impulsados de un pensamiento *político*, y que se propusieron
armonizar la unidad religiosa con la unidad política." (Ed. Madrid, 1852,
tom. ix. ut supra.)

† This is the case with Count de Maistre, in his "Letters on the Spanish
Inquisition ;" with Dr. Hefele, &c.   See also an article on the subject in the
"Dublin Review" (No. LVI. June, 1850).   The writer has made a few
mistakes.

‡ "De Origine et Progressu Officii Sanctæ Inquisitionis" (Matriti, 1598).

for Aragon? And when Torquemada established various courts in different parts of the country, was it not principally ecclesiastics who transacted the business of the said courts? A few years later, when the Catholic sovereigns, with the object of securing the interests of the crown in the confiscated property, established a court of supervision, under the name of "El Consejo de la Suprema,"* it is remarkable that the grand-inquisitor was appointed president, together with three other ecclesiastics. But though latterly those were appointed by the crown who were to decide all cases connected with the Inquisition; though they were responsible to the crown, and removable at its pleasure; yet as all the leading officials were ecclesiastics, and the whole machinery for the most part ecclesiastical also, how can the Inquisition be called a purely royal or political constitution? But it is said that Pope Sixtus IV., hearing in 1482 of the great severity which had been used by the inquisitors in the exercise of their office, loudly complained that Ferdinand and Isabella had not sufficiently informed him of the nature of the powers which had been sought from him, and that he had been betrayed into concessions " which were at variance with the decrees of his predecessors," &c. That such a complaint was made, cannot be denied. But what does it prove? Not that the pope considered the Catholic sovereigns had assumed any undue authority, in opposition to his own, but that he was both surprised and displeased at the severity which was used, towards the relapsed Jews and the Christians who had apostatized.

But whatever may have been the cruelties or undue severity exercised by the different tribunals, they cannot be imputed to *the Church*,† but solely to the individuals who composed those tribunals. Dr. Hefele shows that the number of those executed at Seville and other places has been

---

* Council of the Supreme.

† That is, the Holy See did not authorize or approve the excessive cruelties which were often used.

exceedingly exaggerated by Llorente, and that Ximenez endeavoured, in every possible way, to lessen the sufferings of
the unfortunate victims. Those sufferings we now deplore, and
regret that, both under Isabella and Philip II., some other
means could not have been found to preserve the country
from the machinations of Jews, Moors, and Protestants.
However, no one can deny that *Rome* was always inclined to
the side of mercy. Whoever appealed to Rome was sure to
better his condition. Hence, as Balmes well observes, "the
number of cases commenced by the Inquisition, and summoned from Spain to Rome, is countless during the first fifty
years of that tribunal. But I do not know that it would be
possible to cite *one* accused person who, by appealing to
Rome, did not obtain indulgence and relief. . . . . We constantly find, on the part of the Holy See, a desire to restrain
the Inquisition within the bounds of justice and humanity."
("The Inquisition in Spain," chap. xxxvi. p. 165.)   Indeed,
throughout the whole history of the Inquisition there exists
abundant matter to prove, that the great object of the popes
was to mitigate the rigour of its exercise. But at the same
time I will remark, that we of the present day can form no
conception of the terrible dangers that surrounded the throne
of Ferdinand and Isabella in the fifteenth century, and that,
therefore, it is difficult for us to decide how far they were
justified, or how much to be blamed for the exercise of the
severity to which they resorted. All Protestants condemn
them for the expulsion of the Jews.* But contemporary
writers, who are generally the best judges, took a different
view of the matter.   To me it seems undeniable that the
sovereigns were animated by the purest motives of religion,
and an anxious interest in the welfare of their country;
and that they had no desire to erect the Inquisition into
a great state political-engine. The well-known piety of
Isabella especially forbids such a supposition. Still, I admit
that it was more or less dependent upon the crown, and that

---

* That is, of those who refused to be baptized.

the popes had not that full control over its proceedings which they so often endeavoured to acquire. But it does not follow that *therefore* the Inquisition was purely a political institution, as Dr. Hefele endeavours to prove. Its history may be divided into three epochs: the *first* extends from the time of its establishment till about the middle of the reign of Charles V.; the *second* embraces the period from the middle of the reign of Charles V. till the accession of the Bourbons; and the *third* extends from the last-named period till its abolition in 1820. During the first period. the efforts of the Holy Office were principally directed against the relapsed Jews and the Christians who had apostatized; during the second, under Philip II., all its energies were concentrated towards preventing the introduction of Protestantism; while, during the third, the Inquisition contented itself with punishing infamous crimes, and repressing the circulation of infidel and immoral publications.

III. As, then, the institution has evidently been modified according to circumstances, so also must it be judged.* Under Philip II. the peculiar dangers which threatened Spain from the insidious attacks of Protestantism, induced that monarch to employ and direct all his powers and severity towards its repression. He knew what fatal effects Protestantism had produced in Germany and other countries, and therefore both he and the whole nation concluded, that if it were allowed to gain ground in Spain, the same, if not *greater*, disasters would infallibly happen, the terrible consequences of which it was awful to contemplate. Philip, however, did not establish a new Inquisition; he only continued what Ferdinand and Isabella had commenced: why then should

---

* As I am now leaving the reign of Isabella, I here wish to protest against the violent and unjust manner in which Prescott and others endeavour to blacken the character of Fray Tomas de Torquemada, the queen's confessor. As Zurita, Pulgar, and all the ancient Spanish writers speak of him with the highest respect for his zeal and piety, we must conclude that *they* had better means of appreciating his character than Mr. Prescott, even though he was an inquisitor!

Protestant writers condemn him so severely, when, at the same time, they are inclined to make every allowance for the conduct of the Catholic sovereigns, though *they* were far more severe than Philip? The reason is evident. Protestants adopted every expedient to gain a footing in Spain; but because Philip and the Inquisition baffled them, therefore are they hated, denounced, vilified, and held up in countless publications to universal execration. Prescott, in his Life of Philip II., has done great injustice to that monarch. Even amongst Catholics there seems to exist a certain amount of prejudice against him. His history has yet to be written ; * and when examined from a Catholic point of view, I am confident that his policy with regard to Protestants will be found to have been influenced more by *religious* motives than by political ones. He was a pious Catholic,† most anxiously bent upon the maintenance and preservation of a religion in which he so firmly believed. Protestantism, then, he must have considered to be false, and dangerous by its principles to the peace and welfare of his country. Hence, he was bound to preserve the faith and welfare of his dominions at every cost. Now, as he found the Inquisition already established, it was natural he should make use of it to promote the important objects he had in view. Had he *not* done so, Protestantism would infallibly have entered the country; a civil war would have ensued, and probably the throne itself would have been overturned.‡ But by these observations, I do not mean to approve or justify *all* the acts of Philip's policy. As we regret that Queen Mary

---

* Balmes has a most valuable chapter on Philip II. and the Inquisition in his "Protestantism and Catholicity compared" (English ed. p. 167).

† See a curious volume in Spanish, entitled "Dichos y Hechos de el Señor Rey Don Philipe Segundo, &c., por el Licenciado Balthasar Porreño" (Madrid, 1784). Many of his sayings are remarkably good and witty.

‡ See Stirling's "Cloister Life of Charles V." (chap. viii. p. 159), where he mentions how Protestants endeavoured to disturb the kingdom. Prescott, in his "Life of Philip II." (chap. iii. book ii.), shamefully perverts historic facts connected with Protestantism in Spain ; so also does M'Crie, in his "History of the Reformation in Spain" (Edinburgh, 1829).

of England was forced, in a manner (though some Spanish
friars protested against the act), to burn Cranmer, Ridley,
and Latimer; so do we deplore, with Balmes, that Philip
allowed so many to be executed in Valladolid,*˙when perpetual imprisonment might, perhaps, have equally served the
ends of justice. Though the Inquisition was not a mere
instrument of Philip's policy; yet it experienced more or less
the influence of that policy; and hence, had it been during
his reign exclusively under the direction of the Holy See, it
seems certain that those executions would never have taken
place. Those who suffered (an Englishman named Nicholas
Burton was amongst the number) are extolled as Protestant
martyrs !† Be it so. But have Protestants never persecuted,
never imprisoned, never tortured, never put to death any
unfortunate beings? Let history answer the question.
Protestants, with all their boasting about " liberty of worship
and the inalienable rights of conscience," have persecuted
others who differed from them, in a manner that ought to
make them *blush* when they object the same to us. What
fierce contests did not Luther carry on with the Sacramen-
tarians, and still *more* so with the Anabaptists, whom he

* The spot on which the house of the unfortunate Dr. Augustine Cazalla stood
is still pointed out in Valladolid. Even the street still bears his name—Calle
de Cazalla. His secret conferences with the Protestants were discovered by
the wife of a silversmith, who immediately denounced him to the Inquisition.

† The generality of Protestants have very imperfect ideas of the Spanish
auto de fé. They imagine it must be a huge bonfire, round which the
Spanish kings, bishops, nobles, and ladies assembled on Sundays and holidays,
like so many cannibals, to behold a number of poor wretches roasting and
broiling; and that they enjoyed the execution of heretics with as much pleasure
as they would a bull-fight ! The truth is, that an *auto de fé* (act of faith) consisted neither in burning nor in putting to death ; but partly in the acquittal
of those who had been falsely accused, and partly in the reconciliation of those
who repented to the Church. At other times, sentence was pronounced on
the prisoners who continued obstinate, and these were delivered over to the
secular authority. Many executions did certainly take place in Seville,
Toledo, Valladolid, &c. But we should remember that Llorente himself
mentions several *autos de fé* when *not one* single person was executed. Hence,
in many cases, these *autos* were so many acts of mercy, so many religious
spectacles, at which devout Spaniards might well love to be present. Such
scenes Protestants cannot understand, unless to denounce them as " bloody
and cruel in the extreme." Might not such epithets be applied, with *much*
more propriety, to the execution of many priests under Elizabeth ?

endeavoured to repress more promptly and severely than
his own rebellion was by Catholic Princes ? The history of Calvinism is equally significant. The religious
despotism exercised by Luther was continued by Calvin in a
form more complete, violent, and systematic. The direct
object of one of his treatises is to prove " that heretics should
be repressed by the sword ; " and upon this principle we
know how he acted with regard to Castalio, Ochino, and
Servetus, &c. In the burning of the latter, not only
individual divines concurred—such as Beza, Bucer, and the
" mild Melancthon "—but the great synods of Zurich, Berne,
Schaffhausen, and Basel expressed their approbation also.
But in no country did religious persecution and intolerance
attain to such a fearful height as in England and Scotland.
Dr. Lingard's " History of England," and Bishop Challoner's
" Missionary Priests," show too well the sanguinary and
unjust enactments to which Catholics were subjected for
their faith. In Scotland, Tytler* has proved that Knox was
implicated in the murder of Rizzio ; in a word, that he was
an avowed persecutor, and this too upon principle ; for did he
not proclaim that it was the duty, not only of the civil
magistrate, but even of private individuals, to exterminate all
idolators—that is *papists ?* If such then be undeniable facts,
why should Protestants say a word on the subject of the
Inquisition ? Even Prescott, with all his violent denunciations against it, is forced to make the following admission :
" However mischievous the operations of the Inquisition may
have been in Spain, its establishment, in point of principle,
was not worse than many other measures, which have passed
with far less censure, though in a much more advanced and
civilized age. Where, indeed, during the sixteenth and the
greater part of the seventeenth century, was the principle of
persecution abandoned by the dominant party, whether

---

* " History of Scotland" (vol. vi. p. 215).

Catholic or Protestant."*   (Character of Isabella, chap. xvi.
p. 471 ; ed. London, 1854.)

The famous trial under Philip II. of the archbishop of
Toledo, Fray Bartolomé Carranza de Miranda is frequently
cited by nearly all Protestant historians as a demonstrative
proof both of the injustice and cruelty of Philip, and of the
arbitrary character of the Inquisition. Space will not allow
me to enter into all the details of this celebrated case.† A
statement of a few of the principal points will be sufficient.
Carranza was born at Miranda (in the kingdom of Navarre),
in the year 1503. He studied philosophy at Alcalá, and
theology in Salamanca ; and thence, after a few years, he
was sent to the Dominican convent in Valladolid, where he
taught divinity for some time. He was so highly esteemed
by Charles V. for his knowledge and eloquence, that he was
sent to assist at the council of Trent. Philip II. chose
him for his confessor in 1548, and soon after appointed
him archbishop of Toledo. It is said that this elevation
excited the hatred and envy of the grand-inquisitor, Fernando
Valdés, archbishop of Seville. Carranza was in England at
the time of his appointment. When he came to Spain, to
take possession of his see, he remained a few weeks at
Valladolid, in the noble convent of San Pablo,‡ with his
brethren of the order of St. Dominic. But having written
a tract on the " Residence of Bishops," he was anxious to

---

* In a note the author also remarks : " I borrow almost the words of
M. Hallam, who noticing the penal statutes against Catholics under Elizabeth,
says, 'They established a persecution, which fell not at all short, in principle,
of that for which the Inquisition became so odious.'"

† See his life, by Salazar de Miranda (Madrid, 1788) ; also, " Documentos
Inéditos" (tom. v. p. 389); and " Noticia de la Vida de Bart. Carranza de
Miranda," por D. M. S. (Madrid, 1845). Don Vicente de la Fuente has likewise given a few interesting details of him in his " Historia Ecclesiastica de
España" (tom. iii. p. 123). But the most valuable is the notice of the case,
and the observations upon it, by Balmes, in his chapter on the Inquisition
(xxxvii. p. 169, English ed.).

‡ Now destroyed. The church remains, and is one of the finest Gothic
buildings in Valladolid.

practice what he had inculcated; he therefore hastened to Toledo as soon as circumstances allowed. In August, 1559, while visiting his diocese in Torrelaguna, he was suddenly arrested by the officers of the Inquisition, and conducted under a strong guard to Valladolid. The arrest of such a person naturally caused a great sensation throughout the country.

(1.) Why was he arrested? Not, as Prescott asserts, because he adhered to the doctrine of justification by faith alone, but because both his discourses and his writings* afforded some grounds for suspicions against his faith. (2.) In those times the mere imputation or suspicion of heresy was considered a sufficient reason to justify the arrest of any one, however exalted his station might be. (3.) It seems certain, that Carranza was treated with extreme and unnecessary rigour. (4.) No contemporary historian asserts that Philip acted towards him from *personal hatred* or *resentment.* (5.) It seems almost certain that the king was induced to treat Carranza so severely from the suspicion, or rather conviction, he had of his being heretical. (6.) When the case was summoned to Rome, where an impartial examination of it took place, he was not acquitted on all the points—having been obliged by the Pope to abjure sixteen propositions found in his writings; he was also suspended from his episcopal duties for five years, and required to perform several penances. A few days after the sentence had been pronounced, Carranza died. A monument was erected to his memory by the Pope.† On his deathbed, he protested that he died a true son of the Catholic Church. His great fault was that, considering the critical times in which he lived, he was not cautious in his

---

* He wrote "Commentaries on the Catechism," and also "Summa Conciliorum," which are now seldom referred to in Spain. His "Summa" was printed at Salamanca in 1551.

† An immense mass of documents exists in one of the libraries of Madrid connected with the trial of Carranza. Llorente fortunately did not burn *them*, as he did others.

words; and did not explain himself with sufficient clearness in his "Catechism," when treating of justification. Philip's hatred of heresy—or what might even lead to it—was, no doubt, the true cause of the excessive severity with which he treated him.

Balmes positively asserts that the Inquisition was *not* a mere instrument of Philip's policy. To support his assertion, he mentions how Don Antonio Perez, in his "Relations," answers a letter of Fray Diego de Chaves, who believed that secular princes had power over the lives of their subjects and vassals. These are the words of Perez: "I shall not undertake to relate all that I have heard said, on the subject of the condemnation of some of these propositions. Those who are concerned in this matter will at once understand the import of my words. I shall content myself with stating that, when I was at Madrid, the Inquisition condemned the following proposition. A preacher (whose name I need not mention) maintained in a sermon at St. James's church, in Madrid, in presence of Philip II., 'that kings had an absolute power over the persons of their subjects, as well as over their properties.' These words the preacher was obliged to retract as erroneous, which he did publicly, and with all the form of a juridical act, saying from a paper: 'Kings have no other power over their subjects than what is given them by Divine and human law: they possess none which comes from their own free and absolute will.'" ("Relaciones de Antonio Perez." Paris, 1624; quoted by Balmes. Notes, p. 399.) This passage seems to have been overlooked by Dr. Hefele.

Another objection often brought against the Inquisition, both under Isabella and Philip, is, that it crushed the intellect of the Spanish people, and consequently destroyed in them a love and cultivation of learning and science. Such an assertion has not the slightest foundation in truth. The whole reign of Isabella was a remarkable development of the national enthusiasm for learning and science. It was pre-

d

cisely at the period when the "Inquisition" began to be
consolidated that learning began to flourish. A number of
schools and universities were erected; the art of printing
was introduced; every species of poetry was cultivated;
celebrated scholars, such as Peter Martyr, Lucio Marineo
Siculo, &c., were invited into Spain from foreign parts;
while the Spanish nobility themselves, by the example and
encouragement of Isabella, turned from the art of war to the
more ennobling pursuits of literature. Even a lady—Doña
Lucia de Medrano—publicly taught classics in the university
of Salamanca; and another—Doña Francisca de Lebrija—
occupied the chair of rhetoric at Alcalá de Henares.* Philip
also showed a laudable zeal for the advancement of learning.
When he erected the Escurial, he took care to order Doctor
Benito Arias Montano "to be very diligent in collecting all
the choice books, printed and manuscript, which he should
think proper, in order to place them in the library of the
said monastery. Indeed, it is one of the chief possessions
which I wish to leave to the religious who are intended to
live there . . . . . I have also commanded my ambassador in
France, Don Francisco de Alaba, to collect the best books he
can meet with in that kingdom. You will communicate
with him on the subject," &c. (Quoted by Balmes, notes,
p. 399.) His majesty also ordered Ambrosio de Morales
to undertake a literary journey into the kingdoms of Leon,
Galicia, and to the Asturias, in order to procure relics of
saints and *manuscripts*, and examine the royal sepulchres.
The result of his journey, with the notes thereon, forms a
curious volume, an edition of which was published by
Florez.† Cabrera de Cordova, in his "Life of Philip II.,"
proves that his majesty erected and founded many schools

---

* See "Memorias de la Real Acad. de Historia" (tom. vi. Ilust. 16); also,
Nic. Antonio, "Bibliotheca Vetus et Nova" (Matriti, 1783).

† It is entitled "Viage de Ambrosio de Morales, por orden del Rey D.
Phelipe II. á los Reynos de Leon, y Galicia, y Principado de Asturias, para
reconocer las Reliquias de Santos, Sepulcros Reales, y Libros Manuscritos de
las Cathedrales y Monasterios" (ed. Madrid, 1765).

and monasteries for the education of ecclesiastics, amongst which the English college of Valladolid, though established by Father Persons, was at first entirely dependent on the funds generously given for its support by Philip, who may be called its founder. Several celebrated Spanish writers lived under the reign of Philip II.; and their works were printed with the permission of the Inquisition.* But if we include the *whole* period from the time of Ferdinand and Isabella till the end of the reign of Carlos III., what brilliant names in Spanish literature, both sacred and profane, present themselves before us !—Juan Boscan, Garcilaso de la Vega, Diego de Mendoza, Montemayor, Herera, Luis de Leon, Juan de la Cueva, Bermudez, Cervantes, Lopez de la Vega, Calderon, Pulgar, Zuñiga, Zurita, Mariana, Blancas, Santa Teresa, San Juan de la Cruz, Luis de Granada, El Venerabile Padre d'Avila, &c. But, above all, it is to Spain, under the rule of the Inquisition, that we are indebted for the first Polyglot, published at the sole expense of a grand-inquisitor — the immortal Cardinal Ximenez ! All readers of Spanish history know what a splendid revival of learning took place, and how many magnificent editions of old writers were published in the reign of Carlos III. Surely, then, it cannot be maintained for a moment that the "Inquisition" was opposed to the development of the human mind, or to the cultivation and progress of literature.

With regard to the use of "torture" by the Inquisition, no one can deny but that its frequency and its severity are *grossly exaggerated* by Protestant writers. Besides, it is ungenerous, as well as unjust, to make the Inquisition solely answerable for the use of torture, when at the same time it formed the ordinary part of all criminal proceedings in secular tribunals in nearly all the states of Europe, especially

---

* The committee which drew up the official report respecting the Inquisition, and abolished it in 1812, had the boldness to assert, "that all learning vanished when the Inquisition appeared." (See "Informe sobre el Tribunal de la Inquisicion," &c. ; Cadix, 1812.) The members of the committee were "liberals" of the worst sort.

in England, France, and Germany. It must also be borne in
mind that torture could only be used under certain restrictions, and never by the local tribunals, without the consent
of the grand-inquisitor, or of the supreme court. The
regulations for its exercise, as laid down in the "instruc-
ciones" of Torquemada, are remarkable for their leniency
and caution. Additional precautions were introduced by
Philip II. Llorente acknowledges, "that for a long time
the Inquisition did not make use 'of torture, and that at the
commencement of the present century we may consider it as
totally abolished." Balmes also observes: "Thus we see
the *auto de fé* becomes more and more rare as we approach
our own times; so that at the end of the last century the
Inquisition was only a shadow of what it had been"
(chapter xxxvii. p. 175).

Many more observations might be made on this important
subject; indeed, a complete history of the Inquisition has
yet to be written. But Dr. Hefele has done a great deal
towards exposing the lies and inaccuracies of Llorente.
An immense mass of papers and documents connected
with the Inquisition still exist in the archives of Simancas.
Though I was assured by the keeper of them that
little or nothing was to be found amongst them respecting
Ximenez, yet I have reason to believe that, if the papers
relating to the Inquisition under Philip II. were properly
examined and digested, a new light would be thrown
on many points which are now but imperfectly known or
understood.*

With regard to the university of Alcalá,† little remains

---

* The correspondence which passed between Charles V. when at Yuste,
and his son Philip II., respecting the Inquisition, is very curious. A great
number of letters from Charles and Philip are preserved at Simancas. The
emperor was horrified when he discovered how Protestantism had secretly
spread in Valladolid. He urged his son to execute speedy justice upon
heretics, and to spare no one. Lafuente, in his " Historia General de España,"
tom xii., quotes a few of the letters.

† Alcalá de Henares, so called from the river Henares. It was named
Complutum by the Romans.

to be added by me, as Dr. Hefele has already given so many
interesting details respecting its foundation by Ximenez. So
far back as the year 1498, the Cardinal seems to have conceived the idea of such a noble and gigantic undertaking;
but he was unable to commence it till the year 1500, when
the first stone of the Colegio Mayor de San Ildefonso was laid
by his Eminence in person, with all due solemnity. Amidst
all his distracting duties, the Cardinal never lost sight of
his beloved building. When circumstances allowed him to
remain at Alcalá for a short time, often was he seen with
rule and plummet in his hand, taking the measurements of
the edifice, and encouraging the industry of the workmen.
At length, after the expiration of about eight years, he had
the inexpressible joy of beholding his glorious undertaking
nearly completed. The first professors came from the
University of Salamanca.* A code of studies and discipline
was drawn up by Ximenez, remarkable for its wisdom and
religious spirit. Chairs were established for nearly the
whole circle of sciences which were taught at that time,
special attention being directed to those studies which tended
to elucidate the Holy Scriptures. In 1508 the university
was opened for students, who soon flocked from all parts of
Spain to its academic halls. Different popes, and especially
Leo X., bestowed many privileges on the rising university,
which afterwards became so renowned that when Francis I.
visited it a few years after the Cardinal's death, it is said
that near *seven* thousand students came out to meet him. A
history of the great men who were educated there would fill
several volumes. Well may the ancient biographers † of
Ximenez love to dwell on its literary glories, and the munificence of its illustrious founder, to whom too much praise

---

* The university of Salamanca was founded by Alfonso IX. in the twelfth
century. Before this period, one existed in Palencia where St. Dominic was
educated. Salamanca is now a mere wreck of what it once was. The school
of medicine has been removed to the university of Valladolid.

† Robles calls the university " octava maravilla del mundo" (cap. xvi.
p. 127).

cannot be given for so noble a memorial of his love for the arts and sciences. Our admiration increases when we remember, that the University was erected at his *sole* expense!

But, alas! all its glories have now passed away. Revolutionary governments have committed sad havoc with Alcalá. The university was suppressed in 1822, but re-established the following year, until, at last, it was transferred to Madrid by a royal decree, in the year 1836, and now forms what is called "Universidad Central." Thus have all the ancient associations—so honourable and glorious to Spain—ceased to have any connection with the "Colegio Mayor de San Ildefonso" in Alcalá. This building was sold by Señor Quinto to a committee, composed of the principal inhabitants of the town, who nobly resolved to prevent its entire destruction, by making some repairs which were absolutely necessary. The chapel, however, is in a great measure destroyed, the beautiful ceiling having fallen in. The ancient lecture-rooms and halls are completely stripped of their furniture and ornaments, though the courts and front of the building are in a good condition. But the remains of the Cardinal, having been solemnly translated to another sepulchre in 1857,* still render Alcalá, and the collegiate church wherein they repose, spots that will ever be dear, not only to true Spaniards who love the memory of their great prelates, but to men of every clime, who remember what the arts and sciences owe to Cardinal Ximenez. The town itself contains a population of about 7,000. It is celebrated as the birthplace of Cervantes and Catherine of Aragon. It is only a few leagues from Madrid. The whole now presents a desolate aspect, sad to look upon.†

On the merits of the Complutensian Polyglot, I do not

---

* An interesting account of the translation has been kindly sent to me from Madrid, by the Marqués de Morante. I shall notice it in the Appendix.

† The best history of Alcalá (Complutum) is by Miguel de Portilla y Esquivel" (2 vols. 4to. Alcalá, 1725).

consider myself competent to pass a critical judgment, especially as I have good reasons for believing that the remarks which Dr. Hefele has made upon it are, on the whole, correct and satisfactory. He has given the best description of the Polyglot, from an actual inspection of its contents, in opposition to some writers in Germany and other places, who have ventured to copy one from another, without having either seen or examined it themselves. Le Long, in his "Bibliotheca Sacra" (ed. Masch, part i. p. 332—339), mentions most of the authors who have written on the Complutensian Polyglot. Goeze's * defence of it, against the attacks of Semler and Wetstein in the last century, should also be read by those who wish to see the answers to all the objections that can be urged against the work. Dr. Hefele enters into a few valuable details connected with the subject, and proves that the Complutensian editors did *not* alter their Greek text, to support or exalt the Vulgate. Their rejection of the words following the "Our Father" ("for Thine is the kingdom, the power, and the glory") has been completely justified by modern biblical critics. The celebrated text of the three witnesses (1 St. John, v. 7) is found in the Complutensian Polyglot.†

Whether the codices were ancient or modern,—what particular manuscripts were sent to Ximenez by Leo X., or whether the celebrated Codex Vaticanus ‡ was used by the editors, are questions which have not as yet been satisfactorily settled. It seems certain that other manuscripts were used besides those which had been sent from Rome. D. Michaelis mentions that the Codex Rhodiensis and Codex Bassarionis, were given to the Cardinal as presents; and

---

* Vertheidigung der Complutensischen-Bibel, insonderheit des Neuen Testaments, gegen die Wetsteinischen und Semlerschen Beschuldigungen" (Hamburg, 1765).

† See Cardinal Wiseman's valuable dissertation on this celebrated text, reprinted in his "Essays on various subjects" (vol. i. Dolman, 1853).

‡ Known as the Codex B. It is now happily printed, and so accessible to all scholars. "Vetus et Novum Testamentum ex Antiquissimo Codice Vaticano, edidit Angelus Mai, S. R. E. Card.; Romæ, 1857."

Gomez states that Ximenez spent large sums in the purchase of Hebrew manuscripts. It is to be regretted that the editors were not more careful in describing the manuscripts which were used by them; and yet ought not every allowance to be made, considering that the art of criticism was then in its infancy, and the antiquity of manuscripts but little understood?

It is asserted by many writers that the manuscripts lent to Ximenez were either destroyed at Alcalá, or were never returned. To support the first assertion, Dr. Hefele repeats the story so often mentioned by biblical critics, how Dr. Holdenhawer undertook a journey to Spain in the year 1784, and went to Alcalá for the purpose of discovering and examining the Greek manuscripts which had been used by the editors of the Polyglot. But on his arrival he was informed that, about thirty years before, they had all been sold by the librarian to a person named Toryo, who used them for making rockets! Professor Tychsen, the companion of Dr. Holdenhawer, confirms the above statement, according to D. Michaelis, who gives the whole account in his "Introduction to the New Testament." (Part i. vol. ii. p. 440, Marsh's translation; ed. Cambridge, 1793.) The same story is given by Mr. Ford, in his "Hand-book for Spain." (See Alcalá de Henares.) Bayer, Puigblanch, De Castro, &c., repeat the same statement.

But it is only just to mention that the whole account is considered inaccurate, if not altogether false, by Spanish writers. I have been assured by one of the most learned professors [*] in the "Universidad Central," that he has taken the greatest pains in examining the papers and documents that were brought from Alcalá when its university was suppressed, and could find nothing to justify such a supposition. On the contrary, it now appears certain that the "Greek codices" were *restored*, as Father Vercellone

---

[*] Señor Don Vicente de la Fuente, author of the "Historia Eclesiastica de España."

has found and published the papal acknowledgment of their having been returned. The following are the words of the receipt:—

"Aug. 23, 1518. Pope Leo X. motu proprio, &c. We acknowledge to have received from the venerable brother John, archbishop of Cosenza, our nuncio to Spain, two volumes of the Mosaic Bible, written in Greek, which we had formerly commanded to be lent to the cardinal of Toledo, of happy memory, during his lifetime, by the hands of our beloved son, Eneas de Blandrata, subdeacon and our friend, ordering the librarian that it be registered in the book and certified, and that it should also be registered in the Apostolical Chamber.

"Given at Rome, at St. Peter's, Aug. 23, 1518, in the seventh year of our Pontificate. Thus we acknowledge and command. I, L. Parmenius, custodian, acting as librarian, have written and certify on the day and year as above. I, Paul Morelli, of Lucca, carried and presented the said mandate." (Translated from the Prolegomena to the published Codex Vaticanus. Romæ, 1857.)

This receipt seems to set the matter at rest, regarding the supposed destruction of the manuscripts. Lafuente mentions that, about the period of Dr. Holdenhawer's arrival in Alcalá, a rumour was current that some *Arabic* manuscripts had been burnt there ; and this may have led him into the mistake of *supposing* they must have been the Greek codices, which the ignorant people called "Arabic."

Ximenez, as Gomez * relates, intended by the publication of his Polyglot, to follow the plan first conceived by Origen in his Hexapla, of exhibiting the Holy Scriptures in their ancient languages. Another object was to revive biblical studies, and especially the knowledge of Hebrew and Greek, of which the clergy of that period seem to have been generally ignorant. The Cardinal foresaw, also, that men would

---

* "De Rebus Gestis," lib. ii. fol. 37, &c.

arise, who, pretending to have studied the Scriptures profoundly, would impiously turn their knowledge against the
Church of Christ, taking advantage, in the mean time, of the
ignorance of the clergy to spread their corrupt and poisonous
doctrines. Hence this great man spared no pains or expense,
to provide his clergy with the means of becoming proficients
in Biblical knowledge.

Alfonso de Zamora, professor of Hebrew, and one of the
editors of the "Polyglot," often related in presence of Gomez
that *seven* Hebrew manuscripts cost Ximenez 4,000 golden
ducats; and that the expense of the whole "Polyglot,"
including the payment of salaries, the purchase of manuscripts, the casting of new types, travelling expenses, &c.,
amounted to more than 50,000 ducats;* a sum which,
estimated according to the value of money at that period,
must have been immense. Though the work consisted of
six volumes in folio, a copy could be purchased at the low
price of only six ducats and a half. The editors commenced
their labours in the year 1502. After twelve years the first
volume (including the New Testament) was completed,
January 10th, 1514. The last volume was finished July
10th, 1517. Only 600 copies were printed off. The printer
was a German, named Arnauld William Brocar, whom
Ximenez had invited to Toledo, in order to superintend and
publish an edition of the Mozarabic Breviary. He afterwards
went to Alcalá to print the "Polyglot." When his son,
John Brocar, clad in his festal garments, carried the last
sheets to Ximenez, the Cardinal, then almost on the verge of
the grave,† exclaimed, "I give Thee thanks, O Lord! that
Thou hast enabled me to bring to the desired end, the great
work which I undertook." Then turning to those around
him he said, "Of the many arduous duties which I have
performed for the benefit of the country, there is nothing,

---

* About £25,000 sterling.
† The cardinal died in November, 1517, four months after the completion of
the Polyglot.

my friends, on which you ought to congratulate me more
than on the completion of this edition of the Bible, which
now opens to us the sacred fountains of religion, when they
are most needed." (Gomez, fol. 38.) Some difficulties
delayed its publication; until at length Pope Leo X. issued
a brief (dated March 22, 1520) authorizing Francisco de
Mendoza, bishop of Avila, to allow the sale of the work in
all parts of the kingdom.

Several copies of the "Polyglot" are to be found in the
Spanish Libraries, though many of them are imperfect.
There is a magnificent copy on vellum, preserved at Madrid,
which was brought from Alcalá. Some of the universities of
Germany and the colleges in England possess copies, amongst
which there is a beautiful one (I believe perfect) in the
noble library of St. Mary's College, Oscott.

Making every allowance for the blemishes or imperfections
necessarily belonging to such a gigantic undertaking as the
Complutensian "Polyglot," we must yet acknowledge, in
the words of Mr. Prescott, "That the Cardinal's Bible has
the merit of being the first successful attempt at a Polyglot
version of the Scriptures, and consequently of facilitating,
even by its errors, the execution of more perfect works of the
kind.* Nor can we look at it in connection with the age,
and the auspices under which it was accomplished, without
regarding it as a noble monument of learning, piety, and
munificence, which entitles its author to the gratitude of the
whole Christian world."† (Character of Ximenez, chap. xxi.
p. 522; ed. 1854.)

The account given by Dr. Hefele of the conquest of Oran,
is most interesting. Such an enterprise, though apparently

---

* The Complutensian was followed by the Antwerp Polyglot, the Paris
Polyglot, and the London Polyglot. Several minor polyglots have also
appeared at different times, the chief of which is known as Bagster's Polyglot,
with a prolegomena by Dr. Lee.

† Ximenes had also a number of religious works published for popular
reading, corresponding with the "cheap publications" of the present day.
Amongst these was a life of St. Thomas of Canterbury, to whom the cardinal
was exceedingly devoted. (See Gomez and Dr. Hefele.)

inconsistent with the peaceful pursuits of a primate, was
undertaken by Ximenez in a purely Christian spirit; he
sighed for the day when the banner of the Cross should sup-
plant the proud Crescent, in a country where such men as
St. Cyprian and St. Augustine lived, and where the Catholic
faith once flourished so gloriously. The undertaking as well
as the execution of that celebrated expedition, reflect the
highest lustre on the military talents of the Cardinal. It was
with difficulty that he obtained the consent of Ferdinand,
who dreaded the expense; but Ximenez generously contributed a large sum from his own revenues, while the
chapter of Toledo granted a considerable loan. It was he
who allayed the jealousy of the military commanders, appeased
the dissensions of the officers, established discipline in the
army, supplied all its wants with foresight and promptitude,
and enflamed the religious ardour of the troops before the
attack with a few burning words, such as Napoleon or
Wellington might have pronounced.*   It was only by the
urgent entreaties of the officers, that he was prevented from
exposing himself in the ranks of his soldiers to the fire of
the enemy.   Oran was taken.   The standard which was
carried before Ximenez, is still preserved in the library of the
" Universidad Central " of Madrid.

But it is time to bring this long preface to a conclusion,
though much more might be said on other points, especially
on the boldness and vigour of his measures when *regent*.
During a period of nearly two years Ximenez displayed to the
fullest advantage all his great stateman-like talents. Indeed,
it was only by his consummate prudence, foresight, and
courage, in resisting the intrigues of the grandees, as well as
the ambitious designs of others, that he was enabled to save
his country from the terrible dangers that threatened it on

---

* See his address in the chapter on the conquest of Oran. Gomez states
that the Cardinal often acknowledged "that the smell of gunpowder was more
grateful to him than the sweetest perfumes of Arabia." Doubtless, because
Ximenez wished to destroy the power of the infidel, and was glad whenever
he had an opportunity of attacking the Moors.

every side. His policy, however, as a statesman has been attacked by some French and English writers, especially with regard to his treatment of the Moors after the conquest of Granada. But as the observations of Dr. Hefele on the subject are very just, I refer the reader to the translation, without offering any remarks of my own.

The part which Ximenez took in the conversion of America was so slight, or, rather, all the documents which could throw any light on the subject having either perished or been destroyed, the biographers have not given us any details respecting so interesting and important a matter. Only a few *allusions* to the subject are given by Gomez; according to whom it seems that Ximenez, after the death of Ferdinand, sent a number of Hieronymite monks on a mission for America, nominating Las Casas as the head of them. The instructions which he gave them were most admirable, and the effects of the mission highly beneficial to the poor Indians, and thus were thousands of souls indebted to the Cardinal for their happiness, both in this life and the next.* (See Dr. Hefele's chapter on the " Solicitude of Ximenez for America," chap. xxviii. German ed.)

Ximenez spent the last few months of his life, in the year 1517, in making preparations for the arrival of Charles V. in Spain. But that monarch, at the instigation of his treacherous Flemish advisers, who were jealous of the power of Ximenez, protracted his residence in the north in order to avoid meeting the regent. He had even the ingratitude to address a letter to him, in which, after thanking him for his former services, he dismissed him not only from his office as regent, but from all political duties likewise. Ximenez, however, had already been preparing himself to appear before another royal master, who he hoped would reward his services better a thousand-fold than any earthly monarch could do. The

---

* See Herrera, " Historia de las Indias Occidentales," Madrid, 1730. For an account of Las Casas the reader may consult Irving's " Life of Columbus," or Colon, as the Spaniards call him.

account of his death which is given by Dr. Hefele is most edifying; the news of it filled all Spain with mourning, and never has that Catholic land seen his equal since. To do justice to his exalted character needs no words of mine. As a statesman, he was far superior to Richelieu; * as a prelate, he was the model of bishops; as a monk, full of the spirit of his order; as a patron of learning, he could not be surpassed. Not only was he irreproachable in his morals, kind and generous to the poor, severe to himself alone, zealous beyond conception for the advancement of the Catholic faith, a father to his clergy and canons of Toledo, devoted to the Holy See; forgiving and even kind to his enemies; but, in addition to all this, he is the only prime minister mentioned in history, who was considered to be a *saint*, both living and dead.† Well may Spain be proud of such a prelate, whose history, together with that of Isabella, throws such glory around the period in which they lived, and which, alas! at the same time, forms such a painful contrast with the present degenerate race of statesmen, in whose hands unfortunately are placed the destinies of the noble Spanish nation.

If I can inspire my readers with the same love and admiration for the character of Ximenez that I feel myself, and induce them to take an interest in a country with which we ourselves were once closely united, and which often assisted English priests when persecution drove them from their homes, then will the labour of the translation be fully repaid.

The will of Ximenez is still preserved with great care in

---

* Dr. Hefele devotes a chapter to a comparison between Ximenez and Richelieu. But why do so, when every writer is forced to give the palm to Ximenez? The difference between the two is immense.

† Though the Church has not as yet pronounced any decree respecting the sanctity of Ximenez, he is still called a saint by many Spanish writers. The cause of his canonization was anxiously pressed by the Spanish sovereigns in the sixteenth and seventeenth centuries; but the Holy See has not thought fit to enrol him amongst the saints. Whether she considered the miracles recorded of him not to have been sufficiently proved, or his virtues not to have been *heroic*, I am unable to say. (See Quintanilla, " Archivo Complutense," at the end of his " Archetypo de Virtudes," &c.)

the university of Madrid, and some interesting memorials of him are shown in the chapter-room of the cathedral of Toledo, especially three fine pictures, one of which is said to be a likeness. A volume of letters, written by the Cardinal on various subjects, is also preserved at Madrid, in the Royal Library; but I was unable to discover anything among the documents at Simancas, except a curious account of the expenses of the troops that were sent to the siege of Oran. Many of the papers and documents connected with Ximenez were unfortunately lost or destroyed during the French invasion, which was in so many respects disastrous to Spain.

One relic, however, of the Cardinal, and that, too, exceedingly precious, and which I have had the happiness of seeing, is now in possession of the illustrious archbishop of Burgos, who was educated at Ushaw College. It is the identical ring which the Cardinal wore, with his name, Ximenez, inscribed inside. This ring was presented to his grace the archbishop of Burgos (Fernando de la Fuente) by the right Rev. Dr. O'Connor, bishop of Pittsburg, in America, when they met in Rome in the year 1854. Dr. O'Connor received it from the late bishop of Philadelphia, to whom it was given by Joseph Napoleon, the intruded king of Spain, and he was presented with it by the university of Alcalá, on occasion of a visit which he paid to the place. The archbishop has assured me, that there is no doubt of its authenticity.

I cannot conclude, without expressing my gratitude and thanks for the kind assistance given to me by the archbishop of Burgos, while translating this work, in sending me letters of introduction to Salamanca and Toledo. I also feel exceedingly indebted for much valuable information, which I have received from Senor Don Vicente de la Fuente, professor in the royal University of Madrid; from the Marqués de Morante, of Madrid; from the senator Señor Don Pedro Gomez de la Serna; and from the illustrious rector of the University of Salamanca. I am likewise bound to express my thanks for the assistance afforded to me by the respected rector of St. Alban's College, Valladolid, the very Rev. Dr. Guest, and the vice-rector of the Irish College in Salamanca, the Rev. J. Mooney. I owe many thanks also to the librarians of the university of Valladolid, and the college of Santa Cruz, in the same city, for the facilities they have afforded me of consulting books. It is my duty, moreover, to state, that in consequence of my time being much occupied while here, that portion of the work which embraces the refutation of Llorente's one-sided and inaccurate view of the Inquisition, as well as from page 285 to the end of the volume, has been translated by the accurate hand of Mr. Meno Haas.

JOHN DALTON.

St. Alban's College, Valladolid,
        1859.

In the Appendix will be found an account of the translation of the Cardinal's remains to a new sepulchre at Alcalá de Henares, which solemn ceremony took place April 27th, 1857.

Laus Deo Semper.

LIFE OF CARDINAL XIMENEZ.

CHAPTER I.

THE BIRTH AND YOUTH OF XIMENEZ.

AFTER Spain had been for a long time in a miserable state, Cardinal Ximenez no doubt holds the first rank amongst those who were preparing for her better days, at the end of the fifteenth and the commencement of the sixteenth century.

As a priest, he was pious as a saint; as bishop and primate, he was very remarkable for his great charity to the poor, and indefatigable zeal in the cause of morality and the pursuit of knowledge; as a statesman, few were so active and wise: so that to his very name is attached an undying remembrance of justice and honour. A Spaniard even now blesses his memory; and although since his birth more than four hundred years have passed away, yet writers both of profane and ecclesiastical history, politicians, too, and theologians, still speak of him with the highest esteem.*

Many biographers† have laboured in vain to trace

---

* For the history of Spain from the eighth to the fifteenth century, see Prescott's "Ferdinand and Isabella," vol. i.

† Eugenio de Robles, "Compendio de la Vida y Hazañas del Cardenal Fray Francisco Ximenez de Cisneros" (Toledo, 1604).

his origin from the famous counts of Cisneros.
Ximenez, however, was perhaps more than any one
else indebted to his own deeds, without depending
on or requiring the splendour of ancestry.

The celebrated cardinal belonged to the family of
Ximenez, which came from the decayed nobility of
Castile. The surname Cisneros was derived from the
town where the family dwelt. His father, Alphonso
Ximenez, discharged the humble office of receiver of
tithes for the king,—a tax which was levied by permission of the pope, in order to assist the kings of
Spain in their wars against the Moors. Alphonso
had espoused a lady named Doña Marina de la
Torre,* who was descended from a decayed, though
renowned, family, the name of which, together with
the arms of the noble house, were given on account
of the valour of one of her ancestors who took by
assault a strong tower in Madrid.† Ximenez was
the eldest son, born in the year 1436,‡ at Torrelaguna, a small town in the province of Toledo. At
his baptism he received the name of Gonzalés,
which he changed into Francis, after he entered the
Franciscan order. His parents wishing their son to

Also Quintanilla, "Archetypo de Virtudes, Espejo de Prelados,
el Venerable Padre y Siervo de Dios, Fray Francisco Ximenez de
Cisneros" (Palermo, 1633, fol.), p. 5.

Prescott, though a very agreeable writer, has fallen into several
mistakes respecting the cardinal, and misunderstood many of his
greatest actions.—*Trans.*

* See Fléchier, "Hist. du Cardinal Ximénes" (Amsterdam,
1700), liv. i. p. 4.—*Trans.*

† The city was besieged by King Ramiro, who was on the
point of retiring, when one of the strongest towers was unexpectedly taken. (See Eug. de Robles, cap. 8.)—*Trans.*

‡ Prescott accuses Fléchier of making a mistake of twenty
years in the date of Ximenez' birth. But the mistake seems
evidently to be a mere misprint for 1437, instead of 1457, which
is on the margin of some editions. In the very first sentence
Fléchier mentions that Ximenez was born in the reign of John II.
of Castile.

dedicate himself to the Church, and having trained him to exercises of piety at an early age, soon sent him to Alcala, in order to study grammar under able masters. He afterwards was removed to the renowned university of Salamanca, where he continued his studies, and began to learn canon and civil law, philosophy, and theology; the two last of which he acquired under a celebrated professor named Roa. Here it was that he first manifested that preference for biblical studies which afterwards produced such abundant and fruitful results. By giving private lessons on civil and ecclesiastical law, Ximenez was enabled to support himself for six years at this university; after which period he left Salamanca and returned to his native town, having acquired a good stock of knowledge, and taken his degree of bachelor in canon and civil law. Poverty and the advice of his father induced him soon after, in the year 1459, to seek his fortune in Rome.* On his way, he was twice plundered by robbers, of his money, clothes, and horse: being unable, therefore, to continue his journey, he was obliged to stop at Aix, in Provence. Here, however, he had the good fortune to meet with an old friend, named Brunet, formerly a schoolfellow with him at Salamanca. He, too, was on his way to Rome; and having been informed of the misfortune which happened to Ximenez, he liberally assisted him, and accompanied him to the capital of Christendom.†

At Rome, Ximenez, while pursuing his studies, undertook the office of consistorial advocate in the

---

* Fléchier gives the reason of his journey: "De peur de luy être à charge," &c. (liv. i. p. 6).—*Trans.*

† Gomez (a cotemporary of Ximenez), "De Rebus gestis Francisci Ximenii," lib. i. in "Hispaniæ illustratæ Scriptores" (Francof. fol.), tom. i. p. 932.

ecclesiastical courts. After six years' residence, he soon attracted the notice of his superiors; but the death of his father recalled him to Spain, in order that he might take care of the family, now almost reduced to poverty. With a view of being some assistance to them as soon as possible, he had asked and obtained of the pope letters called "Expectativæ," which gave him the first vacant benefice in the diocese of Toledo.

During several centuries, and especially in the twelfth century, the spiritual lords and civil patrons had introduced the evil custom of granting these letters "expectativæ," for benefices not yet vacant. Although provision was thereby made for men of merit, yet the custom was opposed to the ancient laws of the Church, besides opening a door to simony and every other disorder. The third general council of Lateran, held under Alexander III., considered it necessary absolutely to forbid such kind of promises.* This zealous pontiff not only reserved to the Holy See the collation to benefices already vacant, by the decree "Mandata de providendo:" he also, on the other hand, strictly suppressed the said letters altogether, and forbade any regard to be paid to them. Still, his successors, viz., Celestine III., &c., from the year 1191 to 1198, again renewed the permission, as may be seen from a decree of Pope Innocent III.† Innocent himself, it is true, adhered to the letter of the decree of the third council of Lateran, and forbade all letters "expectativæ," under the form "Promitto præbendam, cùm vacabit;" but by allowing another form, "Promitto præbendam, cùm potero, seu cùm facultas se obtulerit," he weakened the force of his first resolution. About ninety years

---

* Harduin, Collect. Concil., tom. vi. p. 1677, cap. 8.
† Corp. Jur. Canon., cap. 4, de Concessione, &c.

later, Boniface VIII. withdrew again the power of conferring benefices not yet vacant, even under the form " Cùm potero," &c., on account of the abuses which (he says) had crept in. But he himself, by making use of a sophistical distinction,* whilst he condemned letters " expectativæ " as regards a particular benefice, granted them for any benefice in general which might first become vacant.† Thus was the enemy of ecclesiastical order driven out on one side, but he was admitted on the other : hence it was, that during the great schism in the West in the fourteenth century, a favourable opportunity was afforded of exercising fully this pernicious power. Both parties, viz. the popes of Rome and the antipopes at Avignon, sought thereby to enrich and multiply their adherents, by granting permission to possess these benefices. When the vacancies were not sufficient, these letters " expectativæ " were granted without number ; they were often sold at a fixed price, in order to replenish the exhausted coffers.‡

At last, Pope Martin V., importuned by complaints from various quarters, solemnly declared in the council of Constance, that henceforth he would not grant letters " expectativæ," except for inferior benefices,§ and one only for each diocese; Italy and Spain, however, were excepted, because in these countries the benefices being very poor, more were allowed. In the thirty-first session of the council of Basle (1483) a general law was made against

---

* This expression is disrespectful, and not at all just. (See Hurter's Life of Innocent III.) The letters complained of were given with great reluctance by most of the popes, and only in favour of those who deserved well of the Church. (Thomassin, " Discip. de l'Eglise.")—*Trans.*

† Corp. Jur. Canon., cap. 2 et 3, de Concessione, &c.

‡ Theodore de Niem. de Schismate, ii. 7, 8.

§ " Auf niedere Pfründen," &c. p. 13 (German ed.).—*Trans.*

all these " letters " above named; but as this council is considered to be schismatical from the twenty-
sixth session, the regulations of Martin V. alone
remained in force. The pope, therefore, and
Ximenez were both in the same circumstances, on
the ground of historical right; viz., one by seeking
the letters, and the other by granting them. The
council of Trent, by the command of Pius IV.,
absolutely suppressed the " Gratiæ expectativæ."*

The first benefice which became vacant in the
diocese of Toledo, was that of the archpriest of
Uzeda : the revenue was not indeed great, but
Ximenez was in a special manner satisfied with it,
because his native town of Torrelaguna was included
in the limits of the benefice. In the mean time,
Alphonso Carillo, archbishop of Toledo, had already
promised this benefice to an ecclesiastic of his household : he was, therefore, exceedingly angry that
Ximenez laid claim to it. Milder bishops than
Carillo had often resisted the like concessions of the
popes ; much more opposition, then, was to be expected from a prelate whose ambition and inflexible
obstinacy were well known throughout the whole of
Spain.† For a long time, being all-powerful as
minister under Henry IV. of Castile, he had often
placed himself at the head of the rebels; and exchanging the rochet for a coat of mail, had boldly
headed an insurrection, and commanded at the
bloody battle of Olmedo, in 1467. Seldom did any
one venture to resist such a prelate : but from that
day Ximenez began to exhibit that remarkable

---

* Sess. xxiv. cap. 19, de Reform.—(Pallavicini, Hist. Conc. Trid.,
lib. xxiii. cap. 6.)

† Mariana, speaking of this prelate, says, " Magno vir animo,
turbido tamen et inquieto" (Hist. de Rebus Hispan., lib. xxii.
cap. 4). Fléchier mentions him as a bishop "qui étoit
naturelment sévère" (liv. i. p. 9). It is to be hoped that the
character given of this prelate is somewhat exaggerated.—*Trans.*

feature in his character to which he was indebted afterwards as the means of his exaltation—I mean, that unalterable, unshaken firmness which no danger could subdue, when there was any occasion of defending right against might. Ximenez, then, in accordance with his character, persisted most resolutely in pressing his claim to the vacant benefice; but the more he persisted, so much the more haughtily did the powerful archbishop withhold the benefice from him. The result was, that Ximenez, instead of becoming the parish priest of Uzeda, was detained a prisoner there, closely confined in one of the strongest towers. Some time afterwards, when he had arrived at the height of his greatness, this same place was chosen by him for his treasury.* Here it was, according to the relation of his ancient biographers, that a priest, who was his companion in captivity, announced to him his future greatness, and even elevation to the archiepiscopal see of Toledo. "My father," calmly replied Ximenez, "such a commencement does not certainly promise so happy an end;" and thus he continued, without making any complaint against his oppressor, manfully to endure the severity of his imprisonment.†

After a few years, he was removed to the fortress of Santorcaz, which was then the usual place of confinement in the diocese of Toledo for contumacious ecclesiastics. Here he resolutely rejected— as he had done before—the repeated attempts which were made in order to induce him to renounce his benefice. At last, after Ximenez had been deprived of his liberty for more than six years, Carillo being convinced that force was powerless in bending such

---

* Gomez, lib. i. p. 932; Robles, c. 2, p. 40; also Fléchier, who adds, "that he kept here the money which he intended for his expedition into Africa" (liv. i. p. 8).—*Trans.*

† Fléchier, liv. vi. p. 518.

a character, and being also influenced by the entreaties of his niece, the countess of Buendia, gave him his freedom, together with the possession of his benefice.

Ximenez, however, having but little confidence in the future goodwill of Carillo, wished to leave the diocese of Toledo. He exchanged, therefore, in the year 1480, his benefice of archpriest for the first chaplaincy of Sigüenza; but as the revenues of the latter were greater than those of Uzeda, he made an engagement to restore the difference to the former head chaplain of Sigüenza.

At Sigüenza, his virtues soon acquired for him the general esteem and friendship of many illustrious individuals; amongst whom was the rich archdeacon of Almazan, Juan Lopez de Medina-Cœli. By the advice of Ximenez, this ecclesiastic was induced to found the academy of Sigüenza, which was unfortunately suppressed in the year 1807.* Ximenez himself ardently devoted all his time to his biblical studies, and learned the Hebrew and Chaldaic languages.

Such a man could not long remain unknown to the bishop of Sigüenza. From the year 1468 this see had been occupied by Pedro Gonzalez, of the illustrious house of Mendoza, a prelate of great prudence and high attainments, and one, too, who exercised an important influence over the history of Spain and the destiny of Ximenez. In the year 1474 Gonzalez was honoured by the pope with a cardinal's hat, with the title in addition of cardinal of Spain: he had also received from King Henry IV. the dignity of archbishop of Seville; but as the diocese of Sigüenza was intrusted to him at the

---

* I am unable to state whether the seminary has been since restored.—*Trans.*

same time, the* archbishop was anxious to find an able and trustworthy administrator of it. He soon discovered "the right man" in Ximenez, whom he appointed to be his grand-vicar, and honoured with his fullest confidence, rewarding him at the same time with the possession of several benefices. How long Ximenez exercised his zeal in such a wide field, cannot be discovered with any degree of certainty, as all his ancient biographers seem very careless about dates. Quintanilla gives the year 1484 as the probable date. It seems, however, certain, that Ximenez governed the diocese in 1483; for it was about this time that the Count Silva de Cifuentes, having been taken prisoner by the Moors, confided to him the administration of his estates (which were considerable) in the diocese of Sigüenza.

In the mean time, the vicar-general pleased every one better than he pleased himself. He was not happy. He longed to withdraw from the harassing duties and worldly cares of his office. He sighed for the calm of holy contemplation and the study of theology. In vain did friends endeavour to change his mind; he gave up all his benefices to them, recommending to their care and protection his younger brother, Bernardin, then addicted to a worldly life—on the condition, however, that he became virtuous. Ximenez soon retired as a novice into a convent belonging to the Observantines of the Franciscan order. It was called the convent of San Juan de los Reyes, and was founded at Toledo by Ferdinand and Isabella, in consequence of a vow.†

---

* Mariana assures us that this plurality of benefices was contrary to the practice of the Spanish church (Hist. Hispaniæ, lib. xxiii. cap. 19).

† This vow was made in consequence of the successful issue of the War of Succession, by the defeat of Alphonso, king of Portugal. (See Robles, Gomez, and Quintanilla.)

Ximenez chose it, because it was celebrated for the strict observance of the rules.

Scarcely had he finished his noviciate and made his profession, when the fame of his piety spreading far and near, numbers of the inhabitants came to confess to him, asking for advice, comfort, and instruction from him. His interior life being hereby disturbed and interrupted, Ximenez begged his superiors to send him into some lonesome and distant monastery. He was accordingly sent to the small convent of Our Lady of Castañar, which derived its name from its pleasant situation, in the midst of a forest of chestnuts, near Toledo. Ximenez himself assures us, that in this tranquil oasis he spent the most pleasant days of his life, which were equally divided between study and religious duties, with the Bible and the scourge in his hand, and his body covered with a hair shirt. There, after the example of the ancient anchorites, he spent many days and nights in a lonely hermitage which he had built with his own hands, by the permission of his superiors. He loved this retreat to such a degree that afterwards, in the midst of all his grandeur, he said he would willingly exchange for it his see of Toledo, and also his cardinal's hat and the ensigns of the regency which he held. All the religious brethren of his order esteemed his prudence and piety; and often was he sent for by his superiors to Toledo, in order that they might have the benefit of his advice in all important matters connected with the good of the order.

In one of these journeys to Toledo, his exaltation to the see of Toledo was again foretold. Being once, with another companion, overtaken in the night, he was obliged to sleep on the grass with his fellow-brother, Pedro Sanchez. The latter awoke suddenly, and exclaimed, "I dreamt only a moment ago, Father Francis, that you were arch-bishop of Toledo, and that I saw a cardinal's hat on your head." Ximenez, whatever he thought of this dream, did not long enjoy his peaceful re-treat of Castañar; for the rule of the order required the religious often to change their residence. The pious father was accordingly sent to Salzeda, a less rigorous solitude than the former, where he con-tinued his mortified life, and even redoubled his austerities. He was soon unanimously chosen by the religious as their guardian.* Whilst he was fulfilling the duties of this humble office, with the same exactitude which he had shown in the adminis-tration of an extensive diocese, many events had taken place which influenced his future life, and clearly pointed him out as destined to become one of the most active instruments in the regeneration of Spain.

* Prescott, speaking of this period of the cardinal's life, says: "It is no wonder that he should have indulged in ecstasies and visions until he fancied himself raised into communication with celestial intelligences" (vol. ii. p. 338, 5th edit.). Where does the writer of these lines find his authority for such assertions?

CHAPTER II.

FERDINAND AND ISABELLA ASCEND THE THRONE.—CONQUEST
OF GRANADA.

THE greatness of Ximenez, as well as the future destiny of Spain, depended on Ferdinand and Isabella coming to the throne. Two things were absolutely necessary, in order to deliver Spain from the miserable state in which she groaned about the middle of the fifteenth century, and to restore once more that beautiful land to glory and power; viz. sovereigns able to rule, and the union into one kingdom of the Spanish states, which hitherto were so often opposed to each other. Ferdinand and Isabella seemed destined to fulfil these two conditions. But at their birth no one could certainly have anticipated such a blessing, so far distant did the crown seem to be from their heads.* The sceptre of Arragon belonged to Ferdinand's elder brother, Carlos, prince of Viana, who was then in the bloom of age and the strength of his manhood. But he died unmarried, 23rd of September, 1461; thus unexpectedly leaving Ferdinand heir to the throne. Isabella, however, appeared even more unlikely to succeed to the crown of Arragon; for, before this could be effected, it was necessary that death should remove both her brothers, viz., Henry IV. and Alfonso; and also that

---

* Ferdinand was born March the 10th, 1452, and Isabella April the 22nd, 1451. The date of Isabella's birth rests on the authority of the learned Spanish historian Clemencin. (See tom. vi. "Memorias de la Real Academia de la Historia," Madrid, 1821.)

Beltraneja* should be declared by her father incapable of succeeding to the throne.

Yet even supposing that this almost impossible union of events should be effected, another condition was requisite for the future prosperity of Spain; viz. the union of Arragon and Castile, two powerful states, by the marriage of Ferdinand and Isabella. But a thousand obstacles appeared in the way of this consummation, which for a long time seemed insurmountable. It is true, that Isabella, when yet a child about six or seven years old, was betrothed to Ferdinand; but political motives soon dissolved this proposed union. Her hand was then solicited by Ferdinand's elder brother, Carlos, the prince of Viana, before she had reached her tenth year. After his death, she was promised to Alfonso of Portugal (1464); but in spite of threats and entreaties, this proposal did not succeed; for the princess, now only in her thirteenth year, was quite opposed to it. Some time afterwards she was exposed to the still greater danger of becoming the victim of the base political artifices of her brother. The king† wished to give her in marriage to the Grand Master of Calatrava, Don Pedro Giron, brother of the marquis of Villena, and uncle to the powerful Archbishop Carillo. The object of the king, by this proposal, was to weaken the power of his enemies by attaching to himself these three men from the rank of the insurgents. The Grand Master had even obtained a dispensation from his vows. But Isabella was horrified at the mere idea of being united with a man who was

---

* So called from her reputed father, Beltran de la Cueva. Her baptismal name was Joanna. She was supposed to be an illegitimate daughter, though Henry IV. wished her to be considered as presumptive heir to the crown.—*Trans.*

† Her brother, Henry IV.—*Trans.*

considered to be a depraved character.[*] She
therefore besought Heaven, by prayers and fasting,
to deliver her from such a fate; while her faithful
friend Beatriz de Bobadilla was resolved to murder
him, should he make his appearance. Giron,
however, died[†] (May 2nd, 1466) on his way to
celebrate the marriage; and thus was the princess
delivered from her fourth intended spouse.

When at last Isabella was declared heir to the
throne, by the treaty which was drawn up at a place
called Toros de Guisando,[‡] there came again fresh
suitors from the royal families of England and
France.[§] But she had already cast her eyes on her
cousin, Ferdinand of Arragon,[||] a young prince about
the same age as herself, distinguished for the
comeliness of his person and his chivalrous qualities, as well as renowned for many noble deeds of
valour which he performed while serving in the
battles carried on by his father. This time
politics and inclination agreed, while the people
already rejoiced in anticipation of such a happy
union between two such regal personages. But in

---

[*] So Prescott represents him, asserting "that his private life
was stained with most of the licentious vices of the age" (p. 163,
fifth edit.). Isabella certainly disliked the man exceedingly.—
Trans.

[†] Some attributed his death to poison; but not a shadow of
suspicion was ever cast on Isabella, as having caused his death.—
Trans.

[‡] So called from four bulls, sculptured in stone, which were
discovered there. (Prescott, p. 172, note.)

[§] The one from England was a brother of Edward IV., but
which of the brothers seems uncertain. The other suitor, from
France, was the duke of Guienne, brother of Louis XI. (Prescott,
p. 173.)

[||] I refer the reader to Mr. Prescott's "History of Ferdinand
and Isabella" for all the details connected with Ferdinand, which
Dr. Hefele merely touches upon. Dr. Hefele, however, corrects
some mistakes into which Mr. Prescott has fallen. These I shall
notice later.—*Trans.*

order to effect the marriage, the consent of Henry of Castile was necessary; for by the treaty of Toros it was settled, that Isabella should not be forced to marry against her will, nor without the consent of her brother.

Henry, however, was secretly plotting to annul the above treaty, and deprive his sister of the throne.* In order, therefore, that Isabella's claims might not receive any strength and support from an alliance with Arragon, he endeavoured to marry her to Alfonso, the old king of Portugal, and to unite his daughter Beltraneja (Joanna) with the son and heir of the Portuguese monarch, who, it was supposed, would, for his son's sake, espouse the claims of Beltraneja and reject those of Isabella.† But what at last constituted an open violation of the treaty, which Henry swore to observe, was a threat of force and imprisonment, unless she agreed to a union that was hateful to her, both on political and personal grounds. Isabella now considered herself freed from all her engagements, and she accordingly married Ferdinand publicly, on the 19th of October, 1649, without the consent of her brother.‡ Ferdinand, in the true style of a gallant

---

* Of Castile and Leon. The marquis of Villena had, perhaps, more to do with this plot than Henry. The marquis considered the union of Castile and Arragon would be opposed to his interests.—*Trans.*

† Dr. Hefele seems to forget that it was the marquis of Villena who revived the pretensions of Alfonso; and when the princess absolutely refused the king's hand, it was Villena, in reality, who tried to force her by threats of violence and imprisonment. (See Prescott.)—*Trans.*

‡ "Ferdinand was at this time in the eighteenth year of his age. His complexion was fair, though somewhat bronzed by continual exposure to the sun; his eye quick and cheerful; his forehead ample and approaching to baldness. His muscular and well-proportioned frame was invigorated by the toils of war, and by the chivalrous exercises in which he delighted. He was one of the

knight, had exposed himself to a thousand dangers from the soldiers of Henry, on his way from Arragon to Valladolid.

Though King Henry declared his sister had lost all right and title to the throne of Castile, yet the people and the Cortes continued to regard Isabella as the lawful heir to the crown. In proportion, too, as Henry, now lingering under an incurable disease, was approaching the grave, so did most of the families belonging to the high Spanish nobility hasten to enrol themselves under the standard of his sister, together with the celebrated Cardinal Mendoza,* and all his numerous and powerful adherents.

Thus when Henry died (11th of December, 1474), Isabella was immediately proclaimed queen, and solemnly acknowledged by the Cortes as sovereign in February, 1475. Ferdinand received the title of king, but the exercise of the royal power in Castile belonged solely to the queen, as *reina propietaria*.† Whatever part Ferdinand took in the government of the state, was supposed to emanate from her, and to have her consent. To her exclusively belonged the highest prerogatives, such as the nomination to military commands and ecclesiastical dignities; while on the other hand,

best horsemen in his court, and excelled in field sports of every kind. . . . . . Isabella was a year older than her lover. In stature, she was somewhat above the middle size. Her complexion was fair; her hair of a light chestnut colour, inclining to red; and her mild blue eye beamed with intelligence and sensibility. She was exceedingly beautiful: 'the handsomest lady,' says one of her household, 'whom I ever beheld, and the most gracious in her manners.' The portrait still existing of her in the royal palace is conspicuous for an open symmetry of features, indicative of the natural serenity of temper, and that beautiful harmony of intellectual and moral qualities which most distinguished her."—Prescott, pp. 184-5.

* Archbishop of Toledo.   † Queen proprietor.

public notifications, seals, and the current coin, bore the likeness and the arms united, of both the sovereigns.*

Isabella, in the mean time, did not long occupy the throne in peace; for Archbishop Carillo, who once laboured so much for her exaltation, seeing his hopes frustrated of being able to rule the young queen, owing to the rising influence of Cardinal Mendoza, was resolved to take vengeance. Accordingly, following the example of Oppas, archbishop of Seville, who, in the eighth century, introduced the Moors into Spain, so did Carillo, traitor-like, now invite the Portuguese into his native land, and thereby enkindled the War of Succession, which was as bloody as it was of long continuance. The same Alfonso of Portugal who, eleven years before, was anxious to marry Isabella, now sought the hand of Joanna Beltraneja, who had scarcely reached her thirteenth year. Supported by Carillo and other rebels, he endeavoured by the sword to advance and support her pretended claims to the throne of Castile. Fortune favoured him in the beginning, and already the old archbishop boasted that " he had raised Isabella from the distaff, and would soon send her back to it again." But through the untiring activity of Ferdinand and Isabella, through the generosity of the clergy, who offered half of the ecclesiastical revenues for the defence of the country, and also through the enthusiasm of the people for their sovereign queen, joined to the hatred of the Castilians against the Portuguese, Alfonso was defeated and completely routed at the bloody battle of Toro, in the year 1476. Carillo and the other traitors were obliged to sue for pardon, on most humiliating terms. But peace was not fully

---

* The original marriage contract is in the archives of Simancas, which are now, happily, thrown open to the public.—*Trans.*

established till September, 1479. Ferdinand, by the death of his father (1479), then became king of Arragon, to the great advantage of Castile. Alfonso renounced all claims to the latter kingdom, and to any union with Joanna, to whom the choice was given, either to take the veil or marry Don Juan, the infant son of Ferdinand and Isabella,* as soon as he was of a proper age. On the other hand, a marriage was resolved upon between the young Alonso, son of the prince of Portugal, and the eldest daughter of the Castilian sovereigns, the Infanta Isabella (born 1470) : this union was effected later. Beltraneja, after she had taken the veil in a convent at Coimbra, soon left her cell, in order once more to assert her claims to the throne and the royal dignity; but little attention was paid to her words. She died in the year 1530.†

Thus, while Ximenez was part of his time a prisoner, and during another period of his life ruled the diocese of Sigüenza, there came to the throne of Castile a queen who, with the assistance of Ximenez, was destined by Providence to advance the glory and prosperity of their beloved land.

The first event which promoted the elevation of Ximenez was the capture and conquest of the Moorish kingdom of Granada, in the south of Spain.

The happy issue of the War of Succession had put Isabella in quiet possession of the throne, while numerous reforms in the state, the public prosperity continually on the increase, the consolidation of the regal authority, and the improvement in the

---

* Their son was born June 28th, 1478. (Prescott, note, p. 241.)

† Prescott says that she left her convent, not once only, but several times. She affected a royal style and magnificence, subscribing herself to the last, " I, the queen." She died at Lisbon, in the sixty-ninth year of her age. Señor Clemencin gives many details connected with her history after taking the veil. (Mem. de la Acad., tom. vi. Thes. 19.)

revenue, together with the extinction of the deadly feuds between the nobility,—all these blessings enabled the queen to aim at a still higher object— a nobler enterprise. Assisted by the military experience of her spouse, Isabella now began to direct her thoughts towards the accomplishment of a work which would confer numberless benefits on the Catholic Church, as well as honour and glory on the Spanish crown. It was only with feelings of bitter grief that a Christian could behold the beautiful lands of southern Spain, where the Cross was supplanted by the Crescent, and the Gospel by the Koran; while the Spanish patriot, too, must have wept with no less sorrow when he cast his eyes on the fair city of Granada, then a standing monument of the weakness and degradation of his father-land. Hence it was that for some time the young sovereigns, conscious of their strength, had been maturing their plans for the conquest of the south, and feeding their minds with the hopes of success. The commencement of hostilities, on the part of the Moors, soon gave Ferdinand and Isabella the much wished-for opportunity of accomplishing their designs and realizing their hopes. "I will pick out the seeds of this pomegranate one by one,"* said Ferdinand; and he kept his word.

Muley Abul Hassan† was the first to interrupt the friendly relations hitherto maintained with Castile. In 1481 he surprised the fortress of Zahara, which had been left in a careless state of defence, and carried away the inhabitants as captives to Granada. The capture, by the Castilians, of the rich and strong Moorish fortress of Alhama (in

---

* Granada is the Spanish word for pomegranate. (See Washington Irving's most interesting "History of the Conquest of Granada.")

† He succeeded his father, Aben-Ismael, in 1466. Zahara was a small fortified town on the frontier of Andalusia. (Prescott.)

1482) was the first reprisal for the loss of Zahara.
From this event many far-seeing Moors clearly
perceived and acknowledged that this misfortune
would not be the last punishment inflicted on
them for the violation of the treaty of peace; but
rather that it was the forerunner of still greater
evils: and so it happened. Ferdinand had, indeed,
been repulsed with great loss the same year (1482),
from an attempt made to take the fortress of
Loja,* while a more terrible disaster befell his
little army (in the month of March, the following
year), which caused their almost total destruction,
amongst the defiles of the Axarquia, near Malaga.

These reverses, however, were of short duration.
The Moors were at war amongst themselves. Abu-
Abdallah, or Boabdil, as he is called by the Spanish
writers,† revolted against his own father, Abul-
Hassan, and deprived him of the greater part of his
kingdom, together with the capital. Thus, while
Boabdil reigned in Granada, his father ruled in
Malaga; and thereby the strength of the kingdom
was weakened by such discord.

It was only a month after the defeat of the
Christians in the defiles of Axarquia, that Boabdil
was taken prisoner at the battle of Lucena‡ (21st of

---

* It is not many leagues from Alhama, on the banks of the
Xenil. The city was deeply intrenched among hills, and under
the Moors was defended by a strong fortress. Ferdinand seems
not to have made sufficient preparation for the attack. (See Prescott, vol. i. p. 390.)

† Boabdil was surnamed "el Chico," *the little,* to distinguish
him from an uncle of the same name. (Prescott, note, p. 398,
vol. i.)

‡ "He was discovered after the battle hidden among the reedy
thickets of the river, by a common soldier named Martin Hurtado.
The prince, being instantly attacked, defended himself with his
scimitar, until Hurtado, being joined by two more of his countrymen, succeeded in making him prisoner." (Prescott, p. 422,
vol. i.; and Irving.)

April, 1483). Isabella gave him his liberty, but only on these conditions: "That he should pay a yearly tribute as vassal of Castile; and that he should grant a free passage to the Spanish soldiers, and furnish them with supplies on their march against his father."

His return to Granada renewed the civil war;[*] even in the capital itself, the blood of Moors, shed by Moors, flowed for fifty days and fifty nights successively! "El Zagal," that is, *the Valiant*, had deposed his brother, the old king, and made a violent attempt upon the life of his nephew, Boabdil; while, in the mean time, the Spanish arms began at last, though late, to be crowned with success in every direction. One fortress after another fell into the hands of Isabella; and in August, 1487, Malaga, "the beautiful," was obliged to yield to its conquerors. Two years after, Baza followed the example of Malaga; it was the capital of "El Zagal," who, despairing of any more success, renounced, in December, 1489, the throne of his ancestors. By this event a part of the Moorish kingdom was recovered; the Christians took possession of all the strong cities, and left to the Moors the suburbs and the open plains; and also their property, laws, and customs, as well as allowing them the free exercise of their religion; but only on condition of their paying to the crown of Castile the tribute which their sovereigns had paid before.

To this fortunate success of the war Isabella had contributed as much as the most skilful general.

---

* "The Moors became separated into two hostile factions, headed by the father and the son, and several bloody encounters took place between them; yet they never failed to act, with all their separate force, against the Christians as a common enemy." (Washington Irving's "Conquest of Granada," to which I refer the reader for all the details, which are merely alluded to in the text.)—*Trans.*

Often did she clothe herself in armour, and by her presence inflame the courage of her soldiers; she even surpassed many of the chiefs themselves, by her penetration and invincible perseverance. With indefatigable energy she provided for every necessity, and pledged more than once her very jewels, to provide for the expenses of the war, and levy fresh troops. She took care of the poor, assisted the wounded in their sufferings, and was the first to provide for them what are now called "ambulances"* As this war was not merely political, but also a religious one, Isabella knew how to impress on all hearts the same devout feelings which in past ages animated the soldiers who fought in honour of the Cross. Prayer and religious ceremonies were used, both at the commencement and the close of a battle; no noisy quarrels were ever heard, or gambling allowed, or any "bad character" permitted to be seen in the camp.

Of the entire powerful kingdom that the Moors possessed, the weak Boabdil now retained only half of what it once was. Depending, too, on the crown of Castile—to which he was subject for his protection,—this prince had already promised to deliver up Granada; on condition, however, that "El Zagal" should be obliged to surrender his portion of the kingdom;† Boabdil being reminded by Fer-

---

* What the French style "*hospices ambulans.*" This encomium on Isabella is true to the very letter. At the siege of Baza, Peter Martyr (or, to use his Italian name, Pietro Martire), who was present, speaks in raptures of the order that Isabella preserved in the camp. See his Epistles, lib. ii. epist. 73.—*Trans.*

† Prescott, in his "History," falls into some mistakes respecting this event. These I have pointed out and corrected, in an article which appeared in "Der Tübinger Theol. Quartalschrift," 1843, s. 447. I do not know to what mistakes Dr. Hefele refers.—*Trans.*

dinand that, as the conditions (made at Loja) were fulfilled, the time was now come to surrender Granada. The weak king, however, returned an evasive answer—"That he was no longer free, and could not therefore keep his promise." No doubt there was some truth in these words; for the Moors had all risen up, inspired with new enthusiasm against the Christians; while Granada, protected by its numberless* towers, seemed to bid defiance to the most powerful army.† Indeed, Ferdinand himself, in the first expedition undertaken in 1490, attempted nothing of a decisive character. But in the following year, when the Moors beheld the town of *Santa Fé* ‡ rising opposite to Granada with marvellous rapidity, the presence of the Spaniards clearly convinced them that they were determined not to raise the siege : then it was that the courage of the Moors failed, and all hopes of deliverance vanished.

Isabella had named the new city Santa Fé; because, on the one hand, she looked upon the war as a contest in behalf of the Christian *faith* (fé); and because, on the other, she had a pious and strong *belief* that the whole of the enterprise would be brought to a successful issue. Her hopes were realized ; for, on the 2nd of January, 1492, she entered the capital of the Moorish kingdom, to receive the homage of the

* The text mentions the number at 1,030.

† Washington Irving gives a very beautiful description of Granada.

‡ "The holy faith." In less than three months the town was erected, consisting of solid structures made of stone and mortar, and including, besides, stables for a thousand horses. The town was quadrangular in its form, two spacious avenues intersecting each other at right angles in the centre. The whole army was anxious that the new city should bear the name of their illustrious queen, but Isabella modestly declined the honour, and gave it the name which it still bears.—*Trans.*

last of its sovereigns.* With a heavy sigh, Boabdil bade adieu to the land of his fathers, and looked for the last time on beautiful Granada from an eminence near the city. This place is still called by the Spaniards, " El ultimo Sospiro del Moro."† Boabdil departed on his way to a small principality in the mountains of the Alpuxarras, which was appointed for his abode. But he soon left this place, and returned to Africa—to die amidst his friends.

The remaining population obtained similar, and even milder conditions than did the subjects of " El Zagal " a few years before. Their property, religion, mosques, national manners, customs, and government, remained untouched. The tribute was the same as it was under their own sovereigns; and for the first three years no tax whatever was levied: in addition to these advantages, all who wished to emigrate were at liberty to do so. Thus, after eight hundred years had passed away, the object which every Spaniard most ardently wished for was now attained; the long-standing ignominy of his ancestors was effaced ; and the power of the Moors destroyed —after a war of ten years' continuance, which was compared to that of Troy. The whole of Europe shared in the joy of Spain ; and even secular princes vied with the Holy See in celebrating, with the utmost magnificence and pomp, an event which both interested and gladdened the whole of Christendom. The Pope granted to the two sovereigns,

---

* See all the details in Irving.

† "The last sigh of the Moor." Boabdil did not long remain in Spain. The next year he passed over to Fez with his family, having commuted his petty sovereignty for a considerable sum of money paid him by Ferdinand and Isabella. He soon after fell in battle, in the service of an African prince. (Prescott, vol. ii. p. 85.)

Ferdinand and Isabella, the title of " Catholic Majesties "—Los Reyes Catolicos,—a name which has spread their glory throughout the world.*

* Prescott (vol. ii. p. 87) gives an interesting quotation from Lord Bacon, showing what joy was experienced in England when the news arrived of the conquest of Granada, in the reign of Henry VII.

CHAPTER III.

DURING the ten years of the Moorish war, which had occupied Spain so much, Ximenez had been spending his days in the calm retirement of a monastery: the termination of it was the means of drawing him from his peaceful cell. Indeed, amongst the numberless remarkable consequences of this war, not the least was the fact that Isabella's attention was thereby directed to three illustrious men, destined afterwards to become her greatest and most faithful subjects, and to contribute so much to the undying glory of her reign, as well as to the welfare of Spain itself. The men to whom I allude were,— *Columbus*, who discovered America; the great warrior *Gonsalvo de Cordova*, and *Cardinal Ximenez*. Isabella, rejoicing over the conquest of Granada, and thus encouraged to undertake still greater and nobler enterprises, at last heard the prayers of Columbus, which had remained so long unheeded; and on the 17th of April, 1492, presented him with that small fleet at Santa Fé, which was destined soon to discover a new world.

No less illustrious in history is Gonsalvo de Cordova, truly called " El gran capitano," the great captain. For the first time in the Moorish wars, he it was who displayed those extraordinary talents and that rare genius whereby he performed wonders with such slender resources; and, relying on the strength of his undaunted soul, as well as on the magic influence he possessed over his troops, he it was too who knew, not only how to conquer Naples, but also how to retain it in possession of Spain.

The rise of Ximenez is no less intimately connected with the Moorish wars, though not in such a direct way as those were whom I have already mentioned. An archbishopric had been established in Granada—not only for the benefit of the new Christian colonists who might settle in the conquered land, but also for the conversion of the Moors. The dignity of archbishop had been given by Isabella to her confessor, Fernando de Talavera. If personal virtues, unspotted purity of life, and a remarkable gentleness of character, could enable any one to become the apostle of the Moors, this religious was the man. He was of the order of St. Jerome, and had exchanged his rich bishopric of Avila for the poor see of Granada, generously refusing every indemnification which was offered to him.

Just at this time, Isabella was thinking of choosing another confessor, as pious and prudent as her former one was. Cardinal Mendoza, who had been primate of Toledo since the death of Carillo, now directed the attention of Isabella to Ximenez, whom he had already known and esteemed at Sigüenza. He therefore considered him quite capable of directing the conscience of the queen, and even giving her prudent and wise counsel respecting the affairs of the kingdom, on which it was known that she frequently consulted her confessor. By her particular desire to see this remarkable man, and personally judge of him herself, Cardinal Mendoza ordered Ximenez, under pretence of some urgent business, to hasten to court immediately. The poor Franciscan of Salzeda obeyed the summons;

and after the cardinal had been speaking to him for a long time on various matters, he introduced Ximenez, as it were by accident, and without his suspecting anything, into the apartment of the queen. His modest and recollected appearance, so full of dignity at the same time,—his candour of soul, and the noble sentiments which he manifested in his words,—all tended to fill Isabella with the highest esteem and admiration for Ximenez. But he was still ignorant of the intentions of her majesty, until two days after, being again introduced to the queen, he was informed of her wishes. But he modestly declined an office which he considered both too weighty for him, and also in direct opposition to the plan of life which he had laid out for himself. Isabella, however, insisted on his accepting the office of confessor; and hence Ximenez could no longer refuse. But he obtained permission to remain in his monastery, and to appear at court only when he should be sent for.*

The learned Peter Martyr, of Arona,† who was resident in the court at this time, mentions that this choice gave the queen the greatest pleasure and satisfaction; the Spaniards themselves called their sovereign "happy" in having appointed such a man to be her confessor,—one, too, who "was equal in wisdom to St. Augustine, to St. Jerome in austerity of life, and in zeal to St. Ambrose." Even on the courtiers, the venerable appearance of the pious father made a profound impression, which is thus expressed by Alvarez, the royal secretary of Ferdinand, in a letter written to his friend Peter

---

* See Gomez, lib. i. p. 935; Robles, p. 56; and Fléchier, liv. i. p. 15.

† Dr. Hefele mentions in the text Anghiera; but it is perhaps more correct to say that Peter Martyr was a native of Arona, situated on the borders of Lake Maggiore, in Italy.—*Trans.*

Martyr: "A man of great sanctity," he says, "has come from the depths of a lonesome solitude; he is wasted away by his austerities, and resembles the ancient anchorites, St. Paul and St. Hilarion. He has succeeded the archbishop of Granada." *

The more Ximenez endeavoured to abstain from all interference in political matters, so much the more frequently did Isabella seek his advice, until at last she resolved to execute nothing of importance without having beforehand heard his opinion.

A short time after Ximenez had been chosen the queen's confessor, he was also elected, by the chapter of the Franciscan order, provincial of Old and New Castile. He consented with pleasure to bear the burden of this dignity for the usual term of three years, in order to be able to labour more effectively for the restoration of monastic discipline and austerity; while, at the same time, it would give him an opportunity of not appearing frequently at court.

Upon the recommendation of the guardian of Alcalá, Ximenez had chosen for his secretary and assistant a young and well-informed Franciscan, named Francisco Ruyz. He accompanied Ximenez in his journeys, which he made with untiring zeal and energy through the different parts of his vast province, in the visitation of the monasteries of the order. In performing this duty, Ximenez corrected whatever abuses† had crept in, and by word and

---

* Pietro Martire, Epist. 105 et 108, ed. 1670. In chap. ix. of this work, I shall speak more at length of Peter Martyr. His Italian name is Pietro Martire. (See Prescott's note on him, vol. ii. p. 63.)

† Prescott, it seems to me, greatly exaggerates, as most Protestant writers do, the abuses which had crept into the religious orders previous to the Reformation.—*Trans.*

example encouraged the religious to aim at a more
austere life. All his journeys he made on foot: it
was only when sickness compelled him, and then it
was but seldom, that he made use of a poor mule
to assist him. Faithfully keeping to the strict letter
of his rule, the provincial himself often begged
what was necessary to support him on his journey;
and so often was he obliged to be content with a few
raw roots, that Brother Ruyz once said to him,
with a smiling countenance, — "Most reverend
father, you will certainly be the cause of our dying
through hunger! God gives to every one his particular talent. Do you meditate and pray for me,
while I am begging for you."*

Ruyz, however, understood something more than
begging; for Ximenez soon honoured him with
his friendship, and afterwards recommended him
for a bishop.

On one occasion, when they had arrived at Gibraltar, Ximenez conceived an ardent desire, after
the example of his founder and model, St. Francis
of Assisium, to pass over into Africa and become an apostle, and perhaps a martyr, among the
infidels. But a pious woman, belonging to the
class called "Beatæ,"† appearing to have had
some revelation of his future greatness, advised
him to renounce such a thought, and rather await
the glorious career which was reserved for him in
Spain.

The queen soon recalled him to court, in order
to hear his opinion, and support her in the project
she had formed for a general reformation of all the
religious orders. Ximenez approved of the pro-

---

* Gomez, p. 936; Quintanilla, lib. i. cap. 10; Fléchier, liv. i.
p. 16.

† So the Spaniards called those who belonged to the third order
of St. Francis.

ject with all the energy of his character; and this he did the more willingly because the religious orders in Spain stood in great need of a thorough reform.

The Franciscan order was the first to which he immediately directed his attention, for his recent visitation had shown him into what a deplorable state it had fallen. Not only were most of the monasteries in the hands of the " Conventuals,"* who were considered very lax, but the greater part of the religious seem to have entirely forgotten the practice of penance and apostolic poverty, in order to lead an idle and luxurious life in magnificent houses. Supported by the royal authority, Ximenez especially endeavoured to transform the Conventuals into " Observantines," so called because they adhered to the primitive rule. He then took away from the monasteries all the possessions which they were not allowed to retain: he expelled the unworthy members, and endeavoured to induce the better disposed to embrace the reform. To many he offered pensions, if they should wish to leave the order, and make room for others who would be willing to lead an austere life. This offer was accepted by the Franciscans of Toledo, who, as if in mockery of Ximenez, solemnly sang, on leaving their monastery, the psalm, " In exitu Israel de Ægypto,"† &c.

A thousand calumnies would be sure to assail a reformer placed in such circumstances, engaged

---

* Those who did not adhere to the primitive rule of the order.

† " Y he oido a personas muy graves, que los Frayles Claustrales de San Francisco de Toledo, el dia que salieron desterrados de aquella Ciudad, llevavan una Cruz delante, y iban cantando el Psalmo (113) 'In exitu Israel de Ægypto,' &c."— (Robles, " Compendio de la Vida y Hazañas del Cardenal Don Fray Francisco Ximenez de Cisneros," Toledo, 1604, p. 68.)

in a contest against relaxed orders, and with men who preferred the good things of this life to the austerities of their rule. But Ximenez pursued his path unmoved, until at length his elevation to the archiepiscopal see of Toledo gave him opportunities of attaining his object.

CHAPTER IV.

XIMENEZ BECOMES ARCHBISHOP OF TOLEDO.

WHILE Isabella and her pious confessor were zealously carrying on the reform of the Franciscan order, Cardinal Mendoza fell ill; in consequence of which he retired to his native town, Guadalaxara, in order to enjoy its invigorating air, and to have some repose away from the cares of state. Not long after, towards the end of the year 1494, Ferdinand and Isabella paid a visit to their sick minister. They had a long interview with him, during which he left them, as it were, his last political will; for he spoke to them on the future government of the kingdom, as well as leaving them excellent rules to be followed out after his death. Amongst other matters, he told them, in an especial manner, what his ideas were respecting his successor in the see of Toledo.*

The archbishop of Toledo was both primate of Spain and chancellor of Castile: his revenues † were immense, his vassals numerous; while the towns and fortified places belonging to him were no less so. Possessing this double capacity, the archbishop was, no doubt, after the king, the first and most influential personage in the kingdom; and when he placed himself at the head of the nobility,

---

* Gomez, p. 938.

† Prescott estimates the revenue at 80,000 ducats, in the beginning of the sixteenth century. Isabella annexed the dignity of High Chancellor to that of Archbishop of Toledo; but, in later times, it seems to have been a mere honorary title. (Vol. ii. note, p. 343.)

in opposition to the throne, then the king himself frequently had cause to tremble. In a kingdom so completely aristocratic as Castile was, at the time of Isabella coming to the throne,—when the sovereign did not surpass the grandees in their revenues, and was but a little above them in power and importance,—the primate and chancellor held as high a position as did formerly the archbishop of Guesen in Poland. Hence it was that Mendoza, though belonging himself to the highest nobility, advised the queen not to appoint, for the future, to such an important see any one of a noble family, but only a person of great virtue belonging to the respectable middle class. As a confirmation of his opinion, he mentioned the example of Alfonso Carillo, his predecessor, who at one time was feared both by Isabella and her brother Henry, and had shaken even the throne itself. It is supposed that Mendoza recommended to the queen, as the fittest person to succeed to the see of Toledo, her present pious confessor. A few days subsequent to this interview, the great cardinal died (January 11th, 1495),* after a year of sufferings. For a period of twenty years he had served Isabella and her consort as a faithful minister; and had exercised such great influence over the affairs of the kingdom, as to be playfully called " the third king of Spain."

In his youth his manners were not irreproachable; for, alas! at that period the Spanish clergy were somewhat lax : but his numerous virtues afterwards blotted out every stain : his immense revenues were devoted to the advancement of science and the comfort of the poor; while he himself laboured with all his strength, and with

---

* Both Gomez and Peter Martyr, not to mention other writers, give the highest character of the illustrious cardinal. (See Gomez, " De Rebus Gestis," fol. 9 ; also, Peter Martyr, Epist. 158.)

an admirable sagacity, for the prosperity of the State : in a word, his sweetness and modesty gained for him every heart. Hence his name was no less loved in Spain, than it was celebrated in foreign countries; while the queen herself showed the illustrious dead the greatest mark of her respect, by undertaking in person the execution of his will.

The necessity of appointing some one to occupy the archiepiscopal see was now the object of Isabella's serious consideration; for, since her marriage, she had reserved to herself the nomination to all ecclesiastical dignities. She felt, therefore, the deep responsibility which was attached to the exercise of a right that was so frequently dangerous in the hands of sovereigns. Though she did not forget the advice which Mendoza had given her, yet, in a matter of such great consequence, she was anxious to hear the opinion of her prudent confessor. Ximenez differed widely from the advice given by Mendoza. It was his decided opinion, that for such a dignity only a person belonging to the highest class of the nobility should be chosen : he accordingly advised the queen to appoint the nephew of the late archbishop of Seville, Diego Hurtado Mendoza. Ferdinand, on the other hand, was most anxious to have the rich dignity bestowed on his natural son, Alfonso of Arragon, who, from the time he was six years old, occupied the archiepiscopal see of Saragossa, in spite of every remonstrance;* having been appointed by Ferdinand himself, in his hereditary states of Arragon. Though

---

* Mariana (lib. xxiv. cap. 16) mentions that Sixtus IV. had made great opposition to the appointment, and had even refused the dispensation; but that Ferdinand and the king of Naples had compelled him to acknowledge the Infant as perpetual administrator of the archbishopric. (See also Ferrera's " History of Spain," tom. vii.)

Isabella was, on the whole, careful to pay every deference to the wishes of her consort, and though there could be no doubt of the talents of Alfonso, yet his youth (he was only in his 24th year), and his somewhat scandalous life, forbade Isabella from agreeing to the wishes of Ferdinand : hence every entreaty, and even flattery and indignation, on the part of the king, were all unable to alter the resolution of the queen. She placed more confidence in a lawyer, named Oropesa, who had resigned a place in the cabinet of her majesty, in order the more easily to spend his days in prayer and meditation. Ximenez also spoke in favour of this person. The decree for his nomination was already drawn out, and even a courier had been sent to Rome to solicit the confirmation, when Isabella suddenly changed her arrangement. This was accounted for, either from the great age of Oropesa, which probably influenced the decision of the queen, or from the fact that the good old man himself, as some writers mention, requested to be exempted from the dignity. At the same time, Isabella now immediately resolved to raise her own confessor to the vacant see. She therefore sent, without his knowledge, a second courier to Rome, with an order to her ambassador there not to forward the first appointment, but to obtain the necessary bulls for the elevation of Ximenez. A short time after the pope held a consistory, and acceded to the wishes of Isabella : the bulls were accordingly despatched to Madrid, in the Lent of 1495, where the court was then residing. On Good-Friday, Ximenez, after he had heard the confession of the queen, was preparing himself to leave his convent at Madrid, in order to spend the holy days in retirement at Ocaña, when one of her majesty's chamberlains unexpectedly summoned him to the palace.

He immediately obeyed, hoping soon to obtain leave of absence. Isabella, however, to his great astonishment, after speaking with him for a long time on many indifferent things, presented the papal bulls to him, with these words: "Reverend father, you will see by these letters what are the commands of his holiness." Ximenez kissed them with the greatest reverence (as is the usual custom in the Catholic Church) before he began to read them. When he opened them and saw the superscription, running thus—"To our venerable brother Francisco Ximenez de Cisneros, archbishop elect of Toledo," he changed colour, and immediately left the chamber, saying, "These letters are not for me," without even taking leave of Isabella, who contented herself with replying in a kind manner: "Allow me to see what his holiness has written to you." She wished the first emotions of surprise to subside, in order to give Ximenez an opportunity of more easily collecting his thoughts. He hastened, however, to Ocaña, without saying anything to his companion, Ruyz, but these words: "Come, brother, we must leave here as soon as possible."*

A short time after, the queen, supposing that Ximenez was still in Madrid, sent two of the head chamberlains of the court to his Franciscan convent, in order to induce him to accept the offered dignity. When, however, they were informed that the provincial † had already departed for Ocaña, they hastened after him with all speed, and overtook him about three miles from Madrid. Though they succeeded, after a long interview, in persuading the good father to return, yet he persisted again, with

---

* Gomez (pp. 10, 11), Robles (cap. xiii. pp. 76, 77), and Fléchier (pp. 35, 36, 37) give a few more interesting details, which Dr. Hefele omits.—*Trans.*

† Ximenez, who was then provincial of his order.

the greatest firmness, in refusing the dignity. The "Nolo episcopari" has indeed passed into a proverb. But the resolution of Ximenez to remain a religious, and to work out his salvation in the solitude of a monastery, was so clearly without the affectation observable in others, and his refusal of the dignity was so long maintained, that the queen considered it necessary to complain to the pope on the subject. Six months had already passed away; and in the mean time, while the court had fixed its residence in Burgos, there arrived a new papal brief, which commanded the provincial, by virtue of canonical obedience, immediately to accept the archbishopric. Thus a very unworthy pope* (Alexander VI.) was instrumental in commanding one of the most eminent men of the time to occupy the primatial see of Spain.

As further opposition was no longer permitted, Ximenez allowed himself to be solemnly consecrated on the octave of the Feast of St. Francis, October 11th, 1495, in a convent of his order, at Tarazona, in the presence of the two sovereigns, and amidst the acclamation of all good people.

After the ceremony was concluded, the newly consecrated prelate, according to custom, went to kiss the hands of Ferdinand and Isabella. In doing so, he used these few but memorable words: "I come to kiss the hands of your majesties,† not because they have raised me to the first see in Spain, but because I hope they will assist me in supporting the burden which they have placed on my shoulders." Full of emotion, the two sovereigns, and after them all the grandees of the court, respect-

---

* This expression I consider uncalled for, as it is not used by any of the biographers of Ximenez.—*Trans.*

† Charles V. was the first king of Spain who took the title of "Majesty."

fully kissed in their turn the anointed hands of the new prelate, who devoutly gave them his blessing. He was then conducted with great pomp to his palace.

It is remarkable, that while Ximenez in his youth sought after humble ecclesiastical dignities, they seemed to fly from him, and were even the cause of his being confined in a prison. But when, on the other hand, he began to despise them, then the highest honours followed his steps, and were forced upon him quite in opposition to his wishes. Scarcely had twelve years passed away since the death of the proud Carillo, and already had that poor priest, whom he detained in prison for six long years on account of a paltry benefice, inherited the power and the dignity of his persecutor. And now, again though more than three hundred years have passed away, the name of Ximenez is still remembered by every well-informed person with respect, while that of Carillo has long since been forgotten.

CHAPTER V.

MATURED by experience, and with a soul strengthened by mortification, Ximenez took possession of
the archiepiscopal see of Toledo, in the fifty-ninth
year of his age. As bishop, reformer of religious
orders, promoter and patron of science, and a great
statesman, Ximenez was destined to effect immense
good in all these different capacities. Like all true
reformers, he began by reforming himself, and so
giving in his own life and conversation an example
and a pattern to others. "A bishop," says St. Paul,
" is one that ruleth well his own house (1 Tim.
iii. 4). Ximenez so faithfully followed this injunction, that we may, without the least hesitation,
compare him to St. Charles Borromeo, and other
heroes of the Church, who were poor in the midst
of riches, hermits in the midst of the world, and
models of mortification amidst pomp and luxury.

Let us, then, contemplate this extraordinary man
in the interior of his house, before we consider
him and his actions on the great theatre of the
world.

Being a Franciscan heart and soul, Ximenez was
anxious, in his present new dignity, to realize in his
own person the apostolic poverty and religious
austerity of the glorious founder of his order, and
thus to combine the dignity of a bishop with the
simplicity of a monk. No silver, therefore, adorned
his table, nor was any ornament to be seen on the
walls of his apartments : nowhere could be found

the least trace of luxury,—nowhere the least symptom of pomp or riches. His garment was the Franciscan habit, and his food only such as the poorest monastery affords. The journeys which he was obliged to make were always performed on foot, though occasionally he made use of a mule, as most poor Spanish priests do. His palace was changed into a monastery, while only ten Franciscan monks composed the staff of one who was both primate and chancellor.*

But as wasps settle on the ripest fruit, so great fault was found with the archbishop's manner of life. Some blamed him for not having correct notions of his high dignity, while others accused him of pride and hypocrisy : both parties, however, agreed that his dignity and the respect which was due to the high rank he held in church and state were considerably diminished by his present mode of life. The good and the evil-disposed carried, at last, their complaint before the Holy See ; in consequence of which Alexander VI., in a brief, which, perhaps, is the only one on record of its kind, dispenses a follower of the apostles from his apostolic poverty and simplicity.†   It runs thus :—

"*To our well-beloved Son Francis, Archbishop Elect of Toledo, health and apostolical benediction.*

" You are not ignorant, venerable brother, that the holy and universal Church is decorated with many

---

* Prescott relates the following anecdote from Quintanilla. " On one occasion, as Ximenes was travelling, and up, as usual, long before dawn, he urged his muleteer to dress himself quickly : at which the latter irreverently exclaimed—' Cuerpo de Dios ! does your holiness think I have nothing more to do than shake myself like a wet spaniel, and tighten my cord a little ?' " (See Gomez, Robles, and Fléchier, for further particulars of his life.)

† This expression is hardly correct, as is evident by the Pope's brief.—*Trans.*

and various ornaments, like unto the heavenly Jerusalem, in which, if excess is blamable, one may err by trying to avoid the opposite extreme. A due observance of what belongs to each one's state of life is pleasing to God, and consequently deserving of praise. Every one, therefore, and especially prelates of the Church, ought so to regulate their mode of life, their dress, and whole exterior, that no one may be able to accuse them either of pride through an excessive magnificence, or of an abject mind through too great plainness and simplicity, inasmuch as both these faults weaken the authority of ecclesiastical discipline.

" Wherefore, as the Holy See hath raised you from an inferior state to the archiepiscopal dignity, and as we greatly rejoice to hear that you lead a life according to God and your conscience, we now exhort you, venerable brother, outwardly to conform yourself to the dignity of your state of life, in your dress, attendants, and everything else relating to the promotion of that respect due to your authority.

"Given at Rome, under the Fisherman's seal, the 15th of December, 1495, in the 4th year of our pontificate." *

It was with great reluctance that Ximenez changed his mode of life, in obedience to the exhortation of the pontiff. But because he thought it his duty to obey, and nothing was further from his intention than to do anything injurious to the dignity

---

* This brief is found in Gomez (fol. 13), Quintanilla, Raynald's Continuation of Baronius (ad annum 1495), and Wadding, "Annales Minorum," tom. xv. I suspect that the date, 15th of December, is incorrect; for Ximenez had then been consecrated two months. Fléchier is certainly mistaken in assigning the 15th of September, 1496, as the date of the brief; for Ximenez had then been consecrated more than a year. Perhaps, if we were to assign the 15th of September, 1495, as the date, it would be more in accordance with the word "elect," found in the address.

of his ecclesiastical position, hence, for the future, he was resolved to display in public a certain magnificence, more in accordance with his high office. But at the same time he preserved in private all his former austerity. Towards the end of the Middle Age, a fondness for pomp, dress, and luxury seemed to prevail more than at any other period. This was especially the case with the Spaniards, who, having been accustomed under the Moors to a quasi-Asiatic pomp, carried outward magnificence beyond all bounds. Even the greatest men of the time, like the " Great Captain," were persuaded that they could only uphold and strengthen the fame of their illustrious deeds by an extravagant display of pomp and boastful splendour. Only a few exalted minds, like Isabella and Ximenez, remained uncontaminated by the general contagion. But as the queen did not hesitate to appear in public with royal pomp whenever the respect due to her rank seemed to require it, so did Ximenez, after he had received the papal injunction, and heard the complaints made against him, consider it necessary to yield in some degree to the weakness and prejudices of his countrymen. He accordingly now appeared clad in furs and silk garments, though under his splendid robes he always continued to wear, close to his body, the coarse garment used in his order; and this he himself repaired from time to time, that so he might always be reminded of his own nothingness. In like manner did Pius VII., when a captive in France, practise the same humility; but while the French ridiculed the virtue of the pontiff, the contemporaries of Ximenez knew how to appreciate this same virtue more sincerely; for, after his death, a small box, in which Ximenez kept his thread and needle, was found, and was carefully preserved as a relic.

In the archbishop's palace were indeed to be seen

magnificent beds, covered with silk and purple, the posts of which were richly ornamented with ivory and gold. The archbishop, however, was accustomed to sleep either on the bare floor or on a plank, with his habit on; and this austere practice he carefully concealed from his domestics, by never allowing any one of them to enter his sleeping-room. But an accident once led to the discovery of his secret; so that the mortification which the holy man practised upon himself was thus very soon known throughout the country.

Magnificent banquets were now more frequently given by the prince of the Church; but, whilst his table could scarcely bear the multitude of good things provided for his guests, he himself partook very sparingly of food, and that was of the plainest kind. Pages belonging to the first families of the Spanish nobility constantly attended the illustrious prelate; but for his own immediate wants he had, according to his former custom, no other servant but himself. He also took especial care of the proper education of these young nobles.

He filled up all his time with labour, prayer, and study.* After attending to state affairs, he returned again to his breviary with fresh vigour and devotion; he offered the holy sacrifice every day, was frequently present in the choir, and gave the preference to the plain chant before every kind of harmonized music; he was particularly fond of praying in a small dim chapel, the stillness of which penetrated the depth of his soul. Daily did he peruse, on his knees, some chapters of the Holy Scriptures; and numberless times in the day did he also gaze on a crucifix which was attached to his

---

* These and other edifying details are taken from Gomez, Fléchier, and Quintanilla. The Spaniards, at the present day, revere Ximenez as a saint.— *Trans.*

arm by a string: he considered it as a preservative against sin. A promenade was the only relaxation which he allowed himself, and this he took but seldom; while, on the other hand, he daily entertained himself with pious conversations, which he held with his religious brethren around him, and other theologians. He likewise, from time to time, renewed his fervour by making a retreat in some monastery of his order; and there, like the humblest of the brothers, he performed with them all the religious exercises, made his confession, and took the discipline. In a secret chamber of his palace he also frequently used the discipline with such severity on his body that Pope Leo X. was obliged to interfere. He seldom wore anything but a hair-shirt next his skin.

As his poverty had been blamed before, so many now found fault with the splendour of his appearance in public; so much so that Father Contrera once forgot himself to such a degree as to make, in his sermon before Ximenez, a bitter and improper allusion to a. rich fur which he wore at the time. After he had finished his discourse, Ximenez, having shown the preacher his hair-shirt with his usual calmness, the officious accuser was confounded.

But all the discontented were not so easily reduced to silence; even from the religious of his own order Ximenez had to endure many contradictions, and especially from those who composed his household. A deep pride often lies concealed under the poorest habit; and this pride had accordingly so far deceived many Franciscans as to raise in them great expectations of receiving from their brother, now so highly exalted, all kind of favours, honours, dignities, bishoprics, &c. The inmates of his palace were in a particular manner so bent upon realizing their projects as to have recourse to mean intrigues.

Ximenez alone was so much opposed to any blind partiality for his order, that on the contrary, through a real love for its welfare, he was anxious to remove far from it all honours and dignities, because he considered them as so many "rocks" that were dangerous to the monastic life. He was also very careful not to allow his brethren in religion the least influence in the management of his diocese; and hence, while he often spoke with them in the most friendly manner on the affairs of the order, he constantly preserved a strict silence in their presence respecting his plans and affairs. As was to be expected, the complaints of humbled pride and disappointed hopes were loud and constant. It was said, "that he was a hard man, incapable of friendship, and distrustful, whose high position did a great deal more harm than good to the order." Ximenez, however, remained silent and immovable. The only step he took was to send seven out of the ten Franciscans who composed his household, one after the other, quietly back to their monastery, and to retain only three, one of whom was Francisco Ruyz. One was appointed his almoner, another his confessor, and the third his chaplain. They afterwards became bishops, by the recommendation of Ximenez, united with their own virtues, and attained, besides, other ecclesiastical dignities. We shall see, a little further on, how the Franciscans whom he had dismissed wickedly sought to be revenged upon him.

But amongst all his domestics, none gave him so much trouble as his own beloved brother, Bernardin. At the time when Ximenez lived in his monastery, Bernardin was wandering round the world without any employment. At last he entered, as it were by chance, into the Franciscan order, wherein he displayed such great fervour, that Ximenez not only

forgave his past errors, but granted him considerable authority in his palace. But his violent temper
soon changed him into a despot, and urged him on
to a series of most foolish and ill-judged actions.
By his coarseness he offended the archbishop, as
well as his friends and officers of the household ; by
his own authority he drove the servants from the
palace ; and when Ximenez remonstrated with him,
he became insolent, and more than once retired in
his passion to his monastery till the heat of his anger
had cooled. Ximenez, however, always received him
back again with renewed kindness and friendship,
without adverting in any way to the past. But on
one occasion Bernardin left the archbishop's house
in such a passion that, having arrived at Guadalfa-
jara, he there published a libel against his brother,
with the intention of presenting it to the queen on
the first opportunity. Ximenez, on receiving information of his design, immediately ordered him to be
arrested, confiscated all his papers, suppressed the
libel, and imprisoned the calumniator for two years,
until at last he began to show signs of repentance,
and promised to amend for the future. This severe
lesson, however, did not tame the spirit of Bernardin ; on the contrary, it left such feelings of hatred
in his heart, as to urge him on to still deeper crimes.
Once, when Ximenez was ill at Alcalá, Bernardin
mixed himself up, against the express command of
his brother, with a lawsuit that was carried on in
the archbishop's court ; and so violent and over-
bearing was his conduct, that he induced the judges
to pronounce an unjust sentence. Ximenez, having
been informed by the injured party of what had
taken place, immediately ordered the acts of the
process to be brought before him ; he annulled the
sentence, dismissed the judges, and resolved to
punish his peevish brother. The displeasure which

he felt at this event had evidently increased his sickness, and so preyed upon his feeble frame that, when Bernardin came into his presence, Ximenez forgot his usual calmness of mind, especially when he heard his brother assert that he was in the right, and even accuse the archbishop of injustice. Angry words arose; and when Ximenez threatened to imprison Bernardin, his anger knew no bounds; and, not being master of himself, he seized his sick brother by the throat, with both hands endeavouring to choke him. Whether it was that he supposed he had murdered him,* or that in some degree he began to be conscience-stricken, leaving the archbishop half-dead, he quietly left the chamber, commanded the servant outside not to make any noise, lest the archbishop might be disturbed in his sleep, and concealed himself in a cave, awaiting the result.

One of the pages, however, named Avellaneda, having heard the dispute, and noticed an extraordinary agitation in Bernardin, immediately hastened into the chamber of his master. Finding him in a senseless state, he instantly summoned the physicians. Under their treatment, the archbishop soon came round; but he solemnly assured them, that it was far better for him to have been exposed to such imminent danger of death, than to have tolerated an act of injustice. He then mentioned the guilty party, ordered him to be sent in chains to Turrigio, near Toledo, and there shut up in a poor monastery. Bernardin never afterwards dared to appear in the presence of his deeply injured brother, though some time after the latter restored him to liberty, at the request of King Ferdinand, and bestowed on him a

---

* Fléchier seems to attribute to Bernardin the intention of really murdering his brother, as if he had harboured it for a long time. But the supposition is not well founded, besides being very improbable. (See Gomez, fol. 16.)

handsome pension.* His faithful page he took care of, by giving him an excellent education, and providing for him during the rest of his life. Bernardin survived the archbishop several years. Gomez, the historian of Ximenez, mentions, that when he was a boy, he once saw Bernardin at Alcala (Complutum); he was then a very old man, and was living quietly in that place; he was of slender stature, had a bold look, and eyes particularly red and inflamed, with a long crooked nose.†

Ximenez received more consolation from his second brother John, who, in accordance with the wishes of Ximenez, married an excellent lady belonging to a noble family. Don Juan Zapala, brother of the Count Barajas, having died an early death, left behind him a daughter who had received a very good education: her name was Eléonore; and her mother was anxious to form an alliance with the family of the great cardinal, who, as he was not opposed to the union, permitted the marriage to take place, soon after, between his brother John and Eléonore. The archbishop provided the new family with everything necessary, though without any superfluities. This same family still exists in Spain; and not long ago an illustrious descendant of it, Lieutenant-General Sir David Ximenez, died in the English service, in Berkshire, August, 1848, aged 71.‡

* Gomez mentions the sum; viz. "Octogena numûm millia," which probably amounted to 800 ducats.—*Trans.*

† "Hunc ego Bernardinum extremam penè senectam agentem puer olim Compluti vidi; molli otio et genio indulgentem. Erat staturâ procerâ, fronte perfricta, vultu mirum in modum rubro flammeoque, naso prælongo et incurvo; oculis introrsum reductis, totiusque corporis firma quidem compactione, sed macra." (Gomez, "De Rebus Gestis," fol. 16.)

‡ Dr. Hefele refers to the "Augsburg Allg. Zeitung," No. 246, p. 3917. I have endeavoured to discover some further particulars respecting Sir David Ximenez.—*Trans.*

E

CHAPTER VI.

THE FIRMNESS OF THE NEW ARCHBISHOP, WHO TAKES A PART IN THE AFFAIRS OF STATE FOR THE FIRST TIME.

FIFTEEN rich cities, besides a considerable number of small towns and villages, formed the princely domain of the archbishop of Toledo; in consequence of which, he had many civil officers and judges under him. But, as after the death of Cardinal Mendoza the privileges and functions of these persons ceased, so the new archbishop took the opportunity of sending certain experienced delegates around the province, for the purpose of establishing in all the fortresses, castles, and towns, faithful governors, besides conscientious judges and administrators; and also that they might receive their oaths of fidelity in his name.

It was about this time that Ximenez exhibited such a remarkable proof of the independence with which he intended to act in all affairs. This determination was so much the more necessary, as men are naturally inclined to impose all kind of claims on a poor *parvenu*. And, moreover, amongst many abuses which then prevailed in Spain, a very bad custom had crept in, of bestowing dignities and employments, not on account of personal merit, but through the protection of exalted grandees and the intrigues of favourites. Being justly grieved at such a monstrous abuse, Ximenez was resolved to turn a deaf ear to all entreaties from such quarters; and hence he seized upon the first opportunity of publicly manifesting his dislike, by an example that would plainly deter others from following it.

One of the most honourable and lucrative posts which it was in the power of the archbishop to bestow was the government of Cazorla, which the late cardinal had given to his brother, Pedro Hurtado Mendoza. He was a man of great merit, honesty, and talent; having besides every reason to expect kindness and favours from the new archbishop, who was much indebted to his late brother. However, he thought proper to seek the goodwill of the queen first; and then he sent some of his friends to Ximenez to remind him of the wish of Isabella, that he should continue to hold his present office; and also to recall to his mind the many acts of kindness which he had received from the late cardinal. But Ximenez received the deputation in such a manner, that he clearly and firmly declared to them, " He would rather renounce his see itself, than lose the free choice of his officers and servants." The members of the deputation, sent by Mendoza, returned disappointed and exasperated, and related the cardinal's reply to the queen. She calmly listened to what they said, appearing to understand well what were the intentions of her pious but firm archbishop.

Some days after, Ximenez met Don Pedro Hurtado at court, and remarking that he tried to avoid him, he went up to him in a friendly manner, and saluted him as governor of Cazorla, saying :— " As I am now perfectly free, I confirm you in your office, and am confident that for the future you will serve the queen, the state, and the archbishop with the same fidelity that you formerly displayed under your illustrious brother." From that time both continued to live on the best of terms, and Ximenez honoured and loved his faithful governor during all his life.[*]

But, in other matters, the affairs of state began to occupy the attention of the new chancellor soon after his elevation to the title. Just at this period, events of the greatest importance for the future of Spain, as well as for the history of the world itself, were on the point of taking place. Ferdinand and Isabella had already concluded those historical alliances with Maximilian I., emperor of Germany, the result of which in a short time was to unite in the person of Charles V. the Spanish and Austrian crowns, and thus form one of the greatest European powers. Don Juan, the Spanish prince, and eldest son of Ferdinand and Isabella, was united with Margaret, the daughter of Maximilian; while, on the other side, the Archduke Philip le Bel, son and heir of the same Maximilian, was espoused to the Spanish Infanta, Joanna. From this last marriage came Charles V., who, after the death of all his near relations, succeeded to the inheritance of both his ancestors.

It is now impossible to ascertain what part Ximenez took in the final adjustment of these alliances. But there is no doubt they occupied his attention very much; for it was only after their arrangement that he was able to proceed to Toledo, and take possession of his cathedral. It seems certain that he was present with Ferdinand and Isabella at Tortosa,[†] where, in the year 1496, the last clauses of the alliances were agreed upon; at least, it is certain that about the middle of July, in the same year, he accompanied the queen to Burgos, in order to make the necessary arrangements for the departure of the Princess Joanna to Flanders. But

---

[*] Fléchier, liv. i. pp. 40, 41.   [†] See Ferreras, tom. viii. c. 11.

as the queen conducted her daughter to the port of Laredo, Ximenez then obtained permission (which he had long desired) to spend some time in his diocese, and then to proceed to Alcalá, the usual residence of the archbishops of Toledo. When, however, the queen returned to Burgos, her grand chancellor was obliged to come there also, in order to perform the solemn ceremony of the marriage of Prince Juan with Margaret of Austria : this took place April 3, 1497. Ximenez had before obtained permission to remain a little longer in his diocese ; but the queen was unwilling that so important a marriage should be performed by any one, except by the primate of the kingdom.

An unfortunate accident, however, detained Ximenez at Burgos longer than he expected. During one of the magnificent tournaments, Alonso de Cardenas lost his life through a fall from his horse. The archbishop was accordingly compelled to console both the deeply afflicted father and the queen herself, who was overpowered with grief for the poor father. Few crowned heads ever took such a deep and sincere interest in their servants as this admirable queen did. She had a particular esteem for the father of the unfortunate Alonso, whose fidelity towards her she experienced when his services were required, in order to hasten her marriage with Ferdinand of Aragon, and to overcome the difficulties which opposed it.

After Ximenez had fulfilled his duties at Burgos, he went to Toledo, and thence to Alcalá, in order at last to take solemn possession of his cathedral church, and to draw up some useful regulations for his diocese.* In the mean time, he always had his attention fixed on the affairs of state ; and every one

* These we shall speak of more at length in Chapter XIV.

was convinced that when he came to court, he came only for the good of the people; indeed, their welfare was the object of his constant care and vigilance. As far as his power extended, he removed all the abuses which were made known to him, while others he mentioned to the queen herself; he protected the poor and the weak against oppression and injustice; he was also in a special manner the terror of corrupt officers and servants, whose arbitrary conduct and illegal acts he denounced to the queen, without the least scruple. Amongst the numerous benefits which he conferred upon the country, an alteration in the mode of collecting certain taxes drew down blessings upon him from the people.

The Moorish wars had introduced some necessary but extraordinary kinds of taxation in the kingdom of Castile, which had now continued for about a century. The most burdensome of all, and that which completely clogged all commercial business, was a tax called Alcavala. The law was, that the tenth part of everything sold or exchanged should be given to the exchequer. This unjust tax was rendered still more burdensome by the manner in which it was collected; the constant intrigues of the functionaries, and also by the tricks, the lies, and false oaths of the buyers and sellers. It was impossible at that time totally to abolish the hateful impost, however earnestly Ximenez may have wished it; nevertheless, at his suggestion, it underwent an important alteration,* which was this:—the whole revenue of the tax was fixed at a certain sum, and an equitable distribution of it made amongst the

* Ximenez, a short time before his death, sent a pressing letter to Charles V. for the abolition of the Alcavala, but without success. It was, doubtless, in accordance with the suggestions of the cardinal that Isabella recommended in her will the speedy abolition of this tax. (See Prescott, vol. ii.)

towns and villages, according to their relative size and condition; while the citizens themselves collected the tax in their own localities, and the whole band of publicans were dismissed from their office. This excellent plan Ximenez was enabled to carry out by the help of Don Lopez de Biscaja, one of the most illustrious and clever financiers of that time. Both the citizens and the exchequer gained by this arrangement; while an immense number of odious salaries were suppressed, and a multitude of vexations and contentions ceased; so that by this happy change every one rejoiced that a new era of prosperity and happiness had dawned.

In the mean time, while Ximenez was holding his first synod,—of which we shall speak a little later,—events of the gravest importance happened in the royal family, which required the particular attention of the great chancellor, and also his presence at court. On the 3rd of April, he had blessed the union of Don Juan with Margaret of Austria; and only six months after, the prince died, in the 19th year of his age,* having raised the highest expectations of his future greatness. A fever which seized him at Salamanca, immediately after his marriage, overpowered his weak constitution, and caused his death, October 4th, 1497; an end being thus put to a life which was adorned by a love for the arts and sciences. The physicians ascribed the origin of the malady to a too great fondness for the company of his beautiful consort.† His preceptor, Peter Martyr, who gives us these details with tears, adds that Queen Isabella would never consent to a separation of the newly married

---

* He was born 30th of June, 1478.
† "Die Aerzte wolten die Quelle des Uebels in dem zu häufigen Umgange des jungen Prinzen mit seinen Schönen Gemahlin gefunden haben," &c. (p. 50).

couple—contrary to the wishes of the physicians, to whom she replied :—" What God has joined together, let no man separate." The prince gave up all hopes of recovery after the first attack ; he was also the first to console his afflicted parents.*

A short time after, Margaret gave birth to a dead child ; and thus the right of succession to the Spanish throne passed to the eldest daughter of Ferdinand and Isabella, whose name was the same as that of her mother ; not long before, she had been espoused to Don Emanuel, king of Portugal. In the mean time, it seemed as if the Archduke Philip, who was married to the second daughter of Joanna, wished to assert his claim to the title of " Prince of Castile," in consequence of the death of his brother-in-law. In order to have a proper understanding on the subject, and that all troublesome disputes might be avoided, Ferdinand and Isabella immediately summoned the Cortes of Castile to meet at Toledo, and that of Aragon to meet at Saragossa. They also invited the Queen of Portugal and her consort to come and receive in person the homage of the States.

Ximenez, in accordance with his dignity as High Chancellor, took a considerable part in all these proceedings : he assisted at both the meetings of the Cortes ; and at that which was held at Toledo on the part of Castile (April 29, 1498), he received the customary oaths, in concert with the grand constable of the kingdom.†

It was more difficult to obtain the homage of the inhabitants of the kingdom of Aragon than that of Castile, because in the former the laws forbade the succession of women. As soon, therefore, as the

* Petrus Martyr, Epp. 176—182. The Epistles of this celebrated scholar are very valuable.—*Trans.*
† Ferreras, book viii. tom. ii. p. 190.

Cortes at Toledo was dissolved, Ferdinand and Isabella took Ximenez with them to Saragossa, although his authority as Grand Chancellor extended only to Castile, not to Aragon. They were unwilling, however, to be deprived of the advice of their wise minister; for, just at this time, they indeed stood in greatest need of it. Opinions were divided; and no decided advance towards an arrangement seemed likely to be made, when the object of all the contention, the young Isabella, died in child-birth, August 23, 1498. Ximenez had prepared her for death. The last words of the noble princess were a request to the archbishop not to forget to give all the consolation he could to her parents. This mournful duty he fulfilled; he also used the greatest diligence in procuring the homage of Aragon for the young motherless Infant, named Miguel. In accordance with the advice of Ximenez, the prince was conducted with royal pomp, in a litter, through the streets of Saragossa, and thus shown to the people. The Cortes immediately paid him their homage, and appointed Ferdinand and Isabella as the guardians of the young heir to the throne. Ximenez returned with the court to Castile, where Miguel received the homage of that state at Ocaña, in January, 1499. He died, however, July 20, 1500, before he had reached the second year of his age.

CHAPTER VII.

XIMENEZ AT GRANADA.—THE CONVERSION OF THE MOORS.

AFTER the Cortes held at Ocaña had been dissolved, both the sovereigns went to Granada, in September,[*] 1499, in order to see with their own eyes the state of the late conquered kingdom of the Moors, and also with the view of putting an end both to the dangerous intrigues of the Spanish Moors with their brethren in Africa, and to prevent for the future the hostile attacks of the latter. Seven years had already passed away since the last Moorish prince, Boabdil, had lost the kingdom and all his authority, though the conquered people were allowed by the treaty [†] to retain their mode of worship, their mosques, their property, laws, customs, and civil tribunals. They also possessed certain privileges which even Spaniards themselves were deprived of.[‡]

After the taking of Granada, Isabella appointed Mendoza, count of Tendilla, chief governor of the city. Under his wise, benevolent, but firm administration, the Moors enjoyed an amount of happiness

* This is the date given by Peter Martyr (Epist. 211), who accompanied them on the journey. Ferreras is mistaken in placing it in March.

† The whole of the treaty made between Ferdinand and Isabella and the Moors is given at length by Marmol, "Historia del Rebelion y Castigo de los Moriscos," &c. Madrid, 1797.

‡ For example, the commerce of the Moors was not subject to the same restrictions as it was in Castile. Every Moorish slave, too, who fled to Granada from any part of Spain recovered his liberty. (See Prescott.)

and prosperity to which people so lately reduced to subjection could hardly aspire.

The queen was no less fortunate in her choice of the good and pious Talavera* as archbishop of Granada. It was natural that Catholic sovereigns should be anxious to re-establish the archiepiscopal see, which existed in Granada before the invasion of the Moors. Their religious feelings also imposed this step upon them as a matter of duty, while another motive was no less powerful; viz., a regard for the welfare of those Spaniards who settled in the conquered kingdom. Political reasons likewise had their influence with the sovereigns, who were anxious to bind the Moors to the rest of Spain by the introduction of the Christian religion amongst them. Whilst, therefore, Ferdinand and Isabella repudiated every intention of compelling by force the Moors to embrace Christianity, as contrary to the treaty made between them, and while they were also unwilling to interfere with the customs † of the people, on the other hand, they considered themselves perfectly justified in trying to establish at Granada a bishopric, and likewise a mission for their peaceful and voluntary conversion.

Fray Fernando de Talavera, a monk of the order of St. Jerome, was born of poor and obscure parents at Talavera. But, owing to his virtue and wisdom, he was in time chosen confessor to their Catholic majesties, and afterwards bishop of Avila. After the conquest of Granada, he begged of his sovereigns

---

* He had previously been for twenty years prior of the monastery of Santa Maria del Prado, near Valladolid. (See Oviedo, " Quincangenas," MS. dial. de Talavera.)—*Trans.*

† Exemptions from the laws were made in favour of the Moors. For example, in order to put a stop to the extravagance of dress so prevalent at this period, Isabella forbade her subjects to wear silk dresses. The Moors, however, were allowed to do so, through deference to their national customs. (Prescott.)

to allow him to resign his dignity, in order to be able to dedicate his whole life to the conversion of the Moors. This proof of self-denial induced the pious queen to recommend him to the pope as a fit person for the newly-established see of Granada; and though it was poorer in worldly means than the bishopric of Avila, yet Talavera firmly refused every offer of an increase in his revenue, which Isabella considered proper to make the worthy prelate.*

We have seen above how the translation of this prelate to the see of Granada was the cause of Ximenez being chosen to succeed him as confessor to the queen. It is also worthy of notice, how these two prelates, so eminent by their virtue and piety, resembled each other in this respect particularly, that though they had large incomes, yet, as far as regarded themselves, they were poor and economical, while they were noble and generous in the extreme when the public good was concerned. Indeed, the new archbishop of Granada devoted the greater part of his revenues to works of charity; and frequently did he, like St. Martin, divide half of his garment with some poor person.† Such friendship existed between him and the count of Tendilla, that, according to the testimony of Peter Martyr, "they both formed one soul in two bodies."‡ But Talavera must have felt, both as a Christian and a bishop, a great interest in the spiritual welfare of the new arch-diocese; while the conversion of the Moors no doubt formed the subject of his most ardent wishes. This was the reason why he learned, in an advanced age, the Arabic language: he required the same thing of his clergy; and caused some of the most

* Marmol Carvajal, "Historia de los Moriscos" (Madrid, 1797), tom. i. p. 105.
† Prescott, vol. ii. p. 362.   ‡ Petrus Martyr, Ep. 219.

beautiful parts of the New Testament, the Liturgy also, and Catechism, to be translated into the same language. It was on this solid foundation that he hoped to be able to establish a mission among the Moors.* No force, or commands, or threats can convert a conquered people to Christ. This object can only be accomplished gradually, by gentle instructions and the inward force of Christian truth, accompanied by the spectacle of a sublime ritual. But the best recommendation of the new faith was the archbishop's irreproachable purity of morals, his angelic sweetness of disposition and great charity, the powerful influence of which produced numerous conversions. Hence the number of new Christians daily increased; and in the whole of Granada no one was so much beloved as the "great Alfaqui of the Christians;" for so the Moors were accustomed to call him.†

The government supported the mission, by granting certain advantages to those who were converted, and also by protecting them from all threatening losses or dangers. But towards the end of the year 1499, the Catholic sovereigns, during their short residence at Granada, directed their particular attention both to the development of the material prosperity of the country, and to the progress of the mission among the Moors. For this object they were now anxious to invite Ximenez to Granada; and most probably it was by his suggestion that, in October, 1499, a law ‡ was made, the wisdom and moderation of which are praised even by Llorente himself. By virtue of this law, no Moor was allowed to disinherit his converted son merely

---

* Marmol Carvajal, p. 108; also Prescott, vol. ii. p. 363, &c.
† Marmol Carvajal, p. 107.
‡ This law (or pragmática, as it is called) is dated October 31st, 1499. ("Pragmáticas del Reyno," fol. 5.)

on account of his change of religion; while the daughters of the Moors who embraced Christianity received a dowry out of the property acquired by the state from the conquest of Granada. From the same fund, converted Moorish slaves were enabled to regain their liberty.

Ximenez now took part for a time with Talavera in the business of the Moorish mission; while the gentle archbishop of Granada gave his consent the more willingly, because he was more concerned for the glory of God and the salvation of souls, than to be sole master in his diocese. When the Catholic sovereigns were about to leave Granada for Seville, in November 1499, they commanded both the prelates to continue their peaceful and pious exertions; and, indeed, these archbishops were as anxious to remove from the Moors all grounds of complaint connected with their religious feelings, as they were zealous in wishing to continue the work of conversion. To attain this object, Ximenez had recourse to means as novel as they were efficacious. He frequently invited to his palace some of the principal "alfaquis," or Moorish priests and doctors, where he held a conference with them almost daily on matters of religion; and thus he sought to gain their hearts by his kindness and friendship towards them. But at the same time, in order that his instructions might make some impression on their sensual minds, he did not hesitate to make them agreeable presents, chiefly consisting of costly articles of dress, silks, &c. For this object, he encumbered the revenues of his see for many years. The conversion of some of the alfaquis was quickly followed by the conversion of great numbers of other Moors; so much so that, after labouring for two months only, Ximenez was able to baptize in one day four thousand people: this took place on December 18th, 1499.* The holy sacrament was administered as is usual in large missions, not by immersion, but by aspersion. The anniversary of this great event continued afterwards to be celebrated, in the dioceses of Toledo and Granada, every year as a festival.

The result corresponded with such a happy commencement; so that, in the course of a short time, a great number of the inhabitants of Granada had embraced Christianity, and the place had already begun to assume the appearance of a Christian city. The sound of bells, forbidden by the laws of Mahomet, was now constantly heard; so that Ximenez, to whom this introduction was attributed, received from the Moors the surname of "Alfaqui Campanero." †

All this success, however, tended, as a matter of course, to excite a reaction amongst those Moors who were more strict in their religion. Hence, many of the more educated, being grieved to the heart at beholding their national faith on the decline, endeavoured with all their strength to prevent any further conversions amongst the people, and to excite in them a hatred of Christianity, and also dissatisfaction against the government.‡ There is no doubt but that these acts were unjust in a great measure, inflammatory, and therefore deserving punishment: hence, Ximenez had right on his side, when he ordered the most clamorous to be arrested. But he overstepped, on the other hand, in the height of his zeal, the bounds of the treaty which the

* Robles assures us that he baptized all these with his own hand:—"Y alfin con halagos, dadivas, y caricias, los truxo a conocimiento del verdadero Dios; y por esto medio vino a convertir mas de quatro mil Moros, y baptizarlos por su propia mano," &c. ("Compendio de la Vida," &c. pp. 100, 101.)

† Prescott, note, vol. ii. p. 367.

‡ Marmol Carvajal, p. 114; also Fléchier, liv. i. p. 87.

government had made with the Moors, by trying to impose on the prisoners the obligation of receiving instruction from his chaplains on the Christian religion. Those who refused he even punished very severely. Amongst this class was a noble Moor, named Zegri, who belonged to the illustrious family of Aben-Hamar, so renowned in Moorish song. He had acquired great glory in the late wars of Granada against the Spaniards, and was also held in much esteem by his own countrymen. Ximenez confided him to the care of one of his chaplains, named Pedro Leon, with the hope of his being converted. But, finding every gentle means useless, he had recourse to severity in such a manner, that Zegri, playfully alluding to his name,* said, some time afterwards, "that Ximenez had only to let his Leon loose, and in a few days the most obstinate Moor would be converted." And, in truth, Zegri himself was obliged to fast for some days, and to wear heavy irons; till, suddenly, he expressed a wish to be introduced to the great "alfaqui" of the Christians. Having had his request granted, he assured Ximenez how, in the preceding night, Allah had commanded him in a vision to become a Christian. Ximenez rejoiced exceedingly on hearing these words, and immediately baptized the new convert, who took the name of Fernando Gonsalvo, in honour of the "great captain," for he had once fought with him on the plains before Granada.

During the remainder of his life, he continued to display such Christian zeal, that many believed he had been called by God, in a miraculous manner, to embrace Christianity.† Zegri also attached himself to Ximenez with an inviolable fidelity, was constantly by his side, and was employed by him in a

---

* Leon, a lion.

† Marmol and Gomez are of this opinion.—*Trans.*

multitude of affairs, which required both great zeal in the cause of Christianity, and the most delicate tact and sound judgment. He likewise found him very useful in the conversion of the Moors ; and, indeed, Zegri was instrumental in conducting many to the Church, both by word and example.

These conversions tended more and more to confirm Ximenez in the hopes he had conceived of soon putting an end to Islamism in Granada : hence, he no longer considered it necessary to listen to the advice of those who, less zealous than himself, were willing to leave to the future the complete triumph of Christianity. On the contrary, he seemed persuaded, that any delay in the matter would be ruinous to the spiritual interests of the Moors, as well as highly culpable ; and that the work of conversion would be likely to advance more by pressing it forward, than by any tedious delay.*

Wishing then to annihilate Islamism by one blow, he caused several thousand copies of the Koran to be burnt in the public square, together with other religious books of the Moors, which their " alfaquis " had delivered up to him.† Works on medicine only escaped the flames : these were afterwards removed to the library of the University of Alcalá, founded by Ximenez.

It would be a mistake to form any comparison between this action and the burning of the library at Alexandria by Omar ; for the archbishop was not an unlettered barbarian, but one of the greatest promoters of knowledge at the time of the destruction of the Moorish books, which was effected just

* Gomez, ed. Francof. fol. p. 959.
† According to Robles, the number amounted to a million. Gomez mentions only 5,000, and Conde 80,000. Prescott seems to think that the last writer is the most correct, as being better acquainted with Arabic lore. (Vol. ii. note, p. 369.)

about the period when, at his own expense, he was founding the new university of Alcalá, and was also publishing the most learned and admirable work of the age.* In the life of Luther, a parallel may be found to the act related of Ximenez, but with this difference, that, in the fire kindled before the east gate of Wittenberg,† Luther caused the books of canon law belonging to the *Christian Church to be burnt;* while Ximenez, on the other hand, was anxious in his zeal to promote the extension of the said Christian Church. Still, some contemporaries of Ximenez had a perfect right to condemn all violence, and to appeal to the synods of Toledo, which strictly prohibited any one to be forced to embrace Christianity.‡ Ximenez, however, persevered in the course he had entered upon, and left nothing untried in order to make the whole of Granada Christian; his courage increased in proportion as did the great dangers which surrounded him. The means which he made use of for the conversion of the infidels could not fail to produce an immense amount of discontent. Nothing, however, so much excited the hatred of the Moors against the archbishop as the violence which he employed against those who were descendants of renegades from Christianity : these he forcibly received into the Church, against the wish of their parents.§ On this account, feelings of animosity had for some time been nourished against Ximenez, when suddenly, towards the end of the

* It must be remembered, that it was principally the copies of the Koran which were burnt; which Ximenez justly considered would be, if read, an obstacle in the way of the Moors being converted.—*Trans.*

† See Audin's "Life of Luther," vol. i. pp. 234-5, ed. Dolman, 1854. Mr. Prescott's use of the word "bigotry" is more applicable to Luther than to Ximenez.—*Trans.*

‡ Gomez, fol. 959, &c.

§ Mariana, lib. xxvi. cap. 5, p. 238.

year 1499, a very terrible outbreak occurred. Sal-zedo, major-domo of the archbishop, attended by an officer of justice and another younger servant, went into the Abaycin (a quarter inhabited exclusively by Moors), in order to arrest the daughter of an apostate from Christianity. The young woman, however, raised such a great outcry, and exclaimed with such vehemence against the violation of the treaty, that numbers of the infidels rushed to her rescue. The officer of justice, whose profession rendered him doubly odious, and who answered the abusive language of the Moors with threats of punishment, after he had been ill used, together with his companion, was at last killed by a stone thrown at him. The major-domo of Ximenez was saved from a similar fate only through the com-passion of a Moorish woman, who concealed the poor trembling man under her bed until he found an opportunity of returning back in safety to the city.

After the murder of the officer, the whole of the Albaycin, containing five thousand houses, seized their arms; the infidels in the other parts of the city also joined in the mutiny, and rushed in a tumultuous crowd, heated with passion, towards the palace of the archbishop, in order to murder him whom they esteemed the "destroyer" of their liberty, together with his officer. A few days before, the streets resounded with songs in praise of the liberality of Ximenez, whilst now the multitude were thirsting and crying out for his blood.

The heroic courage of the archbishop appeared in strong contrast with the fickleness of the multi-tude. His friends were anxious to conduct him by a secret passage into the fortress of Granada, the celebrated Alhambra; but he assured them that he would never desert his servants in the hour of danger, while he encouraged them by his example

to make a vigorous resistance, making every arrangement at the same time for the defence of his palace :
this he did with wisdom and calmness. During the
whole of the night, they succeeded in repelling the
attacks of the Moors ; at the break of the day, however, the noble count of Tendilla appeared, with an
armed force from the Alhambra ; and thus he saved
the archbishop from the danger which threatened
him. The revolt continued, nevertheless, nine days
more.*

The count of Tendilla now sent a herald to the
rebels, in order to induce them to yield, but they
broke his staff of office on his body, and at last even
murdered him.† Ximenez himself made another
attempt, by summoning all the Moorish priests
around him, and trying to pacify the multitude by
words of peace ; but it was to no purpose. At length
the Archbishop Talavera adopted an experiment
which was most dangerous, though fortunately it
succeeded. Attended only by his chaplain, who bore
the archiepiscopal cross before him, he went forth on
foot towards the rebellious multitude (as Pope Leo
once did to meet the terrible Attila) ; and so calm did
he appear, that it seemed as if he were going to preach
the truths of Christianity to willing crowds. The
appearance of the mild and universally beloved
prelate immediately calmed their heated passions ;
while crowds pressed round the man of God, in
order to kiss the hem of his garment.

The count of Tendilla took advantage of this
momentary calm in the midst of the storm ; for he
presented himself before the rebels as a messenger
of peace, in a civil costume ; and, as a proof of his
friendly intentions, he threw his scarlet bonnet
amongst the crowd,—an act which was received with

---

* Gomez, p. 960. Carvajal, pp. 116—120.
† Peter Martyr, Ep. 212.

shouts of joy. Both of these popular men now represented to the Moors " how useless it would be to continue the contest against the power of Spain, and that their obstinacy would only bring on themselves new miseries; but if, on the other hand, they would return to their duty, that both the count and the archbishop would make use of all their influence to obtain the royal pardon for the repentant."

The count, as a proof of his sincerity, left his wife and two children as hostages in the Albaycin. This had the effect of restoring something like tranquillity.*

Whilst these events were taking place in Granada, the Catholic sovereigns were residing in Seville, to whom Ximenez, after the third day of the revolt, hastened to send an account of what had already happened. The letters were already written when a grandee of Granada came to him, and offered him the services of his Ethiopian slave, as a bearer of the letters, assuring him that he could run fifty leagues in two days. Ximenez accepted the offer; but the slave got drunk on the way, and was thus delayed; so that he arrived at Seville five days after, when the report of what had happened in Granada, with the usual exaggerations, had already reached the ears of the sovereigns before his arrival: the report was, that Granada was entirely lost to Spain. The whole of the court was completely terrified; the king especially blamed Ximenez exceedingly, as having by his indiscreet zeal lost the fruit of so many bloody battles in one hour.† An old

---

* Peter Martyr, Epist. 212. Mendoza, " Guerra de Granada," lib. i. p. 11. Mariana, " Hist. de España," tom. ii. lib. 27.

† Robles quotes the words he makes use of: " Que os parece, Señora, en que nos ha puesto vuestro Arçobispo, que lo que los reyes nuestros predecessores y nosotros, en tan largo tiempo, y con tanto trabajo y sangre temos ganado, el lo ha puesto en una

" grudge " against Ximenez having rankled in his breast at the same time : he bitterly reproached Isabella for having raised to the see of Toledo an incompetent monk, instead of his natural son, Alfonso of Aragon. Isabella herself was now beginning to doubt the prudence of Ximenez, whose mysterious silence on the events she could not understand. She therefore ordered Almazan, her secretary, to write to the archbishop, and demand an immediate account of his proceedings; and to blame him also for his negligence in not having written before.

Ximenez in the mean time was free from any anxiety on the matter, supposing that the slave had certainly delivered his letters. Now, however, having received the queen's despatch from her secretary, he repented having intrusted so important a letter to such a man as a slave ; he therefore sent to Seville Francisco Ruyz, one of his own household, and a religious of his order, to inform his sovereigns of the true state of affairs; and also to announce to them that when the revolt was put down, he should appear at court in person and vindicate his conduct. This he did soon after, and defended himself with such success, that not only were Ferdinand and Isabella appeased, but they expressly thanked him for his services, and gave him their confidence even more than ever.* By his advice, this alternative was offered to the savage inhabitants of the Albaycin and its neighbourhood,—either to undergo the punishment of high treason or to receive baptism. In consequence of this, nearly all the Moors of Granada

hora a riesgo do perderse ? La reyna le disculpava todo quanto le era posible " (cap. xiv. p. 107).

* " Non solùm omnis indignatio discussa est, omnisque ratio offensionis abolita; verùm magnæ illi actæ sunt gratiæ, quòd rem tam difficilem animo primùm concipere ausus, ad exitum tam felicem perduxisset." (Gomez, fol. 32.) The testimony of Robles is almost similar (cap. xiv. p. 108).—*Trans.*

and its environs embraced Christianity; the remainder retired to the mountains, or crossed over to the coast of Barbary, so as to be able to retain the faith of their ancestors.

Peter Martyr, however, justly remarks, that their conversion was only exterior, because it was forced; and hence, that Mahomet was still in the hearts of those who with their lips professed to call upon Christ. But the learned writer adds very properly, that from the conversions which were effected among the present generation little fruit could be expected; but that their posterity would reap all the advantages.*

A modern American writer, Mr. Prescott, passes a harsh and severe judgment on the conduct of Ximenez, with respect to these Moorish conversions.† He calls it a "master-piece of monkish casuistry," because the archbishop, by the rebellion of the Moors, considered himself justified in breaking the treaties which already existed. But the fact is, that the infidels themselves were the very first to violate the treaty; and surely no government in the world would consider itself bound to accord to its rebellious subjects advantages which were granted only on condition of their remaining true and faithful to the said government.

From the court at Seville, Ximenez returned to

---

* Opus Epist. (epist. 215). The number who were converted is variously estimated; some writers making it amount to 50,000, others even to 70,000.

† Mr. Prescott is certainly too fond of using the word "bigotry," which often has no definite meaning in the mouth of a Protestant. Ximenez may have been wanting in prudence, sometimes; but all must admire the zeal of a man who, in such a short period, effected the conversion of so many infidels. Granting that the conversion of hundreds was not sincere, yet must we not allow that many others *were* sincere in their profession of Christianity? —*Trans.*

Granada, in order to take part with the archbishop
of the city in instructing the newly-baptized Christians, and accustoming them to the use of holy
ceremonies. It was truly a touching sight, to behold these two illustrious prelates catechising the
poorest persons, and working together in the sweetest harmony. It was only on one point that there
was a difference of opinion. Talavera, as we have
already noticed, had some time before caused certain
portions of the Holy Scripture and some religious
works to be translated into Arabic; he also wished
to prepare for publication a complete version of the
Bible. Ximenez, on the other hand, would only
allow books of devotion and edification—not the
Bible—to be placed in the hands of the new converts;* drawing the attention of Talavera, at the
same time, to the evils and dangers likely to arise
from the mere reading of the Bible, in the minds of
those who were rude and ignorant. His opinion
was followed, and the proposal of Talavera was
therefore rejected; but the prelates still remained
united in the bonds of friendship, and the good
Talavera was heard to say, "that Ximenez had
gained greater triumphs than even Ferdinand and
Isabella, since they had conquered only the soil,
while he had gained the souls of Granada."

The fame of Ximenez began to spread more and
more throughout Spain. Those even who were the
most indifferent to the principles of religion must
have been forced to appreciate the great temporal
advantages which the conversion of the Moors to
Christianity promised for Spain. It is true that

---

* "Ximenius indignum esse dicebat, margaritas ante porcos
projicere; hoc est, hominibus nondum benè in religione con-
firmatis, sacra nostra irridenda, aut contemnenda proponere."
(Gomez, fol. 40. See also Fléchier, "Hist. du Card. Ximénès,"
liv. i. p. 97.)

Granada only had embraced the faith, while the remaining part of the Moorish kingdom still adhered to Mahometism; but these provinces in a short time violated the terms of the treaty, and thereby forfeited, like the rebels of the Albaycin, the free exercise of their religion.

Ximenez, after his mission to Granada had terminated, returned to his diocese, where he ordered a solemn mass of thanksgiving to be celebrated for the events which had taken place;[*] he also made a visitation of his diocese, and carried on with energy the building of the university of Alcalá. His health, which had been weakened by his recent labours, was now beginning to be restored, when his sovereigns unexpectedly summoned him to return to Granada, on account of an outbreak amongst the Moors who dwelt in the mountains of the Alpuxarras.[†] This happened in the year 1500.

The wild range of the Alpuxarras Alps extends in a south-easterly direction from Granada, for the kings of which it had furnished in ancient times the very best warriors; and even in their late engagements with Ferdinand, they had not lost their ancient renown. In the year 1492, they had, it is true, fallen under the Spanish dominion; but their love of freedom and of their ancient institutions was stronger and more intense than that of the inhabitants of the plains.

Many of those who fled from Granada had informed the Moors of the Alpuxarras how the inhabitants of the ancient capital had been forced to renounce their faith. This news exasperated

---

[*] Robles says, " La fiesta desta conversion celebran las Iglesias de Toledo y Granada siete dias ante de la Natividad de Cristo nuestro Señor" (cap. xiv. p. 108).

[†] This word means, in Arabic, " pasturage," according to Conde (" Descripcion de España," p. 187).

them; and hence, fearful of a similar violence, the
wild sons of the mountain flew to arms (anno 1500),
and took possession of the Spanish fortresses: they
also, according to their ancient custom, made in-
cursions upon the habitations of the Christians;
not remembering that thereby they brought upon
themselves those very evils which they seemed so
anxious to avoid.

The count of Tendilla immediately hastened to
unite himself with the " Great Captain" (Gonsalvo
de Cordova), who was once his pupil, but now
might well be his master in the art of war, and at
this time was residing in Granada. They attacked
the fortress of Huejar,* and soon took it from the
rebels. Afterwards, King Ferdinand himself found
it necessary to take the field in person, when he
captured the haughty and almost impregnable
fortress of Lanjaron, on March 7th,† 1500, while
his generals seized upon other important places,
and inflicted terrible punishment on the rebels.

At last, the inhabitants of the whole of the Alpuxarras, being discouraged and disheartened, gradually
surrendered themselves in the course of the year
1500, and were mercifully dealt with by Ferdinand
and Isabella. They were obliged to deliver up their
arms and fortified towns, contribute to the expenses
of the war, and receive Christian missionaries
amongst them. But no one was forced to receive
baptism, though many advantages and material
benefits were bestowed on those who became Christians of their own free choice. "The wisdom of
these temperate measures," says Prescott, "became

* Situated in one of the eastern ranges of the Alpuxarras.
(Prescott, vol. ii. p. 381.)   (See also Marmol, "Rebelion de
Moriscos," tom. i. lib. i. cap. 28; and Mendoza, "Guerra de
Granada," p. 12.)

† Prescott gives as the date March 8th (vol. ii. p. 383).

every day more visible, in the conversion not merely of the simple mountaineers, but of nearly all the population of the great cities of Baza, Guadiz, and Almeria, who consented, before the end of the year, to abjure their ancient religion, and receive baptism"* (vol. ii. p. 385).

In the mean time, a fresh revolt broke out in another part of the Moorish mountains. The inhabitants of the Sierra Vermeja (Red Sierra†), which lay to the west of Granada, being exasperated by the apostasy of their countrymen, took a horrible vengeance on the Christians, in spite of every friendly assurance on the part of the government: they murdered the missionaries; plundered men and women, and sent them to be sold as slaves in Africa. Ferdinand himself, therefore, marched against the rebels; but, though he was successful at the commencement,‡ the greater part of his forces were terribly cut up in the mountain-passes by the Moors; so that the red rocks of the Sierra were made redder still by the blood of the Spaniards. The universal grief for this day of sorrow is still preserved in some most plaintive romances.§ Alonso de Aguilar, elder brother of the "Great Captain," whom Ximenez loved so tenderly, fell in this engage-

---

* See also Carvajal, "Anales MS.," anno 1500.

† So called from the colour of the rocks rising to the east of Ronda. The river Rio Verde divided the Spaniards from the Moors. Percy has given a translation of the romance commencing,

> " Rio Verde, Rio Verde,
> Tinto va en sangre viva," &c.

‡ Dr. Hefele here omits many interesting details, which may be read in Prescott, especially the account of the death of the brave Alonso de Aquilar.—*Trans.*

§ The Spanish "romances" correspond with our ballads. (See the "History of the Civil Wars of Granada,"—" Hist. de las Civiles Guerras de Granada." Madrid, 1694).

ment—a perfect model of a hero* (March, 1501). There were but few of the Spanish nobility who were not now obliged to put on mourning.

But at last the Moors themselves, being terrified at the thought of the vengeance that was quickly coming upon them, and alarmed even at their own victory, hastened to sue for peace. Though Ferdinand's Spanish heart was most deeply wounded, yet the dictates of prudence induced him to impose no other conditions than these, either to embrace Christianity or to leave Spain, on the payment of ten doblas of gold per head. The few who had the will or the means to leave the country, had a free passage to Africa; for Ferdinand was faithful to his royal promise. The majority, however, declared themselves willing and ready to embrace Christianity; and thus, throughout the whole extent of the ancient Moorish kingdom of Granada, there was no one who had not received baptism; while those who were established in the other provinces of Spain were allowed to profess their religion without any hindrance.† Henceforth, the Christian descendants of the ancient Moors now appear under the name of *Moriscos ;* but though their various misfortunes have made them objects of pity, yet it cannot be denied that they brought on themselves many of their miseries, through

---

* He fell, fighting with a Moor of immense strength and size, named Feri de Ben Estepar, after having performed prodigies of valour. His body was interred with great pomp in the church of St. Hypolito, at Cordova.—*Trans.*

† About seventy years after this rebellion (in 1570), another insurrection broke out, which was put down by the count of Ureña. Many of the soldiers were descendants of those who had fought under Alonso de Aguilar. This revolt called forth the admirable work of Diego Hurtado de Mendoza, who is justly called the Spanish Sallust. The title of it is "Guerra de Granada."—*Trans.*

their obstinate adherence to Islamism and their repeated acts of treason.*

When peace was re-established, Ximenez was summoned to Granada by his sovereigns. The sorrow which he experienced at the death of his friend Aguilar detracted somewhat from the joy which he felt at the rapid progress that Christianity had made. Ferdinand and Isabella received him with the greatest friendship ; and, to testify the high esteem in which they held him, they appointed him apartments in the fortress of the Alhambra itself, and at the same time consulted him in every important and secret business. It seems probable that to his advice is to be ascribed an edict which appeared in July, 1501, forbidding any intercourse of the Moors of Granada with those who still remained unconverted in other provinces of Castile, in order to remove all danger of a relapse from them.

It is doubtful whether Ximenez had anything to do with the edict (Pragmática) published in February 1502. Under this date, the Catholic sovereigns issued that well-known Pragmática, whereby all unbaptized Moors in the kingdoms of Castile and Leon, above fourteen years of age if males, and twelve if females, were commanded to leave the country by the end of the following April. They were, however, allowed, as the Jews were before, to sell their property, and to emigrate into any country, except the territory of the sultan, and such parts of Africa as Spain was then at war with.† But a later edict, issued on September 17th, 1502, confined their choice almost exclusively to Aragon and Portugal. If we may judge from the silence of the Castilian writers, very few of the Moors made use of the

---

* More will be said about the Moriscos in Chapter xviii.
† See " Pragmáticas del Reyno," fol. 7.

permission granted them; on the contrary, they preferred following the example of their brethren in Granada, and consented to receive baptism. In the kingdom of Aragon, however, Islamism seems to have been tolerated till the time of Charles V.

If we are to believe the Chronicle of Bleda, the grand inquisitor, Torquemada, was the first who induced the Catholic sovereigns to publish the severe edict of the 12th of February, 1502; but, according to the just remark of Prescott,[*] Torquemada had already been dead some years before. With more reason does Llorente attribute its publication to the influence and advice of the second grand inquisitor, Deza, who at that time was the confessor of King Ferdinand, and formed one of his attendants at court.[†]

Whilst Ximenez was attending the court at Granada, several important events took place, in which he no doubt took part, by his advice respecting them. I allude especially to the treaty connected with the partition of the kingdom of Naples, a project which, though planned and talked of some time before, was finally resolved upon at Granada in the month of August, 1501.[‡]

Besides the isle of Sicily, which, after the massacre known under the name of the "Sicilian Vespers,"[§] passed into the royal house of Aragon, King Alfonso V., of Aragon, had also in the fifteenth century obtained possession of the kingdom of Naples, partly by inheritance, and partly by the force of arms: thus both kingdoms were united with Aragon. On the death of Alfonso

---

[*] Note, vol. ii. p. 400.

[†] "Histoire de l'Inquisition," tom. i. p. 335. Paris ed. 1817.

[‡] Ferreras, vol. xii. p. 242.

[§] So called from the signal of the bell tolling for vespers. The massacre was caused by the unjust claims of Charles VIII. of France to the crown of Naples.

(May, 1458), the succession of the whole belonged of right to his brother John, the father of Ferdinand the Catholic. But Alfonso had made an arbitrary partition of his states : he gave the crown of Naples to his natural son Ferdinand, whilst his other Italian possessions were united with Aragon, and left to the rightful heir. Neither John his father, nor Ferdinand the Catholic, gave their consent to this division of the kingdom ; and it was only very perplexing events which prevented the latter from depriving the bastard line of their unjust possessions, and of reuniting to the crown of Aragon, Naples, which had been conquered by the blood of the Aragonese. Ferdinand the Catholic had indeed, in the year 1496, supported and defended his cousin, Ferdinand of Naples, against the claims of Charles VIII. of France ; but only four years after, the same Ferdinand consented to take away Naples from his cousin, and to divide it with Louis XII. of France.

Ferdinand has often been reproached for this act, as a proof of his want of good faith ; but powerful reasons can be adduced to justify him, according to the remarks of his contemporary, Peter Martyr.*

For a long time, Ferdinand had endeavoured to prevent the French king from seizing upon Naples ; but when Louis XII. had positively resolved upon war, Ferdinand had only these two alternatives remaining, either to see the whole of his kingdom taken away from him, or by some combination of circumstances to try and obtain at least half of it for himself, though by right he could have claimed the whole of it.

This object, however, applied only to the kingdom of Aragon, not to that of Castile, and Ximenez

---

* Epist. 218.

exercised his office of grand chancellor merely for the benefit of the latter; hence, the archbishop took at most only a confidential, not an official part in these affairs.

In the same month wherein this treaty had been concluded, the Catholic sovereigns made another political move of great importance. This was intimately connected with the conversion of the Moors, and very probably Ximenez had some share in promoting it. The sultan of Egypt, Syria, and Palestine, hearing that the professors of his religion in Spain had been oppressed, threatened reprisals, and seemed determined to force all his Christian subjects to embrace Islamism. In order to prevent so great a misfortune, Ferdinand and Isabella sent (in August, 1501) Peter Martyr as special ambassador to the sultan. He was a very learned man, and prior of a church in Granada.* He has left us an account of his dangers and adventures encountered on the journey, in a work entitled, "De Legatione Babylonicâ,"† and also in his admirable letters. He passed through France, and arrived at Venice by land, having a commission to fulfil with the senate on the part of his sovereigns; thence he embarked for Alexandria in Egypt, where he arrived after a voyage of three months, which had been full of perils and tempests; he then sailed up the Nile, attended with a guard of Mamelukes, as far as Cairo, which was the residence of the sultans, and was then called Babylon, on account of its proximity to the ancient Babylon.‡ The object of the voyage was accomplished, the sultan was pacified, and confirmed and insured not only the free ex-

---

* Peter Martyr, Epist. 224.

† It is appended to his more celebrated work, "Decades de Rebus Occanicis et Novo Orbe."

‡ Epist. 235.

ercise of religion to his Christian subjects, but also permitted pilgrimages to be made to the Holy Land. Peter Martyr left Egypt towards the end of April, 1502 : returning to Venice, he entered into fresh negotiations with the senate, in order to obtain for his sovereign the friendship and assistance of Venice against France. He at length arrived in Spain, in the month of August, 1502, after a year's absence.*

Ximenez, besides taking a part in these and other affairs of state, and giving his counsel and advice in the most confidential and secret negotiations of the sovereigns, carried on, during his residence at Granada, frequent intercourse with the Moorish chiefs, and laboured with untiring zeal to instruct the newly-converted Christians. Having endured for two months these numerous labours, his strength failed him at last, and a severe illness brought him almost to the grave : he was then in his sixty-fourth year. It was then that Ferdinand and Isabella showed the tenderest sympathy with his sufferings ; they honoured him, too, by frequently coming to see him. The queen, especially, evinced the deepest solicitude for his recovery, and asked the physicians if a change of place would not be very beneficial for the invalid archbishop. He was accordingly removed from the fortress of the Alhambra (which was too much exposed to the wind) to the royal summer-house of Xeneralifa, not far distant. But after he had spent a month at this villa, no change for the better took place in his health ; and though the physicians employed all their skill to cool his burning fever, Ximenez was now nearer death than before. Already his complaint was declared to be incurable, when fortunately Francisca, a Moorish woman and a convert, who was married to the head

* Epist. 249.

G

cook of the archbishop, said that she was acquainted with an old dame, eighty years old, who had in her possession a quantity of ointment and herbs of great virtue. She was accordingly sent for at night ; and in eight days the fever had so far abated, that Ximenez was able to leave his bed. The pure and bracing air of the river Darro, which flowed near, on the banks of which he walked every forenoon, was the means of hastening his recovery ; and when, some time afterwards, he was enabled to return to his beloved Alcalá, he found himself restored once more to perfect health.*

* The account of this illness is taken from Gomez, lib. ii. fol. 35.

CHAPTER VIII.

NARRATIVE OF EVENTS CONNECTED WITH THE ROYAL FAMILY.
—DEATH OF THE QUEEN.

WHILE Ximenez was recruiting his health at Alcalá, amidst the air of his native climate, and enjoying a repose so seldom granted to him, Ferdinand and Isabella arrived at Toledo, in the year 1502, in order to attend the meeting of the Cortes, and definitely to settle for the future the succession to the throne.

In September, 1498, and in January of the following year, the new-born prince, Miguel,* was acknowledged by the Cortes of Aragon and the kingdom of Castile as heir to the throne. The Catholic sovereigns loved this prince with such sincere love, that they wished to have him always by their side. Accordingly, they took him with them to Granada, in the summer of 1500 ; but a few days after their arrival, the poor weak child died.† Peter Martyr—being an eye-witness—describes the deep grief which this affliction caused to Ferdinand and Isabella, and which was the more intense in proportion as they endeavoured to conceal it from the eyes of the world.‡

Soon was Isabella's prophecy accomplished. In a short time, at the commencement of the year 1500

---

* This prince was the son of the queen of Portugal, who was a daughter of Isabella.—*Trans.*
† The mother of the child died an hour after her delivery, August 23rd, 1498.
‡ Epist. 216.

(February 24), her daughter Joanna gave birth to another grandson of Isabella, who afterwards became the illustrious Charles V. At the news of this event, Isabella was heard to exclaim,—" As the lot fell upon the apostle Matthias, so will crowns also one day descend upon this child."* And, in reality, Charles became some time after heir to the crowns of Castile, Aragon, Sicily, Austria, and the Low Countries. Such a political position required that his claims, and those of his mother, to the Spanish throne, should be acknowledged by the Cortes. For this purpose, the sovereigns requested their daughter Joanna, and her consort, the archduke Philip, to hasten to Spain. At the same time, anxious for the welfare of their other children, they married their third daughter Maria" (born in 1482) to her brother-in-law Emanuel, king of Portugal, the widower of the deceased infanta Isabella. The fourth daughter, Doña Catherina, was united with Prince Arthur, heir to the throne of England. Maria died in Portugal, universally regretted and beloved, in the year 1517. But Catherina lived, to her great misfortune, a much longer period, being divorced from Henry VIII. of England, to whom she had been married, after the early death of his brother Arthur. The whole world knows how this marriage was, in one sense, the occasion of England being lost to the Church.

When these marriages, in which Ximenez had probably a share, were accomplished, the archduke Philip and his consort Joanna arrived in Spain, January 28th, 1502. Out of regard to his wife, and at the same time to satisfy his own excessive love for amusements, Philip's journey through France was prolonged to a considerable time: at

---

* Ferreras, lib. viii. cap. 11.

the court of Blois, he took part in the banquets and
all kinds of amusements which had been prepared
for him; he even sat in the parliament of Paris,
as a peer of France, and swore homage to King
Louis XII. for his possessions in Flanders.* The
Spanish historian Mariana blames, in few but
severe words, as is usual with him, this servility of
the prince; while, on the other hand, he praises the
consort of Philip for having been mindful of the
honour of her country, by refusing to acknowledge
the sovereignty of the king of France, and taking
no part in the acts of the archduke. King Ferdinand the Catholic was also very displeased with his
son-in-law for being on such terms of friendship
with the court of France. Nevertheless, he ordered
Philip and his consort to be received with all due
honour when they arrived at Fontarabia, the frontier of Spain, and that thence they should be conducted to Madrid.†

In the mean time the States of Castile met at
Toledo, in order to offer their homage. Ferdinand
and Isabella arrived at the same city April 22nd,
1502. The queen immediately summoned Ximenez
from Alcalá to meet her there, in order that he
might take part in the business which would be
brought forward. He arrived towards the end of
April, about eight days before Philip and Joanna.
He prepared everything himself on the most magnificent scale for their entrance into the city. On
the 7th of May, the archbishop, clothed in his
pontifical robes, received the royal visitors at the
porch of the church, where a cross was placed,
resplendent with gold and precious stones. After
Philip and Joanna had testified, on their knees,
their respect for the emblem of our redemption,

---

* Mariana, lib. xxvii. c. 11.   † Ibid.

they were conducted by the archbishop to the high altar; and thence, after remaining a short time in prayer, they proceeded to the state apartments of the sovereigns.

The festivities continued for more than fourteen days, till the 22nd of May. The solemn ceremony of paying homage took place on a Sunday, in the metropolitan church. The Cardinal Diego Hurtado Mendoza,* archbishop of Seville, nephew of the illustrious cardinal deceased, officiated at this solemnity, and was the first who took the oath of fidelity to the archduke and the princess. After him came Ximenez; next followed the other bishops; and lastly the civil authorities—all of whom swore to be faithful.†

During the five months which the archbishop spent with the court at Toledo, he was occupying himself with the formation of those great plans for the advancement of the sciences, of which we shall treat in the succeeding chapters. Towards the end of August, 1502, the court went to Aranjuez, and thence to Saragossa, in order to receive the homage of the States of Aragon, in case the king should die without a male heir to the throne.‡ Isabella, however, went to Madrid, in order to meet the Cortes of Castile assembled there: after a short time, the other members of the royal household joined her, with the intention of spending the winter in that city. All of a sudden, to the great surprise of every one, the archduke Philip declared his intention was to leave Spain immediately, and return to Flanders. He was displeased with the stiff manners of the Spaniards; but especially was this vain and fickle prince apprehensive of being brought under the

---

* See what Peter Martyr says about this prelate (Epist. 222). The cardinal died soon after these festivities.

† Mariana, lib. xxxii. c. 11.　　　　‡ Ibid. c. 14.

tuition of his wise relations. It was in vain, therefore, that Isabella represented to him that the future sovereign of Spain should make himself well acquainted with the manners and customs of the country; in vain did she try to convince him that the prosperity of his future government would necessarily depend on this knowledge, and that, therefore, it was his duty to remain longer; in vain did she call his attention to the state of his wife, now near her confinement, who would be unable to undertake so long a journey in the winter, and that were she separated from him she would be most miserable. Philip alleged, "that the climate of Spain was very bad for his health, and that his former preceptor, Francis Basseidan, archbishop of Besançon, had already sunk under it." On the other hand, his love for his wife was so cold, that it could not detain him in the country, since for a long time it was evident (and he himself felt it) that he was justly to be blamed for his groundless jealousy of Joanna.

His departure was accordingly resolved upon. He justified his obstinacy by an assertion, which was no doubt untrue, that before his departure from Flanders, he had promised his subjects and attendants to return within a year, and that he was obliged to keep his word as a prince. He also added, that war having broken out between France and Spain, his dominions stood in need of his presence and assistance.* He further declared it was his intention, in spite of the war between Ferdinand and Louis XII., of travelling back through France: nothing could turn him from his resolution; he even offered himself as a mediator between the two sovereigns, which offer Ferdinand accepted; not, however, without

* Peter Martyr, Epist. 250.

some mistrust, knowing the preference which Philip had for Louis, and that his attendants were bribed by the gold of France.* His misgivings were soon confirmed; for on the 5th of April, 1503, Philip concluded, at Lyons, a foolish treaty with Louis XII. and with his clever minister, Cardinal D'Amboise; by virtue of which Prince Charles (Philip's son), then three years old, was some day to espouse the Princess Claudia of France; while the kingdom of Naples, then an object of dispute between France and Spain, was to belong to both these children. But, on other points, this treaty was prejudicial to the rights of Spain; and hence, Ferdinand considered himself bound not to acknowledge it. This step he took without much hesitation, because Philip had evidently overstepped his power. After this declaration, the war again resumed its course, and, after many vicissitudes, ended at last (thanks to the military genius of the "Great Captain") in the reunion of the kingdom of Naples with the crown of Spain.

The fears of Isabella respecting the fatal consequences likely to follow from Philip's departure were soon to be confirmed. Joanna, so unlike her illustrious mother in the endowments of her mind, that Peter Martyr said of her, "Simplex est femina, licet a tantâ muliere progenita,"† had concentrated her whole existence in her "beautiful" consort, whom she loved most passionately. Being overpowered then by the pangs of separation from him, she began to exhibit those symptoms of deep melancholy which very soon terminated in a complete derangement of her mind. The world had lost all its charms for her; she showed as little concern for the tenderness of her mother, as she did for the affairs of the kingdom. She spent whole days, as

---

* Peter Martyr, Epist. 253.　　　† Epist. 250.

if lost in silent reverie, immovable, and with her
eyes fixed motionless on the ground; her body
seeming to be in Spain, and her soul in Flanders.
But when Philip's name was mentioned, she immediately awoke from her dream, and ordered the
fleet to be got ready, which was to convey her to
her beloved as quickly as possible. Such is the
account which Peter Martyr gives us of this unfortunate princess; for he was an eye-witness both
of her affliction and that of the Queen Isabella,
who resolved to send her daughter back immediately after her confinement. But this event not
taking place so soon as she expected, caused more
affliction to Joanna: the queen herself, too, began
to be unwell.*

Sighing for a milder climate, and seeking too for
more comfort and consolation, Isabella returned to
Madrid in the beginning of January, 1503; thence
she hastened with her daughter to Alcalá, where
Ximenez was then residing. With a zeal inspired
by religious and other good motives, the archbishop
endeavoured to soothe the sorrows of both mother
and daughter by frequent interviews.† He was
soon able to strengthen and console the great mind
of Isabella, and to induce her again to occupy
herself with the cares of government, especially
with reference to the French war. As to Joanna,
she was safely delivered of a second son at Alcalá,
March 10th, 1503. Ximenez baptized him with
great solemnity, and called him Ferdinand, after
his grandfather. He was afterwards known in history under the name of the Emperor Ferdinand I.
Ximenez, having met, on the birthday of the young
prince, a poor criminal going to be executed,
obtained a royal pardon for him, in memory of

* Peter Martyr, Epist. 253, 255.
† Gomez, lib. iii. fol. 44.

the auspicious event, to the great joy of the people.

After the confinement of the archduchess, the heat at Alcalá became so overpowering, that in the beginning of June the queen was obliged, together with her daughter, to leave that city and hasten to Segovia, the air of which seemed more suitable for her health, which was always delicate. When there, Isabella would be near the coast, where every preparation could be made for the departure of her daughter. But, unfortunately, it was necessary to defer it from month to month; for the king of France, being exceedingly angry that Ferdinand refused to acknowledge the treaty of Lyons, seemed determined to invade Spain with a numerous force, and thus take a terrible vengeance on his rival.* Under these circumstances, the voyage to Flanders would be as dangerous by sea as it would by land; Isabella was consequently obliged to detain her daughter. But, on the other hand, symptoms of derangement in the mind of the archduchess again began to show themselves; she left her mother, and hastened to Medina del Campo, that so she might at least be near the coast, and near the fleet also, which was intended to convey her to Flanders.

Joanna, having received a letter from her husband Philip in the month of November, expressing a wish that she should return, as he had obtained a free passport for her through France, was anxious to depart the very same day. But Juan Fonseca, the excellent bishop of Burgos, who was intrusted with the care of the archduchess, immediately sent information to the queen of her daughter's resolution; and at the same time implored the princess,

* Prescott, vol. ii. p. 296.

by the most tender and powerful entreaties, to delay the journey until the arrival of her mother. But in vain; she heeded not the wishes either of the governor of the town, Juan de Cordova, or of the bishop. To prevent her, therefore, from leaving the place, the governor was obliged to order the gates to be closed, although she threatened both the bishop and himself with death whenever she attained power. Furious on beholding her plans frustrated, " tanquam Punica leœna," as Peter Martyr expresses it, she obstinately refused to return to her apartments, and spent a day and a night in the open air, in the court of the castle, half naked, and almost benumbed with cold.* The next day, she was with difficulty persuaded to enter a cook-shop near at hand, in order both to warm herself and get something to eat. There she remained, in spite of all representations, until the arrival of her mother, who had already sent Ximenez and the high admiral of the fleet to try to calm her.

When the court left Alcalá in the month of June, 1503, Ximenez went to Brihuega, on account of illness. It was in a pleasant place, situated in a mountainous country, and was originally given to the archbishops of Toledo, by King Alfonso VI. Ximenez soon left this retirement and went to Santorcaz, where he had formerly been a prisoner, when contending for his right of archpriest of Uzeda. Hardly had he recovered sufficient strength to return to Alcalá, towards the end of the year, when he was obliged to hasten to the unfortunate princess. Isabella arrived very soon after him; and, by the advice of the archbishop, she commanded the fleet at Larido, which was intended to

* Peter Martyr, Epist. 268.

convey the archduchess to Flanders, to be prepared as soon as possible. It was then only that Joanna consented to return to her apartments.

On the 1st of March, 1504, Joanna was at length enabled to set sail, by virtue of an armistice concluded between Spain and France. She arrived quite safe at the residence of her consort, to be more miserable than ever.

Philip received her indeed, in spite of his frivolity, with every mark of friendship; but Joanna soon perceived that he loved one of the noble dames whom he had brought with him from Spain; and hence the most furious jealousy now arose within her breast. The whole palace resounded with her complaints, reproaches, quarrels, and curses. Being informed that the flaxen locks of the young lady particularly captivated Philip, Joanna on one occasion suddenly rushed upon her, cut off her beautiful hair to the very roots, and cruelly tore the flesh of her face. Philip's indignation could not contain itself within bounds; he treated the unfortunate princess with open contempt, reproached her in the most cutting language, and rejected her company for a long time.*

The news of these unfortunate events in Flanders made a most painful impression on both the Catholic sovereigns, and seems to have thrown them into a fever at Medina del Campo, where they were residing in the beginning of July, 1504.† Ximenez immediately hastened to them, comforted them, instructed them one after the other in their duties, and assisted them by his advice in those affairs which their illness did not allow them fully to attend to. He was also indefatigable in procuring for them everything which could contribute to their recovery.

* Peter Martyr, Epist. 272.   † Epist. 273.

Isabella's solicitude for the state of her husband augmented her own sorrows; but while Ferdinand happily recovered his health at the end of a few months, the queen's illness became more and more critical—a strong fever was wasting away her strength. In October, symptoms of dropsy showed themselves, and the physicians began already to give up all hopes of her recovery. The consternation of men at this sad news was great and universal, both on account of the veneration in which the illustrious invalid was held, as well as through fear for the future welfare of the kingdom.*

The mind of the queen, however, was still vigorous, in spite of the infirmity of her body; so much so, that Prospero Colonna, an Italian noble, told Ferdinand, " that he had come to Spain to see a woman who from her sick bed ruled the world." † She very frequently received visits from her friends and relations. She took a great interest in all the affairs of the kingdom, especially in the war with Naples, and the heroic deeds performed by the " Great Captain," who commanded the Spanish army. Among the foreigners who were introduced to the queen at this time, was a Venetian traveller, named Vianelli, distinguished for his bravery, who was the first person that suggested the expedition into Africa, which was afterwards so gloriously accomplished by Ximenez. Vianelli, during his residence at court, gave the archbishop an opportunity of expressing himself in words that were both beautiful, and at the same time in accordance with his own character. The traveller was anxious to sell a diamond ring of extraordinary value; he offered it to Ximenez, who having asked the price of it, and being told that it was worth 5,000 ducats, replied, " With such a

* Peter Martyr, Epist. 274.
† Prescott, note, p. 465, seventh edit. London, 1854.

sum, it would be infinitely better to do good to five thousand poor people, than to possess all the diamonds of India."*

Another stone, more precious in his eyes, came into his possession at this time. A religious of the order of St. Francis, warden of a convent in Jerusalem, was sent by the sultan of Egypt as his envoy into Spain. He had brought with him a stone slab from the Holy Sepulchre, and had it divided into five parts, so as to make five altar-stones. One he intended to present to the pope; one to Queen Isabella; one to Emanuel, king of Portugal; one to Cardinal Carvajal, who took his title from the holy cross; and the other to Ximenez. As Isabella received her present of the altar-stone from our Lord's sepulchre with the deepest veneration, so also did Ximenez resolve henceforth never to say mass on any altar, except on this stone. At his death he bequeathed it, as a most precious stone, to his cathedral at Toledo.

I must not here omit making mention of another circumstance. Ximenez, during his residence at Medina del Campo, visited the neighbouring town of Cisneros, where his parents were born, and many of his ancestors were buried. His object was to have masses and anniversaries fixed for the eternal repose of their souls.

Soon after, the archbishop was obliged to take leave of the queen, in order personally to attend to his diocese. She graciously dismissed him with these words:—" I hope very soon to be able to follow you to Toledo." But Ximenez was destined never more to see her alive in this world; for she died at Medina del Campo on the 26th of November, 1504, in the fifty-fourth year of her age, and the

---

* Prescott gives a somewhat different version of this story, and sneers very unjustly at the answer of Ximenez.—*Trans.*

thirtieth of her reign. * According to her directions, her body was laid in a plain coffin, and interred at first among the Franciscans of Granada, in the ancient Moorish fortress of the Alhambra. She wished to repose in the ground which she had won for Spain and for Christendom. But after Ferdinand's death, as she desired not to be separated from her husband, her corpse was translated to the cathedral of Granada.† There may still be seen the two superb monuments raised by Charles V. (in the Renaissance style) to the memory of his ancestors. Laborde, in his admirable work, " Voyage Pittoresque," gives a very beautiful plate of the tombs.

Such was the sovereign who, through her knowledge of men's character, raised Ximenez, once a simple monk, to the highest ecclesiastical dignity in Spain ; and chose him also for her adviser in all the most important affairs of the kingdom. To her he was indebted for all the greatness which he possessed, and for all the opportunities of doing the good which he effected. When Ximenez, therefore, received from King Ferdinand the sorrowful news of the queen's death, he broke out into loud lamentations ; his grief overcame those feelings which, before, were wont to be so strictly repressed. " Never," he exclaimed, " will the world ever again

* Prescott gives many interesting details about the queen's death and funeral, and pays a high compliment to her noble character, so different from that of our English Elizabeth. Dr. Hefele mentions in a note, that Cæsar Borgia, after the death of his father, Alexander VI., was deprived of all his possessions, and being taken prisoner at Naples by the " Great Captain," was sent to Medina del Campo. There he was imprisoned for three years ; but having made his escape afterwards, he was killed in battle in the year 1507.—*Trans.*

† See Ford's " Handbook of Spain," where an account is given of the present state of the royal tombs at Granada.—*Trans.*

behold a queen with such greatness of soul, with such purity of heart, with such ardent piety, and such zeal for justice."

Thus did he give a true portrait of the queen's character. Peter Martyr, who was an eye-witness of her life and death, comprises a sketch of her in these few but eloquent words : "The world has lost its noblest ornament; a loss to be deplored not only by Spain, which she has so long carried forward in the career of glory, but by every nation in Christendom; for she was the mirror of every virtue, the shield of the innocent, and an avenging sword to the wicked. I know none of her sex, in ancient or modern times, who, in my judgment, is at all worthy to be named with this incomparable woman." *

Indeed, if, with respect to the art of governing, Elizabeth, her namesake,† of England, may be compared with Isabella, the latter is infinitely superior to the great sovereign of Albion, in the good qualities of her heart and the accomplishments of her mind.

* Epist. 279.
† Isabella is synonymous with Elizabeth, in Spanish.

CHAPTER IX.

HISTORICAL PARALLEL BETWEEN ISABELLA OF SPAIN AND ELIZABETH OF ENGLAND.

THE two queens arrived at the throne by the road of adversity and of trial. But whilst these impediments were raised against Isabella by the injustice of her brother Henry, who wished to crown the bastard Beltraneja, Elizabeth had only to suffer in her youth for having been implicated in a dastardly conspiracy against Queen Mary, her own sister; so that the crime fell back upon herself, but Isabella was only unfortunate by the crime of another.

The effects which misfortune produced upon their minds were not less different. It hardened and froze for ever the heart of Elizabeth; it made her truly cruel, and so far extinguished in her gentleness and mercy, the natural appanage of woman, that in the transports of her rage she would go so far as to box the ears of her counsellors and ministers, and spit in their faces, not to mention the torrent of coarse insults with which she overwhelmed them.* Isabella came forth from adversity mild and benevolent; even in punishments and acts of necessary rigour she never forgot either religion or humanity.†

During a long and fortunate reign, both increased the prosperity of their country, and added a fresh lustre to its glory; but Elizabeth will never

---

* Lingard, History of England, vol. vii. (6th edition), *passim.*
† Prescott, vol. ii. pp. 380-2, note 65.

be admired except as a queen, whilst the personal virtues of Isabella secure to her the veneration and affection of posterity. One of the modern historians of Spain, Muñoz, calls her "the incomparable Isabella," and the memory of that glorious era draws from him the exclamation: *O ! si renaciera el spiritu de los reyes catolicos, autores de la grandezza del imperio español !* (Oh ! that the spirit of the Catholic sovereigns would revive, the authors of the greatness of the Spanish kingdom).[*]

Both exercised over their subjects an extraordinary influence, enchained them to their wills with a singular power; during many years they maintained peace in their kingdom, subdued every party rebellion; but the Englishman bent his head before the pride and despotic will of his queen, and the Spaniard obeyed with reliance the inspirations of the genius and the heart of a sovereign whom he loved as a mother.

Both found a kingdom in the second rank among the states of Europe, and, undeniably, raised it to the first, by the wisdom of their internal institutions, by the formation of a powerful navy, and by successful wars. But Isabella, in politics as in her private life, never lost sight of honour and justice; whilst Elizabeth, although superior to Isabella by the impulse which she gave to commerce, rested her policy upon cunning and insincerity, scattered the seeds of discord among neighbouring nations, fostered in other states rebellion and civil war, and, to fix her own crown upon her head, had basely recourse to the murder of a queen, her cousin and her guest.[†]

Elizabeth and Isabella equally held the sceptre with a powerful hand, and lived in an age when the

[*] Memorias de la Real Academia de la Historia, tom. iii. p. 29.
[†] Lingard, vol. iii. *passim.*

absolutism of monarchs was at its height. But the queen of Spain respected the liberties already acquired by her people, as well as the voices of the Cortes, and in her will she requested, moreover, that certain revenues should be sanctioned by the consent of that assembly. Elizabeth, on the contrary, in spite of her seeking for popularity, her pretended demonstrations of friendship for the peasantry and farmers,[*] was a despot in the full sense of the word: for her was absolute power, for all others passive obedience: she reduced Parliament to be nothing more than the shadow of a deliberative assembly, and despised it in that abasement; she instituted arbitrarily new courts of justice worthy of a nation of slaves, and by them, at her pleasure, disposed of the lives and the liberty of her subjects. In that respect nothing is more characteristic than the reply which she made one day, when informed that the court had refused to condemn Norfolk: "Well," she exclaimed, inflamed with rage, "if the laws are insufficient to condemn him, my royal authority shall be large enough."[†] The right of pardoning the guilty is for all sovereigns the finest prerogative of the crown: Elizabeth rejoiced in the power of delivering over to the executioner those whom the law had acquitted. History has recorded a thousand freaks of her arbitrary and despotic will: thus it was that she ordered the destruction of woad, because the scent of that useful plant was disagreeable to her. As for the religious belief of her subjects, she arrogated to herself the right of ruling it with a power more absolute than ever did her contemporary Philip II., king of Spain.[‡]

---

[*] Lingard, vol. iii. *passim*.
[†] Historisch-politische Blätter, vol. iii. p. 700.
[‡] See Rottek, Weltgeschichte (zweite auflage, 1826), p. 7, s. 311.

Isabella displayed the greatest zeal that justice should be equally dispensed without respect to persons : never did corruption the most seductive arrest the execution of the law ; never did any influence, not even that of her husband, divert her from what appeared to her to be her right and her duty.* "The justice which each enjoyed under her happy government," says Marineo Siculo, "was the same for all, for the noble and for the knight, for the citizen and for the countryman, for the rich and for the poor, for the master and for the servant."†

Under the reign of Elizabeth, on the contrary, these sorts of complaint were so frequent, the tyranny, injustice, and rapacity of the public functionaries excited so many murmurs, that a justice of the peace was openly described in Parliament as " an animal who, for half a dozen of chickens, would dispense with a dozen of laws."‡ By the famous Court of Star Chamber, by the Court of High Commission, the queen herself threw trouble and uncertainty in all the laws; she extended with unexampled rigour the martial laws to ordinary offences, arbitrarily recalled magistrates, for money interrupted the course of justice; permitted the lords and ladies of her court to accept of presents as the price of their interference in the suits of private individuals : so that the French ambassador might with truth assert that the administration of justice was more corrupt under Elizabeth than under her predecessors.§ " Another, and intolerable grievance," says Lingard, " was the discretionary power assumed by the queen, of gratifying her caprice or

* Prescott gives many examples of this (vol. ii. p. 376.)
† Cosas Memorables, p. 180; in Prescott, ibid. p. 588.
‡ Lingard, vol. iii. p. 323.   § Ibid.

resentment by the restraint or imprisonment of those who had given her offence."* Elizabeth never forgave a personal wrong, and punished without mercy the slightest offence to her vanity;† whilst Isabella willingly forgot the faults which only were directed against her person, without injuring the welfare of the public.‡

Both queens acquired large possessions in America: Isabella testified the greatest solicitude for the condition of the poor Indians, and never permitted them to be illused; § and we find, in 1567, on the coast of North America, two large English ships engaged in the slave-trade for the special service of the queen of England. ‖

Both queens rewarded genius and talent; they sought for and found great men, who made the immortal glory of their government. But whilst Isabella, gifted with singular prudence and great knowledge of mankind, selected only ministers capable of promoting the welfare of her people, Elizabeth, with as much perspicacity, permitted herself frequently to be guided in her choice by the external advantages and corporeal qualities of the candidates; she often desired to have favourites and lovers in the persons of her ministers.

Isabella treated her councillors with kindness,

---

* Lingard, vol. iii. p. 324.

† The least criticism upon her pronunciation of the French language irritated her excessively; and the French ambassador, Buzenval, could not negotiate with the English cabinet on account of his having allowed himself, *several years previously*, to make use of criticism of this sort (Bayle, Dict. Hist. et Crit., art. "Elizabeth," note E.)

‡ Prescott, vol. ii. p. 383.

§ In 1500, Columbus having sent two natives as slaves to Spain, the queen indignantly demanded *by what right Columbus dared thus to treat her subjects,* and instantly set them at liberty. (See chap. xxvii.)

‖ Lingard, ibid. p. 235.

confidence, and friendship. She took a sincere interest in their welfare; rewarded them worthily; protected them against hatred and envy, as Ximenez and the Great Captain experienced; comforted them in misfortune; visited them when sick; and sometimes herself undertook the office of testamentary executor, as she did, for instance, on the death of Cardinal Mendoza and the great commander Cardenas. She showed the same familiarity, the same kindness, to the ladies of her court; forgot among them the differences of rank; took advantage of all occasions to make them delicate presents; and testified to them, whenever they met, the frankest cordiality, especially to the friend of her youth, Doña Beatrix Bobadilla, afterwards marchioness of Moya.*

Elizabeth never admitted familiar and kindly relations between her and her circle: she passed incessantly from one of two extremes to the other, sometimes playing the part of coquette in her own court, at others indulging in the irritable disposition which she inherited from Henry VIII., so far as to swear at and box the ears of her maids of honour and her ministers. She trusted no one around her, and did not believe any person capable of a sincere devotedness; but she was as much deceived on all sides, and more than once the craft and lies of her ladies and her ministers impelled her to false steps. Another capital evil of her court had its rise in her avarice and parsimony towards her servants and the members of the royal household. Hence arose an odious corruption: to indemnify themselves, the courtiers sold places, monopolies, patronages; law-suits themselves became an object of traffic. The queen, on her part, loved to receive

* Prescott, vol. ii. p. 381.

presents; she knew adroitly how to provoke generosity and make her gracious visits productive.*

Both sovereigns were gifted in their youth with extraordinary beauty; but whilst Elizabeth suffered herself to be governed by a foolish vanity, by a love of ornaments, a desire to please carried to ridiculous excess, Isabella displayed none of these feminine weaknesses.† When the English *Thetis* gave audiences, she constantly was pulling off and putting on gloves to draw attention to her fine hands.‡ No flattery more agreeable could be addressed to her than praising her *celestial* beauty: almost a septuagenarian, she yet desired that homage should be paid to her faded charms with the pomp of Oriental style.§ Still more, she boasted of her own attractions: she one day announced to her faithful subjects that none of the portraits which had hitherto been taken of her person did justice to

---

* "At her first lighting at the lord keeper's she had a fine fanne, with a handle garnisht with diamonds; in the middle was a nosegay, and in yᵗ a very rich jewel, valued at £400 at least. After dinner in her privy chamber, he presented her with a fine gown and a juppin (petticoat), which things were pleasing to her highness; and to grace his lordship the more, *she of herself tooke from him* a salte, a spoone, and a forcke of faire agatte." (Sidney Papers, vol. i. p. 376.) On the 6th of December before her death, she dined with Sir Robert Cecil, and accepted from him presents to the amount of 2,000 crowns, &c. (Lingard, vol. iii. p. 321.)

† Isabella, in stature, "was somewhat above the middle size. Her hair of a bright chesnut colour, inclining to red; and her mild blue eye beamed with intelligence and sensibility. She was exceedingly beautiful; 'the handsomest lady,' says one of her household, 'whom I ever beheld, and the most gracious in her manners.' The portrait still existing of her in the royal palace is conspicuous for an open symmetry of features, indicative of the natural serenity of temper, and that beautiful harmony of intellectual and moral qualities which most distinguished her." (Prescott, vol. i. p. 190.)

‡ Bayle, Dict. &c. "Elizabeth," note D.

§ Lingard, ibid.

the original; that, at the request of her council, she had resolved to procure an exact likeness from the pencil of some able artist; and that all the previous portraits must be reformed after the new one.[*] However exalted the opinion which she had of her person, she did not disdain the aid of foreign ornaments, and at her death there were found in her wardrobe two, some say three, thousand dresses. She covered herself with such a mass of trinkets of gold and precious stones, that the verse of the poet might have been applied to her :—

" Gemmis auroque teguntur
Omnia; pars minima est ipsa puella sui."[†]

The bishop of London having one day, in his sermon, endeavoured to raise the thoughts of the queen to the care of the beauty of her soul, her coquetry was so much offended by it, that she threatened the preacher with death if he should again take a similar liberty. [‡]

Very different is the portrait of Isabella drawn by Prescott, her latest biographer. " She was equally simple and economical in her apparel. On all public occasions, indeed, she displayed a royal magnificence; but she had no relish for it in private, and she frequently gave away her clothes and jewels as presents to her friends."[§]

Prescott relates that Isabella manifested little taste for those frivolous amusements that occupy so large a place in the life of courts.[||] Elizabeth, by the admission of her panegyrist Leti, took great pleasure in them : she loved balls and other such

---

[*] Lingard, vol. iii. p. 321.

[†] She is so covered with gold and jewels, that the smallest part of the girl is the girl herself!

[‡] Lingard, ibid.   [§] Prescott, vol. iii. p. 175.

[||] Prescott, ibid. p. 371.

merriments ;* even at a far advanced age, dancing was her favourite pleasure, to which she daily devoted herself.†

The finest ornament of Isabella, was the purity and innocence of her morals, in which envy itself never found a stain, and which caused Peter Martyr to say, that she not only was a living model of chastity to wives, but might justly be called chastity herself.‡ Is it necessary to add that the *Virgin Queen* cannot here be compared with her? The shameful part which Henry VIII. had played with his wives Elizabeth in her time played with her lovers,§ and, more faithfully to resemble her father, she put to death the dearest of her favourites, the Earl of Essex. Every one admits that the outward charms of Isabella concealed a lofty soul and noble mind; and when age had wrinkled the face of Elizabeth, Essex, the friend of her advanced years, might say with truth that she had a soul as crooked as her body; an expression which, perhaps, contributed more to his ruin than all his political errors.||

The court of Isabella was for the young nobility of both sexes a school of discipline, of good morals, and of polished manners.¶ Cotemporaries designate the court of Elizabeth as " a place in which all enormities reigned in the highest degree, a place where there was no love but that of the lusty god of gallantry, Asmodeus." "The only discontent I have," says a correspondent from the court of England, "is to live where there is so

---

* Bayle, Dict. "Elizabeth," note N.
† Lingard, vol. iii. p. 320.   ‡ Pet. Mart. Epist. 279.
  § An Act of Parliament conferred the right of succession on the natural children of the *Virgin* Queen. (Cobbett, " History of the Reformation of England," lett. 10.)
|| Lingard, ibid. 302.   ¶ Prescott, vol. ii. 371. ; i. 562.

little godliness and exercise of religion, so dissolute manners and corrupt conversation generally, which I find to be worse than when I knew the place first."*

In addition to the royal diadem, Elizabeth aspired to place upon her brow the laurel of science. And, indeed, she possessed more knowledge than any other woman of her time: she understood five foreign languages, and read with ease the Greek text of the New Testament. But she made no use of her learning, except for the purposes of ostentation, and sought, with offensive affectation, on all occasions to display her intellect, her abilities, and acquaintance with languages. Isabella also, although in this respect inferior to the queen of England, possessed more than ordinary acquirements: she spoke Latin with equal fluency and eloquence; but she rarely used it, being in this, as in all the rest of her behaviour, modest and unpretending. She introduced printing into Spain, established libraries, founded and endowed schools, and laboured in the advancement of all the sciences. As for Elizabeth, she wished to confine learning to herself, and, as Hume admits, showed more vanity of her own knowledge than real love for the sciences;† but whilst she protected them to satisfy her vanity, sentiments far more noble instigated a similar conduct on the part of the queen of Spain; she bestowed her protection upon them because she honoured

---

* Lingard, vol. iii. p. 322. Raumer's statement is therefore a colossal falsehood, when he says of the court of Elizabeth, " Hitherto there had never been seen a court so learned and so moral, so intelligent and romantic." (Gesch. Europa's, ii. 618.) The romance, according to the " Historisch-Polit. Blätter," ii. 701, doubtless lay in those boxes on the ear which Elizabeth so liberally dispensed to the people of her court.

† Prescott, vol. ii. 386.

them, and because she was convinced of their powerful influence upon the welfare and prosperity of the
people.

Both sovereigns showed themselves intolerant in
regard to heterodoxy : but in Elizabeth it was policy,
and not the warmth of sincere conviction, which
dictated the penal enactments : Isabella, on the
contrary, proved the sincerity of her religious zeal
by her tender mercy, by the innocence of her life
and innumerable works of charity ; and her severity
towards the Moors and the Jews is a thousand
times more easy to be justified than the cold and
atrocious persecution exercised against the Puritans and the Catholics by a queen who, probably,
herself had neither faith nor conviction. Under the
reign of Mary she had solemnly embraced Catholicism ; she had, on her accession to the throne,
sworn to maintain that religion ;* and, on more
than one occasion, had hypocritically received the
Catholic communion to deceive her subjects who had
returned to the Church of Rome under the preceding reign. But as soon as she had thrown off the
mask, she issued against the Catholics laws so barbarous, and caused them to be enforced with so
much cruelty, that she left very far behind even
the excesses of the Spanish inquisition. The first
refusal to acknowledge the queen as spiritual head
of England was punished with confiscation of property, the second with death.† Crowded prisons,
horrible torture in constant use, gibbets incessantly
erected, the bodies of Catholics true to the ancient
faith cut to pieces, quartered, and disgracefully
mutilated, are, for posterity, irrefutable proofs of
the religious despotism of Elizabeth.‡ Assuredly,
if the inquisition under Isabella killed one thousand,

---

* Lingard, vol. iii. p. 4.   † Ibid. p. 7.   ‡ Ibid. p. 162, &c.

the Reformation by Elizabeth slew ten times the number !

Finally, the latter days of both queens were clouded with cares; but it was solicitude for the future of her kingdom that weighed upon Isabella; she gave her last commands with a firm and tranquil mind, and, like a pious Christian, fortified by the blessings of the Church, she awaited death with calmness and fortitude. Elizabeth, on the contrary, plunged in profound melancholy, a prey to the bitter reproaches of her conscience for the murder of her favourite, Essex; heart-broken at seeing the popular favour estrange itself from her old age; became, by the caprices of her ill-temper, the torment of the servants who waited upon her. In place of seeking for the consolations and the support of the sacraments for the sick, she ordered a sword to be placed by her table, and thrust it with violence into the tapestry of her chamber. Afraid of death, she refused, in the latter days of her existence, to go to bed; she remained seated in the middle of her apartment upon a stool, bolstered up with cushions, with her eyes fixed on the floor, in the attitude of despair. In vain did the archbishop of Canterbury pray beside her, her heart seemed insensible to the consolations of religion.* In this manner she died, on the 24th of March, 1603, nearly a century after Isabella. Prescott, who has also endeavoured to draw an impartial parallel between the two queens, remarks that "the masculine genius of the English queen stands out relieved beyond its natural dimensions by its separation from the softer qualities of her sex; while her rival's, like some vast but symmetrical edifice, loses in appearance somewhat of its actual grandeur from the perfect harmony

* Lingard, vol. iii. p. 316.

of its proportions."* However accurate this remark of the American historian may be, it is far
from expressing the entire truth. It is not only
the absence of the gentle qualities of her sex, but
the positive existence of the worst qualities in the
character of Elizabeth, which justifies the severe
judgment which cotemporary history, in its learned
impartiality, has begun to bring upon that queen ;†
whilst Isabella finds the same respect, the same
veneration, in all historians, to whatsoever nation
they belong, or opinions that they represent.‡

The death of Isabella was for Spain the source of
numerous political difficulties, in the solution of
which Ximenez had the principal part. But before
following him upon that theatre, we proceed to study
the other works of this illustrious prelate.

---

* Prescott, vol. iii. p. 192.

† Schiller puts this menace in the mouth of Mary Stuart :—
" Wo to you, if the world shall one day raise the mantle of
honour with which your hypocrisy covers the horrible fire of your
secret pleasures." Besides, Elizabeth did not appear to care much
for this revelation of her secrets, and for her reputation in that
respect.

‡ Havemann also draws a fine portrait of Isabella in his
" Darstellungen," &c. p. 134—137.

CHAPTER X.

FOUNDATION OF THE UNIVERSITY OF ALCALA.

SPAIN, like other western states, beheld, in the middle of the fifteenth century, a new era of learning dawn, especially in philological and classical studies. John II. was then king of Castile, which formed the principal province of Spain, though it had not yet been united with the other states : he was the father of Queen Isabella the Catholic. During his long reign (from 1406 to 1454) nothing was attended to in the kingdom but the arts and sciences. While, therefore, all other business was neglected, learning began to flourish; and the hearts of the Castilians, especially the nobility, were soon captivated with it. But all these tender blossoms were crushed by civil war, under the inglorious and disturbed government of the dissolute Henry IV.; and when Isabella ascended the throne of her brother (in December 1474), almost every vestige of what her father had established was destroyed. The schools were reduced to a very small number, and of these Salamanca only deserved to be named. But the illustrious queen had inherited from her father a great love for the arts and sciences; and with this love were also united the most noble qualities and the grandest regal virtues, though they may seem incompatible with her sex : these endowments were totally wanting in her father, to his own great misfortune and that of his people. Following the example of King John II., she also made a collection of books, and thus contributed to the foundation of a library.* Even when seated on the throne, amidst all the cares of government, she found time to learn Latin, and in the course of a single year she acquired a solid knowledge of it; while Ferdinand, her spouse, whose education was far from being complete, was entirely ignorant of it.†

Isabella was unable during the first years of her reign, on account of her contest for the crown with Beltraneja and with Portugal, to make any exertions on a large scale for the advancement of learning; but as soon as she was firmly seated on the throne, she directed all her zeal and penetration to this object, and so gave such a powerful encouragement to learning, that under her protection there arose a new epoch in Spanish literature. But above all, the art of printing, then but lately invented, was introduced into Spain, encouraged, extended, and liberally supported by the queen.‡ Civil advantages and freedom from taxation, &c. were the rewards and encouragement bestowed on the most eminent printers, whether natives or foreigners. The liberty of introducing foreign works excited a still greater desire for them, and sharpened the diligence of collectors.§ Hence, Spain soon possessed poetry, classics, and works of piety; and in the year 1478, there appeared a translation of the Scriptures at Valencia, by the brother of St. Vincent Ferrer.|| Often

---

* Prescott mentions that there are still to be seen in the royal library of the Escurial many books in manuscript which belonged to Isabella; others, no doubt, are among the archives of Simancas. —*Trans.*

† Marineo Siculo, De Rebus Hisp. lib. xxi. p. 506. (See "Hispaniæ Illustratæ Scriptores;" ed. Francof. 1603.)

‡ "Archivo de Murcia," apud Mem. de la Acad. de Hist. tom. vi. p. 244.

§ Mendez, "Typographia Española," p. 52, &c.

|| See Mendez, in the work already cited (pp. 61—63); also

did the queen herself furnish money for the publication of good works; while Ximenez also published a great number at his own expense,* distributed prizes to the best workmen, and so generally encouraged the art of printing (then only in its infancy) that in a short time printing-presses might be seen in all the principal towns of Spain.†

Isabella had invited many German printers into Spain: to Italy, also, she was indebted for the presence of many learned men in her dominions—Italy, which then far surpassed every other country by its literary glory and renown. Thus, there came to her court the two brothers Antonio and Alessandro Geraldino,‡ both conspicuous for their classical erudition. Peter Martyr,§ named Anghiera, likewise, a native of Arona, on the borders of the Lake Maggiore, descended from one of the noblest families in the north of Italy, and closely related to the Borromeos, was brought to Spain from Rome in the year 1487, by the count de Tendilla, Isabella's ambassador. The admiral Henriquez was the means of inducing Marineo Siculo to leave Sicily, and accompany him to Spain. The queen received all these learned

---

Le Long (tom. ii. p. 145). Cyprian de Valera assures us that he saw this version. Consult Calmet; art. "Bibles Espagnoles."

* Ximenez also composed books, as well as published them. They consisted chiefly of theological treatises on the nature of sin, on angels, &c. (See Fléchier, liv. vi. p. 504).—*Trans.*

† Such as Toledo, Seville, Granada, Valladolid, Burgos, Salamanca, Barcelona, Valencia, Murcia, Alcalá, Madrid, &c.—*Trans.*

‡ Antonio died in 1488. Some of his Latin poetical works were printed in 1505, at Salamanca. The younger brother, Alessandro, after serving in the Portuguese war, embraced the ecclesiastical state, and died Bishop of St. Domingo, in 1525. (Prescott, note p. 165, vol. ii.)

§ Celebrated for his "Epistles" and other works. His "Epistles" were first published at Alcalá, in 1530; but a second edition, in a more beautiful form, was issued from the Elzevir press in 1670, folio.—*Trans.*

men with the greatest kindness and affability, and considered them as most precious seed for the improvement and renovation of the national literature. Neither were those Spaniards forgotten who sought to collect rare and rich treasures of knowledge in foreign lands: after their return to Spain, the queen appointed them professors in the public schools. Such were Antonio de Lebrija* (Nebrissa), and Avias Barbosa.† It was principally to the brothers Antonio and Alessandro Geraldino that she intrusted the education of her children, who became, under such masters, more learned than any other prince or princess in Europe at that period. Erasmus himself was astonished at the knowledge of Isabella's youngest daughter, who was afterwards married to Henry VIII. of England; while the great Spanish classical scholar Vivés ‡ mentions with admiration how the unfortunate Joanna, mother of Charles V., was able to deliver a Latin speech extempore.

Such examples tended to inspire the nobility especially with a love for learning; for the queen was particularly anxious for the improvement of their education. For their instructor she appointed Peter Martyr, who, soon after his arrival in Spain, took part in the Moorish war, exchanging literature for the military life; but after the conquest of

* He spent ten years in Bologna, and returned to Spain, laden with stores of erudition, in 1473. He published several works, mentioned by Prescott (vol. ii. p. 175).—*Trans.*

† This learned man was a Portuguese; but he spent most of his life in Spain. Like Lebrija, he studied in the schools of Italy. (See Nic. Antonio, "Bibliotheca Nova," p. 170.)

‡ The passage comes in his treatise "De Christianâ Feminâ," cap. 4, apud "Mem. de la Acad. de Hist.," tom. vi. Erasmus calls Catherine of Aragon "egregiò doctam" (Epistolæ,—Londini, 1642, Epist. 31).—*Trans.*

Granada (in 1492) he wished to receive holy orders.[*] Having been introduced to the queen by means of the great Cardinal Mendoza, she offered him to undertake the education of the young nobility attending her court, on condition of receiving valuable remuneration from her, and also for the sake of promoting a good work.[†] Peter willingly agreed to her proposals. The queen accordingly, after the example of Charlemagne, instituted a " Schola palatina;" that is, a school which was to accompany the court wherever it went. The commencement was indeed difficult; for the young grandees prized nothing but the art of war, and considered, therefore, that the arts and sciences were incompatible with their profession. However, in the month of September, 1492, Peter Martyr begins to speak of his success: he tells us how his house was filled every day with crowds of young Spanish nobles; and that Isabella herself daily sent her relations and those of Ferdinand to hear his lectures.[‡]

Although he was canon, and afterwards prior, of the church of Granada,[§] he still remained at court. His efforts, however, were so successful, that the young nobility made most rapid progress in learn-

---

[*] Epist. 113, ed. Elzevir, 1670.   He was not made priest till a much later period; viz. 1505.

[†] This is his own account, as related in Epist. 102.

[‡] " My house," he says, " swarms all the day long with noble youths, who, reclaimed from ignoble pursuits to those of letters, are now convinced that these, so far from being a hinderance, are rather a help in the profession of arms. . . It has pleased our royal mistress, the pattern of every exalted virtue, that her own near kinsman, the duke of Guimaraens, as well as the young duke of Villahermosa, the king's nephew, should remain under my roof the whole day," &c. (Epist. 115.)—*Trans.*

[§] Fléchier and some other writers call him dean of Granada; but they are incorrect; for Peter Martyr styles himself " prior " of Granada, which dignity seems to have been the same as provost of the chapter. (See Peter Martyr's Epist. 345.)

ing; and, even after several years, the worthy scholars highly esteemed him as a father. He says himself, " that all the Castilian nobles had sucked his literary breasts."

In union with Peter Martyr other illustrious scholars worked; such as Lucio Marineo, the Sicilian. He was first professor at Salamanca; then, in the year 1500, he was invited to court, where he laboured with such success for the education of the Spanish nobility that " no Spaniard was considered noble who showed any indifference to learning." Erasmus also declares " that the Spaniards had attained such eminence in literature that they not only excited the admiration of the most polished nations of Europe, but served likewise as models to them."[*] Many belonging to the first houses of the Spanish nobility—once so high and so proud—now made no hesitation in occupying chairs in the universities. Thus Don Gutierre de Toledo, son of the duke of Alva and cousin of the king, lectured in the university of Salamanca; as also did Don Pedro Fernandez de Velasco, son of the count of Haro.

Noble dames likewise vied with illustrious grandees for the prize of literary pre-eminence; while many even held chairs in the universities, and gave public lectures on eloquence and classical learning.[†]

With such a zeal for knowledge, the old schools now began to be filled and newly endowed; but Salamanca excelled them all. It was called the Spanish Athens, and was said at one time to have

---

[*] Epist. 977.

[†] Some of the names of these literary Spanish ladies have been preserved; viz., the marchioness of Monteagudo, Doña Maria Pacheco, and the queen's instructor in Latin—Doña Beatriz de Galindo. Doña Lucia de Medano and Doña Francisca de Lebrija are also mentioned.—*Trans.*

seven thousand students! It was there that Peter
Martyr gave lessons on Juvenal (1488) before such
an immense audience that the entrance to the hall
was completely blocked up, and the lecturer had to
be carried in on the shoulders of the students.[*]

But at the commencement of the sixteenth
century, there entered the lists with the ancient
university of Salamanca the new university of
Alcalá, which owed its magnificent establishment to
Ximenez, and was called by the Spaniards the
" eighth wonder of the world."[†]

When Ximenez was head chaplain of the church
of Siguenza, he already showed a great esteem and
love of learning; while he not only endeavoured by
diligent study to supply any deficiency in his own
education, but he also prevailed on his rich friend,
Juan Lopez de Medina Cœli, archdeacon of Almazan, to found the academy of Siguenza.

But not only did the queen herself see the necessity
of providing a higher education for all classes of
her subjects, and especially for the clergy, but
many prelates, and other illustrious individuals in
the kingdom, had the same convictions. About a
year before Isabella ascended the throne, the
council of Aranda found it necessary to make a law,
that no one should be allowed to receive holy orders
who was unacquainted with the Latin language.[‡]
Wherefore, in order to afford every one the means
of acquiring a good education in all the provinces
of the queen's vast dominions, a number of schools
were established about this period; viz., that of
Toledo, by Francisco Alvar; that of Seville, by
Roderigo de San Ælia; that of Granada, by the

---

[*] Peter Martyr, Epist. 57.

[†] " Octava maravilla del mundo." (Robles, p. 127, ed.
Toledo, 1604.)

[‡] Harduin, " Collect. Conc.," tom. ix. p. 1504.

Archbishop Talavera; that of Ognate, by Mercato, bishop of Avila; Ossuna, by Giron, count of Ureña; and Valencia, by Pope Alexander VI.

But all these schools were far excelled by the foundation of Ximenez at Alcalá. As soon as he had been raised to the archiepiscopal see of Toledo, he resolved to devote the immense revenues which he possessed to found a sanctuary where the arts and sciences could be taught. As a place most suitable for this purpose, he chose Alcalá de Henares, the ancient Complutum,* where, for two hundred years, there had already existed a school, which the archbishops of Toledo often honoured with their presence. Its pure air, its atmosphere always serene, and its pleasant situation on the banks of the Henares, recommended the spot to Ximenez. In the year 1498 he had already taken the first step towards carrying out his magnificent design; he then fixed on the spot where the building was to be erected, and adopted the plans which were drawn out by Pedro Gumiel, who at that time was the most celebrated Spanish architect. At length, in in the year 1500,† the foundation-stone of the college of San Ildefonso‡ was laid by the archbishop himself, with great solemnity. He delivered an eloquent discourse on the occasion, blessed the place where the building was to be raised, and offered up public prayers for its happy completion. Gonsalvo

---

* "Quæ dicitur esse Complutum; sit vel ne, nil mihi curæ," says Peter Martyr (Epist. 254). Consult Ford's excellent "Handbook of Spain," on the present state of Alcalá. I believe the university was suppressed in 1850.

† Gomez and Robles agree in placing the foundation of the university in the year 1500. But the first writer falls into serious mistakes in his chronology relating to this event.

‡ So named from the patron saint of the cathedral in Toledo. Ximenez had a particular devotion to St. Ildefonso. (See F. Florez, "España Sagrada," tom. v.; and also Alban Butler, Jan. 23.)—*Trans.*

Zegri, whom Ximenez had baptized some time before in Granada, and who was tenderly attached to the archbishop, placed in the foundation-stone, according to the ancient custom (as Gomez mentions in the sixteenth century), gold and silver coins, together with a brass image representing a Franciscan monk, in the middle of which was placed the deed of the foundation, written on parchment.

Just at the time when Ximenez was commencing the foundation of the university, the revolt amongst the Moors broke out in the mountains of the Alpuxarras : on this account, therefore, the archbishop was summoned again to Granada by the Catholic sovereigns.   Scarcely had he fulfilled his duties there, and recovered his strength after a severe illness, when he immediately hastened back to Alcalá, in order to continue the good work, and to adorn the town itself with several new streets.*   Towards the end of the year 1501, and in the beginning of 1502, these works were going on.   He remained at Alcalá till the end of April, 1502 ; but he was obliged to hasten to Toledo in the month of May, the same year, in order to be present at the solemn recognition of Joanna and Philip as heirs to the throne.   He made a good use of his five months' residence in that city, in order to mature his plans still more, and to obtain for his new university an annual and considerable revenue from the royal treasury.   He was also able to obtain new privileges ; for on the 10th of March, 1503, Prince Ferdinand— afterwards emperor of Austria—was born at Alcalá, and on the fifth day after was baptized by Ximenez.

---

* These details are all taken from Gomez, who tells us that some of the people blamed the cardinal for being too fond of building, jocosely observing, "that the church of Toledo never had a bishop of greater *edification,* in every sense of the word, than Ximenez."

On this occasion the queen bestowed so many fresh favours on the new university, that great numbers both of teachers and scholars crowded to it. As a memorial of this event, Alcalá has ever since preserved, as a precious relic, the cradle of Ferdinand.

When the court left Alcalá, Ximenez (as we have already seen), hastened, in the summer of 1503, to breathe the pure air of Brihuega, the Tivoli of the archbishops of Toledo; illness, however, detained him at Santorcaz, where he had once been a prisoner; whence he returned restored to health to Alcalá on the vigil of the Nativity, in 1503. Soon after his arrival he was summoned to Medina del Campo, in order to console the unfortunate Princess Joanna. There he remained after her departure, on account of the illness of Isabella, till the affairs of his diocese recalled him to Toledo. Thence he hastened back to Alcalá, with the intention of forwarding the work he had commenced there. Often was he seen on the ground with the rule in his hand, taking the admeasurements of the works, and stimulating the men by his example, and also by suitable rewards.[*]

About this time—viz. towards the end of the year 1503, or the beginning of 1504—a brief arrived from Rome authorizing the erection of the new university. With a view of obtaining this authorization, Ximenez, four years before, had deputed Francisco Ferrera to Rome (he was attached to the church of Alcalá); but the business was unaccountably delayed, till Alexander VI. (who died August 18th, 1503) and Julius II. (who was elected November 1st of the same year) at last granted the most exten-

---

[*] "On le vit plusieurs fois la règle à la main, visitant ses bâtiments, prenant lui-même les proportions, et les mesures, et animant les ouvriers par sa présence et par ses bienfaits." (Fléchier, liv. vi. p. 504.)

sive privileges and liberties to the new foundation :* these were afterwards still further augmented by Leo X.

The college of San Ildefonso was the head of the new university. The name was taken from the patron saint of the cathedral of Toledo, to whom Ximenez had an especial devotion. On the 26th of July, 1508 (or, according to others,† in 1510), seven students arrived at the university from Salamanca.‡ Their names were—Pedro Campo, Miguel Carasco, Fernando Balbas, Bartolomeo Castro, Pedro de Santa Cruz, Antonio Roderigo, and Juan Fontius.§ It was enacted, that for the future the college should consist of thirty-three professors, according to the number of years our Saviour lived ; and that twelve priests (who were called chaplains) should be added, in remembrance of the twelve apostles. These latter were not allowed to take any part in the teaching of the students, but were merely to dedicate themselves to the divine service and their

---

* Both Gomez and Fléchier place the bull of erection in the year 1502 ; but they are certainly mistaken ; for Julius II. did not ascend the pontifical throne till towards the end of the year 1503. It was only in the year 1513 that the statutes of the new university, having the approbation of Julius II., were promulgated among the professors of San Ildefonso. They were printed at Complutum in 1560, under this title: "Constitutiones Insignis Collegii Sancti Ildefonsi." In addition to this note of Dr. Hefele, I may remark, that Prescott mentions the year 1508 as the date when the university was opened for the admission of pupils.— *Trans.*

† Garibay, "Compendio Historial de las Chronicas," &c. (Anveres, 1571, fol. lib. xv. c. 10).

‡ "Studiosorum juvenum colonia, à Salmantica Complutum Ximenii jussù deducta," &c. (Gomez, lib. iv.)

§ Neither Gomez nor Robles gives the names in Spanish. I cannot, therefore, be certain whether I have spelt the names properly. All the account respecting the university is taken from Gomez, who had every opportunity of collecting materials for his History of Ximenez.— *Trans.*

pastoral duties; to recite the canonical office together, and distribute amongst the poor whatever remained after meals. The professors, properly so called, who were all theologians, occupied for the most part the academic chairs; or merely prepared themselves, like the "fellows" in English universities, to fulfil the duties of high and important offices; while some amongst them appear to have been intended for the post of administrators. It was, in effect, to these latter that the administration of the whole university was confided. When they appeared in public, they were distinguished from the other academic members by their imposing dress, which consisted of a long red robe, closely fitted to the body, together with a kind of scarf of the same colour, and about three inches in breadth. It was thrown over the left shoulder, and reached almost down to the ankles, hanging on the back in large folds.*

Besides this head college, Ximenez founded several other institutions, adapted to all kinds of wants. For poor young students in the classics, he endowed two boarding-schools,† where forty-two scholars were supported for three years free of all expense: they were dedicated in honour of St. Eugenius and St. Isidore. The students attended the lectures given by the six professors of languages, who were attached to the university; at their houses, however, special exercises were given, and disputations held for fourteen days. Strict examinations were required before any one could be admitted to a higher class, or to a particular course of lectures on any science. All these regulations were followed by such great results,

---

* " Hæc autem est veluti insigne Collegii Primarii; cæteris enim non licet sic vestiri." (Gomez, lib. iv.)

† Convicta, or, as the Germans call them, " Contubernien."

that, according to the judgment of Erasmus, "Alcalá was especially distinguished by its able philologists.*

Two other colleges—that of St. Balbina (from whom Ximenez took his title of cardinal) and that of St. Catherine—were intended for students in philosophy. In the first logic was studied for two years, and in the other physics and metaphysics for the same term. Each of these institutions numbered forty-eight scholars, the elder of whom were obliged to take care of the younger. All attended the lectures given by the eight professors of philosophy in the university; while, for the period of fourteen days, public disputations were held in presence of the rector and chancellor of the university; after which diplomas were given to the successful candidates for the degrees of bachelor, licentiate, and master of arts.† Another building, dedicated to the Mother of God, was provided for students who fell ill. But as the architect made it smaller than Ximenez wished, the archbishop erected a much larger one for the same object, in the year 1514; and appropriated the other building for eighteen poor theological students and six students in medicine: the course of whose studies was to continue for four years. A sixth college, named the "Little School," was founded in honour of the apostles St. Peter and St. Paul, where twelve Franciscan scholars, under the authority of a warden, and separated from the convent of St. Francis, in the city, devoted themselves entirely to their studies. According to the testimony of Wadding, from this house came forth a great

---

* "Academia Complutensis non aliunde celebritatem nominis auspicata est, quàm a complectendo linguas ac bonas literas." (Epist. 755.)

† Gomez, "De Rebus Gestis," &c. lib. iv.

number of generals of different orders, provincials, bishops, and learned men.*

The College of Three Languages, for thirty scholars, dedicated in honour of St. Jerome, was also founded by Ximenez; in this ten were taught Latin, ten Greek, and the same number learned the Hebrew language,† and all thoroughly.

Thus by degrees there arose such a number of buildings connected with the university in Alcalá, that many *bon-mots* were made at the expense of their founder.‡ But, besides these foundations of the archbishop, many other institutions arose, which owed their origin to the renown of the university; for all the monastic orders in Spain, with the exception of the Benedictines and Jeronymites, established houses of their own in Alcalá, in order to give the young religious an opportunity of studying in such an illustrious place.§

The superintendence over all these colleges, from which that of San Ildefonso made up the number of its staff, was confided to the rector of the university, who was also assisted by three counsellors; and to these was given the power of admitting the stipendiary professors. Ximenez reserved only a few free places for his relations, and other persons, besides some particular corporations. He placed the whole of the university under the perpetual patronage of the king of Castile, of the Cardinal de

---

* "Annales Minorum," tom. xv. p. 143.

† "Tambien el Colegio Trilingue, con titulo de San Geronymo, con treynta colegiales. . . . . . en quien se ha fundado la puridad de las lenguas, y elegancia de la retórica." (Robles, p. 132.)

‡ The play upon the word "edification" has already been related.—*Trans.*

§ Robles, p. 133.

Santa Balbina, the archbishop of Toledo, the duke del Infantado, and the count of Coruña.

Ximenez wished that the rector of the university should be at the same time rector of the college of San Ildefonso. Herein he deviated from the custom followed at Salamanca and other universities, even out of Spain, of appointing as " Rector Magnificus " (honorary rector) a student who might belong to a royal family, or at least to some noble house.* Ximenez appointed three counsellors for the rector, to assist him; and these were chosen from the professors of San Ildefonso. Their business was to consult together on all affairs of minor importance connected with the university, without being obliged to trouble the other professors. Hence they formed a kind of august senate, being chosen, like the rector, from the professors of San Ildefonso : they were changed, however, every year. Matters of importance were submitted to the " fellows " of San Ildefonso, and sometimes were discussed by all the professors of the university. By means of papal indults and royal privileges, the rector was invested with the right of correcting the faults of all persons belonging to the university. He also possessed great influence, and his dignity was highly respected ; for, in union with his three counsellors, he had the power of nominating persons to nearly all offices, and even to the professorial chairs.

The first rector was chosen on the feast of St. Luke, 1508; his name was Pedro Campo, one of those academicians who were summoned from Salamanca, and who were the first that were received in the college of San Ildefonso.

Besides the rector, the university of Alcalá,

* Voight, in his trentise "Ueber Fürstenleben und Fürsten-sitte im 16 Jahrhundert," mentions several princes who, whilst students, were rectors of the university of Wittenberg.

following the example of the university of Paris, had also a chancellor, who conferred academic degrees, and took part in examinations, disputations, and scientific exercises. Ximenez chose the learned Pedro Lerma for the first chancellor, having invited him from Paris, and appointed him abbot of San Justus, and pastor in Alcalá. He made a rule, that for the future the dignity of chancellor should always be united with the office above named.

Ximenez invited professors, partly from Salamanca, and partly from Paris; and so numerous were the excellent and learned men whom he collected around him, through his immense liberality, that on the opening of the university, which took place October 18th, 1508, (only eight years after the foundation-stone had been laid,) all the chairs of the professors were found to be occupied. Their number amounted to forty-two: of these six taught theology; six, canon law; four, medicine; one, anatomy; one, surgery; eight, philosophy; one, moral philosophy; one, mathematics; four, the Hebrew and Greek languages; four, rhetoric; and six, grammar.* The following are the names of the first professors of theology:—Gonsalvo Ægidio de Burgos, the Franciscan Pedro Clemente, and Pedro Sirvel de Daroca; for philosophy were Miguel Pardo de Burgos and Antonio Morales de Cordova; medicine was taught by Torracona and Cartagena; and philology by Demetrio Ducas of Crete, and Nuñez de Guzman,† or Pinciano. Hebrew was taught by Paulo Coronel, a converted Jew; canon law by Loranca and Salceo, and rhetoric by Fernando Alfonso Ferrara. There was no chair

---

* Robles, p. 133.

† This was a very celebrated scholar, belonging to the ancient house of that name. He was the author of the Latin version in the polyglot of Ximenez.—*Trans.*

appointed for civil law, as this branch was studied with success at Salamanca and Valladolid. Ximenez himself had no taste for this science, although he had profoundly studied jurisprudence.

In order to excite the zeal of the professors, he made a law that their period of holding office should not continue longer than four years, at the end of which a fresh concursus was to be held. For the like object Ximenez made a law, that if a professor had no audience, he was not to receive the emolument attached to his chair, and that his salary was to be confined only to his benefice, or to some office he might have in the college. This regulation is similar to one which now prevails in the colleges of many universities.

The archbishop adopted other no less efficacious means of exciting the zeal of masters and of scholars. Thus he often attended the lectures, and presided in person at the academic exercises and disputations.* He obtained for the university the right of conferring degrees in philosophy, medicine, and theology; following herein the rules of the Paris university as his pattern. But the theological honours were far more solemn, and much more difficult to attain. No one could venture any claim to them before he had devoted ten years to the study of theology. Hence it happened, that well-deserving persons, and even priests, who had been in office and dignities for years, were yet obliged to undergo a rigorous examination in theology. Gomez relates, that Fernando Balbas, a professor in San Ildefonso, was obliged to wait till the expiration of his rectorship before he could receive his degree of licentiate in theology.

The annual revenues with which Ximenez en-

* Gomez, lib. iv.

dowed the university amounted at first to 14,000 ducats; but in the time of Robles (anno 1600) they had risen to 30,000.* This writer also remarks, with particular emphasis, that of all the foundations made by Ximenez, not one had failed.

Quickly there hastened to Alcalá an immense number of students† from all parts of the Peninsula. The university itself counted in a short time as numerous a body as any of its elder sisters in Spain. But amongst so many, it was to be expected that sometimes there would occur outbreaks of juvenile rashness; as, for example, in the following case :— One day the students rescued an unfortunate man, who was going to be hanged,‡ and insulted the police.§ Ximenez pardoned them, and obtained their pardon from the king also; but reprimanded the offence so firmly, that the like never happened again in his lifetime. About six years after, Ximenez had to bear another severe trial, on seeing many of his most able professors leaving Alcalá for the rival university of Salamanca, and even taking with them many of the students. They were seduced by promises of all kinds from the authorities at Salamanca.‖ Amongst the

* Robles, p. 129. I do not exactly know the amount in English money; no doubt it was equal to several thousand pounds.— *Trans.*

† Prescott mentions, that 7,000 students came out to meet Francis I. when he visited Alcalá, only twenty years after the university had been opened.

‡ This case is mentioned by Gomez, who states that the students attacked the mayor and the executioner. Nothing is said about the police, if there were any such body in those days.— *Trans.*

§ " Und die Polizei dabei insultiren." (Hefele.)

‖ Gomez gives more particulars :—" Nam viri illi præstantes, quibus munus docendi datum diximus, partim Ximenii favore abutentes, partim Salmanticensis Academiæ pollicitis invitati (verebantur enim Salmanticenses, ne sua schola non ita floreret,

professors whom Ximenez lost at this time, was Ælio Antonio de Lebrija (Nebrissa), a town in the neighbourhood of Seville. He was born* of a noble family, in the year 1442. He studied five years at Salamanca and ten in Italy, with extraordinary success, having acquired vast stores of knowledge, especially in languages. About the year 1470 he returned to his native country, and was appointed tutor to the nephew of the arch-bishop of Seville. Soon after, he was named to a chair in the university of Salamanca,† where his lectures, and especially his works on philology, gained him an extraordinary reputation. In order, however, to be able to devote all his time to the composition of a Latin lexicon, he resigned his public professorship about the year 1488, and lived in retirement with the grand master of the order of Alcantara, who was afterwards known as Cardinal Zuñiga. At the cardinal's death, Lebrija accepted the office of preceptor to Prince Juan, the heir to the throne; and was also appointed the "historio-grapher" under Ferdinand and Isabella. After the queen's death, he returned, in 1505, to his professor-ship at Salamanca, where he remained till 1508, when Ximenez induced him to become professor in

si Complutensis tam insignes haberet professores), salaria sibi majora dari poscebant. Id cùm Ximenius, ad eos provehendos alioqui munificus, indignum esse et impudens duceret, semper enim vir in promittendo parcus, benè de ipso sperarent edixerat—cœpit animo nonnihil commoveri." (Lib. iv.) Dr. Hefele omits mentioning that the professors wished their salaries to be raised. —*Trans.*

* Prescott states that he was born in 1444. But Señor Muñoz proves the date to be incorrect. (See his life of Lebrija, tom. iii. "De las Memorias de la Real Academia de la Historia," p. 2. Madrid, 1799.)

† Prescott states that he was appointed to the *two* chairs of grammar and poetry, a thing unprecedented in the university. (See his notice of Lebrija, vol. i. p. 451.)

his new university at Alcalá, and to assist him in the great work of his Polyglot Bible. It is uncertain in what year Lebrija left Ximenez, to return to Salamanca. But in 1513 the archbishop had the consolation of beholding this learned professor returning to him once more, never again to leave him.* Ximenez rewarded him with princely generosity, and testified the highest esteem for him. Often did he pass before his residence, and converse with him through the window, sometimes on difficult points which he could not understand, and at other times on the affairs of the university. Lebrija on his part deserved so well the gratitude of Alcalá, that for several years after his death (which took place in 1522) his anniversary was commemorated by the university with a solemn service, as a mark of respect for his memory. According to the opinion of Gomez,† Spain owes to Lebrija almost all the glory of her classical knowledge. His two "Decades" on the reign of Ferdinand and Isabella, composed at Alcalá in 1509, contain most valuable stores for the history of that period.‡

In the beginning of the year 1514, the new university was highly honoured by a visit from King Ferdinand, who personally inspected all the institutions, attended some of the lectures, and admired

---

* The real motive which induced Lebrija to leave Salamanca seems to have been this. The first chair in Humanity being vacant, Lebrija was most anxious to occupy it. But the students of Salamanca had then the right of election: they entered into a plot, and rejected the learned professor. This so displeased him, that he abandoned the university for ever. (Muñoz, "Memorias de la Acad. de la Hist." p. 22.)

† "Cui Hispania debet quicquid habet bonarum literarum." (See also Antonio, "Bibliotheca Nova," tom. i. pp. 132—139.)

‡ Thus his new biographer, Juan Bautista Muñoz, speaks of him as, "El restaurador del gusto y solidez en toda buena literatura," and "Maestro por excelencia de la nacion Española." ("Memorias," &c. tom. iii.)

the grandeur and beauty of the buildings.* Having
noticed that one of the walls was made merely of clay,
the king remarked, "that such a wall but ill corresponded with a building which was destined to last for
ever." "It is true," replied Ximenez; "but a man,
who is mortal, should make haste to see the termination of his labours. I am consoled by the reflection,
that what is now made of clay will one day be made
of marble." And his words came true; for forty-
three years after, by order of the rector Turbalano,
the whole wall alongside of the Franciscan convent
was built of marble. While the king was conversing
with the archbishop, Fernando Balbas, the rector
of the university, came from the college of San
Ildefonso, attended by his beadles, who carried their
maces with great gravity. The rector invited his
majesty into the college. But when the attendants
of the king perceived the pomp and state of the
beadles, they called out to them to lay aside those
insignia, as unbecoming the presence of kingly
power. Ferdinand, however, blamed the zeal of his
attendants, and commanded that respect should be
shown to the customs of the university, adding
these words: "Here is the residence of the Muses,
where the learned are kings." † The rector then
threw himself at the feet of Ferdinand, who received
him kindly, and heard with interest the details which
he gave him respecting the state and progress of
the university. In the mean time night came on,

---

* Fléchier (liv. iii. pp. 302, 303) and Prescott also assign the
date 1513 for this event. But Balbas was not elected rector till
October 18th, 1513: and Ferdinand did not arrive at Alcalá till
January in the following year.

† Gomez gives the answer somewhat differently: "Musarum,
inquicus, illas œdes esse, in quibus fas poscebat, ut Musarum
sacris initiati regnarent"—This is the seat of the Muses, and
those have a right to reign there who are initiated in the mysteries of the Muses.—*Trans.*

and the young pages of the king were waiting to accompany his majesty back with torches. But, on a sudden a quarrel arose between them and the students, which ended in violence.* When the king arrived and heard of the tumult, he was very angry, and bitterly upbraided Ximenez in these words:—" If the first excesses which the students committed had been punished as they deserved, the present insolent proceedings would not have occurred." † The bishop replied by making an allusion to the provocation which had been received from the pages : " O king, even an ant has its gall, and every one will be revenged when he is oppressed." These words calmed the anger of the king.

Some years after the death of Ximenez, the university received a visit from another no less illustrious personage,—Francis I., king of France. After he had visited all the various institutions, he uttered these remarkable words : " Your Ximenez has undertaken and accomplished a work which I myself could not attempt. The university of Paris, the pride of my kingdom, is the work of many sovereigns. But Ximenez alone has founded one like it."

After Ximenez had made every regulation connected with the course of studies in the university, his solicitude also provided for aged and infirm professors. On this subject he consulted with the plenipotentiary of Charles V., afterwards known as

---

* " His vero fustibus et saxis se ulciscentibus," &c. (Gomez), show how the quarrel was carried on.

† " Hæc sunt (inquit) præmia meæ semper lenitatis. Nam si isti tui scholastici, cùm primum in regios ministros irreverenter se gesserunt, fuissent ut merebantur mulctati, non pervenissent ad tantam impudentiam, ut, me præsente, in meam familiam tam procaciter irruerent." (Gomez, lib. iv.)

Pope Adrian VI., and who was associated with the archbishop in the regency of Castile. Adrian was then not only professor in the university of Louvain, but he was also honoured with the dignity of "Dean" of the church of St. Peter in that city. Now, there a custom prevailed of providing for aged professors, the same as was done for the canons. Ximenez approved of this custom, and therefore he solicited Pope Leo X. to incorporate with the university of Alcalá the collegiate church of SS. Justos and Pastor.* His petition was granted; and hence he was empowered to bestow canonries on professors of theology; while lesser benefices were given to the professors of philosophy.

The academy of Siguenza, after the death of its founder, expressed a desire to be united with the university of Alcalá; but Ximenez would not consent to the proposal, out of respect to the memory of his friend who had founded the college at Siguenza. Neither would he give his consent that his university should be incorporated with that of Salamanca.

But it was reserved for the 19th century (1807†) to behold this magnificent home of the arts and sciences, together with the academy of Siguenza, and many other colleges in Spain, completely dissolved and suppressed.‡

---

* These were two martyrs, whose bodies reposed in the church of Alcalá. (See Robles, who gives many interesting details connected with the university, cap. xvi.)—*Trans.*

† Dr. Hefele refers to the invasion of Spain by the French, when religion and literature were alike outraged.

‡ The *Univers* of the 6th of June, 1857, speaking of the translation of the remains of Cardinal Ximenez, refers to a much later date the suppression of the university of Alcalá:—" Tout demeure dans le même état jusqu'en 1850, où l'Université d'Alcalá se trouva supprimée par la création de l'Université Centrale, et

ses bâtiments vendus au Comte de Quinto. Les habitants de cette ville, voyant que l'édifice allait être détruit, sans respect pour les souvenirs qui s'y rattachent, et pour le mérite artistique de sa construction, résolurent de sauver au moins le riche tombeau du Cardinal Cisneros," &c. A more detailed account of the translation of the cardinal's remains is given in the Preface.—*Trans.*

CHAPTER XI.

THE COMPLUTENSIAN POLYGLOT.

THE greatest literary work published at Alcalá is the cardinal's celebrated Polyglot; the name "Complutensian" being added from Complutum, the place of its publication. It was the ancient name of Alcalá.

The impetus that was given to philology at the commencement of the 15th century, exercised a very beneficial influence on the progress of biblical studies, and especially with reference to biblical criticism and hermeneutics.* Even in the middle ages there were biblical critics; such as abbot Stephen, of Citeaux, who received the vows of St. Bernard, and the learned Dominican, Hugo de Santo Caro (1236).† There was also the famous Sorbonne of Paris, that attempted to correct the text of the Vulgate, not merely from ancient Latin manuscripts, but also from a comparison with ancient Greek and Hebrew ones.‡ But the incapacity of copyists, and the ignorance of many who undertook the correction of Scripture, were so many obstacles which prevented

---

* It treats of the principles of biblical interpretation. (See Dr. Dixon's "Introduction," &c. vol. i. p. 270. Duffy, 1852.)— *Trans.*

† The writer's account, in this introduction to the polyglot of Ximenez, is very meagre. He passes over the labours of St. Jerome, Origen, Eusebius, Lucian, Cassiodorus, and Alcuin. Reference should also have been made to St. Augustine's treatise "De Doctrinâ Christianâ," where he insists on the necessity of procuring a correct text as far as possible.—*Trans.*

‡ See Welte's "Kirch. Ansehen der Vulgata," Quartalschr. 1845.

the full growth and development of critical investigation.[*] Hence, at the commencement of the fifteenth century, Cardinal Pierre d'Ailly complained bitterly, but very justly, of the deplorable state of the original text of Scripture.[†]

But just at the period when in the West the new impulse given to philological studies had revived the long-delayed hopes and wishes of at last beholding an emendated text of Scripture, then it was that Germany gave to the world a new instrument of power, applicable to all branches of literary knowledge and science. This was the art of printing, whereby books, beautifully got up, could be multiplied a thousandfold, and sold at a comparatively low price.[‡]

It was but natural that the newly-invented art should immediately have given its services to the Holy Scriptures; and in reality we find, that from the year 1462 to the year 1500, no fewer than eighty complete editions of the Vulgate appeared, of which the Roman edition of 1471 had been corrected from ancient manuscripts by the learned bishop Joannes Andreas of Aleria.[§]

Soon did the zeal of the pious and learned extend to the original text of the sacred books. The Jews were the first who endeavoured to multiply copies

---

[*] The reader will not fail to peruse Cardinal Wiseman's tenth lecture, on oriental studies, in his "Lectures on Science and Revealed Religion," where an immense mass of information will be found on the history of biblical criticism.—*Trans.*

[†] It is now, however, acknowledged that the Hebrew and Greek manuscripts of the Scripture have not been wilfully corrupted, and that no material or substantial interpolation has found its way into them. The accuracy of our ordinary text is wonderful.—*Trans.*

[‡] See Charles Knight's interesting volume, "The Old Printer and the Modern Press." (London, Murray, 1854.)

[§] A town in Corsica. There is a short account of this bishop in Watt's "Bibliotheca Britannica." Edinburgh, 1824.—*Trans.*

of the Hebrew Bible. After several attempts had been made upon the Psalms and other single books of Scripture, a Jew published the first complete Hebrew Bible, in the year 1488,* at Soncino, a town in Lombardy, between Cremona and Brescia. Several other editions followed, especially that of Brescia, in the year 1494,† all being edited by Jews. Up to this period there is no question but that Christians were behind others in biblical emendations. But there now appeared a man who was destined to restore to the Christians their ancient renown in scriptural knowledge; and this personage was Cardinal Ximenez. No one lamented more bitterly than he had done the miserably low position which biblical studies held in the theological course of studies pursued at that time. We have already noticed how he himself, in riper years, and when he was head chaplain of Siguenza, learned the Hebrew and Chaldaic languages through his love of the Bible. Often was he heard to say that he would willingly give up all his knowledge of civil law (which was then considered essential to a theological education), to be able to explain only a single verse of the Bible.‡ Gomez assures us that Ximenez had two especial reasons for lamenting the neglect of biblical science in the clergy of his time, and also their ignorance of Hebrew and Greek. The first was, because such neglect closed up the principal source of sacred learning, viz., the Bible and the works of the

* Abraham Ben Chajim seems to have been the name of the editor. The third and last of the Soncinates editions was printed in 1517, folio. (See Le Long, "Bibliotheca Sacra." Paris, 1723.) —*Trans.*

† Herbst, "Historisch-Kritische Einleitung in's A. Test.," herausgegeben von Dr. Welte, 1840, thl. i. ss. 128—132.

‡ Gomez, lib. i. p. 933 (in "Hispaniæ illustratæ Scriptores," Francof. 1603, fol.)

fathers; and secondly, they at the same time made themselves incapable of offering any opposition (which was so necessary to be done) to those impious heretics who either abused the Holy Scripture or perverted it.

Scarcely had the archbishop been elevated to the primatial see of Spain, when he began to show his early love for learning, not by the foundation of the university of Alcalá only, but he also at the same time resolved to give a new impulse to biblical studies, by the publication of a work equal to the "Hexapla" of Origen, now unfortunately lost.* His ideas on this subject are thus expressed in the prolegomena to the Polyglot: — "No translation can fully and exactly represent the sense of the original, at least in that language in which our Saviour himself spoke. The manuscripts of the Latin Vulgate differ so much one from another that one cannot help suspecting some alterations must have been made, principally through the ignorance and negligence of the copyists. It is necessary, therefore (as St. Jerome and St. Augustine desired), that we should go back to the origin of the sacred writings, and correct the books of the Old Testament by the Hebrew text, and those of the New Testament by the Greek text. Every theologian should also be able to drink of that water 'which springeth up to eternal life,' at the fountain-head itself. This is the reason, therefore, why we have ordered the Bible to be printed in the original language with different translations . . . . . To accomplish this task, we have been obliged to have recourse to the knowledge of the most able

* Gomez, p. 966. One of the most learned amongst the members of the Spanish academy, Señor J. B. Muñoz, pays a just tribute to Ximenez for the services he rendered to learning. (See his article in "Memorias de la Historia," &c., tom. iii. p. 18.)

philologists, and to make researches in every direction for the best and most ancient Hebrew and Greek manuscripts. Our object is, to revive the hitherto dormant study of the Sacred Scriptures."*

During the summer of 1502 Ximenez was obliged to spend five months in Toledo, on account of Joanna and Philip being acknowledged as heirs to the crown of Spain. But while the court of grandees were rejoicing amidst the splendid *fêtes* which followed the act of homage, the archbishop was preparing a more magnificent feast for sacred theology. It was then that he conceived the plan of his great Polyglot, that he chose learned men to help him, that he procured the manuscripts, and fixed upon his new university to be the place where this gigantic work was to be prepared and completed.†

The men to whom this undertaking was intrusted were the celebrated Antonio de Lebrija, of whom mention has been made; Demetrius Ducas, of Crete, who had been invited by Ximenez to Alcalá, to teach the Greek language; Lopez de Zuñiga (Stunica or Astuniga), so well known by his discussions with Erasmus; Nuñez de Guzman (Pintianus), of noble extraction, professor at Alcalá, and author of several commentaries on the classics. With these Ximenez associated three learned Jews, converts to Christianity; viz., Alfonso, physician at Alcalá; Paul Coronell, of Segovia (he died, in 1534, professor of theology at Salamanca); and Alfonso de Zamora, who was specially appointed to compose a grammar and Hebrew dictionary for the Poly-

---

* " Ut incipiant Divinarum Litterarum studia hactenus intermortua reviviscere," &c. — (Prolegomena, inserted in vol. i. of the Old Testament.) If this introduction was not written by Ximenez himself, it certainly expresses his ideas and sentiments.
† Gomez, p. 965.

glot. Demetrius of Crete, Zuñiga, and Nuñez de Guzman, occupied themselves especially with a Latin version of the Septuagint. They afterward made use of the assistance of their scholars, one of whom, Peter Vergara (who died canon of Alcalá, in 1557), translated the sapiential books of Proverbs, Ecclesiastes, the Canticle of Canticles, Ecclesiasticus, and the Book of Wisdom. It would be quite a mistake to suppose that Ximenez was able to collect all these men together in a day to help him in his work. Alfonso de Zamora, for instance, did not receive baptism till the year 1506, and consequently he did not belong to the learned band till after the others had been connected with it several years.

The whole of the plan for his magnificent undertaking was formed by Ximenez himself, and these learned men worked under his direction, being confident that they would be most liberally rewarded. He himself, with noble generosity and immense zeal, supplied all their wants, and furnished them with every help necessary for the work. Often did he quicken their zeal by such words as these:— " Make haste, my friends; for as all things in this world are of a transient nature, you might lose me as your patron, or I might have to lament your loss."* He made researches on all sides for manuscripts of the Old and New Testaments; and sometimes was obliged to purchase them at an enormous expense, while others generously hastened to lend them for his use; amongst whom was Pope Leo X. This pontiff honoured and revered Ximenez, and still more, he loved the fine arts. He therefore generously supported him in the publication of the celebrated Polyglot. In return, Ximenez dedicated the work to his holiness, and in the introduction

* Gomez, p. 966.

gave him public thanks in these words:—"Atque ex ipsis (exemplaribus) quidem Græca Sanctitati Tuæ debemus; qui ex istâ Apostolicâ Bibliothecâ antiquissimos tam Veteris quam Novi Testamenti codices perquam humanè ad nos misisti."*

I am aware that a doubt respecting the chronology of this event has been raised: Leo X. was only elected pope in March, 1513, while the first part of the Polyglot—the New Testament—was only completed on the 10th of January, 1514. During so short an interval, then, it is asked, how could the Vatican manuscripts have been not merely collated together, but also have been copied? We are inclined to believe, with most biblical critics, that before Leo X. was made pope, when he was only cardinal, he had sent the archbishop the manuscripts † from Rome, and that the public thanks for them were offered by Ximenez (such as we have seen in the preface) after Leo had been elected pope.‡

* "It is to your holiness that we are indebted for the Greek manuscripts. You have sent us, with the greatest kindness, the copies both of the Old and New Testament, the most ancient that the apostolic library possessed." These manuscripts having been unfortunately lost or destroyed, critics cannot pronounce any judgment on their precise date. It seems the editors must have had other manuscripts, besides those which had been sent from Rome. (See Michaelis, "Introduction to the New Testament," vol. ii. p. 433, ed. Cambridge, 1793. Also, Hug's "Introduction to the Writings of the New Testament," vol. i. p. 304. London, 1827.)

† This is the opinion of Marsh, in his "Remarks on Michaelis' Introduction;" Professor Hug, Feilmoser, and others, give the same explanation. See the curious and rare volume of Zuñiga (Stunica), entitled, "Itinerarium dum Compluto Romam proficisceretur." 4to.

‡ Respecting these manuscripts, Michaelis relates ("Introduction to the New Testament," vol. ii. pp. 440—441), that Professor Moldenhawer, who was in Spain in 1784, went to Alcalá, for the purpose of discovering the manuscripts which had been used for the Complutensian Polyglot. It was supposed that very pro-

In the same prologue, Ximenez also mentions what great pains and trouble he took in order to collect from various parts a considerable number of Hebrew, Greek, and Latin manuscripts. He likewise informs us, in the second prologue, that for the Greek text (probably used for both the Old and New Testament) he made special use of the Roman manuscripts,* besides consulting others, particularly one sent by the republic of Venice, which was a copy of a codex that once belonged to Cardinal Bessarion. Mention is also made of some very ancient Latin manuscripts, written in Gothic characters, which seem to have been made use of for the edition of the Vulgate. We learn, too, from Zuñiga,† one of the principal editors of the Polyglot, that a *Codex Rhodiensis* (Griesbach speaks of it under No. 52 of the manuscripts for the Acts

bably the Greek manuscripts were preserved in the library of the university. But on making inquiries, the professor found that about thirty years before his arrival, an ignorant librarian, who wanted room for some new books had sold the ancient vellum manuscripts to a person named Toryo, as "Membranas inutiles"! This man, who made fireworks, used them as materials for his rockets! Michaelis candidly admits that the editors of the Polyglot did *not* alter the Greek text to confirm the authority of the Vulgate, and that when they described their manuscripts as being of the greatest antiquity, the editors were honest, though they were mistaken; the art of criticism being then in its infancy, and the antiquity of manuscripts but little understood. (Vol. ii. p. 434.)

* It is uncertain whether the " Codex Vaticanus " was in the number of the manuscripts which were sent from Rome. The Complutensian Polyglot differs from it very frequently, according to Blanchini:—"Falluntur qui putant ad solum exemplar ex Bibliothecâ Vaticanâ suppeditatum a Leone X., suam editionem exprimendum curasse Ximenius, cum ab ipsâ sæpissime, factâ a nobis collatione, deflectat." (" Evangeliarum Quadruplex," pars i. p. 495.)—*Trans.*

† Lopez de Zuñiga is the same person who has been mentioned before, whose " Itinerarium " is referred to in a previous note.

of the Apostles and catholic Epistles)* was made use of for the Greek text of the New Testament. In a word, Gomez testifies that seven Hebrew manuscripts alone cost no less a sum than 4,000 ducats; and that the total expense of the whole work amounted to 50,000 ducats,†—a sum which, if estimated at the value of money then, could have been expended only by a man who united the wants of a monk to the revenues of a king. The purchase of manuscripts; the remuneration of those engaged in procuring them; the emoluments of the editors, the copyists, and assistants; the expense also of the new letters, which were all to be cast in Alcalá; the bringing over able printers from Germany; the printing itself;—all these required an enormous outlay. The sale price bore no kind of proportion to the expense of publication; for Ximenez had no more than 600 copies taken off, while each copy, though consisting of six folios, cost no more than six ducats and a half.‡ But even the produce of the sale was devoted by Ximenez, in his will, to charitable purposes, as may be seen from the papal bull of confirmation, in the first volume of the Old Testament.

The small number of the copies that were printed accounts for the scarcity of the work and the dearness of the price;§ for at the present day a perfect

---

* See his "Krit. Aus. des N. Test.," 2 band, p. 8.

† This sum would amount in English money to near £25,000 sterling.

‡ This price we know from the declaration of Francisco Ruyz, bishop of Avila, who was an intimate friend of Ximenez; and who, after the death of the cardinal, tried to extend the sale of the Polyglot. His declaration may be found at the end of the preface to the Old Testament.

§ In all Germany there are not more than fifteen copies. (See Hanlein's "Introduction to the New Testament," part 2, p. 260.)

copy cannot be purchased under 500 florins.* The second volume, viz., the Hebrew-Chaldaic Lexicon, is often wanting in many copies. Gomez, the biographer of Ximenez, informs us that in his time it was difficult to find it, even in Spain.

The learned editors commenced their labours in the same year that Ximenez conceived the design of the Polyglot (1502).† But it was not till twelve years after (January 10, 1514), that the first volume was finished, containing the New Testament. This date is evident from the final remarks appended to the Apocalypse.‡

This volume, the first in the order of time, and forming the sixth of the work, contains the whole of the New Testament, and other matter, in the following order :—It commences by a kind of preface in Greek and Latin, explaining why the Greek text of the New Testament has no accents. As the ancient Greeks did not make use of any accents, so also, it seems that the writers of the New Testament did not use them in their autographs: thus the editors of the Polyglot wished to adhere to the ancient custom.§ Their absence, however, can cause

---

* The price varies according to the state of the copy. A short time ago a copy was sold in London for £75. Five hundred florins would amount to about £40, for which I believe a copy could be procured from Mr. C. J. Stewart, of King-William Street.—*Trans.*

† Not in 1505, as Schröckh and others suppose; nor in 1500, as Rosenmüller states in his "Handbuch für die Literatur der Bibl. Kritik und Exegese" (band iii. s. 281).

‡ From comparing each volume, and from the prologue to the whole work added to each volume of the Old Testament, it is very evident that the New Testament was printed first. Many, however, have fallen into an error on this point.

§ We should be mistaken were we therefore to conclude that the Greek copies which the editors had were without accents. Michaelis appears to believe that their manuscripts really had

no difficulty to any one who has a slight knowledge of Greek. Still, the tonic syllable of every poly-syllable is marked with a stroke, resembling our acute accent. As to the Septuagint—the Greek version of the Old Testament,—there is no difficulty with the modern accentuation, since the question is not about the original text, but merely of a translation. In a word, we are assured that only the most ancient and correct copies were made use of,—"Antiquissima emendatissimaque exemplaria," which Pope Leo X. had specially sent to serve as the basis of the Greek text.*

This short preface to the reader is followed by the letter of Eusebius Pamphilus (who died in 340) to Carpianus, respecting the harmony of the Gospels. The letter is in Greek, without a Latin translation. This letter generally precedes the canons of Eusebius, connected with the concordance of the Gospels. But the Polyglot contains the letter only, and simply mentions the order of the canons. They are ten in number. In the first are included all those passages which are found in the four Evangelists; in the second are the passages which are common to St. Matthew, St. Mark, and St. Luke; in the third, those which are found in St. Matthew, St. Luke, and St. John; in the fourth, those which

accents, and that therefore they were not so ancient as the editors supposed.

* These are the words of the preface to the New Testament:— " Illud lectorem non lateat, non quævis exemplaria impressioni huic archetypa fuisse, sed antiquissima emendatissimaque, ac tantæ præterea vetustatis, ut fidem eis abrogare nefas videatur; quæ Sanctissimus in Christo Pater et Dominus noster Leo X. Pontifex maximus huic instituto favere cupiens, ex Apostolicâ Bibliothecâ educta, misit ad Reverendissimum Dominum Cardinalem Hispaniæ," &c. In the letter addressed to Leo X. by Ximenez, to thank his Holiness for sending the manuscripts, he says,—" Qui nobis in hoc negotio maximo fuerunt adjumento " —meaning the manuscripts.—*Trans.*

are common to St. Matthew, St. Mark, and St. John; in the fifth, those which St. Matthew and St. Luke have in common; in the sixth, those of St. Matthew and St. Mark; in the seventh, those of St. Matthew and St. John; in the eighth, those of St. Mark and St. Luke; in the ninth, those of St. Luke and St. John; and the tenth, finally, includes all those passages which belong only to one single Evangelist, and for which no parallel passage is found in the others.*

Then there follows the letter of St. Jerome to Pope Damasus, upon the four Gospels: there are also two prefaces on St. Matthew, together with a dissertation (argumentum) on his Gospel.

After these introductory parts, come the four Gospels themselves, divided into two columns, the largest of which contains the Greek text, and the smallest the Vulgate, with reference to the margin of the parallel places and quotations. The division into verses is wanting both in the Old and New Testament. This division, it is well known, was invented a few years later (1551), by Robert Stephens. The chapters, however, are distinguished from each other according to the manner introduced by Cardinal Hugo in the thirteenth century.

At the end of the Gospel of St. Matthew is introduced the preface of St. Jerome or St. Mark, though, by an error of the press, St. Matthew is put instead of St. Mark. In like manner, after the Gospel of St. Mark, a preface of St. Jerome precedes the Gospel of St. Luke, which is followed by a preface on the Gospel of St. John.

Two dissertations in Greek come after this first part of the New Testament; the shorter one is ano-

---

* These canons (Tabellen) of Eusebius, together with the letter to Carpianus, are printed in Mill's edition of the New Testament.

nymous, though probably composed by the editors themselves : it treats of St. Paul's journeys. The other is much longer : it was composed in the fifth century by the deacon Euthalius, the inventor of stichometry,* and treats of the chronology of St. Paul's preaching, and also of his death.

Then there follows a preface of St. Jerome upon all the epistles of St. Paul, and a particular preface of the same father upon the Epistle to the Romans; after which comes the text of St. Paul's epistles, by the side of the Vulgate. To each epistle is prefixed a preface and a dissertation (argumentum).

The Epistle to the Hebrews closes the series of all St. Paul's epistles ; then come the Acts of the Apostles, with two prologues; and the Acts are followed by the seven catholic epistles; and last of all is the Apocalypse. At the end of the Apocalypse of St. John are added five pieces of poetry, upon the work itself, and upon Ximenez; two of which were composed in Greek by Demetrius Ducas and Nicetas Faustu, who was probably a scholar of Demetrius. The three others, however, are in Latin, and were composed by Juan Vergara, Nuñez Guzman Pintianus, and Maestro Bartolo de Castro. These were doubtless five learned men, who were principally occupied with the labour of preparing the New Testament.†

To these poems succeeds a table, explanatory of all the proper names in the New Testament, ranged

---

* This is a biblical term, from the Greek στιχομετρια. It consists in setting just so many words in one line as are to be read uninterruptedly, so as clearly to give the sense of the author. No punctuation was then used. (See Hug's "Introduction to the New Testament," vol. i. p. 240, &c.)

† There is a very excellent account of the Complutensian Polyglot in Le Long's "Bibliotheca Sacra" (ed. March.), pp. 332—339.

according to the order of the books; there is also a complete, though small, Greek grammar, printed on one single folio leaf; together with a short Greek lexicon, with the meanings in Latin, intended for reading the New Testament, and the books of Wisdom and Ecclesiasticus. The editors inform us, in their "Introductio quàm brevissima ad Græcas Literas," that the lexicon was composed by the express order of Ximenez. To them it appeared "Lexicon copiosum, maximâ curâ et studio elucubratum."

This volume, and all the other copies of the work, though not wholly free from mistakes, are yet very beautifully printed, especially if we consider them as the production of an art which was then only in its infancy. Each title-page bears the arms of the cardinal in red and black letters. The characters are large and clear: the Latin ones are made according to the Gothic form, and the Greek according to the form of letters used in ancient manuscripts, from the ninth and following centuries: those letters were small.*

The Greek text and the Vulgate are indicated by small Latin letters, which point out the corresponding words in both languages. If there come a chasm in the Latin translation, or if the Latin words are not sufficient to complete the line, the open space is filled up with serpentine lines crossing each other. The following example from St. Matthew (xiii. 1) will illustrate this arrangement, and make the mode of accentuation clear :—

b	c	d	e	f		b	d	c	e	f
Εν δε τη ημέρα εκείνη, εξελθών ο ιησούς						In illo die exiens Iesus ☉☉☉☉☉				

g	h	i	k	l		g	h	i	k	l
από της οικίας, εκάθητο παρά την θάλασσαν						de domo sedebat secus mare ☉☉				

---

* See Montfaucon, "Palæographia Græca," pp. 271, 291, 293, 308, 324. Also Marsh's "Remarks on Michaelis' Introduction" (Notes, vol. ii. p. ii. p. 838, &c.).

But while we acknowledge the care and zeal which were bestowed on this great work, we must also so much the more express our regret that the editors did not see the necessity of giving some account of the text, and of entering upon questions of criticism, which seem indispensable in such an undertaking. Hence, in the whole of the New Testament, they considered it necessary to make only four remarks of a critical nature,* with the exception of a few exegetical observations, which are of very little importance.

Moreover, an account of the "Variantes" is entirely wanting, and no manuscript authority is given even for a single reading. There the text stands as if it had dropped down from the clouds, and not once are the codices named from which it has been taken. The preface to the New Testament merely mentions certain manuscripts which had been sent by Leo X. from the Vatican library; but instead of describing them, the writer of the preface contents himself with giving only a vague and presumptuous assurance, that not merely have the best copies been made use of, but also the most ancient and correct—"antiquissima emendatissimaque," &c.; and these were of such great antiquity, that if they could not be trusted, no confidence could be given to any other codex. Whether the letters were uncial or small; of what date the manuscripts were; what was the number used, and to what family they belonged, &c.,—these and other questions remain unanswered.† Hence it is, that the merits of the

---

* Dr. Hefele's note in reference to the nature of the remarks has been omitted.—*Trans.*

† Though these omissions must be lamented, yet, at the same time, allowance should be made for the first attempt of the kind, which, considering the state of biblical studies at that period, claims our highest praise.—*Trans.*

Complutensian Polyglot, as we shall see later, have been often controverted.

A few months after the first volume, the second appeared, in May, 1514, to serve as an introduction to the edition of the Old Testament. This is the work of the converted Jew, Alfonso Zamora. It contains a Hebræo-Chaldaic lexicon on the Old Testament sufficiently extensive : the various meanings of the words are given in Latin, pointing out at the same time all the places in the Bible where they occur. Another small dictionary resembles the index which Gesenius has added in our times to his Hebræo-Chaldaic lexicon. It contains the Latin phrases, and refers the reader to the corresponding Hebrew and Chaldaic words ; so that, as the preface states, by the help of the lexicon and index, the Latin can be translated into Hebrew or Chaldee, and *vice versâ.* This volume also contains an explanatory table of the Hebrew, Chaldee, and Greek proper names both of the Old and New Testament, in alphabetical order ; and likewise a Hebrew grammar, tolerably copious for the period. In the exterior arrangement of the Polyglot, this volume occupies the fifth place. The four following volumes are exclusively devoted to the Old Testament.* The first commences with the prologue of which we have already spoken ; in which Ximenez dedicates his work to Pope Leo X., and gives a short explanation of the plan he has followed in the arrangement of the Polyglot. He speaks of the manuscripts which served as the basis of the text, and also of the happy results which he hopes will follow from the publication of the work. Then there comes, after a second preface to the reader, a direc-

---

* At the end of the last volume we are informed that the printing was finished July 10th, 1517.

tion taken from the grammar of the preceding
volume, upon the method of finding out the roots
of Hebrew words.   There is also a prologue (of
which mention has been made above, and which
belongs to the New Testament): this gives the
reasons why the accents were omitted, &c.   There
is likewise reprinted a kind of introduction to the
Hebrew lexicon.

Then follow dissertations on the origin of the
Septuagint, on the versions of Aquila, Theodotion,
and Symmachus; upon the Hexapla of Origen, and
the biblical labours of St. Jerome.

In the same manner, there is a short treatise on
the four different ways of interpreting the Holy
Scriptures; viz, the historical, the allegorical, the
anagogical, and the tropological, or moral.*   The
definition of these is the same that is usually
given : the character and difference of one from the
other are given in a few words and examples. Thus,
while the " historical " gives the literal sense, the
three other methods aim at the more profound
meaning concealed under the literal sense; and
this they discover either in the " moral " precepts,
or in allusions to the redemption (" allegorical "),
or in some reference to the Church in its glorious
state ("anagogical").   Here, too, are quoted the
well-known verses, which were made use of in the
" middle age " to express the character of these
different modes of interpretation :—

> " Litera gesta docet; quid credas allegoria;
>   Moralis quid agas; quo tendas anagogia."

Then follows a letter of St. Jerome to Paulinus
on all the books of Holy Scripture; and also the
preface of the same father on the Pentateuch.   Be-

---

* See Dr. Dixon's " Introduction to the Sacred Scriptures,"
vol. i. p. 279 (ed. Duffy, 1852).

fore we come to the original text of the Bible, is
found immediately preceding it the brief of Leo X.,
dated March 22nd, 1520, addressed to the bishop of
Avila and the archdeacon of Cordova, Francisco
Mendoza: the brief authorizes the publication of
the Polyglot. In addition to the pontifical letter,
the bishop of Avila makes some short observations
on the price of the work. These two last documents
were naturally printed some years after the completion of the rest of the work, and the death of
Ximenez, which took place in 1517. A glance at a
copy of the Polyglot will be sufficient to show the
reader that the page in which these two documents
appear, was inserted afterwards in the volume.

After these introductions, this volume presents
us with the Pentateuch in Hebrew, Chaldee, and
Greek, together with three Latin translations.

Each page is divided horizontally into two sections.
The higher section is composed of three parts, which
include three columns; the lower section has only
two columns. The three columns of the higher
section contain the Septuagint, the Vulgate, and
the Hebrew text. The Vulgate holds the middle
place; that is, between the other two texts. The
second preface gives the reason of this collocation;
viz. that as our Lord was crucified between two
thieves, so the Latin Church stands between the
Synagogue and the Greek Church. Some writers,
by taking this comparison to mean that the Vulgate
is as much superior to the Hebrew text and the
Septuagint, as our Saviour was above the two thieves,
have been induced to believe that Ximenez was not
the writer of this second preface, since in the first
preface he gave to the original text so decided a
preference. In reality, it is necessary to adopt this
supposition, or to attribute gross inconsistency to
Ximenez, if the words in question have really the

meaning attributed to them. But this is not the
case. Far from giving the Vulgate such an immense preference, the second preface, as well as the
first, calls the Hebrew text the truth, *veritas*,
and this by the side of the other versions. It is,
however, nowhere said that the Latin version
has the same relation to the Greek and Hebrew
text as our Saviour had to the thieves ; but that the
Latin Church stands in the same relation with the
Greek Church and the Synagogue. The question
then is not about the texts, but the relation of the
churches. It was only the exterior arrangement
of the texts—an arrangement very reasonable in
itself, which gave occasion to the remarks on the
relation of the churches ; which remarks were quite
out of place. By adopting this explanation, we free
Ximenez from any imputation of inconsistency, or
from having recourse to a supposition which is far
from probable, because the last words of the first
preface necessarily belong to a second preface,*
which explains to the reader the order and arrangement of the Polyglot. And such in effect is the
object of the second prologue, which, together with
the study of the Bible itself, will be our guide in
what remains to be said respecting this and the
following volumes.

Of the three columns of the upper section of each
folio page, the Septuagint, corrected in many places
from the Hebrew text, always occupies the inner
one, nearest to the back of a bound book, while the
Hebrew text always has the outside place in the
volume.

Above the text of the Septuagint is placed a Latin
interlinear translation, giving the literal sense : this

---

* These are the last words of the first prologue : " Hunc ad
instruendum de operis artificio lectorem convertimur."

is the production of the editors. Each Latin word is placed just over the corresponding word in the Septuagint.

Only two columns fill up the lower section; the larger space is occupied by the Chaldaic text,—that is, the Targum of Onkelos ; and the smaller space contains a Latin translation of the Targum. On the exterior margin of the Hebrew and Chaldaic texts are marked the roots and forms of difficult words in both these languages. When, for example, the word עשׂו occurs in the line, we see in the margin the root of it—עשׂה. It is the same with the Chaldaic. Small Latin letters point to every word of the text which corresponds with the root placed in the margin. The same small Latin letters unite the Hebrew text, as we saw above with regard to the New Testament, with the version of the Vulgate ; but this is not the case with the Chaldaic and Greek versions. Here also ovals (oooo) are made use of, either to fill up chasms in the Latin version, or in the empty spaces at the end of the lines. However, in the Hebrew and Chaldaic text, whatever empty space might remain at the end of the lines, it was not filled up by the enlargement of the final letter, but by a number of jods (·.··). The lines of the Vulgate are only about half as long as those of the Hebrew text ; but as a line in Hebrew, on account of the characters being large, required double the height of the Latin, so it is that each line in the Hebrew corresponds with two lines of the Latin text. The same relation exists between the Chaldaic text and the Latin version belonging to it. The Chaldaic characters, though identical in form with the Hebrew ones, are evidently smaller : the characters of the Latin translation of the Chaldaic are also smaller than those of the Vulgate ; hence it is that one line of the Chaldaic corresponds with two of the Latin version belonging to it.

The Greek characters of the Septuagint are small, and full of volutes and abbreviations, such as we often meet with in the old Greek type. In no way can they be compared, either in size or in form, with the characters of the New Testament. The same height is given to the Gothic letters of the Latin interlinear version, which is placed over the Septuagint; hence one line of this version and the Septuagint form two equal lines, which always correspond with a line of the Hebrew text. Thus the column of the Septuagint necessarily has the same length as that of the Hebrew text.

It may also be well to remark that, in the arrangement of the whole work, the order used in the West is followed, and not the Oriental method; thus the first chapter of the book of Genesis comes, not in the last page of the volume, as is the custom in Hebrew and Chaldaic works, but in the first page.

The type, especially that of the Hebrew and Chaldaic, which are in what are called "Spanish" characters, is very beautiful, though, unfortunately, it is not free from errors. Both texts have the vowel-points and the large accents. Should the accent in the Hebrew words, instead of falling on the last syllable, fall on the antepenultimate, then this tonic syllable receives the grave accent. But the Greek text of the Septuagint is fully accented, the same as the Greek text of the New Testament.

A somewhat different arrangement is found in the following volumes of the Old Testament. As the Targum of Onkelos includes only the Pentateuch; and, moreover, as the Chaldaic paraphrases of the other books seemed to Ximenez or his learned assistants (as is mentioned in the second prologue), either to have been corrupted, or full of fables, so they were accordingly omitted in the whole remaining portions of the Old Testament.* Nevertheless, Ximenez caused these Targums to be translated into Latin; he also ordered these translated to be separated from the Polyglot, and preserved in the university library at Alcalá. It is from the second prologue, so often named, that we have taken these details.

The absence of the Chaldaic text has allowed the second volume of the Old Testament to be divided, not into five but only into three columns. This volume contains the books of Josua, Judges, Ruth, the four books of Kings, the two books of Paralipomenon, and the Prayer of Manasses. The Vulgate occupies its usual place between the Hebrew and the Septuagint; the latter has an interlinear translation with it, as before. The remaining portion resembles the first volume of the Old Testament: the very letters themselves and the general arrangement are the same. The Prayer of Manasses, at the end of the volume, is merely given in Latin.

The third volume of the Old Testament includes the proto-canonical and deutero-canonical books in the following order: Esdras, Nehemias, Tobias, Judith, Esther, Job, the Psalms, Proverbs, Ecclesiastes, the Canticles, Wisdom, and Ecclesiasticus. As we have already mentioned, it was Juan Vergara who gave a new translation of the five last books. The whole arrangement corresponds with that of the preceding volumes, with the following exceptions. The division into three columns, intended to receive the Hebrew text, the Vulgate, and the Septuagint

---

* Indeed, the Targum of Jonathan on the prophets, &c. contains many fables, not to speak of the incorrectness and caprices of the translations. (See Herbst, "Einl. in's A. Test." herausgegeben von Dr. Welte, thl. i. s. 178—187.)

(with their interlinear translation), is only used for the books which belong to the first canon, or the canon of the Jews; but the Hebrew text is wanting in all the deutero-canonical books; viz., Tobias, Judith, Wisdom, and some parts of Esther, which come in various parts of the Septuagint, but were united by St. Jerome; and after him by the editors of the Complutensian Bible. There is, however, in these deutero-canonical pieces a division into three columns; but as the Septuagint, with its Latin version, requires a space double that of the Vulgate, two columns, therefore, are assigned to it, between which the Vulgate always occupies the middle space. Among the proto-canonical, or Hebrew books of this volume, the Psalms have this peculiarity, that the Vulgate is not, as elsewhere, placed by the side of the Hebrew text, but comes as an interlinear version to the Septuagint, with which it corresponds. The middle of the three columns contains the version of the Psalms, made from the Hebrew by St. Jerome: it is by the side of the Hebrew text.

The fourth and last volume of the Old Testament contains Isaias, Jeremias, the Lamentations, Baruch, Ezechiel, Daniel, with the deutero-canonical fragments of the 3rd, 13th, and 14th chapters;* Osee, Joel, Amos, Abdias, Jonas, Mi-

---

* The Complutensian Polyglot has been described by writers who seem never to have examined the work. The celebrated Rosenmüller ("Handbuch für die Literatur der Bibl. Kritik und Exegese," s. 279) gives a description of this Polyglot; but from his account, it is evident he never saw the work: if he had, he would have perceived that the words of the parentheses (in hoc libro habentur libri de Susanna, &c.) are not the words of the editors themselves, but an ancient account of the Polyglot, written in Latin and copied by Rosenmüller. Very recently, another writer, who does not give his name, in an article on the Complutensian Bible, which appeared in the "Zeitschrift" of

cheas, Nahum, Habacuc, Sophonias, Aggeus, Zacharias, Malachias, and the three books of the Machabees. The fragments inserted in Daniel (viz., the prayer of Ananias, the canticle of the three children in the furnace, the history of Susanna, and of Bel and the Dragon), Baruch, and the three books of Machabees, not being proto-canonical, are not found in the Hebrew. The third book of Machabees, not being deutero-canonical, but apocryphal, is not in the Vulgate: hence, the Polyglot has only two columns here, both of which contain merely the Septuagint, with its new Latin interlinear version.

This volume, the last of the Old Testament and of the Polyglot, was issued from the press of Arnold William de Brocario, of Alcalá, July 10th, 1517. As soon as John Brocario, the young son of the printer, clothed in his best attire, ran with the last sheets to the cardinal, Ximenez exclaimed with great joy, raising his eyes to heaven:* "I give thee thanks, O most high God, 'that thou hast brought to the long-wished-for end this work which I undertook."

Thus was Ximenez allowed to behold the printing of his great Bible finished; but four months

Pletz, contents himself with reproducing the manual of Rosenmüller, without examining for himself. The history of Susanna is attributed to Ezechiel, instead of to Daniel. As regards Rosenmüller, I could mention other facts which prove, either that he had never seen the Polyglot, or that he examined it very carelessly.

* "Audivi Joannem Brocarium Comp. excussorem, Arnoldi Gulielmi Brocarii filium, sæpenumero ad æquales dixisse, eo ipso die ultima manus à patre operis excussioni imposita fuit, se puerum eleganter vestitum cum ultimo Bibliorum volumine ad Ximenium venisse; cui impendiò lætatus, ita cœlum suspiciens acclamavit,—'Gratias tibi ago, summe Christe, quòd rem magnoperò à me curatam, ad optatum finem perduxeris,'" &c. (Gomez, lib. ii. p. 38, ed. 1569.)

after he died, November 8th, 1517. The papal permission which authorized the publication of the
work, did not appear till two years after his death,
viz. March 22nd, 1520.* A year passed away
before any copy could pass the Spanish frontier.
The text, therefore, of this Bible could not be made
use of, either for the editions of the Old Testament
by Bomberg (1518), or for the first edition of the
New Testament by Erasmus (1516). But a little
later, the Complutensian Polyglot was not without
its influence on the formation of the text of the
Bible. As regards the New Testament, it is, without
doubt, the "editio princeps" in the order of time
(1514), though the first edition of Erasmus became
public before it (in 1516). But this same Erasmus,
who had devoted only five months of labour to his
work, and that very superficially, and who possessed
but a small number of manuscripts, was fortunate in
the later editions (the fourth in 1527, and the fifth
in 1535), by being able to consult the Complutensian text.†

It is certainly very pleasing to consider the mildness with which Ximenez defended the work of
Erasmus against the attacks of even his own friends
around him. As soon as his edition of the New
Testament appeared, Zuñiga, one of the chief editors of the Polyglot, began to make remarks against
the notes of Erasmus. Ximenez expressed a desire
that the manuscript of this sharp critic should first

---

* The death of Ximenez was the reason why the approbation
was not solicited from Rome. At length, Leo X., in order not to
deprive the world any longer of so great a work, approved the
publication *proprio motu*, as the brief mentions. Hug, in his
Introduction, is mistaken both in the month and the year, by
giving as the date of the brief, March 20, 1525. (See vol. i.
p. 304, English ed.; London, 1827.)

† Griesbach, N. Test. tom. proleg. p. 6.

be shown to the accused author, and then only made public if Erasmus should manifest no inclination to correct his mistakes. But Zuñiga would not agree to the proposal; he even went so far one day as to express, in the presence of Ximenez, a very contemptuous judgment on Erasmus. Then it was that the cardinal answered him with a simplicity combined with earnestness, in the following words:—"God grant that all writers may do their work as well as he has done his. You are bound either to give us something better, or not to blame the labours of others." Zuñiga was silenced: these few words made such an impression on him, that during the lifetime of the cardinal he never indulged in any invective against Erasmus. But after the death of Ximenez, he became still more violent and bitter. At length, however, towards the end of his life, Zuñiga began to relent; for a short time before his death (1530), he ordered that his other manuscripts directed against Erasmus should not be printed, but sent to him for his use.*

From about the middle of the sixteenth century, almost innumerable editions of the New Testament followed,—sometimes that of Erasmus, sometimes the text in the Complutensian Polyglot, and sometimes both together. While the editions printed at Basle gave the preference to Erasmus, the editions issued from the Plantinian press at Antwerp and Geneva followed the text of the Complutensian Bible. The famous Polyglot of Paris, which appeared in 1645, also adopted the same text for the New Testament, in its ninth and tenth volumes. But not to dwell on other editions, the great

* Du Pin, "Nouvelle Bibliothèque des Auteurs Ecclésiastiques," &c. tom. xiv. p. 75. See also Erhard, "Geschichte des Wiederaufblühens der Wissenschaftl. Bildung," Bd. ii. s. 571.

Antwerp Polyglot published in 1569, and edited by Spaniards at the expense of King Philip II., followed the text of Erasmus and the Complutensian compared together.

The Bible of Ximenez had no less influence on the celebrated editions of the Stephens'. The first, published by Robert Stephens, printer, at Paris (1545), adopted the Complutensian text entirely for its basis; and though the third edition of Stephens (much superior to the first) followed the fifth edition of Erasmus, yet it is not to be forgotten that the Polyglot of Ximenez was made use of by Erasmus. It is by this third edition of the Stephens' that the Polyglot of Alcalá is connected with the "textus receptus," which became known by the family of the Elzevirs, who were printers at Leyden. Their press produced from 1624 to 1735 innumerable copies of the text of the third edition of the Stephens', with readings from the edition of Beza. These were so multiplied that they received the name of the " Textus receptus."*

Such was the great influence which the Complutensian edition of the New Testament exercised on the text of the New Testament in the sixteenth and seventeenth centuries, until at length the English Polyglot, by Brian Walton (who was afterwards archbishop of Canterbury)† opened a new era in 1657. Dr. Fell, bishop of Oxford, published his edition

---

* The "received text." Dr. Hefele merely glances at this interesting part of the subject. For further details I refer the reader to Dr. Dixon's "Introduction," or to a similar work in French by Glaire, tom. i. (Paris, 1839).—*Trans.*

† Dr. Hefele is mistaken in supposing Walton to have been archbishop of Canterbury. He was bishop of Chester. The history of the London Polyglot and of the labours of Walton, are most interesting. (See Archdeacon Todd's " Memoirs of the Life and Writings of Walton," 2 vols. 8vo. London, 1821.)—*Trans.*

of the New Testament in 1675 ; and Mill published another, more splendid and accurate, in 1707, at Oxford, where he was one of the professors in the university. These editions, however, were surpassed by those of Bengel and Wetstein.*

The labours of Griesbach and other modern biblical critics have certainly thrown the Complutensian Polyglot into the shade. But we need not wonder at this, when we remember that the editors of that Bible seem to have consulted at the most only about ten manuscripts, while, in our days, through the labours of Scholz,† more than five hundred manuscripts have been collated and classified. Still, the Complutensian text has very lately been made use of by Dr. Gratz, in his edition of the New Testament (Tübingen and Mayence, 1821). The edition by Dr. Van Ess has adopted for its basis the text of the Complutensian and that of Erasmus at the same time. A still later and more widely-extended edition, by Goldhagen, has also followed the Complutensian text.‡

The Complutensian Polyglot has exercised no less influence on the text of the Old Testament. Here, it is true, it is not considered the " editio princeps," as it is in the New Testament. This glory belongs, as we have already remarked, to the

---

* Bengel's edition appeared in 1734. He did not confine himself to the " received text." Wetstein's famous edition appeared in two volumes folio, at Amsterdam, in 1751 and 1752.—*Trans.*

† One of the Catholic professors at Bonn. The work forms two volumes quarto ; it was published at Leipsic, the first part, containing the four gospels, in 1830, and the second part in 1836. Though possessing great merit, the edition has been severely criticised by Catholic writers.—*Trans.*

‡ Among the modern editions may be mentioned the one by the late Dr. Bloomfield (2 vols. 1832). The notes are open to criticism, though the ordinary Greek text is impartially treated.—*Trans.*

M

editions published by Jews at Socino (1488) and at
Brescia (in 1494) : still, the Complutensian forms
the second fundamental basis of the Hebrew text.
The question still remains undecided, whether the
editions of Socino or Brescia were consulted or not.
Many critics have fancied they could discover a
resemblance between the text of the Complutensian
and that of Brescia, but on a closer examination
all traces of resemblance have vanished.* Gomez,
the earliest biographer of Ximenez, mentions that
the cardinal purchased seven Hebrew manuscripts
for 4,000 ducats; but the archbishop himself, or
some of his learned assistants, in the first Prologue
addressed to Pope Leo X., merely state " that they
had collected together a considerable number of
Hebrew, Greek, and Latin manuscripts," without
any further explanations. Quintanilla asserts that
the seven Hebrew manuscripts arrived too late, and
were therefore useless.† But Gomez, who lived at
Alcalá a short time after Ximenez, makes not the
slightest allusion to this circumstance, which, if
true, was certainly of importance to be recorded.
However, he merely states that these seven Hebrew
manuscripts were preserved, in his time, at Alcalá.

Some years after the Polyglot of Complutum,
the celebrated Hebrew Bible of Bomberg was published at Venice (1518),‡ from the press of Daniel

---

* Rosenmüller, "Handbuch," &c., thl. iii. s. 289.

† " Archetypo de Virtudes, espejo de Prelados el Venerable
Padre, y Siervo de Dios, F. Francisco Ximenez de Cisneros "
(Palermo, 1653), lib. iii. cap. x. p. 137. The writer was a
Franciscan, and was employed in procuring the beatification of
Ximenez.

‡ Several editions of this Bible appeared at different times;
the most remarkable is the second of 1526. Some were in folio,
others in quarto. They were called *Rabbinical Bibles*, because
the text is accompanied with Rabbinical commentaries. (See
Calmet, "Bibliothèque Sacrée," 1re partie; "Bibles Hébraïques
et Rabbiniques.")—*Trans.*

Bomberg. But though it appeared before the Complutensian, yet as regards the New Testament, both are on an equality, and both share the glory—Ximenez and Bomberg—of having been the first Christians who gave editions of the Hebrew text of the Old Testament. Hence, the Bible of Alcalá and an edition of Bomberg, viz. that published in folio by the learned Jew Jacob Ben Chayim (in 1526), became afterwards the basis of most of the editions which followed. The Polyglot of Heidelberg, by Bertram, in three editions (1586—1616), borrows not only the Hebrew text of the Complutensian, but also the Septuagint and the Vulgate.*

The Antwerp Polyglot (1569-72) adopts the Hebrew text of the Complutensian, compared with that of Bomberg; and this has been followed by the editions of Plantinus, and also in the celebrated London Polyglot of 1657.

From this time the influence of the Complutensian Polyglot on the text of the Old Testament began to decline. In proportion as the labours of Athias, Buxtorf, Norzi, a Jew of Mantua, John Henry Michaelis of Halle, Professor Kennicott of Oxford, and Rossi,† a professor at Parma, began to throw light on the original text of the Scripture, so much the more did the Complutensian Polyglot fall into the oblivion of libraries. Such is the lot of all human works; even those which are considered the most perfect are in their turn supplanted by others.

But in the last century, the Complutensian Bible was in great danger of being deprived of its ancient and well-deserved merit, through the attacks of an

---

* Herbst, "Einleitung in's A. Test.," thl. i. s. 135.

† For a very interesting account of these biblical scholars, see Cardinal Wiseman's Lecture X., in his " Connection between Science and Revealed Religion."

unjust critic. The Hebrew text was allowed to remain undisturbed: but complaints were made, that alterations had been made in the Septuagint by the editors of the Complutensian, in order to render it more conformable to the original text.*
The Greek text of the New Testament was the object of long and bitter discussions on the part of some learned Protestant writers.†

The first who undertook to controvert the merit of the Complutensian Bible was the critic John James Wetstein, of Basle. In the prolegomena to his magnificent edition of the Bible (1730 and 1751), he brings forward the three following serious objections against the Complutensian text of the New Testament:—

1. "That the Greek text does not rest on ancient manuscripts.

2. "That it has intentionally been altered according to the Vulgate.

3. "That the assertion of manuscripts having been received from Leo X. deserves little credit; because his holiness was elected pope on the 11th of February [read March 11th], 1513, and the printing of the New Testament was finished January 10th, 1514."‡

In the year 1764, Dr. Semler had the pro-

---

* Dr. Michaelis, "Oriental und Exeget. Bibliothek," bd. ix, s. 162; Rosenmüller, "Handbuch für die Literatur der Biblischen Kritik und Exegese," bd. iii. s. 289.

† The details connected with this controversy may be seen in Walch's "Neuester Religions-geschichte," bd. iv. s. 423—490. An epitome of this account is given by Rosenmüller, in his "Handbuch," bd. iii. s. 291.

‡ This last objection we have already answered. To assert, with Semler, that the manuscripts sent from Rome were made use of, not for the New, but for the Old Testament, is grossly to contradict the very words of the editors of the Complutensian Bible, in their Preface to the New Testament.

legomena of Wetstein reprinted at Halle; but although Semler adhered to the principles of criticism adopted by Bengel, and not to those of Wetstein, yet he adopted as his own all the objections of the latter against the Complutensian Bible, and brought them forward again. Wishing, however, to give them still greater force, he published in the same year (1764) a work, entitled "Historical and Critical Remarks on certain Passages brought forward to support Dogmas;" first part, on 1 John v. 7.

" It cannot be denied," the writer says, at p. 77, " that this edition (the Complutensian) has been wilfully altered from the Latin text, and that the whole is the production of men who had but little profound learning." Such is the judgment which Semler dared to pronounce even before he had seen a single copy of the Complutensian Bible; and this reproach he could not help allowing his adversaries to make in the discussion, though at a later period he endeavoured to remove it !

While J. N. Kiefer, rector and pastor at Saarbrück, sided with Semler, another pastor, John Melchior Götze,* of Hamburg, defended the Complutensian Bible. A controversy sprung up; and such a number of treatises, answers, and replies appeared on the subject, that at last the public began to be tired of the discussion. But the character of Semler had received a more severe wound than even his learning. Yet even this was far from being victorious. Semler had commenced

---

* The title of the work by Götze was, "A Complete Defence of the Complutensian Greek Testament, with a collection of the principal differences between the Greek Text and the Latin Text of that edition." (Hamburg, 1766.) " A Continuation of the Defence" appeared in 1769. (See the notes of Marsh, in Michaelis' " Introduction," vol. ii. part 2, p. 813.)—*Trans.*

the discussion by asserting that the whole of the Complutensian Bible had been altered from the Latin text, knowingly and wilfully; but in his second pamphlet against Götze, published in 1768, he was obliged to abandon his position, and maintain that he did not mean that the whole of the Complutensian text had been altered, but only a falsification of it in the "liturgical parts" had been made.

But Kiefer reduced this assertion also to a very small compass, by confining it to two or three passages (St. Matthew vi. 13; 1 St. John v. 7; and in a certain way, 1 St. John ii. 14). Thus it was evident, that Semler, after he had at first undertaken to defend the whole of his fortification, was at last forced to save himself in a small tower.

Götze defended himself in the controversy with much greater success than he did ten years after, against Lessing. He proves, in four works, that the Greek text of the Complutensian differs from the Vulgate in more than nine hundred places, and this too in many of the liturgical parts;* and moreover, that the editors must have followed, generally speaking, their own Greek manuscripts in opposition to the Vulgate :† this furnishes an inductive proof, that the two or three contested passages have their text formed from the Greek manuscripts, and still more that the very important passage (1 St. John v. 7) in the Complutensian Bible is evidently not a translation from the Vulgate.

Thus the objections of Wetstein and Semler against

---

* Walch, "Neuester Religions-gesch.," s. 461.

† For example, in the verse on the resurrection (1 Cor. xv. 51), where the editors of the Complutensian have given the true reading, quite in opposition to the Vulgate.

the Complutensian Bible cannot be considered valid or just; on the contrary, most able critics, like John David Michaelis, have become the defenders of the Polyglot. Amongst these is the celebrated Ernesti, in his "Neue Theologische Bibliothek" (bd. vi. s. 723), and the author of the epitome of the whole controversy, in Walch's "Neuester Religions-geschichte." Griesbach also asserts that Semler went a great deal too far in his attacks against the Complutensian Bible ; and that through the progress which biblical criticism has made, and by the discovery of new manuscripts, many passages which Semler had considered as having been "wilfully altered" were now fully vindicated.* On the whole, a more favourable judgment is, in our day, pronounced on the Complutensian Bible, and with justice ; because, in reality, the complaints respecting an alteration having been made in the Greek text from the Vulgate have been gradually reduced to almost nothing. Hence, one must not for the future be too hasty in condemning the Complutensian Bible.

1. With regard to a passage in St. Matthew (vi. 13), where the editors of the Complutensian have omitted the well-known Doxology after the "Our Father," they have put in the margin the following remark :—" In exemplaribus Græcorum post hæc verba Orationis Dominicæ,—Sed libera nos a malo, statim sequitur,—οτι σου εστιν η βασιλεια κ. τ. λ. Sed advertendum, quod in Missa Græcorum, postquam chorus dicit illa verba Orationis Dominicæ, Sed libera nos, &c., sacerdos respondit ista verba supra dicta : Quoniam tuum est reg-

---

* Griesbach, N. Test. Proleg., p. ix. This illustrious critic, however, seemed to believe that, in some parts of the New Testament, the editors of the Complutensian Bible have given the text different from their manuscripts.

num, &c. Sic magis credibile videtur, quod ista verba non sint de integritate Orationis Dominicæ, sed quod vitio aliquorum scriptorum fuerint hîc inserta, &c."

The editors of the Complutensian frankly acknowledge, then, that here they departed from the Greek codices, and at the same time they give their reason for so doing, viz., that this doxology, which was used in the Greek Liturgy, had crept into the text by an error of the copyists. All critics of the present day consider that the editors had good grounds for departing from the Greek text, while the frankness with which they mention this departure gives us a strong presumption for the correctness of the alterations in other passages.

2. The second objection respects the omission in the 1st Epistle of St. John (chap. ii.), where the editors of the Complutensian, in opposition to their codices, have suppressed the words at the commencement of verse 14 :—" I write unto you, babes, because you have known him who is from the beginning." Such is the objection. But these words are evidently only a literal repetition of the commencement of the preceding verse. It cannot, therefore, have been any great rashness in the editors to ascribe the insertion of the words, in spite of the authority of excellent codices, to the error of some ancient copyist. But it cannot now be decided whether the editors of the Complutensian Bible wilfully omitted the words merely from a conviction that the authority of the Vulgate would thereby be strengthened, or whether the words were really wanting in the manuscripts they used. The editors have no remark whatever in this place. But, in any case, neither doctrine, nor the liturgy, nor any controversial or theological question, depends upon the fact being known, whether the verse is found once or twice

in the Epistle of St. John referred to. Hence, the Catholic Church has no interest in determining whether any alteration was really made from the Vulgate by the editors of the Complutensian Polyglot.

3. The third and last objection refers to what is called the "Comma Joanneum," in the 1st St. John v. 7. It is maintained that the verse was translated from the Vulgate, and introduced into the Greek text, without any authority whatever. The words, "And there are three who give testimony in heaven, the Father, and the Word, and the Holy Ghost; and these three are one " (v. 7), are always quoted by theologians as a proof of the Blessed Trinity; but it is well known, that the passage is not found in any single Greek codex of authority. But as the Greek text of the Complutensian Bible in this passage does not perfectly agree with the words of the Vulgate, hence the suspicion that the editors translated the verse from the Vulgate is considerably weakened. The editors give no explanation whatever; for the half-critical and half-exegetical remark which comes in the margin, and seems to have been borrowed from St. Thomas, gives no data for deciding whether the comma existed or not in any of the Complutensian manuscripts.

The objection against the Complutensian Bible becomes still weaker, from the fact that, up to the present time, three Greek manuscripts of recent date have been discovered, which contain the "Comma Joanneum."* Erasmus had already referred to a " Codex Britannicus," from which he had inserted

---

* By this phrase is understood the controverted parts in the 1 Epist. of St. John v. 7, as if they were a modern interpolation into the text. (See Cardinal Wiseman's learned and satisfactory Letters on the Controversy, published in the *Catholic Magazine*, 1832.)

the passage in his last editions of the New Testament.* The passage is certainly found in the Codex Britannicus, or Codex Montfortianus (No. 34, in Griesbach), and in two other manuscripts compared by Scholz (Nos. 162 and 173); one of which, No. 162, belongs to the Vatican.† The number "three" must be increased, if we may admit that the Codex Britannicus of Erasmus is different from the Codex Montfortianus, as the diversity of the readings allows us to think that it is.‡

As then there are, properly speaking, four manuscripts which contain the controverted passage, and one of them is in the Vatican, may we not therefore conclude, without any rashness, that the editors of the Complutensian Bible might have found the said passage in one or other of the manuscripts which they had? This assertion would be still more undeniable, were there not a possibility that the passage was first copied from the Complutensian Bible into the recent manuscripts (Nos. 34, 162, 173). What took place in the controversy between Zuñiga and Erasmus makes us somewhat suspicious of the Complutensian editors.

Zuñiga had reproached Erasmus with the omission of the "Comma Joanneum" in his first editions; but Erasmus demanded the place to be pointed out to him in the Greek text where the passage could be found. Zuñiga evaded the question,

* See the Dissertation of Griesbach on 1 John v. 7, in his Appendix to part ii. of his New Testament, p. 3.

† See the Annotations of Scholz on 1 John v. 7, in his edition of the New Testament. The "Codex Ravianus," at Berlin, contains also the "Comma Joanneum;" but it is only a copy of the the Complutensian text. (Griesbach, Appendix, pp. 4, 5.)

‡ Griesbach has printed the reading of Erasmus in the third page of his Appendix; and at page 4, the reading of the "Codex Montfortianus."

and confined himself merely to complaints respecting the corruption of the Greek manuscripts.*

This incident may certainly have given rise to the suspicion; but there is no ground for any certainty, when we recollect (what has already been stated), that in the passage the Greek text of the Complutensian does not agree with the Vulgate, and that in almost a thousand other places the editors have neglected to form the Greek text according to the Vulgate. Indeed, it is not at all improbable, but that the editors may have found the passage in question in some recent codex, as Erasmus did. But even supposing they had inserted the " Comma Joanneum " without the authority of any manuscript, relying merely on the Vulgate and the twelfth general council, &c., still even this one fact cannot possibly justify a sweeping and general accusation against their honesty; at a time, too, when men had for their guide, not so much fixed laws of criticism, as vague rules, which were altered according to the caprice of the moment. All that can in any way be objected against the editors amounts to what Griesbach has already mentioned, viz., (1.) That they exaggerated the age of their manuscripts, and asserted that their " codices " were " antiquissimi et vetustissimi,"† when, in reality, they could not have reached beyond two hundred years. (2.) That when the manuscripts differed in their readings, they preferred those which were more conformable with the Vulgate.‡ But this is a circumstance which must not be dealt with too severely, since the result

---

* Griesbach, Appendix, pp. 7, 8. Walch, p. 438.

† The same happened to Erasmus, who also calls his manuscripts "vetustissimos, venerandæ antiquitatis;" and yet they did not date beyond the eleventh or twelfth century. (See Ernesti, "Neue Theol. Bibliothek," bd. vi. s. 718.)

‡ Griesbach, N. Test. Proleg., pp. 6 and 9.

of the labours of our biblical scholars at the present day tends to strengthen the conviction that the Vulgate had for its basis most excellent manuscripts.* In any case, the Complutensian text adheres to the Vulgate much less than that of Erasmus, who, it is well known, in his first editions of the New Testament, translated several passages from the Vulgate through the want of Greek manuscripts.†

It cannot, indeed, be denied, that the editors of the Complutensian Bible possessed none of the best and most ancient manuscripts; for their text is throughout conformable to recent manuscripts,

---

* On the "Comma Joanneum," see the letters of his Eminence Cardinal Wiseman (mentioned in a preceding note); also Perrone, "Prælectiones," tom. ii. p. 294, &c. The following are their principal reasons for supporting the text in 1 St. John v. 7 :—

1. Christianity reached the north of Africa, from Italy, at the commencement of the second century, if not before.

2. With the faith, Rome also sent the Holy Scripture.

3. The Bible was translated into Latin in Africa—*not* in Rome, where every one understood the Greek language; a translation was therefore useless. Lachmann admits this conclusion of the cardinal (Nov. Test. Græcè et Latinè, tom. i. proleg. p. 11, &c.).

4. This translation was made in the second century. Tertullian, St. Cyprian, &c., made use of it.

5. It must have had for its basis a Greek text more ancient than any of the Greek manuscripts known to us at the present day, which at the most do not extend beyond the third century.

6. Now, the "Comma Joanneum" is found in the ancient Latin version made in Africa. It must, therefore, have been in the ancient Greek manuscript sent from Rome to Africa; and consequently its antiquity is greater than the most ancient manuscripts which we possess.

7. The "Comma" is wanting in the manuscripts of later date; which may have happened either through its being omitted by anti-trinitarian heretics, or through the fault of the copyists, by the similarity of words occurring near each other. Thus the "Codex Veronesus" omits verse 8, because it commences and ends like verse 6; and yet its authenticity is acknowledged by critics.

† Hänlein, "Einl. in's N. Test.," thl. ii. s. 260.

when these differ from the ancient, while it never agrees with the ancient in opposition to recent manuscripts.*

It is also proved that the editors had not the use of the venerable *Codex Vaticanus* (B); whether it was not then to be found in the Vatican, or whether the librarian himself did not lend it to them, is now uncertain.† What particular manuscripts were sent to them from Rome cannot be discovered, because hitherto they have not been found in that city; and also because Griesbach, Scholz, and others, who have examined and compared the different manuscripts of the New Testament which are preserved in the Vatican library, assure us that none of them have served as a basis for the Complutensian text. Perhaps—and this is the opinion of Ernesti ‡—the copies sent to Ximenez belonged, not to the Vatican library, but to the pope himself; and after his death they may have passed into other hands.

We may also form another supposition, viz., that after the manuscripts had been consulted, they may have remained at Alcalá, and have shared the sad fate of those others used for the Complutensian Polyglot. In the year 1784, a German professor, named Dr. Moldenhawer, went to Alcalá, in order to inspect on the spot the precious manuscripts; but on his arrival, he found, to his great sorrow, that in the year 1749 the librarian had sold them all, " as waste

---

* Griesbach, Proleg., p. 7.

† The celebrated "Codex Vaticanus" seems to have been written about the fifth century. Its antiquity, however, has been variously estimated by different critics. Mill quite takes it for granted that this codex was used by the Complutensian editors; but he does not prove his assertions, which are mere conjectures. Dr. Hefele seems to have good ground for supposing that the codex was not known to the editors of the Bible of Alcalá.—*Trans.*

‡ " Neue Theol. Bibliothek," bd. vi. s. 725.

paper," to a rocket-maker of the name of Torzo !
In almost the same way did Ludwig of Wurtemberg act, by taking a great number of manuscripts
away from the celebrated monastery of Hirsau, and
putting them in "usum bombardicum."* Professor
Tychsen, the companion of Dr. Moldenhawer, confirms the account about the manuscripts of Alcalá;†
and adds, moreover, that a learned Spaniard, named
Martinez, when he first heard of such vandalism,
endeavoured to save such a treasure from destruction.
But all had perished, with the exception of a few
leaves.   These he preserved, and collecting them
together, deposited them in the library at Alcalá.
Marsh,‡ having given these details, draws the conclusion that the manuscripts, having been written
on paper, must have been of no great antiquity ;
because parchment could not have been made use of
for rockets.

But though the barbarous act of a librarian may
have rendered impossible any further research
respecting the character of the manuscripts used
by the editors of the Complutensian Bible, still I
believe we can form a correct judgment respecting
their antiquity from the nature and form of the
Greek letters employed in the Polyglot.   Ximenez
must first have the types cast, and this was done,
very probably, according to the model which the
form of his manuscripts furnished : hence we may
draw the conclusion that the manuscripts written
in small letters date from the 9th to the 13th

* Feilmoser, "Einl. in's N. Test.," 2te Aufl. s. 625.
† This account has already been given in a preceding note,
taken from Michaelis.—*Trans.*
‡ Herbert Marsh, who died bishop of Peterborough.   He
translated "The Introduction" of Michaelis into English; a
work which, though abounding with much critical learning, is too
full of German rationalism to be safely followed.   The bishop
himself was also unfortunately tainted with it.—*Trans.*

centuries. According to the researches made by critics, it seems that the readings in the Complutensian agree the nearest with those manuscripts which are now designated under the names of Codex Havniensis 1, Laudianus 2, Vindobonensis Lambeci 35, and Codex Guelpherbytanus C.*

There is no doubt but that the modern recensions of texts are far superior to those of the Complutensian Bible; but yet it will always have the honour and glory of having been the " first " among the Polyglots, and the most ancient of the editions of the New Testament.

Time has, indeed, robbed Alcalá of its ancient glory—her university; but the Bible of Alcalá, though so few copies of it were printed, remains for all time in honour and renown, and raises itself aloft untouched amidst the ruin and desolation which for fifty years have laid waste unfortunate Spain. Political revolutionists have, alas ! destroyed or suppressed all those magnificent colleges which Ximenez believed he had established for ever ; but amidst the ruin of his buildings they cannot bury the glorious name of their founder, and much less can they silence the voice of his great Polyglot, which will proclaim to posterity both the glory of its originator, and his undying love for biblical pursuits.

* Hänlein, " Einl. in's N. Test.," thl. ii. s. 259. These manuscripts are described in Michaelis. (See his " Introduction," English ed.)

CHAPTER XII.

As Ximenez intended his Polyglot for theological
studies, so also was he anxious, at the same time,
to promote philosophical pursuits by means of a
great work of a similar character. For this object
he chose Juan Vergara,* and some other learned
men, well skilled in the Greek and Latin languages;
to them he gave a commission to prepare a complete
edition of the works of Aristotle. At this period
the Peripatetic philosophy was held in high repute,
especially in Spain,—an inheritance which had come
down to the Christians from the time of the Moors.
It was, then, but natural that the art of printing, recently invented, after having consecrated its first effort
to the Book of all books, should immediately afterwards offer its services to the prince of philosophers.
Although Aldus Manutius had already published at
Venice, between the years 1495 and 1498, the first
Greek edition of Aristotle, in five volumes folio,
yet Ximenez wished to enrich science with a much
better edition, which, in addition to the Greek text,
and an ancient Latin version of it, was to contain
in a third column a new Latin translation, the object
of which was to correct and elucidate the obscurities
of the first edition. Vergara applied himself immediately to the work, and translated a number of the

---

* He died canon of Alcalá, in 1557. Gomez gives a few details about him, in his "Life of Ximenez," lib. ii.

physical, psychological, and metaphysical treatises of the Stagirite. But as the publication was deferred till the completion of the Polyglot, the death of the archbishop, which soon followed, put a stop to the noble enterprise. The materials, however, which were already complete, were deposited in the library belonging to the cathedral of Toledo. But there appeared no second Ximenez to carry on the work.

The works of the celebrated Spanish critic, Alfonso Tostatus,* bishop of Avila, met with a more fortunate fate; they were printed for the first time, by the order of Ximenez. Other works of less note also appeared, which the archbishop had printed more for the instruction of the people than for the use of the learned. Some of them were in Latin, and some in Spanish; and they were published at the same time that the printing of the Polyglot was going on. Among these were the Letters of St. Catharine of Sienna; the writings of St. Angela de Foligno, and of the holy Abbess Mechthildes; the Ladder of Perfection, by St. John Climacus; the Rule of Life, by St. Vincent Ferrer and St. Clare; Meditations on the Life of Christ, by the Carthusian, Landulph; and a Biography of St. Thomas à Becket, archbishop of Canterbury.†

The intention of Ximenez, in publishing these works, was that they might find their way into domestic circles, and thereby displace all immoral writings: thus, by multiplying at his own expense these good books, he hoped also to increase and

---

* Dr. Dixon gives a short account of this writer, in vol. ii. of his "Introduction," p. 363. He wrote rather diffuse Commentaries on certain books of Scripture, which display great learning. He died in 1454 or 1455.—*Trans.*

† Gomez, ibid. p. 967.

extend piety and devotion in every direction; for
this object he gave away an immense number of
copies of the works referred to above. They were
eagerly received, and read with avidity; so that in
the time of Gomez, fifty years after, very few copies
of them could be found.*

There was also another undertaking of Ximenez
which deserves notice, relating in a special manner
to the good of his diocese. Hitherto the ecclesiastical music-books, especially in Spain, could only be
multiplied in manuscript, and of course were very
dear and scarce. The archbishop, therefore, now
ordered a great number of new works on ecclesiastical music to be published, containing the whole
series of church-offices, together with the notes and
other musical additions, on parchment. These he
distributed to all the churches of his diocese, in
order that the Gregorian Chant, which he loved
exceedingly, might be everywhere known and understood.

Ximenez, being likewise anxious to promote the
material prosperity of the country, procured the aid
of a clever and experienced agriculturist, named
Ferrera, brother to the professor of rhetoric at
Alcalá. He assisted the cardinal in publishing
several popular treatises on agriculture, which he
distributed amongst the country-people. Gomez
assures us that these publications were quite equal
to the ancient classical works on the same subject,
and that many years after several editions of them
were published.†

---

* "Sed hi libri . . paucissimi nunc inveniuntur, et sui
pretium raritate adaugent." (Lib. ii. p. 39, ed. Compluti, 1569.)
These and other interesting details are mostly taken from Gomez.
The account of the Mozarabic Liturgy is given by Florez, in his
"España Sagrada."—*Trans.*

† Hoc ille (Ferrera) argumentum ita feliciter tractavit, ut jure

Another undertaking of Ximenez deserves honourable mention, for its object was to promote not only the interests of science, but also those of literature. Whilst he was residing, in the year 1502, at Toledo, (the city where he first conceived the idea of his Polyglot), having had occasion to visit the library of his cathedral, he found that many of the valuable manuscripts were much injured by the humidity of the place. He immediately resolved to erect an entirely new building for a library, which should be in a better locality, more spacious, and more airy and lightsome. He also intended to have endowed it with considerable funds, so that it might vie with the Vatican itself in its literary treasures. But this and other intended erections at Alcalá were deferred, on account of the enormous expense arising from the publication of the Polyglot; and at last it unfortunately happened, that the death of the archbishop suddenly put an end to everything.

This visit, however, to the library at Toledo, was not without profit both to the Church and to science. Ximenez found, amongst the manuscripts there, several which were written in old Gothic characters. By this discovery, the thought occurred to him of preserving from impending destruction the Gothic or Mozarabic Liturgy.*

The ancient Spanish Liturgy, which was introduced into Spain by the apostles of that country, —viz., St. Torquatus and his companions (called Septemviri Apostolici),—resembled, as Florez† has proved, the Roman Liturgy, at least in all essential

---

cum priscis illis contendat, qui Græcè Latinève de eâ re scripserunt. Quanti vero fiant quæ scripsit, testimonio sunt crebræ illorum voluminum editiones, nostri nimirum hominibus ca semper avidè exoptantibus." (Gomez, lib. ii.)

* Gomez, lib. ii.

† "España Sagrada," tom. iii. pp. 192—198.

points. But this resemblance was soon lost; because in Rome itself various alterations were made in the Sacramentaries by different popes; viz., in the sixth and seventh centuries by Leo the Great, Gelasius I., and St. Gregory the Great.* Then there came into Spain, soon after this period, the Alani, the Suevi, the Vandals, and Visigoths,† all of whom were Arians. Having conquered the country, they introduced their own particular Liturgy, which was in reality like the Latin, though composed according to the model of the Græco-Arian.‡ The Arian and ancient Spanish rite existed together for some time. But the old orthodox Church, through Arian barbarities and intolerance, soon saw herself reduced to such destitution, that nothing but confusion and disorder surrounded her rites and ceremonies. But the evil was still greater: the violent system of proselytism made use of by the Arian conquerors had for its object to make both their religion and their Liturgy dominant in Spain; the consequence of which was, in some places, a mixture at least of the ancient and new rites. Thus certain elements, if not entirely Arian, still foreign and Grecian in their origin, gradually crept into the ancient Liturgy, and developed themselves still more under the influence of Grecian priests who came and settled in the country. Indeed, from the commencement of the fourth century, viz. from the time of Hosius of Cordova, we know that a frequent intercourse subsisted between the Spanish Church and that of Constantinople; while, in the commencement of

---

* Florez, tom. iii. p. 209.

† See Gibbon, for an account of these tribes (vols. ii. and iii. Bohn's ed. 1854).—*Trans.*

‡ In Spanien einfielen und ihre eigene, der Griechisch-Arianischen nachgebildete, aber doch Lateinische Liturgie, nach Spanien mitbrachten." (Dr. Hefele, pp. 150, 151.)

the fifth century, we find that Pope Hormisdas considered it his duty to put John, archbishop of Tarragona, on his guard respecting certain Grecian clergy who were then resident in Spain.* In a word, it is very probable that the heresy of Priscillian,† not yet extinguished at this period, contributed its share towards corrupting the ancient Spanish Liturgy.‡ To such an extent was this evil carried, that, in the year 537, Profuturus, archbishop of Galicia, wrote to Pope Vigilius for advice in this matter. His holiness sent him the canon of the mass according to the Roman rite, together with the entire mass for Easter, that these might serve as models for the reformation of the Spanish Liturgy.

But a very important change took place in this Liturgy when, towards the end of the sixth century, the Visigoth kings were converted to the Catholic faith. In the fourth council of Toledo, held under King Sisenand,§ in the year 633, the Spanish bishops, with St. Isidore of Seville (who died in 636) at their head, resolved to put an end to the diversity of rites which then prevailed, and to establish throughout the whole of the country one and the same Liturgy and Psalmody. For this object, the bishops undertook to give to each priest, at his ordination,

---

* Florez, tom. iii. p. 222.

† See a learned note of Alban Butler, in the "Life of St. Martin" (Nov. 11), on Priscillianism. It was supported in Spain by the severe laws of Honorius, the zeal of St. Leo, and of St. Turibius, a Spanish bishop.—*Trans.*

‡ Florez, tom. iii. p. 219.

§ The learned Jesuit, Mariana, in his "History," gives us most interesting details connected with this and other early kings of Spain, as well as general information, to which modern writers are much indebted. (See "Historia General de España," ed. Madrid, 1623.) Another edition appeared in 1780, which is superior to the former.—*Trans.*

a ritual, to which he was strictly obliged to adhere in the performance of his sacred functions.* It is very probable that St. Isidore† himself, who was then the most illustrious of all the Spanish bishops, under-took the compilation of the new Liturgy; and that he was enabled, from the ancient liturgical books still existing, to collect materials which would be useful to him, and so to compile the work by making certain alterations and additions, or suppressing what was unnecessary. Hence it is that the work often bears his name; and the mistake arose—already refuted by Cardinal Bona—that St. Isidore himself was the author of the new Missal and other works.‡

This Gothic Liturgy, with part of it in Greek and part in Latin, soon came into general use in Spain. It extended everywhere, without being influenced in any way by the reform of St. Gregory the Great, which about this time began to be adopted, when, at the commencement of the eighth century, the Moors conquered the greater part of the country. Every one knows that numbers of the Spaniards remained on the battle-field, while others took refuge in the Sierras of the north, in order to preserve their liberty. But those who were willing to submit to the Moors were allowed to preserve and practise their religion without any danger. Those living under the Moorish power received the name of "Mostarabuna,"§ that

* Harduin, "Collectio Concil." tom. iii. p. 579, cap. 2.

† See a short account of Isidore, in Mariana's "Historia de España," libro sexto, cap. 7; also a note of Alban Butler, in the Life of the Saint, April 4th. There seems to be a great difference of opinion amongst the learned respecting the real origin of the Mozarabic Missal and Breviary. F. Lesley, a Jesuit, gave a new edition of the Liturgy, at Rome, in 1755.—*Trans.*

‡ See Stolberg's "Geschichte der Religion Jesu Christi," continued by Dr. Brischar, of Tübingen. (Bd. xlvi. s. 402—404.)

§ Signifying, "Mixed with Arabs." It is an Arabic participle.

is, Arabizants; while at the same time their Liturgy also was soon called the Mostarabic, the Muzarabic, Mozarabic, or Mixt-Arabic.

Not long after, the rise of the heresy of the Adoptians made this Liturgy suspected of containing false doctrine; for Glipandas, of Toledo, who was the chief of these heretics, had quoted some passages from it in support of his errors. The synod of Frankfort (held in 794) believed his assertions, and therefore showed itself to be very unfavourable to this Liturgy.* Florez, however, tries to prove that the Adoptians quoted, not genuine, but false passages from the Mozarabic Liturgy.† As to the approbation which, about one hundred and thirty years later, Pope John X. (in the year 924) formally gave to the Mozarabic Liturgy, this rests only on a single document, which is certainly not genuine.‡

Whilst the Mozarabians lived under the dominion of the Moors, their brethren, who possessed liberty, were beginning gradually to recover a great part of their native land; until at last Toledo, the ancient capital of the Visigoth kings, was once more conquered. About this period, a change in the Liturgy took place among the Spaniards who were free; for the popes Alexander II. and St. Gregory VII. were enabled by the legates Hugo Candidus and Cardinal Richard to introduce into Castile and Aragon the Gregorian rite, in place of the ancient Gothic one. In Aragon, King Sancho Ramirez§ had effected this change at the Synod of San Juan de la Peña, under Pope Alexander II. But about the same time, Alfonso VI., king of Castile, by the advice of his

---

* Harduin, " Collect. Concil." tom. iv. p. 885.
† Florez, tom. iii. p. 270.
‡ Florez, Appendix, tom. iii. p. 29.
§ Or Ramiro, as Mariana calls him.—*Trans.*

queen, Constantia, who had been accustomed to the
Gregorian rite in her native country of France, and
who now regretted that it was not followed in Spain,
wrote to the Abbot Hugo of Clugny, expressing a
wish for the pope to send into Spain Cardinal
Girald, who was then nuncio in France, in order to
introduce the Roman Liturgy. The violence, however, with which this cardinal conducted matters,
prevented at first any good effect; and though, in
the year 1074, the Castilian bishops promised their
assistance to the newly-elected pope, Gregory VII.,
and Alfonso VI. had even made a law for the introduction of the Liturgy, still the synod held at Burgos, in 1077, offered the most energetic opposition
to it. As, therefore, the two parties could not come
to any agreement, it was determined to decide the
matter by single combat, according to the custom of
the times! The knight of the Mozarabic Liturgy
gained the victory. But King Alfonso then solicited the pope to send another legate; and accordingly Gregory VII. appointed Cardinal Richard,
who was at last enabled, by the support which he
received from the king and most of the bishops, to
introduce the Roman Liturgy into the whole of Castile, in the year 1085. The celebrated council of
Burgos, held in 1085, solemnly sanctioned this
introduction.*

When, a few years later, Toledo was recovered
and annexed to the crown of Castile, the Gregorian rite was adopted in place of the Mozarabic. The choice was confirmed in a council held
in that ancient royal city (which was again honoured
as the primatial see) in the year 1088. But
the approval of the council raised such a powerful

---

* Stolberg's " Geschichte," &c., continued by Dr. Brischar,
bd. xlvi. s. 407—414; also Florez, tom. iii. p. 299, &c.

opposition amongst those who adhered to the Mozarabic Liturgy, that it was considered necessary this time to decide the matter by having recourse to the "judgment of God" (Gottesurtheil). A copy of both Liturgies was accordingly thrown into a blazing fire. The Gregorian copy rebounded from the pile of wood and fell by the side of it, while the Mozarabic remained uninjured in the midst of the flames. The inhabitants of Toledo exulted over the victory. But the king decided, that as both Liturgies appeared to be respected by the fire, so they should both be allowed in his kingdom. This decision, it is said, gave rise to the proverb, " Where kings wish, there the laws go."*

But though the king recognized both Liturgies, he was far from granting them equal rights. The Mozarabic Liturgy was only allowed in Toledo, and in these six parish churches of St. Justa, St. Luke, St. Eulalia, St. Marc, St. Torquatus, and St. Sebastian, in the same city : these parishes were inhabited by Christians living under the Moorish dominion. But all the other churches of the city and of the kingdom were obliged to use the Gregorian rite. But in course of time, when the Mozarabic families died, or, through mixing with strangers, lost all attachment to their ancient Liturgy, then the Gregorian began by degrees to be adopted in the abovementioned six parishes; until, at last, the Mozarabic Liturgy was used only on certain festivals of the year, to keep up the memory of it.

* " Allà van leyes, donde quieren reyes," as quoted by Mariana, who gives the curious details connected with the trial of the two Liturgies (libro nono, cap. xviii. p. 444, ed. Madrid, 1623). According to Archbishop Rodrigo, it seems that the Gregorian or Roman Liturgy was really burnt. The words of the archbishop are quoted by Robles, from a work entitled, " De Commutatione Officii Toletani." (See Robles, p. 235.)—*Trans.*

Such was the state of matters when Ximenez took possession of the primatial see of Toledo. His predecessor, Cardinal Mendoza, had been engaged in the same object, viz. that of restoring the Mozarabic rite. But Ximenez effected what death prevented Mendoza from accomplishing. He carefully collected all the best manuscripts of the said Liturgy, and chose Canon Alfonso Ortiz, together with three parish priests attached to the churches of the Mozarabic rite, to revise the manuscripts; he also changed the ancient Gothic characters (not the language) for the Castilian* letters, and expended a considerable sum in the printing of a great number of Mozarabic Missals and Breviaries : this was done by the assistance of Melchior Gutierrez, of Toledo.†

But, in order that the Mozarabic rite might for the future rest on a more secure foundation, Ximenez erected a very beautiful chapel, called " Ad Corpus Christi," in his own cathedral : he also founded a college of thirteen priests for the Mozarabic rite, who were called " Mozarabes Sodales, or Capellani," with a head chaplain, named Capellanus Major. These celebrated the divine office every day, and recited the canonical hours according to this Liturgy. They also exercised the right of presentation to all ecclesiastical posts in the six parish churches of the Mozarabic rite. The patronage of

---

* Robles says, Ximenez changed the characters "de la letra Gotica en la letra Latina" (p. 236).—*Trans.*

† Gomez, lib. ii. fol. 41. Binterim, in his " Denkwürdigkeiten der Christl. Kirche," bd. iv. thl. iii. s. 116. This last writer gives 1500 as the date of the publication: we certainly read this date at page 474 of the Mozarabic Missal, reprinted in 1755. But if we are to follow Gomez, the most ancient biographer of Ximenez, it seems that the Mozarabic books must have been printed about the period of Queen Isabella's death, viz. in 1504. (See Gomez, lib. iii.)

these institutions was confided to the chapter of Toledo.*

Other bishops followed the example of Ximenez; so that in the 16th century similar institutions arose at Salamanca and Valladolid. The first was founded by Patriz Maldonato de Talavera, and the other by Pedro Gasca, bishop of Sagunto.†

Thus it is to Ximenez that we are indebted at the present day for our knowledge of this Liturgy, so venerable for its antiquity and deep piety. In less than half a century after the death of Ximenez, the books that were published by him became so scarce, that a single copy of a Missal was sold, in the presence of Gomez, for 30 ducats. But now Mozarabic copies of the Missals and the Liturgy may be found in almost every library; for an edition was reprinted in Rome in the year 1755.‡

It would be out of place here to enter into any long details connected with this Liturgy; they may be found in Robles, Pinius, Thomasius, Bona, Martene, Aguirre,§ and others. Still, a short description of the Mozarabic Mass may not be unacceptable to the reader. It commences by a prayer, a little different from the Roman rite, at the steps of the altar: the psalm " Judica" (Psalm xlii.) and the

---

* Robles (p. 237, &c.) gives a long description of this foundation, of its chapels, revenue, &c. He himself was one of the chaplains, and was a curé at the church of the Mozarabic rite of St. Mark, in Toledo, about the year 1600. His " Compendio de la Vida y Hazañas" of Ximenez was published in 1604, at Toledo.

† Binterim, loco citato, p. 117.

‡ By the learned Jesuit F. Lesley.— *Trans.*

§ Cardinal Aguirre died in Rome, in 1699. His celebrated work, entitled " Collectio Maxima Conciliorum Hispaniæ et Novi Orbis," was published in Rome, in 1693, 1694. Another edition appeared in 1753, 6 vols. folio.—*Trans.*

" Confession of Sins" form the principal parts. The " Introit" varies according to the festivals, but differs considerably from ours. The " Gloria in Excelsis" follows, or, on certain days, the canticle of the " Three Children in the Furnace ;" then comes a prayer and a lesson from the Old Testament, amongst which prayers are versicles quite different from those in the Roman Missal. After the gradual called " Psallendum," comes the epistle, properly so called, which is distinct from the lesson, and is always taken from the New Testament, and generally from the epistles. It is announced by the priest or deacon in these words : " Silentium facite." It commences, as our gospel does, with the " Sequentia," * &c. ; to which the choir answers, " Deo gratias," and, at the end of the epistle, " Amen."

The gospel, on the other hand, is announced by the form, " Lectio sancti Evangelii ;" to which the choir answers, as with us, " Gloria tibi, Domine." It generally begins with these words, " In illis diebus ;" and at the end of it the people answer, " Amen."

A second book (which is necessary for the Moz-arabic Mass), called " Omnium Offerentium" (that is, Liber), is placed on the epistle side of the altar. It contains prayers common to all the Masses ; and the " Offertory" commences with prayers similar to those in our Missals, though not alike. After the " Offertory," as is the case in the ancient Greek and Milanese Liturgies, a series of prayers come, the third of which, by its title, " Post Nomina," alludes

---

* On certain days, such as the Ascension and Pentecost, &c., there is read, instead of the epistle, a passage from the Acts of the Apostles, with the initial form " Principium Libri Actuum," or " Lectio Libri Actuum." (See the Mozarabic Missal, p. 250—259, ed. Romæ, 1755.)

to the reading of the dyptichs which preceded the Offertory. After the fourth prayer, entitled " Ad Pacem," the kiss of peace takes place, which is given here, as in the Greek and Milanese Liturgy, not *after*, but *before*, the consecration. The priest kisses the paten, and thus receives the peace; he then gives it to the deacon, and the deacon gives it to the nearest person among the people.

The preface, called the "Illatio,"* that is, the conclusion (viz. of the first part of the Mass), often varies in its form. It begins by the words, " Introibo ad altare Dei;" to which the choir answers, " Ad Deum, qui lætificat juventutem meam." Then come the following versicles. The priest says, " Aures ad Dominum;" to which the choir responds, " Habemus ad Dominum;" the priest, " Sursum corda;" the choir, " Levemus ad Dominum;" the priest, " Deo ac Domino nostro Jesu Christo Filio Dei, qui est in cœlis, dignas laudes dignasque gratias referamus;" the choir, " Dignum et justum est." The preface itself commences, as with us, by the words, " Dignum et justum est, nos tibi gratias agere;" and concludes with the Trisagion, Sanctus, &c.

Up to this part, the Mozarabic Liturgy bears a great resemblance to the Roman; but in the canon of the Mass there is a great difference. After the Trisagion (or Sanctus), and a short prayer called the " Post-sanctus," the consecration immediately follows. It is then, as with us, that the Host and chalice are elevated before the people; while in the Greek Mass this takes place *after* the consecration, immediately before the communion. During the

---

* In a work by Thomasius, entitled " Codices Sacramentorum " (Romæ, 1680), and which contains a " Missale Gothicum," the preface is called " Immolatio Missæ."—*Trans.*

consecration, the priest of the Mozarabic rite uses these words: "Adesto, adesto, Jesu bone, Pontifex in medio nostri;* sicut fuisti in medio discipulorum tuorum : sancti✠fica hanc oblationem :✠ut sancti-ficata✠sumamus per manus sancti angeli tui, sancte Domine ac Redemptor æterne. Dominus noster Jesus Christus in quâ nocte tradebatur, accepit panem; et gratias agens bene✠dixit ac fregit ; deditque discipulis suis, dicens: Accipite et manducate. Hoc: est: corpus: meum: quod: pro: vobis: tradetur." † Then the priest elevates the sacred Host, and thus continues: " Quotiescunque manducaveritis, hoc facite in meam✠commemora-tionem." Taking the chalice, he says: " Similiter et calicem postquam cœnavit, dicens: Hic✠est: calix: novi: testamenti: in: meo: sanguine; qui: pro: vobis: et: pro: multis: effundetur: in: remissionem: peccatorum." The sacred chalice, covered with a pall, called "filiola," is then shown to the people; and the priest adds the words, "Quo-tiescunque biberitis, hoc facite in meam✠comme-morationem." The choir answers, "Amen."

After a few more short prayers, and another elevation of the Host, comes the Credo,‡ which in

---

* These words are used at the commencement of the canon, according to Robles — " Comiença luego el sacerdote consecu-tivamente el sacro canon, con aquellas palabras . . . . Adesto, adesto, Jesu bone, Pontifex in medio nostri," &c. This writer, as one of the Mozarabic chaplains at Toledo, gives a very inter-esting account of the Mozarabic Mass. (See cap. xxvii. of his "Compendio de la Vida y Hazañas del Cardenal Ximenez.)— *Trans.*

† This form of consecration is almost all taken from the words of St. Paul. 1 Epist. Corinth. chap. xi. 24. We have copied the form, word for word, together with the punctuation, from the Mozarabic Missal.

‡ I use the word "credo," but in the Mozarabic Liturgy it is always "credimus." (Robles, p. 289.)—*Trans.*

the Roman Liturgy is recited before the offertory, but in the Greek immediately after. The Creed is that of Constantinople and Nice, with the addition of "Filioque;" but it is translated quite differently from ours. I am convinced, by comparing the symbol of the Mozarabic Liturgy with that which comes in the Acts of the third Council of Toledo (held in 589, when the Visigoths were Catholics), that both rites completely agree with each other, with the exception of a few unimportant parts; and that the Mozarabic symbol is no other than an ancient translation of the old Spanish (Toletana) symbol, remodelled so as to resemble in some respect the Roman Credo. By a canon of the council of Toledo, the Credo has its proper place in the Mozarabic Liturgy.*

The breaking of the Host is a rite exceedingly peculiar. The priest divides the sacred Host into two parts; these are again divided, one into five and the other into four parts.† These he ranges on the paten, on which is engraved a cross formed of seven small circles, in such a manner that each circle receives the first seven particles of the Host. The two other particles are also placed on the paten, to the right of the cross. Each of these nine parts has a name corresponding with some period in the life of our Lord. These are the names in order : 1. Corporatio; 2. Nativitas; 3. Circumcisio; 4. Apparitio; 5. Passio; 6. Mors; 7. Resurrectio; 8. Gloria; 9. Regnum. Their proper

---

* Concil. Tolet. III. Canon 2. Apud Harduin, tom. iii. p. 479. See also Aguirre, Concil. Hispaniæ, tom. ii. p. 349.

† Thus making nine divisions, to correspond with the nine principal mysteries of the Catholic faith, contained in the "Creed" already recited by the priest. (Robles, p. 289.)— *Trans.*

arrangement will be understood from the following figure :*—

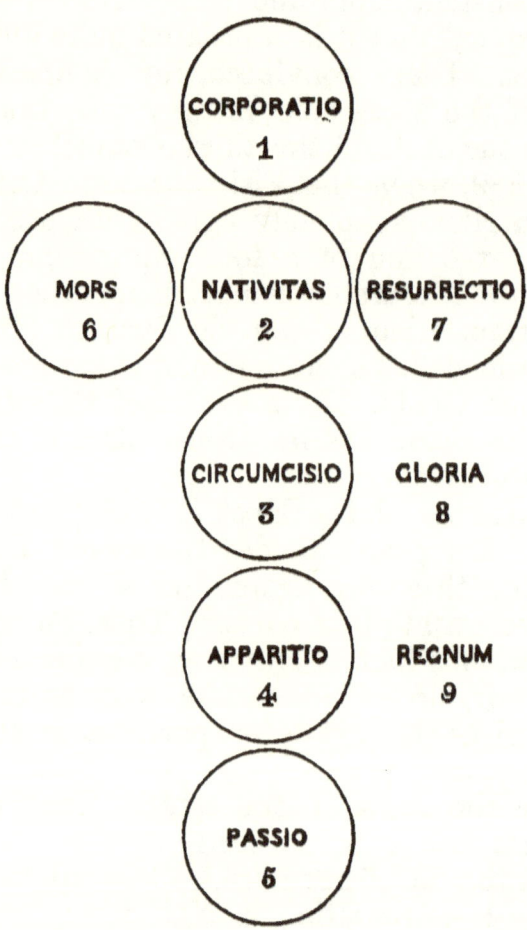

After the breaking of the bread comes the "Pater noster," with a rather long introduction.† To each petition the choir answers, Amen. Then the priest, after having prayed for the afflicted, for

---

* *Corporatio* is the same as *Incarnatio ;* and *Apparitio* the same as *Epiphania.* (Robles, p. 290.)—*Trans.*

† It corresponds with the "Oremus, Præceptis salutaribus moniti," &c. in the Roman Liturgy. (Robles, p. 291.)—*Trans.*

those in prison, for the sick, and for the dead, strikes his breast, as is done with us at the "Nobis quoque peccatoribus." He then takes the particle, "Regnum," and lets it fall into the chalice, saying the proper words* prescribed.

The blessing of the people immediately follows; then comes the communion, during which the choir sings, "Gustate et videte, quam suavis est Dominus," &c. The priest then takes the particle "Gloria," saying, "Panem cœlestem de mensâ Domini accipiam, et nomen Domini invocabo :" he prays for the dead, says the "Domine, non sum dignus," striking his breast three times; he then consumes the particle "Gloria," together with the others, one by one. Then he receives the precious blood, and afterwards the ablutions, and recites another prayer.

The deacon then removes the Liber Offerentium from the altar, and places on the Epistle side the proper Missal, from which the priest reads the post-communion. Instead of our "Ite Missa est," he says, "Solemnia completa sunt, in nomine Domini nostri Jesu Christi; votum nostrum sit acceptum cum pace;" to which the choir answers, "Deo gratias." But on feasts of no particular solemnity, the priest merely says, "Missa acta est, in nomine Domini nostri Jesu Christi; perficiamus cum pace." Then comes the "Salve Regina," after which the priest, turning towards the people,† blesses them in these words,—

---

* Which are, "Sancta Sanctis, Conjunctio Corporis et Sanguinis," &c. Dr. Hefele omits mentioning a very curious ceremony which takes place from Easter till Whitsuntide at Mass; and is also used on Corpus Christi. It is this: When the priest holds the particle "Regnum" over the chalice, he says, three times, in a loud voice, as if singing the victory of our Lord over death—"Vicit Leo de tribu Judæ; Radix David, Alleluia!" The choir answers each time—"Qui sedes super Cherubim; Radix David, Alleluia!" Robles, p. 292.—*Trans.*

† According to Binterim (p. 131), this is the only time that

"In unitate Sancti Spiritus benedicat vos Pater et
Filius, Amen:" after which he leaves the altar, and
unvests in the sacristy.

Having now described the Mass of the Mozarabic
Liturgy, let us return to Ximenez. It certainly
seems remarkable that a man who loved and promoted so much all branches of knowledge, should
himself occupy no considerable place in the rank of
authors. Our astonishment, however, increases,
when we see Ximenez described by his contemporaries as one "Doctrinâ singulari oppletus," and
compared even with St. Austin for the quickness
of his genius.* But without dwelling upon the fact
that Ximenez, though so highly educated, was far
more conspicuous for his virtue than for his learning,† yet it is evident that his natural character
was more practical than theoretical, more formed
for action than for writing. Moreover, his many
important and various duties, both as a bishop and
statesman, could have afforded very little leisure for
literary undertakings, even to one whose talents
were of the first order; hence, he who rules others
well is justly dispensed from the labours of an
author.‡

It is said, however, that Ximenez found sufficient
time to compose several theological treatises; for

the priest turns round to the people; but according to the
Mozarabic Missal (p. 3), he also turns round before the Preface,
when he says: "Adjuvate me, fratres, in orationibus vestris, et
orate pro me ad Deum." These words seem to correspond with
our "Orate, fratres." (See Quartalschrift, 1849, s. 342.)

* Peter Martyr (Epist. 108). It is not the judgment merely of
Peter Martyr himself, but of others also.

† "Aiunt homines esse virum, si non literis, morum tamen
sanctitate egregium," says Peter Martyr. (Epist. 160.)

‡ Dr. Hefele somewhat detracts from the merit of Ximenez by
his remarks, for the cardinal certainly found abundance of time
for the completion of his Polyglot amidst all his other duties.—
Trans.

example, a work entitled "De Naturâ Angelica," and another "De Peccatis." These were never printed, but were preserved in manuscript in the monastery of the Blessed Virgin at Salzeda, where Ximenez was once warden. It has likewise been said that there were found at Alcalá, composed by Ximenez, a biography of the old Gothic king Wamba; and also certain critical treatises and observations on various parts of the Holy Scripture, falsely attributed to Nicholas de Lyra.* It is certainly difficult to determine whether these assertions are correct. Gomez is silent† on the subject, while Nicolas Antonio, the learned editor of the "Bibliotheca Hispaña," expressly says, "that Ximenez was indeed a very learned man, and promoted every branch of knowledge, but that no work of his own was published by him" (s. 11. p. 687). The assertion of Robles, adopted also by Fléchier, that Ximenez *did* compose several works, will lose all authority whatever when we remember that the work "De Naturâ Angelica" was composed, not by our Ximenez (as Robles asserts), but by another, Francisco Ximenez, who lived almost a century before, and was bishop of Elne (or Perpignan), and titular patriarch of Jerusalem.‡

It is no less incorrect to ascribe to Ximenez a biography of king Wamba,§ for the assertion only

---

* Robles (p. 114) says: "Cuyo original se conserva oy dia, escrito de su propria mano, en el monasterio de Nuestra Señora de la Salçeda." This is certainly strong testimony. (See Fléchier, liv. vi. p. 505.)—*Trans.*

† Cave, "Historia Litteraria," appendix, p. 57. Busse, "Grundridtz der Christl. Literatur," bd. ii. s. 331.

‡ Dr. Hefele is mistaken. Gomez expressly says, "Scripsit etiam historiam de rebus gestis à rege Bamba . . . . quæ in Bibliothecis Hispaniæ asservatur" (folio 22, ed. Complutum, 1569.)—*Trans.*

§ He died about the year 680. He seems to have been a most

rests on a mistake made by Robles, and which has
been thoughtlessly copied by Fléchier. Gomez
relates that Ximenez at his first synod—of which
we shall soon speak—ordered the feast of St. Ildefonso of Toledo to be kept as a solemn feast throughout the diocese. On this occasion the historian
(Gomez) remarks, that St. Ildefonso (who died in
667) left amongst his writings a life of king
Wamba. Robles, not understanding this passage
properly, ascribes this biography to Ximenez, instead
of his ancient predecessor.

But Ximenez, after all, has done so much service
to literature, by the foundation of the university of
Alcalá, together with its rich and numerous institutions, and also by the publication of his great
Polyglot and several other literary undertakings,
that his name alone will be immortal. We shall
now see how deserving of our esteem was his zeal
for the good of his diocese and the reformation of
religious orders.

excellent king. Mariana gives some interesting particulars of
his life. (" Historia General de España," lib. sext., cap. xiv.)—
Trans.

CHAPTER XIII.

XIMENEZ IN THE ADMINISTRATION OF HIS DIOCESE.—REFORM
OF THE CLERGY, SECULAR AND REGULAR.—PIOUS FOUNDA-
TIONS.

XIMENEZ, from the time he became archbishop, gave constant and numerous proofs of his apostolic zeal for the good of his diocese. Even in his literary foundations, it is easy to see that he had the best interests of the Church at heart before all things else. But it is the property of true zeal never to be satisfied in doing good, and therefore it is, that we behold Ximenez extending his zeal and activity to different objects at one and the same time. One of the principal objects to which he applied his energies was the reformation of morals, especially amongst the clergy of his diocese.

Many causes had contributed to impair the morals of the Spanish clergy.

1. The bishops possessed great revenues and widely-extended domains; they also took an active part in political matters, and even sometimes exposed themselves personally to the horrors of war.*

* According to Marineo Siculo (" Cosas Memorables de España." Alcalá, 1539, lib. iv.) the archbishop of Toledo had an annual revenue of 80,000 ducats; Seville, 24,000 ducats; Santiago, 20,000 ducats; Granada, 10,000 ducats; the bishop of Burgos, 20,000 ducats; Siguenza, the same; Cuença, 16,000 ducats; and Segovia, 14,000 ducats. The bishoprics in Aragon were not so richly endowed. (Dr. Hefele should have added, that most of the bishops and archbishops belonging to the different sees made a very good use, generally speaking, of their enormous revenues. Now how different is the condition of the Spanish bishops and clergy! God knows they are poor enough,

The consequence was, that they either became very worldly, or were in a great measure incapacitated from properly fulfilling the duties of the sacred office which they had undertaken.*

2. The number of ecclesiastics became so great in Spain, that many of them experienced what dangers to morality arise from idleness.

3. The benefices were numerous and richly endowed; hence, they attracted many to embrace the ecclesiastical state who had not real vocation or sufficient learning. Being thus deprived of two essential elements in the support of a sacerdotal life, they yielded to sensual pleasures, and the enjoyments of a dissipated mind. The evil at length became so great that the council of Aranda (in 1473) made a law that no one should be allowed to receive holy orders who was ignorant of the Latin language. Peter Martyr assures us that in his time a clergyman of noble birth who could preach, "was more scarce than a white crow."†

4. This want of learning in the Spanish clergy favoured the rise and growth of errors under the name of Judaism, which we meet with in the Spanish history of the period; while, during the fifteenth and sixteenth centuries, the opposition which was raised against the Church in Italy took the form of Anti-Trinitarianism (as, for instance,

and yet how patient, how zealous, and exemplary are they as a body; this is evident from the interesting article on "Spain," written by his Eminence Cardinal Wiseman, in the *Dublin Review*, No. XXXVI., June, 1845.—*Trans.*

* The religious wars with the Moors excited for a long time the warlike propensities of several Spanish bishops. Sometimes they took part even in civil commotions. Monks also followed their example occasionally. Clemencin devotes a whole treatise on this subject, viz. the warrior-bishops of Spain, in the "Memorias de la Real Academia de la Historia," Madrid, 1821; tom. vi. ilustrac. 15, p. 388.

† "Alba cornice rarius." (Epist. 356.)

Socinus); in Germany, that of Predestination (Luther); in Spain, on the other hand, learned Jews there were enabled to infect a great part of the clergy with their errors, so that even Christian bishops were secretly attached to Judaism.[*] If one may credit the statement of a recent English traveller,[†] vestiges of this attachment to Judaism are yet to be found in the Peninsula.

5. As in the later period of the middle ages sins of the flesh prevailed to such an extent, so in Spain also they were even more common, because the evil example of the neighbouring Moors exercised a very destructive influence on the manners of the Christians. Another influence, probably no less disastrous, was the corruption of the Castilian court under Henry IV. Cast-off mistresses were made abbesses! The sovereigns themselves shamefully defiled the sanctity of the marriage state, and almost intentionally endeavoured to root out of their people all feelings of modesty and detestation of impurity.[‡] It was no uncommon thing to behold the concubines seated by the side of the lawful wife; while ladies of the highest rank were not ashamed to countenance such a state of things: open concubinage seems to have been almost as freely tolerated: public opinion was silent on the matter. No wonder, then, that this corruption reached even the clergy; and what was a remarkable feature in the

---

[*] Dr. Hefele here refers to a bishop of Calahorra, and gives for his authority Llorente. What credit is due to this writer we all know, who have read his mendacious work on the Inquisition.—*Trans.*

[†] Borrow's "Bible in Spain." For the character of this work see an article in the *Dublin Review*, No. XXVIII. 1843.—*Trans.*

[‡] For example, Catharina von Sandoval, once the king's mistress, became abbess of the monastery de San Pedro de las Dueñas, in order (said King Henry) "that she might reform its morals!" (Becker, "Geschich. Ferd. und Isab.," thl. i. s. 36.)

immorality of this period is the fact, that the concubines were not so much blamed for their wickedness as for the extravagance of their dress.* In a word, the laws of Castile declared that the bastards of ecclesiastics might, in the absence of any will, become lawful heirs.†

Such was the deep degradation into which the inferior clergy were plunged in Spain. But amongst the bishops, though in general they were not so corrupt, yet many were not without reproach. Without recalling the case of Rodrigo Luna, archbishop of Santiago, who was deposed in 1458, for having dishonoured a lady on the day of her marriage,‡ Alfonso Carillo, archbishop of Toledo, of whom we have already frequently spoken, had led an unchaste life, and the people were not ashamed to bury his corpse in the Franciscan monastery at Alcalá, by the side of his natural son named Troilo. But Ximenez, justly indignant at such a proceeding, ordered the body of the latter to be removed.§ Fonseca, archbishop of Santiago, bestowed the right of succession to the see on his own son, not, however, without great opposition on the part of Ximenez, as we shall have an opportunity of seeing later.

6. Another terrible evil was, that very frequently

---

* An ordinance (dated 1405) had commanded all the concubines of ecclesiastics to wear on their head a piece of red cloth, in order that they might be distinguished from others. (Ferreras, tom. vi. p. 162.)

† Dr. Hefele quotes Mr. Prescott for his authority. But the statements of this writer with regard to the Spanish clergy of the period under consideration must be received with great caution. —*Trans.*

‡ Mariana, lib. xxii. cap. 20. Dr. Hefele speaks of Rodrigo as archbishop of Compostella: but Mariana says he was " Arzobispo de Santiago." This wicked prelate came to an untimely end.— —*Trans.*

§ Fléchier, liv. vi. p. 495. See also Moreri, Diction. art. " Carillo."

the bastards of kings and grandees were raised to episcopal sees, there to continue the incontinence of their fathers. Thus, in the time of Ximenez, we see, for example, Alfonso Henriquez occupying the episcopal see of Osma : he was a natural son of the grand-admiral of Castile. Ximenez himself also beheld, in his younger years, the archiepiscopal see of Saragossa, the first in the kingdom of Aragon, occupied by Don Juan of Aragon, the bastard of King John II. On the death of Don Juan, in 1475, Don Alonso of Aragon, a bastard of Ferdinand the Catholic, was raised to the same see (1478) when he was only six years old. Pope Sixtus IV. had long protested against this abuse ; but through political influence, and under a threat of seeing all the church property in Sicily confiscated, he was at last obliged to consent that the bastard should have the perpetual administration of the property belonging to the archbishopric.*

7. This general corruption had also found its way into the monasteries. The vow of poverty was no longer observed by the mendicant orders; their cells were often changed into magnificent apartments, and asceticism exchanged for luxury. That holy see, it is true, which had so often before stirred up new life in the Church, and so severely punished wickedness, was at this period occupied by Innocent VIII. and Alexander VI., whose individual sins forbad them to punish the guilt of others.

A prelate, then, like Ximenez was absolutely necessary for Spain, and also a queen like Isabella ; both of whom exhibited in their unspotted lives the fairest pattern of every virtue. By the purity of their morals they gained the public esteem;

---

* Mariana, lib. xxiv. cap. 16. Zurita, "Annales," tom. iv. lib. xx. cap. 23. Ferreras, tom. vii. p. 550.

and by their wise institutions of every kind, especially the advancement of knowledge amongst the
clergy and people in general, they strove to improve
their manners and to banish vice.

When the chapter of Toledo was informed of the
elevation of Ximenez, they appointed two canons,
viz. Franz Alvar and Juan Quintanapallia, to wait
on the new prelate. The archbishop took that first
opportunity of communicating his views to the
clergy. He did not conceal from them his intention of introducing a more strict discipline amongst
them; and his wish to commence with the venerable chapter itself. Like nearly all other chapters, that of Toledo had widely departed from its
ancient strictness: the canons had formally abandoned all traces of community life, and introduced
that mode of irregular living so opposed to the very
name of canon—that is, a *rule*. Ximenez therefore
informed the deputies from the chapter that it was
his express wish to see all the canons give up, as
soon as possible, their private magnificent dwellings,
and live together in the ancient manner,—" vita
communis;" but above all, he wished that those
who had to attend the weekly services of the Church,
should live together in a house near the cathedral,
so as always to be ready to attend to their sacred
duties. He promised them, on his part, to procure
a suitable dwelling for them. The zeal with which
he immediately ordered the building to be commenced, proved that he had not uttered mere idle
words.

The chapter, having been informed by the deputies of the archbishop's intentions, and seeing very
soon that he was quite in earnest, by the erection of
the building, did not dare, openly, to oppose his
intended reform. But they resolved to prevent him,
if possible, from carrying out his intentions, and

accordingly they secretly sent an agent to Rome for this object. Their choice fell upon a canon named Alfonso Albornoz, who was a clever man, and accustomed to business. He immediately departed for Rome, but as privately as circumstances would allow, pretending that he had some other business. But his real object was, to obtain the papal confirmation of the chapter in its present state, and protection from the reform about to be introduced by the archbishop. In reality, their hopes of obtaining what they wished were sanguine, judging from the character of Alexander VI. Ximenez, also, had too much reason to fear, lest some obstacle might be raised by the pope to his plans of reform. Accordingly, when he first heard of the agent's journey to Rome, he despatched, by the royal authority, a police-officer to the nearest port, in order to arrest the deputy of the chapter, in case he intended to embark: but he had already set sail. Ximenez, however, had provided for this contingency, and sent out a fast-sailing galley to overtake the other vessel. At the same time, he wrote to Garcilasso de la Vega, the Spanish ambassador at Rome, to arrest the said deputy as soon as he should arrive, and to send him back to Spain.

Everything happened as well as could be wished. Albornoz, having been sent back to Spain, was summoned before the archbishop at Alcalá, who kept him in prison for some months, with more or less severity. This punishment so terrified the canons, that for the future no more opposition was made. In this affair Ximenez exhibited a peculiarity in his character which I do not wish wholly to justify, —I mean the use of severe measures in order to promote what one may consider useful objects.

Ximenez, however, thought it necessary to allay any fears which might arise in the minds of the canons. He therefore assured them, that he did not intend or wish to introduce the proposed changes by force, but merely by advice and exhortations thereto. But we are not informed that his wishes and exhortations, as regards living in community, were attended to by the canons, those especially who had to officiate at the services of the Church. Gomez, who lived so near the times of Ximenez, is silent on the subject; on the contrary, we learn from him, that the buildings which were erected by him for the residence of the canons, were some time afterwards added to the archiepiscopal palace at Toledo.*

About the middle of the year 1497, having assisted at the marriage of Prince Juan with Margaret of Austria, he obtained permission to reside at Toledo. This he had for a long time desired, because he had not yet taken possession of his cathedral, having been obliged since his promotion to reside either with the court or at Alcalá, the usual residence of the archbishops of Toledo.

In order to avoid all pomp, Ximenez wished to make his entrance at night and in silence, and so take possession of his cathedral in the ancient capital of Spain. But the inhabitants being so pressing in their entreaties that he would not decline the honourable reception prepared for him, had at last their wishes gratified by the consent of the cardinal to make a public entrance. Accordingly, his reception was most enthusiastic and magnificent; never, indeed, had an archbishop of Toledo been so greeted

---

* Gomez, folio xviii. (ed. Compluti 1569). The reason why Ximenez did not then insist on the canons living together, appears to have arisen from an apprehension that some tumult and disturbance might have taken place : " Cæterum tumultus et turbas emersuras prævidentem," &c. (Gomez). Ximenez, no doubt, gained his object at last.—*Trans.*

by his people. The reason was evident. The fame of his sanctity had already preceded him ; hence, both clergy and people vied with each other in the pomp and splendour of their demonstrations towards him. Having been conducted in triumph to the porch of the cathedral, Ximenez stopped there to venerate a relic of the true cross, which was brought to him in procession. Having entered the cathedral, he prayed before the high altar for a short time, and then took the oath to maintain all the rights and laws of the cathedral church of Toledo. After the ceremony was finished, the archbishop retired to his palace near the cathedral.*

Three days after, he summoned all his chapter around him, and spoke to them in the following words : " None of you are ignorant, my beloved brethren, how unwillingly I accepted my present dignity ; no one knows, too, better than myself, how unworthy I am of the exalted office which I have undertaken, under the weight and responsibility of which I already begin to totter and to groan. I feel, then, that I stand in great need, not only of the aid of Divine grace (which I earnestly implore), but of human help also ; and, above all, assistance from you, venerable brethren, who possess so much piety and prudence, and who can support me by your advice and prayers in carrying on the affairs of the Church. Confidently, therefore, do I hope and trust that you will be of the greatest assistance to me by your co-operation, zeal, and advice, that so we may be enabled to extend and promote, not

* Gomez mentions that the streets and houses were so crowded with people that the lives of many persons were in danger, and that the immediate attendants of the cardinal could hardly push their way through the multitude of men, women, and children. It was the hour for vespers before the procession arrived at the cathedral.—*Trans.*

only in this parish, but throughout the whole of the diocese, the worship of God; the reform of ecclesiastical discipline and morals, if not to their ancient strictness (which would be a difficult task in this corrupt age), at least to something of their former purity and vigour. This object will, I am sure, be accomplished, if I behold in you models of every virtue. It is but just and proper that priests, above all others by their dignity and emoluments, should also surpass others by their merits and the sanctity of their morals. What fruit can we expect from our instructions, advice, or preaching to the faithful, if you neglect your duties, and excite divisions or quarrels amongst yourselves? No; you must rather show your people by your very dress, by the very movements and gesture of your body, by your mutual peace and union one with another, by your holy conversation, and by your good works, that you are interior men, and therefore worthy of the sacerdotal dignity with which you are honoured. As for myself, I will act candidly with you, by assuring you that whomsoever I shall see walking through this life piously, and ascending step by step towards the heavenly Jerusalem, those I shall not only encourage in their efforts, but will watch over their interests, and honour them with my confidence and esteem. But if any amongst you should err from the paths of justice (which God forbid), and walk in the ways of this world, and fall into the abyss of vice, I shall follow in their regard the example of the good Samaritan in the gospel, and pour out on them oil and wine in such proportions that they will feel more the sweetness and refreshment of the oil than taste of the sourness of the wine; unless, however, some deep corruption should require the knife or the fire; then, in spite of my repugnance, I should be obliged to have recourse to these extreme measures, whenever my conscience before God and your good should demand this duty of me. But I am confident that better fruit will come from so venerable and prudent a chapter. Moreover, because I have resolved to hold my first synod at Alcalá, in order to deliberate on ecclesiastical affairs, I earnestly exhort you to send your deputies, according to ancient custom. I shall receive your observations and advice with gratitude in this church, or in any other place within my jurisdiction, and also whatever remarks you may consider fit to make respecting the project of reform." *

After a respectful reply from the dean, the chapter retired. The archbishop devoted a few days for the reception of the magistrates and citizens of Toledo. In order to expedite the reception, he adopted the following expedient. On a table by his side he placed a Bible, opened, before him. If, after the usual compliments had passed, the visitor had nothing of importance to communicate to him, he immediately began to read the book, thus intimating to the troublesome talker that it was time to retire. He kindly received the petitions that were addressed to him, and took a special interest in those which related to the protection and support of the poor. Hence the fame of the new archbishop's generosity attracted round his palace such a number of supplicants and beggars, that on one occasion when he was about to leave home he was unable to pass through the crowd, till by a device of his almoner a sum of money had been thrown amongst them.†

During the few days which Ximenez spent in Toledo, he made rich presents to the churches, and

* This address is translated almost word for word from Gomez (fol. 19). It is indeed worthy of the zeal and eloquence of the illustrious prelate.—*Trans.*

† Gomez, fol. 20.

published many excellent regulations both for the clergy and people. It was discovered on one occasion that the choir of his cathedral was somewhat contracted by a mortuary chapel, which contained the remains of ancient kings. But by removing the tombs into another chapel of the church, he was enabled to enlarge the choir. The queen approved of what had been done, in spite of the opposition of the clergy who were attached to the chapel, and were supported by the chapter. Immediately after, Ximenez went to Alcalá, in order to make preparations for the opening of his first synod there.

Alfonso Carillo, archbishop of Toledo, after the ecclesiastical institution of synods had for a long time become obsolete in Spain, had indeed, in December, 1473, convoked a provincial synod of his suffragans at Aranda, at which many useful regulations were made.

Every two years a provincial council was to be held, and every year a diocesan synod (cap. 1). Every Lent the clergy were commanded to explain to their respective flocks the principal articles of religion (cap. 2). No one was to be admitted to holy orders who did not understand Latin; and when the bishops were unable to be present themselves at the examinations of the clerics, they were to appoint two delegates to examine the candidates, who should attest by oath their fitness (cap. 3). The ecclesiastical vestments were somewhat curtailed of their excessive magnificence (cap. 5, 6, 7). Keeping concubines was punished with loss of the benefice (cap. 9). The game of dice was forbidden (cap. 11). The use of firearms was not allowed (cap. 15). And the permission to preach was reserved for those priests only who were approved of by the bishop (cap. 13). The celebration of marriage was only allowed to take place at certain periods (cap. 16). Secret affiances, unless five witnesses had been present, were punished by excommunication against the parties; while the ecclesiastic who had blessed such affiances was suspended for three months, and deprived of his benefice for the same period (cap. 17). Theatrical plays and representations were strictly forbidden to be held in churches, especially on Christmas Eve and the three following days; while those priests who permitted such unbecoming scenes were heavily fined (cap. 19). Other regulations were made, more or less useful.* But, alas! all these reforms were only on paper, never having been put into execution, for Carillo was not the man to undertake and carry out such important measures.

This glory was reserved for Ximenez, who, amongst other excellent regulations for the improvement of his diocese, held two synods also,† the "acts" of which have not, unfortunately, come down to us. But the decrees have been made known to us both by Gomez and Robles.‡

In the first synod Ximenez gave confessors the right of absolving each other in the sacred tribunal from all cases reserved to the bishop, in order that none of them might be prevented from offering up the adorable sacrifice. He also commanded all who had the care of souls to explain the Gospel on Sundays and holidays of obligation;§ and in the evening, after complin, at the hour of the "Angelus," that the bell should be rung, and all the children of the parish assembled together to recite the "Salve," in honour of the glorious Queen of Heaven. At the

---

* Harduin, "Collect. Concil." tom. x. pp. 1501-1516.
† One was held in Talavera, and the other at Alcalá.—*Trans.*
‡ Gomez, fol. 21, 22. Robles, cap. xv. p. 109.
§ This decree is not found in Gomez, but it is mentioned by Robles (p. 110).

same time, they were to be taught the creed, the articles of faith, the commandments, and other points of Christian doctrine. The archbishop likewise granted an indulgence of forty days to all who should assist at catechism.*. This regulation still existed in the time of Gomez; and was afterwards considered so useful that it came into general use, and served as a model for all catechistical instructions on Sundays.

He also re-established the custom (which had almost entirely fallen into disuse) of taking holy water at the entrance of the church. He likewise ordered, though Carillo had forbidden it, that the paten should be taken to the laity to kiss at mass, as a sign of peace (instrumentum pacis).

In order to prevent many from being impoverished through the expenses arising from cases at law, and to shorten the long duration of judicial proceedings, he enjoined all ecclesiastical and lay judges throughout the diocese to give judgment there and then on all cases of minor importance, without making use of any writ; and in other cases to carry on the proceedings as much as possible by word of mouth. Towards ecclesiastics especially, he wished that every respect should be shown to their character in all cases of trifling importance. If the accusation was light, sentence was to be pronounced by the vicar-general privately, and without any formal proceedings either of acquittal or punishment. If, on the other hand, the accusation was grave and serious, and judicial proceedings seemed unavoidable, still Ximenez recommended the judges to respect as much as possible the honour of Christ's anointed.

* I have added from Robles some additional interesting matter, which Dr. Hefele has omitted, in the last two sentences. The fifteenth chapter of Robles—" De dos Synodos que el Cardenal celebró "—is well worth reading.—*Trans.*

In this synod regulations were also made, which were productive of the greatest good to the diocese, that "registers" of births and deaths should be kept in all churches, in order that a stop might be put to marriages which were null through the relationship existing between the parties; and to criminal divorces often made under pretext of alleged relationship. Many difficulties, too, connected with questions of inheritance were removed. Another decree obliged all curates to keep an account of those who led lukewarm or disorderly lives in the diocese.

In addition to this, all priests were commanded to send information to the bishop of any public and serious scandal which should occur in their parish, in order that he might apply a remedy to the evil as soon as possible; a regulation which, Gomez tells us, was continued to his time in the diocese of Toledo with great benefit, and which other bishops also adopted, especially the suffragans of Ximenez.

Other rules and decrees relate to festivals. The archbishop followed therein the calendar of Pope Sixtus IV. (who died in 1484), who was, like Ximenez himself, a Franciscan. Thus it was decreed, that the feast of the Presentation of our Lady should be fixed on the 21st of November, and the feast of St. Joseph on the 19th of March. It was also ordained that the feast of St. Francis of Assisium should be observed as a festival, and that of St. Julian also, who was bishop of Toledo (he died in 690), be kept on the 8th of March.*

A few years later, in the summer of 1498, Ximenez held a second synod, in the palace† of his

---

* Gomez has made a few mistakes about the calends and nones. For example, he has put "xi. Calendas Octobris," instead of Decembris.

† One would suppose, from the words of the text, that the synod was really held in the palace of Juan Aiala; but Gomez

friend Juan Aiala of Talavera de la Reina, near
Toledo, at the time when the cortes was assembled
in the latter city to do homage to the young Isabella,
then recently married to the king of Portugal.
Gomez mentions that a great number of priests were
present at this synod, and that Ximenez opened
nearly all the sessions with a solemn pontifical
service. Holy and learned men were appointed to
preach upon all the subjects which were to be discussed in the synod; amongst whom Gregorio
Castello, a pontifical judge, particularly distinguished
himself, and gained the admiration and thanks of
every one, especially of Ximenez. The decrees of
the first synod were confirmed in this second; and,
according to Gomez, several new and wise regulations were made and promulgated; but, unfortunately, only one of these has been preserved by
Gomez; viz., that for the future a yearly diocesan
synod should be held for the maintenance of ecclesiastical discipline.* Ximenez was afterwards so
engaged with ecclesiastical and political affairs, that
he was unable to carry out this regulation which he
himself had made. It was only after the council of
Trent that King Philip II. established the custom of
holding provincial and diocesan synods in Spain.†
Moreover, the decrees of both these synods held by
Ximenez were quietly embodied in the "constitutions" of several of his successors in the archiepiscopal see; and thus did they come into active
operation long after the death of the illustrious
cardinal.

only intimates, that many of the clergy were hospitably entertained there, together with Ximenes.—*Trans.*

* Robles, in the fifteenth chapter of his work, seems to unite
both the synods and decrees together (p. 109).

† Gomez (fol. 26). Prescott, in his "History of Philip II.,"
has misrepresented many of this king's actions. See especially
book ii. chap. iii.—"Protestantism in Spain."—*Trans.*

But independent of these synods, Ximenez published many excellent regulations for the good of his diocese. For example, he ordered a list to be made of all the parishes, and of the revenues they possessed ; of the state of morals amongst the parishioners ; of the incomes belonging to particular families and localities ; and of the abuses which prevailed, &c. He also sent round visitors and commissioners, in order to introduce reforms both amongst the clergy and laity. The appointment of persons to ecclesiastical dignities was an object of his particular care and attention. He made choice of those only who were really worthy —that is, virtuous and humble priests, without any regard to rank, birth, or previous condition. With a view of removing any ill kind of intrigue and patronage, he made it a point resolutely to reject every one who, either by himself or by the intercession of others, should seek to obtain benefices. It was generally about the time of Easter that the appointment to vacant benefices was made.*

Already it was evident what great progress discipline and religion had made in the diocese. But in order that Ximenez might labour with still greater effect, and especially that he might be able to conquer the opposition of certain ecclesiastics, who claimed exemption from episcopal jurisdiction, he obtained from Pope Alexander VI. a brief (dated June 23rd, 1497), which invested him, by the

* " Il s'informoit de leurs inclinations; de leurs études; de la conduite de leur vie passée. Il pesoit leur mérite, et ensuite il les plaçoit, selon la proportion de leurs talens avec les besoins des paroisses. . . . . C'étoit sa coûtume de reserver toûjours quelque bénéfice pour ces bons prêtres, qu'on découvre de tems-en-tems, à qui la pauvreté ne permet pas d'attendre les occasions, et qui sont obligez d'aller chercher de l'emploi hors de leurs diocèses." (Fléchier, " Hist. du Card. Ximénes," liv. vi. p. 426—497.)—*Trans.*

authority of the Holy See, with full and unlimited power over all ecclesiastics in his diocese, whatever might be their privileges or dignities.*

Ximenez, being now supported both by the authothority of the pope and that of his sovereigns, formally declared war against all vices and abuses in his diocese. His efforts were crowned with such abundant fruit that, to use the words of Gomez, " Men seemed to have been born again."†

But so confident was he of having right and power on his side, that even out of his diocese he resolved strictly to uphold ecclesiastical discipline, and hesitated not to punish severely and boldly any violation of it. Of this spirit he gave a remarkable proof in the affair connected with the archbishopric of San Jago of Compostella. This see the aged prelate Fonseca had resigned, in favour of his son Alfonso ; hence, with the permission of King Ferdinand, but to the great scandal of the faithful, it came to pass, that a son, who was more distinguished for his warlike than his virtuous habits, was seen to succeed his father in the metropolitan see. Ximenez boldly represented to his sovereign that even kings had no right to violate the laws of the Church, and that the inheritance of Christ ought not to be possessed by a bastard. As Ferdinand, however, refused to recall his consent, Ximenez then uttered these words : " If Fonseca is to possess the revenues of the Church, on your highness must rest the responsibility, the expiation, and restitution."‡

---

* The brief is given by Gomez (fol. 24).

† " Ita in omni disciplinâ et sanctitate diocesim suam continebat, ut homines denuo renati viderentur, et bellum omnibus vitiis indictum, priscamque illam severitatem rediisse" (fol. 24).

‡ Fléchier, liv. vi. p. 495. Zurita, " Annales de Aragon" (tom. vi. lib. viii. cap. v. p. 141), informs us that this event happened

While Ximenez, however, was carrying on these reforms in his diocese with untiring energy, he did not forget at the same time the reformation of the Franciscan order, which he had commenced even from the period when he was chosen provincial and confessor to Queen Isabella. As we have already remarked, his intention was to bring the lax "Conventuals" into a stricter observance of their rule; those, on the contrary, who refused to submit, he endeavoured to remove from the monasteries, partly by mildness, and partly by force, and then to renovate the houses with monks of stricter observance. From the very commencement Ximenez met with powerful opposition. But when he became archbishop, as he strove to accomplish the reform with redoubled energy, so also was the opposition redoubled; for the lax Conventuals found numerous supporters amongst the nobility. Many of the best families had tombs and mortuary chapels in the churches of the Conventuals. But as the "Observantines," who were to be introduced in their place, were not allowed to receive any remuneration for services performed; nor any revenues for pious foundations; so these noble families began to fear that the masses and prayers for their ancestors would cease altogether, especially as a false report had spread that Ximenez intended to divert the foundations to other purposes.

The authority of the pious queen, however, kept down the opposition of the nobility. But Ximenez met with a greater and more serious obstacle on the part of the court of Rome. The reform was considered by many there as a violation of the constitutions of the order, which had been approved of by

in 1507, and that the aged Fonseca, after his resignation, took the title of Patriarch of Alexandria.

Paul II., Sixtus IV., and Innocent VIII., by virtue
of which neither the Conventuals nor Observantines
could take possession of the monasteries and churches
belonging to either, even with the permission of the
Holy See.   Alexander VI. had certainly approved
of the alteration intended by Ximenez.   But afterwards he listened to the complaints and grievances
made by the Franciscan General Samson, who belonged to the Conventuals, as all his successors did
till the year 1517.   The pope, having consented to
the representations of the general, decreed, that
the royal visitors of the monasteries (obtained by
Ximenez) should not undertake the business of
reform alone, but only in union with other delegates, who were to be chosen by the general from
amongst the Conventuals.   But in addition to this,
the pope went still further.   As these delegates were
not respected in Spain, and their advice no longer
listened to, his holiness addressed a brief to Ferdinand and Isabella (dated Nov. 9th, 1496), whereby the continuation of the reform in Spain was to
be suspended for a time : but the name of Ximenez
was not mentioned.*

The queen, almost disheartened, communicated
this intelligence to Ximenez; but he did not give
up all hopes of accomplishing his good intentions,
for he sent such powerful representations to Rome,
that the pope withdrew the prohibition, and committed the carrying-on of the reform to Ximenez
and the two bishops of Catanea and Jaen.   Thus it
came to pass, that, with few exceptions, the strict
rule of the Observantines was introduced into
all the monasteries of the Franciscans in Spain; and
whatever piety, discipline, mortification, and purity

---

* The brief is given in Gomez (fol. 23).   See also Wadding,
" Annales Minorum " (tom. xv. p. 127).

were observable amongst them in the time of Gomez, all, it is said by him, must be ascribed to Ximenez.

But even after the archbishop had obtained the papal permission, many obstacles had yet to be overcome; for about a thousand Conventuals, who were averse to the reform, went over to Africa, and by their apostasy to Mahomedanism freed themselves from the strictness of reform, and gave themselves entirely up to the gratification of their base passions. Such, at least, is the account given by Petrus Delphinus, and after him by Raynaldus,* in his continuation of Baronius. Zurita,† also, and a more recent writer, the Spanish academician Clemencin,‡ give this fact as quite certain. Hence, the assertion of Prescott (which rests only on a single authority), that the rebellious monks did not go over to Barbary, but into Italy and other Christian countries, scarcely deserves credit.§

But amongst all those who opposed the reform of the order, the most determined was the general of the Franciscan order, Ægidius Delphinus. From the time he was raised to this dignity (in 1500), he had been planning how to unite the Conventuals and Observantines together: he came into Spain, a short time after his election (in the same year, 1500), for the purpose, if possible, of supplanting

---

* Raynald. ad annum 1497, n. 34.

† " Hist. del Rey Hernando," lib. iii. cap. xv.   (See Mr. Prescott's note on the subject, vol. ii. p. 350, ed. 1849).—*Trans.*

‡ See his " Elogio de la Reina Doña Isabel," in the " Memorias de la Real Academia de la Historia " (tom. vi. p. 201).

§ Dr. Hefele is here somewhat mistaken. Mr. Prescott does not positively assert that the monks went into Italy. He merely says, in a note: " One account represents the migration as being to Italy and other Christian countries," &c. (vol. ii. p. 350). But in the text he states that " they passed over to Barbary."—*Trans.*

Ximenez.* Soon did all the enemies of the archbishop range themselves on the side of the general;
and zealously did they endeavour to collect together,
for the inglorious campaign, all their griefs, complaints, and accusations. Supported with such arms
and provisions in abundance, the cunning general
first endeavoured to lower Ximenez in the estimation of the queen. For this object he asked for an
audience, which was granted by Isabella. After the
usual greetings and civilities were over, he immediately began to launch forth the poisoned arrows of
his false zeal: "What did your majesty see," he
said, "in brother Francisco Ximenez, that could
induce you to promote him to so exalted a dignity?
What is his origin? What his learning? What
are the proofs of his holiness and virtue? As to
his birth, he is nothing but a poor hidalgo: as to
his learning, an ignoramus. What knowledge had
he of canon law, or what knowledge could the obscure official of Siguenza have acquired in four days,
that your majesty should intrust him now with
affairs of such great confidence? If you chose him
for his holiness and virtue, your majesty should not
trust to a feigned sanctity, which is nothing better
than hypocrisy and deceit. It could not escape his
penetrating eye, that Ximenez was very fickle; and
that he often passed from extreme severity to extreme laxity. He did not wish to dwell on his
rude and melancholy character, on his boorish
manners, and his want of education and good-
breeding. All these were, however, so many proofs
that Ximenez had no true holiness about him, since
real virtue was mild and gentle, serene and uniform.
Even his long refusal to accept his present dignity

* Accusations against Ximenez had been previously sent to
Rome, to the general, who, according to Robles and Gomez,
believed every unfounded report against the archbishop.—*Trans.*

was a proof, not so much of his virtue as of his cunning. Your majesty is still able to heal the wound," he continued, " which you have inflicted on the church of Toledo, since it cannot be difficult for you to deprive a man of his dignity who is in every way so utterly unfit for it."*

To these words he also added other accusations and insinuations; but he so completely failed in his attack, that the queen could hardly restrain her indignation, and prevent herself from ordering him to leave the room immediately. She, however, contented herself with addressing these few but severe words to him: " Are you, father, in your right senses, or do you know to whom you are speaking?" " Yes," he passionately replied; " I *am* in my senses, and I know well to whom I am speaking —to Queen Isabella, a handful of dust and ashes, like myself."†

Having said these bold words, he suddenly arose, and departed like a fury. He continued for a few years throwing the order into confusion, until at last he was deposed in 1506, by a general chapter held in Rome. As to Ximenez, he continued his labours for the reformation of discipline, not only amongst the Franciscans, but also amongst all the other religious orders in Spain, towards the accomplishment of which object he had already made a beginning, with the approbation of the pope, when he was confessor to the queen.‡ If the Franciscans submitted to the reform with great reluctance, the

---

* This impudent address is taken partly from Robles, and partly from Gomez.—*Trans.*

† " Diziendo: Entero juyzio tengo, y bien só que hablo con la Reyna Isabela, un poco de ceniza y polvo, tambien como yo." (Robles, p. 91.)—*Trans.*

‡ Quintanilla, " Archetypo," &c. (lib. i. cap. xi.—xiv. p. 21), gives some details connected with the reform of the religious orders. So also does Robles (p. 67, &c.).

Dominicans, on the other hand, the Carmelites, and
Augustinians, most readily embraced it.*

But while Ximenez was carrying on these affairs,
connected with the good of his diocese and the
reform of the religious orders, so great was his zeal
that he expressed a desire to hasten to Granada,
and remain there some time for the conversion of
the Moors.† After he had satisfied his zeal, the
attendance at court and the ceremonies respecting
the homage which was to be paid to Philip and
Joanna occupied his attention. Scarcely had he
recovered his health at Santorcaz, towards the end
of the year 1503, when he returned to Toledo, in
order to be able to continue the work of reform
with energy. But he had scarcely departed, when
the queen immediately summoned him to Medina
del Campo, where her daughter Joanna was afflicted
with a deep melancholy. The archbishop hastened,
as we have already seen, to console the princess ; but
in the mean time, anxious not to slacken in carrying
out the work of the reform, he commissioned his
vicar-general Dr. Alonso Garcia Villalpando, and
Canon Fernando de Fonseca, to visit the chapter of
Toledo officially. The canons, however, seeing
therein a violation of their ancient right of being
responsible to no one but the archbishop himself,
would not acknowledge or accept the visitation of
the two delegates; they, accordingly, appealed to
Rome.

Three of the most obstinate and clamorous
amongst the canons were arrested by Ximenez, from
the report sent in by the vicar-general : their names
were Sepulveda, Barzana, and Ortiz. The others,
fearful of the same fate, sent a deputation to the queen

---

* Zurita ; Quintanilla.
† The labours of Ximenez amongst the Moors have already
been mentioned in a previous chapter.

at Medina del Campo, where she was then residing with the archbishop. The head of the deputation, Dr. Francisco Alva, assured her majesty " that it was not through any spirit of opposition against the archbishop, or any fear of the reform, that induced them to undertake the journey. They were even ready to submit to the censures of the archbishop, although every one knew that Ximenez was without comparison far more severe than his vicars-general. But the interests and honour of the chapter were at stake, which from time immemorial had never been responsible to any one but to the archbishop himself."

Ximenez, no doubt, perceived that in this matter he had acted with too much precipitation. He accordingly entreated the queen to allow him to visit the chapter in person, and so put an end to the dispute. She granted him leave to do so, for the interest of religion, though she was herself then beginning to be unwell: Ximenez therefore left Medina for Toledo. At his departure she addressed these words to him: " As soon as my health is restored, I shall rejoin you at Toledo ;" but death prevented the queen from ever seeing Ximenez again.*

The visitation of the archbishop to the chapter calmed all their fears. Unfortunately, the particulars have not reached us, or the regulations which he made ; still we know that the relation in which Ximenez afterwards stood towards the canons was most amicable; that he consulted them on all important matters, and often entreated them to remember him in their prayers at the altar.†

---

* She died November 26th, 1504. (See Clemencin's eulogy of this most illustrious and pious queen, in the " Memorias de la real Academica de la Historia," tom. vi.)—*Trans.*

† Fléchier, liv. vi. p. 487.

Ximenez, about this period, founded other very useful institutions in his diocese. He discovered that many young women were driven by poverty to a life of sin and dishonour; and on his visitations as provincial he also found out that several who had taken the veil through necessity, and without having any vocation, became afterwards very unhappy in their convents. To remedy this double evil, he founded at Alcalá the Convent de San Juan, to which he joined a house of charity for poor girls, under the title of " Santa Isabel." Here they lived to a certain age, under the guidance of a spiritual mother and the warden of the Franciscans of the city, with certain rules drawn up for their direction. They had the choice either of marrying or of embracing a religious life. If they chose the former, they received a dowry from the revenues of the house; if the second state, they were received without a dowry into the convent of San Juan.

Ximenez lived long enough to behold the blessings arising from such institutions. He was so pleased with their success, that in his will he left considerable sums to them, though in his lifetime he had endowed them with large donations, which were afterwards considerably increased by Francisco Ruyz* and King Philip II. By these means the establishments became so flourishing that even ladies of respectability and daughters of officers connected with the royal household endeavoured to be educated in them.

Ximenez also encouraged such institutions which were so productive of good, even when they had been founded by other people. Thus two individuals of the middle class, named Jeronymo Madrit and Pedro Zalamea, being grieved that no institu-

* He was bishop of Avila. (See Gomez, fol. 51).

tions for the poor existed in Toledo, resolved to found an hospital which was intended for poor invalids. A considerable number of these were brought to a house, where doctors and other necessary helps were provided for them. The middle age, so fruitful in good works " for God's sake," had scarcely commenced this pious undertaking, when immediately many persons hastened to give it their support. Accordingly Madrit and Zalamea, having united their resources together, soon saw themselves in a condition, not only to provide for poor invalids, but also to take care of widows and orphans who had been abandoned, besides undertaking numerous other works of mercy. Ximenez was the chief patron of these institutions; he invited Madrit to come and see him, and encouraged him to persevere; he gave him also most substantial assistance, assuring him of his willingness always to aid him by his advice, money, and authority. This encouragement excited the zeal of the founders to such a degree, that the undertaking soon assumed the form of a religious congregation, whose office was to take care of the poor and the sick, and especially of those who wished not be known as paupers. Every night during the year, from the 1st of November to the last day of March, two of the members were obliged to walk through the streets of Toledo, with torches in their hands, collect together all the houseless poor, and conduct them to the newly-erected hospital. When Ximenez saw the success of the institution, he gave to it, during the year of famine in 1505, more than 4,000 bushels of corn, to be distributed amongst the poor. Indeed, every year he made valuable presents to it, both in money and provisions. After the death of Ximenez, Pope Adrian VI., as a memorial of the pleasant days which he and Ximenez had spent together in Spain, solemnly approved of the institution. Gomez* seems to delight in describing the blessings which flowed from its establishment, as well as the gratitude which the public felt and expressed towards Ximenez by the celebration of a solemn service on the anniversary of his death and an abundant distribution of alms to the poor.

In addition to these benefactions, Ximenez was also in the habit of performing a number of other works of charity. Thus, he visited the hospitals in person; he gave dowries to distressed women; every day he fed at his palace thirty poor people; he released those who were in prison; and founded four hospitals, eight monasteries, and built twelve churches.†

But while he was thus engaged in promoting the welfare of his diocese, assisting the poor, and endeavouring to lead his clergy along the paths of virtue, the noble Queen Isabella died. By her death the faithful chancellor was again interrupted in the performance of his episcopal duties.

* Lib. iii. fol. 50, 51.
† Fléchier (liv. vi. pp. 499—501) gives these and many other edifying details about the charity, zeal, and devotedness of Ximenez.

CHAPTER XIV.

XIMENEZ TAKES PART IN THE AFFAIRS OF STATE UNDER PHILIP THE FAIR.

By the death of Isabella, who died without a male descendant, Castile came to be settled on the Infanta Joanna, the consort of Philip the Fair; while Ferdinand, by this event, lost all right over Castile, and was therefore obliged to be content with his hereditary states of Aragon. But this posture of affairs, so simple in itself, soon became exceedingly complicated, both by reason of the enfeebled state of Joanna's mind, and the inconstancy of Philip.* Philip seemed to have but little regard for Spain; and so anxious was he to leave the country almost immediately, that people began to doubt whether he intended ever to take up his residence there, and not rather live in the Netherlands, the land of his affection. As to Joanna, who doted upon him with excessive fondness, and whose jealousy was also proportioned to her love, would she in this case consent to remain absent from him, and so leave Castile without a sovereign? No one could be deceived on the question;—she would never remain behind him. But, independent of this consideration,

---

* He was archduke of Austria, and son of the emperor Maximilian. Joanna, to whom he was married, was the second daughter of Ferdinand and Isabella. But Philip being a stranger to Spain, the marriage proved very unfortunate. He treated Joanna with the greatest indifference. In spite of every solicitation on the part of his wife, and of Ferdinand and Isabella, he could not be prevailed upon to remain for any length of time in Spain.—*Trans.*

Q

it was also to be feared, as indeed was afterwards the case, that the disordered state of Joanna's mind would become worse and worse, and so render her incapable of holding the reins of government.

Isabella, therefore, in order to guard against both dangers, viz., either the departure * of her daughter, or her increasing infirmities of mind; and being aware, too, that her own death was approaching, appointed her husband Ferdinand regent of Castile; for in his prudence she could confide. She had already, towards the end of the year 1503, wished the Cortes of Castile to sanction a law, that in case she herself should die in the absence of Philip and her daughter, Ferdinand should be elected *ad interim* regent of the states of Castile. But the queen declared her wishes more clearly in this respect in that admirable will which she dictated in October, 1504, a few months before her death. Foreseeing either the absence or the incapacity of Joanna, she declares, that after mature reflection, and by the advice of several prelates and nobles of the land, she had appointed King Ferdinand, her husband, " to be the sole regent of Castile," until her grandson Charles should have attained his twentieth year. She also bequeathed to Ferdinand a rich income, and bestowed on him during his lifetime half of the revenues which should arise from the newly discovered lands in the Indies, together with the grand-masterships of three Spanish military orders, which a short time before had been united to the crown by a papal indult.† The queen made no

---

* From the time Philip left Spain to return to the Low Countries, Joanna began to sink into a deep melancholy. She was always talking and thinking about her husband; and never recovered her tranquillity till she returned to Brussels, the year after Philip's departure from Spain.—*Trans.*

† Mariana, lib. xxviii. cap. ii.

mention of Philip in her will, and did not confer the regency on him; because he turned a deaf ear to her advice, ill-treated her daughter, and constantly preferred the interests of France to those of Spain.[*]

Isabella had named as her executors King Ferdinand, Archbishop Ximenez, Deza, bishop of Palencia, Antonio Fonseca, and Juan Velasquez, two inspectors of the finances, together with her secretary Juan Lopez Lezarraga.[†] The two first had full powers to act, in conjunction with any one of the others.

Many of the nobles of Castile were, however, exceedingly displeased with these appointments of the queen, for they did not wish to hear anything about the regency of Ferdinand; whether they were blinded by the rivalry so long subsisting between Castile and Aragon, or whether they hoped to exercise greater influence under Philip, a weak and inconstant prince, than under Ferdinand, who was strong and resolute. Scarcely had they heard the will of Isabella read than they broke forth into complaints, and sent messengers forthwith to Flanders to invite Philip to hasten without delay into Spain.[‡]

Ferdinand, on the other hand, instructed by these intrigues, and with the intention of complying with the regulations of the will, solemnly resigned the title of King of Castile, and ordered the heralds publicly to proclaim that his absent daughter Joanna, and her husband Philip, were now the sovereigns; but that he himself, according to the

---

* Peter Martyr, Epist. 277.

† Prescott gives a good epitome of Isabella's will. (See "History of Ferdinand and Isabella," part ii. chap. xvi.) There seems, however, to be a difference respecting the date of the will, between Mr. Prescott and Dr. Hefele: the former mentions as the date, November 23rd, 1504; the latter, October 12th, 1504.

‡ Peter Martyr, Epist. 277.

wish of the deceased queen, was merely the administrator of the kingdom.*

According to ancient custom, he also delivered the standard of Castile to the duke of Alva, and summoned the primate and grand chancellor to meet him at Toro, on the confines of Portugal, in order to deliberate about the affairs of the kingdom and the execution of Isabella's will. In the mean time, while Ferdinand and Ximenez were conferring together on business at Toro, the corpse of Isabella, attended by the faithful Peter Martyr and a great number of cavaliers and ecclesiastics, was borne from the north to the south of Spain, Granada, amidst the most dreadful weather.† The wise Ferdinand surpassed himself in royal civilities towards Ximenez, in order to gain to his side such an influential prelate. He saw clearly that he then stood more in need of Ximenez than Ximenez of him: he accordingly went forth to meet him, welcomed him in the most friendly manner, and offered him a seat, while he himself continued to stand. The executors met and consulted together almost every day. The Cortes was also immediately convoked at Toro

* Peter Martyr, Epist. 279.

† Scarcely had the funeral procession left Medina del Campo, where the queen died, than a tremendous tempest arose, which continued with little interruption during the whole of the journey. Such is the testimony of Peter Martyr and others. The remains of Isabella were first laid in the Franciscan monastery of the Alhambra, at Granada; but on the death of Ferdinand, they were removed to the cathedral, where both now lie, side by side. A magnificent mausoleum of white marble was erected to their memory, by their grandson, Charles V. The sides were adorned with figures of angels and saints, richly sculptured in bas-relief, while on the top reposed the effigies of the illustrious sovereigns. The Capella de los Reyes, though forming a part of the cathedral, is quite distinct in a manner from it. Fortunately, the royal remains have never been disturbed. (See Ford's "Handbook of Spain," Granada; also, "Spain as it is," by Hoskins, vol. i. chap. xiii.; and Laborde's "Itinéraire," ed. Paris, 1827.)

(January, 1505), in order to ratify the wishes of Isabella as expressed in her will, to take the oaths of allegiance to the queen Joanna and her consort, and to acknowledge Ferdinand as the administrator of the kingdom.[*] Unfavourable news, however, having arrived respecting the state of Joanna's mind while the Cortes was holding its sittings, it was declared that the circumstances which were foreseen by Isabella regarding her daughter had arrived; and therefore Ferdinand was expressly requested not to abandon the kingdom, but to carry out the wishes of the deceased queen. At the same time, notice of these proceedings was sent to the court of Philip.[†]

Thus every arrangement was made in accordance with the laws of justice, and with a view to the future welfare of Castile. But many of the nobles seemed as unwilling to comply with the commands of the Cortes, as they did to carry out the last wishes of the queen expressed in her will. They even spread injurious reports about Ferdinand, as if he intended, by a marriage with Beltraneja, to acquire possession of Castile for himself, and also demand half of the kingdom of Granada. Others, likewise, openly declared themselves the friends of Philip; viz, the marquis of Villena, the duke of Najara, and Don Juan Manuel, the ambassador of Ferdinand and Isabella at the court of Maximilian. On being informed of the death of the queen, he immediately hastened to Flanders without the permission of his sovereign, where he gained great influence over Philip by his talents,[‡] increased the ill-will already

---

[*] Mariana, lib. xxviii. cap. xii.

[†] Zurita, "Anales de Aragon," tom. vi. lib. vi. cap. iv.

[‡] "This nobleman, descended from one of the most illustrious houses in Castile, was a person of uncommon parts, restless and intriguing, plausible in his address, bold in his plans, but exceedingly cautious, and even cunning in the execution of them," &c.

existing between Ferdinand and Philip, and openly refused to obey the command of the former to return to his post of ambassador: he also served as a means of communication between Philip in Flanders and the rebellious Castilian nobles.* His insinuations succeeded so much the more powerfully with Philip, as they were supported by the court favourites of the prince, who hoped the more easily to enrich themselves with the gold of Castile, by the removal of Ferdinand out of the way. Philip also, dreading to find in his father-in-law a severe and troublesome tutor, readily came into the plans of Don Manuel to drive Ferdinand from Castile, in spite of the will of Isabella.

Such difficulties were, of themselves, sufficient to damp the courage of Ferdinand. For thirty years he had been accustomed to love Castile as his own father-land; while in union with his wise and faithful queen, he had done innumerable good things for its welfare, and even gained a new kingdom for it by the conquest of Granada. But now it seemed as if he were about to lose the fruit of all his labours, and that the band which had so long united him with Spain would be broken, in case the light-minded Philip should succeed.† Ferdinand, also, began to have some apprehensions about the kingdom of Naples, recently added to the crown of Aragon. Neither could he divest himself of a suspicion which forced itself on him for a long time, that perhaps the " Great Captain " might, as a Castilian, unite himself with Philip, and so deliver up Naples to him.

Ximenez, however, was entirely devoted to the

(Prescott's History of Ferdinand and Isabella," part ii. ch. xvii.) —*Trans.*

* Peter Martyr, Epist. 282. See also Ferreras, tom. viii.

† Such are the apprehensions expressed by Peter Martyr (Epist. 283).

cause of Ferdinand. He advised him to send some persons of tried fidelity to the court of Flanders, in order to inform Philip of the self-interested views and plans of the Spanish nobles; to offer him the friendship of Ferdinand, and to request the young prince (Charles) to come into Spain. Lopez Conchillos and Miguel Ferrera were accordingly sent to Flanders.*

Ximenez, during his stay at Toro, was very anxious to see and venerate the corpse of St. Ildefonso of Toledo (who died in 667); it was preserved in the neighbouring town of Zamora. But the inhabitants of the place refused him permission, through the apprehension they had, that he might perhaps request for himself a portion of the saint's body. Being painfully disappointed at the refusal of the people, Ximenez applied himself again to his episcopal duties; but it seems uncertain whether he returned to Alcalá, and carried on the business of the reform (now for some time interrupted) in his diocese, or whether, as some other writers say, he joined the king at Segovia, and was unwilling to leave him till the aspect of affairs became more settled.

About this time, Philibert de Vera, of Burgundy, and Andrea de Burgo, from Cremona in Italy, arrived in Spain as ambassadors of Philip and the emperor Maximilian. Their object was to repeat by word of mouth what Philip had already expressed in writing to Ferdinand; viz., that Ferdinand should resign Castile, and retire as soon as possible into his own hereditary states. The unfortunate Joanna, in her lucid intervals, saw with grief the blindness of Philip, the cruel treatment shown to her father, and the dangers also which threatened his states of

* Peter Martyr, Epist. 282; Mariana, lib. xxviii. cap. xiii.

Castile. Acting according to the advice of Conchillos, who was her secretary, she addressed the following affecting words to her father :—" If the entreaties of a loving daughter are of any force, do not, my father, resign a kingdom which, in union with Isabella, you delivered from ruin, and made great and powerful. I, the heiress of that kingdom, hereby surrender to you full powers for its government; and when I return to Castile, your counsel shall be my rule of conduct." Conchillos had intrusted this letter to his companion Ferrera, that so he might take it with him to Spain. But Ximenez and others were deceived by this man; for he was base enough to deliver the confidential letter to Philip. When he read it, his rage knew no bounds; he banished all the Spanish ladies and grandees from the court of Joanna, censured her correspondence with Spain, and threw the unfortunate Conchillos into a horrible dungeon as a state criminal. There the miserable young man, probably under the effects of poison, soon lost his hair, and for a time even his reason.* Philip immediately equipped a powerful fleet to drive by force his father-in-law from Castile; and having entered into an alliance with France, it was arranged that Louis XII. should take Naples from King Ferdinand, while Philip at the same time was to land in Spain.†

Oppressed under all these difficulties, Ferdinand summoned Ximenez to Segovia, in order to oppose his authority to the unruly nobles, and to confer with the ambassadors from Flanders. Immediately on his arrival in the city, even before he had any

---

* Gomez, and Peter Martyr, Epist. 286.

† Peter Martyr, Epp. 285, 289, 290, 291. These details are somewhat different from those given by Mr. Prescott, who seems to forget a reference to any authorities. (See chapter xvii. of his History, &c.)—*Trans.*

interview with the king, Ximenez invited both the ambassadors to an audience with him. These, in opposition to the representations of the Spanish grandees, showed such respect for the primate and grand-chancellor, that they at once arose from table, and hastened to Ximenez, who received them in the royal apartments. The archbishop then represented to them, " how deplorable it was, that Philip should mistrust his father-in-law, and deliver himself over to rapacious vultures and hungry wolves. As to the imprisonment of Conchillos, he proved that the punishment was much greater than the fault he had committed; he therefore requested them immediately to send off a courier to Philip, to demand his liberation: above all, he convinced them that it was high time for Philip to show himself more conciliating towards Ferdinand; for should his anger be once roused, he could easily prevent Philip by force from entering Spain."* Alarmed by these words of Ximenez, and also dreading his firmness, as well as fearful of his influence, they immediately sent off —even before they arose from table—a courier to Philip, to inform him of the conference which had just taken place, and to beg of him to come to some understanding with Ferdinand; for that this would be the only means of avoiding great evils. Everything succeeded so well, that Conchillos was released from prison, and fresh negotiations were opened between Philip and his father-in-law.

Another circumstance contributed to make Philip more pacific. At the time when he was making pre-

---

* Robertson, in his " History of Charles V.," is to be blamed for having attributed to Ferdinand the intention of resisting the landing of Philip by force. Ximenez only wished to terrify the ambassadors by such a threat. Peter Martyr assures us that Ferdinand had no idea of employing force against Philip. (See Epist. 291.)

parations for war against Ferdinand, in union with
France, Ferdinand, by his tact and wisdom, had succeeded not only in averting the threatened storm,
but even in gaining over to his cause his hereditary
enemy, Louis of France. Through his hatred of
Philip, he went so far as to marry Germaine,* the
niece of the king, that so he might leave Aragon to
another heir, rather than to the ungrateful Philip.†
Thus, the enmity between the son-in-law and the
father-in-law threatened to undo all that the marriage
of Ferdinand and Isabella had effected for the welfare of Spain. The hatred, too, of Ferdinand had
become so intense, that he sacrificed precious advantages in order to detach France from Philip, and
to gain it over to his cause. While Louis renounced,
in favour of Germaine, all his claims to Naples, Ferdinand engaged himself, in case Germaine should
die without children, to deliver the moiety of the
kingdom of Naples to France: in a word, the
affiance between the young prince Charles and
Claudia (which was not agreeable to the French)
was declared to be of no effect. The two parties
signed the treaty in October, 1505. Peter Martyr
justly calls it "a shameful treaty" (Epist. 292);
but, he adds, that Ferdinand considered it absolutely necessary; and these words explain the reason
why Ximenez gave it his co-operation.‡ France
now took in a decided manner the part of Ferdinand,
and refused Philip an entrance into Spain, so long

---

* She was the daughter of Jean de Foix, viscount of Narbonne, and one of the sisters of Louis XII.; and granddaughter
to Leonora, queen of Navarre, the guilty sister of King Ferdinand. (Prescott, chap. xvii.)

† Dr. Hefele omits here several details connected with the alliance between Ferdinand and France, and also many of the terms
on which this alliance was to be based.—*Trans.*

‡ "Non abnuente Ximenio." (Gomez.)

as he refused to be reconciled to his father-in-law.

The letter in which Ferdinand announced these events to his son-in-law is interesting:—" You have no reason, my son, to be angry with me for having concluded a treaty of peace with your friend of France; since as long as the king was my open and your secret enemy, you eagerly sought to obtain his assistance against me, and even against yourself. In making this treaty, I have not been unjust towards you; but you, by your alliance with France, have treated me with contempt and done me great harm, and also yourself; you have likewise forced me to enter upon this new marriage. Recover, then, yourself. Should you come into Spain as a son, and not as an enemy, I shall forget the past, and receive you as my son; so great is the power of paternal love. Should you listen to the advice of one who knows perfectly both the people and the nobility, your presence in Spain will be happy and welcome. But should you continue to give your confidence to those who think only of their own interest and your destruction, you will certainly fall into terrible misfortunes."*

This unexpected turn of events compelled Philip to become more pacific towards Ferdinand, who, after the treaty with France was arranged, went from Segovia to Salamanca in company with Ximenez. There the archbishop first heard of the death of the governor of Cazorla, Pedro Hurtado Mendoza, brother of the late great cardinal of the same name. He immediately commissioned persons with full authority to confirm the inferior officers in their places, and to provide for the levying of the taxes;

* Peter Martyr, Epist. 293.

but he deferred till a later period the appointment of any one to the late governor's post.

It was during his stay at Salamanca that the affair of the regency was settled,—November 24th, 1505; it was publicly proclaimed on the feast of the Epiphany.　From this date it was settled, that all royal decrees and documents should bear at the head of the page the names of Ferdinand, Philip, and Joanna, together; and that they were to carry on the government in union with each other.[*]　But the friends of Philip amongst the Spanish grandees considered this treaty only as a necessary evil, which was unavoidable on account of the friendship of Ferdinand with France; but that it would be null and void as soon as Philip should once arrive in Castile.　They hoped, that then Ferdinand would no longer occupy the first place, or rather no place at all, in the government of Castile, but that he would be obliged, against his wish, to retire into Aragon.

Their prophecies were correct, because they themselves had a share in the accomplishment of them. Ferdinand, in the mean time, being satisfied with the treaty, left Salamanca, and returned to Segovia, to enjoy the pleasures of hunting, which he loved excessively.　But when he heard that Philip and Joanna had embarked for Spain (January, 1506), he ordered public prayers to be offered up throughout the whole of Castile for their safe arrival.　He himself came more towards the north, as far as Valladolid, in order that he might hasten to the coast as soon as he heard of their arrival in Spain. Peter Martyr mentions with what profound grief Ferdinand was afflicted, when the news reached him,

---

[*] Peter Martyr, Epist. 294.　The treaty was really intended by Philip to lull the suspicions of Ferdinand, who was quite deceived in the matter, as events prove.—*Trans.*

some time after, that a most furious tempest had destroyed part of the Flemish fleet, and a fire broken out in Philip's ship, while the remainder of the vessels were cast on the coast of England.*

Being obliged to remain some time in England, Joanna took the opportunity of visiting her sister Catherine.† Philip at last set sail, and reached the port of Coruña on the 28th April, 1506. Ferdinand hastened to meet them, and sent two envoys to Philip to assure him of his friendly intentions; and that after he had taken part in the government of Castile for two years, he should then retire into his kingdom.‡ Ximenez followed the king by his special command. Gomez relates, that on his journey he obtained for the inhabitants of Villumbrale, by his prayers, a most abundant shower of rain, which had been long wanted.§ Ferdinand and Ximenez arrived together at Molina, while Joanna and Philip proceeded to Compostella. There their arrival was waited for by the ambassadors, who had been deputed by Ferdinand to congratulate them.

But in the mean time, the friendship which had but just commenced between both parties so closely related was soon destined to be broken. Philip was so unwise, and also so presumptuous, as publicly to declare that the treaty of Salamanca was not binding in his estimation; that he should receive no advice from Ferdinand, nor allow Joanna his wife to have an interview with her father.‖ Philip was

---

* At Weymouth. When Henry VII. heard of the shipwreck, he invited the illustrious persons to Windsor, where they were magnificently entertained for three months.—*Trans.*
† Catherine of Aragon, who was then married to Henry VIII. —*Trans.*
‡ Peter Martyr, Epp. 294, 301, 304.
§ Gomez, lib. iii. folio 58.
‖ Peter Martyr, Epist. 305 (also, Epist. 300). The letters of

exceedingly irritated at the marriage of Ferdinand
with Germaine, because such an event threatened
to deprive him of Aragon, Naples, and Sicily. The
Castilian nobility were also irritated at this union,
because it seemed to injure the memory of the great
Isabella, the national honour, and likewise the welfare of Castile. Thus numbers of the grandees were
already deserting the cause of Ferdinand, and going
over to the side of Philip, who was intentionally
endeavouring to avoid an interview with his father-
in-law; he even hastened away from Compostella,
like a fugitive, in order not to meet Ferdinand there
on his arrival. Ximenez, the grand-admiral, the
grand-constable of Castile, the duke of Alva, his
brother, the marquis de Denia, and a few others,
were the only persons who remained faithful to
the king.

One can hardly decide whether it was meanness
or wickedness that induced Philip to hide himself,
like a thief, in the mountains of the north of Spain.*
The words, "odiunt, quem læserint," are certainly
applicable to him; for he must naturally have felt
a strong dislike to appear before Ferdinand, whom
he had lately irritated by his violation of the treaty
agreed upon at Salamanca, and by his refusing
Joanna an interview with her father.

Towards the middle of May, 1506, Ferdinand,
with the object of effecting some good, commissioned
Peter Martyr to have an audience with Philip,
hoping that the archduke would lend a willing ear
to the representations of so learned a man, whom
he had so highly honoured ever since his arrival in
Spain.† But as the visit was useless, Ferdinand
poured out all his grief into the bosom of Ximenez,

this learned man are of great historical value for this period of
our history.— *Trans.*
    * Peter Martyr, Epist. 308.   † Ib. 305, 306.

though he had fortitude enough to conceal it from the eyes of the world. He now regretted having remained so long at Molina, and thus allowed his son-in-law to escape from him. He also reproached Ximenez for not having corrected his negligence; but the archbishop at once replied, "that he had, alas! constantly given advice to his majesty which was never attended to; that he had frequently entreated him, not only to make haste, but also to have recourse to arms to subdue his rebellious nobles, and to keep his evil-minded son-in-law in check: but still, that Ferdinand must not lose courage, and might count for certain on his support and adherence."*

The result of this conversation was, that Ximenez, though now advanced in years, undertook the difficult task of effecting a reconciliation between Ferdinand and Philip. He accordingly hastened to overtake the latter, followed him across the mountains, and ceased not till he found him at Orense, in Galicia.† On the same day of his arrival, he sent his companion Francisco Ruyz to Philip, to offer him his respects and ask for an audience. This was readily granted, while Ferdinand expressed his joy to Ruyz at the arrival of so venerable a prelate, and appointed the following day for the audience. Philip received Ximenez before the whole court with extraordinary marks of respect and kindness; for he had already learned to esteem, not only the ecclesiastical dignity of the primate, and his great political influence, but also the high personal character which he bore. The first interview—which was private—lasted more than two hours. Several other interviews

* Gomez, folio 59.

† Gomez states, that Ximenez commenced his journey at the beginning of May, 1506; but it is clear, from Peter Martyr, that it was at the commencement of June.

followed, and conferences with the ministers of Philip. Hence, the best amongst the Castilian nobles now began to rejoice at seeing Ximenez become the only mediator capable of effecting a reconciliation between the two hostile parties.

The representations which Ximenez made to Philip may be seen in a letter which the archbishop addressed to Ferdinand from Orense. It was to the following effect :—" He assured the young prince, that the Spanish grandees sought only their own interest, even at the risk of the repose and security of the kingdom; that they hated King Ferdinand, because he saw through their avarice, and was determined to put a check upon it. As Ferdinand had rendered great services to Philip, the latter could do nothing better than allow himself to be guided by his wise father-in-law, whose long experience and knowledge of the Castilian people and nobility would be a pledge for promoting the welfare of the kingdom. But should he refuse to confide in Ferdinand, and be resolved to trust himself to Don Manuel, such an act would be nothing more or less than to cut himself off from a strong support, and rest only on a weak reed. Seldom indeed do step-mothers agree with their step-children ; but quite the opposite is the case between a father-in-law and son-in-law, especially in the present case, where the father-in-law, having no male heir, would devote himself to the interests of his daughter and her children."*

But the words of Ximenez were of no avail. Philip could not be induced to allow Ferdinand to retain the provisional government of Granada, which had been conquered by him, and was not yet entirely subdued. Philip persisted in wishing Ferdinand to

* Gomez, folio 60.

remove from Castile, and would allow him to claim nothing but the revenues which his wife Isabella left him in her will.

Ximenez, believing that any further negotiations would be perfectly useless, accepted the conditions mentioned above. But as he earnestly desired that the two princes should have an interview with each other, he resolved not to depart from the court of Philip till he had effected a meeting between them. Ferdinand, on his part, did not delay in expressing to Ximenez his warm thanks for all his exertions : he declared that he was ready even to abandon his kingdom, to govern which he was forbidden by the blindness of his son-in-law.

Thus was an apparent reconciliation effected, principally through the condescension of Ferdinand:* from this period Ximenez seems constantly to have remained by the side of Philip, as he was required by his duties of grand-chancellor of Castile.

It was about this period that Ximenez bestowed the office of governor of Cazorla on his cousin, Count Garcias de Villaroel. It was remarkable that the mode of collation which he made use of, respected at once both the right of confirmation which be-longed to the crown, as well as the liberty of election which belonged to the archbishop. Ximenez one day addressed these words to Garcias in the presence of Philip : " Kiss the hand of the king, our master, for having made you governor of Cazorla." The king, quite taken by surprise, could not refuse his consent, because it seemed as if the appointment had come directly from himself. Thus it was seen, that Ximenez had deferred appointing

---

* Ferdinand, through the love which he had for his daughter, sacrificed his rights, as Peter Martyr remarks: " Ab armis temperatum est a Fernando, quia paternus amor tot opprobria ferre coëgit." (Epist. 309.)

any one to the office till the arrival of Philip, as, indeed, it was the general opinion from the first that such would be the case.

When Philip met the Cortes at Burgos, and thence went to Puebla de Senabria, Ximenez accompanied him, where he at last obtained a promise from him, that he would consent to have an interview with his father-in-law. Philip chose Don Manuel to regulate all the details. But this individual had offended Ferdinand too grievously to dare to appear before him till the duke of Alva and Don Antonio Fonseca had offered themselves as hostages: Ximenez received them in his house. After everything had been arranged, the solemn interview at last took place in an open plain near Senabria, on the borders of Leon and Galicia, June 23rd, 1506. Philip, accompanied by a great number of Belgians and Spaniards, and surrounded by a considerable force, as if prepared for a battle, made his appearance on the plain with royal pomp; Don Manuel being on his left hand and Ximenez on his right. Ferdinand, on the other hand, came without any pomp or military escort, attended only by about two hundred followers, who were mounted, like himself, on quiet mules, without any warlike preparations. Even his very enemies could not help admiring his wisdom and tact, in seeing him thus advance like a father going to meet his children; while Philip hastened to his father-in-law as if he were going forth to encounter an enemy. The pompous parade of the one did not diminish the simplicity of the other.

The military formed an extensive circle round the two sovereigns and their noble attendants, while the Spanish grandees, being now brought so near to Ferdinand, could not help, in spite of their enmity against him, from showing him formal marks of their respect. This ceremony certainly cost their pride a great deal, for many were conscious how grievously they had injured Ferdinand, and, above all, the count of Benevente and the marquis of Astorga, who had refused Ferdinand on his journey to meet Philip a passage through their territory. Ferdinand, however, thanked them all with kindness, and added, moreover, many good-humoured remarks and witty allusions. Several of the grandees wore armour inside their clothes, because they had no faith in the reconciliation of the two princes, and feared the worst from their own guilty conscience. These precautions had not escaped the sharp eyes of Ferdinand : he said, therefore, to Don Garcilasso de la Vega (who was once his ambassador at Rome), while he was embracing him in a friendly manner : " Why, my dear Garcilasso, what broad shoulders you have ! You have grown wonderfully stout since last we met !"

The moment when the two sovereigns were to embrace each other having now arrived, Philip wished outwardly to give a proof of that respect which he really entertained in his heart for his father-in-law. But Ferdinand tried to prevent the exhibition ; he made a sign to him not to dismount, and instead of offering him his hand to kiss, he embraced him, kissing him with great tenderness " on his forehead and cheeks," as well as two knights could do. Almost all the nobles of Castile and a great number of people witnessed this scene. The two kings then dismounted, and entered a small hermitage close at hand, in order to be able to confer more leisurely with each other.

They were followed only by Don Manuel and Ximenez. When they entered, the archbishop, being most anxious to banish the demon of hatred from

R 2

the breast of Philip, suddenly turned towards Don Manuel, and addressed these laconic words to him, uttered with all possible earnestness: "The princes wish to speak to each other in confidence, let us therefore depart; I will remain as sentinel at the door." Manuel accordingly retired. Ximenez closed the door, and then seated himself near the sovereigns on a bench in the chapel.

The interview lasted about two hours. After Ferdinand had complained of the undeserved mistrust to which he had been exposed, he gave Philip a description of the grandees of Spain; told him their real character; dwelt on the amount of their fidelity, and the manner in which he was to treat each one of them. He then recommended Ximenez to the young prince, as one of the wisest and most loyal of all the great men in the kingdom; worthy before every one else of the royal confidence, and deserving to be treated with love and esteem. Philip promised to follow the benevolent advice of his father-in-law; left the chapel with Ferdinand; and renewed before the whole assembly his most friendly intentions.*

A few days after, on the 27th of June, Ferdinand, in the presence of Ximenez and others, solemnly swore to observe the treaty which had been agreed upon; the same was done by Philip on the following day. But Ferdinand went still further; for he executed another instrument, in which he plainly acknowledged the incapacity of his daughter for carrying on the government, and promised to support Philip as sole regent.† But Ferdinand, before signing the document, made a protest in private, before several witnesses, that what he was about to

---

* All these details are taken from Gomez and Zurita, and also from the valuable epistles of Peter Martyr.—*Trans.*

† Zurita, tom. vi. lib. vii. cap. viii. Prescott, chap. xvii.

do was not of his own free choice, but from necessity; and that so far from relinquishing his claims to the regency, it was his intention to enforce them, and to rescue his daughter from captivity as soon as he was able to do so. Philip's conduct, too, was far from being honourable, for under friendly appearances he nourished continually a bitter hatred. This hatred manifested itself on the very same evening of the interview, by his refusing to accompany Ferdinand on his journey to Aragon, and not allowing him to see his poor beloved daughter after such a long separation from each other, though his desire to see her was supported also by the authority of Ximenez. Nay, only a short time afterwards, when Ferdinand and Philip met together in a church at Renédo, near Valladolid, and Ferdinand took the opportunity of again pressing his request, Philip refused permission in a harsh tone,* and repeated several times these insulting words: " The good of Spain requires that Ferdinand should leave Castile as soon as possible." According to Zurita, this second interview took place in the presence of Ximenez, July 5, 1506, and lasted an hour and a half,† though Peter Martyr says it lasted only half an hour. Philip contented himself with merely promising Ferdinand permission to retain the grand masterships of the three military orders for ever, and the revenues secured to him by the will of Isabella. Nothing was said on other subjects. ‡ Ferdinand had now the sorrow to see himself obliged

---

* " Durior Caucasiâ rupe," says Peter Martyr (Epist. 310).

† Zurita, tom. vi. lib. vii. cap. x. Peter Martyr, Epist. 310.

‡ There appears to be some discrepancy in the dates of these two interviews. Prescott seems to take it for granted, that it was on the 27th of June that Ferdinand surrendered the sovereignty of Castile to Philip and Joanna. Altogether three interviews took place between the two sovereigns.—*Trans.*

to depart for Aragon, attended only by the duke of Alva and the marquis of Denia. It was his intention, however, as soon as possible, to visit his states of Naples and Sicily.

Ximenez, in the mean time, was constantly at the court of Philip, and therefore was unable to remain in his diocese for the present, because he wished to guide the young prince in the way of virtue, as far as circumstances would allow. We may relate (in passing), that about this time Ximenez gave a remarkable proof of his courage. The count Pimentel de Benevente, while the young king was on his way from Senabria to Valladolid, had prepared a great bull-fight in his honour. Before the combat commenced, Ximenez, wishing to cross over to the place where the king was sitting, suddenly met one of the beasts, who got free through the carelessness of the keeper. It furiously attacked the attendants of the archbishop, wounded several, and threatened to attack Ximenez himself. But he stood before it calm and tranquil, like a man prepared to fight or to die; the royal guard, however, quickly came, and drove the bull away. When he was praised for his calmness and courage, he jocosely answered: "When the king's guard is near, no one need fear." *

Ximenez now began to excercise his influence, not without fruit, in calming the terrible and often fatal quarrels which soon began to break out in the court of Philip between the grandees, and especially between the houses of Benavente and Mendoza. He also took part in a quarrel with Fonseca, archbishop of Compostella, because as primate he had to receive an appeal against a decision of Fonseca. This last prelate had excommunicated two of the government

---

* Gomez, folio 63, 64.

judges for having imprisoned Francisco Ribas, although he had received minor orders. For this reason the judges appealed to Ximenez. What was the issue we are not informed.

The Cortes soon after took the usual oath of fidelity and homage to Queen Joanna, as " Señora natural," to her consort Philip, and also the Prince Charles, as presumptive heir to the crown. But Ximenez soon had an opportunity of witnessing the evil influence which the Spanish and Flemish favourites began to exercise over Philip. Judges the most faithful and talented, officers the most able, governors, prefects, and other persons in authority, were odious and suspected, merely because they had been appointed by Ferdinand. Even the marquis of Moya was dismissed from his post of governor of Segovia, without any regard being paid to his past fidelity and that of his spouse, Beatriz Bobadilla, in favour of the late queen, Isabella.* Unworthy favourites, and even strangers from Flanders, got possession of the most important offices : often were the posts purchased by money, and even the property of the state sold to supply the excessive prodigalities of a corrupt court. Philip himself said once, " that having been rich when count of Flanders, he became poor when he was the greatest king in Europe."† Complaints the most just, when addressed to the sovereign, remained unanswered; so that it is not wonderful if, as was the case in Andalusia, a revolt broke out in some of the provinces. Ximenez now thought it was his duty to overthrow the pernicious influence of Don Juan Manuel, and to close the too credulous ears of Philip to his advice and suggestions. A

* Peter Martyr, Epist. 312. Prescott, chap. xix. part ii. The government of Segovia was given to Don Juan Manuel.

† Peter Martyr, Epist. 313. Fléchier, liv. ii. p. 181.

favourable opportunity soon presented itself.   In
one of the treaties signed by Philip, he had insured
to Ferdinand, conformably with a clause in the
will of Isabella, the revenues arising from the silk-
manufactures of Granada.   This solemn pledge,
however, did not prevent Don Manuel from farming
out the said revenues to some speculating favourite;
thus making his royal master's words so many lies.
Being prime minister, Don Manuel was also inspec-
tor of finance.   When the contract was found in his
cabinet, signed with his own hand, Bertrand de
Salto, one of the royal collectors, showed it to
Ximenez, without having any suspicion that matters were going wrong.   Ximenez tore it in pieces
immediately, and went directly to the king to
inform him of the disgraceful conduct of Don Juan
Manuel.   Then, taking advantage of this circumstance, the archbishop spoke in a general manner
of the evils which the bad counsellors of the king
had brought upon Spain, &c.   He concluded his
address by imploring his majesty to remove Don
Manuel from court, under some honourable pretext.
Though Philip refused to do so for a long time, he
at last promised to send him as ambassador to
Rome : the promise was not, indeed, fulfilled ; but,
according to the testimony of Gomez, his influence
from that day began to decline.

At the request of the king, Ximenez was soon
after charged with the difficult but important task
of studying the nature of all the different affairs
which were brought every Friday before the council
of state, and then of giving in a report respecting
them to the king.   By this means it was very easy
to show the king everything in its true light and
bearing.   Every Thursday Ximenez gave an audience
to some of the principal ministers, who gave him an
account of the most important matters which were

to be brought under the consideration of the council
the following day. Don Manuel himself was now
becoming more discreet and reasonable than he used
to be : often did he accompany the other ministers
to the house of the energetic prelate, who was the
real cause of the downfall of his influence.

God only knows whether the king would have
continued long in this way ; for, as the Almighty
called him out of this world in the flower of his age,
Philip was unable to give sufficient proof of his
having altered for the better.

CHAPTER XV.

\

AMONGST many other dignities conferred upon Don Manuel by Philip, was that of governor of Burgos. This favourite had therefore prepared a magnificent feast for his royal master in person, as a proof of his gratitude for the honour. The most lively joy and pleasure prevailed at the banquet. The king, however, who had eaten and drunk to some excess, on rising from table wished to take a little exercise. He called for his horse, and rode on the riding-ground with great ease. Then he dismounted and had a game at tennis-ball, which he passionately loved. At this he played for a long time with considerable exertion. But he became so heated that he thoughtlessly drank a jug of cold water, which brought on a fever that very same evening. This happened on the 19th of September, 1506. At first there seemed to be no danger, but it soon increased with fearful rapidity, either through negligence or improper treatment. One only amongst the physicians of Philip (Ludovico Marliano,* from Milan) was aware of the danger in which the prince was ; all the others believed there was no danger whatever. When Ximenez heard of the case, he thought it his duty to

---

* He afterwards became bishop of Tuy, in Galicia. Peter Martyr, who was his friend and admirer, calls him " Lucida lampas inter philosophos et clericos " (Epist. 313). See also Mariana, lib. xxviii. cap. 23.

send his own physician (Dr. Yanguas) immediately to visit the sick prince. Philip received him kindly, and told him all the particulars of his illness. Yanguas saw no remedy but in bleeding. The Flemish doctors, however, were exceedingly opposed to such treatment, pretending to know the nature of the malady, as well as the constitution of the king, better than the Spanish physician. Their opinion prevailed. Yanguas then hastened to inform the archbishop that there was no hope for the king.[*]

As soon as the report spread abroad, the nobles and ministers considered it necessary to deliberate on the present posture of affairs, and consider the best means of providing for the government of the kingdom, in case the king should die. The incapacity of the queen was evident to all. The grand-constable, Velasco ; Henriquez, admiral of Castile ; and the duke of Infantado—the two first of whom were related to the royal family,—declared themselves in favour of Ferdinand, and were of opinion that he ought to be immediately invited to return from Naples, and, as guardian of his daughter, undertake the regency of Castile. But the duke of Najara and the marquis of Villena, two old enemies of Ferdinand, opposed such a motion with great earnestness. The count of Benavente and others sided with them,—mostly through fear, lest when Ferdinand should come into power again, he might revenge on them the injuries which they had committed against him after the death of Isabella. The nobles, being thus divided, put the matter into the hands of Ximenez till the king's death. They conjured him to try and conciliate the two parties, and preserve the peace, in quality of his dignity as grand-chancellor and primate.

* Gomez, folio 66.

In a second conference, held on the 24th of September, just when the king was near his death, Ximenez at last succeeded, by his prudence and wisdom, in effecting a union among the numerous nobility who surrounded him. Many had already spoken in favour of King Ferdinand; and their advice would probably have been followed, had not Pimentel, count of Benavente, opposed the others with all his might. "What!" he exclaimed, "will you all be so mad as to invite back again to Spain one whom you have so lately driven away? Are you not afraid, lest, after being kind to you in the beginning, he may at last exercise all his deep vengeance upon you? This I now tell you openly: I possess at home two new suits of armour; these shall be torn from my body before I suffer the king of Aragon to return to Castile."[*]

These fiery words produced a great effect, for most of the grandees came over to the views of the count of Benavente.

Hitherto Ximenez had not spoken, as he listened in silence to the various opinions which were expressed. Though devoted, as all right-minded persons were,[†] to the cause of Ferdinand, he could only speak under the present circumstances in a general way, invested as he was by the nobility with the character of a mediator. He promoted, then, the interests of his country, as well as the cause of Ferdinand, much better by the way in which he spoke; for he represented to the assembled nobles, that King Ferdinand had indeed a long and practical experience of affairs, and had also displayed talents of the highest order for governing; but, at the same time, that Castile had no need of choosing a regent

[*] Gomez, folio 67.

[†] Peter Martyr says: "Fernandus apertis visceribus à bonis desideratur; is nisi redierit, ruent omnia." (Epist. 317.)

out of the kingdom, because there were so many fit and excellent men within her own bounds. The nobility, therefore, had only to choose some one amongst themselves, who possessed the love and esteem of the people. As for himself, he would honour and support any one they might choose, just as he would the king himself.[*]

Scarcely had Ximenez finished his address, when it was received with the most lively joy by the nobility. Had he taken the part of Ferdinand then, it is very probable, that after Philip's death there would have been a civil war. The only thing for which Ximenez can be blamed is, that he showed himself more politic than candid with the passionate grandees. Some were fearful, that if Ximenez had spoken more in favour of Ferdinand, he might quickly have excited or irritated their minds. The result was, that Ximenez himself, together with the grand-constable, the grand-admiral, the duke of Najara, the duke of Infantado, the ambassador of the emperor of Germany, Andrea del Burgo, and Vere, a Flemish nobleman, were chosen for the provisional administrators of the kingdom, until the Cortes (now near at hand) should pronounce a definitive judgment on the choice.[†] The biographers of Ximenez, with Gomez at their head, who is followed by all the others, seem to think, in their account of these proceedings, that Ximenez was chosen regent of Castile personally, with only two councillors, viz. the grand-constable and the duke of Najara. But Zurita has given us all the authentic documents of the meeting, and from these sources it is that we have taken the above account.[‡]

* Gomez, folio 67. See likewise Fléchier, liv. ii. p. 170.
† Gomez, folio 68. Zurita, tom. vi. lib. vii. cap. xv.
‡ It is certainly true, that Peter Martyr (Epist. 317) speaks merely of Ximenez, the duke of Najara, and the grand-constable.

The following day the fatal event which was
so much feared took place. After an illness of six
days, Philip died on the 25th of September, 1506,
at Burgos, five months after his arrival in Spain,
and in the twenty-eighth year of his reign. Being
the first of the royal family of Austria, he had a
probability of inheriting an almost world-wide monarchy; but it was not given to him to arrive at
such greatness, and much less had he the talents and
capability of Charles, his son and heir. For although
nature had not been backward in her gifts to him,
yet Philip "the Fair"* was too fond of the pleasures of life, too light-hearted and weak, ever to
become a great sovereign.†

Joanna, who was so deserving of pity, being possessed of an invincible love for Philip, would not
for a moment leave the bed of her deceased spouse.
No tears, however, assuaged her sorrow; for, from
the time when she discovered a Belgian maid in the
arms of her faithless husband, terror had dried up
the fount of tears in the eyes of the unhappy woman.
But after the death of Philip, and in spite of her
being far advanced in her pregnancy, she could not
be removed from the corpse, either by the entreaties of the grandees, or even by those of Ximenez
himself. ‡

On receiving the news of the king's death,
Ximenez immediately retired to his domestic
chapel; and there, unseen by men, he wept over

But he, no doubt, only wished to indicate the *principal* personages
who composed the council for the regency.

* Felipe el Hermoso, of whom Mariana thus speaks: " Labium
inferius porrectum cum gratiâ" (lib. xxviii. cap. xxiii.).

† " He was rash and impetuous in his temper, frank, and careless. He abandoned himself to the impulse of the moment,
whether for good or evil." (Prescott, chap. xix.)

‡ Zurita, Anales, tom. vi. lib. vii. cap. xv.

the young prince and recommended his soul to God. After he had performed this duty, he hastened forthwith to the queen, not with the view of addressing useless exhortations to moderate her grief, but to console her by sympathizing with her in the affliction which had just befallen her, and then endeavouring to pour the oil of comfort into her afflicted soul.

The remains of Philip were publicly exposed that day and the following night, according to the Flemish custom. They were covered with costly robes, and all the usual tokens of the royal dignity, and surrounded by a great number of the clergy and laity; amongst whom was Peter Martyr, who gives us the account of the proceedings. In the morning of the same day, the body had been opened by two doctors, embalmed, and then bound round, like a mummy, with cloths, and put into a double coffin of lead and wood. It was then deposited in the Carthusian convent of Miraflores, near Burgos; where it remained till it was removed to Granada, to be interred by the side of Isabella, according to the wish of Philip. But the king had bequeathed his heart to Flanders, to which he had belonged all his lifetime.

The king's death might easily have led to an explosion of hatred (long pent up) on the part of the Spaniards, against the avarice and tyranny of their Flemish masters. To prevent such an evil, the duke of Najara and the grand-constable considered it necessary, by order of the council, to publish in the public square of Burgos, by the assistance of the heralds, "that whoever should be found with arms in the streets would be horsewhipped; and that whosoever should draw a sword would have his hand cut off; and, finally, whosoever should shed even one drop of blood, would be punished on the spot with death."* By this means order was preserved. As soon as the funeral ceremonies were over, the grandees assembled again in presence of Ximenez, on October 1st, in order to confirm his authority of regent, and to compel the nobility to yield obedience to him. The decree is to be found in Zurita, who informs us, that a certain pre-eminence was given to Ximenez over his colleagues in such a way, that none of them could send a deputy into the council of regency without his consent, while he alone was commissioned to receive the adhesion of the nobles and prelates to the new government.†

But before this meeting took place, Ximenez, immediately after Philip's death, wished, if possible, to enter into a correspondence with Ferdinand; he therefore instantly sent a letter to him, hoping it would find him at Barcelona before he set sail for Italy. The following is the substance of it:—A fever carried off Philip in a few days, and so great is the disunion amongst the grandees, that no one knows what to do. The queen, overwhelmed with grief and mourning, has lost the powers of her mind. If, then, you have any consideration for a kingdom once so dear to you; if any love yet remains for a daughter so inconsolable,—let the affairs of Italy stand by for a time, and return immediately to Castile. Ximenez trusts to the magnanimity of the king, which he hopes will induce him to forget all the evils which the grandees made him suffer. But now nothing of the kind need be feared; rather was Ximenez confident that he would be able to surrender the government into the hands of his majesty, and that

* Peter Martyr, Epist. 317.
† Zurita, Anales, tom. vi. lib. vii. cap. xvi.

he would find it in a more tranquil state than it was even under Isabella herself."*

Louis Ferrer, whom the Catholic king had left as his ambassador at the court of his daughter, took charge of this letter, and immediately sent it by a courier to Ferdinand. Letters of similar import were also sent by the grand-constable and the faithful Peter Martyr.† But Ferdinand had already left Spain, and the courier only overtook him at Portofino, near Genoa, October 6th, 1506.

But in spite of so many pressing invitations, the king did not think proper to return immediately to Castile. He probably wished his subjects to taste for some time the bitterness of anarchy, before he offered them any assistance, and thought that it would be the most prudent course for him to return then in the character of a liberator. Moreover, a violent and unjust suspicion of the fidelity of the "great captain,"‡ who was his viceroy at Naples, had tormented him. Ferdinand, in order to diminish the power of this man who had been so useful to him, had already conferred a part of his powers on other magistrates. But his suspicions induced him to proceed to Italy at once, in order to suppress any perfidious attempts which some might be plotting against his statholder. He therefore continued his journey towards Naples, and contented himself with sending kind answers to the grandees, prelates, and citizens of Castile, assuring them in affectionate words of his speedy return to Spain. He begged of Ximenez especially, faithfully to attend

---

* Gomez, folio, 68. A Spanish historian is mistaken in supposing that Ximenez *at first* wished to make himself regent. (See Ascorgorta, "Compendio de la Historia de España," Paris, 1838, p. 229.)

† Epp. 317, 319. Zurita (loco citato), cap. xix.

‡ Gonsalvo de Cordova.

to the affairs of the kingdom; not to abandon the
unfortunate queen, and frequently to inform him
how matters were going on.*

Enmity and disorder soon began to break out
amongst the nobles, while a hatred arose between
the grand-constable and the duke of Najara, which
threatened to end in bloodshed. Ximenez interfered, but his efforts were useless. The queen also
began to thwart him, by her complete obstinacy
in all matters connected with the regency. She
listened, indeed, through a latticed window to the
plans of the archbishop and his colleagues, but she
paid no further regard to them; she even refused
to subscribe to any decree which was presented for
her approval, and neither prayers nor tears had
any effect upon her. She had, however, allowed
Ximenez to dwell with her in the palace, but she
forbad him to speak to her on the affairs of government, considering him "not to be a councillor, but
merely a companion to her." She was exceedingly
angry whenever the prelate ventured to meddle in
" *her* affairs," as she expressed herself.†

The only thing which she did about this time,
was to order payment of the Flemish musicians,
whom, after Philip's death, she had received into
her court. She had loved music from her infancy,
for in that she found her only solace during the
hours of her melancholy.‡ Some time afterwards,
shortly before her departure from Burgos, she
awoke from her apathy, and by an act which tended
to increase still more the public discontent and
confusion, she suddenly recalled, without any
apparent grounds, all the honours and rewards
which her spouse had bestowed on different persons

* Gomez, folio 71.
† Peter Martyr, Epist. 317. Zurita (as above), cap. xxi.
‡ Peter Martyr, Epp. 317—349.

during his regency. In other matters she remained mute and almost inaccessible. To every question she merely answered in these words: "I can only do one thing,—pray for my husband;" or with the remark, "My father will soon return, and he will provide for all." With such words she also put off the Flemish servants, who demanded in vain to be paid, that so they might be able to return home. It was equally impossible to induce her to sign a decree against the duke of Medina Sidonia, who had revolted, or for the appointment to important offices which had been long vacant. Several cathedrals were without their bishops: Ximenez, therefore, conjured the queen to present to the pope any persons who were agreeable to her; but she replied "that her father would know better than herself who were fit subjects." When the spiritual evils were represented to her, that were likely to arise from so many sees being left vacant, she remarked, with a quickness which was not uncommon to her in her lucid intervals, "that the evils would be still greater if she should name unworthy subjects." She remained during the greater part of the day in a dark chamber, with her chin resting on her right hand, quite silent, full of obstinacy towards her attendants, and especially of bitter hatred towards the whole race of women*—only two of whom were allowed to approach her, viz., Doña Maria d'Ulloa, countess of Salinas, who was her lady in waiting, and the wife of the grand-constable. Though this last lady was a natural daughter of Ferdinand, yet she left the palace of her husband when Philip and Joanna came to dwell at Burgos; it was only after the death of the king that she returned:† there the unhappy princess

---

* Peter Martyr, Epist. 318.   † Mariana, lib. xxix. cap. iii.

continued to reside for some time, until, for the sake of her health, she removed to the country house of the Vega, near Burgos.

Her case, however, became worse and worse, until at last it terminated in downright madness. On the feast of All Saints, 1506, she went from Burgos to the convent of Miraflorés, where the body of her spouse had been deposited for a time, in order to convince herself that the body had not been stolen by the Flemish attendants on her husband. She even ordered the coffin to be opened; she gazed upon the corpse for a long time; she touched it with her hand in several places, and always with dry eyes and a calm countenance. She then ordered the lid to be put on again, and immediately returned to Burgos.*

Under these circumstances, and amidst the increasing disorder of the kingdom, it was evident that some one was required to save the country from utter ruin, who should be invested with unlimited power. Some of the grandees cast their eyes upon the German emperor Maximilian, father of the deceased King Philip, and wished the government of the kingdom to be confided to him. Others preferred calling from Flanders the young Prince Charles, who was then in his seventh year, and who could easily choose an administrator and invest him with full power. Another party were anxious that the queen should marry again; but they could not agree respecting the choice of a husband. Some thought of Ferdinand, the young duke of Calabria,

---

* Zurita, cap. xxvi. Mariana, lib. xxix. cap. iii. Fléchier (liv. ii. p. 182) confounds another journey to Miraflorés, which took place later, with that which Joanna made on the feast of All Saints. This mistake probably arose because Peter Martyr speaks only of the last (Epist. 324). But Mariana and Zurita distinctly mention each separate journey.

or Don Alonso of Aragon, both of whom were her uncles. Others wished her to marry the king of England, or the French count Gaston de Foix, brother of Germaine. But Joanna rejected all these overtures with invincible firmness. "She loved her spouse now that he was dead, as much as she did when he was alive."[*] All the best-disposed, however, wished Ferdinand to return; but on this point different opinions prevailed. Some considered it better that Ferdinand should be acknowledged administrator of the kingdom while absent; others wished it to be done only on his return to Spain. Ximenez belonged to the first party: hence it was thought that he wished to confide the government to Ferdinand while he was in Italy, in order that Ximenez himself might be named his representative. But, according to the testimony of Zurita, Ferdinand had in reality bestowed full power and authority on Ximenez to govern Castile during his absence, in concert with other grandees who should seem proper persons.[†] It would, then, be very rash to impute the zeal which Ximenez showed for the interests of Ferdinand merely to motives of self-interest. It is evident that the good of the country dictated to Ximenez the same line of conduct as other less generous motives might have inspired him with. Who can venture to decide that the sole motive of self-interest, gratuitously alleged, produced acts which it is most natural to attribute, if not to the most noble of the two motives, at least to both of them together?

But, however anxious Ximenez was that Ferdinand should return to Castile, this could not be effected in the present state of affairs without a royal decree, and the sanction of the Cortes.

[*] Zurita, cap. xxi. Mariana, lib. xxix. cap. iii.
[†] Zurita, cap. xxv.

Ximenez, then, and his colleagues resolved to assemble the Cortes at Burgos, in November, 1506, in order, by a solemn decision, to settle the question of the regency. But the archbishop had wisely taken the precaution beforehand to induce the various parties into which the nobility were divided to make a solemn promise not to enter into negotiations with any prince in the mean time.

But while Ximenez was thus exerting himself to assemble the Cortes, the other friends of Ferdinand, and especially the duke of Alva, were endeavouring to prevent the meeting. This party had on its side the express declaration of the Catholic king (Ferdinand), who derived his right to the regency from the last will of his spouse, and the decree of the Cortes held at Toro, without there being any necessity for a new decision on their part. But Ximenez and the other adherents of the king, and, lastly, his majesty himself, clearly saw that the right acquired by the will of the queen, and through means of the Cortes held at Toro, had been made null by his treaty with Philip.*

Nevertheless, under such circumstances, the universal and peaceful acknowledgment of Ferdinand could not be made without the ratification of the Cortes. The decree was therefore prepared, according to the wish of Ximenez, for the convocation of the Cortes. Soon was there a general agitation visible amongst all parties, who were anxious to direct the choice of the provinces and cities so as to promote their own views. The provinces of Guipuscoa and Biscay, which had not been accustomed to send deputies to the Cortes, now demanded to be represented for this time only.†

---

* All these details are principally taken from Zurita, "Anales de Aragon," so often quoted.—*Trans.*

† Zurita, cap. xxii.

Ferdinand's party gained great advantages in the elections, for the people universally wished his return, as the only means of recovering tranquillity.[*] To complete the victory, there were only wanting two points, viz., the opening of the Cortes, and its being acknowledged by the queen. To obtain this result, the grandees, the council royal, and the governor of Burgos hastened to the palace, where Ximenez pressed the queen to accede to the wishes of the deputation, representing to her that the welfare of the kingdom depended on the Cortes being convoked.[†] But no efforts or motives could induce the queen to give her consent. In this extremity Ximenez, contrary to all custom, and in spite of the protestation of the duke of Alva, and without any order from the queen, convoked the Cortes by an edict of the council royal. But as it did not obtain the necessary approbation in all the provinces, only a very small number of deputies arrived at Burgos towards the middle of November; the meeting, therefore, was soon dissolved.[‡]

It was then that the provisional government of Castile ceased, and Ximenez, the duke of Alva, and the grand-constable obtained from King Ferdinand full power to conduct affairs.[§] Ximenez, with an eagerness peculiar to him, now took advantage of the meeting of the Cortes solemnly to declare— what the whole of Spain already knew—the incapacity of the queen. His object was that Ferdinand, on his return, might be spared the pain of being obliged to adopt this measure against his own daughter, and by this means, to avoid any obstacle in his administration. No doubt this arrangement of the archbishop was good, but it is no less certain

---

[*] Zurita, cap. xxv.   [†] Ibid. cap xxi.
[‡] Ibid. cap. xxviii.   Mariana, lib. xxix.   [§] Zurita, cap. xxxii.

that the compassion which every one felt for the
unfortunate Joanna made it useless : neither the
people nor Ferdinand himself approved of it.*

But though Ximenez at first was so determined
on convoking the Cortes, yet he began a little later
to change his opinion on the subject, when he saw
how, in the course of their proceedings, they did
nothing but quarrel more and more amongst themselves, and suffered themselves more than ever to
be influenced by the Austrian party. Hence it was
that Ximenez, the duke of Alva, and the grand-
constable considered it necessary to adjourn the
States. They also heard with joy that the queen,
the day before her departure from Burgos, had
ordered a deputation from the Cortes to retire to
their homes. A royal decree prorogued the Cortes
for four months.

After the prorogation of the Cortes, the queen at
length yielded to the entreaties of those around her,
and left Burgos, which was then ravaged by a
pestilence. Having dwelt in the neighbouring Vega,
not far from the city, for a few weeks, she resolved
to leave that part of the country altogether. A
number of the nobility, through the hope of acquiring
greater influence over her, offered her their mansions
for her habitation, as soon as they heard of her
intention to leave the neighbourhood of Burgos.
Ximenez himself, if we may trust the assertion of
Zurita,† had recourse to this expedient; while
Gomez, on the other hand, assures us that Ximenez
endeavoured to dissuade the queen from her intended
departure, on account of her being pregnant. But
Joanna obstinately refused to listen to any advice,
whether good or bad; she was resolved to follow
only her own will. Accordingly, on the 20th of

* Zurita, cap. xxi. xxxii.   † Cap. xx.

December, 1506, she went to the convent of Miraflorés, in order to disinter the body of her husband,
and take it with her on her journey. In vain did
the bishop of Burgos represent to her that such a
proceeding would be contrary both to the laws of
the Church and to the will of Philip himself;
and that, moreover, no corpse could be removed
during the first six months after its burial. This
opposition threw the queen into a fearful passion;
she uttered the most terrible threats in case her
orders were not obeyed. Fearful lest some dangerous
consequences might follow from her passion, and
considering, too, the state she was in, the bishop
complied with her wishes. Accordingly, all the
grandees present, the papal nuncio, the ambassadors
of Maximilian and Ferdinand, the bishops of Burgos,
Malaga, Jaen, and Mondoñedo, as also Peter
Martyr, were summoned to view the body, in order
to testify to its identity. But, according to Peter
Martyr,* nothing could be seen save a form enveloped
in cloths, and totally incapable of being recognized.
Joanna, however, ordered the coffin to be ornamented
with gold and silk coverings. She then placed it
on a car, which was drawn by four Flemish horses,
and ordered it to be conveyed before her to the town
of Torquemada, which lay between Burgos and
Valladolid. At this last city she stopped, the journey
having taken two days, though the distance is so
short; because the queen travelled only at night,
by the light of torches. " A respectable woman,"
she said, " after the death of her husband, who was
to her a sun, should shun the light of day, and
travel only in darkness."†

At Torquemada she ordered the body to be

---

* Epist. 324.
† Peter Martyr, Epist. 359. Mariana, lib. xxix.

taken into the principal church, and be surrounded by numerous guards, as if she wished to
repel the attack of an enemy. But her object
was to prevent any woman from approaching the
royal coffin; for the jealousy of the afflicted queen
still troubled her, even after the death of her
husband. Every morning a funeral service was
performed in presence of the corpse, and in the
evening vespers of the dead were recited. Neither
these nor the watching of the guards were interrupted during the whole of the journey. Ximenez,
at first, had remained at Burgos, with the grand
admiral and the duke of Najara; but he soon
hastened to join the queen at Torquemada, in order
not to be absent a moment during the approaching
" confinement" of Joanna. He feared—and his fears
were shared by all the friends of order—lest, if the
queen should die during her delivery, the guardian-
ship of Charles, the heir of Castile, together with the
regency of Spain, should pass into the hands of the
emperor Maximilian I. But these fears of Ximenez
were the result of his zeal for the interests of
Ferdinand, as well as for the good of the country.
Fortunately, they were not realized, for, on the 14th
of January, 1507, Joanna gave birth to a princess
at Torquemada. She was baptized by Ximenez, and
received the name of Catharina. She was afterwards
married to the king of Portugal.* The queen soon
recovered her strength, though her reason was far
from being restored; on the contrary, her mind was
more and more filled with delusions.

Under such unfortunate circumstances Ximenez
considered it his duty, in virtue of the authority
with which he was invested, to transfer the royal

---

* Gomez, by an error, says the princess was born on the
nineteenth calends of *January* instead of *February*. (See Zurita,
cap. xliii., and also Peter Martyr, Epist. 331.)

council, and also the office of the Inquisition, to Palencia; while he himself remained near the queen, who became every day more and more incapable of governing. Whenever she was called upon to sign any document, says Peter Martyr, it seemed as if her fingers were glued together.* She cared very little what became of the kingdom, provided she was not disturbed in the deep apathy that had possession of her; and this prevailed to such an extent, that when once she was seized with it she was unable to raise herself up.† In the mean time the hatred of the nobility one towards another, and especially between the grand-constable and the duke of Najara, arose to such a height that at Torquemada they would have come to blows, even in the palace of the queen herself, had not the queen, or rather Ximenez by means of the queen, sent some mediators to appease the strife of the parties.

No wonder, then, that the return of Ferdinand was anxiously and daily hoped for; though Peter Martyr complains that the promises he made of returning were empty and deceitful.‡

During the stay of the court at Torquemada, Ximenez visited the small town of Cisneros, from which his family originally came. There he saw his parents, paid his respects to them, and gave them many tokens of his affection. The inhabitants of the town received him with great honour, and as a return for what they had done to testify their esteem for him, he granted the favour they had asked, viz. that for the future the civil officers were not to be chosen from Castile, but they them-

---

* Peter Martyr, Epist. 331.   † Ibid. 332.

‡ Prescott seems to think that Ferdinand showed a "discreet forbearance," in not immediately returning to Spain. He used, however, the most courteous style in his communications to the nobles. (See chap. xx. part ii.)—*Trans.*

selves were to elect two adelantados, or municipal officers, who should have the power of settling all their disputes.

Towards the end of April, 1507, the queen, at last, left Torquemada, which was not healthy; but, as Peter Martyr remarks, she only exchanged Scylla for Charybdis, by choosing for her residence the small town of Fornillos, which scarcely contained sufficient houses for her attendants. In vain was she exhorted to proceed to the neighbouring city of Palencia, where the royal council had already arrived: she resolutely replied, " that widows ought not to dwell in large cities and magnificent houses." Many of her attendants were obliged to erect small cabins for themselves, in order to have some place in Fornillos wherein to dwell.*

The principal object, in the mean time, which Ximenez zealously aimed at, was, by negotiating with the grandees, gradually to unite all the parties, and so prepare them for acknowledging Ferdinand, so that on his arrival in Spain he might find order everywhere re-established.† Sometimes even his own friends put obstacles in his way, viz., the duke of Alva and the grand-constable; partly because they considered his negotiations and compacts as disgraceful for Ferdinand to accept; and, above all, because they considered themselves justified in complaining that favours were promised to their adversaries, which ought to have been the reward of their own fidelity. Another obstacle to the complete success of Ximenez was his want of the authority with which Ferdinand had invested him the preceding year, during his negotiations with Philip. Still

---

* Peter Martyr, Epist. 339.

† Ximenez was unwilling to employ any severity, except against the two most obstinate enemies of Ferdinand, viz., the duke of Najara and Don Manuel.

Ximenez succeeded in gaining over the most bitter enemies of Ferdinand; viz., Garcilasso de la Vega, the marquis of Villena, the count of Benavente, and the duke of Bejar. But the duke of Najara and Don Manuel remained inflexible.*

Ximenez derived great assistance from Ferdinand's ambassador, Louis Ferrer, who used his utmost endeavours to keep the archbishop, the duke of Alva, the admiral, and grand-constable united together.

As a recompense for so many services on the part of Ximenez, Ferdinand endeavoured to show his gratitude to the archbishop. Hence, during his residence in Italy, a report was spread through Spain that Ferdinand had obtained the cardinal's hat for Ximenez from Pope Julius II., and also that he had reserved for him the dignity of grand inquisitor of Castile.† Zurita insinuates that these two dignities were objects of ambition with Ximenez; he likewise mentions, in another place, that Ferrer had made proposals on the subject to Ximenez in the name of Ferdinand, and at the same time had promised a bishopric to his friend Ruyz.‡ These promises were fulfilled on the arrival of Ferdinand in Spain.

In the mean time Ferdinand, having left Naples, set sail for the port of Savona, instead of Ostia, where Julius II. had been expecting him in vain.§ At Savona, Ferdinand and Louis XII., king of France, met together amidst great pomp. The "great captain" also was amongst Ferdinand's attendants, though he was once deprived of his dignity of viceroy over Naples by the suspicious monarch; but

---

* Zurita, cap. xxxix.; also lib. viii. cap. vi.
† Peter Martyr, Epp. 340, 343.   ‡ Zurita, cap. xxii.
§ It seems as if Ferdinand had designedly avoided having an interview with the pope. (See Peter Martyr, Epp. 352, 353.)

now the illustrious warrior was loaded with the highest honours by the king of France, against whom he had so often fought in battle.*

At length, after having enjoyed the splendid hospitality of Louis for four days, Ferdinand and his queen re-embarked, and reached their own port of Valencia on the 20th of July, 1507. After a short repose, he proceeded by slow journeys towards Castile, while all the grandees and nobility came forth to meet him with great pomp. His daughter Joanna was also anxious to meet him on the frontier of Castile; but Ximenez, at the suggestion of Ferdinand, dissuaded her from the undertaking, and advised her to remain in some town not far from Fornillos, where sufficient room could be found for the residence of both courts. Joanna accordingly set out on her journey in the middle of the night of August 24th, accompanied by the corpse of Philip, and attended by Ximenez and the other officers of the court. She reached Tortolés, which was about fifteen miles from Fornillos. A few days before (August 21st), Ferdinand had arrived in the territory of Castile, where the duke de Infantado, the admiral, and a crowd of grandees and cavaliers, received him most solemnly and cordially.

On the 27th of August he entered Tortolés, and embraced his daughter with tears of joy, though he was exceedingly shocked by Joanna's outward appearance, which was wild and haggard.†

After a long interview, at which Ximenez only

---

* The "great captain" was also exceedingly honoured by Ferdinand himself, who now studied to efface from his mind every uncomfortable impression. (See Prescott, chap. xx.)—*Trans.*

† She survived forty-seven years after this meeting, but took no part in public affairs. Philip's remains were finally removed to the cathedral church of Granada, where they were deposited with those of his wife Joanna, in a magnificent sepulchre erected by Charles V. (Prescott.)

was present, it was resolved that the court should remove to Santa Maria del Campo. The king departed in the morning, but Joanna, as usual, would travel only by night, taking along with her the corpse of Philip. On his arrival Ferdinand assumed the reins of government with a firm hand, and also with the full consent of his daughter. So confident, too, was he in the justice of his cause, that he took no trouble to have his " right and title" ratified by the approbation of the Cortes, which was only convoked three years after, on the 6th of October, 1510.

CHAPTER XVI.

XIMENEZ IS NAMED CARDINAL, AND GRAND INQUISITOR OF CASTILE AND LEON.

ONE of the first acts of Ferdinand, the new regent of Castile, was to procure the cardinal's hat for Ximenez. For a long period the Spanish episcopacy had been honoured by having several cardinals in its ranks. The kings themselves generally solicited this dignity from the pope in favour of those amongst their subjects who had served the State more than the Church. It was during the time when Ferdinand was residing in Italy, that he proposed to the holy father to invest Ximenez with the purple, alleging most powerful reasons for wishing to honour him with this distinction; amongst which were the great services he had rendered to himself, to his deceased queen, and to the kingdom of Castile.

Often had the Holy See been obliged to accede with regret to solicitations of this kind. But, in this case, Pope Julius II. and the Sacred College were exceedingly delighted to be able to accord such an honour to a man who was one of the most illustrious prelates of his time. Nay, so loudly and frequently did the cardinals express their joy at this new creation, that a great number of letters having been sent from Rome by the resident Spaniards there, the news quickly spread through Spain. Gomez assures us that he himself found several of these documents in the archives of the church of Toledo. After all the negotiations and necessary formalities had been completed at Rome, on the 17th of May,

1507, the brief was published, which raised Ximenez to the dignity of a cardinal of the Roman Church.* With the title of St. Balbinus, was also united the honourable appellation of "Cardinal of Spain," which his immediate predecessor in the primatial see of Toledo had also borne, as well as Pedro Frias, bishop of Osma, in the fourteenth century.†

On the very same day, after the publication of the pontifical brief, Ferdinand, who was still at Naples, wrote a letter to Ximenez, in which he assured him, "that his numerous and extraordinary virtues, as well as the important services which he had rendered to Spain and to himself personally, had induced him to solicit the holy father to confer the dignity of cardinal upon him, and that he, Ferdinand, hoped the archbishop would accept this favour with the same kind feeling and sentiments that had inspired him with the idea of obtaining it for him," &c. This letter, written by the king's own hand, contained something still more honourable and important. He was named, at the same time, grand-inquisitor of Castile and Leon, in place of Deza, archbishop of Seville, who had just resigned that dignity.

Though the papal brief and royal letters had been

---

* " Venerabili Fratri nostro Francisco, S. R. E. Presbytero Cardinali, Julius II. P. M. :—

" Dilecte fili, Salutem et Apostolicam Benedictionem.—Inducti præclaris meritis et virtutibus tuis ; contemplatione etiam carissimi in Christo filii nostri Aragonum, Siciliæ, Regis Catholici, qui hoc à nobis per literas et oratores instantissimè petiit, hodie in consistorio nostro secreto, S. R. E. Cardinalium consortio et collegio te aggregavimus ; sperantes quod eidem S. R. E., cujus tam honorabile membrum es, utilis eris et honorificus, illiusque authoritatem pro viribus conservabis, et augebis.

" Datis Romæ, apud Sanctum Petrum, sub annulo Piscatoris, die XVII. Maii, MDVII. pontificatus nostri anno quarto." (See Gomez, folio 76 : Alcalá, 1569.)

† Mariana, lib. xxix. cap. x. p. 34.

T

for some time previously received in Spain, it was ten months before Ferdinand returned. He brought with him the red cap or birretta belonging to the dignity of cardinal, in order that he might solemnly place it on Ximenez, in the place of the pope; a function which the Catholic sovereigns themselves very frequently fulfilled.* It was the original intention of Ferdinand that the solemn ceremony should take place in presence of the court, at Santa-Maria del Campo: Joanna, however, who seemed to view with displeasure the honours which had been conferred upon Ximenez, absolutely refused her consent, remarking, "That such a festivity was quite inconsistent with a widow's sorrow; that some other place ought to be chosen; and if so, that she would undertake to provide the tapestries and other ornaments necessary for the solemnity of the function, from the royal treasury." Ferdinand, yielding with regret, fixed upon the neighbouring town of Mahamud† for the ceremony, which, he considered, ought properly to be performed before the court. However, many grandees of the kingdom were present. The papal nuncio, Giovanni Rufo, bishop of Bertinovo, near Ravenna, celebrated mass; the pontifical brief being publicly read, Ximenez was then decorated and honoured by receiving the red birretta, in September, 1507. Soon after, he sent official notice to the chapter of Toledo of his election, and of the honour which had been conferred upon him by Ferdinand, entreating the canons at the same time

---

* Her majesty Isabel of Spain performed the same solemn ceremony at Madrid, on the 6th of April, 1858, by placing the red birretta on the recently-elected cardinals of Toledo and Seville.

† The modern name of this place seems to be unknown. It was called "Mahamudum" by the inhabitants, according to Gomez. Robles names it Mahamuz.—*Trans.*

to pray for him, and also for the good estate of the whole of Christendom.*

The second dignity of grand-inquisitor, which was bestowed on Ximenez in the same year (1507), invites us to direct our especial attention to the history and nature of the Spanish Inquisition. The importance of the subject in itself, towards enabling us to draw a correct portrait of the cardinal, demands of us so much the greater diligence in the examination of the question.

* Gomez (folio 76) ; Peter Martyr (Epist. 340—343, 364) ; Zurita (tom. vi. lib. viii.) ; Robles (pp. 161, 162).

CHAPTER XVII.

THE SPANISH INQUISITION.—THE LITTLE TRUST WHICH IS TO BE PUT IN THE STATEMENTS OF LLORENTE.

IT often happens, that one and the same word points out two similar things, though essentially different in their meaning; and hence the similarity of expression is calculated, by degrees, to confound the radical diversity of the things themselves. Such has been the case with the word " Inquisition," which at first was used to designate an " ecclesiastical tribunal" in matters of faith ; but afterwards it meant a " political institution," which became the terror of Europe by its cruelties, real or imaginary. There is sufficient evidence to prove, that from the very commencement of Christianity, an ecclesiastical tribunal existed in matters of faith. It is also certain, that the punishments inflicted on heretics in the first ages of the Church were, like the tribunal itself, purely ecclesiastical and spiritual, without any effect in the department of the State. Thus obstinate heretics were banished from the society of the faithful, or, in other words, "excommunicated;" for the Church could not act otherwise, without losing her right as guardian of the doctrines of Christ.

A new order of things opens before us, when the emperor Constantine united the Church and State together, and made regulations himself which, at first, were in a great measure ecclesiastical. The emperor, in virtue of being the " protector and secular arm" of the Church, now assumes the title of "Episcopus ad extra," and considers himself absolutely bound to punish by exile and other penalties those heretics who should disturb the peace of the Church. Two motives justified, in his eyes, these severe proceedings against heresy. The one was, that, being the "first son" of the Church, he was bound to protect her for the future against her open enemies; the other, that, being head of the State, he was obliged to preserve order and tranquillity in the kingdom, by the removal of the disaffected; for when religious strife and dissensions prevailed, then order was at an end.

When, however, Constantius and Valens came to the throne, much more cruel punishments than banishment were directed by the Arians against the Christians. By the first they were imprisoned; by the second, they were drowned in the sea.* All the Arian princes in the new Germanic empire successively followed this cruel example towards those who differed from them in religion. At the end of the fourth century, we meet, for the first time, with the fact of Catholics punishing heretics. This happened under the emperor Maximus, who, in order to suppress the Priscillianists, commanded the leaders amongst them to be executed at Treves, in the year 385. But the most illustrious bishops of that time, viz. St. Martin of Tours, St. Ambrose of Milan, Pope Siricius, and others, and later St. Leo the Great, all loudly condemned the shedding of the blood of heretics. St. Augustine himself was of the same opinion, though he did not disapprove of the use of force as a means of correcting error. This opinion gradually gained ground, and afterwards served as a basis for the civil laws under Theodosius II. and Valentinian III. These sove-

* Socrates, " Hist. Eccl." lib. iv. cap. xvi.

reigns considered heretics as enemies of the State, and disturbers of public order and morality; and accordingly they excluded them from all posts of honour, and deprived them of the rights of succession, besides the loss of many other civil privileges; but at the same time, they did not punish them with death.

In the middle ages the union of Church and State was much closer than it was under Constantine. A grand idea then began to be entertained,—of which Pope Gregory VII. was the originator,—of uniting the whole of the West into one vast theocratical alliance; the Pope, under God, was to be its protector, while those only were to be members who belonged to the Church. From this point of view heretics evidently became guilty of high treason, because by their errors they rose up in rebellion against God, who was considered to be the head of the alliance. Hence the civil legislation of the middle ages always threatened heretics with death. The teaching of several illustrious theologians of the period accords with this legislation. Thus, for example, St. Thomas of Aquin, in his celebrated "Summa," does not hesitate to defend the punishment of death: "To corrupt the faith," he says, "is a crime much greater than that of corrupting the coin, and therefore it ought to be punished as the latter always is. But in order to win over the guilty, the Church does not immediately pronounce the excommunication. It is only after the heretic, having received several warnings and admonitions, still remains obstinate, that then she pronounces the sentence and delivers him over to the secular arm, in order that by his death the other members may be preserved sound." St. Bernard, however, thought otherwise; and many other lights of the Church, also continued, like the ancient fathers, to protest against the punishment of death being inflicted on heretics.*

Thus, while on the one hand civil punishments were inflicted on heretics by princes from the time of Constantine, on the other, the Church from the very commencement decided cases of heresy by means of her bishops and synods. Hence, if we wish to have a clear idea of the real object of the Inquisition, viz. the seeking out of heretics and their punishment by the ecclesiastical authority, sanctioned by the civil power, we shall find that the Inquisition in its first form dates its origin from the time of the Apostles, and in the second from the reign of Constantine the Great.

But, according to the usage of language, the Inquisition was not yet properly organized, until special courts and tribunals had been established for the discovery and punishment of heretics.

This organization took its rise in the eleventh and twelfth centuries, when a prodigious number of sects arose in the West, like a destroying pestilence, and infected all classes of society, penetrating even amongst the chapters of cathedrals and the cloisters of monks.

The first celebrated edict issued against these sects does not belong, properly speaking, to the history of the Inquisition, inasmuch as it appointed no special court for the examination of heretics. It contented itself with recommending, in general, to the civil power the obligation incumbent upon it of punishing them. The third general council of Lateran, held in the year 1179, under Pope Alexander III., issued the following decree against the heretics residing in Gascony and about the borders of Albi and Toulouse. These sects were called

---

* Hurter, " P. Innocenz III." (Hamb. 1834), bd. xi. s. 245.

Cathari, Pateri, or Publicans. The decree, though cited by Llorente in his "History of the Inquisition," is mutilated by him. The following is the decree:—
"As these heretics no longer remain in obscurity, but boldly proclaim their errors, and try to seduce the weak and simple,* they and their abettors are hereby excommunicated. None of the faithful are allowed to associate with them any more, or to hold any intercourse with them." The same punishment was inflicted on the heretics and their abettors who then desolated Aragon, Navarre, and the Basque provinces in the Spanish peninsula, "because they practised great cruelties on the orthodox, and spared neither churches, widows, nor orphans.† It is decreed, therefore, that the faithful are freed from all obligations towards them, until they shall have been reconciled to the Church. Force may be opposed to force; their goods can be confiscated, and Christian princes can even reduce these heretics to slavery."‡

Though these decrees against the heretics are severe, yet no mention is made in the council of any tribunal for the Inquisition. But a few years later we see traces of such a tribunal under Pope Lucius III. and the emperor Frederic Barbarossa. At a council held at Verona, in presence of the said emperor, and in concert with the bishops, his Holiness decreed as follows, with the consent of the emperor:
—" (1.) That the Cathari, the Pateri, the poor men

---

* These words, so necessary for understanding the true nature and history of the Inquisition, are entirely omitted by Llorente in his "History of the Inquisition." (Paris, ed. 1817, tom. i. p. 28).

† This passage also is omitted by Llorente.

‡ Harduin, "Collect. Concil," tom. vi. para. ii. p. 1683. Respecting these decrees against heretics, compare Van Espen, "Commentarius in Canones et Decreta Juris Veteris ac Novi" (Colon. ed. 1755, p. 557).

of Lyons, &c., were excommunicated. (2.) That all others who should preach without permission, and try to propagate their errors, were also liable to the same punishment. (3.) So were those, too, who encouraged such people. (4.) The council, moreover, decrees, that as mere ecclesiastical punishments are often despised by such persons, an heretical cleric shall first be degraded, and if he do not retract, that he shall be delivered over to the secular power ; that heretical laymen, if they continue obstinate in their errors, shall be given up to the civil authorities in order to be punished. (5.) That those who are 'suspected,' and who hesitate or delay in appearing before the bishop to clear themselves from all suspicion of heresy, shall be treated as heretics. (6.) That all who have renounced their errors, and have again relapsed, shall have an opportunity given them of renouncing their errors a second time; but if they refuse the offer, they shall be delivered to the secular power."

So far these decrees of the council of Verona are only applications of what were decreed in preceding synods. The following decrees, however, of the said council show a transition towards the establishment of a tribunal, properly so called. The pope decreed, with the consent of the prelates and the emperor assembled,—" That all bishops should make, at least every year, either in person or by means of their archdeacon, a visitation of those parts of their diocese which were inhabited by the heretics; and that the bishop should bind by oath three or four respectable and virtuous persons to denounce the different heretics, and those also who held secret meetings, and separated themselves from the rest of the faithful; after which the bishop or archdeacon shall summon the said persons before his ' tribunal' and examine them."

Here we see, for the first time in history, bishops making visitations connected with the Inquisition : these journeys were regulated according to certain rules, and the bishops had assistants to attend them. Here was the commencement of tribunals in tho proper sense of the word. 'Other decrees of the same council were as follows :—" (1.) That all civil magistrates shall be bound by oath to obey these decrees made against the heretics, and to enforce the punishments directed against them. (2.) That all those magistrates who favour or protect the heretics shall at once be deprived of all their honours and dignities."

All the measures which were in the mean time adopted against heresy took as their base these decrees of the council of Verona. But the twelfth general council (the fourth of Lateran), held under Pope Innocent III., in the year 1215, renewed the decisions of the council of Lateran held in 1179, and particularly enjoined on the bishops to make visitations of the diocese connected with the heretics, and to take with them assistants.

By the war carried on against the Albigenses, the character and nature of the Inquisition began to be more and more developed.

Towards the end of the twelfth century, the numerous sects, which we have already mentioned, began to infect almost the whole of Europe. As their principles were Manichæan, they committed the most frightful disorders. The contagion principally prevailed in the south of France, where the powerful barons on the one hand (like the Count Raymond of Toulouse), either adhered to the heresy themselves or were its supporters ; while, on the other side, the ignorance, the apathy, and even sometimes the vices of the bishops and the clergy, opposed but a feeble resistance to the errors and disorders of the heretics. Nay, even many of the clergy of the higher and lower orders were secret adherents of the sects. Pope Innocent III. was accordingly obliged to appoint legates, with a view to extirpate this heresy from the south of France. But being convinced that error cannot be overcome by force alone, except the clergy are models of learning and virtue, the pope confided the mission to members of the Cistercian order, because, though it was still, as it were, in its infancy, it possessed men who were eminent for their learning and virtue. Peter de Castelnau, Brother Rodolph, and Arnold, abbot of Citeaux, were appointed the apostolic missionaries and legates for the south of France. Scarcely had these commenced their labours, when twelve more Cistercian abbots joined them, together with the pious bishop of Osma, in Spain, Don Diego de Azevedo, and a priest named Domingo Guzman.* This took place in the year 1206.† The latter personage, who afterwards became the celebrated St. Dominic, is considered by many writers to have been the first grand-inquisitor. But there is no evidence for such a supposition; for the fact is, that St. Dominic, while in the south of France, exercised no other office but that of a missionary: even in the whole history of his life there appears no trace of his having ever acted as a judge in the tribunal of the Inquisition; on the contrary, he always appears as a travelling preacher of the faith. But if we wish to speak of the " inquisitors " of this period, we must cast our eyes on Peter de Castelnau and the other papal legates, who possessed, together with the power of teaching, the power also of compelling

* St. Dominic. (See the interesting life of this great saint published in the " Popular Library." Burns and Lambert: London, 1857.)—*Trans.*

† Hurter, Band ii. p. 276.

bishops and civil magistrates to drive out of their territories those who were heretics; to excommunicate all who were negligent in complying with this command; and who, in a word, had full power to do whatever they thought proper for the success of the mission and the extirpation of heresy. Indeed, the author of the "History of Languedoc"* dates the origin of the Inquisition from this very mission to the south of France, which was authorized by Pope Innocent III. But though the legates were connected with the Inquisition, properly so called, in the capacity of special judges for discovering and examining heretics, yet there is a difference between the one and the other, inasmuch as their office of legates was only transitory, while the Inquisition was something permanent—a regularly-established tribunal. The mission to the south of France would not have been organized had not the obstinacy of the Albigenses forced the pope to send it. Indeed it may be said that the war against the Albigenses arrested the commencement of that organization which the Inquisition had already received; the suppression of the heretics by means of the tribunals was changed into a war of religion; thus making the legates no longer inquisitors, but the leaders of a crusade that deserves to be called, not the Inquisition, but a thirty years' war. As at the conclusion of a civil war the conquerors erect tribunals before which those are tried who persist in exciting rebellion, so the natural result of the crusade against the Albigenses was something similar: a tribunal was considered necessary for the suppression of those who, though defeated in battle, did not cease to carry on their rebellion against the Church.

* Dom. Vaissette, "L'Histoire du Languedoc," tom. iii. p. 131.

Indeed, the Inquisition may be considered really to have commenced at this period. In the year 1229 the great council of Toulouse, embracing the ecclesiastical provinces of Auch, Bordeaux, and Narbonne, was convoked, under the presidency of the cardinal legate Romanus. It was attended by many bishops, as well as a considerable portion of the nobility of the South of France, amongst them the counts of Toulouse and Foix, who had formerly supported the heretics. This council not only *exercised an act of inquisition*, by inquiring into the orthodoxy of numerous accused persons, and by enjoining penances of various kinds and degrees upon those who repented, confessed, or were convicted, but took also for the future measures against heresy, chiefly by the institution of special tribunals. The following is an abstract of the decisions:—" Chap. I. orders the archbishops and bishops to appoint in all the parishes a priest and several laymen of good repute, and to bind them by oath zealously and faithfully to search for the heretics in their districts, and to report them as well as their abettors to the bishop, the lord of the district, or to their representatives. The same measures are in Chap. II. enjoined upon the exempted abbots for their districts; and Chap. III. calls upon the secular lords to find out the heretics, and destroy their hiding-places. Chap. IV. threatens those with the loss of their dominions who harbour heretics knowingly; but a lesser punishment is imposed, according to Chap. V., upon those by whose negligence the heretics find refuge in their dominions. Chap. VI. The house to be rased in which a heretic is found. Chap. VII. Negligent officials to be severely punished. Chap. VIII. shields the innocent and calumniated by enacting that no punishment be imposed before the bishop, or those authorized by him, have found the accused guilty. Chap. X. Heretics whose native places are infected with heresy, are, on renouncing their doctrines of their own free will, to be removed to other places not infected; to wear two coloured crosses fastened upon their dress, and to be disabled from holding public offices, until the Pope or his legate have with due solemnity received them again into the Church; whilst, according to Chap. XI, those who abjure heresy only from fear are to be kept imprisoned by the bishop, so as not to infect others, and their maintenance to be defrayed either out of their own property, or by the bishop. Chap. XII. All males of fourteen years and upwards, and all females of twelve years and upwards are to swear that they will remain faithful, and denounce all heretics to the authorities; which oath is to be repeated every two years. Chap. XIII. Such as omit going to confession and communion three times a year, at Christmas, Easter, and Whitsuntide, to be suspected of heresy. Chap. XIV. No layman to have a Bible, or any portion of the same, except the Psalms, nor any other books, save the Breviary and the offices of St. Mary in the original. Chap. XV. Persons branded with or suspected of heresy not to be permitted to attend as physicians, nor any one suspected of heresy to be allowed to visit sick persons.[*]

Thus the council of Toulouse instituted the first real Inquisition, leaving, however, to the bishops, as in former times, the power of sitting in judgment upon heretics.

Shortly after we find special inquisitors in Italy, where heresy had spread considerably, and become so dangerous as to induce Frederick II., who

---

[*] Haurdin, tom. vii. p. 173—178. The remaining decrees of this synod refer to other matters, such as the public peace, the keeping of the Lord's day, &c.

certainly cannot be accused of bigotry, at his coronation, and repeatedly afterwards, to decree capital punishment against the heretics in his dominions. Llorente ascribes to him even the nomination of special inquisitors from the Dominican order *before* the sitting of the council of Toulouse. But the edicts of the earlier years of the emperor* make no mention of this, and the document upon which Llorente bases his opinion is not dated 1224 but 1239, as he might have learned from Rolandini " in Muratori Scriptores."†

But in Italy we meet with the first special inquisitors two years after the council of Toulouse, introduced by the same Gregory IX., whose legates presided at this council. In his bull of the year 1231 he anathematizes all heretics, as well as their abettors, brands the obstinate ones with infamy, declares them unable to hold public offices, to act as witnesses, to be testators, or inheritors, &c., whilst he excommunicates such as are suspected and cannot sufficiently clear themselves, and punishes as heretics those that remain under the ban for one year.

In consequence of this bull, which makes no mention yet of the Inquisition, the senate of Rome, and its president, Annibald, issued on their part decrees for the persecution of heretics within the jurisdiction of the Roman territory. Those decrees, which speak for the first time of " inquisitores ab

* The edict of the year 1224 is given *in extenso* in Raynaldi " Contin. Annal. Baronii," ad ann. 1231, n. 18.

† The edict in question is to be found in Harduin, tom. vii. p. 370, and in the letters of Petrus de Vircis, i. 25, but without a special date. It was signed at Padua, the 22nd February of the twelfth indiction, the year 1224 being designated by the twelfth indiction, Llorente hastily places the document in this year, forgetting that the year 1239 bears the same number, and that Frederick did not visit Padua before the year 1239. See Rolandini, lib. iv. c. 9, and Pertz, vol. iv. p. 326 et seq.

ecclesia dati," were, together with his own bull, sent by Gregory to the archbishop of Milan and his suffragans, as well as to other parts of Italy, to be acted upon.

Shortly after we find the Dominicans at the side of the *episcopal* inquisitors charged with the duties of the inquisitions, but it is impossible to determine when they first took place; it probably happened in the following manner.

The chief object of the order being the conversion of heretics by preaching (whence it was also called the order of the Preachers), Hadrian III. recommended the bishops to avail themselves of the aid of its members. They showed great zeal in their exertions, and were probably charged with extraordinary inquisitorial functions even before the institution of regular tribunals. When these were established, in 1229, many bishops selected, doubtless, also priests of the Dominican order for their inquisitors and *officers*.

There can be no doubt about Gregory IX. having done so. He greatly befriended both the Dominicans and Franciscans. The former had, in 1233, zealously laboured to extirpate heresy from Milan and its environs, and, two years after, were specially sent to several towns charged by Gregory with the reconciliation of a number of persons guilty or suspected of heresy. But besides the Dominicans, other priests and members of other religious orders were labouring in the cause of the Inquisition, as, for example, in France, in the year, 1233, Stephen, prior of the Benedictine abbey of Cluny.

Under Pope Innocence IV. (1243-54), however, the influence of the Dominicans began to develop itself more fully, and, as we believe, first in Spain. Aragon was, of all the Spanish provinces, the one nearest to those parts of southern France, where

heresy had established its head-quarters. That part
of it situated on the other side of the Pyrenees
belonged even to the ecclesiastical province of Narbonne in France. Heresy had, therefore, infected
Spain, especially Aragon, where King Alfonse II.
had already, in 1194, put into execution the above-
mentioned bull of Lucius III. against heresy.

Peter II. of Aragon, at first followed in his
footsteps, but shortly after joined the count of
Toulouse, and other nobles of the South of France,
who fought in the ranks of the Albigenses, against
the crusaders. His death (he fell in the battle of
Muret, 1213) re-established the former state of
things in Aragon, and Gregory IX. summoned, in
1232, the archbishop of Tarragona, Esparraga and
his suffragans, to search for heretics themselves, or
to have them searched for by the Dominicans.
Indeed in a few years we find the latter at the head
of an inquisitorial tribunal at Lerida.

What had hitherto only been exceptional, became
now a rule. Innocent specially invested the Dominicans with full inquisitorial powers, equal to those
of the bishops. In his brief of the 20th October,
1248, addressed to the great Dominican, St. Raymond of Pennafort, he declares: "The Dominicans
having, as it were, been sent to him by Providence to assist him in the extirpation of heresy,
and their zeal remarked by him, he had decided
upon intrusting these affairs to them . . . ipsis
hujusmodi negotium providimus specialiter commit-
tendum." He orders, therefore, Father Raymond
to send several Dominicans, as inquisitors, to that
part of Aragon which belonged to the ecclesiastical
province of Aragon, and to give them the decrees
issued by Gregory, which were confirmed by
himself.* Innocent, doubtless, meant by this the

* The decree of the Pope is recorded by Mansi, tom. xxiii.

U

decrees of the council of Toulouse, for his own inquisitorial statutes, divided into thirty-eight paragraphs, were only issued several years after this brief. In these statutes, dated the 15th May, 1252, we find the Dominicans mentioned as regular inquisitors for Lombardy, the Roman States, and the province of Treviso.

Thus the Inquisition was gradually transferred from the bishops to the Dominicans, who introduced it into almost all parts of Europe.

In the peninsula, to which we must confine ourselves, it soon extended from Aragon to Castile, Navarre, and Portugal. The former province counted many tribunals, over which several celebrated inquisitors presided, as for instance, Nicolas Eymerick, author of the "Directorium Inquisitorum," and which, on account of the close proximity to southern France, where heresy prevailed, had from time to time to renew their activity.

In Castile, however, the Inquisition fell gradually into disuse about the middle of the fifteenth century, so much so, that, in the year 1460, Father Alphonse Espina, who, as a Franciscan, was antagonistic to the Dominicans, complained of the absence there of an inquisitor delegated by the pope, which allowed heretics and Jews to scoff at the Christian religion.

Anton Riccio, provincial of the Dominicans, is said to have in consequence been nominated grand-inquisitor of Castile by Pope Paul II. But though this may be true, it is certain that no successor was appointed to him; for, at the commencement of Ferdinand and Isabella's reign, no inquisitor was to be found in Castile for the trial of Peter of Orma, which had to be conducted before the archbishop of Toledo, and to be confirmed by Pope Sixtus IV.

It is, however, remarkable, that Castile became the home of (as Llorente calls it) the modern, or rather, the political inquisition, owing to peculiar circumstances belonging exclusively to Spain.

In the very first centuries of the Christian era, the Jews became so numerous and powerful in Spain, that they were even emboldened to believe they might attempt to "judaize" the whole country. Some records of doubtful authority state that they came into Spain about the time of Solomon ;* but it seems much more probable that they entered the peninsula from Africa, about a century before the birth of Christ. By degrees they became very numerous, obtained considerable power and influence, and carried on the work of proselytism with exceeding zeal and perseverance. So far back as the commencement of the fourth century (303—313), a synod held in Illeberis,† considered it necessary to decree, "that no Christians possessing estates should have their lands blessed by Jews; that neither priest nor layman should hold any intercourse with them ; and laymen were especially forbidden to contract marriage with them." But it was no easy matter to uproot the evil; for it is certain that at this period (as Jost positively asserts) many Spanish Christians were addicted to the practices and doctrines of Judaism. The third council of Toledo, held in the year 589, considered it absolutely imperative to renew the decree which we have just cited regarding marriage. Moreover, as the Spanish Jews carried on a considerable traffic in slaves, whom they frequently circumcised, the same council forbad this traffic, and declared

* Jost, " Geschichte der Israeliten, seit der Zeit der Maccabäer bis auf unsere Tage " (Berlin, 1825), vol. v. p. 13.

† Or Elvira, supposed to have been where Granada now stands.

every slave to be free who had been circumcised.[*] Several other decrees of the same character were issued against them; but they appear not to have been carried into effect. Many of the Jews purchased by their gold the protection even of several amongst the Spanish clergy: against this evil the fourth council of Toledo, held in 633, issued severe decrees.[†]

The Visigoth kings, on the other hand, were at the same time endeavouring to convert the Jews by force; but the same fourth council of Toledo expressly forbad any violence to be used: "For the future" (these are the words of the 57th canon), "no Jew must be forced to embrace Christianity; but those who have already been converted, even should it have been done by force, and have received the holy sacrament, shall be obliged to preserve their faith, and on no account dishonour or despise it."[‡] Respecting baptized Jews, the 59th canon further decrees: "A very great number are still Jews in secret; but as King Sisenand commands, they must be induced to embrace Christianity again." In order to avoid the guilt of apostasy, the 62nd canon forbids all intercourse whatever between Jews baptized and non-baptized.

Thus this ancient council made an essential difference between Jews who had been baptized and were yet secretly attached to their old religion, and real Jews. This distinction must, in our future remarks be always carefully borne in mind.

In the mean time the number of Jews apparently converted to Christianity, but still secretly attached to their former practices, considerably increased by the severe laws of the Visigoth kings against them in the seventh century. These laws, first made by

---

[*] Harduin, tom. iii. p. 481, can. 14.   [†] Ibid. p. 590, can. 58.
[‡] Ibid. tom. iii. p. 590.

the civil power, were confirmed by the ecclesiastical authority in the fourth, sixth, twelfth, and sixteenth councils of Toledo, and tended to deprive the Jews of many of their civil rights, in order more effectually to force them to become Christians.

The consequence was, that amongst these pretended Christians a terrible plot was secretly and silently extending on all sides, which had for its object the downfall of the Christian kingdom of the Visigoths by the assistance of the Saracens in Africa, and the erection of a new Jerusalem in Spain.* But the deep-laid plot was discovered by King Egica, and the originators severely punished. The seventeenth council of Toledo alludes to this event, where it says (speaking of the baptized Jews, " qui tunicam fidei, quâ eos per undam sacri baptismi induit sancta Mater Ecclesia, maculaverint"), "Ausu tyrannico inferre conati sunt ruinam patriæ et populo universo . . . . . et regni fastigium sibi per conspirationem usurpare maluerint." The guilty were condemned to slavery, and the incursion of the Saracens was, fortunately, repulsed.

Prescott, who mentions this event in his "History of Ferdinand and Isabella," falls into a serious mistake on this point, for he positively asserts, "that no sooner had their Arian masters (the Visigoths) embraced the orthodox faith, than they began to testify their zeal by pouring out on the Jews the most pitiless storm of persecution;" and he adds the words, "one of their laws alone condemned their whole race to slavery" (vol. i. p. 296, ed. 1849). He supports his assertions by referring to the seventeenth council of Toledo. But he, unfortunately, seems to have forgotten that both the real Jews and pretended converts were the very persons

---

* Jost, loco citato, p. 147.

who drew down upon themselves these severe laws by their secret machinations, and especially that the council expressly states—" Slavery was to be the punishment, *not of the whole* race, but only of the chief conspirators." *

But the Jews soon recovered from the adversities and punishments which they were forced to endure in the seventh century. After the invasion of the Arabs, they again acquired riches, power, influence, and honours ; they established flourishing schools and academies in Cordova (anno 948), Toledo, and Barcelona. Several learned men arose amongst them, until at last the Jews reached a degree of importance and literary eminence in Spain which they never acquired in any other part of Europe.

They suffered also greatly by the religious wars of the Spaniards against the Moors, many Spanish knights seeing in them nearer and consequently more dangerous enemies to the Christian faith. In these difficult times it was the clergy and the popes who (though they are seldom given credit for it) protected the Jews. This is clearly proved by a brief of the predecessor and friend of Hildebrand, Alexander II., in which he applauds the Spanish bishops for having protected the Jews and prevented their massacre. In the same manner and for the same reason he wrote to Viscount Berengar of Narbonne, but to the archbishop of that province he wrote, censuring him : " Your prudence will know that all ecclesiastical and civil laws condemn the shedding of blood." One hundred and fifty years later, Pope

---

* These are the words of the council, as given by Florez :—
" Que todos los Judios sean hechos esclavos, y confiscados todos sus bienes, pues no solo havian judaizado despues de bautizados sino que havian conspirado contra el reyno " (tom. vi. p. 229, ed. 1751). The words certainly seem to imply, that the whole race was condemned to slavery.—*Trans.*

Honorius III. imitated the example of Alexander by guarding the Jews from brutal treatment.* On the other hand, the popes, without being inconsistent, demanded,—as, for instance, Gregory VII. of King Alphonse VI., of Castile,—that the Jews should not be allowed to hold power over Christians, either as their masters or as their judges. We nevertheless repeatedly find them holding public offices, especially since Alfonse X., the astrologer, who esteemed them highly for their astronomical learning, had collected around him many learned Jews.

It was no uncommon thing to see them employed as governors, administrators, and treasurers, both to the kings and the grandees of Spain. Many of them, by practising the art of medicine, gained access into private families, and thus learnt every domestic secret. Most of the dispensaries in the country were in their hands. They had their own judges, and were tried by laws and rights peculiar to themselves, often to the prejudice of the Spaniards. They also possessed several privileges which the Christians did not enjoy; for instance, that of not being imprisoned (which privilege belonged only to the nobility) without the express command of the king. We even find Jews at this period as ministers of finance, and favourites with kings to such a degree as to hold the reins of government in their own hands. The consequence was, that often, in the fourteenth century, the Cortes and different councils were obliged to send remonstrances to the government on the subject of these privileges enjoyed by the Jews; while several civil commotions proved what were the feelings of the Spanish people towards these dangerous foreigners.

---

* The clergy of France, too, in the thirteenth century, protected the Jews against the severity of the civil courts.—Jost, vi. 302.

But those who *pretended* to be converts to Christianity were far more dangerous than the real Jews. The number of the former had increased exceedingly since the persecutions at the end of the fourteenth century. The real Jews had indeed monopolized a great part of the national property and commerce, while the pretended converts threatened to uproot the Spanish nationality itself and the Christian faith, because, on the one hand, they were raised to several ecclesiastical dignities, and even to bishoprics;*

---

* Jost, vol. vii. p. 100. Borrow, in chap. xi. of "The Bible in Spain," tells a very remarkable adventure bearing on this subject. On his way to Talavera, in the beginning of the year 1836, he met a man, dressed in a manner strange and singular for the country, who appeared to be half Spaniard, half foreigner, and in reality was a disguised Jew. After a short discourse, the man, believing to have discovered in Borrow another son of Abraham, opens his heart to him, tells him that his family had always remained faithful to the creed of their forefathers, that he was possessed of great wealth, and had large sums employed in usury, &c. "My grandsire was a particularly holy man," he continues, "and I have heard my father say, that one night an archbishop came to his house secretly, merely to have the satisfaction of kissing his head. He was one of us, at least his father was, and he could never forget what he had learned with reverence in his infancy. He said, he had tried to forget it, but he could not; that the truth was continually upon him, and that even from his childhood he had borne its terrors with a troubled mind, till at last he could bear himself no longer; so he went to my grandsire, with whom he remained all night; he then returned to his diocese, where he shortly after died, in much renown for his sanctity." On Borrow expressing his surprise, and questioning him as to whether he had reason to suppose that many of his people were to be found among the priesthood, the Jew continued: "I not only suppose, but know it. There are many such as I amongst the priesthood, and not amongst the inferior priesthood either; some of the most learned and famed in Spain have been of us, or of our blood at least, and many of them at this day think as I do. There is one particular festival of the year at which four dignified ecclesiastics are sure to visit me; and then, when all is made close and secure, and the fitting ceremonies have been gone through, they sit down upon the floor and curse." In chapter xvii. Borrow repeats his assertion that many disguised Jews were then still to be found amongst

and, on the other, not only possessed many civil posts of importance, but intermarried with noble families, and used these advantages and their riches as so many instruments to erect Judaism in place of the Spanish nationality and the Christian faith. It is a well-known fact, admitted even by Llorente himself in a work prior to his "History of the Inquisition," and denied by no one, that in the time of Ferdinand the Catholic the proselytism carried on by the Jews had reached an alarming degree.* And the Cortes, too, of 1812, of philosophical memory, who legally suppressed the Inquisition, positively asserted that the Jews were at this period " a people within another people ;" and that, in the year 1473, they even tried, by means of their money, to obtain possession of the fortress of Gibraltar, the key of Spain.

Under these circumstances, many of the clergy and laity, seeing the great danger which the Jews threatened to bring on the nation, and being also

the clergy in Spain, saying that he derived his information from a priest formerly belonging to the Inquisition at Cordova. Dr. Kunstmann in the " Münchener Gelehrte Anzeigen " (1845, No. 97), remarks with reference to this: " This report is to be accepted with caution, not only because it is highly improbable that a stranger on the first meeting would be initiated into the secrets of crypto-judaism, the adherents of which were liable to severe punishment, but also because in the very year of Borrow's tale, 1836, nearly the half of the sixty-two episcopal sees of Spain were vacant, and a meeting of four bishops in one and the same house impossible without causing great sensation. It is true, that a tendency towards Judaism is still to be found in some Spanish families, but not a single instance can be found, either in former days, when the usual inquiry, de genere, was rigorously conducted, or in modern times, of a priest of Jewish extraction, having been raised to the episcopal dignity.

* Don José Clemente Carnicero, " La Inquisicion justamente restablecida; ó, Impugnacion de la Obra de Don Juan Llorente, Anales de la Inquisicion de España, y del Manifesto de las Cortes de Cadiz." (Madrid, 1816, tom. i. p. 61.)

convinced that the evil could not be averted without
the assistance of the government, several times
solicited Ferdinand and Isabella to proceed with
severity against the disguised converted Jews.*
It was *these* that the "Inquisition" afterwards
punished, and not the Jews properly so called, which
is carefully to be borne in mind.†

The young sovereigns received an address of this
kind while they were residing at Seville, during the
years 1477 and 1478. Philip de Barbéris, inquisitor of Sicily, had arrived at that city about this
time, in order to obtain from his sovereign, Ferdinand
the Catholic, the confirmation of an ancient privilege
for his institution in Sicily. Both he and the prior of
San Pablo in Seville, Alonso de Ojeda, who belonged
to the Dominican order, as also Diego de Merlo, a
respectable magistrate of the city, represented to the
sovereigns the necessity of re-establishing in Castile
a tribunal to judge heretics. If we may credit the
assertion of Llorente, Nicolas Franco, the pope's
nuncio, supported their representations. According
to the same author, the queen was at first quite
opposed to the introduction of the Inquisition. If
this assertion be correct, she must soon have seen
by the course of affairs the absolute necessity of
such a tribunal, for in her last will she expressly
recommended her heirs to favour and uphold the
Inquisition. These are her words : " E que siempre
favorezcan mucho las cosas de la santa Inquisicion,
contra la herética pravedad,"‡ &c.

* Pulgar, " Crónica de los Reyes Católicos," &c. (ed. Valencia, 1780).

† Neither the unbaptized Jew nor the unbaptized Moor could
be brought before the Inquisition, but only those of these two
creeds who had relapsed. Maistre, pp. 49—53.

‡ Carnicero, pp. 229, 230. The will is still to be seen in the
archives of Simancas.—*Trans.*

Soon after Ferdinand and Isabella had resolved to introduce the Inquisition into Castile, Pope Sixtus IV. authorized (November 1st, 1478) the sovereigns to establish a tribunal for searching out and punishing heretics, which was to consist of two or three dignitaries of the Church, who might be either seculars or regulars, according to the wish of the sovereigns, provided the said dignitaries were at least forty years of age, of pure morals, bachelors of theology, or doctors of canon law.*

The sovereigns, however, before establishing the tribunal, tried some other means of arresting the progress of concealed Judaism. It was no doubt with their consent that Mendoza, the great archbishop and cardinal of Seville (and afterwards of Toledo), published a catechism, in which the principal duties of a Christian's life from the time of his baptism till his death were briefly explained. This little work the cardinal not only circulated in Seville, but had it also posted up on all the church doors throughout his extensive diocese, commanding all the curates to make it known to the faithful, to exhort them to live according to its maxims, and to teach their children to do the same. This measure,

* According to Bernaldez and Zuñiga the papal bull is dated 1480, but Llorente and his usual opponent Carnicero place it and the introduction of the Inquisition in the year 1478. The date matters little. Of greater importance is, that Pope Sixtus shortly after declared the bull, confirming the Spanish Inquisition, had been obtained of him by an imperfect representation of the royal intentions. Through a misconception of these, he had confirmed the royal plan, which, as it now appeared, was contrary to the decrees of the holy fathers and the general practice of the church. (Llorente, tom. iv. p. 347 in the documents.) This observation is for those who believe that the pope was overjoyed at the political inquisition of Spain. We shall see later how different it was from the ecclesiastical one, and how it became an institution for the absolutism of the king.

so wise and so gentle, was afterwards made the occasion of accusing the noble cardinal of having been instrumental in establishing the Inquisition. But no contemporary writer makes any mention of his participation; and even modern historians* consider the accusation devoid of truth.

In order to render this measure of the archbishop more successful, Ferdinand and Isabella ordered several regular and secular priests to endeavour to wean back to the Church, by public preaching and private discourses, such as had been misled; and on leaving Seville requested the vicar-general Don Pedro (Llorente says Alonso) de Solis, the corregidor Merlo, and the above-named father Alphonse, to watch the results of this peaceful mission.

But these efforts could not bend the obstinacy of the Judaists. Far from being induced to become sincere Christians, they published a cutting and bitter pamphlet against the conduct of the government, and even against the Christian religion. This publication, however, soon drew down upon the heretics themselves the severest punishments. It was not answered with such a friendly spirit by the sovereigns as Isabella's confessor, the mild Ferdinand of Talavera, would have wished. By virtue of the papal bull, two royal inquisitors were immediately nominated for Seville, both of whom were Dominicans, viz., Miguel Morillo and Juan Martin; the first was the provincial of his order, and the last the vicar. With these were united Dr. Juan Ruiz, counsellor of the queen, and her chaplain, Juan Lopez del Barco.

Such is the origin of the modern, or rather of the Spanish state Inquisition, between which and the

---

* Prescott, for instance.

ecclesiastical Inquisition there is this difference,
that in the former, the persons, whether clerical or
lay, appointed to seek out and punish heretics, were
not employed as servants of the church, but as
functionaries of the State, and received from the
sovereigns their appointment and instructions.

The ancient Spanish writers do not agree as to
the exact date of the commencement of the modern
Inquisition.* Some see its rise in the institution
just named; others refer its beginning to the period
of Torquemada's nomination as grand-inquisitor.
This last opinion is supported by the authority of
Zurita;† while the first, on the other hand, is confirmed by an ancient inscription on the tribunal of
the Inquisition at Seville, which mentions 1481 as
the year of its establishment.

The Inquisition of Seville, immediately after its
establishment (January 2nd, 1481), issued a decree
wherein a number of "signs" were given, by which
the secret Judaism of a pretended Christian could
be detected; this decree also contained a general
order to every one to denounce those who showed
these "signs" of Judaism. Llorente attacks this
decree with his usual violence, asserting that twenty-
two of the signs indicated in the edict would scarcely
be sufficient at the present day to establish a mere
suspicion of Judaism.‡ Prescott maintains the
same opinion.§ But it is easy to prove what *little
honesty* the first writer possesses, and what little

---

* Similar reasons called the Portuguese state inquisition into
existence.

† "Anales de la Corona de Aragon," tom. iv. lib. xx. cap. xlix.

‡ The edict itself is to be found in Llorente, tom. i. pp. 153—
158.

§ "Hist. of Ferdinand and Isabella," vol. i. p. 311, ed. 1849.
Mr. Prescott is exceedingly incorrect and unjust in his remarks
on the Spanish Inquisition.—*Trans.*

judgment and want of criticism the other shows. If, for instance, the pretended convert would not allow, after his baptism, any fire in his house on the Sabbath-day, and if on that day he wore better clothes than usual, would there not be in such conduct, as the edict asks in the fourth section, matter sufficient for a just suspicion, however ridiculous Llorente may consider it? And again : who would not suspect a secret relapse into Judaism on beholding the practice of those who, after the baptism of their infant, hastened to wash those parts of the body which had received the unction of the holy oil? (Section 24.)

Llorente and his followers might have borne in mind the axiom : duo si faciunt idem non est idem —and that one born of Christian parents may, without being suspected of crypto-judaism, do many things which one of Jewish descent may not. Yet were the former to show many of the signs indicated in the decree, even he would not escape from being gravely suspected of apostasy.

But the dishonesty of Llorente does not stop here. A little further, he asserts (p. 160), that in the year 1481 alone, the Inquisition of Seville ordered no less than two thousand persons to be burnt in the two dioceses of Seville and Cadiz. In order to strengthen the faith of his readers in such a monstrous assertion, he appeals to the authority of the celebrated Spanish historian Mariana. Now, if we peruse his work, we shall certainly find the number two thousand mentioned.* But it is

---

* Mariana thus approves of the modern Inquisition : " Remedio muy á propósito contra los males que se aparejaban . . . . Dado del cielo, que sin duda no bastará consejo, ni prudencia de hombres, para prevenir y acudir á peligros tan grandes como se han experimentado, y se padecen en otras partes." (Lib. xxiv. cap. xvii. ed. Valencia, 1795.)—*Trans.*

expressly mentioned that this was the number of those who were burnt under Torquemada. Therefore not during the year 1481 alone (when Torquemada was not grand inquisitor *yet*), and not in these two dioceses only, but throughout the whole provinces both of Castile and Aragon.* What Mariana says, Llorente might have seen in Pulgar also, who was contemporary with these events; for after having mentioned that Torquemada established tribunals in the provinces of Castile, Aragon, Valencia, and Catalonia, he thus continues:—"These tribunals now conducted the Inquisition against heresy . . . they summoned all the heretics to appear before them of their own accord . . . About fifteen thousand responded to the call, and, after having done penance, were reconciled with the Church. Those who waited to be accused, were tried, and, if convicted, delivered over to the secular power. Of these, about two thousand men and women were burnt *at different* times, and in certain cities and towns."†

Llorente, who so often quotes Pulgar, must have seen this passage; but in *his* estimation, it seemed more dramatic to make his readers suppose that so great a number were burnt in *one* year, and in *one single* province. The boldness and indifference with which he misquotes and falsifies Mariana is still less excusable.‡

* The jurisdiction of the tribunal of Seville was not confined to Andalusia alone, but extended over the whole of Castile and Leon. The bull of Sixtus IV., of the year 1483, clearly proves this, as therein mention is made of several bishoprics, in which these two inquisitors exercised their power and functions. The bull is to be found in Llorente, tom. iv. p. 357.

† " Destos fueron quemados en diversas veces, y en algunas cibdades ó villas, fasta dos mil homes ó mugeres " (ed. Valencia, 1780, p. 137). In this beautiful edition, the ancient orthography of many words is preserved.—*Trans.*

‡ Prescott also acquiesces in the assertion of Llorente; but he has the candour to acknowledge that L. Marineo, also a contem-

I am, however, far from praising the inquisitors of Seville for their mildness and indulgence: on the contrary, they deserved the just reproaches and complaints which were abundantly heaped upon them by Pope Sixtus IV., in a brief dated January 29th, 1482, in which he complained that the bull of confirmation had unfairly been obtained from him. "It was only through regard for Ferdinand and Isabella," he says, "that he had not deposed the two inquisitors against whom complaints were made, of having condemned even persons who were not guilty of heresy."* Prescott represents the matter in such a manner as to lead the reader to suppose "that the pope was for a moment touched with something like compunction; that he rebuked the intemperate zeal of the inquisitors, and even menaced them with deprivation. But these feelings were but transient; for we find the same pope in 1483, quieting the scruples of Isabella respecting the appropriation of the confiscated property, and encouraging both sovereigns to proceed in the great work of purification," &c. (vol. i. p. 313.) The brief, dated February 23rd, 1483, in which the pope is represented as having made use of such language, may be seen in Llorente (tom. iv. p. 352). As far as regards the assertion of Prescott that the pope endeavoured to calm the scruples of the queen respecting the confiscated property, the truth is, that, "he assures her majesty he fully credits the assurance she gives him, that she had *not* persecuted the heretics through any motives of self-interest." In a second brief, dated August 2nd of the same

porary, diffuses the two thousand capital executions over *several* years. Why does not Mr. Prescott say the same of Mariana and Pulgar ?

* The brief may be seen in Llorente, tom. iv. The date (1481) which he gives is incorrect. It ought to be 1482.

year, the pope requires* "that all those who repent of their heretical doctrines shall be allowed *to retain possession of their property.*"

But if Sixtus praises the queen, he does so on account of the Inquisition in Sicily, and not that in Spain; he approves of the Inquisition as such, but not of the political one, as may be seen from his brief of February 25, 1483, in which he expresses to her doubts of his ability to grant several requests concerning the Inquisition. Moreover, his aversion against the political Inquisition is shown by the nomination of the Archbishop of Seville, Don Inigo Manrique, as papal councillor of appeal, to whom appeals could be made against the sentences of the royal inquisitors. And when he found that this measure neither lessened the severity of the latter, nor was respected by them, he received himself appeals of the persecuted, declaring in his edict of the 2nd August, 1483, that he was forced to this step not only by the contempt shown to the power intrusted to the Archbishop of Seville, but especially by many of the accused having been prevented from appealing to the papal judge.

He further cautions therein strongly against too great severity, takes the repenting heretics under his protection, demands pardon for them, though their time of grace may have elapsed, and enjoins the sovereigns to leave them in the quiet possession of their property.

If so mild an edict had been issued by a secular prince, or better still, by a republican senate, Llorente could hardly have praised it enough; but, coming from the pope, he sees therein nothing but contradiction and violation of the Archbishop of Seville's rights; he would rather have recorded

---

* Llorente, tom. iv. p. 357.

X

that a few thousand additional heretics had been burned than that their appeals went to the Holy See. Nay, even the merciful benevolence which dictated to the pope to absolve such in private, and not to proclaim their offence as had addressed themselves to him of their own accord, is in his eyes nothing more than a desire to extort increased fines.*

The brief of August 2nd, 1483, had no effect in dissuading Ferdinand and Isabella from their design of converting the Inquisition into a *political* institution.† A short time after, Pope Sixtus authorized them to name as grand-inquisitor for the whole of Castile the Dominican Tomás Torquemada, prior of the convent of Santa Cruz, in Segovia, with the power invested in himself of choosing other inferior ministers.‡ In a second brief, dated October 17th, 1483, the pope consented that Torquemada should unite with his other powers that of grand-inquisitor of Aragon also.

It was not without strong opposition that the other inquisitors of Aragon accepted the authority of their new head, who had been invested by the crown with such extensive powers : from his appointment, the Spanish state Inquisition dates its full organization. In a short time, Torquemada established four tribunals, at Seville, Cordoba, Jaen, and Villa-Real; the last of which was afterwards

---

* Several mistakes of this nature, made by Llorente, were ably refuted by a writer in the " Theologische Quartalschrift," published at Tübingen in the year 1820.

† Both the " Univers " and the Spanish " Esperanza " blame Dr. Hefele for representing the Spanish Inquisition as a *purely* political institution. (See preface to the translation.)

‡ Paramo, " De Origine Inquisitionis " (Matriti, 1598), lib. ii. cap. iii. p. 137.

removed to Toledo : for these tribunals he drew up several rules and statutes.*

Ferdinand placed under his presidency a council, consisting of theologians and jurists, who lent him their advice in all matters purely religious, but whose majority decided in all cases of a civil and juridical nature. It is evident that these councillors, more still than the great inquisitor, were functionaries of the state, whose nomination required not even the sanction of the pope, or any other ecclesiastical power. Whether they were ecclesiastics or laymen is a question of no import, as modern times furnish many similar cases, in which civil offices were filled by members of the Church. We shall, moreover, see later that Ferdinand acted upon his principle of laymen also being able to hold places in this council.

While the organization of these tribunals was going on, Pope Sixtus IV. died. His successor, Innocent VIII., approved of the tribunals and statutes in a brief, dated February 11th, 1486. Soon did the new Inquisition behold its power extend more and more, when Ferdinand and Isabella, in the year 1492, immediately after the conquest of Granada, issued a decree for the banishment of *all* those Jews who refused to be baptized. But the causes and circumstances connected with this event have no direct connection with the history of the Inquisition, and it may therefore suffice to say that various reasons tended to occasion that decree. The inquisitors and other zealous persons saw the impossibility of suppressing crypto-judaism as long as the Jews remained in Spain. It needed little

* There is a copy of these " Statutes " in the public library of Valladolid. They seem to be drawn up with great care and moderation.—*Trans.*

sagacity to see the indefatigable proselytism of the
Spanish Jews, whose aim was not only to bring
back to their faith the Maranos,* but also to convert
the *old* Christians and to judaize the whole of
Spain.   Hence the warnings of the inquisitors were
listened to by the statesmen, who for some time
previous had looked with suspicion upon the grow-
ing national wealth of the Jews, in whose hands
were the most lucrative trades of the country.
The public weal, this word whose magic power must
also in our times cover many a violation of justice
and religious liberty, demanded, therefore, imperatively the expulsion of the Jews ; and this the more,
as, perhaps, through the great severity used against
them, there seemed little hope of converting them
into peaceful subjects, and of deterring them from
their desire to make converts.

However reluctantly these measures were resorted
to, they were hastened on by several ill-timed
brutalities and acts of revenge on the part of the
Jews. They defaced crucifixes, profaned consecrated
Hosts, and were gravely suspected of having, at La
Guardia, in the Mancha, in the year 1490, and
elsewhere, crucified Christian children, and attempted the same crime at Valencia. In 1485 a
conspiracy of the Jews was discovered in Toledo,
the object of which was nothing less than the
seizure of the town on Corpus Christi day, and the
murder of all the Christians.†

All this, and the wealth of the Jews, had so

---

* So called from Maranatha: "The Lord is coming." —
1 Corinth. xvi. 22.

† See Jost, Ferreras, Carnicero, and Balmes, all of whom
prove that the Jews at this period were guilty of most terrible
crimes.   The chapter of Balmes, on the " Inquisition in Spain,"
is most valuable.   (See English ed. London, 1849, chap. xxxvi.
p. 161.)—*Trans.*

exasperated the Christian population of Spain, that government could rely upon their co-operation in the expulsion of the Jews. In vain they endeavoured to ward off the blow by offering to Ferdinand the sum of 30,000 ducats, at a time when, still engaged in his war against Granada, he stood greatly in need of money. The latter is indeed said to have nearly yielded to temptation, and to have intended to relinquish his plans against the Jews. But Torquemada appeared before him and Isabella, holding in his hands a crucifix. "Judas sold our Saviour for thirty pieces of silver, but your highnesses will sell Him for 30,000. Here He is, sell Him." So saying, he laid the crucifix before them and retired. This bold behaviour made such an impression upon the sovereigns, that they immediately after issued at Granada the memorable edict of the 31st March, 1492, which commanded all the Jews to leave the country who, up to the 31st July, had not become converts. They were allowed until then to sell their possessions, and to take with them their property in bills or in goods, but not in specie, whilst the sovereigns provided them with a pass and vessels for their transport.* The Spanish preachers used their utmost exertions to win over many Jews before the expiration of the term of emigration, and Torquemada in particular charged the Dominicans to devote their utmost zeal to this cause. Many thousands, however, preferred exile to conversion, and left the country in large masses at the end of July, having been compelled to sell their property at very low prices, as, for instance, a house for a mule, &c.

* Ferdinand and Isabella say in this edict, " that they had been advised to it by many wise and distinguished men, and adopted it only after long and profound reflection."—Carnicero, tom. i. p. 273.

Llorente assures us that, according to the calculation of Mariana, about eight hundred thousand
Jews were banished. But the *conscientious* historian
of the Inquisition forgets to remark that Mariana
declares the number to be *exaggerated*, and indeed
almost incredible.* He also neglects, according to
his usual custom, to acknowledge that Ferreras,
another Spanish historian, after having given the
number of those who were exiled throughout the
provinces, makes them amount to about thirty thousand families, and one hundred thousand souls.

Although many of the emigrants acted against
the prohibition of taking precious metals with them,
and sewed gold-pieces in the saddles and halters of
their mules, or swallowed them in small pieces, and
hid them on parts of their body where delicacy
forbade to search for them, Ferdinand kept his
word and let them pass unmolested. Most of them
wandered to Portugal, Italy, France, or to the
Levante, and to Africa. But their misfortunes did
not end here. Many were carried off in Italy by
epidemics; and in Africa, they were robbed and
murdered by the Moors, who defiled their wives and
daughters, and cut their bodies open in search of
the gold-pieces they had swallowed. Many thousands returned then, in the greatest misery, to
Spain, submitting to baptism. Those who had
from the beginning declared their intention to
remain, had had to do the same, but their conversion
was only outward. They continued in their old

---

* These are the words of Mariana:—" El número de los Judios
que salieron de Castilla y Aragon no se sabe...... No falta
quien diga que llegaron á ochocientos mil almas; gran muche-
dumbre sin duda," &c. (lib. xxvi. cap. i.) Prescott himself candidly owns that the calculation made by Llorente is exaggerated:
—"A review of all the circumstances," he continues," will lead us,
without much hesitation, to adopt a more moderate computation."
(" Hist. of Ferdinand and Isabella," vol. ii. p. 130.)—*Trans.*

Jewish rites, and, as a necessary consequence, fell a prey to the Inquisition, whose functions were thereby greatly extended.

The tribunals of the Spanish Inquisition were, to a much less degree, called into requisition by the Moriscos, or baptized Moors. Ferdinand and Isabella, after the conquest of Granada, in 1492, solemnly confirmed to the Moors, besides their civil privileges, the retention of their mosques and the free exercise of their religion, and authors who have taken only this into consideration stigmatize severely the subsequent proceedings against them. The facts, however, are as follows.

The sovereigns did not consider that they broke their word, by appointing Talavera and Ximenez, the two most virtuous bishops of their state, to win the Moors over to Christianity by persuasion and instruction. Nor can it be called a violation of their promise, to have conferred special civil and material privileges upon those who were converted.

We have seen, in the tenth chapter, what threatening revolts were caused by these attempts at conversion, by the exasperated Moorish population of the Albaycim, the Alpuxarras, and the Sierre Vermeja. No wonder that the sovereigns considered themselves no longer bound by their treaties of 1492. Had not the Moors, by their rebellion, broken them first? They henceforth treated them, therefore, as rebellious subjects, and thought it but a merciful and lenient exercise of their rights, instead of arraigning them for high treason, to compel them either to be baptized, or, without confiscating their property, to allow them to emigrate on payment of a fine of ten gold florins for every head. The greater part of them remained, and embraced Christianity, so that, soon, not a single unbaptized Moor was to be found in the entire old kingdom of

Granada. Many lived, however, still in the provinces of Castile and Leon, which had been subjugated before by the Christians; and to guard the Moriscos of Granada against a relapse, an edict, of the 20th July, 1501, forbade all communication with their co-religionists. By a second edict, dated but a few months later (12th February, 1502), the more rigorous measures used against those of Granada, to be baptized or to emigrate, were also extended to them. Many preferred the former alternative, were baptized, and remained in Spain.

Diego de Deza, a Dominican, successor to Torquemada (who died 16th September, 1498) in the office of grand-inquisitor, confessor to Ferdinand, and Bishop of Jaen, afterwards Archbishop of Seville, is said to have been the chief instrument in causing these severe measures to be taken against the Moors.* It is also he who induced the sovereigns, to introduce the Inquisition into Granada, to prevent the Moriscos from returning to Islamism. Isabella, however, granted him only the permission of extending the jurisdiction of the tribunal of Cordova to Granada, forbidding, at the same time, to molest the Moriscos on any other ground than that of apostasy. Under the same condition, the Moriscos residing in Castile, Leon, and Aragon, were placed under the Inquisition, and a declaration of theirs, of the year 1524, shows that they were not treated harshly. In this document, which is addressed to the fifth grand-inquisitor, Manrique, they say: "We have always been treated justly by your predecessors, and properly protected by them." Manrique did not change this policy, even when a visitation of the kingdom of Granada, in 1526, showed that almost all the Moriscos had renounced

---

* Several historians wrongly attribute this measure to have originated with Torquemada, who died several years previously.

Christianity, and that hardly seven had remained faithful to it. The consequence of this visitation was, indeed, the erection of a special tribunal for Granada, but it was conducted with great leniency towards those that had relapsed. Pope Clement VII. made it his special care to provide for the Moriscos a sound instruction in the Christian religion, and the Emperor Charles V. ordered that the possessions of apostates could not be confiscated, but were to be retained for their children; nor could they be handed over to the civil authorities, still less condemned to death.

They fared similarly under Philip II. Not one was condemned to capital punishment for apostasy, and harsher means were resorted to against them only after the inhabitants of Granada had revolted again, proclaiming as king a descendant of one of their former rulers. Several popes, especially Gregory XIII., tried unsuccessfully to win the Moriscos over by kindness. They were never thoroughly converted, nor for any length of time, but revolted and revolted again, conspiring with the Moors in Africa, until at last, in the year 1609, Philip III. issued a decree for their expulsion from Spain, a measure which Francis I. of France had recommended before to the Emperor Charles V.*

The Inquisition has hitherto appeared to us only as a barrier against the encroachments of Judaism

---

* Llorente, tom. i. p. 429. The decree of expulsion is to be found in Carnicero, tom. i. p. 289, and also in Balmes, p. 218. The Spaniards have frequently been reproached for this expulsion of the Moriscos, but the Göttinger Gelehrte Anzeigen (July 28, 1842) have already pointed out correctly how it was considered an urgent necessity by the most enlightened and liberal contemporaries, such as Cervantes and others. The "Ausland," too, in its number 146, for 1845, acknowledges that the unity of the state was, by the open and secret partisans of the Moors, much more jeopardized than is generally believed.

and Islamism.* We shall now see what further political reasons induced the Spanish kings to favour an institution, which, though apparently of an ecclesiastical nature, was constantly complained of and combated against by the popes and bishops. The reign of Ferdinand and Isabella was, in Spain, the phase of transition of the old state into the modern one, of the primitive and free state into the abstract and absolute one, as Ranke has clearly shown in his "Princes and People of the Sixteenth and Seventeenth Centuries." In the old state, the central or monarchical power was restricted by three tolerably independent corporations: the aristocracy, the clergy, and the towns. Their close connection with foreign countries—of the clergy with Rome, of the aristocracy and the towns with the aristocracy and towns abroad—prevented the concentration of the state in itself, and the royal power from gaining too much ascendancy. But nowhere in Europe was royal power so limited as in Castile and Aragon; hence we find the sovereigns here, earlier than elsewhere, striving to lessen the independence of the three states and to increase the central power. They succeeded sooner in Castile than in Aragon, but in both countries the Inquisition was the most efficient instrument for subjugating entirely to the crown all the subjects, in particular the nobility and clergy, and completing the absolute power of the monarch.†

* De Maistre, in his Letters on the Spanish Inquisition, observes very justly with reference to this: "Great political evils, and especially violent attacks on the state, can only be prevented or repulsed by means equally violent. This is an irrefutable principle in politics. The Judaists and disguised Moors necessarily either inspired fears or had to fear for themselves."

† Ranke, vol. i. p. 248. "The Inquisition was the means of completing the absolute authority of the king." Very remarkable is what Count Alexis de St. Priest, in his history of the banish-

Hence the two upper classes were the fiercest opponents of the Inquisition, and oftener persecuted as enemies of the same, than as heretics. The prelates in particular soon saw themselves entangled in numerous suits with the new tribunals. The popes, too, could not fail to discover that the Spanish Inquisition served more as a means to consolidate the absolute power of the monarch than to purify the Church, and therefore endeavoured to thwart it in the same degree in which they favoured the ecclesiastical Inquisition. Nor were the Castilian people blind to the fact that the tribunals of the Holy Office were the rock against which the power and authority of the nobles and the clergy would be shattered.*

ment of the Jesuits from Portugal ("Revue des Deux Mondes," April, 1844), observes, with reference to the relation of Piombal to the Inquisition. This minister, the destroyer of the Jesuits and apostle of absolutism, an enemy of Rome and the hierarchical power like no other, recognized in the Inquisition the best means for the accomplishment of his plans. "He had found," says St. Priest, "this formidable institution a convenient and safe weapon, a sort of committee of public safety; hence he also spoke of it always in terms of the greatest admiration." One day he said to the French ambassador: "I intend to reconcile your country with the Inquisition, and prove the utility of this institution to the world. It was established under the authority of the most faithful king, for no other reason than to exercise certain functions of the bishops, which are much safer in the hands of a corporation chosen by the sovereign, than in those of a single individual, who can deceive himself or others." It was Piombal who persecuted the Jesuit P. Madrigal for his connection with the family Tanora, and accused him of heresy before the Inquisition. He was sentenced to be strangled, and afterwards burned in a solemn *auto-da-fé*.

* Philip II., in particular, used the Inquisition to act against the Jesuits and reduce their privileges. This is clearly shown by the famous bull, "Dominus ac Redemptor," by which Clement XIV. suppressed the order of the Jesuits in 1773: "Multæ hinc ortæ adversus Societatem querimoniæ, quæ nonnullorum etiam principum auctoritate munitæ ... fuerunt. In his fuit claræ memoriæ Philippus II., Hispaniarum rex Catholicus, qui tum

The Inquisition, therefore, found great favour with the lower classes, and the Castilian even boasted of this institution of his country. But there is still one other reason, mentioned also by Ranke, which made it really popular in Spain. There, more than elsewhere, a marked distinction existed between persons of pure and impure blood, and the Inquisition, by making this opinion her own, became the most powerful weapon against the latter. National hatred divided in Spain the sons of the Germanic Visigoths from the descendants of the Jews and the Moors, so that the most severe laws against these were joyfully received by the former. It was consequently natural that, urged on by the sovereigns, who were struggling for absolutism, and considered as a national institution by the people, the Inquisition spread rapidly, and without much opposition, throughout the whole of Castile.*

In Aragon, the endeavours to change the old state into the new one were less successful and less complete than in Castile. We find here rather a a fierce opposition against the *new* tribunals on the part of the nobles and the representatives of the towns, although the *ecclesiastical* Inquisition had, for centuries, continued to exist there unattacked. Similar events took place in Sicily and Naples, where the inhabitants, accustomed since time immemorial to the old Inquisition, could only by main force, and

---

gravissimas, quibus ille vehementer impellebatur rationes, tum etiam eos, quos ab Hispaniarum Inquisitoribus adversus immoderata societatis privilegia ac regiminis formam acceperat clamores .... Sixto V. Prædecessori exponenda curavit." (Nat. Alexander, Suppl. II. p. 134. Venet. 1778.)

* Balmes coincides with this view, and is moreover of opinion that Ferdinand and Isabella followed, in their introduction of the measure, more the general voice of the nation than their own political views.

after the suppression of several insurrections, be brought to submit to the political Inquisition.*

But the irritation of the nobles of Aragon against the Inquisition was raised to such a height, that, on the 15th September, 1485, they assassinated the first royal inquisitor of Seville, Dr. Peter Arbues, of Epila, canon of Saragossa, whilst singing the matins in the church. This outrage was, however, the very cause of the political Inquisition taking a firmer footing in this country.†

Modern historians, whose researches have at once been more accurate and impartial, have thoroughly recognized the political character of the Spanish Inquisition. Ranke testifies to it in the following words :—

"We have a celebrated book on the Inquisition by Llorente, and if I am so bold as to say anything in opposition to him, it is only because this well-informed author wrote in the interest of the Alfrancesados and the government of Joseph. He, consequently, contests the privileges of the Basque provinces, although they can hardly be denied, and considers the Inquisition a usurpation of the spiritual power over the political. But I must be much mistaken if, on the contrary, the result of the facts adduced by him does not show that the Inquisition was only a royal tribunal, furnished with spiritual weapons. In the first place, the inquisitors were royal officials. The king had the right

---

* They fared in this similarly to the Templars in the fourteenth century, who insisted upon being tried by the old Inquisition, well aware, as the historians of the order say, that they could expect milder and juster treatment of this institution than of Philip the Fair of France.

† Blancas, p. 264, calls Arbues and his colleague the Dominican, Caspar Inglar, " duo egregii et præstantes viri ;" and Arbues especially, " vir justus, optimus, singulari bonitate et modestia præditus, imprimisque literis exaltus et doctrina."

to appoint and dismiss them, and, independent of the
other councils belonging to the court, had a council
of the Inquisition. The tribunals of the Inquisition
were subject to the same royal visitations as other
bodies, and their assessors were often men who held
seats in the highest court of justice of Castile.
Ximenez in vain opposed the introduction of a
layman into the council of the Inquisition, who had
been nominated by Ferdinand the Catholic, 'Do
you not know,' said the king, 'that if this council
has any jurisdiction whatever, it is only owing to
the king?' As regards the measures which, Llorente says, were projected against Charles V. and
Philip II., it is indeed evident, from his own
account, that Paul IV., then in open war with
emperor and king, proposed proceedings against
them, but we cannot learn from him if their proposals were accepted, or even attempted to be carried
out.* Secondly, the profits from the confiscations
of this tribunal fell to the king . . . the proceeds of
these confiscations formed a sort of regular revenue
for the royal treasury. Thirdly, the state was first
rendered entirely independent by the Inquisition,
the king thereby becoming the master of a tribunal
from which neither grandee nor archbishop could
withdraw. Foreigners were particularly shocked
by this. 'The Inquisition,' says Segni, 'has been

---

* Ranke states the facts incorrectly. It is true, Paul IV., embittered against Charles, threatened him and his son Philip with
the Inquisition ; but, of course, he intrusted the inquiry not to the
Spanish State Inquisition, but to the Roman tribunal, which had
to declare whether the emperor had not made too great concessions to the Protestants of Germany. Paul charged the Spanish
inquisitors only with the trial of those theologians, who, like
Melchior Carus, had advised Charles " to force the Pope to yield."
But Charles protected Carus, and his Inquisition had to act after
his will.—(Llorente, tom. ii. p. 172—176.)

invented to rob the rich of their possessions, and the mighty of their authority.'

"When Charles knew no other means of arraigning the bishops who had lent assistance to the committees in their revolt, he ordered the Inquisition to try them. When Philip despaired of his ability to punish Antonio Perez, he called the Inquisition to his aid. Accordingly, as this tribunal reposed on the authority of the king, its administration turned to the profit of the royal power. It belonged to those spoliations of the Church by which this reign became powerful, for instance, the management of the grand-mastership, the appointment of the bishops—but in its spirit and aim it was intrinsically a political institution. It was of importance to the popes to throw obstacles in its way, and they did so as often as they could. The kings, on the other hand, were interested in advancing its power constantly."*

The opinions of Henry Leo on the Inquisition are similar to those of Leopold Ranke. "Isabella," he says, "knew how to break the nobles and the clergy of Castile by means of an ecclesiastical institution entirely dependent on her, and equally directed against laymen and clergy;" and further—"These sovereigns knowing how to employ, as political agents, other and similar institutions in the rest of their dominions, in the same manner in which they had made use of the Inquisition in Castile, to undermine the power of the nobles and the clergy, the greater part of the peninsula advanced, under their rule, at the end of the middle ages, towards absolute monarchism."

* Ranke, vol. i. p. 245. " It is evident from the letters of Visconti, the papal nuncio, of the year 1563, that Rome ascribed to the Spanish Inquisition a great decrease of the papal authority (gran diminuzione dell' autorità di questa santa sede)."

Guizot's opinion coincides with the above : " The Inquisition was, at first, more political than ecclesiastical, and destined rather to uphold order than to defend the faith." Professor Havemann expresses himself much in the same manner in his "Essay on Ximenez:" " Royalty and the Inquisition have frequently been regarded as, two distinct powers to which Spain was then subjected. Yet the Inquisition has, at no time, occupied here a position independent of the crown, although in the days of Ferdinand it was not as much a political instrument as it became during the reign of Philip II. Avarice, and the desire to undermine the national freedom of Spain, were no less the causes of the establishment of this institution than zeal for the Church. The king appointed the president, and himself prepared his instructions, whilst the ratification of the Holy See was only sought to save the forms in the eyes of the Church : the assessors were sometimes nominated by the king, sometimes by the president in his name. Neither grandee nor archbishop could withdraw from this tribunal, nor even the three powerful knightly orders, which, by virtue of their ' fueros,' had long maintained an independence difficult to be reconciled with the power of royalty."

To these opinions of eminent Protestant scholars we add a few from the writings of not less distinguished Catholics. Lenormant, formerly substitute for M. Guizot in the professorship of history, speaks in the following terms : " The Inquisition, in its original conception and its essence, was not an ecclesiastical, but a political institution ; and far from abhorring the enormity of a justice which covered her mysteries with an impenetrable veil, the Spaniard felt even proud of possessing so excellent an institution. The very fact of this secret tribunal having been principally composed of civil functionaries* is a decided proof of its character; and the Inquisition was nothing more than a police excellently served, admitting no distinction of persons."†

The celebrated Count de Maistre observes: "Many believe the Inquisition to have been a tribunal purely ecclesiastical; this is false . . . . the tribunal of the Inquisition was purely royal. It was the king who appointed the Inquisitor-general, who, in his turn, nominated the councillors, subject to the approval of the king. The rules for this tribunal were issued in the year 1484 by Cardinal Torquemada, in concert with the king."‡ In the same manner, the ultra-liberal Cortes of 1812 expressed themselves: "The Spanish kings have always rejected the advice given to them against the Inquisition, because they could in all cases, and at their pleasure, nominate, suspend, or remove the councillors."§ It is, therefore, not without reason that Charles V., who knew how to govern, and loved absolute power, recommended the Inquisition so warmly to his successor in his will, *that he might be able properly to discharge his duties as sovereign.*

The correctness of these opinions of the political character of the Inquisition is clearly shown by the very statutes of the year 1484. All the paragraphs stamp the Inquisition unmistakably as a political

---

* This is incorrect. Most of the members were priests, but *secular* priests; hence the misconception of Lenormant.

† Spittler, in his interesting preface to Reuss's collection of the instructions of the Spanish Inquisition, bears testimony to this truth when he says, p. xiv.: "It was an instrument in the hands of the kings who sought to establish absolutism on the ruins of the great national liberties." P. xv.: "The new tribunal was merely a royal one." P. xviii.: "Everything to the interest of the king and—not the Church."

‡ Lettres sur l'Inquisition, pp. 11, 12.   § Pp. 37, 38.

Y

institution, and expressions like the following recur constantly :—"*Their Highnesses* [that is, Ferdinand and Isabella] will, ordain, command ;" — " *their Highnesses* pardon ;"—" it is not at all the intention of *their Highnesses ;*"—" the Most Serene Sovereigns the *King and the Queen* ordain, approve, &c. ;" whilst no mention is made of the will and the dispositions of the ecclesiastical power.

The Portuguese Inquisition was equally considered a political institution by the sovereigns of that country. This is evident from the decree of the minister Piombal, of the 20th March, 1769. " I have been informed," says King Joseph I., "that, contrary to the usage of all other tribunals, which have at all times taken, and still take, the title of Majesty, because they represent my royal person, an abuse has crept into the Holy Office to adopt a different address, *though this tribunal, by its organization and its service, is immediately and more than any other attached to my royal person.*" The king proceeds farther on—" As the members of the council of the Holy Office exercise my royal jurisdiction not only in criminal and disciplinarian matters against all who offend against religion, but also in civil matters against the privileged classes, as I am further acquainted that the intrigues of the so-called Jesuits profit by this abuse (namely, the suppression of the title of *majesty* by the council of the Inquisition) to lower the authority of this tribunal, I ordain that the general council (of the Inquisition) be, in all addresses, writings, and petitions, treated as *majesty.*"*

But for that very reason that the Inquisition, as we have seen, was closely connected with political absolutism, and perhaps its most powerful weapon,

* Colecção de Legislaçao Portugueza (Lisbon, 1829), tom. ii. p. 379, et seq.

the Inquisition was necessarily compelled to die as soon as the absolute power of the monarch vanished. This is, in few and striking words, said already in Art. II. of the decree of suppression, issued by the Spanish Cortes on the 22nd February, 1813 :—" El tribunal de la Inquisicion es imcompatible con la constitucion." And when, on the return of Ferdinand VII., in the year 1814, the old monarchy was re-established, the Inquisition was immediately revived to keep down the demagogues ; but as soon as Ferdinand, in the year 1820, had been compelled to grant again a constitution, the Inquisition was once more suppressed. Similar events happened in Portugal and other states; the Inquisition stood and fell with political absolutism.

This correct estimate of the object and political character of the Inquisition has, in our times, produced a more just appreciation of this institution and its effects. History, which, in general, of late has been freed from many often-repeated falsehoods, has also learned better to appreciate facts connected with the history of the Inquisition. Before, therefore, we proceed to examine what part Ximenez took in the proceedings of the Holy Office, truth, not the desire to defend that institution, induces us to make the following observations :—

1. The Inquisition has often been unjustly judged according to the principles of the *nineteenth* century, instead of those of the *fifteenth* and *sixteenth*. Whilst many, for the last hundred years and more, were inclined to see in heretics and infidels of all kinds the most enlightened and honourable citizens of the state, the Inquisition, in direct opposition, was based on the opinions of the Middle Ages, according to which heresy was high treason, and only such subjects were safe and worthy of confidence as conformed to the religion of the state. It is natural

that the defenders of modern ideas cannot appreciate
and judge impartially facts which find their reasons
in those of former ages, if they are unable to divest
themselves of the ideas of the present time, and to
think themselves into those of the past. Every true
historian does this.   But the Inquisition has mostly
been described by such writers as tried to substitute
mere words and assertions for sound and conscientious researches; gave romantic descriptions for real
facts, and hid their want of absolute knowledge under
liberal phrases.   Persons of this kind understood of
course not the maxim, cujus est regis, illius est religio,
—on which the whole Inquisition is based, and which
formerly was thoroughly and universally recognized,
and so little contested, that Protestants in particular
have defended it and carried it into practice.   The
Palatinate may serve as an example.   Here the
Elector Frederick III., who had been a Lutheran,
after having turned Calvinist in the year 1563,
forced all his subjects to do the same; and expelled
from his country all who would not adopt the
Heidelberg catechism.   Thirteen years later, in the
year 1576, his son Ludwig re-established the old
Lutheran confession, drove away the Calvinistic
preachers and teachers, and forced his subjects to
become Lutherans again. In 1583, the Elector John
Casimir, in his office of guardian to Frederick IV.,
introduced Calvinism once more, and with equal
severity; so that the Palatinate has sufficiently
experienced that conformity to the religion of the
state and court was enforced not in Spain only, and
by Ferdinand the Catholic, but also in Germany
and by Protestant princes, and that the severest
civil punishments were inflicted by them upon dis-
senters. Spain has indeed not acted otherwise than
the Lutherans and Calvinists in Germany. The
Peace of Religion, concluded at Augsburg 26th

September, 1555, gives, in paragraph 24, to every state of the empire full powers to put to their subjects the alternative either of adopting the religion of the state or emigrating, on payment of a certain fine; just as the Jews and Moors were treated in Spain. It is well known that precisely to this lenient Spanish measure the Reformation owes much of its extension in Germany. It can, moreover, not be doubted that mild treatment was not to be expected in Germany by those who, obeying outwardly only the dictates of their Protestant princes, and adhering to the old faith, sought to re-establish it again in the dominions of their masters. But it may be doubted whether it was worse to fall into the hands of the Spanish Inquisition than into those of a zealous Lutheran prince.

2. It is, further, often forgotten, in judging the Inquisition, that the criminal law of those days was frequently more cruel and bloody than that of the present century. Many offences which now are punished but slightly, called formerly for blood. The most striking proof of the criminal justice of those times to which the Inquisition owes its origin, is the Carolina, or penal code of Charles V., of the year 1532. Blasphemy against God and the Blessed Virgin is therein (in sect. 106) punished with mutilation and death; (sect. 116), pederasty and sodomy with death on the stake; (sect. 106), sorcery with death. Even purely civil offences are visited with similar severity. So coiners and persons circulating base coin knowingly are (sect. 111) condemned to the flames; (sect. 113), defaulters of measures and weights to flogging, or, if the offence be great, to death; (sect. 159—162), burglars, however large or small the thefts might be, to death by hanging, to blinding, to the chopping off of the hand, &c.; whilst repetitions of the same crime

were punished with death. In a similar manner the smallest offences against the safety of the roads were punished with death in France; and the cruel measures used formerly against poachers are well known.

On looking further back in history, we do not meet with greater mildness in the laws, but, on the contrary, find that the penalties were even more severe *before* the compilation of the Carolina, especially in the application of torture; so that the penal code of the great emperor may be called mild if compared to the earlier practice. Nay, in the very century which gave birth to the Inquisition, one of the wisest and most liberal men of Europe, the celebrated Chancellor of Paris, Gerson, recommended pain of death to be applied even to pope and cardinals, if their actions were detrimental to the interests of the Church. If Gerson did not recoil from advising such stringent measures against the highest authorities of the world, what could heretics of impure blood expect in Spain?

But in the same degree in which the treatment of heretics bore relation to the criminal justice of those days, in the same degree their treatment became less severe under the milder laws of subsequent times. Llorente even acknowledges this; nor are his followers in the Cyclopædia of Ersch and Gruber silent upon it.

3. It must further not be overlooked, that *pain of death* against heretics was not decreed by the Inquisition only, but was common to all countries and to all confessions. We have before, at page 277, adduced the ancient code of Suevia as testimony; but a better witness still is *Michael Servetus*, of whom the well-known reformer Bucer said, in 1531, whilst delivering, at Strasburg, a public sermon from the pulpit, that he deserved the most miserable

death for his work against the Trinity. And Calvin showed, twenty-two years later, that this was not idle talk of the reformer, by having, on the 27th October, 1553, the "heretic" burned at the stake by a small fire. To justify which act the great reformer wrote his work : "Fidelis Expositio Errorum Michælis Serveti, et brevis eorum Refutatio, ubi docetur, jure gladii coërcendos esse Hæreticos." And to place it quite out of doubt that the Protestants of those times wished to have capital punishment inflicted upon heretics, the "mild" Melancthon wrote to Calvin : "*I have read thy book in which thou hast fully refuted the horrible blasphemies of Servetus, and thank the Son of the Lord for having awarded thee the victory in the contest thou hast sustained. The Church owes thee now and for ever eternal gratitude for this. I quite agree with thy opinion, and maintain that thy tribunal has acted in accordance with justice, in having, after due investigation, put to death a blasphemer.*"* For superabundance I may add that also Theodore Beza composed a work : "De Hæreticis a Magistratu civili puniendis ;" and that, besides Servetus, many others, as for instance, Valentine Gentilis, Bolsec, Carolstadt, Castello, Judge Ameaux, by their imprisonment, banishment, or death, learned that the Inquisition of the Protestant church was not less severe than that of Spain. Many Protestants, as for instance, Prescott, in his "History of Ferdinand and Isabella," acknowledge this. But there is no need for going back as far as the sixteenth century, or even for recalling the horrible atrocities committed against the Catholics in England, to furnish pendants to the Spanish Inquisition among the Protestants. A singular case of this kind is recorded by Pfeil-

---

* Schröckh : Neuere Kirchengeschichte, vol. v. p. 517.

schifter of a young soldier, who, convicted of having entered into a pact with the devil, was, at Rendsburg, in Holstein, in the year 1724, *decapitated* by the mercy of the king. Nay, even in our days, that is, on the 3rd April, 1844, the painter J. O. Nilson, for having apostatized and embraced a heretic religion (the Catholic), was banished from Sweden, his civil and hereditary rights declared forfeited, and this judgment confirmed by the highest tribunal of the land. The unfortunate Nilson died in misery at Copenhagen, in February, 1847. This is not intended as a reproach. Our only object is to show, that the Protestants had also adopted the sanguinary principle, that "deviation from the Church of the country is to be punished by death;" and that Sweden adheres to this doctrine, slightly modified, to the present day. If the sixteenth and seventeenth centuries had doubted the correctness of this principle, the Protestants ought necessarily to have been the first to raise scruples, as their own apostasy should have made them indulgent towards other converts.

4. Amongst the victims of the Inquisition, the so-called *witches* and *sorcerers* form a considerable portion. It is needless to prove at length, that these unfortunate persons were persecuted just as much in Germany as in Spain, and as mercilessly by Protestants as by Catholics. Not Torquemada only, but two hundred years later, Benedict Carpzov also delivered them to the flames. The Reformer Beza reproaches the French parliaments with negligence in the persecution of witches; and Walter Scott owns that, the more Calvinism extended in England, the more numerous became the trials for witchcraft. Seventy years before the Protestant *Thomasius* shook the belief in witches amongst his co-religionists, the Jesuit *Frederick Spee, of Langen-*

feld,* had done so amongst the Catholics. As late as 1713, the Faculty of Law at Tubingen condemned a witch to death; and, one year later than in Spain, in 1782, the last witch was burned in the canton of Glarus, tried and condemned by a *reformed* tribunal. In general, a comparison of the German trials of witches with the proceedings of the Spanish Inquisition, would hardly be to the advantage of the former.

5. Moreover, it must not be forgotten that the tribunal of the Inquisition confined itself to *the* sentence, that the accused be more or less, entirely, partly, or not at all, guilty of heresy, blasphemy, or other crimes. The tribunal has never pronounced pain of death, but its sentence was, nevertheless, followed by this punishment; those found " guilty of heresy " by the Holy Office, being handed over to the secular arm, which, and in particular the Council of Castile, the highest Spanish court of justice, condemned them to death or prison. We learn from the sentence of the Inquisition, cited by Count de Maistre,† that the tribunals always pleaded in behalf of the convicted heretic. This document is the more trustworthy, as it was first published by the author of the book, " The Inquisition Unmasked," one of the bitterest enemies of the Inquisition.‡ He thinks, it is true, that this intercession was mere idle form, and to strengthen his assertion, cites the canon law of the celebrated Van Espen (tom. i. pars ii., tit. x. ch. iv. & xxi.), but, apart from this author treating there of something totally different,

---

* Leibnitz, in his Theodicée, I., secs. 96, 97, has erected a beautiful monument to this noble and zealous priest.

† Lettres, p. 32.

‡ Don Antonio Puigblanch, under the pseudonym Nathaniel Jomtob. See Balmes about this incorrect and fanatic Spanish writer.

namely, the intercession of the bishop in behalf of a priest about to be handed to the secular arm, such forms, even if they at last became mere phrases, which we will not deny, unmistakably had originally a real meaning; which opinion is held also by Van Espen in the passage just quoted.

6. The Spanish Inquisition is generally represented as an offshoot of Romish intolerance; but the popes, especially, were least favourable to this institution, and have at all times tried to reduce its power and influence. Even Llorente, who can as little be called a partisan of Papacy as a Jacobin can be called a friend of royalty, shows in almost numberless cases and examples the truth of this assertion.

a. From the very beginning, Pope Sixtus IV. was little pleased with the royal plan of the new Inquisition, and the relations between the Spanish and Pontifical courts became, in consequence, so constrained, that the ambassadors of both were imprisoned, and Ferdinand's subjects recalled from Rome. We know that Sixtus at last yielded to the impetuosity of the king, by granting the bull of the 1st November, 1478. But when complaints of the severity of the first inquisitors reached the Holy See, he issued, on the 29th of January, 1482, the energetic brief, of which we have spoken before, in which he declared the preceding bull as surreptitiously obtained, and notified to the inquisitors, under strong censure, that nothing but his regard for the sovereign deterred him from dismissing them. To put a stop for the future to similar excesses of the inquisitors, he further ordered in this brief, that they were henceforth only allowed to proceed against heretics in concert with the bishops of the diocese. And further on, he opposes the intention of Ferdinand and Isabella to introduce the same Inquisition into other provinces of their dominions, because the old, namely the ecclesiastical and episcopal tribunals, already existed. And when Isabella, not long after, desired the abolition of the concurrence of the bishops being obligatory in the proceedings of the Inquisition, Sixtus, in many polite phrases, again sent a refusal.

b. At about the same time, in the year 1483, the Pope tried further to diminish the severity of the Spanish inquisitors, by appointing the archbishop of Seville, Manrique, judge of appeals, to whom such as were treated with too great severity by the Holy Office, could address themselves.

c. But when the Pope found that these were not better protected by the archbishop than before, he received himself the appeals against the sentences of the Inquisition, suppressed numerous cases, modified certain punishments, and demanded milder treatment for those who repented and abjured heresy. He even went so far as to implore the king and queen, by the mercy of Christ, to be merciful and lenient towards such of their subjects as had fallen into error.* Ferdinand, however, and afterwards his grandson, Charles V., endeavoured to frustrate all these appeals to the Papal court, causing thereby many disagreeable embroilments with the Holy See. They demanded that all those against whom the Inquisition had pronounced sentence, should address their appeals to the royal minister of justice, and not to the Papal court. And as they had from the beginning considered the Inquisition only a political institution, the consistency of their demand cannot be called into question.

d. The popes endeavoured, besides, to mitigate the severity of the Inquisition by trying to regain

---

* The edict is to be found in Llorente, tom. iv. p. 365.

the restitution of the property and civil rights of
many condemned persons, preventing by this the
impoverishment of numberless families.   We know
this from the best source; for anything advanced by
Llorente in *favour* of the popes, must of necessity be
an undeniable fact.

e. The children of the condemned were a matter
of special solicitude to the popes.   They endeavoured
to shield them from suffering together with their
parents, and from being punished with infamy
and confiscation of their property.   Unfortunately,
numerous Papal edicts to this purpose were disregarded by royal command.*

f. The benevolence of the popes did not end here.
To guard repenting heretics, they repeatedly ordered
the inquisitors to absolve such penitents secretly,
in order to save them from civil punishments and
public shame.   Thus *fifty* heretics were secretly
absolved by virtue of an order of the Pope, of the
11th February, 1486; another fifty by an order of the
30th May, of the same year; an equal number on
the following day; and again fifty by a fourth brief
of the 30th June.   One month later, on the 30th
July, 1486, the Pope issued a fifth edict for secret
absolution.   Llorente does not state the number to
whom the favour was extended, but he does say
that these Papal edicts of grace were very frequently
disregarded on the part of the Spanish government.

g. Under Julius II. and Leo X. the appeals to
the Papal court not only continued, but we learn,
even from Llorente, numerous cases in which these
popes appointed special judges to rescue the appel-
lants from the hands of the Inquisition.   Frequently,
also, the popes notified their will to the grand inqui-

---

* In a similar manner Pope Clement IV., in the thirteenth
century, endeavoured to mitigate the severity of the French laws
against blasphemers.—De Maistre, p. 23.

sitors, in special edicts and strong terms, to liberate less guilty prisoners. To others they remitted the punishment of carrying the san benito, or shirt of penitence; removed this sign from the graves of persons over which it had been hung as an addition to their punishments, and, in general, saved the memory of numerous deceased from ignominy. Many of these Papal mitigations had the intended effect, but many miscarried, because the Spanish kings, Ferdinand the Catholic, and Charles V., in particular, frequently intimidated the judges delegated by the Pope to replace the inquisitors, or opposed the execution of the Papal briefs. Sometimes the Spanish inquisitors suppressed the Papal edicts of mercy, or had their sentences so quickly executed, that the protests of the pope arrived too late, or even went so far as formally to refuse to obey them. But the soul of this opposition was always the Spanish government, bent upon rendering null the Papal mediation, frustrating the appeals, and making the Inquisition entirely independent of the Church.

h. The inquisitors were often called to account by the Pope, or his nuncio, or his delegate, and threatened with excommunication if they persisted in persecuting persons who had sought aid at the Papal court. This excommunication was repeatedly carried into effect, as, for instance, by Leo X. against the inquisitors of Toledo, to the great annoyance of Charles V.

i. Sentences pronounced by the Inquisition, and already half carried out, were at times cancelled by the popes. For instance, that against Virues, the preacher to Charles V., who, being suspected of holding Lutheran views, was condemned to be imprisoned in a cloister, but by Pope Paul III., in the year 1538, declared innocent, and able to fill all

ecclesiastical offices. Virues became afterwards
bishop of the Canary Islands.

k. To deter witnesses from giving false evidence
in the tribunals of the Inquisition, Leo X. decreed,
on the 14th December, 1518, pain of death against
them.

l. Leo X., irritated by the disregard shown to
several of his edicts of mercy, purposed, in the year
1519, an entire reorganization of the Inquisition.
All the inquisitors then in office were to be removed,
and two canons to be presented by each bishop to
the grand-inquisitor, one of whom was to be appointed provincial-inquisitor; but even this nomination to be subject to the approval of the Holy See,
and the new inquisitors to be carefully visited every
two years. But Charles strained every nerve to
frustrate this intention of the Pope, and to prevent
the three briefs already issued by the same, from
being carried into execution. And as during the
negotiations Charles had become emperor of Rome,
the Pope desisted from pressing the matter further,
in order to avoid the dangers of a rupture. To
frighten the Pope, the Spanish ambassador even
advised his master apparently to favour Luther,
which, however, did not deter Leo from declaring
that the Spanish Inquisition worked much mischief.

m. We have seen above, how in later years the
popes, especially Gregory XIII., continued their
efforts to soften the rigorous measures of the Inquisition. Llorente supplies us with more ample
information. Paul III. in particular complained
bitterly of the Spanish Inquisition, and protected
those who endeavoured to hinder its introduction
into Naples. Pius IV. and his nephew, the great
St. Charles Borromeo, acted similarly by opposing
the introduction of the Spanish Inquisition into
Milan. Llorente avows openly that the Spanish

government had long made it their special business always to take the part of the inquisitors whenever the Papal court decreed anything which was displeasing to them.

A convincing proof of the little influence possessed by the Holy See over the Spanish Inquisition is furnished by the trial of the celebrated Bollandists. Since the year 1683, complaints had been made in Belgium against the learned Jesuit Daniel Papebroch, and the works of the Bollandists, then edited by him. These complaints found their way to Spain, and were brought before the Inquisition of Toledo, which, in the year 1695, issued an edict, condemning the first fourteen volumes of the "Acta Sanctorum," on account of alleged heretical propositions, although popes, cardinals, bishops, and other distinguished Catholic notabilities, had constantly praised and in every way supported the work. Father Papebroch in vain defended himself and his work in various Latin and Spanish pamphlets, as well as in a special letter to the grand-inquisitor. He received no answer, nor were the heretical propositions pointed out to him. When the matter was brought to Rome, Pope Innocent XII. did not hesitate calling the decree of the Inquisition a *fiera censura*, and several cardinals, amongst them the celebrated Cardinal Henry Noris, declared themselves decidedly in favour of the learned Jesuit. The Congregatio Indicis, however, would not pronounce either of the two contending parties wrong, but in the year 1698 imposed silence on both, which did not prevent Cardinal Noris from openly saying that regard for Spain had been the only reason for not pronouncing the Bollandists entirely innocent.*

* The complete history of this trial is to be found in Bollandi Thesaurus Eccles. Antiquitatis ... seu Præfationes, Tractatus, &c. tom. i. pp. 92, 95, 97, 350; tom. iii. pp. 149, 150, 152, 305. 306, et seq.

All this shows that the Papal See has acted an honourable part in the history of the Inquisition, and was, as it has at all times been, a protector of the persecuted.

But the Inquisition has also to be cleared of many unjust reproaches, which we will endeavour to do here.

7. The cruel *tortures* and *torments* of all kinds to which prisoners were subjected in the prisons of the Inquisition, are particularly dwelt upon. But let us recall to those who shudder at the bare mention of them, that the torture in those days was used *by all civil courts of all countries*—nay, that it legally existed in many German states as late as the present century, and fell practically into disuse only about the middle of the last, *simultaneously in the Inquisition and the civil courts*. It is certain, says Llorente, that the Inquisition has long ceased to condemn prisoners to the torture; so that this punishment may now (writing at the beginning of this century) be considered abolished. As long as the torture was not abolished by *law*, the *fiscal* of each tribunal had, in certain cases, to propose its application; but the judges never sanctioned it, and Llorente observes justly: "The fiscal would have been sorry had his proposition been complied with." This is common to all courts of justice in all states. Severe legislation, as, for instance, the Carolina in Germany, existed still as law when it had long ceased to be carried out in practice.

The above remarks of Llorente explain and confirm also an anecdote told by the Count de Maistre in his "Letters on the Inquisition." He relates that he had, in the year 1803, met two distinguished and well-informed Spaniards, with whom he conversed on the Inquisition and the application of the torture. They looked at each other in astonishment, he continued, and assured me most positively never to have heard anything about it in their own country. Quite natural; for, according to Llorente's own confession, the torture had long ceased to exist.

It requires but little love of truth to convince oneself that the Inquisition used at least not more severity in the treatment of its victims than the other courts of justice of those times, both in Catholic and Protestant countries. A simple comparison with the Carolina will suffice to dispel all doubts on the subject. The penal code of Charles V. not only speaks of execution by fire and sword, of quartering, the wheel, the gibbet, and death by drowning, but also of burying alive, of tearing with red-hot pincers, of the loss of the tongue, the ears and hands, &c. The Inquisition knows absolutely *nothing* of all these barbarous and painful punishments. Add to this, that at a time when the prisons in the whole of Europe were damp, impure holes, into which neither air nor light penetrated, veritable graves, full of putrefaction and pestilential atmosphere, those of the Inquisition were, to speak with Llorente, "well-vaulted, light, and dry rooms."* "No prisoner of the Inquisition"† (we quote him again) "ever sighed under the weight of chains, handcuffs, iron collars, &c. ; he knows of one only who was put in fetters, and he to hinder him from committing suicide. The prisoners were asked if they were treated well by the gaoler; the sick were properly nursed. For the prisoners for life, special buildings, called penitentiaries, were erected, which were periodically the object of scrupulous investigation.

* The same assurance was recently given to Ferdinand III. by his grand-inquisitor.—De Maistre.

† The statutes of the year 1484 admitted the repetition of the torture ; but this severity was soon after abolished.

We must, moreover, not omit to mention that the civil legislation, the Carolina in sections 55 and 57, admits the repetition of torture to extort confession, whilst, again according to Llorente, the great council of the Inquisition from time to time impressed on the provincial inquisitors that the torture was admissible but once in one and the same trial, and always to cease as soon as the physician in attendance considered the life of the prisoner in danger. It is true, Llorente adds, that the sub-inquisitors often evaded these benevolent orders of their superiors, by having the torture applied a second time, under the pretext that it was only a continuation of the first ; but everybody knows how frequently inferior functionaries, even in the present century, are severer than the stern law itself. We must, besides, take into consideration that the Inquisition, at its very commencement, often threatened with the torture without applying it, and that the grand council of the Inquisition, as early as the year 1537, forbade almost every application of this punishment against the Moriscos.* No other court of justice of that time can boast of similar benevolence. Other wise and precautionary measures were soon introduced. According to one, the provincial tribunals had no power to impose the punishment of torture, but only the grand council of the Inquisition. According to another, this power was vested in the bishop of the diocese, acting in concert with the councillors and the inquisitor ; but the punishment could be inflicted only after the accused had exhausted all means for his defence. In this case, to avoid all brutal treatment, the bishop, the coun-

---

* The torture was, in the civilized states in general, legally abolished only in the present century, in the Inquisition by a decree of Pope Pius VII. of the year 1816.

cillors, and the inquisitor were necessitated to attend each application of the torture.

So sure, therefore, as it cannot be denied that the torture was a stain on the old criminal legislation, so unjust it would be to blame the Inquisition exclusively for proceedings which were admitted, and unhappily too often carried into effect by enlightened Athens, by Rome, learned in the law, and by all the courts of justice of all countries in ancient times, and during the middle ages.

8. It has further grown customary to look upon the Inquisition as a rapacious monster, constantly lying in wait for its victims, ready and eager, on the slightest suspicion, to snatch them up. This representation, which works so powerfully in historical romances and romantic histories, is totally wrong and perverted, and must be altogether dismissed, if Llorente is not to be accused of being a partisan of the Inquisition.

a. Each tribunal began its activity by promulgating a *time of grace*, announcing publicly that "every one would be absolved and saved from heavy punishments who, conscious of apostasy, presented himself within the limited time, and did penance."

Such penitents had, of course, to undergo smaller, and especially ecclesiastical punishments, and their penance was required to be public if their apostasy had been also public. These measures, though based on the old discipline of the Church, are, nevertheless, commented upon by Llorente, who certainly, as priest, ought to have known from his own experience, that ecclesiastical punishments, vindicativæ as well as medicinales, are imposed even upon those who confess of their own free will. Besides, the statutes of the Inquisition ordered the mildest possible treatment for such penitents.

Although after the expiration of the term of grace,

the rigour of the law was to be resorted to against the apostates, these terms were repeatedly renewed and prolonged. So, on the occasion of the removal of the tribunal from Villareal to Toledo, a time of grace of forty days was fixed. Llorente relates—"A great number of new Christians were seen hastening to confess of their own accord their relapse into Judaism." And he continues, "The term having expired, the inquisitors accorded an extension of *sixty* days and another of *thirty* days."

b. The statutes of the Inquisition, referring to youthful heretics, merit our full attention. By a decree of Torquemada, the sons and daughters of heretics who had not yet reached their *twentieth* year, and who, through the advice and instruction of their parents had fallen into error, were, if they presented themselves for absolution of their own free will, to be kindly received, even *after the expiration of the term of grace;* their exercises of penitence to be less heavy than those of grown-up persons; and their instruction in the faith and the sacraments of the holy mother Church to be properly cared for. Boys under fourteen and girls under twelve years of age were unable solemnly to abjure heresy. This, because the punishments for relapse being severe, the Inquisition wished to guard young people against the possibility of a relapse, by allowing them only to renounce heresy when their understanding had become more mature.

c. The slightest and most innocent expressions, it is asserted, were sufficient to throw the unfortunate persons into the prisons of the Inquisition. But the second grand-inquisitor *Deza,* whose severity is considered to have surpassed that of Torquemada himself, decreed, on the 17th June, 1500, "that nobody could be arrested for matters of slight importance, nor even for blasphemies, if uttered in a fit of anger.

d. If any one was accused of having spoken heretical language, the Inquisition first inquired of the physician if debility of mind might not be the cause of the punishable expressions of the prisoner. Llorente does not allude to this precaution; but in a trial of the Inquisition in Sicily, where, at the beginning of the sixteenth century, the ecclesiastical Inquisition had made way for the Spanish one, express mention is made of the tribunal having consulted, under oath, several medical men on the mental condition of the accused.

e. The tribunals of the Inquisition were not disposed to listen indiscriminately to every denunciation. Llorente relates, on the contrary, many cases in which only *repeated* accusations could induce the Inquisition to proceed against a person. They were more inclined to consider the mad behaviour of many of the heretics the result of mental derangement.

f. It may in addition be boldly asserted that no other court of justice of that time was bound by so many restrictions and conditions in the grant of orders for arrest. Torquemada, in the first article of his statutes of the 25th May, 1498, decrees, "At each tribunal are to assist two inquisitors, the one a jurist,* the other a theologian, who are forbidden to issue an order for arrest otherwise than by mutual consent." Article III. of these statutes declares, "No person can be imprisoned whose crime is not placed beyond doubt by sufficient evidence." If the inquisitors did not agree, or the suspected was a person of some importance, for instance, an eccle-

---

* This jurist was generally also an ecclesiastic.

siastic, the arrest could be ordered only by the grand council. Philip II. extended this even more, and King Charles IV. decreed that the Inquisition was not allowed to arrest any one without first having acquainted the king. The tales of secret arrests, according to which persons had suddenly disappeared without leaving a trace behind, are therefore mere fables, the more so, as each prisoner had a special administrator appointed for his property, and the arrest itself was subject to numerous formalities.

The right of the Inquisition to imprison was still further restricted. If any one was accused of heretical expressions, and his heresy not quite clear, the tribunal had to obtain the opinion of a commission of learned theologians, professors, &c., called *qualificators*, who, without being directly connected with the Inquisition, indorsed their opinion in a document signed by them, and decided whether the suspicious (spoken or printed) propositions were really heretical or not. In the latter case, the arrest could not take place, unless other qualificators, consulted before, had given a different decision. Llorente, indeed, complains that these qualificators were principally *scholastic* theologians, but *freemasons*, which he probably would have preferred, they certainly could then not have been.

9. Many accuse the Inquisition of barbarous cruelty; of having in its trials sought not truth, but the conviction of the prisoners; and of having used all manner of cunning and intrigue to find even the most innocent guilty.

a. Llorente, for one, pretends that the Maranos and Moriscos were interrogated on points which so little support a suspicion of heresy, that the most orthodox Christians might permit themselves to do things for which those unfortunate persons were condemned by the Inquisition. Prescott echoes this assertion; but we have already alluded to the invalidity of the accusation, and shown that many actions of converted Jews or Mohammedans would raise just suspicions, which a Christian by birth might do with little danger of seeing them misconstrued. It is, for instance, very harmless to wash a child immediately after baptism on those parts of the body where it was anointed with the holy oil. But this action assumes a different aspect if done by a convert from Judaism, especially if his conversion seems not to have been very sincere. Most of the points, however, on which the Maranos and Moriscos were questioned were really such as would prove apostasy, among which may be reckoned the circumcision of a child, the assertion that the Mosaic law possessed the same efficacy for salvation as the gospel, and other matters.

Prescott imagines that he has discovered, in a glaring case, the most monstrous tyranny in the proceedings of the Inquisition. "The Christian Jew," he says, " became suspected of relapse, if he gave his children names from the Old Testament, whilst he was forbidden to give them such as belong to the New." Our indignation would be just, if this assertion were true; but it is utterly false, because Prescott confounds Jews with *Christian* Jews. Those Jews who adhered to their religion were forbidden to give *Christian* names to their children, but not so those who had been converts to Christianity. Whilst the former were punishable for giving their children names from the New Testament, the latter became equally so for choosing for theirs names from the Old.

b. Every court of justice is exposed to receive false witnesses against or in favour of the accused, but a tribunal loving justice will punish them equally; the former one because it aims at truth, and not at the conviction of the criminal; the latter one because it cannot suffer justice to yield to falsehood. The Inquisition acted in this respect the same as other courts. Article VIII. of its statutes of the year 1498 decrees that false witnesses are to be publicly punished. Llorente makes use of a wrong artifice in trying to make us believe that by false witnesses such were principally understood as spoke in *favour* of the accused, whilst those who made *calumnious* accusations passed almost unpunished. Llorente not only omits substantiating this assertion by facts, but is compelled to confess, in another place, that Ximenez, in a celebrated trial, rejected as suspicious a number of witnesses who spoke *against* the accused persons, and that in the year 1559 at an *auto-da-fé* in Seville a false witness received not less than *four hundred* lashes, and was besides condemned to the galleys for *four years*. We have already cited the instructions of Leo X. to the inquisitors, in virtue of which false witnesses were punished by death.

c. The mode and manner in which the Inquisition had to proceed in its interrogatories, equally contradicts the assertion that it intended to find even the most innocent guilty.

α. The interrogatory was conducted by the secretary of the tribunal, in presence of two of the provincial inquisitors and two priests in no way connected with the Inquisition, who, in the office of assessors, had to guard the prisoners against ill-treatment and arbitrary power.

β. Valdés, the eighth grand-inquisitor, described by Llorente as one of the severest, decreed further, that the accused was to be treated *with benevolence* and to be left sitting, except during the reading of the act of accusation, to which he was to listen standing.

γ. By the same instruction the inquisitors are enjoined to mistrust the accuser as much as the accused, and carefully to guard against embracing the side of either beforehand, as this would easily lead them into error.

δ. Article XXIII. decrees, "the inquisitors are to let the accused choose an advocate amongst those of the Holy Office (who were all bound by oath to silence), and to administer an oath to the one chosen, faithfully and loyally to defend his client." The fiscus paid the fees of the advocate, if the prisoner was poor.

ε. The accuser, in his turn, was obliged to swear that he was not moved by private hatred, and was threatened with the severest punishments on earth, as well as eternal damnation, if he gave false evidence.

d. The solicitude of the Inquisition, shown by the revision of the protocols, also merits our attention. The protocols were not only read to the prisoner immediately after the interrogatory, in presence of the two priests above named, in order to establish the identity of the depositions, but they were, four days later, subjected to a second revision, in presence of the same priests, when such remarks were added as had the first time been omitted. If the prisoner had not yet reached the twenty-fifth year, a special procurator was selected for him from the most honourable inhabitants of the town, especially the jurists, whose business was to assist during the trial, to correct the protocol, &c.

Llorente complains that these precautions were often rendered useless by the great ignorance of the accused, which prevented him from comparing his depositions with the protocol. But let us not forget that ignorance may also in our days make a protocol a dangerous instrument, and that the two ecclesiastical assessors before mentioned were specially appointed for the benefit of these ignorant persons. As regards the alleged *alterations* of these protocols, which the enemies of the Church reprove with so much energy, they consisted simply in translating the depositions of the accusers and witnesses from the first into the third person, and suppressing such points as would have revealed the names of the accusers to the accused: this was done to avert *Spanish* vengeance.

e. The inquisitors, furthermore, received instructions to be zealous and careful in collecting all the materials which might serve for the defence of the accused, and after obtaining them, to inquire of him if he desired other researches to be made; in which case his wishes were to be complied with as far as possible.

Llorente, we see, has hitherto given us the best weapons to defend the Inquisition against unjust accusations. He will still continue to do so in our subsequent observations.

10. The sentences of the Inquisition were surrounded by equally great precautions.

a. Each sentence of the provincial tribunals was subject to the revision and consent of the superior authorities, the grand-inquisitor, and the grand council, and only acquired legality after being confirmed by them.*

b. The grand-inquisitor had to transmit the original documents, sent to him by the lower court for revision, to a number of jurists, who, under the title of counsels, were advocates to the upper court, but in no wise functionaries of the same. Llorente regrets that they could not participate in the ulti-

---

* In the commencement, the upper tribunal revised only such sentences as had not been come to unanimously; afterwards all, without discrimination.—Llorente, tom. i. p. 221.

mate voting, but to my knowledge such practice exists nowhere in the world.*

c. In the same manner in which, *before* the imprisonment of suspected persons, impartial theologians were consulted for their opinion on the alleged heretical expressions, so, in the same manner, after the interrogatory and the depositions of the witnesses had thrown more light upon them and defined them more clearly, the qualificators were referred to a second time, in order to declare if they still adhered to their former opinion.

d. The accused had the right to object to the judges of a provincial tribunal, in which case the grand-inquisitor was compelled to appoint others. (Statutes of the grand-inquisitor Valdés, of the year 1561.)

e. In the absence of the prisoner's own confession, conviction for heresy was rendered extremely difficult. Torquemada already recommended in this case the utmost circumspection and care.

f. Many passages of Llorente's work prove that the bishop of the diocese for the time, or his substitute, had to assist in the passing of the sentence of the Inquisition; but his illogical style makes it impossible for us to determine what share they had therein.

g. Besides all this, we have shown before that the popes ordered Spanish archbishops to receive appeals against the sentences of the Inquisition, and that the papal court itself received numberless cases of this kind.

11. The Inquisition has been bitterly reproached for never revealing to the accused the names of the witnesses who bore testimony against them. This

---

* These counsels seem, in later days, to have been abolished, and their functions transferred to members of the upper tribunal qualified for the purpose.—Llorente, tom. i. p. 319, No. 3.

was said to be opening a door to numerous denunciations; but the real state of the matter is
different.

a. Already the statutes of Torquemada, of the
year 1484, allude to this in the following manner:—" It has become notorious that great damage
and danger would accrue to the property and person
of the witnesses, by the publication of their names,
as experience has shown, and still shows, that several
of them have been killed, wounded, or maltreated
by heretics."

b. Leopold Ranke has also seen and explained
the real motive of this measure, when he says that
the Inquisition introduced the concealment of the
names of witnesses and accusers, in order to save
them from the persecutions of the culprits, who were
often rich and powerful.*

c. Lenormant expresses himself in the same
manner: "the accusers mostly belonged to the lowest
class, and were, therefore, by this law (the suppression of the names) protected against the revenge
and persecution of distinguished and powerful
families."

d. The correctness of the views of these eminent
historians is corroborated by Llorente's statement,
that under Charles V., the Cortes of Valladolid demanded the publication of the witnesses at the
Inquisition, as this would no longer be attended
by disastrous results, *except if the accused were a
duke, margrave, count, bishop, or prelate.*

e. The danger caused by the suppression of the
names of witnesses was to a considerable extent
neutralized by another measure, according to which
the accused had the right to name such persons as
he considered his enemies, and whose testimony he,

* Vol. i. p. 247.

therefore, rejected. It may often have happened, as Llorente observes, that the accused mentioned persons who had never appeared against him; but this did not much matter, as they were simply passed over. On the other hand, it was of considerable importance to the prisoner to have thereby the legal means of excluding his personal enemies from being witnesses against him. It is self-evident that he was required to support his rejection of the witnesses by sufficient reasons and other witnesses; in the like manner as it was the duty of the tribunal to inquire if the witnesses not excluded by him were not animated by personal hatred.

The accused had, moreover, the right of naming a number of witnesses in his favour; the Inquisition was obliged to hear them, even if they were to be fetched from America, as is proved by a case related by Llorente.

12. We are asked—" But has not the Inquisition cruelly protracted its trials?" The statute of the year 1488 says in reference to this—"Those who have been imprisoned are not to be tormented by detention, but tried at once, so as not to have cause for complaint." The statute of Torquemada, of 1498, equally demands precaution and *precision*. If, in spite of these regulations, the trials of the Inquisition lasted a considerable time, the reasons must be sought for in the delays occasioned by the qualificators in giving their opinion; by the revision of the protocols, the examination of all the witnesses, who, at times, had to be summoned from distant countries, by the transmission of the acts to the upper tribunal, their revision by the counsels, and the final confirmation or modification of the sentence by the grand council of the Inquisition. Sometimes the proceedings were purposely protracted, not with the intent of tormenting the

prisoner, but of giving him time for reflection and repentance, the Holy Office never handing any penitent to the secular arm for capital punishment except in cases of relapse. "From the moment the accused confessed and repented," says De Maistre, "the *crime* changed into *sin*, and *punishment* into *penance*. The culprit fasts, prays, and mortifies himself. Instead of being led to the place of execution, he sings psalms, confesses his sins, listens to the holy mass, is made to do spiritual exercises, is absolved, and restored to society and his family."

As we have seen before, the Holy Office was not permitted to condemn an accused as long as a witness for the defence remained unexamined, even if this witness lived in America; it was equally forbidden to protract the imprisonment by awaiting evidence *against* the prisoner from distant countries. The statute of 1488 says expressly that the sentence is not to be deferred under pretext of awaiting the completion of the evidence of the crime, that, on the contrary, the prisoner is only to be judged according to the evidence produced, and, if insufficient, to be released. The proceedings could be recommenced if fresh proofs turned up; in other words, the detention of the prisoner ceased from want of evidence, and the inquiry against him was resumed with the arrival of fresh proofs, similarly to the absolution of prisoners *ab instantia.*

13. There exist fabulous accounts of the enormous revenues of the inquisitors, who are alleged to have condemned many prisoners in order to enrich themselves by the confiscation of their property. Justice would indeed be badly administered by that judge who derives pecuniary advantages from his sentences, and the Holy Office would assuredly have been a dangerous and abominable institution had

the income of the inquisitors depended upon the number of the condemned. But notwithstanding the insinuations of Prescott, we know from Llorente that the confiscated property of the condemned fell to the royal fisc, whilst all the officers of the Inquisition received a fixed salary quarterly. This is the reason why Llorente accuses the Spanish kings of cupidity, and not the inquisitors; in which opinion Ranke coincides.* Similar reproaches were made to Ferdinand and Isabella already, soon after the institution of the tribunals. In a letter to Pope Sixtus IV. Isabella complains of the accusations made against her, of having, in the establishment of the Holy Office, been actuated by motives of cupidity, rather than zeal for religion. It is well known that the first statute of Torquemada, of the year 1484, declares the confiscated property of heretics to be employed by the Spanish sovereigns in the cause of God, especially in the war against the Moors.

Ferdinand was often so embarrassed in his finances, that the public treasury could not pay even the salaries which were due. The archbishopric of Granada, then newly established, furnishes a striking and deplorable example: this see, not being endowed with lands, could not obtain all its revenues, although Peter Martyr, as many of his letters still show, warmly urged at court the cause of his colleagues and the archbishop. In consequence of the functionaries of the Inquisition frequently being left unpaid, Torquemada, on the 27th October, 1488, intended to establish a rule for having the confiscated property of the condemned handed over to the royal fisc, only after the deduction for the salaries of the officers and servants of the Inquisition had been made. This project was rejected by King

* Page 244.

Ferdinand, but he devised some other plan to supply the necessary expenses of the Inquisition. Already, in the year 1486, he had obtained a bull authorizing the inquisitors to enjoy the revenues of their former benefices, for an additional five years, even should they be prevented by their new office from residing in them; thus maintaining the royal inquisitors at the expense of the church livings. But in the year 1501, the acute monarch gained from the pope another concession, by which each episcopal church of Spain had to cede one canonry to the Inquisition, to enable the latter to defray the expenses of its administration.

But Llorente acknowledges that even the royal fisc derived little financial benefit from the Inquisition. The first years during which the rich Maranos were brought to punishment, may have yielded considerably, but the moneys were spent in the national war against the Moors.

About fifteen years after the establishment of the institution, Llorente tells us, Ferdinand complained to the pope, that the decisions of the inquisitors on the confiscated property had repeatedly been prejudicial to the royal fisc. The pope immediately, on the 29th March, 1496, charged Archbishop Ximenez with the investigation of the causes of these complaints; but Llorente gives us no further details, and leaves us to guess the real state of affairs. There is, however, no difficulty in divining it, for we know that in another case, when the inquisitors wanted to appropriate some confiscated property to their own use, Ferdinand quickly interposed, without imploring the assistance of the pope. It is natural to think that he would again have known how to help himself, and not have required a papal delegate, if the inquisitors had repeated their attempt to enrich themselves. We must, moreover, remember that the popes constantly exerted themselves in behalf of the penitents, and the children of the condemned heretics, and tried to preserve their property for them. If the inquisitors, in consequence of the papal bulls to that effect, wrested at different times a long-coveted prey from the royal fisc, it is clear why Ferdinand preferred complaining at Rome, to taking the law in his own hands. The Inquisition is, therefore, also in this respect better than its repute.

Besides, the law for the confiscation of the property of convicted prisoners existed in Castile long *before* the establishment of the Inquisition, and the time of grace granted by each tribunal before the commencement of their proceedings was specially devised for the saving of the property, fortunes, &c., of heretics.

From the Moriscos the royal fisc derived no revenue, because the property even of those who were condemned, fell to their children, and not to the State; the fisc was, on the contrary, compelled to cede part of the confiscated property to the minors of the other condemned, and to provide for their education. Moreover, Ferdinand and Isabella restored the whole, or part, of the confiscated property to many widows and orphans.

14. We have been accustomed to consider the *autos-da-fé* (or acts of faith) enormous fires, round which, every three months, the Spaniards assembled to watch, like cannibals, the roasting and toasting of several hundred heretics. The purport of the *autos-da-fé* was, however, neither to burn nor to murder, but, on the contrary to procure the release of such persons as were falsely accused, or to reconcile penitents with the Church. Numerous *autos-da-fé* have passed without the burning of anything but the candles which the penitents carried in their

hands as a symbol of the resuscitation of their faith. Llorente, to prove the great zeal of the Inqusition, describes an *auto-da-fé* which took place at Toledo on the 12th February, 1486, at which not less than 750 culprits were punished. But *not one* of all these was executed; their punishment consisting merely in a public penance. Another great *auto-da-fé* was held in the same town on the 2nd April of the same year, when not one of the " 900 victims " suffered capital punishment. A third and fourth *auto-da-fé* took place on the 1st May and 10th December of the same year, at which 750 and 950 culprits were present; but again not one was put to death.

The number of persons at Toledo who at that time were condemned to do penance, amounted in all to about 3,300; of which twenty-seven were executed. Llorente, our authority for this, is not one who would have altered figures for the benefit of the Holy Office.

We find elsewhere in his work, the description of another *auto-da-fé* held at Rome, with 250 Spaniards, who had appealed to the Pope. None were put to death; but all, after having performed the prescribed penance, were at the *auto-da-fé* reconciled with the Church. They afterwards walked two and two to the Basilica of the Vatican, there to offer their prayers; thence in the same order to S. Maria Minerva to take off the *san-benito*, or shirt of penitence; and ultimately returned to their homes, abandoning for the future every sign of the sentence previously passed upon them. Another *auto-da-fé* is described by an English ecclesiastic, Townsend, in his "Voyage in Spain" (during the year 1786), and cited as an example of the horrors of the Inquisition. An impostor, speculating on the credulity of persons, having sold love-philters, was publicly whipped and condemned to do penance. The inquisitor who read the sentence to him, addressed him in terms such as we should like to hear from the mouth of every judge.

Of all the trials recorded by Llorente, very few terminate with the death of the culprit. No one will accuse him of having selected the mildest cases and suppressed the most gloomy ones; for it is well known, his aim was to paint the Inquisition in the darkest possible colours.

The above facts explain the reason why the Spaniards, as Llorente even confesses, regarded the *autos-da-fé* rather as acts of mercy than of cruelty.

After the reconciliation of the penitents with the Church, the obstinate heretics, and such whose offences were partly civil, were transferred to the secular power.* Llorente omits mentioning that the *auto-da-fé* was then at an end, and the inquisitors retired. We learn this, however, from Malten's "Library of Cosmology," published in 1829. A trial is therein reported at full length, which took place in Sicily in the beginning of the eighteenth century, and at which the civil punishment was inflicted only the day after the *auto-da-fé*.

15. It is further not to be overlooked, that the persons condemned by the Inquisition were far from being all heretics. They included—(*a*) sodomites, such as carried on infamous intercourse with animals; (*b*) polygamists, who, owing to the example of the Moors, were rather numerous, and are said still to be so at the present day.† (*c*) The

---

* Llorente, tom. i. p. 321. "La condamnation au feu par la *justice du roi.*"

† Llorente, tom. ii. pp. 338—341. At an *auto-da-fé* held at Murcia on the 8th September, 1560, seven bigamists were burnt; three years later, at the same place, thirteen others; and there

jurisdiction of the Inquisition was also extended to those who had committed ordinary carnal sins, if the seducer had made the girl believe that their action was not sinful. (*d*) The same punishment awaited the ecclesiastic or monk who had married, having concealed their station from the girl, or persuaded her that, although ecclesiastics, they were permitted to marry. In the like manner were punished—(*e*) confessors who had seduced their female penitents; (*f*) priests who had dissuaded the women, with whom they had sinned, from confessing their fault; (*g*) laymen who had exercised ecclesiastical functions; (*h*) deacons who had heard confessions; (*i*) persons pretending to be agents of the Inquisition, which, as we know from Gil Blas, frequently happened; (*k*) blasphemers; (*l*) church-robbers; (*m*) usurers; and (*n*) even murderers and rebels, if their deeds were in some way connected with the affairs of the Inquisition. Thus, for instance, the murderers of Arbues, the inquisitor of Saragossa, and the rebels of Cordova, who had liberated the prisoners of the Inquisition, were judged by the Holy Office. Even (*o*) the servants of the Inquisition were not exempt from punishment, but sentence of death was passed upon those who had violated female prisoners of the Inquisition. In the like manner smugglers were punished, who during war, in particular that with France, sold horses and ammunition to the enemy; and lastly, an immense number of witches, sorcerers, mixers of love-potions, pretended saints, and, in fact, all who speculated upon the credulity of the people.

The Inquisition was charged by the Spanish

was hardly a large *auto-da-fé* at which not one or more sinners of this kind appeared. If they repented, and had not relapsed, they received only ecclesiastical punishments.

monarchs with the prosecution of all these numerous and various crimes, partly contrary to the will
of the grand-inquisitors.* If we remember the
number of witches only, burnt in Germany, that
of heretics, sorcerers, witches, murderers, usurers,
sodomites, fornicators, smugglers, church-robbers,
and other criminals condemned by that institution,
will no longer appear extravagant.

Soldau, in his "History of the Trials of Witches,"
narrates that in the little Protestant town of
Nördlingen, in Bavaria, numbering, in his lifetime,
about six thousand inhabitants, not less than thirty-
five witches were burnt during the years 1590—1594.
Applying this scale to Spain, the number of witches
executed during four years would amount to
50,000, or, according to Llorente, to 20,000 more
than there were criminals of all classes executed
by the Holy Office during the 330 years of its
existence.

Taking further into consideration, that in Germany the criminal code of Charles V. pronounced
capital punishment against blasphemers (sect. 106),
sodomites (sect. 116), sorcerers (sect. 109), church-
robbers (sect. 172), and similar criminals, and de-
ducting the probable number of all these, as well
as the other criminals quoted above (such as
witches, bigamists, usurers, smugglers, &c.), from
the thirty thousand condemned to death by the
Inquisition, the number of persons executed in
Spain for heresy decreases considerably, even if we
accept Llorente's computations as by no means
exaggerated.

16. But we assert that they are exaggerated, and
will endeavour to prove this.

* The grand-inquisitor Aveda, for instance, would allow no
other persons to be tried before the Inquisition but such as had
sinned against religion.—De Maistre, pp. 92, 93.

It must always be borne in mind that Llorente has derived his statistics neither from official registers nor even private sources; but that they are solely and entirely the result of calculations of probability based on wrong premises. He himself at different places (tom. i. pp. 272, 406; tom. iv. p. 242) avows this openly and candidly, and describes the method adopted by him; the fallacy of which is evident.

a. Llorente starts with the assertion that, according to the Jesuit Mariana, two thousand victims were given to the flames at Seville in the first year of the Inquisition, 1481. On referring to the work of this historian, we find, however, that the passage (lib. xxiv. c. 17) referred to by Llorente, runs as follows : " A Turrecremata edictis proposita, spe veniæ homines promiscuæ ætatis, sexus, conditionis, ad decem et septem millia ultro crimina confessos, memorant duo millia crematos igne, &c." Mariana says, therefore, expressly, that two thousand were burnt *under* Torquemada. Llorente, fixing himself 1483 as the year of the installation of Torquemada as grand-inquisitor, could not say that the two thousand mentioned by Mariana, were executed by him, in Seville alone, in the year 1481 only, when Torquemada had as yet no participation in the proceedings of the Inquisition. He ought, on the contrary, to have known, from the works of Marineo Siculo and Pulgar,* that this number was to be distributed over several years, and included the executions of all the tribunals of the kingdom under Torquemada.

To our question, how many were really executed in the first year of the Inquisition, Llorente himself

* Marineo Siculo, " Cosas Memorabiles," p. 164. Pulgar, " Crónica de los Reyes Católicos," p. II. ch. lxxvii. p. 137.

supplies us, in another place, with the correct answer. He states that the tribunal had, up to the 4th November, 1481, burnt already 298 persons; but, as if feeling his own contradiction, adds that these were executed in Seville alone, the remaining 1,700 in its environs and the bishopric of Cadiz. Unhappily for him, he had closed a back-door by asserting elsewhere that *before* Torquemada, or 1483, only one tribunal existed for the whole of Andalusia; and, consequently, also for Cadiz. This was at Seville, where the suspected persons were brought from all parts of Andalusia, and if convicted, executed on the Quemadero, the only place of execution so long as no other tribunal was erected.* It is therefore evident the right number is 298, and the statement of 2,000, wrongly based on Mariana, utterly erroneous.

b. Llorente pretends to know from Bernaldez, that, during the years 1482—1489, eighty-eight persons were annually executed at Seville. We cannot verify this assertion, as the work of Bernaldez, who was chaplain to the second grand-inquisitor, exists only in Spain in manuscript; but must object to the conclusions which he has drawn from it. He reasons thus:—In Seville the delations were more numerous than elsewhere; the number of persons condemned by each of the other three tribunals may therefore be calculated at forty-four, or half the number of those at Seville. So far his hypothesis seems admissible. But he retains this figure even after

---

* Llorente, tom. i. p. 150. At page 160 Llorente relates that on the stone scaffold at Seville, called Quemadero, four large statues of plaster, under the name of the Four Prophets, were standing, in which the unfortunate victims of the Inquisition were broiled to death in the manner of Phalaris. He retracts, however, this assertion afterwards, observing that the condemned were tied only to these statues. Jost, in his "History of the Jews," vol. vii. p. 77, still repeats the false assertion of Llorente.

the tribunals were increased to eleven, allotting to each forty-four sentences of death. Hence, according to his theory, criminals would augment in proportion to the establishment of new courts of justice; and a country, possessing at first only one court of justice would, if eleven more were added, produce as many more criminals.

c. Another flaw in the calculations of Llorente has already been indicated by Prescott,—that of reckoning the same number of condemned for the five tribunals of Aragon, as for those of Castile; although the latter province contained five times as many Jews as Aragon, and for that reason, certainly, also many more judaizing Maranos.

d. Prescott adds the following words:—"One might reasonably distrust Llorente's tables, from the facility with which he receives the most improbable estimates in other matters, as, for example, the number of banished Jews, which he puts at 800,000. I have shown, from contemporary sources, that the number did not probably exceed 160,000, or, at most, 170,000."

e. If Llorente, therefore, states the number of persons burnt under Torquemada during the eighteen years of his administration to be 8,800, we have more than one just reason to doubt the correctness of his assertion. Having shown him wrong in his premises, on which his fabric of numbers is built, we ought, by rights, to oppose our own calculations of probability to his, which would run as follows:— Llorente having sextupled the actual number of persons condemned at Seville in 1481, and quintupled that of the Jews expelled from Spain, we are justified in taking for granted that he has in the same ratio multiplied the number of victims of the Inquisition. But we are not minded to adopt this in earnest : we intend only to prove how easily

Llorente's system of calculation may be turned against him.

f. His arbitrary reasoning and his incorrectness are more particularly evident in his statements respecting Ximenez. He expressly tells us, as we shall see hereafter, that our archbishop endeavoured to lessen the severity of the Inquisition, deposed bad functionaries, pardoned numerous accused persons, &c. Not one of the special sentences recorded by him of the administration of the third grand-inquisitor, is a death-warrant. Yet he hesitates not to include this period in his calculations, and to assure us that, under Ximenez, as many prisoners were executed as under Deza and his auxiliary Lucero, both of whom he accuses of the most barbarous cruelty and the greatest severity. Are stronger proofs needed to show the fallacy of his theory?

17. Those who would apply modern notions to the estimation of the minor punishments of the Inquisition imposed on the penitents and less guilty, would necessarily conceive a wrong and exaggerated opinion.

Numerous persons were found guilty only in a minor degree (*de levi*), and in that case not even submitted to ecclesiastical punishments. They were merely, as it was then termed, absolved *ad cautelam;* that is, the excommunication was not pronounced against them, though they might have deserved it. The same practice is to the present day adhered to by the Catholic Church in the confessional, the penitent being absolved by the confessor, even if he had incurred excommunication through his sins. Llorente himself acknowledged that since the middle of the last century, all the sentences of the Inquisition belonged to the class *de levi,* but regrets that the prisoners were acquitted without being indemnified for loss of time, &c. I cannot say whether future generations will adopt what Llorente claims from the Inquisition; up to the present time it has not, to my knowledge, been the practice of any court of justice.

We have now arrived at the *san-benito*, or dress worn, we are told, by all suspected persons, one which was in itself a stigma and an indelible mark of ignominy on the wearer. The history of the Church, as well as Llorente, provides us with the facts necessary to dispel this illusion. *San-benito* is a corruption of the Spanish words *saco bendito*, the name of the dress which, in conformity with the early usages of the Christian Church, was worn by penitents, to show their repentance and contrition also by outward signs. To appear in court dresses embroidered with gold and diamonds, was unknown to the Church, and consequently not allowed by the Inquisition, which Llorente considers very hard and cruel. The *saccus*, mentioned already in the Old Testament, was subjected during the Middle Ages to benediction for the use of penitents; hence its name of *saccus benedictus*, or in Spanish, *saco bendito*. The colour of this dress was blue in some countries, in others grey or black; in Spain, yellow.

Those who were absolved *de levi*, had to wear it during the act of reconciliation, but only then, and without any other sign or figure; many were altogether dispensed from it; and those who confessed of their own free will, entirely escaped the publicity of their penance, their reconciliation with the Church taking place in secret *autos-da-fé* in the interior of the tribunals. Penitents who had to abjure, wore a *san-benito* with half a cross fixed on it if gravely suspected, and an entire one if they had been decided heretics. Such, however, and only such, as showed no repentance whatever, were handed over to the secular arm, dressed in a *san-benito*, painted all over with flames and figures of demons, carrying besides in their hands a cap (*caroza*), painted in the same manner. Spain, like all other countries, has had a dress for criminals—the *san-benito*, in which they were led to the place of execution. In states which are justly reckoned amongst the most civilized of Germany, they were, even in the present century, dragged thither in hides.

With regard to the *penance* of those who were reconciled with the Church, we have to consider two things. Firstly, that the very statutes of the Inquisition command the exercises of penitence to be as merciful and mild as is compatible with conscience; secondly, that the ancient Church and the Middle Ages looked upon penance as a matter of devotion rather than of disgrace. Whilst, in former days, thousands thought nothing of confessing their sins before the whole community, few are now found who will do so in private. Kings left their thrones to do penance in sackcloth and ashes; as for instance, Theodosius the Great, for his cruelty to Thessalonica. His subjects did not consider him dishonoured by this act, nor when St. Louis submitted of his own free will to the discipline of his confessor, did France lament the disgrace of her sovereign; on the contrary, millions admired him for his piety. Numerous examples from history could be added; but these suffice to show that formerly sin, not penance, was looked upon as a disgrace, and the latter merely regarded as an atonement for the former.

In this light we must also view the penances imposed by the Inquisition. Indeed Llorente himself furnishes several instances of persons, who, having been punished *de levi* by the Inquisition, were thought so little disgraced, that they married into the highest families, and even into that of the king. Nor were such as were gravely suspected, and had done penance, excluded from again attaining the highest civil and ecclesiastical dignities. The prisons of persons who, on account of their greater culpability, or to prevent their infecting others, had been condemned to confinement for life, were either their own houses, as decreed by the Statutes of Valladolid, or penitentiaries similar to those of the Beguines or the houses of the Fugger at Augsburg, where they could follow their former occupations and trades.*

18. Several writers have asserted that the Inquisition has smothered the genius of the Spanish nation, retarded the progress of intellect and the cultivation of sciences. They find this a very natural and necessary consequence of such an institution, but do not stop to inquire whether history has no objections to make, and does not teach differently. Now, it is an indisputable fact, that during the reign of Ferdinand and Isabella, with whom the Inquisition originated, science began again to flourish in Spain; numerous schools and universities were established, and the classical studies pursued with unusual vigour ; *belles-lettres* and all kinds of poetry revived, celebrated *savants* of foreign countries were invited to come to Spain and well rewarded, the nobility was reinspired with love for the productions of the mind, even ladies of high rank taking professorships in the universities. In short, Spain was then the theatre of a scientific life, incomparably more active than it is in the present day. We are far from attributing these noble results to the Inquisition. Our aim is only to show that this institution was not the violent storm which swept away the precious buds and blossoms of science. We hold this opinion, in

* Torquemada already ordered small buildings surrounded by a common wall, as it were a little town in the town, to be erected for the penitents.

spite of the committee of the Cortes of 1812, who, misguided by modern doctrines, strove to engraft on Spain, then at war with France, a constitution fashioned after the French, and declared, in their report, that the writers disappeared the moment the Inquisition was introduced. They have by this shown themselves utterly unworthy of the praise generally bestowed upon Spaniards, and recently repeated by Arndt in his "Comparative History of Nations," that of having a thorough contempt for falsehood. The most brilliant epoch of Spanish literature extends from the end of the 15th to the middle of the 17th century, and embraces just the very period during which the Inquisition was most powerful. All the writers through whom Spain has become famous, lived during this time; and their works were printed with the consent of the Holy Office.

Spain's three great poets, Cervantes, Lope de Vega, and Calderon, as well as her eminent historians, F. de Pulgar, Zurita, Mariana, not to mention a host of other authors of less note, belong to this period. Llorente, it is true, enumerates in the second volume of his History, 118 learned men who were prosecuted by the Inquisition, but omits adding that they escaped without personal injury.

19. We cannot pass over in silence the opinions pronounced on the Inquisition by the greatest and most cultivated minds of Spain. Llorente, who likewise devotes a special chapter to this subject, lays particular stress upon the celebrated historian Pulgar having expressed himself against the Inquisition, which was established during his lifetime. It is true Pulgar blames the Inquisition for the application of capital punishment against heretics, but no one will ever be able to prove that he spoke against this institution in *general*. From Mariana, Llorente prudently quotes only such passages as

arc introduced by that author, into his history, as
the opinions of others. He forgets to give Mariana's
own, which is the more weighty, as he was himself
once the object of the persecutions of the Holy
Office. Mariana says that the Inquisition had been
" reipublicæ universæ majori commodo," and " præ-
sens remedium adversus impendentia mala, quibus
aliæ provinciæ exagitantur, cœlo datum; nam hu-
mano consilio adversus tanta pericula satis caveri
non potuit."—Lib. xxiv. ch. 17.

Let us now listen to what Peter Martyr says, a
philosophical writer, whose candour is praised by
Llorente, and whose letters, he adds, are so liberal
that they had to be published abroad. The latter
assertion is incorrect, as the first edition of this
celebrated collection of letters was printed at
Alcala de Henares, in the year 1530. True it is,
that Peter Martyr repeatedly and openly passed
very strong censures on the inquisitor Lucero
and his conduct, calling him Tenebrero (man of
darkness) instead of Lucero (man of light). The
opinion which this great humanist and avowedly
liberal writer passes on the Inquisition itself is quite
different. In his 279th letter, addressed to an
intimate friend, he says, with reference to Queen
Isabella, who had just died,—" Qualem una cum
viro se gesserit ad exstirpandas hæreses, purgandam
religionem . . . . nemo ambigit;" thus reckoning
the zeal of the queen against the heretics as one of
her *virtues*. In his 295th letter he censures Lucero,
but calls the Inquisition itself a " præclarum in-
ventum, et omni laude dignum opus, ut omnis
religione labes tollatur." This was written at a
time when the persecutions of Lucero against the
archbishop of Talavera, a friend whom he greatly
esteemed, had already begun, and in a letter to so
intimate a friend, that reserve, much less dissimu-

lation or falsehood, is out of the question. Peter Martyr refers several times to the trial of Talavera, without once attacking the Inquisition, but only the person of Lucero. Yet it must not be supposed that his pen was chained by fear. His vehement expressions against Lucero, and his courageous behaviour before the judges of the Inquisition, in favour of Talavera, disprove this. (Ep. 334.)

Of Zurita, the celebrated historian of Aragon (died 1580), Prescott speaks as more free from religious prejudices than any other Spanish writer, and Llorente calls him the trustworthy and truthful author of the "Anales de Aragon." But what does the liberal Zurita say:—"For this reason they [Ferdinand and Isabella] established the holy office of the Inquisition against heresy. It was the best means which could be devised for the protection of our holy faith, and seems to have been a divine inspiration to guard Spain against numberless errors and heresies by which the rest of the Christian world has been disturbed."* At the end of the chapter, and elsewhere† in his work, he regards the Inquisition as a benefaction for Spain.

A younger contemporary of Zurita, and his successor in the office of historiographer of Aragon, was Hieronymus Blancas (died 1590), distinguished both by his elegant Latin and his high-minded love of liberty. In his principal work, "Commentaria Rerum Aragonensium," of which the beautiful edition of Saragossa, published in 1588, lies before me, he speaks, at page 263, in the following manner of the Inquisition :—"The greatest proof of the wisdom and piety of Ferdinand and Isabella is to be found in their having, for the purpose of turning the minds of heretics and apostates from

* Tom. v. lib. i. ch. vi.
† For instance, tom. iv. lib. xx. ch. xlxix.

fatal errors, and breaking their boldness, established the office of the Holy Inquisition, an institution the utility of which is readily acknowledged,
not only by Spain, but the whole Christian world."
Blancas repeatedly returns to his praises of the
Inquisition—for instance, at page 274; and it is
unmistakable that he, like Zurita and others, valued
the Inquisition the higher the more he saw the
horrors produced in other countries by the wars
of religion consequent upon the Reformation.
Hence, also, he assures us, at page 346, that the
Inquisition was held in the highest regard by his
contemporaries.   His opinions are embraced by
more modern writers, who agree with him that the
Inquisition was a preventive measure, by which
Spain, for a considerable time, was saved from civil
and religious wars.

20. We have but one more duty to perform,—to
investigate whether Llorente, whose history is
considered by many as irrefutable, is a witness
worthy of credit or not.   Having been a functionary
of the Holy Office, he is generally believed to have
made revelations.   We would wish he had done so,
and instead of empty tirades and long declama-
tions, given us plain sterling facts.   True, he frequently quotes documents to support his assertions; but they have reference mostly to minor
punishments only, whilst we should have greatly
preferred to learn the entire decisions and sentences
of the tribunals, on which the large *autos-da-fé*
were based.

As it is impossible for us to examine the secret
documents which Llorente professes to have used,
and thereby be enabled to form a judgment on
their value, it is the more necessary to inquire
carefully into his own moral and scientific character,
to enable us to find in it either a guarantee for his

truthfulness or reasons for doubting the correctness of his assertions.

Happily we possess an interesting biographical sketch of him, written by two of his Paris friends,—Mahul and Lanjuinais, and inserted in the April number of the " Revue Encyclopédique " for 1823, to which he was himself a contributor for many years. In spite of the partiality for the friend, they have given therein sufficient truthful matter for us to pass a correct judgment on him.

Juan Antonio Llorente was born March 30th, 1756, of a noble family in Aragon. He studied civil and canon law at Saragossa, was ordained priest in 1779 for the diocese of Calahorra, and made a doctor of canon law in Valencia. He belonged then already to that class of the clergy who were called *éclairés;* and as the Spanish government favoured at that time persons of such tendencies, a path to civil and ecclesiastical honours was soon opened for Llorente. Only two years after his ordination, he became at Madrid a counsellor in the High Council of Castile, and was elected a member of the Academy of San Isidoro, which had been established after the expulsion of the Jesuits, and favoured Jansenism from the very commencement of its career. In the year 1782, we find him, though hardly twenty-six years old, acting as vicar-general of the bishop of Calahorra; and in 1784, according to his own testimony, entirely and completely " purified from the last remains of the leaven of ultramontanism." For this change he was indebted " to a very learned and intelligent friend." From that period (Llorente tells us so) he became intimate with the Freemasons, to whom, no doubt, the same " learned and intelligent friend " belonged, who convinced him how full of errors and prejudices his knowledge had hitherto been, and taught him to throw off the yoke of authority, and to listen only to the voice of reason! We have no cause for calling in question the assertion of his panegyrists, that Llorente made rapid progress in this new path; it was to this fact that he owed his nomination by the king to a canonry in the cathedral of Calahorra; that he was chosen by the minister, Count Florida-blanca, a member of the new Academy of History; and by the grand-inquisitor, Señor Don Augustin Rubin de Cevallos, bishop of Jaen, appointed secretary-general of the Inquisition at Madrid in the year 1789. Since the days of Aranda and Piombal, it was no uncommon thing to behold Jansenists and Freemasons occupying the most important ecclesiastical offices, both in Spain and Portugal. The university of Coimbra, for example, was full of theologians, who were members of the fraternity of Masons.*

Llorente was secretary to the Inquisition of Madrid till the year 1791; he was then banished from the capital and sent back to his canonry of Calahorra. Being recalled, however (1793), by the enlightened grand-inquisitor, Don Manuel Abad y la Sierra, he laboured with him, and after the fall of Don Manuel was associated with the minister Jovellanos, the Countess Montijo, and others, in endeavouring to introduce liberalism into the religious and political institutions of Spain. But some of his letters, having been intercepted, compromised him; and though his name was on the list of candidates for a bishopric, he was arrested, deprived of the office which he held in the Inquisition, and condemned to do penance for a month in a monastery.

He was in disgrace till the year 1805, when the

---

* Pfeilschifter, " Politische Studien," vol. i. p. 7.

notorious " Prince of Peace," the Spanish minister
Godoy, endeavoured to deprive the Basque provinces
of their ancient rights and privileges,* and to bring
them under his own despotism.

In order to facilitate the success of this tyrannical
enterprise, the violent act was to be accompanied by
a so-called historical and scientific exposition.

For this business Godoy selected Llorente, who
was recalled to Madrid, and for writing his work,
" Noticias Historicas sobre las tres Provincias Bas-
congadas " (Madrid, 1806-7, in 3 volumes), in
which he attacked the privileges of these provinces, successively named canon of the cathedral of
Toledo, scholastic of the chapter, chancellor of the
university in the same city, and knight of the order
of Charles III. Llorente, who thus had become
the pliant instrument of despotism, was in consequence, as if in mockery to the provinces, named
a member of the " Patriotic Association of the
Basque Provinces." The improper conduct of
Llorente is also reproved by Ranke.† To us it furnishes a proof how the writer could make history
bend to his own views and plans; and if we had no
other work by him but this unjust attack on the
Basque Fueros, in which history is violated and
perverted, it would suffice to justify our suspicions
against his mode of writing history.

Every one knows how Napoleon (May 10th, 1808)
forced Ferdinand VII., then a captive in Bayonne,
to resign his crown, in order that he (Napoleon)
might bestow it on his brother Joseph. The Spanish
patriots courageously rose up against the stranger
who was forced upon them. There was, however,
a party so forgetful of the national honour as to
sell themselves to the French; in the ranks of this

---

* " Fuéros," as they are termed in Spanish.
† " Fürsten und Völker," vol. i. p. 242.

party was to be found Llorente. The religious orders were suppressed, the monasteries robbed of their property, while to Llorente was confided the honourable mission of putting the sacrilegious decrees into execution, of extending a system of rapine and spoliation throughout the whole country, and of administering the "secularized" property, not, it is said, without enriching his private purse with many a precious jewel stolen from the churches. Indeed, he exhibited so much ability in the art of confiscation, that he was very soon raised to a " director-general" of the *national property*,—a name by which his patrons were pleased to designate the confiscated property of the patriots who were opposed to France.

Having been accused of the embezzlement of eleven millions of reals, Llorente shortly after lost his office; but, as the crime could not be proved, was appointed instead commissary-general of the bull "de la cruz," a bull by which, in former days, the popes allowed the Spanish kings to raise certain funds for the purpose of defraying the expenses of the Moorish wars. Though the object had ceased to exist, the contribution still continued.

Since the year 1809, Llorente, by order of King Joseph, was engaged in the publication of several pamphlets in support of the French cause, but especially in writing his history of the Inquisition, for which, in conjunction with others, he collected documents. Being, after the fall of Joseph, banished from Spain on a charge of high treason, he repaired to Paris, in the year 1814, where he edited his famous " Histoire Critique de l'Inquisition," four vols. 8vo, originally written by him in Spanish, and, under his own superintendence, translated into French by Alexis Pellier (1817-18). In consequence of the appearance of this work, the archbishop of Paris interdicted him both to hear confessions and to read mass, and when he endeavoured to support himself by giving private lessons in the Spanish language, the University of Paris forbade him to teach in private educational establishments; so that he was forced to live partly by his pen, partly by the charity of the Freemasons of Paris. Though comprised in the amnesty of 1820, Llorente remained in Paris, translated about this time the immoral adventures of Faublas, and published in 1822 his equally exceptionable "Portraits Politiques des Papes," which latter work determined the French government to banish him from France in December, 1822. Shortly after his arrival in Madrid, death overtook him on the 5th February, 1823.

Having given this sketch of Llorente's life, the question naturally arises—Can a man who sold himself to a tyrannical minister, and, by the perversion of history, aided him to extinguish the ancient liberties of a brave people; a man who proved himself a traitor to his country, and sold his soul and body to a foreign oppressor; a priest, who lent himself as the instrument of violence and the sacrilegious robbery of church property; who, on account of his principles, was by the ecclesiastical authorities forbidden to exercise his sacerdotal functions, and to teach youth; can such a man be worthy of our confidence, can we put faith in such an historian?

Nobody will be tempted to give an affirmative reply to our first question; for a writer who perverts the history of the Basques can also falsify that of the Inquisition. We have Ranke's testimony that he has done this.* So much for Llorente as an historian. It remains for us now only to inquire what he was as a priest and churchman. The above-mentioned

* Fürsten und Völker, vol. i. p. 242.

stains on his sacerdotal character were allied to an
uncommon enmity for the Church, which drew from
his pen a series of falsehoods and mistakes.   We
will not repeat that he falsely represented the Inquisition as a usurpation of the ecclesiastical over the
civil power, although the document brought forward by him shows clearly that this institution was
nothing but a royal tribunal armed with spiritual
weapons.   His hatred for the popes is vented against
them even when they endeavoured to mitigate the
severity of the Inquisition and to protect its victims,
and with marvellous ingenuity he discovers the
worst motives in their best and kindest actions.
As an instance of the misrepresentations which
hatred caused him to make, we will cite the following :—Charles V. desired to obtain a living for
one of his favourites, which before had been given to
a monk by the Pope.   When Leo X. in consequence
persuaded the latter to renounce his rights, the
Spanish ambassador, who reported it to his master,
added that the monk was said formerly to have
been a Jew, but this did not signify much to Rome.
Llorente on this exclaims : "What a singular state of
things ! the court of Rome does not care much if a
monk *is* a Jew or not, whilst the Spanish Inquisition
is so scrupulous and severe in this respect."   It is
manifest how perfidiously Llorente here perverts the
fact of the monk having formerly *been* a Jew, in
order to enable him to accuse the Papal See of the
most culpable indifference.   How much history
becomes caricature under his pen, may also   be
seen in what he says concerning the crusades :—
"This war [speaking of the first crusade] and the
subsequent expeditions of the same kind, would, by
their injustice, have been revolting to Europe, had
she not before been carefully indoctrinated with the
absurd notion, that war was allowable if carried on

for the glory and honour of Christianity." What other author would not shrink from and feel ashamed of writing in this vein?

In another work of Llorente's, "Project of a Religious Constitution," which, according to the title, was only edited by him, but from the testimony of his biographers written by him, we find the assertion—"The advantages humanity has derived from Christianity are counterbalanced by the many evils which the change of the primitive constitution of the Church brought with it." After this confession, which for every Catholic amounts to nothing less than self-excommunication, Llorente strives to place the Church again on that footing on which she was two hundred years after Christ. The supremacy of the Pope—such is the opinion of our Catholic priest and canon—is therefore to be rejected as a mere human institution, and no one to obey the decrees of the head of the Church if they are not in accordance with the decisions of the tribunal of individual reason. The "pious priest" further rejects the obligation to confess and take the sacrament of the holy supper once a year, at Easter; to hear mass on Sundays, specially to confess one's sins, &c.; and adds that the priest is not bound to press the performance of these exercises. Our doctor of canon law considers divorce allowable, demands the abolition of the obstacles to marriage, of religious vows, celibacy, and the suppression of the four minor orders of priesthood, &c. In short, he proposes such a number of anti-ecclesiastical and anti-catholic changes, that already, in 1822, the Tubingen Theological Quarterly found it necessary sharply to censure his doctrines, and point out his numerous contradictions and errors against history.

But Llorente's hatred for the Church and her head, shows itself most glaringly in his "Portraits of the Popes" a work, of which even his Jansenistic friends say, that " the author not only accepted as authentic, a mass of things of doubtful truth, as for instance the fable of the so-called Popess Joanna, which has sufficiently been proved quite apocryphal, but also, we grieve to say, the subject, tendency, and even tone of the work, are such as to be incompatible with the character of a Catholic priest." And further on they proceed : " He has also attacked those traditions of apostolic origin which every true Catholic respects as the dogmas of his faith."

We add, Llorente, after having in his work exhausted the repertory of old reproaches against Rome, is at no loss to invent new accusations. Thus, for instance, he reproaches, at page x. of his preface, most of the popes with having, for the extension of their power, taken the title of Œcumenic or Universal Bishop. We can scarcely suppose that Llorente was ignorant enough to believe in his own assertion. With great affected simplicity he continues: " If the popes were really the vicars of Christ on earth, Divine Providence would never have permitted the succession of the first popes to be left in doubt, but made it a matter of certainty whether Cletus and Anacletus were one and the same person or not. This being left doubtful, the popes could not be the vicars of Christ." * Gregory the Great is to him (i. p. 166) the most venal flatterer; and in his wrath he calls Gregory VII. the greatest monster ambition ever engendered, the cause of a thousand wars and murders, a man who has done more mischief in history than any other, who lived in concubinage with Mathilde, poisoned his predecessor, &c. † Rome is to Llorente the centre of intrigues (i. 241), and history, he assures us, will never par-

* Portraits Politiques des Papes, tom. i. pp. 11, 12.
† Pp. 344—350.

don the sovereigns of Europe the re-establishment of the States of the Church.

This will, I believe, suffice to enable us to pass a judgment on Llorente's sentiments towards the Church. Let us, however, put aside his ecclesiastical character, and consider him in his capacity of profane historian. Here his incorrectness is not less apparent, and no confidence can be placed in him. His little pamphlet on the constitution of the Church furnishes abundant proofs. Llorente has absolutely fixed the year 200 after Christ as the normal one for the regeneration of the Church. All the changes in the Church since this year are to be put aside; but he is so illogical or thoughtless as immediately after to speak of the prescriptions of the general councils to be retained for the regenerated Church, and yet the first general council was held only in the fourth century, in the year 325.

It is of little moment whether the Apostle Paul was married or not; but a theologian who, in the face of the Bible, furnishes him with a wife, is either an incorrect writer, or worse still, an intentional forger; and who, like Llorente, gives as a fact, that the Apostles, before their separation, together composed the Apostolic Creed, is not only little versed in theology, but shows also great audacity in propounding as certain and indisputable, what he could only know from hearsay.

The " Portraits of the Popes " are not less rich in historical blunders. Vol. i. p. 66, Llorente relates in the most serious manner that Paul of Samosata adopted the heresy of Sabellius,—an assertion which will cause the least tyro in church history to smile. Page 9 we are told that St. Justin had written his works *before* Ignatius of Antioch, that is, whilst he was still in his cradle. On the same page we find the celebrated heathen Apollonius of Tyana amongst the ancient heretics ; the well-known persecution of the House of David is placed under the emperor Vespasian instead of Domitian, and the most confused and irrational trash is written about the ancient heresies. His equal also is not to be found in the treatment of modern history and statistics. "The consequence," he says, "of the refusal of Leo X. to reform his court, was that England, Switzerland, Saxony, Bavaria, Holland, Germany, Wurtemberg, Hanover, Prussia, Sweden, Denmark, and Russia are now Protestant countries." * Yes, Llorente goes so far as to be of opinion, Russia and Greece would still belong to the Roman Church if Leo X. had been more yielding.†

After all these specimens, we will throw a last glance on Llorente's "History of the Inquisition." He there makes Gregory VII. go to war with the emperor Henry III. (i. 23) ; the Pseudo-Isidorian decrees are composed in the eighth century (i. 15) ; the Crusaders take Antioch before laying siege to Nicea and Edessa ; and the Protestants receive their name from their protesting against a decree of the *Pope.* At page 196 of the same volume he raises by his own power the monk Peter of Castelnau to the dignity of Abbot of Citeaux, and as a set-off assassinates him four years too early. His blunders in the history of his own country are equally gross. Thus, he repeatedly speaks (i. 145, 150) of the count of Arcos and margrave of Cadiz as of two distinct persons, although one and the same famous warrior, Ponce de Leon, to whom to a high degree Spain owes the conquest of Granada, united both these titles. The mistake here committed is at least

* " Portraits," tom. ii. pp. 198 et seq.   † P. 200.

as great as if a French historian made Marshal Ney and the duke of Elchingen two generals of the French empire.

Another mark of the greatest carelessness is, for a Spanish historian, to prolong the life of Philip I., the father of Charles V., to the year 1516 and 1517 (i. 421), when he had been dead ten years, and his death caused such disturbances and commotions in Spain as we have seen in chapter XIV. We shall take occasion, in the following chapter, to point out other gross blunders of Llorente, even in the history of Spain.

If we sum up, after all that has been said concerning the life and character of Llorente, and his mode of writing history, our verdict will be considered mild, when we say, that he is an author not to be depended upon, and unworthy of our confidence. The artistic part of his history does not concern us. But we will insert the criticism of his Paris friends. They say: "The good which this work has produced, is not owing to the style in which it is written, being devoid of all colouring and elegance; nor to a skilful and judicious arrangement of the materials, nor to the clearness of the descriptions or the depth and beauty of the views and reflections—no, the art of being able to write history is not revealed by this work." Whoever has read the four volumes of the history, will agree that this criticism is by no means exaggerated.

Before concluding this chapter, we must add that we are far from wishing to be the champion of the Spanish Inquisition as such. On the contrary, we entirely deny the right to the secular power of ruling over consciences, and are, from the bottom of our heart, averse to every religious oppression on the part of the temporal power, no matter whether perpetrated by a Torquemada in the cowl of a Dominican, or by a minister of the nineteenth century in his court dress. Our intention was only to show that the Inquisition was not that abominable monster which party passions and ignorance have often represented it. We are obliged to do this, in order to be able properly to appreciate the man who for ten years presided over this institution as grand-inquisitor. If the Inquisition in reality had been what it is frequently depicted—an institution more blood-thirsty than the legislation of the times, a colossus of injustice, all the brilliant virtues and eminent qualities of Ximenez would not have availed to wipe out this stain on his character.

We have proved that it was not so, and can now turn to the great Cardinal in his new office.

CHAPTER XVIII.

XIMENEZ AND THE INQUISITION.

In many historical works it is asserted, repeated also by Rotteck in his work on Spain and Portugal (published in 1839), that Ximenez, in union with Cardinal de Mendoza, was instrumental in advising Queen Isabella to establish the Inquisition. But Llorente himself declares this assertion to be without foundation; indeed, a simple examination of dates and facts will suffice to show that Ximenez appeared at court *ten years after* the tribunal of the Inquisition had been established, and that he was only an obscure priest when it was first introduced.

The first participation of Ximenez in the affairs of the Inquisition dates from the year 1496, after Ferdinand the Catholic had complained to the Holy See that the inquisitors had, without his knowledge or consent, been disposing of the property of the condemned, and thus deprived the revenue of considerable sums. We have before expressed our opinion, that the Inquisitors very likely robbed the royal fiscus of many a prey by preserving the paternal property to the children of condemned persons, thereby incurring the displeasure of the king. Alexander VI., who governed the Church at that stormy period, considering it necessary to gain the friendship of Ferdinand, appointed the Archbishop Ximenez (March 29th, 1496) to examine the matter; and at the same time gave him power to demand restitution, if necessary, of whatever had been unjustly taken away from the revenue of the king. The result of this inquiry is unknown.

What connection Ximenez had with the Inquisition under Deza, the second grand-inquisitor and successor of Torquemada, we have no means of ascertaining. It was the vast knowledge of Deza that caused him to be chosen to occupy the high dignity of grand-inquisitor, and which afterwards was the means of his being elevated to the archiepiscopal see of Seville, as well as being ranked amongst the most illustrious theological writers of Spain.

Prescott seems to consider it "worthy" of a grand-inquisitor, that Deza should constantly have a tame lion at his feet. Llorente also represents him as a man possessed of a savage and austere nature, who surpassed in cruelty even Torquemada himself, and introduced the terrors of the Inquisition into Naples and Sicily. But this judgment is annulled by the Spanish academician Muñoz, who wrote a eulogium on Lebrija,* with whom Deza once had some misunderstanding. Muñoz, however, gives Deza the character " of a great and good prelate and a learned theologian." We ourselves may also add, that he was amongst the small number of those enlightened men who, by having encouraged and assisted Columbus, had a share in the glorious discovery of the New World.

The person who contributed most to injure the reputation of Deza as grand-inquisitor, was his assistant Diego Rodriguez de Lucero, scholastic of Almeria and inquisitor of Cordova, who, it must be owned, persecuted innocent persons, perpetrated barbarities of all kinds, and abused the confidence of Deza. As early as January, 1506, Peter Martyr describes him as " severus et iracundus a natura,

---

* " Memorias de la Real Academia de la Historia," tom. iii. p. 17.

judaico nomini et neophytis infensissimus,"* and one year later he repeatedly declares that his name Lucerius was a lie, and should be Tenebrerius.†

One of the most odious trials commenced at the instigation of Lucero, was that against Talavera, the archbishop of Granada, which brought Ximenez again in connection with the Inquisition. We have, in a former chapter, spoken of the virtues of Talavera, and his labours for the conversion of the Moors. But Lucero conceived the idea of accusing this noble prelate of judaizing tendencies, because he had from the beginning opposed the introduction of the Inquisition, protected the suspected neophytes, and was, on his mother's side, of Jewish extraction. The grand-inquisitor was soon won over for the prosecution, especially as Lucero produced a sufficient number of witnesses, who were probably bribed.‡ As early as the commencement of the year 1506, Peter Martyr began to complain of the insult offered to the most holy man in Spain.§ But not Talavera only was accused of heresy; several relatives of his fared the same, and were even imprisoned, particularly his nephew, Francisco Herrera, dean of the cathedral of Granada, and the sisters and mother of the latter.‖

We learn from Llorente, that Deza at first intended to intrust Ximenez with the examination of the orthodoxy of the archbishop of Granada.¶

---

* Epist. 295. † Ib. 333, 334, 339, 342. ‡ Ib. 333, 339.
§ Epist. 295. According to Llorente (i. 341), Lucero conferred first with Isabella concerning the suspicion against Talavera; but Isabella had then already been dead one year and a half. Leonce de Lavergne (in his Essay on Ximenez, "Revue des Deux Mondes," 1841, May) represents this matter as if Talavera had been attacked by the Inquisition on account of his intention of preparing an Arabic version of the Bible for the Moors.
‖ Epist. 342.
¶ When Talavera learned that Ximenez, and not the Inquisi-

But Ximenez reported the whole affair to Pope Julius II., and by following this course was instrumental in bringing about the speedy deliverance of, and tranquillity to the accused. The Pope, namely, took the inquiry entirely out of the hands of the grand-inquisitor, confiding it to the care of his legate in Spain, John Ruffo, bishop of St. Bertinoro, in the Romagna, and to a special commission, as Peter Martyr informs us.*

The history of this memorable trial is much curtailed by Llorente, but the details are happily supplied by Peter Martyr, himself one of the chief actors in the affair. The inquiry was opened in the spring of 1507, either at Torquemada, where the unfortunate Queen Johanna resided for some time after the death of her husband, or in the vicinity of this little town, at Palencia. Talavera sent a special representative to the court in the person of the canon Gonzalez Cabecas to conduct his case. He found, besides, an energetic defender in Peter Martyr, who warmly pleaded the cause of his venerable and well-beloved friend the archbishop, reminding the judges in particular of the venerable age of the man, who was then eighty years old, of his universally admired holy life, as well as of the zeal he had shown in the conversion of the Moors.† The legate, himself a friend of Peter Martyr,‡ showed much benevolence for the accused, interceded for them with the Pope,§ and sent the papers to Rome, whence the complete acquittal of Talavera and his relatives soon arrived.‖

---

tion, was to conduct the inquiry, he became somewhat reassured, as well as the people who loved him. Talavera says so himself in his letter to King Ferdinand of the 23rd January, 1507, reprinted in the " Memorias," &c., tom. vi. p. 489.

* Epist. 334. Llorente, i. p. 342, wrongly calls the nuncio bishop of Bristol, although he might have known from Peter Martyr, Letter 428, that Ruffo was Episcopus Britonoriensis.

† Ep. 334.   ‡ 328—330.   § 334, 335.   ‖ 342.

Talavera did not long enjoy his liberation; in a letter dated the last of May, 1507, Peter Martyr mourns the death of this wise and pious prelate, whom he elsewhere compares to King Solomon, and the patriarch of monachism, St. Hilario.*

Another trial, if possible, still more scandalous, instituted by Lucero, led to the nomination of Ximenez as grand-inquisitor.

Several persons in Andalusia accused of heresy, had falsely denounced a great number of others in the hope of saving themselves and seeing their trials suppressed by a general amnesty, which they thought might be obtained if the number of suspected were increased. Lucero was credulous and suspicious enough, on their report, to threaten a great number of persons of all ranks, ages, and sexes; nobles, ladies, priests, monks, nuns, and other persons of distinction. Deza gave his consent; but Ximenez raised his voice to oppose it, and entreated King Ferdinand to assist him, by writing to the pope and requesting him to deprive Deza of his office of grand-inquisitor. According to Zurita, who gives us this account,† Ximenez himself was then aspiring to this dignity. Ferdinand, however, would not agree to the proposal: it was only after the arrival of King Philip in Spain that Deza was ordered to confine himself to his diocese; his jurisdiction was suspended, and the affairs of the Inquisition were confided to the royal council. Zurita informs us that this proceeding was severely commented upon by the nation.

But when Philip died, Deza appeared again in

---

* Petrus Martyr. Ep. 334. Llorente (i. 342) wrongly states the trial to have lasted three years, whilst in reality it lasted only one year and a half. He further makes the archbishop live several months after his liberation, which took place on the 21st May. On the last of the same month he was already dead.

† "Anales," tom. vi. lib. vii. cap. 29.

public, and protesting against what had been done in opposition to him, reinstalled himself in his former dignity. His return encouraged the inquisitor of Cordova (Lucero) to recommence proceedings against those who had been falsely denounced. An insurrection was the consequence, for on the 6th of October, 1506, the whole population of Cordova rose. Lucero was forced to fly for his life; the buildings of the Inquisition were seized, and the prisoners released by the Marquis de Priego, who, in conjunction with the chapter of the cathedral and the magistrates of the city, required Deza to depose Lucero. The grand-inquisitor refusing to comply with their request, the insurrection became more threatening, and extended throughout the whole of Andalusia. Ferdinand now began to be convinced that Deza, his friend and confessor, against whom the public dislike was so clear and intense, could no longer preside over the Inquisition. He therefore made, during his residence in Italy, every requisite arrangement with Pope Julius II. for transferring the dignity of grand-inquisitor to Ximenez. Deza submitted, and resigned his office. Ximenez succeeded him, and his appointment was confirmed by a royal edict dated May 18th, 1507. There was, however, this alteration made, that his jurisdiction (contrary to what his predecessors enjoyed) should be confined only to Castile. Another grand-inquisitor, Don Juan Enguera, Bishop of Vich, was appointed for the kingdom of Aragon. But as both he and his successor, Don Luis Mercader, a Carthusian, died very soon after each other, the dignity of grand-inquisitor for Aragon was offered to Ximenez. He refused to accept it, and recommended Adrian, the dean of Louvain, in his place, who after the cardinal's death united both dignities in his own person, and afterwards became celebrated under the name of Pope Adrian VI.

Ximenez, immediately after his elevation to the dignity of grand-inquisitor, drew up several regulations, which were ordered to be published and observed as laws throughout the whole of Castile. They applied especially to the new converts, regulating the manner in which they themselves, their children, and all belonging to them, were to conduct themselves and observe the practices of the Christian religion, in order not to incur any suspicion of apostasy, witchcraft, blasphemy, &c.* At the same time, the cardinal commanded more complete instruction to be given them in religious matters, and particularly that they should be put on their guard against every form of superstition and blasphemy. Indeed, he adopted every expedient which justice and humanity dictated, in order to diminish the number of judicial cases reserved for the tribunal of the Inquisition. Llorente himself acknowledges that Ximenez exerted all his energy in providing for the instruction of the converts, for which object priests were appointed in all the large towns, with special injunctions to visit the new Christians in their houses, and warn them not to commit any act which might make them amenable to the Inquisition.

Another important matter which occupied the attention of the cardinal, was the trial of the inquisitor of Cordova.† Ximenez lost no time in ordering his arrest. Having been suspended from his functions, he was conducted to Burgos, and there imprisoned and ordered to give an account of his stewardship.

* Gomez gives us all these particulars ("De Rebus gestis," lib. iii.; Compluti, 1569). † Lucero.

All suspected witnesses were likewise arrested. Ximenez, considering the serious nature of the case and the great number of the accused, appointed, with the king's consent and approbation, a commission, under the name of "Catholic Congregation," which, as Llorente acknowledges, consisted of twenty-two of the most respectable personages that could be found ; these were to preside and take cognizance of the case, the cardinal himself being the president of the "commission." The names of the members were—the bishop of Vich, who was grand-inquisitor of Aragon ; the bishops of Ciudad-Rodrigo, of Calahorra, and Barcelona ; the mitred abbot of the Benedictine convent in Valladolid ; the president of the council of Castile, together with eight of his counsellors ; the vice-chancellor and president of the chancery of Aragon ; two provincial inquisitors ; two counsellors belonging to the higher court of the Inquisition, and an auditor of the chancery of Valladolid.

The reason why Ximenez named so many in the " commission" who belonged to Aragon was, that Castilian families had an interest in the case, and therefore it was necessary to obtain impartial judges.

In November, 1507, Peter Martyr, who was then residing at court, sent several particulars connected with the trial to his friends in Granada; viz., to Count Tendilla, viceroy of the city, and to the dean of the cathedral. "Lucero," he says, "stoutly asserts his innocence, but the judges suspect he has been guilty of great cruelty." (Epp. 370, 372.) In the month of March of the following year, this writer remarks, " that the judges, having carefully examined the sentences pronounced some time before by Lucero, were convinced that he had too

easily believed improbable accusations, and consequently punished the innocent." (Epist. 375.)

On the 9th of July, 1508, the "commission declared the witnesses brought forward by Lucero
to be unworthy of credit or confidence, both on
account of their bad character and contradictory
depositions. What they had asserted was, therefore,
inadmissible as proof against the prisoners, who
were accordingly liberated. The memory of those
who had already perished was honourably mentioned; the houses which had been pulled down,
under the pretext that they were private synagogues,
were rebuilt; while the defamatory "notes,"
which had been supplied by the inquiries of Lucero
and his agents in the books of the Inquisition,
were erased.

On the 1st of August, 1508, the judgment of the
"commission" was published with great solemnity
in Valladolid, in presence of the king, and a crowd
of prelates and grandees.

With regard to Lucero, Llorente informs us that
after he had been confined for some time in prison
at Burgos, he was, by an excess of indulgence,
ordered to return to his diocese of Almeria. Certainly Peter Martyr (Ep. 393) and several others
regretted that Lucero had been treated with such
mildness. But since he seems to have acted more
from excessive credulity and false zeal than from
any real wickedness of heart, and since the trial had
not revealed any "mala fides" in his conduct, as
Gomez observes, it seemed but natural that he
should be released after a year's imprisonment. He
was also deprived of his dignity, and reduced to his
former rank of canon, though Llorente erroneously
makes him a bishop.*

* He is simply called "canonicus" by Gomez.

About this period, Ximenez also acquired great
renown by the protection he gave to the celebrated Antonio de Lebrija, or Nebrissa, so called
from a town in the neighbourhood of Seville. In
the two chapters which treat of the foundation of
the university of Alcalá and the Complutensian
Polyglot, we have already said sufficient to prove
that Lebrija was one of the most distinguished
scholars of his time in Spain. The freedom with
which he spoke, in a work entitled "Critical
Remarks on some Passages of Scripture," respecting
a few mistakes in the translation of the Vulgate,
roused the indignation of several theologians, who
accused him of rashness and presumption.* Deza,
taking advantage of these complaints, condemned
his two first commentaries on the Bible, in consequence of which Lebrija suspended the publication of other works which he had prepared,
until Ximenez became grand-inquisitor, to whom
he then addressed an apology in self-defence,
written with considerable boldness and independence. Such is the account given us by the academician Muñoz,† and Nicolao Antonio, the historian
of Spanish literature.‡ Llorente is quite mistaken,
however, when he speaks of unkind treatment
shown to Lebrija. The fact is, that in spite of his
books being condemned, he continued to live undisturbed by Deza, sometimes at Salamanca as professor, and at other times at court as the royal
historian, until the year 1508, when Ximenez made
use of his labours in the publication of his Polyglot,
appointed him professor in the new university of

* Du Pin, "Nouvelle Bibliothèque des Auteurs Ecclésias-
tiques," tom. xiv. p. 121.
† "Memorias de la Real Academia," tom. iii. p. 17.
‡ "Bibliotheca Hispana Nova," tom. i. p. 132 (Madrid, 1783).

Alcalá, and honoured him with his particular friendship. In chapter XI. we have already seen how Ximenez consulted him in all important matters connected with the university; and how familiarly he often spoke to him from the balcony of his palace. To the end of his life, the archbishop also accorded his support and protection to many other learned men, who were thereby freed from the examinations of the Inquisition; amongst these may be mentioned the first chancellor of Alcalá, the abbot Lerma, and the learned Vergara.

Llorente relates many other events, all of which tend to the honour of Ximenez; amongst these we may mention the scrupulous care with which he watched over the officers of the Inquisition. The details connected with the case at Cordova show to what extent the officers of that tribunal abused their power by violence and oppression. Ximenez, therefore, endeavoured to diminish their influence by depriving them, amongst other things, of the right of permuting works of penance for some others which were imposed; he also closely watched their conduct, and even deprived many of their office altogether. In vain did these protest against his proceedings; in vain did they appeal to the pope himself. The Holy See confirmed all the acts of Ximenez, and resolutely maintained his authority.*

The cardinal, however, could not carry into effect, his project of having only ecclesiastics admitted to the grand-council of the Inquisition. The reply Ferdinand gave him on the 11th February, 1509, respecting this, shows clearer than anything else, the political character of the Inquisition. Ximenez protested against the nomination of Hortugno

---

* Llorente, tom. ii. p. 358.

Ybagnez d'Aguirre as member of the grand-council, on account of his being a layman. But Ferdinand told him that the grand-council was indebted solely to the king for its jurisdiction; the king had therefore a right of appointing for it and every other court of justice any one he chose. Ximenez was forced to yield during the lifetime of the king; but when, after the death of Ferdinand, he became regent of Castile, Aguirre was excluded from the grand-council. Charles V., however, reappointed this otherwise very worthy layman, after the decease of the cardinal.

Llorente does not tell us why Ximenez deposed also Antonio Ruyz de Calcena, the secretary of the grand-council, but relates other details which are not without interest.

At Toledo, the assistant of the gaoler of the Inquisition had had culpable connection with several of the imprisoned females; this crime had caused great sensation and general indignation. Doubtless the letter of Gonzalo de Ayora, cited by Llorente elsewhere (i. 349), in which the knight speaks in the strongest terms of such scandalous conduct, has reference to this case. Ximenez immediately recognized the greatness of the evil and the urgency of prompt remedy, and with his usual energy and severity did not hesitate, in concert with the grand-council, to decree pain of death against any functionary of the Inquisition found guilty of carnal connection with female prisoners.

We have before mentioned several beneficial measures of the new grand-inquisitor framed with the view of procuring better religious instruction for the newly-converted, and of guarding them against the danger of drawing on themselves a suspicion of apostasy. To these belong the foundation of special parishes for the new Christians, and the rules of conduct which the cardinal issued for them to preserve them against the suspicion of the inquisitors.

Unlike the above, and in itself of no importance, is the decree of Ximenez, of the year 1514, by which in future the crosses fixed in certain places of the Sanbenito were no longer to be of the usual form, but in the shape of a cross of St. Andrew, in order, says Llorente, that the cross of Christ might not be dishonoured by being represented on the dresses of the condemned.

The receivers of the revenues of the confiscated estates, generally obtained assistants at the expense of the fiscal; Ximenez abolished this custom, made the receivers pay for their assistants, and demanded of them to render an exact account of the possessions confided to their administration. In order to have their accounts properly examined, he issued special instructions for the use of the receivers and the persons charged with the revision of their management.

It is much to be regretted, that of all the cases examined and adjudged by Ximenez, Llorente gives us an account of only four. The details, however, connected with them, show us at once how careful and exact that great prelate was in the discharge of the duties of an office which has been so much calumniated and misunderstood.

The first of these trials took place in the year 1511, and concerns a so-called saint, the daughter of a peasant from Piedrahita, in the diocese of Avila, who wore the dress of the third order of St. Dominic, pretended to be in relation with Christ and the Holy Virgin, held frequent conversation with both, and called herself the bride of Christ. She held, besides, the opinion that she was constantly accompanied by the Holy Virgin, for which reason, out of politeness, she remained at the doors, offering the precedence to Mary, &c. Ferdinand ordered her to be brought to Madrid, and he, as well as Ximenez, conversed with her.

The opinions of the most learned theologians differing greatly on her account, one party declaring her a self-deluding visionary, the other party recognizing in her a saint, the Pope ordered his nuncio and two other bishops to inquire into the matter; whilst on the other hand, also, the Inquisition, as in duty bound, tried the girl. Ximenez, for his part, believed her to be inspired, and as the tribunal could not discover anything dangerous, heretical, or deceptive in the person, she was spared further molestations.

The second trial related by Llorente, concerns Juan Henriquez de Medina. The Inquisition of Cuenca had, after his death, declared him guilty of heresy, and purposed to confiscate his property; Ximenez, on the appeal of the heirs, appointed commissioners to revise the trial. When these, according to the established usage, refused to communicate the names of the witnesses to the relatives of the deceased, the interested parties appealed to Leo X., who, by his briefs of the 8th February and 9th May, 1517, ordered, under pain of excommunication, the communication of the acts and an equitable judgment; Henriquez was in consequence entirely absolved. Ximenez, who was then near his death, seems to have had no other share in the proceedings than the nomination of the commissioners for the revision.

The third trial ended only after the cardinal's death. John of Covarrubias, of Burgos, who had once before been absolved, was after his death again denounced to the Inquisition by the fisc. Leo X., from the very beginning, interested himself the more warmly in behalf of the accused, as Covarrubias had been his schoolfellow. By a letter dated 15th February, 1517, he recommended to Ximenez a quick conclusion of the inquiry, and shortly after translated the case to the court of Rome. Ximenez remonstrated against this, and Charles V., after the Cardinal's death, in the autumn of the same year, protested so strongly against this pretended encroachment of the Roman court on the rights of the Holy Office, that the Pope handed the matter over to Cardinal Adrian, the successor of Ximenez in the office of grand-inquisitor; Llorente does not tell us the ultimate result.

We cannot gather from Llorente that Ximenez participated at all in the fourth trial. The superiors of the Augustines had complained of the prosecution of several members of their order by the Inquisition, and obtained by a brief of Leo X., of the 13th May, 1517, the privilege for the order of its members being in matters of faith judged by their own superiors, and not the Holy Office. We do not learn whether Ximenez regarded this exemption favourably. If we did not know Llorente better, the selection of these trials would induce us to believe that he intended to show the solicitude of the Holy See to lessen the severity of the Inquisition. A decree of Ferdinand, of the 31st August, 1509, specially directed against these endeavours of the Pope, is very remarkable; he therein threatens with death all those who obtained of the Pope or his legate, a bull or other document directed against the Inquisition; Llorente, of course, finds this sanguinary measure in favour of the Inquisition very rational and just, because it is based on the principle of *opposition to Rome*, nor does it shake his opinion that the Inquisition was an *ecclesiastical* institution.

How easily the most astonishing contradictions are made to agree by Llorente is strikingly illustrated by the following example:—He is of opinion that Ximenez is the real author of an anonymously written allegorical novel on the Inquisition, discovered in the library of St. Isidor, at Madrid, and entitled "Of the Government of Princes." He asserts that it furnishes clear proof of the cardinal's aversion to the Inquisition, as well as of his demands for numerous important changes, for instance, publicity of the debates, &c. This curious work is addressed to Charles V., when still prince of Asturia, and partly reprinted amongst the documents in vol. iv. of Llorente's History. Llorente presumes it to have been written by Ximenez himself, or at his instigation, before his nomination as grand-inquisitor, and after the death of Isabella, that is between the years 1504 and 1507, forgetting that a few pages before (iv. 389) he has fixed 1516 as the year in which it was written ; this date is probably correct, for during the years 1504—1507 Charles, then only four to seven years old, was in no wise capacited for the consideration of such important topics.

Although we would gladly accede to Ximenez the honour of such liberal principles as are expressed in the book in question, yet we cannot help strongly doubting the admissibility of Llorente's opinion. Prince Charles is therein urged to introduce several important changes in the Inquisition, more especially publicity of the inquiry ; but, in reality, it was Ximenez who determined King Ferdinand not to yield to the clamour of the new Christians, and is said even to have sought to indemnify him from his own purse for the refusal of 600,000 ducats, which the new Christians had offered him, to tempt him to grant their request.* When, after the death of Ferdinand, they repeated their offer to Charles V., raising the sum to 800,000 gold ducats, and were even backed in their petition by Chièvres, duke of Croy, the instructor and confidant of Charles, Ximenez protested once more against the grant of publicity, addressing the following letter to the king :—

"Most high and mighty Catholic King, most gracious lord !—The Catholic kings, as your Majesty is aware, have bestowed so much care upon the Holy Tribunal of the Inquisition, and examined its laws and institutions with so much prudence, wisdom, and conscientiousness, that modifications of the same are not needed, but would rather be prejudicial than otherwise. At the present moment such changes would fill me the more with sorrow, as they would assuredly tend to increase the defiance shown to the Inquisition by the Catalonians and the Pope. The pecuniary embarassment of your Majesty is, I confess, very great, but certainly that of Ferdinand the Catholic, the grandfather of your Majesty, was greater, when the newly converted Christians offered him six hundred thousand gold ducats to carry on the Navarrese war. He did not accept their proposals, because he preferred the

* Llorente, tom. i. p. 367. Flechier, liv. vi. p. 492. Jost, vol. viii. p. 237. Ximenez would probably have heard of this offer only after the acceptance of it by Charles, if Cardinal Pucci, whose nephew was destined as nuncio for Castile and therefore wished to ingratiate himself with Ximenez, had not given him timely notice. Gomez, p. 1104.

purity of the Christian religion to all the gold of the world.* With all the true devotion of a loyal subject, with the zeal which I must have for the office to which your Majesty has raised me, I beseech you to open your eyes and follow the example of your Majesty's grandfather, and consent to no changes in the proceedings of the Inquisition. All the objections raised by its adversaries have before been refuted, under the Catholic kings of glorious memory. The modifications of even the most unimportant law of the Inquisition could not be done without betraying the honour of God and insulting that of your most illustrious ancestors. If this consideration has not sufficient weight with your Majesty, may it please you to recall the deplorable occurrence which has lately taken place at Talavera de la Reina, when a newly-converted Jew, who had learned the name of his accuser, searched for him and stabbed him. The hatred against these informers is indeed so great that, if the publication of their names is not prevented, they will not only be assassinated in private and public, but even at the foot of the altar. No one will be found in future willing to risk his life by similar denunciations; this would be the ruin of the Holy Tribunal, and the cause of God would be left without a defender. I live in confidence your Majesty, my King and Lord, will not become unfaithful to the Catholic blood which runs in your veins, but be convinced that the Inquisition is a tribunal of God, and an excellent institution of your Majesty's ancestors."†

After this it was impossible that Ximenez should

---

* Ximenez does not speak here of his own offer to Ferdinand, and we cannot vouch that he ever made it.

† Carnicero, tom. ii. p. 289—293. Gomez gives only an abstract of this letter.

have written or been the instigator of the allegorical novel mentioned by Llorente. It must, on the contrary, be attributed to one of those whose influence he opposed in the above letter.

In the computation of the victims of the Inquisition under the administration of Ximenez, Llorente has evidently done injustice to the cardinal. Llorente's usual practice of basing his calculations rather upon probabilities, the fallacy of which we have demonstrated before, than upon documents, is in this instance specially invalidated by other circumstances. According to his own confession, the administration of Ximenez commenced on the 1st of October, 1507, and lasted therefore little more than ten years, whilst Llorente's calculations are based upon eleven years. Besides this, he makes Ximenez responsible for the condemnations of all the twelve ancient tribunals instead of only seven, Ximenez being only grand inquisitor of Castile and not also of Aragon. The hypothetical number of two thousand executions would consequently be reduced by half.

In the year 1514 Ximenez established a new tribunal at Cuenca. Llorente here again commits the same error which we have exposed before, that of increasing the number of criminals with each additional court of justice. And lastly he starts in his calculations with the entirely arbitrary assumption that Ximenez, whose benevolence he admits, executed every year as many persons as his predecessors, Torquemada and Deza, whom he describes as cruel.

We know nothing certain or even probable of the number of trials conducted under Ximenez; but this we know, that our cardinal more clearly circumscribed the jurisdiction of each separate tribunal, by dividing them according to the provinces and bishoprics and introduced tribunals in Oran in Africa, which he had conquered, as well as in the Canary Islands and America. These latter held, however, as we shall see hereafter, jurisdiction only over the old Christians who had settled there, and not over the indigenes. Ximenez has, in all these affairs of the Inquisition, shown himself the same straightforward and thoroughly just, though severe man, which he was in all his other actions. We shall find him the same again on a field on which the former Franciscan monk will hardly be expected —that of battle.

CHAPTER XIX.

THE CONQUEST OF ORAN.

MILITARY events have always occupied a more prominent place in history than other more important facts that occur in time of peace. Thus, more abundant details have been preserved connected with the part Ximenez took in the Spanish conquests in Africa than respecting other events in his life, however important.

So far back as the year 1505, when the " Great Captain " (Gonsalvo de Cordova) returned to Spain from his glorious Italian campaigns, crowned with honour and accompanied by his victorious legions, Ximenez advised the king to employ these troops in the conquest of some strong fortress in Africa. As a bishop, he sighed for the day in which he should see the cross replanted in that country, where once the Church flourished so prosperously, and where prelates, like St. Cyprian and St. Augustine, displayed such genius, learning, and piety : as a statesman, too, Ximenez had not forgotten his interview with the famous Venetian traveller Vianelli; hence, he saw at once the immense advantage that would be gained by Spain, both in a strategic and commercial point of view, if she had a station on the coast of Africa.

Directly opposite to the Spanish port of Carthagena, was a large and strong fortress called by

2 D

the Moors Mazarquivir. It stood on the sea, and had become, in consequence, a nest of pirates, who spread terror in every direction. Some years before (1501), the Portuguese had attempted, but in vain, to gain possession of it. However, in September, 1505, Ferdinand, assisted by the munificence of Ximenez, sent a fleet against the place under the command of Diego de Cordova and Raymund de Cardona. The expedition succeeded. Cordova was appointed governor of the conquered city, and remained there with a strong garrison, whilst his companions in arms returned to Spain.*

About this period Ximenez conceived a still vaster plan; viz., a new crusade against the infidels for the recovery of the holy sepulchre in Jerusalem. For this object, he entered into negotiations with the kings of Spain, Portugal, and England. Gomez has preserved a remarkable memorial of these negotiations: a letter addressed by King Emmanuel of Portugal to Ximenez, in which his majesty expresses the most profound respect for the cardinal, and the hope that his pious desires for the recovery of the holy places and the overthrow of Mahometanism may speedily be realized. At the same time he assures Ximenez, that every day he fancies himself in the holy sepulchre receiving from his hands the true and real body of our Lord; and that he counts more on the part which Ximenez takes in the enterprise than upon the efforts of the most powerful kings in Europe, because the presence of so holy a man would be sure to draw down most abundant blessings from heaven. Moreover, that the pecuniary assistance offered by the cardinal, his high character, zeal, and

* Gomez, Zurita, Ferreras, &c.

geographical knowledge, would be a certain pledge of success.*

But in spite of so much ardour and enthusiasm, all this beautiful project fell to the ground, in consequence of the political events which quickly followed, by Philip becoming regent of Castile, and afterwards quarrelling with Ferdinand. Ximenez, too, experienced profound grief on beholding the small Christian colony of Mazarquivir exposed to the greatest danger of being lost. The circumstances are as follows :—In the same month that king Ferdinand returned from Italy, to assume the government of Castile after the death of Philip (August, 1507), a terrible misfortune happened to the Spanish garrison in Africa. The governor, Cordova, being most anxious to extend his conquests further, had fortunately succeeded in taking two small places from the Moors. He was returning with a considerable booty of men and beasts, when his troops, having halted to take some repose, were suddenly attacked by the enemy and completely routed ; the governor himself escaped with difficulty. Gomez, while mentioning the great grief which filled the heart of Ximenez on hearing the account of this terrible disaster, adds, that it only served to confirm the cardinal the more in the plan he had conceived, of extending the Spanish conquests in Africa still further. His character, indeed, was such, that the more obstacles he met with to oppose his designs, the stronger his resolutions became to carry them into execution.

The arrival of Ferdinand, however, and the events which followed therefrom, delayed for a time the accomplishment of the cardinal's project. In

* Gomez, " De Rebus gestis," p. 78 (ed. Compluti, 1569).

August, 1507, the king arrived at Tortoles with his
daughter Johanna (called " loca "*); and thence
hastened with the court to Maria del Campo, and
sent the cardinal's hat to Ximenez, who was then
residing in a neighbouring town, named Mahamud.
After Johanna had taken up her residence at Arcos,
in company with Ferdinand's second consort, Germaine, his majesty and Ximenez proceeded together
to Burgos, in order to devise some remedy for the
evils that afflicted the kingdom.†

As many of the grandees viewed the return of
Ferdinand with regret, they publicly evinced their
hostility to him in many ways. But the king conducted himself towards them with as much prudence as mildness. He endeavoured rather to win
them to his cause than to punish them; and if he
sometimes spoke of their past conduct, it was not
by way of reproach, but as it were in joke. However, with regard to some of the nobles who continued
obstinate in their refusal to submit, Ximenez
advised Ferdinand to be firm and severe. Hence,
the duke de Najara and the marquis de Priego,
who were amongst the most turbulent, were severely
punished; so also were the bishops of Badajoz and
the young duke de Medina-Sidonia. Ximenez was
of great assistance to Ferdinand in his work of
pacification and in the humiliation of the grandees.
It is uncertain whether the cardinal took any part
in the formation of the league of Cambray, which
was directed against Venice, and concluded, December 10th, 1508, between Ferdinand, Louis XII.,
king of France, the emperor Maximilian, and Pope
Julius II. That which gives some ground for the

* That is, deranged, mad.
† Peter Martyr, epp. 367, 368.

uncertainty is, that Ximenez did not assist at the negotiations. He was then too much occupied with the expedition to Africa. The league of Cambray reconciled Ferdinand with two of his most dangerous enemies, the king of France and the emperor Maximilian; the latter renounced all his claims to the regency of Castile.

A short time after, Ferdinand was delivered from another source of trouble. His unfortunate daughter Johanna at last consented (March, 1509) to reside at Tordesillas, a pleasant and healthful spot, whither she took the remains of her deceased husband. There most of her former follies disappeared, that profound melancholy only remaining which adhered to her till the end of her days.*

Matters being now quietly settled in the kingdom, Ferdinand at last yielded to the prayers and representations of the cardinal, and resolved to fit out a considerable fleet for the expedition to Africa. The object was the conquest of Oran. This city, situated at a short distance from Mazarquivir, was one of the most important of the Moorish possessions, being very populous and strongly fortified. It was a kind of republic, under the protection of the king of Tremesen, and had acquired considerable opulence by its extensive commerce with the Levant. Oran was also as powerful as it was rich, having at its command an immense number of cruisers, which swept the shores of the Mediterranean and committed fearful ravages. This stronghold Ximenez was most anxious to take ever since the Spaniards gained possession of Mazarquivir: Vianelli had already furnished him with plans of the city and its environs; but the political state of

* Peter Martyr, epp. 410, 411.

affairs in Spain had hitherto delayed the fulfilment
of the cardinal's anxious desires. The cardinal was,
however, now resolved, though in his seventy-second
year, to march in person to the conquest of this
important place, and even to furnish himself all the
necessary expenses, so that the king might incur no
risk or suffer any loss, should the enterprise not
succeed.* In vain did many of the grandees ridicule the whole affair, exclaiming " that the world
was turned upside down; and that while the Great
Captain was telling his beads in Valladolid, the
Franciscan father was preparing himself for battles
and sieges !"†

But impartial observers thought otherwise; for
Gomez assures us, that they considered, Ximenez
possessed all the requisite qualities of a general:
an invincible courage and an admirable prudence,
united with a mind fruitful in resources. Such,
too, was the conviction of Ferdinand himself, who
immediately placed all the forces that could be
raised, at the disposal of Ximenez, and left him to
choose any Spanish port he thought proper for the
equipment of the fleet. He also gave him a number
of blank papers (signed with Ferdinand's name)
which could be filled up by Ximenez, when circumstances required any orders to be carried out in the
king's name. Two military judges were likewise
annexed to the expedition to punish military offences.
In a word, orders were issued throughout the whole
kingdom for the levy of troops, and the purchase of

---

* Zeal for the propagation of the faith and the conversion of
the Moors, were the chief motives that enkindled the zeal of
Ximenez. (Robles, cap. xxii. p. 246.)—*Trans.*

† " Gonsalvum Fernandum, orbiculos quibus preces annume-
rari solent, Pintiæ volvere; antistitem vero Toletanum cædes et
lanicnam optare," &c. (Gomez, p. 100.)

everything necessary for so important an undertaking.*

Ximenez would willingly have named his friend the "Great Captain" commander of the forces; but through regard for King Ferdinand, who for some time had not been on terms of friendship with Gonsalvo, he intrusted the post to Count Pedro Navarro, who was brought up in the school of the illustrious warrior during his Italian campaigns. Navarro had also recently acquired great glory in Africa, having conquered for the Portuguese, in 1508, by the permission of Ferdinand, the strong city of Arzila, in the kingdom of Fez. Troops now came pouring in from the provinces of Castile and Aragon, amongst which Alcalá especially distinguished itself by its zeal and energy; hence, in a short time, four thousand horse and ten thousand foot were under arms,† and officers appointed to command them who were already illustrious for their bravery. Gomez gives us the names of several of them; amongst whom we find a titular bishop, named Bustamante, at the head of one of the divisions. Garcias Villaroel, a cousin of the cardinal and prefect of Cazorla, commanded the cavalry; whilst Vianelli, being perfectly acquainted with the locality of the country, was named one of the staff.‡

---

* Leonce de Lavergne highly praises the military talents of Ximenez, in an article on the conquest of Oran, inserted in the "Revue des Deux Mondes" (tom. xxvi. p. 536; Mai, 1841). See also an article on the subject, by Vincente Gonzalez Arnao, in the "Memorias de la Real Academia de la Historia," tom. iv. pp. 2—15.

† The numbers are variously stated. Fléchier says the whole of the forces amounted to about 16,000; while Robles estimates the cavalry at 2,000.—*Trans.*

‡ Peter Martyr, ep. 413; Mariana, lib. xxix. cap. 18; Zurita, tom. vi. lib. viii. cap. 30.

For some years before, the cardinal had been carefully husbanding his revenues with a view to this
expedition, so that Peter Martyr and others were
almost inclined to accuse Ximenez of avarice, saying
"that he was richer than Crassus himself." The
metropolitan chapter of Toledo, having been requested by Ximenez to assist him in his expedition,*
sent him a considerable sum " for the success of a
war in which the honour and extension of the Christian faith were interested." Many of the canons
even wished to accompany the cardinal to Africa, if
he would allow them to do so. Pecuniary assistance
was sent from other dioceses also, as Gomez makes
mention of a letter addressed by Ximenez to Ferdinand, wherein he expresses his delight " that other
churches and dioceses had followed the example of
Toledo."

Though everything was now ready for the expedition to sail, it was delayed under various pretexts,
by false reports and base insinuations. At the
head of the intrigue against Ximenez were the
senator Varga and his friend Villalupo, who had
charge of the commissariat and stores. Navarro
himself, by continually proposing new plans, endeavoured to obtain the sole command. But Ximenez
satisfied all the scruples and calmed all the fears of
the king, whilst he reminded him with great wisdom
and judgment, and in words as powerful as they
were worthy of an archbishop, "that his promise
had already been given, and the honour of the
Christian name, as well as the good of the kingdom
were at stake," &c. By these and other pressing
arguments Ferdinand was induced, towards the end
of the year 1508, to renew his promise of supporting
the expedition.

* Ximenez addressed a very interesting letter to the chapter
on the subject, the substance of which is given by Gomez.—*Trans.*

But new difficulties arose, on the part of Varga and Villalupo, who refused, on various pretexts, to deliver the munitions provided by them, alleging that it would be better to forward them to Mazarquivir in transport vessels rather than intrust them to the fleet. The folly of such a proposition was evident, and Ximenez terrified his two enemies into submission by threatening them with the king's anger. Matters seeming now to be more quiet, the cardinal, in the spring of the year 1509, summoned Navarro and the other principal officers around him, in order to arrange with them the plan of the expedition. He afterwards went to Toledo, and confided the temporary government of his diocese to the bishop of Calahorra; he also collected together the prefects and governors of various towns and cities, to the number of twenty-four, each at the head of his division of troops, and addressed many encouraging words to them. Public prayers were likewise ordered for the success of the enterprise. At length, at the commencement of the year 1509, Ximenez hastened to join the army, being attended by two of his canons; viz., Francisco Alvar, theologian of the chapter; and Carlo Mendoza, abbot of St. Leocadia: these followed him to Carthagena, where the fleet, together with the forces, awaited his arrival. He arrived there March 6th; Navarro had previously ordered the vessels to sail from Malaga to Carthagena to receive Ximenez. Some more levies had also been raised by Colonel Spinosa, at the expense of the cardinal; while relays of horses were distributed at certain distances, so as to connect Carthagena with different parts of Spain, that the king might receive immediate information of what had passed.

Just as the fleet was about to sail, a mutiny suddenly broke out in the army. Ximenez had wisely resolved not to give any pay to the soldiers till after the expedition, in order to be able the more easily to keep the military in his power. But now they refused to embark, declaring "that they would take no part in the war unless they received the whole of their pay in advance." In every direction was heard the wild exclamation :, "The monk is rich— let him pay—let him pay us." A great number of soldiers left the camp, and occupied a neighbouring hill, threatening at the same time to proceed to extre- mities. Vianelli, instead of suppressing the mutiny, only enflamed it the more, by executing some of the ringleaders.* Ximenez, who perceived the threat- ening aspect of affairs, immediately deputed Garcia Villaroel, prefect of Cazorla, to command Vianelli to use some mildness. Villaroel probably discharged his commission somewhat rudely. The consequence was, that a violent altercation took place between them. Vianelli spoke contemptuously both of Ximenez and Villaroel. The latter immediately drew his sword, and severely wounded Vianelli on the head. He fled for refuge into the citadel, fearing the indignation of Ximenez, who, however, soon reconciled the two combatants by the valuable services of an officer named Salazar. Being a po- pular speaker, he also harangued the seditious soldiery, and soon quelled the mutiny. Ximenez, too, having promised the troops to advance a portion of their money as soon as they had em- barked, they hastened to the vessels to the sound of trumpets, bags of gold crowned with boughs of laurel being carried before them. The pay was dis- tributed according to the cardinal's directions, and order completely restored. Ximenez, on this occa- sion, deemed it prudent to use mildness and modera-

* Vianelli is supposed to have encouraged the revolt.

tion, especially as he suspected that General Navarro had excited the revolt, through the hope either of delaying the expedition or of breaking it up altogether.* In a confidential letter addressed to his faithful friend Ruiz, he complained bitterly of the perfidy he had to endure, together with numerous other trials and vexations ; but he suffered all things patiently (he said) in order to avoid greater evils.

At last, on the 16th of May, 1509, the fleet weighed anchor. It consisted of ten galleys, eighty large transports, besides a large number of smaller vessels.† The forces amounted to four thousand horse and ten thousand foot, as we have already mentioned. The following day, being the feast of our Lord's Ascension, the fleet reached the coast of Africa. Fires were soon observed blazing along the Moorish hills, announcing the arrival of the enemy, and calling the infidels to arms. All the Spanish vessels safely entered the port of Mazarquivir, without having suffered the least injury. Ximenez was received by the governor of the city, and conducted to his apartments in the castle. But he spent the night without sleep, occupied in giving instructions for the following day. All the cares and troubles which he had lately undergone, had evidently affected his health. But though his body was weak and emaciated, his mind still possessed its wonted vigour ; while he knew well how to infuse into his soldiers the courage which animated his own breast, and to elate them with the hope of victory.

---

* These and other details connected with the expedition are all taken from Gomez, lib. iv.

† "Classis ergo octoginta actuariis navibus, decem maximis triremibus, quas nunc regias galeras vocant, constabat ; præter permulta navigia minora, et scaphas majoribus servientes." (Gomez, p. 107.)

He summoned Navarro in his presence, and assured him, before all the officers, " that the glory of this expedition would belong to him alone; and that as regarded himself, he only undertook to furnish the expenses of the war, to encourage the troops, and to acquaint the king with their exploits."

No time was now to be lost. A council of war having been held, it was resolved to gain possession as soon as possible of a hill situated between Mazarquivir and Oran, and which was the key to the latter; if there were any delay, the Moors would probably hasten to defend it; and therefore the galleys were to drop down under the walls of Oran in the morning, and attack the city both by sea and land.*

As soon as the army had landed and formed in order of battle, Ximenez left the castle. He was clothed in his pontifical robes and mounted on a mule, with a belted sword at his side. A number of priests and religious surrounded him. Before him rode, on a white charger, a Franciscan friar of immense stature, bearing aloft the silver cross of the primate as the standard;† a scimitar hung from his girdle, and all the other ecclesiastics wore their swords, according to the directions of Ximenez. As it was Friday, the cardinal dispensed the soldiers from their accustomed fast.

As the cavalcade advanced, the priests and other religious sang, with great devotion and enthusiasm,

---

* The hill being the principal point of attack, Oran was at first assaulted merely to divert the attention of the inhabitants. Quintanilla gives the best account of the attack in his " Archetypo," lib. iii.

† Robles thus speaks of it: " Un estandarte que de la una parte llevava un santo Crucifixo, y de la otra las armas de los Cisneros " (p. 252).

the hymn "Vexilla regis prodeunt, fulget Crucis mysterium," &c. The cardinal rode along the ranks, and imposing silence, addressed the following harangue to the troops:—" If I thought, my brave Spanish soldiers, that your courage and confidence stood in need of being excited by any words of mine, it is not I, without eloquence and unskilled in the art of war, who would have ventured to address you. This duty I leave to one of your valiant captains, whose stirring eloquence has often led you on to victory, and who has won your confidence by sharing in your toils and triumphs. But knowing your ardour to prosecute this holy war, in which both the glory of God and the welfare of our country are interested, I wish to be a witness of your bravery and magnanimity now that the die is cast, as the proverb expresses it. For many years you have heard the words repeated: ' The Moors are ravaging our coasts; they are dragging our children into slavery; they are dishonouring our wives and daughters; they are insulting the Christian name.' These crimes and evils you have long thirsted to avenge. Soldiers! you I have chosen, to give to our country this consolation. The mothers of Spain have seen us pass through towns and cities; prostrate before the altars of God, they have entreated the Most High to bless our undertaking. They are already anxious to behold us returning victorious; already, in imagination, they behold us breaking the chains of their captive children, and restoring them once more to their loving arms. The day so long desired has at length arrived. Soldiers! behold before you the accursed land: behold the proud enemy who insults you, and now thirsts for your blood. Prove to the world this day, that hitherto it has not been lack of courage on your part, but only the want of a fitting opportunity to avenge the wrongs of your country. As for myself, I wish to be the first in facing every danger; for I have come here with the resolution to conquer or to die with you, which God forbid. Where can the priests of God find a better place than on the battle-field, fighting for their country and religion? Many of my noble predecessors in the see of Toledo have given me an example, and have died a glorious death on the field of battle."*

After this address, Ximenez was about to place himself in the foremost ranks of the soldiers, whose enthusiasm had reached the highest pitch on hearing the stirring words of the cardinal. They were deeply affected at beholding a prelate in his seventieth year, worn out with fatigues and watchings, so anxious to expose his sacred person to danger. But both men and officers pressed around him, conjuring him, for the common good and his own safety, to retire from the field. Ximenez very unwillingly yielded to their entreaties, and retired into the fortress of Mazarquivir, after having given his blessing to the whole army. In the citadel was an oratory dedicated in honour of St. Michael. There, on bended knees and with his arms uplifted towards heaven, the cardinal offered his prayers, that the God of battles would grant victory to the Christians.†

Ximenez had, however, scarcely entered the fortress, when he was informed that Navarro thought the cavalry would be useless in a country so hilly as that around Oran appeared to be, and,

---

* This address is almost a literal translation from Gomez (lib. iv. p. 109). Fléchier has also given a translation of it (liv. iii. p. 241). Robles gives merely a short epitome.—*Trans.*

† Gomez adds, that he also prayed, "multis lachrymis."

therefore, intended to employ only the fleet and the infantry. Ximenez, who was quite opposed to such a measure, immediately left his apartments, and ordered the cavalry to support the infantry in the engagement. He also gave orders for the troops to occupy the defiles of the sierras around Oran, so as to be out of the reach of any sudden attacks from the Moors. This double precaution contributed considerably to the success of the day.

But another difficulty presented itself to Navarro. Perceiving an immense number of the enemy occupying the heights which he had resolved to attack first; seeing also the exhausted state of the troops, who had hardly recovered from the effects of their voyage, and that the day was far advanced, Navarro began to doubt which would be the best plan to adopt, whether to defer the attack to the following day, or to profit by the enthusiasm of the troops and commence the attack immediately. In this perplexity he hastened to Ximenez to ask his advice. The cardinal, after a few moments' reflection, replied in the following words :—" Navarro, in this engagement, Christ, the Son of the Most High, and the impostor Mahomed, are about to contend. To defer the battle, would, I consider, not only be injurious and dangerous, but also sinful ; therefore, be not fearful, but lead your men on to battle ; for I am confident that this day you will gain a glorious victory over the enemy."* The wisdom of this advice was afterwards seen, for only three hours after the capture of Oran, the messuar, or chief visir of Tremesen, arrived with powerful reinforcements ; but seeing the city already in the

* Gomez, p. 109. Prescott and others sadly curtail these words, which seem to have been, as it were, inspired.

hands of the Christians, immediately returned, without attempting its relief.

Navarro, returning to the camp, gave instant orders for the troops to advance. He divided the infantry into four battalions, placing the artillery and cavalry in the rear. When the trumpet sounded for the attack, the troops raised the national shout, "Santiago, Santiago!" and began their ascent up the sides of the sierra, amidst a shower of stones and arrows which were hurled down upon them by the Moors. But the Spaniards pressed forward with such impetuosity, that some of the foremost soon came in contact with the enemy, with whom they fought, contrary to the commands of their officers, hand to hand, according to the chivalrous custom of the time. Luis Contreras was killed in one of these single combats, and his head, having been cut off, was carried to Oran and shown to the populace as the first trophy of victory; after which the children kicked it about in the streets like a ball. The Christian captives were told that the head belonged to the "great alfaqui," that is, to the cardinal; but the falseness of the report was detected by one of the prisoners, who had been a servant of Ximenez. The Spaniards gradually became masters of the lower part of the sierra, where they found a stream of clear water that restored their exhausted strength. The attack was again renewed, while the Moors, rushing down, endeavoured to drive back their assailants. The position was disputed with fearful obstinacy, until at length Navarro placed a battery of guns in such a position as to operate on the dense masses of the enemy. Their flank being attacked, the enemy began to waver, seeing themselves decimated both by the sword and the fire of the Spanish artillery. A retreat was made, which soon ended in a confused flight. The heights being abandoned, the Spaniards pursued the flying enemy, without paying the least regard to the commands or menaces of their officers; a circumstance which might have proved fatal, but fortunately only tended to increase the terror of the Moors, who supposed the Spanish army to be much more numerous than it really was.

The fleet, in the mean time, had anchored before the city, and opened upon it a heavy fire, which was answered with great spirit and vigour from the Moorish battlements, until at last a Spanish gunner, by a well-directed shot, destroyed one of the principal batteries. The fire of the enemy beginning to slacken in consequence, the troops on board made good their landing and soon joined their comrades, who, pushing forward with all haste towards Oran, resolved to carry the place by escalade: though but ill provided with ladders, they overcame every obstacle. In a short time the Spanish colours floated from the walls. The first who gained the summit was Sousa, a captain of the cardinal's guard, who, having planted the standard of his master on the highest tower of the fortifications, exclaimed with a loud voice, *Santiago y Ximenez!* The soldiers, rushing into the city, obtained possession of the gates, and threw them open to their comrades. For some time the enemy continued the engagement with obstinate fury: seeing themselves, however, pressed on all sides by the Spaniards, they fled in confused masses towards Tremesen; but being met by the Spanish cavalry, they were all cut to pieces. Though the victory was glorious, it was stained with cruelty and unnecessary bloodshed. All were massacred within the walls, without distinction of age or sex. In vain did Navarro call the troops off; in vain did he strive to restrain their fury. They returned to the slaughter with renewed

madness, until at last, wearied with plundering and
butchery, and gorged with wine, the greater part
of the soldiers sank down in the streets to sleep
by the side of the bodies they had slain.

Navarro, fearing an ambuscade on the part of
the Moors, kept watch all the night with some
troops under arms. The following day, when the
sun rose on the scene of carnage, the Spaniards
were thoroughly ashamed of their previous excesses.
The general placed guards at all the important
points, and summoned the Moors, who had fled to
the mosques and other places, to surrender ; his
object was to have everything quiet and secure
in the city before the arrival of the cardinal.
Force, however, was necessary, in order to gain
possession of the mosques, which were only taken
after considerable difficulty and labour. Four
thousand Moors are said to have fallen in the battle,
and from five to eight thousand were made prisoners;
while the loss of the Spaniards is said to have
amounted only to thirty,[*] an assertion which can
scarcely be believed. The spoil was estimated at
about five hundred thousand golden ducats ; in consequence of which many of the soldiers returned to
Spain exceedingly rich with their share of the
booty.[†]

When Ximenez received, the same evening, the
news of the glorious victory, he spent the whole
night in acts of praise and thanksgiving to God.
The following day he proceeded by sea to Oran,
where he made his solemn entry, preceded by the
archiepiscopal cross, and surrounded by his victo-

---

[*] The number certainly seems incredible ; but both Gomez
and Robles state that it amounted only to *thirty* slain.—*Trans.*

[†] Several minor particulars of the engagement have been
omitted by Dr. Hefele ; while Prescott gives several details which
are not found in Gomez.—*Trans.*

rious troops, who received him with loud acclamations of joy, declaring "that he alone was the real conqueror of the infidels." But the cardinal, humbly disclaiming any merit on his part, was heard to repeat aloud the words of the Psalmist: "Non nobis, Domine, non nobis, sed nomini tuo da gloriam."

Ximenez immediately proceeded to the fortress called Alcázava, where, having received the keys from the governor, he had the inexpressible happiness of setting at liberty three hundred Christians, who had been taken captives to Oran. The spoil found in the city was presented to him, as being the commander-in-chief; but though it consisted of a great number of most valuable objects in gold and silver, he took nothing for himself, but merely reserved a part for the king, and divided the rest amongst the army. He thanked publicly the whole of the forces, including the generals and officers, for the signal courage they had displayed in the capture of the city; and distributed decorations and presents to those who had particularly distinguished themselves. Fearing a pestilence might arise, he also ordered the bodies of the slain to be removed and interred as soon as possible. Such a quantity of provisions were found in the city, and especially so many engines of war, amounting to more than sixty pieces of cannon,* that every one was astonished such a strong place could have been taken in a few hours. Some believed a miracle had been wrought by the piety of the cardinal; whilst others, and especially the Moors themselves, suspected treachery on the part of some of the inhabitants of Oran, who shut the gates of the city against the Arabs that were coming to their

---

* "Plusquam sexaginta sunt capta." (Gomez.)

assistance, and opened them for the Spanish troops. Another account is also given by Gomez, of the cardinal having gained over to his side, by means of two individuals, named Alfonso Martos and Martin Argoto, some of the principal inhabitants in Oran, who acted as spies, and gave Ximenez secret intelligence of the movements and plans in the Moorish camp.*

Ximenez remained in Oran for some time. The day after his entry, he visited the city on horseback, in order to examine its situation, and give the necessary orders for the repair of the fortifications. He was especially assiduous in dedicating the mosques to the worship of the true God, having converted them into churches. The principal one was consecrated in honour of the Blessed Virgin, under the title of the Annunciation. He ordered a solemn festival to be celebrated every year, in memory of the conquest of Oran. Another mosque was dedicated in honour of St. James, the patron of Spain, and an hospital established and dedicated to St. Bernardin of Sienna. He also founded two monasteries, one for Franciscans and the other for Dominicans. And as he was fearful lest many of the converted Spanish Jews might hasten to Oran, in order to renounce the Christian religion with impunity, he established a tribunal of the Inquisition there, appointing as the chief officer over it a priest named Yiedra, who was as pious as he was learned.

The cardinal immediately sent a courier to Ferdinand, to give him all the necessary information respecting the capture of Oran. Fernandez de

* M. Leonce de Lavergne maintains, as an undeniable fact, that a Jew and a few Moors were induced by Ximenez to assist him in the capture of the city. ("Revue des Deux Mondes," tom. xxvi.; Mai, 1841.)

Vera was chosen to carry the despatches; but the thoughtless young man, more intent on enjoying himself during the journey than on minding his errand, allowed a soldier, who perceived his negligence, skilfully to steal the despatches from him, and on their delivery to Ferdinand, to receive the presents which were intended for Vera. Ximenez afterwards deputed his faithful friend, Francisco Ruiz, to repair the negligence of the first messenger.

The cardinal now began to deliberate about the propriety of advancing still farther into Africa with his victorious army. An event which happened about this time had some weight with Ximenez. The inhabitants of Tremesen, being exasperated at the capture of Oran, seized their arms, and massacred all the Christian merchants in the town, in spite of the efforts of the king to restrain them, and although they were living under the royal protection. The Jews shared the same fate. But when the first transports of their fury had passed away, the Moors were seized with terror. Fancying that the Spaniards were already at the gates, they abandoned their homes, and retired into the kingdom of Fez. But if this could be considered a favourable circumstance for the continuance of the war, other reasons induced Ximenez not to carry it on in person. Navarro began to be very jealous of the cardinal's fame; and on one occasion publicly said, "that he never could have thought an old captain like himself would have been obliged to receive orders from a monk." When one of Navarro's soldiers had killed a domestic of the cardinal, and the latter was about to order instant punishment to be inflicted on the culprit, Navarro interfered, and insolently addressed the following unbecoming language to Ximenez: "Whatever disorder arises, comes from you. No army ever knew two masters. Had I the sole command in Africa, I could subdue the country in a few months. The king nominated you generalissimo solely for the siege of Oran : with the siege, therefore, your power expires. Return to your diocese, and there reap the fruits of your victory ; but if you remain here, know that henceforth you shall be treated as no other than a private individual."* This threat was no sooner pronounced than executed.

Ximenez, however, preserved his composure, and made no reply. On the following day he sent for Navarro, and issued his orders as usual, mildly but firmly. Navarro obeyed, and also acknowledged his fault. But what contributed more than anything else to induce Ximenez to return to Spain was a letter which fell into his hands, addressed by the king to Navarro, in which Ferdinand requested him "to detain Ximenez in Africa as long as his presence was necessary." The old prelate's feelings were hurt, for he began to suspect that the king wished him to die in a foreign and burning climate. The jealous mind of Ferdinand seemed to justify this suspicion, for he could not endure to see the glory of his friend, the " Great Captain," dimmed by that of Ximenez.

The cardinal immediately resolved to hasten his return to Spain. Before his departure he appointed Navarro commander-in-chief of the army, observing at the same time, that "old men were usually timid and circumspect, and that he was convinced he could be of more service to the war in Africa by returning to Spain than by remaining in the camp." He then gave Navarro much good

* One can hardly believe such language could have been used by Navarro, had not Gomez given us the very words themselves. —*Trans.*

advice respecting the government of the new ac-
quisitions, entreating the general especially not to
allow any fraud or embezzlement by his officers.
For the maintenance of the army, he left an abundant supply of stores, consisting of fruit, wine, and
biscuit; and for the revictualling of the fleet, a large
sum of money. He also appointed Villaroel governor of the fortress Alcazava, and promised to send
him from Spain, as soon as he arrived there, an
abundant supply of provisions.

All the officers were so much affected by the
cardinal's kindness and attention, that they immediately entreated him not to abandon them in a
strange land; for as fortune had so wonderfully
favoured them under his guidance, they were
afraid that if he now left them, it would fare
ill with them. Navarro himself joined his entreaties with those of the soldiers, and appeared
exceedingly grieved for his past conduct towards
Ximenez.

The cardinal set sail from Oran on the 23rd of
May (1509), and with a favourable wind arrived the
same day at Carthagena, accompanied by a few
attendants. He remained there a week, solely occupied with providing for the necessities of the army,
and establishing a line of transports to run between
Carthagena and Oran. He also addressed a letter
to Ferdinand, entreating him to send royal commissioners to Carthagena, with powers to provide
everything requisite for Oran and the troops quartered there. Towards the end of May, fearing he
might suffer from the excessive heat of the place,
he departed for Alcalá de Henares. Before the
harvest commenced, he most kindly sent to their
homes all the labourers whom he had enrolled for
the war; and afterwards, in his will, appointed
two canons of Toledo to visit all his subjects, and

repay them for whatever losses they had sustained from the expedition to Oran.

The rector of the university of Alcalá, Don Pedro Campo, hearing of the cardinal's approach, deputed two of the most distinguished doctors to advance a day's journey, and meet his eminence. The cardinal received them with exceeding joy, like a father receiving his children after a long absence. Whilst taking refreshments with them, he asked many questions respecting the state of the colleges, the progress of the new buildings, the state of discipline, and the number of students. The two professors were utterly astonished on hearing Ximenez speak only of the Muses, instead of dwelling upon his African conquests and brave Spanish soldiers. One of them, named Fernando Balbas, playfully alluded to the cardinal's pale looks and emaciated frame. Ximenez, roused by the remark, as if it were a reflection upon his indolence or cowardice, replied with warmth: "You do not know, Fernando, the strength and vigour which God has given me. Had my army been faithful to me, pale and emaciated as you see me, I should have hastened at this moment to plant the Cross of Christ in all the chief cities of Africa."*

The next day he made his entry into Alcalá, where he was greeted, both by the citizens and the students of the university, with extraordinary acclamations. A part of the walls had been broken down, in order to receive him as a conqueror in the most solemn manner; but Ximenez refused this honour, preferring to enter through the usual gate. He was preceded, as in the triumphs of ancient times, by a body of Moorish slaves, leading camels loaded with the

---

* Translated from Gomez (lib. iv.), but almost wholly omitted by Dr. Hefele.—*Trans.*

booty* destined for the king. For himself the cardinal had reserved some rare curiosities, with which he intended to enrich his beloved university; viz., several Arabic manuscripts on astrology and medicine; the keys of the gates and citadel of Oran; some chandeliers and basins from the mosques; Moorish colours which had been taken; besides several other things—all of which Ximenez ordered to be preserved in the church of San Ildefonso.† To Talavera he sent the key of Oran, which had for a long time been called the "key of Talavera," because it was taken by a captain of that city, named Bernardin de Meneses. He also presented a red standard, in the middle of which figured an azure crescent. Both these gifts were deposited in a chapel of the Blessed Virgin.

In order to perpetuate the memory of the capture of Oran, a large tablet was placed in the Mozarabic chapel of the cathedral of Toledo, containing the following inscription, which gives an epitome of the events already related in this history. It is taken from Robles (p. 143) :—

" Anno salutis Christianæ millesimo quingentesimo nono, pontificatus domini Julii papæ secundi anno sexto, regnante serenissima domina Joanna regina Castellæ, relicta quondam Philippi Burgundi, unici Maximiliani imperatoris nati, ac pro ea Ferdinando ejus genitore Aragonum et utriusque Siciliæ rege Catholico regnorum gubernacula gerente : reverendissimus pater et dominus frater Franciscus Ximenez de Cisneros, cardinalis Hi-

* " Cameli auro argentoque ex prædâ Africana onustæ." (Gomez.)

† Gomez says that they were to be seen in his time. "Quæ adhuc Compluti magno studio visuntur." At the present day, a few curiosities are still shown in the sacristy of the cathedral at Toledo, which are said to have been brought from Oran by Ximenez.—*Trans.*

spaniæ et archiepiscopus Toletanus, ex portu Carthaginensi cum ingenti armatorum classe, tormentis et commeatibus refectissima, movens, in biduo ad Mazarquibir, die decimo octavo Maii appulit, et ea nocte in classe pernoctato, sequenti die egresso e navibus exercitu, cum hostibus conflictum habuerunt, quibus, ultra urbis Aurensis ambitu expulsis et profligatis ad portas usque impune preventum est, ubi picas pro scalis ad muros exponentes, in urbem primi congressores ascenderunt, et elevatis ad mœnia signis Christianorum ac portis undique reseratis, cuncti fideles pariter intraverunt, et cæsis passim iv. mill. hostium, urbs ipsa cum arce infra quatuor horas capitur, triginta de nostris solum desideratis, annuente Deo, qui in Trinitate perfecta vivit et regnat in sæcula sæculorum. Amen."

Ximenez remained a few months in Alcalá, in order to recruit his health. But he declined going for the present either to Toledo or to the court at Valladolid, to receive the congratulations which he heard awaited him there. However, at his request, the chapter of Toledo ordered public prayers to be offered, to thank God for the success of the expedition and his safe return to Spain. But the sad news which Ximenez received from Oran about this time considerably lessened his joy. Zarata, one of the chief judges there, had informed him that Navarro and Vianelli, by acts of the most revolting avarice, were actually causing a famine in the city, in spite of the abundant supply of provisions which Ximenez had sent from Spain. They had monopolized all the corn, and forbidden any to be introduced into the place. In vain Zarata endeavoured to put an end to such disorders. He was only answered by threats; and when he offered to resign his office and return to Spain, was not allowed to do so, lest he should inform the king of their conduct. Ximenez then considered it his duty to inform Ferdinand of the disgraceful proceedings of Navarro. He requested his majesty to exclude him from all authority in the civil government, and confine him to his military command. Moreover, in order to introduce more unity in the operations of the military power in Africa, Ximenez pressed upon Ferdinand the necessity of placing Oran and the citadel of Mazarquivir, under the authority of one and the same governor. He proposed Don Fernando de Cordova, the then prefect of Mazarquivir, as the person most capable, in his opinion, of fulfilling the duties of that important post. " It is also necessary," continued Ximenez, " to send a certain number of priests to Oran with fixed salaries, and to establish colonies, in order that the fertile soil of the country may be cultivated." In a word, Ximenez reminded Ferdinand, if he wished to preserve the Spanish conquests in Africa, it was of the highest importance that the defence of Oran should be committed to the knights of the order of St. James—each knight being required to spend at least twenty years in the country—just as the knights of St. John of Jerusalem had done for the defence of Rhodes against the Turks.*

Ferdinand complied with the whole of this advice, except the latter part; but Ximenez did not live to see it fulfilled, not daring during his regency to attempt so important an undertaking without the consent of Charles V., and died before he had an opportunity of conferring with the young monarch

* Gomez, lib. iv. Mariana, lib. xxix. cap. 18. Fléchier, liv. iii. pp. 259-260.

on the subject. In accordance with the pressing
solicitations of the wise statesman, Ferdinand in
the following year ordered Navarro to attack the
strong and important Moorish city of Bugia, which
the Spaniards took on the 5th of January, 1510,*
after having performed prodigies of valour. The
joy over the victory, however, was lessened by the
death of Count Altamira, who, in charging boldly
the ranks of the enemy at the head of his troops,
was mortally wounded by a poisoned arrow. When
he perceived his end to be near, he lifted up his
eyes towards heaven, and thanked God that he died
fighting in His cause. His death was universally
regretted by the whole army, and by none more
than Ximenez, who had raised the young hero to
the rank of lieutenant-general during the expedition to Oran, on account of his bravery.

Five months later, the king of Bugia endeavoured
with a powerful army to retake his capital; but he
was repulsed with great slaughter by Navarro.
Algiers, Tunis, and Tremesen soon became subject
to the Spanish crown; while, towards the end of
July, Navarro became master of Tripoli.† Such
unexpected successes caused the greatest joy, not
only to Ferdinand and Ximenez, but also to the
pope and the sacred college. A solemn act of
thanksgiving was performed in Rome, and in a
consistory held by Julius II. the highest eulogiums
were passed upon Ximenez as the first author and
soul of these successful expeditions.‡

In the mean time, a fatal accident happened in

---

* Peter Martyr (epist. 434). Fléchier is mistaken in the date
1511; it ought to be 1510.

† Gomez (lib. iv.).

‡ Peter Martyr (epp. 435, 436, 437, 440, 442).   Gomez
(lib. iv.).

Africa to the illustrious Vianelli and Don Garcias de Toledo. The first perished through the treason of an officer whom he had injured. One day he went to dig a well at some distance from the fortress, without having any guard with him but a few servants. The officer secretly conducted some armed Moors to the place; where they suddenly attacked Vianelli, and massacred both him and his servants.

Garcias de Toledo, son of the duke of Alba, and father of the celebrated captain of the same name, had attacked, by the orders of Navarro, the isle of Gerbe or Zerbi,* near Tripoli. Being the month of August (1510), the heat was excessive. The soldiers, oppressed by a devouring thirst, hastened in disorder to the different wells in the island. But whilst quenching their thirst, they forgot to take the requisite precautions against the enemy, who suddenly emerging from a wood of palm-trees, assailed the Spaniards, and killed Garcias and four thousand of his soldiers. Those who escaped the sword died through thirst. This was the commencement of Navarro's misfortunes. Losing the favour of Ferdinand, he renounced his allegiance, and served in the armies of France. But being afterwards taken prisoner by the Spaniards, he was confined in a dungeon, where he soon died; or, as some assert, put an end to his existence. With him terminated Ferdinand's conquests in Africa.†

Ximenez was at last induced to visit Toledo, in order to fulfil the vows he had made during his

---

* Prescott and Fléchier call the island Gelves.—*Trans.*

† Villaroel returned from Oran to enjoy a life of repose. But having ill-treated a respectable citizen, he lost the favour of Ximenez, and died in obscurity.—*Trans.*

expedition to Oran, and to gratify the wishes of his venerable chapter. He was received with unbounded joy. He ordered two annual masses to be solemnly celebrated by the chapter (for which he left sufficient funds), in memory of the day on which the Spanish army took Oran and he made his solemn entry into the captured city. As long as he lived, he never ceased to take the deepest interest in his " dear Christian oasis," that lay amidst a desert of infidelity : even death itself, if we may credit some of the cardinal's biographers, could not lessen his affection or solicitude for it. The tradition is, that the Moors often beheld the gigantic form of a Franciscan wearing a cardinal's hat, some times riding on a mule, and at other times fighting against them with a sword in his hand at the head of his troops. It was in the year 1643, at the time when the Moors of Algiers were besieging Oran, that the form of the cardinal was seen last, infusing new courage into the Spanish soldiers and promising them victory. Other prodigies are mentioned by Quintanilla,* who seems to be too fond of the marvellous.

But without our being obliged to give credence to these, or deciding on what foundation they rest, it is certain, that for some centuries the Spaniards retained possession of their African conquests, until the year 1790, when an earthquake occurred and destroyed nearly the whole of the city. It soon after fell into the hands of the dey of Algiers. But in our time Oran and the north of Africa fortunately again belong to Christians, and form an important colony of the French empire.

The plan which Ximenez had conceived, of plant-

---

* "Archetypo," &c., lib. iv. cap. 21.   (Ed. Palermo, 1653.)

ing Christianity in Africa, and there establishing
the power of Spain, was full of grandeur and wisdom.
Charles V. hoped to see it realized.   But it was not
the fault of these two great men, if the daily decay-
ing state of the monarchy, so far from extending its
conquests, was at length unable even to preserve
them.   With the Spanish lion, the cross of Christ
also disappeared from the soil of Africa.

CHAPTER XX.

XIMENEZ ATTENDS TO HIS DIOCESE. — HIS MUNIFICENCE. —
TERESA ANTIQUES. — THE UNKIND TREATMENT WHICH HE RE-
CEIVED FROM FERDINAND, ETC.

AFTER the death of Isabella, Ximenez, being engaged in many important matters, could not bestow so much attention to his diocese as he desired. But when the regency had been secured to Ferdinand, the troubles in Castile settled, and the conquest of Oran achieved, Ximenez considered it his duty to visit his diocese, and provide for its necessities. The first object of his solicitude was the church of Baza. It was originally under the jurisdiction of the bishop of Toledo : in the eighth century it was taken by the Moors, and reconquered by Isabella in 1489. The church was then incorporated by the queen, as part of the diocese of Cadiz, by and with the consent of Mendoza, who was primate of Spain. Ximenez, wishing to have it restored to the diocese of Toledo, referred the matter to his chapter, and ordered the archives to be examined, in order to prove his claim. The Holy See, also, having been consulted, gave its decision in favour of Baza being restored to Toledo.

Ximenez soon after founded a convent for nuns at Illescas, which was dedicated to the Blessed Virgin ; and another Franciscan convent at Torrelaguna,* the place of his birth. Hearing that a

---

* Ximenez endowed these convents with ample revenues. Don Antonio Ponz speaks of a Franciscan monastery being in existence there, when he visited the town in the last century : " Fabrica

monastery, not far distant from that town, had become disorderly, he visited it to restore discipline. Once, when a great scarcity of provisions occurred in his diocese, he ordered public granaries to be erected; and from his own revenue settled upon the poor an annual donation of forty thousand measures of wheat. He committed the distribution of it to the magistrates, who, in order to testify their gratitude, raised a fund for the performance of an annual service, in the chapel where the Mozarabic Liturgy was celebrated in Toledo, at the conclusion of which a panegyric was to be pronounced in honour of Ximenez. In proportion to their extent, the cardinal bestowed the same relief, under certain conditions, upon the towns of Cisneros and Alcalá de Henares. In Torrelaguna, he also erected a magnificent church,* and endowed it with ample funds. For the convenience of the building, as well as for the benefit of the public, he constructed an immense aqueduct, for the formation of which passages were opened through rocks and mountains. The expense is said to have amounted to a million of English money.

But, in the midst of his pastoral solicitude, an event happened about this time which caused Ximenez great trouble and vexation. Several of the grandees, whom he had been instrumental in humbling, had long sought an opportunity of making him lose the favour of Ferdinand. When the cardinal was in Oran, he ordered that all the correspondence between Spain and Africa should pass through his hands; hence, he opened the king's letter to Navarro, of which we have already spoken in the

grande y solida, que fundó el Cardenal Cisneros," &c. (" Viage de España," ed. Madrid, 1781, carta. iii. tomo decimo.)—*Trans.*

* Described by Ponz, ut supra.

preceding chapter. When Ximenez returned to
Spain, the circumstance of the letter having been
opened was eagerly laid hold of by the nobles, who
denounced the act to the king as a public outrage,
and an attempt upon the rights and privileges of
his majesty.

But, not content with seeking the ruin of the cardinal, they also wished to deprive him of the greater
part of his property, hoping that this would result
from his losing the king's favour. Knowing the
royal exchequer to be almost exhausted, and
Ferdinand ready to seize any pretext in the hope
of freeing himself from his obligations, they represented to him that the cardinal could not demand
payment of the money which he had lent for the
conquest of Oran; for though they could not
positively deny the engagements to which the king
had pledged himself before the expedition, yet
they maintained that the cardinal had acquired so
much glory as well as booty in Africa, that he lost
all right to demand any other compensation. The
conditions to which the king had acceded were, that
he should either annex Oran to the archbishopric
of Toledo, or refund from the treasury the expense
incurred by Ximenez. Ferdinand seemed unwilling
to fulfil the contract. The cardinal, however, both
asserted his claim, and refuted the objections
urged against him. "As for the booty," he said,
" all that he had reserved for himself were a few
books and manuscripts, which he had bestowed
upon his university; a gift which would tend rather
to the benefit of the country at large than to his
own profit."

Ximenez, finding that he gained no redress, wrote
a letter to the king, in which he reminded him of
his promise, and alleged in excuse for his application the demands of the Church upon the money

expended on the expedition. The king referred the matter to his council, and proposed for their deliberation, whether it would be better to grant the jurisdiction of Oran to the cardinal, or to reimburse him. Some gave it as their opinion, that the first proposition was the best, because the maintenance of the garrison of Oran would then belong to the archbishops of Toledo. But others objected to the offer, because thereby an important position, the key of the whole kingdom, would be placed at the discretion of individuals,—a measure at all times dangerous, as the treason of Count Julian, assisted by Archbishop Oppa, had proved. The king agreed with this opinion, and accordingly decided on repaying the money, but with conditions exceedingly hurtful to the feelings of the cardinal. A commissioner was appointed to examine all his private apartments, to see what he had reserved for himself from the spoils of Oran. The soldiers, too, whom Ximenez had levied for the expedition, were commanded to show to the commissioner the carpets, silks, and other articles distributed amongst them, a fifth part of which was to be set apart for the king. But Ximenez refunded to these poor men the amount of what they had forfeited, and consoled them under their trial. As for himself, being conscious of his rights, he bore the indignity in silence, contenting himself with merely producing his account-book.

About the same time, the king proposed to him, to cede the archbishopric of Toledo to his natural son, Alonso de Aragon, in exchange for the archbishopric of Zaragoza. Don Alonso was a worldly prelate, a skilful politician, and an intrepid warrior, exceedingly beloved by his father. Ximenez declined the offer, with as much dignity as firmness : " Never will I leave my spouse," he replied, " in exchange for another; I would rather return to my former

2 F 2

state, the poverty and solitude of which have always been dear to me. I will not give up my see to any one, except to the church and the poor." Here the matter ended. Ximenez heard no more from Ferdinand on the subject.*

In the year 1510, when Ximenez was in Alcalá, he received information of the death of the bishop of Salamanca. No one appeared more worthy to occupy the vacant see than Francisco Ruiz: but every one knew in what horror the cardinal held all intrigues for obtaining ecclesiastical dignities. This time, however, Ximenez appeared really anxious that his old and dear friend should obtain the bishopric. He, therefore, commissioned one of his domestics to have an interview with Ferdinand and to solicit the dignity in favour of Ruiz. But as Ferdinand had previously nominated Francisco Bo-badilla, son of the celebrated countess de Moja, who was a particular friend of Isabella, he sent word to Ximenez, that Ruiz might, if he chose, succeed Bobadilla in the bishopric of Ciudad-Rodrigo. He did so. Some years after, on the death of the bishop of Avila, Ruiz was translated to that see: this was done, however, without the consent of Ximenez, who was opposed to bishops changing their sees.

Though at this period Ferdinand showed a certain coldness towards the cardinal, yet all was forgotten by him when his interests or the welfare of the kingdom were at stake. As he had espoused the cause of Pope Julius II. against the king of France, he applied to Ximenez for his co-operation, and desired him to meet him at Seville. The Cardinal immediately obeyed the summons, though it was in the depth of winter (January, 1511). It was necessary

---

* This circumstance is related by Pulgar, in his life of the cardinal. (See Fléchier, " Histoire du Cardinal Ximénes," liv. iii. p. 272.)—*Trans.*

for him to pass through a small town in Castile, called Torrijos, where lived a pious lady, named Teresa Antiques. Ximenez had been her confessor when he was a simple religious. She was very anxious to receive and entertain him in her house, on account of the great esteem she had for him, and her desire to profit by his instructions and advice. But knowing how particular Ximenez was with regard to females, she caused a report to be spread that she was obliged to leave home on account of urgent business. In the mean time the cardinal accepted her invitation, supposing that she had really left the town; but he was hardly a few hours in the house before the lady returned, and requested an audience of him. Ximenez, however, was so angry with her, on discovering the ruse, that he instantly left the house, without even attending to the usual rules of politeness, and took up his residence in a neighbouring Franciscan monastery. The next morning he departed at an early hour.*

In order to satisfy his piety he remained a few days at Guadaloupe, a place celebrated for the number of pilgrims resorting there in honour of our Blessed Lady. Ximenez left behind him many proofs of his munificence and veneration for the Mother of God. Continuing his journey along roads that were almost impassable, he arrived at the town of Fornillos, where he had formerly resided for some time with Queen Johanna, after the death of her husband. The inhabitants, who had preserved a grateful remembrance of his kindness, showed him the greatest marks of respect. On the way the cardinal lost a great number of mules belonging to his retinue, through their having eaten a poisonous plant which grew in that part of the country. As he approached

* The account is taken from Gomez, lib. v.

Seville, towards the end of February, 1511, he sent word to his representative at court, Lopez Ayala, that he should arrive the following evening. When Ferdinand heard this, he went out several miles with his court, to meet a man whom he loved not, but of whose advice and assistance he stood much in need. The compliment, however, gave great offence to the courtiers.

CHAPTER XXI.

THE CARDINAL SUPPORTS THE CAUSE OF POPE JULIUS II.

On the death of Pius III., Julius II. was elected to succeed him, a pontiff who possessed both military and political talents of the highest order, which threw into the shade all his predecessors. He was an enemy of all nepotism; but, being more of a secular than an ecclesiastical prince, he directed his efforts, not to the aggrandisement of his family, but to the extension of the temporal power of the Church.* Above all, he was most anxious to reconquer the territories which had been wrested from the states of the Church, to force his vassals into obedience, and to put an end to the depredations which his enemies were continually making upon the inheritance of St. Peter. He was also the declared enemy of Venice, which was then at the height of her power, and mistress of almost all the seaports in the pontifical states.

The first years of his reign were occupied in subduing the pride and insolence of the Baglionis, Bentivoglios, and other intractable vassals. At last an opportunity presented itself of humbling the "Lion of St. Mark." The republic had recently gained a brilliant victory over the emperor Maximilian, and imposed upon him most humiliating conditions. But this triumph was the subsequent cause of all its misfortunes. The king of France, Louis XII., viewed with a jealous eye the strength

* See Peter Martyr, ep. 577.

and power of Venice increasing more and more every day; hence he began to fear for his states of Milan, seeing they were near so dangerous a foe. Under the frivolous pretext that his dignity had been wounded, in the treaty concluded between the republic and the emperor, he formed the celebrated League of Cambray* with Maximilian, the pope, and the king of Spain, with the sole object of enfeebling Venice and depriving her of her possessions. This design was accomplished by the allies during the years 1509 and 1510, when Julius II. recovered the rich domains of which the republic had despoiled the states of the Church.

But the political views of the pope did not rest here. Though Venice was weakened, France, on the other hand, was all-powerful in the south of Italy, where she had possession of Milan: might she not, therefore, become a dangerous enemy to the pontifical states? Whatever may have been the motives of his holiness, he separated himself from his former allies, and took part with the Venetians against France. The king of France was naturally exceedingly surprised and irritated at the sudden change in the sovereign pontiff's politics, which thus destroyed all his plans and designs with regard to Italy. He immediately vowed vengeance, and even resolved to overthrow the pope himself, if possible. Two methods were devised for effecting this object; viz., the force of arms, and the convocation of a council in opposition to the Holy See. The first was very soon carried into execution, for in the summer of 1510, while the French prelates were assembled at Tours, a French army seized upon Bologna. About the same time the emperor Maximilian and Louis XII., in concert with several cardinals, at the

---

* December 10th, 1508.

head of whom was the Spanish cardinal Bernardin de Carvajal, convened a council at Pisa. There the pope was accused of having disturbed the peace of Europe, of having gained the tiara by simony, and neglected, in spite of his solemn promise, to assemble a general council.

Surrounded by these difficulties, and confined to his bed by an attack of fever, Julius II. wrote to the king of Spain. His letter arrived at Seville (May 18th, 1511), where Ferdinand and Ximenez were then residing. The pontiff explained to his majesty the deplorable state of affairs, especially lamenting the conduct of the cardinals, almost all of whom had abandoned the cause of the Church. His holiness concluded by imploring the assistance of Ferdinand against their common enemy, the king of France.*

The king, as Fléchier justly remarks, always considered it an honour to protect the Holy See when his own interest was concerned. He therefore summoned a council of all his ministers in the palace, at which also Ximenez was present, together with all the bishops then at court. The subject was discussed with considerable care and earnestness. The unanimous opinion was, " that it would be folly to fight the enemies of the Christian religion in Africa, when the head of the Catholic Church was attacked in Rome.†" Ferdinand resolved, accordingly, to send into Italy all the forces at his disposal ; while, at the same time, he deprived cardinal Carvajal of his bishopric by the express desire of the pope.

Ximenez was the principal person that induced Ferdinand to adopt this resolution. To Julius he

* Fléchier gives the letter at greater length, liv. iii. p. 284.—
—*Trans.*

† Peter Martyr, ep. 468.

had been indebted for his dignity of cardinal, and the university of Alcalá for numerous privileges. For these and many other reasons Ximenez loved his holiness, and admired his unbending and energetic character. But this was not all. The cardinal wrote a letter to the pontiff to encourage his holiness to persevere in his efforts, sending him at the same time a considerable sum of money for the wants of the Church.

Ferdinand now began in earnest to prepare himself for carrying on the war against France. He summoned, for this object, the cortes to meet him in Burgos: Ximenez, also, who had returned to his diocese from Seville was invited to attend; but fearing the heats of summer, and not having quite recovered the fatigue of his journey to Seville, he begged to be excused till the end of August. He then hastened to Burgos. Hardly had the cortes commenced its deliberations, when the pope's nuncio arrived with the information, that an alliance had been concluded between Julius II. and Venice. Ferdinand also joined the alliance, and published the bull for the convocation of the fifth general council of Lateran. The proceedings of the schismatical meeting at Pisa are well known. Louis XII. easily gained over the Emperor Maximilian to his cause, both of whom were anxious to have the pope deposed. Besides seven refractory cardinals, twenty bishops (chiefly French) assisted at the opening, which took place November 1st, 1511. But the clergy of Pisa refused to take any part in the proceedings, and even refused to lend the prelates the chalices and vestments necessary for saying mass. The pope, too, threatened to excommunicate the inhabitants if they gave any support to the schismatics. The assembled prelates themselves were seized with a sudden panic; and fearing to fall into the hands of the pope, they soon removed from Pisa to Milan, in order to be under the protection of France. Here they continued their sessions, amidst the contempt and derision of the people; and in the eighth and ninth sessions, had the audacity to declare the pope "deposed." But Julius, on the other hand, lost no time in convoking a general council to meet in the Lateran palace at Easter (1512), at which he invited all the princes of Christendom to attend, and gave thus the death-blow to the schismatical assembly.*

Such was the state of affairs when the pope's legate arrived in Spain. Gomez, unfortunately, does not give us any details connected with the subsequent events. We are therefore obliged to depend upon the account given us by Peter Martyr, who was then in Burgos at the court of Ferdinand. Ferreras has also inserted in his "History," the chronicle of a contemporary ecclesiastic named Bernaldez,† who gives some interesting details relating to the publication of the bulls for the council. The pope had named as his legate in Spain one of the judges of the rota, named Casadorus, who arrived at Burgos at the beginning of November (1512). By the king's desire, the bull for the convocation of the council was published with great solemnity in the cathedral on Sunday, November 16th. After the gospel, in presence of Ferdinand, of all the prelates, the grandees, and an immense number of the faithful, the legate read from the pulpit the pontifical bull in Latin; then

* Peter Martyr, epp. 469, 470. See also Harduin, "Collect. Concil." t. ix. p. 1584.

† Andres Bernaldez was curate of a town near Seville, named Los Palacios. He was a native of Fuente, in Leon, and died about the year 1513. His "chronicle" is still in manuscript.—Trans.

he explained it in Spanish, and gave many reasons
to prove the necessity for calling the council, inviting
the king at the same time to send as many prelates
as possible to assist at it. The legate afterwards
adressed Ximenez and the other bishops, begging
them to be present in person at the council, if circumstances permitted. He concluded his discourse
by exhorting the grandees, and the laity in general, to
defend, if necessary, by arms, the unity of the Church.

By the order of Ferdinand, Valerian de Villa-
quiran, bishop of Oviedo, ascended the pulpit after
the legate. Being an excellent popular speaker,
he addressed the people at considerable length, and
explained the meaning of the bull, enlarging also
upon the words of the legate. But suddenly
changing his style, he inveighed with great force
and earnestness against those cardinals who had
proved traitors to the sacred college and the Church.
He also denounced the king of France as the head
of the revolt, and as guilty of great wickedness in
having opposed the pope and seized upon Bologna,
&c. Ferdinand, moved by these burning words,
assured the legate that he would joyfully devote
all his power and resources to the defence of the
Church, and commission a certain number of prelates to assist at the council. The legate respectfully
thanked the king in the name of the pope. About
this time Ferdinand had the good fortune to gain
over to the cause of the pope and the council his
son-in-law, Henry VIII. of England. Even the
Emperor Maximilian himself was induced to detach himself from France and declare war against
that country; while, to justify his conduct before
Europe, Ferdinand addressed a remarkable letter to
Ximenez, which is preserved by Gomez.*

* Lib. v. p. 138; ed. Compluti, 1569.

The dissolution of the cortes and the commencement of the Italian campaign, allowed Ximenez an opportunity for returning to Alcalá to attend to the affairs of his diocese and family.* On his return, he found that Cabrera, archdeacon of his cathedral, had, on account of his advanced age, obtained from the Holy See powers to nominate a co-adjutor. But this proceeding being contrary to the statutes of the chapter of his cathedral, he forbad the canons to agree to the powers he had received. At the same time, he wrote to the pope and the king, entreating them to revoke the permission which had been granted. He remained at Alcalá till the matter was satisfactorily adjusted.

His university now occupied his principal attention. For its better regulation, he enforced the observance of two decrees, which had lately been promulgated by the council of Lateran. The first required every master, besides instructing his pupils in profane literature, to be exceedingly careful in teaching them the duties of their religion and the rules of ecclesiastical discipline; also the Holy Scriptures, the articles of faith, the forms of prayer, the traditions of the Church, and the examples of the saints. It particularly enjoined, that on Sundays and holidays the students should diligently perform the exercises of devotion, hear mass, attend a sermon, and read good books. The second decree forbade all students in holy orders to spend more than five years in the study of grammar, logic, and philosophy. Rectors were not allowed to permit them to remain longer in the college, unless it was the intention of the students to apply to canon law or theology.

In order to make the professors attached to their

---

* He married his niece, Joanna de Cisneros, to Alfonso de Mendoza.

office, Ximenez afforded them every comfort and
convenience, and built three country-houses for
their recreation during the vacations. In the
chapter on the university of Alcalá, we have
already described the royal visit of Ferdinand to
that noble seat of learning, and the manner in
which he was received (anno 1514). Leo X. had
a very high esteem for the cardinal, whom he often
consulted by letter, as he was unable to attend the
council of Lateran ; while Ximenez, on his part,
endeavoured to enforce throughout his diocese all the
most important decrees. The project which Leo X.
had conceived (realized two centuries later by Gregory XIII.) of reforming the Julian Calendar, met
with a warm supporter in Ximenez, who often
declared that the Church would derive great benefit
by the alteration.

Though Ximenez was so devoted to Leo X. and
the Holy See, yet he opposed the introduction into
his diocese of the papal bull relating to the completion of St. Peter's Church in Rome, which had
been commenced under the pontificate of Julius II.
Leo X., in order to be enabled to continue the
work, renewed the indulgences which had been
granted (1509) by his predecessor, to all those who
should contribute to the expenses of the pious
undertaking.* The bull was published in Spain by
the permission of Ferdinand. Ximenez, however,
though he commended the liberality of those who
devoted their property to the promotion of works
of piety, and especially to the erection of churches,
yet freely expressed his regret both to the pope and
the king, that the liberality of the faithful was
encouraged by means of "privileges."† In this

* Pallavicini, "Hist. Concil. Trident."
† "Ximenius, ut erat priscæ religionis tenacissimus, laudabat
quidem eos, qui in templi Apostolici constructionem suas pecunias

relaxation of temporal punishments imposed upon sinners, the austere prelate perceived a dangerous custom introduced, which might tend to enervate ecclesiastical discipline.

On another occasion, his zeal for the maintenance of discipline placed him in opposition to Rome. A canon of Avila had obtained a brief from Rome, dispensing with his attendance at choir, but allowing him at the same time the usual remuneration " distributiones quotidianæ." The cardinal, fearing lest this dispensation might become a dangerous precedent for others, commanded the canon to resign his privilege; this he did in obedience to the authority of Ximenez, as metropolitan. The cardinal also advised Ferdinand to enact a law, that for the future all bulls which came from Rome should be inspected, before their publication, by the minister of state.* This advice may be excused, though it cannot be justified, on the ground, that at this period a great number of dispensations were granted by the Holy See with little or no difficulty.

largiebantur, sed privilegia ob id dari, contra vetustos Ecclesiæ ritus, numquam probare voluit; et quid de hâc re sentiret, ad pontif. max. prudentissimè scripsit, et regi Fernando in privatis colloquiis, sine ullo fuco declaravit." (Gomez, lib. v. p. 143.)— *Trans.*

* This advice one would hardly have expected from Ximenez, who was so devoted to the Holy See. But his object was no doubt good—to prevent abuses. Gomez mentions the fact.— *Trans.*

CHAPTER XXII.

DEATH OF KING FERDINAND.

Since the end of the year 1513 the health of Ferdinand gradually gave way, and in November of the following year, Peter Martyr predicted his speedy end, unless he immediately abstained from two things,—the continual connection with his wife and the immoderate exercise of the chase, in which he indulged now, during the most inclement weather, even to a greater degree and with more passion than in his early days.* Restlessness of the mind constantly drove him from town to town in the northern provinces of his realm; and this man, formerly so active in the conduct of state affairs, felt now a real aversion to them. This made him and his councillors wish more for the presence of the Cardinal. But Ximenez showed little inclination to share the restless life of the king in his old age, and desired, as Gomez tells us, to reserve his remaining strength for the probable speedy end of Ferdinand.† He was, however, obliged to yield to the desire of the king, when the latter convoked the Cortes of Castile to Burgos for the purpose of obtaining subsidies for the war, which, after the death of Louis XII. and the succession of Francis I. to the throne, threatened to break out with France. At the same time the queen was forced to depart for Calatayud, in order to conduct the negotiations with the Cortes of Aragon assembled there.

* Petrus Martyr, ep. 542.   † Gomez, p. 1066.

Whilst at Burgos, Ferdinand, during one night of the month of July, was attacked by such a violent fit of vomiting that, unable to call for aid, he was nearly suffocated. Happily, a soldier on guard in the anteroom heard the groaning, and hastened with his comrades to the assistance of the king. They raised him up, and, by rubbing him and sprinkling water in his face, restored him to consciousness. Ferdinand, believing his death near at hand, made his will, appointing, in case of his decease, his second nephew, Ferdinand, regent until the arrival of his elder nephew Charles, and repaired for the better preservation of his health to Aranda de Duero, a quiet and secluded place.* Ximenez in this extremity could no longer refuse to comply with the request of the king, and accordingly arrived at Aranda in the month of August. Ferdinand, though still very feeble, received him solemnly before the town gates in his sedan-chair, showing him the same honours which he had almost always accorded him.

Shortly after, at the end of the same month, Ximenez accompanied the sovereign to Segovia, whence Ferdinand suddenly started for Aragon, because the states of that kingdom had shown themselves intractable, and refused the subsidies. Ferdinand, having already ordered the imprisonment of their chancellor, Anton Augustin,† hastened to Calatayud in the hope of suppressing the opposition by his personal authority. During his absence from Castile, the reins of government were intrusted to

---

* Ferreras wrongly gives the 27th July as the date of this attack. Petrus Martyr mentions it already in his letter of the 18th of the same month.

† Liberated by Ximenez in the following year, after his accession to the regency. Gomez, p. 1068.

Ximenez, who was to act in concert with the members of the royal council.*

The king was deceived in his hopes : the states adhered to their refusal, and were dissolved. Ferdinand, greatly annoyed, returned to Castile, in order to reside at Madrid. Ximenez repaired again to Alcalá. But the king could find no rest at Madrid. The ill-omened bell of Vellala, a village of Aragon, is said to have at that time struck of its own accord, thus prophesying the speedy death of the king. In mortal anguish he was again driven from town to town, and removed in the winter to the provinces of the south, there to equip a powerful fleet against Africa or Italy. At the end of November he arrived at Plasencia, having on his way again indulged freely in the pleasures of the chase. Here he received in December the dean of Utrecht, Hadrian (afterwards Pope Hadrian VI.), the preceptor of the Infant, Charles, whom his illustrious pupil had sent there, under the pretext of negotiating the marriage of Charles with a French princess: in reality, however, for the purpose of inquiring into the condition of things in Spain, and of taking possession of the realm as soon as Ferdinand had breathed his last. Ferdinand, who divined his motives, endeavoured to keep him away from court. He granted him, however, an audience, and received him with all due honour. But when Hadrian asked for a second interview, the king exclaimed angrily—"Does the spy want to see whether I am already dying? Tell him that I will not receive any one." Nevertheless, on the representations of his ministers, he allowed Hadrian to enter his chamber, and politely dismissed him, saying that his health was at present too much shaken to permit the discussion of state affairs, and

* Petrus Martyr, Ep. 552.

that the dean might meanwhile repair to the monastery at Guadaloupe, where he would follow him when better, and hold conference with him. The king ordered him also a guard of honour, evidently for no other purpose than to keep from Hadrian persons with whom the king did not wish him to confer.*

At the same time Ferdinand again invited Ximenez to Plasencia. But the cardinal had now even stronger reasons than before for evading the request, pointing out in particular that in the absence of the king from Castile his own presence was imperatively called for by the unsettled state of that province. He pleaded, moreover, heavy rains, and the consequent inundations, as obstacles to his journey; adding that in January he would be ready to come to Talavera, the farthest limit of his diocese towards Plasencia, there to receive the orders of the king. In the same letter he took occasion to speak of the conduct of Ferdinand towards Hadrian, praised him for having received the ambassador with so much honour, but blamed him for the undisguised mistrust shown to that worthy man in giving him a guard of honour which almost amounted to imprisonment. In conclusion, he warned the king, "for reasons explained before," but which have not come to our knowledge, to extend his journey farther south.† Ximenez also addressed a very friendly letter to Hadrian, in which he congratulated him on his arrival in Spain, and expressed his regret at not yet having been able to make the personal acquaintance of so virtuous and learned a man. It was natural that the wise cardinal should endeavour to win the favour of a man who had educated the future sovereign and was deep in his confidence.

* Petrus Martyr, Ep. 561, 565.　　† Gomez, p. 1068.

Ximenez here, as on many former occasions, had
the good sense to adopt a course dictated equally by
prudence and good breeding, for Hadrian deserved
indeed, in no slight degree, the praise and mark of
respect bestowed upon him by the cardinal.

Meanwhile Queen Germaine had returned to
Alcalá from Aragon, to forget there, in the beautiful
regal palace, surrounded by merry companions, the
dulness of her stay at Calatayud. There Ximenez
conferred with her on the affairs of the state, the
health of the king, and his reasons for postponing
his journey to him.

Fresh news of a more alarming nature having
arrived, the queen hastened to her husband, promising Ximenez to excuse him with the king for his
non-appearance. She travelled day and night, but,
in spite of her haste, found the king dying, incapable
of speaking with her.

In consequence of a prophecy made to the king
many years before, that Madrigal would be disastrous to him, Ferdinand had always avoided this
town, situated in the vicinity of Avila, and the
birthplace of the celebrated theologian, Alphonse
Tostatus. Suddenly attacked by a severe illness
on his way to Guadaloupe, he was obliged to
be taken to the nearest village, which, as chance
would have it, bore nearly the same name as
the above-mentioned town. It was called Madri-
galejo, and became indeed the place of the king's
death. A visionary saint from Avila having shortly
before predicted him long life, he refused at first to
see Hadrian, who had hastened from Guadaloupe,
and even his pious confessor, the Franciscan Mati-
enso. But his principal physicians and councillors
directed his attention to the danger in which his
life stood, and the violence of the evil itself reminded
him that his end was near: he therefore received

Hadrian with kindness, promising him a longer audience if he recovered from his illness. After this he remained for several hours in secret converse with his confessor, and, at his advice, turned his mind once more to the consideration of the affairs of the state. Above all, he communicated now to the councillors most in his confidence the contents of his former will, according to which the temporary regency of Castile and the grand-mastership of the three knightly orders were assigned to the Infant Ferdinand. By advice of his ministers this will was annulled, as there were fears of its becoming a cause of discord between the brothers, and as it would have weakened the crown too much by severing from it the grand-masterships. They contended that one grand-master was already sufficient to involve the king in many unpleasant affairs, how much more a man who united in his hands the highest dignity of the three powerful knightly orders?* The question who, in the place of the Infant Ferdinand, was to become regent of Castile until the arrival of Charles, presented greater difficulties. The bitter hatred existing between the grandees of the kingdom made the choice of any of them for this office impossible. When, in this emergency, Doctor Carvajal, a learned jurist and councillor of the king, proposed Ximenez, the king at first turned away with a discontented air, saying that the cardinal was too austere to be able to manage properly the different characters as regent. The councillors were silent: but after further reflection Ferdinand proceeded— "If he were but a little more pliable, I could not wish a better regent, as he would also be the best man to re-establish discipline, order, and morality; and as you seem to persist in your vote for him, I

---

* As regent for Aragon he nominated his natural son Ferdinand, the archbishop of Saragossa.

will accede to your proposition, on account of his virtues, and his love of justice. Not being the descendant of a noble family, he will be able to conduct the administration with more impartiality than others; besides his attachment for the royal house, increased by many favours, especially from Isabella, has always been most sincere and devoted." The ministers thanked the king for this decision, which was annexed to the will. He then received the Holy Sacraments, clad in the Dominican cowl, and before the break of the following day, the 23rd January, 1516, breathed his last, in the sixty-fourth year of his life, and the forty-first of his reign.

The news was at once conveyed to Hadrian who was already on his way to pay another visit to the king. On the same day the will was opened in the presence of the ambassador, and a great number of high personages, civil and ecclesiastical. A copy was sent to Flanders, and Ximenez, by a letter from the royal council, invited to take upon himself the reins of Government, until the arrival of Charles. Misled by the ill advice of his courtiers, particularly Gonsalvo Guzman, the commander of the order of Calatrava, and the Bishop of Astorga, Prince Ferdinand attempted to take possession of the regency. He sent a haughty message to the royal council, ordering them to assemble at Guadaloupe, and to await there his further orders. But the council replied in a short and energetic letter that Charles was master, not he; * upon which he desisted from his pretensions. The remains of the king were taken to Granada by Peter Martyr and others, and interred at the side of Isabella, in the town conquered by them for Spain.

---

* The council having made use of the words of the Bible, "Non habemus alium regem nisi Cæsarem," these were afterwards considered as a kind of prophecy of the future dignity of Charles.

CHAPTER XXIII.

XIMENEZ TAKES POSSESSION OF THE REGENCY, AND EXERTS
HIMSELF IN FAVOUR OF CHARLES.

WHEN Ximenez received the intelligence of the decease of Ferdinand, and of his own nomination to the regency, the recollection of his obligations towards the royal house, together with the thought of the frailty of all human greatness, so overcame him, that the man, usually so stern and austere, burst out into tears. In order to provide for the necessities, and, above all, for the tranquillity of the state, he at once hastened to Guadaloupe, where the royal council had met, paid the dowager-queen the honours due to her, and assured himself of the person of the Infant Ferdinand. This young prince was acquainted with the contents of the former will, by which he had been nominated regent of Castile, and, misguided by his advisers, endeavoured, as we have seen in the preceding chapter, to frustrate the subsequent arrangement of his grandfather, to declare the nomination of the cardinal an injustice, and possess himself of the reins of the government. His first attempt had miscarried. To forestall a repetition, and insure the tranquillity of public order, Ximenez henceforth kept him under his eye, without forgetting the respect due to his royal origin.*

* Gomez, p. 1071. Vinc. Gonzalez Arvao,"Elogio del Cardinal" in the " Memorias de la Real Academia," tom. iv. p. 20. Here a sketch is also given of the difficulties Ximenez had to contend with on entering the regency. Lavergne (" Revue des Deux Mondes," tom. xxvi. pp. 542—544) blames Ximenez for having secured Spain for the elder brother instead of the younger, or rather for having done his duty.

When the cardinal proceeded to take possession of the regency, Dean Hadrian presented a document previously signed by Charles, by virtue of which he, the dean, in the event of the death of King Ferdinand, was appointed regent of Castile in the name of the hereditary prince. A quarrel was unavoidable, but the jurists consulted on the question, decided in favour of Ximenez. They contended that King Ferdinand was, by the will of Isabella, and the consent of the Cortes, sole and legitimate regent of Castile until Charles had attained his twentieth year. Consequently, every arrangement made by him during his lifetime had the force of law, and was binding, whilst Prince Charles, who during the life of his grandfather had been invested with no authority to govern, could not transfer or cede this to any one.

Ximenez, desirous of settling the dispute amicably, proposed to his rival to conduct the affairs and sign the decrees conjointly, until Charles himself, having by the death of Ferdinand become absolute master of his will, should decide which of the two competitors he selected as regent during his absence.

Even before a reply had arrived from Flanders, Ximenez saved for Charles and the crown the grand-mastership of the order of San Iago di Compostella. Ferdinand and Isabella had, as we know, by the consent of the Pope, succeeded in uniting with the crown the grand-mastership of the three great knightly orders of Spain, in the person of the king. During the lifetime of the latter the Spanish nobles endeavoured to wrest this again from the crown, and the "Great Captain" is said to have entertained hopes of becoming grand-master of San Iago after the death of Ferdinand. But Gonzalvo died before the king; and Pedro Portocarrero, brother of the duke of Escolano, obtained from Rome the promise of this dignity. The death of Ferdinand seemed to offer a favourable opportunity for his being elected by the commanders of the order, and then maintaining himself in his position by force of arms. His arrangements were already made, and several districts secretly excited to rise, when Ximenez received intelligence of the conspiracy, and in concert with Hadrian sent Villafagne, one of the four criminal judges, with full powers, to the disturbed provinces. Simultaneously he placed a body of troops ready for marching, in order to suppress the whole undertaking, if need be, by force. Portocarrero, however, perceiving the energetic measures of the cardinal, thought it wiser at once to submit, and relinquish his pretensions ; whilst the commanders in all haste returned to their districts, and never attempted again to meet without the consent of the cardinal.

This matter terminated, the necessity was felt of transferring the seat of the regency and the council from Guadaloupe to a more suitable place. Ximenez selected Madrid as being more central, and not far from his own possessions. By this, he explained to the royal council, he would always be enabled easily to raise a sufficient force to suppress any insurrectionary movement, whilst in other places his power was likely to be neutralized by the grandees who owned property in the neighbourhood. Thus Madrid became, through Ximenez, the seat of government, and, as the sovereigns confirmed his choice, since Philip II. the capital of the kingdom.*

Whilst these events were taking place in Spain, the envoys despatched by Ximenez and the royal council, brought Charles at Brussels the intelligence

---

* Lavergne, who finds fault with Ximenez almost in everything he has done, blames him also for his choice of Madrid as capital.

of the death of Ferdinand, and the quarrel about the regency. The Flemish advisers of the young prince, more especially his former instructor, the Duke William of Croy, lord of Chievres, his chancellor Jean Sauvage, lords de la Chaux, Amerstorf, Lanoi, and others, were ill-disposed towards Ximenez. They saw, with displeasure, at the head of affairs in Spain, a man who was likely to become a powerful barrier against their culpable designs of using this state for the enrichment of their own finances. Nevertheless Charles, perceiving, doubtless, that a foreigner like Hadrian would be odious to the Spaniards, and for other reasons which will become apparent hereafter, returned in very flattering terms a decided answer in favour of the cardinal. In his letter to the royal council, he expressed his great grief at the death of his grandfather, who had loved him so dearly, and guided him so faithfully and devotedly. He proceeds to say that his sole consolation for this loss, but this only a partial one, could be the cardinal, whom Ferdinand had appointed to reign temporarily as regent of Castile; a man the fame of whose consummate wisdom, experience, and eminent virtues had reached even Flanders. In conclusion, he confirms to its full extent the authority given to Ximenez, desiring Hadrian to be considered only as his ambasssador.[*]

At the same time, he addressed letters to his brother Ferdinand, to the dowager-queen Germaine, to Ximenez, the grandees and prelates, acquainting them of his intention to come to Spain in the course of the following summer, and exhorting them to obey Ximenez and the royal council as they would

---

[*] Prescott, who seems to have known this letter only from the manuscript annals of Carvajal, might have found it also printed in Robles, p. 181, whom he often quotes.

himself.* The letter directed to Ximenez was couched in the following terms:

" Most Reverend Father in Christ, Cardinal of Spain, Archbishop of Toledo, Primate of Spain, Grand-chancellor of Castile, our most esteemed and dearly-beloved friend! Most Reverend Sir:

" We have received the news of the decease of his Royal Highness, the most powerful Catholic king our lord, whom God will receive in his glory. It has caused us great grief, because Christendom in general has lost in him an illustrious defender, and our kingdoms in particular are thereby deprived of a wise administrator and good king. This loss is particularly painful to us, who are fully aware of the great benefit and advantages we could have derived from his kind advice and vast experience. But as God has so ordained it, we must submit to his decrees and his will. In the will of our grandfather we have everywhere recognized his good and holy intentions, and the thought that for their sake God will be merciful to him, is a great consolation to us. The most excellent clause we have found in the testament is that by which you, Most Reverend Sir, are during our absence invested with the government of the kingdom and the administration of justice. It was the best the late king could do, for he thereby insured the peace and tranquillity of our states. Indeed, Most Reverend Sir, if this had not been done already, we could, considering your integrity, wisdom, and zeal for God and ourselves, not have selected for this office a man who would give greater satisfaction to our conscience, and in whose hands the weal of our kingdoms could be safer. We therefore have written to several prelates and lords, as well as to our principal towns, requesting and enjoining them to obey

* Petrus Martyr, Ep. 569. Gomez, p. 1073.

you, and make others obey you, and to execute your
orders as well as those of the royal council.

"We now beseech you most earnestly to undertake the administration of justice, and to apply
yourself to the preservation of peace amongst our
subjects, until we ourselves, if it be God's will, soon
shall come in proper person to console and rule
them. We further request you to write us constantly, and acquaint us of all that may happen,
giving us, at the same time, your advice, which we
shall receive as that of a father, not only from
gratitude for the eminent services you have rendered
to King Philip, our much-esteemed lord and father,
but also from our warm friendship for you and our
confidence in your excellence. Most Reverend
Father in Christ, Cardinal of Spain, our very dear
friend, may God have you constantly in his holy
keeping! Brussels, the 14th February, 1516.

I, the Prince.*

At the end of the letter addressed to the royal
council, the prince intimated that he had intrusted
a secret commission of the highest importance to
his ambassador, Hadrian, on which he wished them
to deliberate without delay, and give their opinion
as soon as possible. Pope Leo X. and the Emperor
Maximilian, in their letters of condolence and congratulation, had already addressed him by the title of
King of Spain, and Charles himself, spurred by his
Flemish courtiers, greatly desired to obtain this title,
although, during the lifetime of his mother, he
could lay claim only to that of Prince Regent in
Castile and Aragon. To insure the success of his
wishes he had prudently signed his letters "El Prin-
cipe," and charged Hadrian to lay them before the

---

* Sandoval, "Historia de Carlos V.," lib. ii. Flechier, liv. iv.
p. 357.

nobles of Castile. His letter to Ximenez, the esteem
he professed for him, and the quickness with which
he confirmed his nomination, owed much to the
same cause, as Charles knew well that the powerful
cardinal was sufficient to insure the success, or cause
the defeat, of his projects. But Ximenez and the
councillors earnestly implored the prince to desist
from his plan, as he could not gain any increase of
real power by it, and would only thereby give to the
discontented nobles of Castile occasion for complaining of the infringement of the laws of the
country, and an apparent reason for civil dissensions.
Their letter was sent off to Flanders in March of the
year 1516, but could not shake the resolution of
Charles. He wrote back to Ximenez and the council, saying, the pope, the emperor,* and the cardinal
having already given him the title, it would be incompatible with his honour to relinquish it, and he
confidently hoped they would obtain its recognition
from the nobles of Castile. He, moreover, requested
the cardinal to have him proclaimed King of Castile, if
necessary, even without the concurrence of the council and the grandees. Ximenez, conceiving that he
could no longer disobey the express orders of the
prince, in conjunction with Hadrian assembled, in
the royal palace at Madrid, the royal council, the
nobles and bishops then present in that town. The
meeting was attended by the grand-admiral, the
duke of Alba, the duke of Escalona, the count of De,
the archbishop of Granada, Antonio de Rojas, the
bishops of Burgos and Siguenza, Francis Ruyz de
Avila, and other personages of less distinction.†
Ximenez notified to them the will of the prince ; but,
undecided what reply to give, they called upon Dr.

---

* "Cæsaris est reges creare," says Peter Martyr, Ep. 572.

† Lavergne wrongly asserts that Ximenez convoked the States.
(" Revue des Deux Mondes," xxvi. 545.)

Carvajal, one of the most learned members of the royal council, to give them his opinion on the subject. Carvajal, in a long and detailed speech, represented to them that the royal council had at first advised the prince to desist from his intention, but having, at the instigation of the two great heads of Christendom, the pope and the emperor, already accepted the title of king, Charles could not now retrace his steps with honour. He added, even if Charles had the intention of doing so, the duty of the Castilians was to oppose it, in order to prevent their sovereign from being considered rash and inconstant. The kingdom could, in his opinion, only benefit by Charles being invested with the full dignity of a king, and by being no longer, even in appearance, dependent upon his mother, who was incapable of conducting the affairs; for the greater his authority, the prompter also the obedience of his subjects. He cited examples from Spanish history, showing that not only sons, but even brothers and cousins, had been appointed regents and kings conjointly with the legitimate sovereigns. Lastly, he concluded, Charles did not intend to submit his proceedings to the investigation and approval of his subjects, but simply demanded their recognition of and congratulation on his elevation. In confirmation of what he had said, Carvajal read to them a letter of Charles, couched in imperative terms. The grandees were silent for a considerable time, evidently perplexed by the speech, but, partly from interested motives, unwilling to agree with its purport. Seeing their minds wavering, Ximenez, together with the bishops and several of the nobles, declared themselves for Prince Charles, whilst the grand-admiral, the duke of Alba, and others, defended the opposite opinion, and denied that the examples adduced by Carvajal proved the validity of the case. The duke of Escalona returned an evasive answer, saying, that as Charles, according to the words of Carvajal, did not seek their advice, he would not press his upon him, and therefore abstain from declaring himself. Under these circumstances it was to be feared that the meeting would be dissolved without any result. Ximenez, with knitted brow and raised voice, then addressed them in the following manner :—" The matter under consideration is indeed one in which your advice is neither asked nor required, for the prince is not dependent upon that of his subjects; but having your interest at heart, I called you hither to enable you to win the good graces of the king, by respectfully acceding to his wishes, and congratulating him. As you have not understood this, I will this very day order Charles to be proclaimed king in Madrid as an example to the other towns." With these words, which taste pretty strongly of absolutism, he dismissed the meeting. Immediately after, he sent for the prefect of Madrid, Pedro Correa, to give him the necessary orders for the solemn proclamation of Charles, which was celebrated with all pomp at Madrid, on the last day of the same month. The nobility, seeing further resistance was unavailing, joined in the universal joy at the accession of the new king. On the succeeding day Ximenez wrote to the magistrates of the towns, and to all the grandees, summoning them also to acknowledge the royal title of Charles, declaring at the same time that in all public documents the name of Queen Johanna was to precede that of her son.

The severity of the Cardinal was so much dreaded that every one obeyed promptly and without opposition. But Toledo surpassed all the other towns by the zeal and splendour with which the ceremony of homage to the new king was celebrated. The

Aragonians, however, over whom the archbishop of
Saragossa was regent, stoutly refused to acknowledge Prince Charles as king, until their Cortes
had deliberated on the question whether the title
could be acceded to him during the lifetime of
his mother; and imitated the example of the
Castilians only after the ᴗarrival of Charles in
Spain, at the diet of Saragossa.*

* Petrus Martyr, Epp. 568, 572, 590, 603, 605, 617, 618, 624.
Robles, p. 183.   Gomez, p. 1077, is mistaken when he asserts
that Charles obtained in Aragon the title of king only after the
death of his mother (1555).

CHAPTER XXIV.

XIMENEZ' SOLICITUDE FOR THE PEACE, ORDER, AND SECURITY
OF THE STATE.

XIMENEZ had scarcely entered upon the duties of
the regency, when he was called to repress numerous
attempts against public order. The first and almost
the most serious one was made by Pedro Giron, eldest
son of the count of Ureña. We have seen before how
this bold and energetic nobleman was exiled from
Spain by Ferdinand, together with his ward and
brother-in-law, the young duke of Medina Sidonia,
who owned large possessions in the south of Spain.
Soon after their return to the country, in the year
1513, the young duke died without issue. Giron
forcibly took possession of his estates, on the plea
that the inheritance belonged to his wife, a sister of
the deceased. Alvar, half-brother of the duke, protested against this, and became possessor of the
whole property by a feudal sentence of Ferdinand.
As long as Ferdinand lived, Giron yielded to force;
but the regency appeared to him a favourable moment for the recovery of these rich domains. On the
news of King Ferdinand's death, he immediately
invaded the duchy of Sidonia, with open force, and
besieged San Lucia, a strongly-fortified place on the
sea, and the key of the whole duchy. He justified
his conduct, by alleging that the *old* Duke of Medina
Sidonia had, after the death of his first wife, married her sister without a proper dispensation; consequently only the children by the first marriage
were entitled to inherit him, but not those by the

2 H

second marriage. Duke Henry and Mencia, Giron's wife, were the only issue of the marriage; hence, after Henry's death, the latter, and not Alvar, his half-brother by the second marriage, was entitled to the inheritance. The sentence of Ferdinand, he maintained, was not only unjust but also partial, Alvar having married Anne of Aragon, daughter of the archbishop of Saragossa and grandchild of the king.

Ponce, duke of Arcos and Cadiz, and Gomez Salis, commander of the order of St. Jago, repulsed the first attack of Giron on the duchy, and communicated these events to the cardinal and the Council of Castile. Ximenez immediately ordered the inhabitants of Seville and Cordova and the surrounding country to aid against Giron, declared the latter guilty of high treason, and sent an able general, Anton Fonseca, at the head of a considerable force, to Andalusia, to quell the revolt. At the same time he despatched Cornejo, one of the four criminal judges, to institute the necessary proceedings against the rebels. Giron, terrified by these preparations, dismissed his army, and, through the intercession of his father and the archbishop of Seville, obtained pardon. But the ambitious count could not rest long. Perceiving the great dissatisfaction which the question of the royal title had provoked amongst the nobility, he renewed his secret intrigues, and, backed by his uncle, the grand-constable of Castile, endeavoured to form the nobles into a league sufficiently formidable to set the cardinal openly at defiance. In his boldness, he ventured into Madrid, there to continue his canvass, as it were under the eyes of Ximenez, and to consult with his partisans; and carried his audacity even so far as to send a message to the cardinal to inform him that he had come for the purpose of conferring with his friends. Ximenez contented himself with replying that he hoped his affairs would end well, but kept a watchful eye on the movements of the nobility.

A considerable number of the nobles were, for some reason or other, hostilely inclined towards Ximenez. Several were won over by Giron's representations that prudence advised opposition to the cardinal, for Charles would set but little value on the allegiance of those who so readily obeyed his vicar. Others, amongst them the grand-constable, had different motives. Knowing that it was the intention of Ximenez to reunite with the crown all briefs and revenues to which no sufficient legal title could be shown, they resolved to resist the man who threatened to dispossess them of their property. The grand-constable, in particular, exerted himself to the utmost in uniting all the hostile grandees for the overthrow of the cardinal. He directed his special care to win for the cause the Count Pimental of Benevente, the Duke Cueva of Albuquerque, the Duke Cerda of Medina Cœli, the bishop of Siguenza, and the duke of Infantado. These he addressed, representing to them that they ought no longer to tolerate the rule of a monk of base extraction over the nobility of Spain; that it was not for him to command princes, but to obey them; that the will of Ferdinand had certainly intrusted the regency to Ximenez, but that their fear of their late king, who had treated them so cruelly, should now cease. For his part, he added, he was resolved no longer to obey Ximenez, unless he could produce the most absolute powers signed by the hand of Charles himself. These words raised the indignation of the nobles against the cardinal to the highest pitch. The duke of Infantado alone appeared more prudent than his friends. He, in his turn, represented to them that none had greater cause for being discontent with Ximenez than he himself, inasmuch as the cardinal

had prevented the marriage of his niece with the
house of Infantado, and was now desirous of depriving him of his possessions. Nevertheless he did not
concur in their views, being well aware of the great
power and still greater obstinacy of the cardinal, and
considering a political rising a very hazardous and
dangerous undertaking; if, however, they could
devise some other means to guard their authority
and break the power and pride of the monk, they
might rely, this he swore on his honour, upon his
hearty co-operation. These words having somewhat
cooled the ardour of the other grandees, it was ultimately decided formally to accuse the cardinal before
the king, and to send Don Alvar Gomez, a well-
informed and sensible man, son-in-law of the duke
of Infantado, to Flanders, to demand the dismissal
of Ximenez.

The cardinal received intelligence of all these
machinations and plans, but was nothing daunted.
To some of his friends, who expressed their alarm, he
laconically replied—" These men have only words,
not money to raise a revolt."   At the same time he
gave the conspirators to understand that it would
be for their own interest to abstain from causing
disturbances, as otherwise they would soon learn
who was the stronger.   Frightened by this language, almost every one of them tried to clear
himself in the eyes of the cardinal, even the duke
of Infantado and the grand-constable assuring him
by letter and through the medium of friends, of
their submission and respect.   It is related that, at
the instigation of the grand-constable, several grandees had previously waited on the cardinal to request
the presentation of the documents upon which he
held the regency.   Ximenez invited them for the
following day, when, taking them to the window,
and showing them his soldiers and artillery, he
said—" Behold the powers by which I govern Cas-

tile, by the will of the king, my lord and master." But Gomez was unable to authenticate this anecdote, and reports it only as a tradition.

The grandees, notwithstanding, persisted in their former resolution, and sent several ambassadors to Brussels to accuse the cardinal. Ximenez, for his part, sent Diego Lopez to procure more extended power for him, and place him in a position to suppress more effectually any attempt at rising on the part of the nobles.

Without waiting for the return of his ambassador he now set vigorously to work to introduce a new system in the recruiting of the army with the object of securing the peace of the kingdom against every contingency. Peter Martyr informs us that Ximenez had always taken great interest and pleasure in discussions on war and armaments.* In one of his familiar conversations with Ferdinand, the king had intimated that armies recruited from different countries offered more danger than security to a state, and that a kind of standing militia would be infinitely preferable to the system then pursued. He argued that citizens fighting for their own home would be more faithful and brave, while their better education would be a pledge for their better conduct and greater mildness to the enemy. Ferdinand had, to the confession of Ximenez, once drawn up the plan for such a military organization, but been prevented by illness and other occupations from carrying it into effect. Ximenez now bethought himself of putting this great and important plan into execution, for which purpose he had already (in April, 1516) demanded from Charles the fullest powers for the administration of the kingdom in all its branches: but he was too impatient to wait for their arrival. After a long conference with the royal senate, and

---

* Petrus Martyr, ep. 573: "Bellicis colloquiis et apparatibus gaudet."

an experienced warrior, he issued a proclamation to
all the towns and cities in Castile, promising important privileges to the inhabitants, and in particular
to the citizens who inscribed their names in the
lists of troops about to be levied.   They were to be
exempt from lodging the king and his retinue, as
well as from all taxes, socages, and other charges.
In return they were to serve without pay, the officers
and musicians only receiving a remuneration.   The
proclamation at first met with universal approbation.
In a very short time not fewer than 30,000 citizens
had voluntarily enlisted, who were daily drilled
before their fellow-townsmen, thereby inducing a
great number of young men to follow their example.
Ximenez was highly pleased at this success. Foreign
princes looked with envy and suspicion upon this
new institution, capable of making Spain so powerful, while the anger with which it filled the king of
France was one of the greatest proofs of its utility.
The cardinal of Guise, a relative of Charles, who
visited Madrid in June of the year 1516, avowedly
for the purpose of paying his addresses to Ximenez,
but it is supposed on a secret mission of the Emperor Maximilian to observe affairs in Spain, thanked
him in the name of Christendom for a work which
would more effectually protect Spain against the
attacks of the infidels.

Opposition, however, was not wanting, especially
on the part of those who, either for gain or pleasure,
delight in disturbing the public peace. They endeavoured by every means in their power to cast aspersion and contempt on the new scheme, representing
it as a dangerous innovation, calculated to ruin the
citizens by taking them away from their employments. The nobility, moreover, perceived in the
arming of the citizens an encroachment upon their
privileges, and an attempt to deprive them of their

political influence. Hence, the introduction of the new system found powerful opposition in Leon, Burgos, Salamanca, Medina del Campo, Arevalo, Madrigal, Olmedo, and Valladolid.* In the latter town the excitement was so great that the inhabitants imprisoned the envoy of the cardinal, one Topia from Segovia, declared Ximenez an oppressor of liberty, and fortified the town in all haste to be prepared for resistance in case of need. One of the principal instigators of the revolt was Antonio de Rojas, archbishop of Granada and president of the royal council, a man who secretly worked against the cardinal, and is even said to have incited the deputies of Valladolid against the "*tyrant*." The grand-admiral, the bishop of Astorga, and other grandees who owned possessions in the neighbourhood of Valladolid, were also implicated in the revolt; and, partly from interest, partly from revenge, encouraged the citizens in their opposition to Ximenez. Although the number of towns which defied the cardinal was comparatively small, it was to be feared that their example would work injuriously upon the rest. Ximenez endeavoured therefore to gain Valladolid by promises and kind remonstrances. But the inhabitants rejected his proposals; replying haughtily that he might say and do what he liked; they knew well how to defend themselves and their liberties until the arrival of Charles. Ximenez, hesitating to adopt rigorous measures against the town without the consent of Charles, meanwhile contented himself with collect-

* Peter Martyr shared the universal dissatisfaction. Ep. 575. As usual, Lavergne blames the cardinal for these reforms. According to his opinion, Ximenez had, in introducing them, only the intention of humbling the nobles. His leading idea was, therefore, not the regeneration of the commons, but the advancement of despotism.—"Revue des Deux Mondes," tom. xxvi. p. 545.

ing, under another pretext, more troops in its
neighbourhood, at the same time urging Diego
Lopez, his agent at Brussels, to obtain from Charles
as quickly as possible express powers for the reduc-
tion of the rebellious cities and grandees. Moreover, to counteract the false reports which several
nobles had sent to Charles and the duke of Chièvres,
he addressed a letter to Charles himself, in which
he explained the utility of the system, and asked for
the transmission of arms and ammunition from
Flanders. Ximenez gained his point. Charles sent
the powers; and in a special letter summoned the
rebellious towns to render prompt obedience to
Ximenez, the depository of his authority. They all
obeyed, even Valladolid not excepted. After their
resistance was broken, Ximenez showed every kindness and indulgence : to Valladolid he prudently
granted the privilege which best secured the future
obedience of the town. The grand-admiral and the
count of Benevente, having succeeded in introducing
many of their partisans into the municipality of
Valladolid, Ximenez, in order to counterbalance
their influence, permitted the citizens to elect two
procurators, with the power of veto in the sittings
of the municipality, similar to the ancient tribunes.
With regard to the military organziation introduced
by him, it has served as the model for the standing
armies : it is not for *us* to decide whether the model
is better than the imitation.*

Simultaneously with these changes in the army,
Ximenez effected important improvements in the
maritime power of Castile. He added twenty
trireme galleys to it, and equipped the entire
fleet to resist the attacks of the Moors and pirates,
the most famous of whom, Barbarossa, then ra-

* Gomez, pp. 1081—1084. Mariana, p. 3. Arvao, in the
" Memorias," tom. iv. pp. 22.

vaged the coasts of the Mediterranean, carrying terror in every direction. The usefulness of these arrangements soon became evident. In July, 1516, a number of Spanish vessels encountered five Turkish ones of considerable size, near Alicante, attacked them, and, after great slaughter, sank two, while the remaining three were towed in triumph into the harbour of Alicante. This success, and the congratulations which he received from Leo X., encouraged him to continue his exertions to strengthen the navy. He accordingly, in the following year, ordered the restoration of the dock-yards near Seville, which long neglect had rendered almost useless, hereby providing the means of permanently supplying Castile with a sufficient number of vessels ready for sea.[*]

Events at the other extremity of Spain now equally claimed his attention. Shortly after the death of Ferdinand, the young king of France, Francis I., began to raise an army, the destination of which was at first not known. It became, however, soon apparent. Jean d'Albret, the exiled king of Navarre, thought the moment favourable for the recovery of his dominions; considering this an easy matter whilst the reins of government were in the hands of a monk. The faction of the Agramonts had declared for his cause,[†] and many Navarrese fled across the Pyrenees to enlist in the army which he formed in all haste. On the receipt of the ntelligence of his march against Navarre, in conjunction with a French army, Ximenez, in concert with the royal council, appointed the duke of Najara, a man experienced in arms and owner of considerable property in Navarre, governor of this

---

[*] Gomez, p. 1084. Miniana, p. 3.
[†] That of the Beaumonts sided with Castile.—Petrus Martyr, ep. 570.

province, in the stead of the actual viceroy, who was
considered no match for the emergency.   The grand-
constable, the old enemy of Ximenez, was so embittered by this choice, that he threw every possible
obstacle in the way of the duke, nearly enabling
Jean d'Albret thereby to regain Navarre.   But the
Colonel Ferdinand Villalba, after encountering terrible fatigues, boldly attacked the enemy in the
gorges of the Pyrenees, totally defeated him, and
made a great number of superior officers, belonging
to the first families of Navarre, prisoners.   Amongst
them, in particular, the Marshal Pedro of Navarre,
Diego Velez, the favourite of Albret, the lords of
Garri and Gambra, and many others, all of whom
Ximenez ordered to be confined in the castle of
Atienza, and carefully guarded.   King d'Albret,
having now lost all hope of reconquering Navarre,
retired under heavy losses across the Pyrenees into
his principality of Béarn, where he and his wife
died shortly after.   Villalba was treated with great
respect by Ximenez, and ever after consulted by him
on the military affairs of Navarre.   The consequence
was that Ximenez ordered many of the fortresses of
the province to be rased, as he could neither afford
to garrison them sufficiently with Castilian troops,
nor dared leave them in the hands of the Navarrese,
who still remained attached to the house of their
former king.   These measures highly exasperated
the Navarrese, who shed bitter tears at the sight of
the demolition of the walls, and the dismantling of
the castles.   But Ximenez swerved not from his
resolution, he only exerted himself in expediting the
necessary though painful work.*   The enemies of
the cardinal of course found in these measures fresh

* Villalba soon after died; it is supposed, poisoned by the
Navarrese, because he advised the rasing of their fortresses.—
Gomez, p. 1088.

occasion for complaints and accusations, and were naturally supported by the enraged Navarrese. One of their chief accusations consisted in reproaching the cardinal with having profaned religion by the destruction of a convent of the Franciscans and the church belonging to it. But the Castilians universally approved of the steps taken by him, to which Spain in subsequent wars owed much of the preservation of Navarre.*

The war of Navarre was hardly ended, when fresh complications arose in another quarter. A courier of the king of Portugal, destined for France, having, through his own imprudence, drawn suspicion on himself, had been taken prisoner by the governor of Salces, then a Castilian fortress: despatches written in cipher were found on him, revealing the negotiation of a marriage and alliance between France and Portugal to the detriment of Castile. These the governor forwarded at once to the government at Madrid. In the absence of Ximenez, who had gone to Alcalá to superintend the building of the university, the letters were opened by Hadrian, who still took part in the affairs of the government. Frightened by their dangerous contents, and perceiving their importance, he immediately sent the courier to Alcalá, with orders to deliver the despatches to Ximenez, without loss of time, and even to have him awakened in the night if necessary. Ximenez read them indeed at midnight, and replied to the messenger: "Tell Hadrian that he may rest in peace, I undertake to face the danger." He forthwith acquainted Charles with these secret intrigues, and gave orders to his ambassador at Lisbon to watch carefully the steps of the king of Portugal.†

---

* Gomez, pp. 1086—1088. Petrus Martyr, epp. 569, 570, 571. Miniana, p. 3.

† Gomez, p. 1089.

Meanwhile the affairs of Navarre claimed once more the attention of the cardinal. Ferdinand had confided the government of Pampeluna, the capital of this country, to an Aragonian of the name of Ferrara, whom Ximenez considered unfit for this important post, partly from his not being a Castilian, partly from his excessive severity. Ximenez resolved therefore to replace him by a Castilian of tried fidelity, who would win the affection of the people by kindness and benevolence. Charles gave his consent, but the choice of the cardinal is not known, Gomez having already endeavoured in vain to learn the name of the person on whom it had fallen.*

But an affair of still greater annoyance awaited the cardinal. For many years the supreme council of Navarre had been equally divided between the two rival factions of the Beaumonts and Agramonts. The nomination of the president had given rise to constant quarrels. To whichever of these families he belonged, he was sure to be the object of the fiercest opposition on the part of the other faction. D'Albret, and after him Ferdinand the Catholic, to obviate these constantly-recurring quarrels, had introduced the practice of appointing a foreigner to this dignity. The Navarrese now exerted themselves to re-establish the former institution, and unknown to Ximenez, had, probably by a bribe, won over to their cause the duke of Chièvres and other councillors of the court of Charles. They entertained already sanguine hopes for the success of their plans, when Ximenez became acquainted with their intrigues, and frustrated them by representing to Charles the danger of such an innovation.†

At the same time, the pope demanded of Ximenez

* Gomez, p. 1089. † Ibid.

to reinstate Cardinal d'Albert, brother of the former king of Navarre, in his bishopric of Pampeluna, from which he had been ejected. Ximenez consulted the duke of Najara, then still viceroy of Navarre, on the matter, and on his representations that it was dangerous to provide so powerful a political adversary with influence and money for fresh revolts, refused to grant the request of Leo.[*] The tranquillity of Navarre was thus preserved, affording Ximenez leisure to turn his mind to the consideration of other very important matters.

In Malaga a revolt had broken out against the jurisdiction of the grand-admiral. By the ancient laws of Spain, the grand-admiral not only held the command of the naval powers, but was also intrusted with the supervision of the coast, and the jurisdiction over all the persons belonging to the fleet, official and private, whose disputes he had to settle. Special judges had accordingly been appointed in all the sea and mercantile places. But this institution, though it may have worked well in the beginning, had in the course of time, engendered numberless abuses. Thus, if the town alguazils had taken up one of those rogues and idlers with which seaports abound, he disputed the competency of the ordinary courts to try him, and demanded to be transferred to that of the grand-admiral, on the plea of being a discharged sailor, or something similar. The soldiers, who were stationed at the coast for its defence, acted in a like manner. If brought before the royal courts, they insisted upon belonging to that of the admiral, or *vice versâ*, according to which of them offered the greatest chance of escape. Hence a deplorable delay in the procedure, and what is still more pernicious, the impossibility of quickly punishing offences against

---

[*] Gomez, p. 1089. Fléchier, liv. iv. p. 372.

order and the police; or the impunity of criminals
who escaped through these quarrels about the competency of the courts.

By these means, the tribunals of the admiralty had,
for a long time, become exceedingly odious to the
inhabitants of the coast.   Having in vain solicited
their suppression of Ferdinand, they now, after his
death, endeavoured to right themselves, as they
called it.   The inhabitants of Malaga rose in open
rebellion, effaced all the outward emblems of the
jurisdiction of the admiral, expelled his officers, and
refused him obedience.   Ximenez, on learning these
disorders, exhorted them in a pastoral letter, to
return to their allegiance, pointed out to them the
course they were to pursue to obtain redress against
the admiral, and assured them, that as long as he
lived, justice would not be influenced by the authority of any grandee, however noble he might be;
this letter produced but little effect.   Incited by
several hot-headed persons, and even by Flemish
nobles, they rejected the authority of the cardinal-
regent, appealed to King Charles himself, armed
the whole town, and mounted as many pieces of
artillery as they could obtain on the ramparts, in
order to resist all attacks of the cardinal.   Ximenez, on hearing this, immediately despatched Don
Antonio Cueva, with 6,000 infantry and 400 horse,
against the rebellious town, choosing soldiers from
the recently-organized militia for the expedition,
and thereby testing, for the first time, the merits of
the new military system.   At the same time, he
summoned the inhabitants to surrender, threatening
them, in case of refusal, to regard them guilty of
high treason.   The army moved in forced marches
towards the south.   When arrived within two days'
march from Malaga, the inhabitants began to
tremble, and to open their eyes to the impending

danger. They accordingly deputed two of their chief magistrates to Cueva, to assure him of their willingness to lay their complaints against the grand-admiral before the cardinal, and to accept his decision. Cueva hastened to convey the news to Madrid; and soon received orders to spare the city, and punish only the principal ringleaders. Ximenez sent an account of the whole affair to Charles, acquainting him that Malaga had returned to order without the shedding of blood, and would have done so sooner, had the rebels not been encouraged in their proceedings by letters from Flanders, which he enclosed. He gave, by these, fresh proofs to his majesty, of how little the real wants and necessities of Spain were understood and cared for in Flanders, and how necessary it was, therefore, to guard the regent against these influences and intrigues; his authority being so closely allied to the king's that it could neither rise nor fall without increasing or injuring the other.*

Another revolt at Arevalo terminated in an equally happy manner. King Ferdinand had bequeathed a yearly income of 30,000 gold florins to his wife Germaine, to be derived from the revenues of the kingdom of Naples. But as the dowager-queen intended to remain in Castile, Ximenez proposed to exchange the dowry for the Castilian towns and villages of Arevalo, Almedo, Madrigal, and S. Maria de Nieve, considering this arrangement, to which both Germaine and King Charles gave their consent, at once more honourable and safe. Arevalo formerly belonged to the widow of John II. of Castile, the mother of Isabella, whose grand-master of the household, Count Gutierre Velasquez of Cuellar, had been appointed prefect of that town. His son

* Gomez, p. 1090. Fléchier, liv. iv. pp. 372—376. Miniana, p. 3.

had retained this office after the death of the princess, but feared now to lose it through the intended exchange. At the instigation of his wife, a bitter enemy of Germaine, after having been her intimate friend, he determined to maintain himself in the possession of Arevalo. Ximenez, who greatly esteemed this otherwise very worthy man, endeavoured, by friendly letters and exhortations to dissuade him from his undertaking, and induced even Charles to address a very kind and gracious letter to him. But the grand-admiral, who hated the queen, and liked the cardinal but little, having, together with several other grandees, offered their assistance, Cuellar and the inhabitants of the town were easily encouraged to persist in their hostile intentions. When Ximenez perceived the fruitlessness of further efforts to bring about an amicable arrangement, he sent, in the summer of 1517, one of the higher judges, Cornejo, with an armed force against the rebellious town. His instructions were, once more to offer pardon and mercy to the inhabitants and the count, and to threaten them in case of continued resistance, with confiscation of their property, with branding, and all the pains of high treason. As in this extremity, neither the grand-admiral nor any of the other grandees sent the promised assistance, Cuellar, seeing himself abandoned, dismissed his troops, and sent his submission in to Cornejo. The city gates were thrown open, the commissary of the cardinal entered the town, and occupied the citadel. Ximenez forthwith interested himself, like a friend, in behalf of the count, interceded with Charles for his pardon, and at his decease, which happened shortly after, recommended his family to the mercy of the sovereign, and his eldest son to the succession of the offices and possessions of his father. As regards the admiral, Ximenez requested Charles to reprimand him severely for his conduct, as otherwise the example of so high a personage and relative of the royal family might have a dangerous influence over the rest of the nobility.*

The submission of Arevalo accomplished, the cardinal refused to deliver this and the other fortified town, Olmedo, to Queen Germaine. A Spanish proverb says : "Arevalo and Olmedo, afterwards the whole of Spain." Ximenez remembering this adage, and knowing the queen to have sided with the Infante Ferdinand, and participated in the plans to raise him to the crown of Castile in place of his brother Charles, feared to see these important fortresses in the hands of a woman who, little inclined towards the king, could give courage and help to the discontented party to rise in open rebellion. In vain did Germaine complain, in vain attempt to take possession of Olmedo by force; in vain were her threats to leave Spain and return to her native country. Ximenez, provided with full power from Charles, remained inexorable. She was forced to content herself with Madrigal until the arrival of the young king, and obtained possession of these towns only when the presence of Charles dispelled all fears of pretensions to the throne.†

About the same time another royal widow, Johanna, the mother of Charles V., occupied the care and solicitude of the cardinal. Her father, Ferdinand, as we have observed before, had brought her to the castle of Tordesillas, a pleasant and healthy retreat, but her mind, constantly occupied with the death of her late husband, found there no relief. She obstinately refused to exchange her dark and un-

---

* Gomez, pp. 1091, 1092. Miniana, p. 4. Fléchier, liv. iv. p. 376—379.

† Gomez, p. 1092 et seq. Miniana, p. 4. Fléchier, liv. iv. pp. 379, 380.

clean room for a lighter and better apartment, or
leave it to enjoy the fresh air. In the like manner
she dispensed with a bed, rejected during winter the
warmer clothing provided for her, and often passed
two or three days without taking either food or
drink. Ximenez, being of opinion that her major-
domo, Luis Ferrier, a man, advanced in years and
of a serious disposition, was incapable of exercising
the necessary influence over the unfortunate queen,
still less to exhilarate her and dispell the clouds
which hovered over her mind, removed Ferrier from
his office, and appointed in his stead Fernando
Ducas, surnamed Strata, a prudent and cheerful
man. The choice turned out a happy one; Ducas, by
kindness and artifice, gained such an ascendancy
over the queen, that she not only consented to have
her room cleaned and to sleep on a bed, but
attended also at the public offices of the church.
This produced so visible an improvement in her
mental and bodily condition, that Charles took
occasion to express his gratitude to Ximenez in the
warmest terms.*

Old Ferrier was not the only one whom Ximenez
removed. Many other useless or unjust public
functionaries were dismissed or punished by him.
Thus, shortly after his father, young Ferrier, prefect
of Toledo, was deposed and replaced by Portocarrero, count of Palma. A severer punishment
awaited several of his subordinates, who, taking
advantage of his careless administration, had been
guilty of gross malpractices. The commissary of
the regent ordered them to be led through the
streets of the town by a herald proclaiming their
misdeeds and the executioner flogging them with
rods.†

* Gomez, p. 1093. Fléchier, liv. iv. p. 382.
† Gomez, p. 1094.

Arovia, the prefect of Zorita, a knight of the order of Calatrava, who had committed violence on the wives and daughters of his subjects, escaped similar or severer punishment by flight. Ximenez placed in his stead an honest man, Sancho Cabrero, and wrote to Charles to hang the fugitive if he should find his way to Flanders.* He further dismissed the secretary of the grand-council of the Inquisition, Calcena, and a judge of the same tribunal, d'Aguirre: the latter, however, only because he was a layman, and Ximenez would not suffer any but priests to be members of the grand-council of the Holy Office.†

All this, as well as the many proofs of his wisdom and power, tended to raise the authority of the cardinal. At the end of the first year of his administration his authority had increased so much that even those grandees who had been most opposed to him, recognized the necessity of submitting to him and seeking his friendship. The duke of Infantado, the grand-constable, and the duke of Alba, were the only ones who continued their resistance, but they feared Ximenez too much to show it in more than words, or to disobey his orders. On the other hand, Ximenez had, by a wise distribution of the public offices and dignities to able members of high families, succeeded in attaching to himself a large portion of the nobility, often winning the good will of the whole kindred by showing honour to one single man.‡

Order at last being restored, Ximenez directed his attention to the reformation of abuses, and the introduction of useful institutions. To guard the kingdom against disturbances from within and without, he ordered the three strategically most

* Gomez, p. 1094.   † Ibid.   ‡ Ibid. pp. 1094, 1095.

important towns of Castile—Medina del Campo, Alcalá, and Malaga—to be supplied with the neces- sary material for war, especially with cannons of large calibre. But, according to the testimony of Gomez, he lived only to see the armament of the first of these towns completed. The accusation of his having intended during his regency to issue coin bearing the effigy of St. Francis, and having aban- doned the plan only on the representation of the royal council, requires confirmation.*

Another intention of the cardinal, and one of much greater importance, was frustrated by his death : that of having a list drawn up of all the revenues of the crown, as well as a description and statistical tables of the kingdom. Only portions of this useful work were completed, and it is to be regretted that it was left unfinished. He was more fortunate in the execution of a similar plan with reference to the three military orders. By the desire and in the name of Charles, who was their grand- master, Ximenez ordered an exact list and account to be prepared of their revenues, institutions, fi- nances, laws, and administration. The commanders resisted at first, but by the able management of Ximenez, were soon brought back to obedience, without violence having been necessary. The result of the investigation was the discovery that these orders had annually wronged the royal treasury to a considerable extent, and, besides that, the order of Calatrava was in possession of two towns belonging to the king. Ximenez abolished these abuses. On the other hand, he returned several privileges to the orders, of which they had been unlawfully and unjustly deprived by Ferdi-

* Gomez, pp. 1094, 1095. Fléchier, liv. iv. p. 384.

nand, and at their request dismissed several officers who had been forced upon them. One of these, the treasurer Ciaconio, King Charles reinstated in his former office, in spite of all the representations of Ximenez.*

At about the same time another measure of considerable delicacy drew upon Ximenez the hatred of a great number of persons. The wars of Ferdinand had not only emptied the royal treasury, but burdened it largely with debts. Nevertheless the court at Brussels was constantly sending for fresh supplies of money, ostensibly for the equipping of the fleet which was to convey Charles to Spain. But it was openly said that Chièvres and Sauvage retained considerable sums for themselves, and purposely protracted the departure of the king, in order to be able to ask for further remittances from Spain.† In this financial embarrassment Ximenez, probably by the orders of Charles, cancelled a great many salaries paid to different noblemen and courtiers without their doing any actual services for them. To show his impartiality he commenced with his own friends, such as the heirs of the great captain. Gomez supposes this and similar matters to have occasioned the complaints of the cardinal that he was burdened with the most odious commissions from Flanders, and passed in Spain as the evil spirit of Charles, who had originated and advised them.‡ This supposition is strengthened by the fact that Ximenez for a long time vainly endea-

---

* Gomez, pp. 1095, 1096. Fléchier, liv. iv. p. 385, 386.

† On the cupidity and avarice of these two first judges of Charles, see Petrus Martyr, epp. 576, 577, 582, 594, 614. They protracted the king's journey, partly because they thought, as foreigners, they would in Spain be less able to govern the country than from Brussels.—Petrus Martyr, ep. 580.

‡ Gomez, p. 1097. Fléchier, liv. iv. p. 386.

voured to prevail upon the king to continue the pension of the learned Peter Martyr.*

At the same time Ximenez proposed to the king a new method of levying taxes, cheaper and safer than the one before in use. He also boldly and frankly remonstrated with Charles for his lavishness with the public money, telling him that he had, during the four months of his being king, given away more money than had his grandparents, the Catholic kings, during the forty years of their reign. If Charles was desirous of exercising liberality, that noble virtue of kings, he should rather bestow it upon true and faithful servants and friends than upon those whose services were null, and whose fidelity was doubtful. In his opinion three things were essential to consolidate the power of a king—uniform justice to high and low, generosity towards deserving warriors, and carefulness to keep the finances in good order.†

These internal reforms of Ximenez were interrupted by fresh armaments. In consequence of the conquest of Oran, Algiers had, as we have seen before, acknowledged the supremacy of Spain, and consented to pay a yearly tribute. Shortly after, the young and daring pirate, Horac Barbarossa, from Mitylene, in the island of Lesbos, began to make his name terrible in the Mediterranean and on its coasts. He had hardly reached his twentieth year when he already commanded a piratical fleet of forty galleys. As early as 1515, when Ferdinand was still alive, he attempted to take Bugia, a fortress in Africa which was then in the hands of the Spaniards. Though a cannon-ball had carried away

---

* Petrus Martyr, ep. 581. Peter Martyr says nothing of Ximenez having been the originator of the cancelling of these salaries.

† Gomez, p. 1098. Fléchier, liv. iv. p. 389.

his left arm in the first attack, he returned to the assault, and having gained possession of the smaller citadel of Bugia, put the whole Christian garrison of the same to death. On the 25th of November of the same year he attacked the principal fortress, but failed in the attempt, and retired.[*] He was more successful in his exertions to excite the Moors in Africa to shake off the Spanish yoke. He roused the fanaticism of their holy tribe, the Morabites, by representing to them that it was a crime and a shame for a Mussulman to pay tribute to a Christian. The consequence was, that the king of Algiers, Selim Beni Timi, asked his assistance to enable him to withdraw his allegiance from Spain and refuse to pay the tribute. Barbarossa responded to the call, but treacherously murdered his friend in a bath, seized the throne, refused the tribute, and not only menaced the neighbouring fortified towns of the Spaniards, but also those of the Moorish princes allied to Spain.[†] He threatened Tunis, took the king prisoner and put him to death. The heir to the throne fled to Spain to implore the assistance of Ximenez against the robber. The cardinal immediately sent, at the end of September, 1516, eight thousand men and the requisite vessels to Algiers to regain the place and punish the pirate. Ferdinand Andrada, to whom the command was first offered, refused it, on the ground that the army contained too many in whom no reliance could be placed. The cardinal then fixed upon Diego Vera, a general of artillery, a choice which from the beginning was regarded as hazardous by many, and amongst them also by Peter Martyr, who calls him "magis loquax et jactabundus quam strenuus" (ep. 574).

---

[*] Petrus Martyr, ep. 571.
[†] Ibid. ep. 574. Gomez, p. 1099. Fléchier, liv. iv. p. 390.

Early in October the fleet landed on the coast of Algiers, and found the town vigorously defended and skilfully fortified. In order to be enabled to attack it from all sides, Vera, in opposition to the advice of his officers, divided his army into four bodies, thus weakening his strength considerably. The officers, obeying reluctantly, showed little zeal, and Vera himself committed many other blunders. The expedition having miserably failed, he was forced to return to Spain, covered with shame, where he became an object of ridicule to all the children, and lampoons were made on him, in which he was taunted with having been unable with his two arms to overcome the one-armed Barbarossa. The sad intelligence reached Ximenez at the end of October, at an hour when, according to his usual wont, he was seated in the midst of a number of theologians, discussing theological matters. After having perused the letters, he calmly said to those around him : "Our army has been defeated and partly destroyed. There is, however, one consolation in it : Spain is thereby ridden of a great many idle and bad characters." He then resumed the discussion, admired by all for his coolness and self-possession. His enemies failed not to take advantage of this reverse, representing to Charles that the cardinal only was to be blamed for the disaster. Ximenez defended himself against these accusations in a special letter, in which he stated the number of Christians slain to be one thousand. He seems also to have acquainted Leo X. of the event, for this Pontiff expressed to him, through Cardinal Bembo, his regret at the calamity, urging him at the same time to prepare another attack against Algiers, and assuring him of his willingness to exhort the Christian princes to a war against the Turks. The cardinal, however, died before a second expedition against Barbarossa could be carried out. The latter met his death in the year 1518, in a war with Spain and the king of Tremesen, by the stone-throw of a Spanish ensign.*

Shortly after these events, Ximenez, in union with the royal council, issued an edict against the Genoese merchants in Spain, ordering them, under pain of confiscation of their property, to leave the kingdom by a given time. This severe measure was occasioned by the following circumstance:—A valiant mariner, John del Rio, native of Toledo, impatient at the inactivity to which peace condemned him, secretly carried on piracy on his own account, and had a short time previous to the sailing of the fleet destined for Algeria, done considerable damage to the Genoese. These resolved to revenge themselves at the first opportunity. Accordingly they waited for him in the Spanish harbour of Carthagena, with three war-gallions, and three merchant vessels which were taking in wool. Del Rio arrived with his gallion, but in company and under the protection of Don Berenguel of Omus, who returned richly laden with spoils from a successful expedition against the African pirates. Berenguel having refused to comply with the just demand of the Genoese to deliver Del Rio over to them, they took the matter into their own hands, opened fire on the vessel of the pirate and sank it. Enraged at this, Berenguel attacked the Genoese in his turn, firing on them not only from his own ships, but also from the heavy guns of the port. The slaughter was great on both sides. After an obstinate resistance the Genoese were forced to retire, not without first having destroyed the principal houses and towers by a well-directed cannonade, and caused such havoc in the town that the inhabitants lamented and com-

* Gomez, pp. 1099, 1100. Petrus Martyr, ep. 621. Fléchier, liv. iv. pp. 391—394.

plained, saying the Turks could hardly have carried devastation further. The indignation against the Genoese was universal. Ximenez shared it, as is proved by his severe and cruel edict. On the other hand, he was highly and justly irritated against Berenguel, whom he immediately dismissed from his command of the fleet. But Berenguel found friends at the court of Flanders who interested themselves in his behalf and obtained his reinstallation in his former dignity, much to the annoyance of the cardinal. We must add, that he shortly after retrieved his offence to a certain extent by his success in a naval engagement, in which he captured four three-oared galleys from the Turks.* The Genoese soon felt the disastrous effects of the edict upon their commerce. They consequently sent an embassy to Flanders to excuse themselves with the king, and assure him of the deep regret, which the occurrence had caused to the republic, contending, however, that the chief blame rested not with them, but with Berenguel. They further stated, to satisfy the Spanish crown, the senate had pronounced sentence of death against the captains of the three war-gallions, and condemned the inferior officers to other severe punishments. These sentences would have been carried out, had not providence forestalled them by all but utterly destroying the vessels in a storm near Nice. Charles pardoned the Genoese, and promised to revoke the edict of the cardinal. But Ximenez remonstrated and gave reasons why the sequestration of their property should continue, assuring Charles of having in the interval received intelligence of an alliance between Genoa and France, the purport of which was nothing less than to wrest from Spain

---

* Gomez, pp. 1100, 1101. Petrus Martyr, cp. 573, 576.

her possessions in Italy. As long as such an alliance existed, the property could not be restored, in order to be able, in case of a rupture, to fight the Genoese with their own money. The Genoese, however, soon removed these suspicions, and, with the consent of Ximenez himself, entered again into the possession of their property.[*]

The solicitude of Ximenez was not merely confined to Castile, but embraced all the dominions of his king, whose interest he had constantly at heart. The following is an instance :—The duke of Najara, viceroy of Navarre, informed the cardinal that he had received orders from King Charles to send the cavalry under his command to Italy, and place them at the disposal of the emperor, Maximilian, then engaged in the siege of Brescia. France had lately gained considerable ground in Italy; the war of Maximilian against this power was therefore as much in the interest of his grandson as in his own. Convinced that it was his duty not to withhold his advice in so grave an affair, Ximenez despatched in all haste a courier to Charles, urging him to induce his grandfather to abstain from continuing the siege of Brescia, a place which nature and art had made almost impregnable, and persuade him to lay siege to Milan instead, as the fall of the capital would necessarily draw after it that of Brescia and the rest of Lombardy. If the king of France attacked Naples, he, for his part, would, with Charles's consent, make a diversion into France, and order his soldiers to march direct upon Paris. As regards the Neapolitan nobles, who were living at the court of Brussels, Charles would do well to forbid his courtiers to treat them with insolence as heretofore, and to settle their affairs as quickly as possible,

[*] Gomez, pp. 1102, 1103. Petrus Martyr, ep. 585. Fléchier, liv. iv. pp. 394—399.

that they might not be affronted, but become attached and remain faithful to their allegiance in case of war. Above all, he advised Charles no longer to withold the pay due to the Spanish troops stationed in Naples; it would be better to postpone the payments to his household than those to the soldiers. In order easier to suppress the movement by which Italy was agitated, Charles should endeavour to gain the goodwill of the pope. Although Leo X. professed the greatest friendship, his political intentions could not implicitly be trusted, the less so because only recently he had sanctioned in France the levying of the tax for the holy war, whilst it was evident that the plans of the king were not directed against the Turks, but against Germany and Spain. For this reason the pope should be kept a little in fear. He himself (Ximenez) had, a short time ago, acted in this spirit, by addressing a letter to Leo in which he had candidly spoken his mind, and invited him to more friendly dispositions towards Spain. It was therefore of the greatest importance that Charles should be particularly careful in the choice of his ambassador to Rome, and select only such a man as was likely easily to obtain considerable influence with the diplomatic body at the court of Rome. This admonition was the more needed as Charles, on the advice of his friends in Flanders, had, in the person of Don Pedro Urreo, appointed an adjunct to Hieronymus Vict, till then his only ambassador at Rome, and these two men, instead of working in concert for the interest of their master, constantly opposed each other, and paralyzed their actions. Equally important, continued Ximenez, was the choice of the papal nuncio, upon whose reports to the pope depended much of the amicable relation of the two courts, the most violent quarrels and agitations having resulted from the incapacity or arrogance of a nuncio. According to recent information, the pope had destined Lawrence Pucci, a nephew of the cardinal of the same name, as nuncio for Castile : Charles should endeavour to prevent this choice, as the young prelate was frivolous and the uncle proud and of insatiable avarice.* The pope sent, indeed, not Pucci, but the cardinal Aegidius of Viterbo, general of the Augustins, but not until after the death of Ximenez, in the spring of 1518.†

During these events, Ximenez exerted himself strenuously in behalf of his former opponent, the Cardinal Carvajal. This prelate had been the chief of the league of the cardinals against Pope Julius II., and had in consequence been excommunicated. Yielding to the desire of this pope, King Ferdinand, as we have seen before, had deprived Caravajal of his bishopric of Siguenza, and given it to Prince Frederick of Portugal. After the death of Julius, Caravajal, having become reconciled to Leo X., and been reinstated into his dignity of cardinal,‡ solicited the restitution of his bishopric of Siguenza, backed by Ximenez in his request. But difficulties arose which prevented the settlement of the question. The partisans of Caravajal, and those of Bishop Frederick came even to blows, and the affair was arranged only after the death of the bishop of Plasencia, whose seat was given to Caravajal as indemnification for that of Siguenza.§

Ximenez rendered a similar service to Hadrian, in the summer of 1516, by proposing him to Charles for the vacant bishopric of Tortona, and the place of grand-inquisitor for Aragon. Hadrian obtained

---

* Gomez, p. 1104. Fléchier, liv. iv. pp. 399—401.
† Petrus Martyr, ep. 616, 621.
‡ Raynaldus, ad. ann. 1513, n. 47.
§ Gomez, pp. 1104, 1105. Fléchier, liv. iv. p. 402.

these two high offices, but nevertheless continued to reside in Castile, and remain in his former relations to this kingdom.* Ximenez procured also for Mota, the celebrated preacher and secretary to Charles, the bishopric of Badajoz, the former occupant of which, Manrique, received that of Cordova instead.†

* Gomez, p. 1107. Miniana, lib. i. c. i. p. 4.
† Gomez, p. 1107. Petrus Martyr, ep. 576.

CHAPTER XXV.

SOLICITUDE OF XIMINEZ FOR AMERICA.[*]

THE new world had, shortly after its discovery, been the object of the pious zeal of our cardinal. He did not neglect it when he became regent.

About the time when Christopher Columbus made his first voyage of discovery, and on the 12th of October, 1492, saluted the land so long wished for, Ximenez was first called from the solitude of his cloister to the brilliant court of Isabella. Born in one and the same year, one and the same event determined the career of these two great men. Full of joy at the conquest of Granada, Isabella granted to the intrepid mariner the vessels which he had solicited for so many years, appointed her former confessor, the virtuous Talavera, to the new archiepiscopal see of Granada, and summoned Ximenez in his place to the court. During the time that the pious Franciscan guided the conscience of the queen, Columbus returned from his first voyage on the 15th March, 1493, full of the glorious news of his discoveries, and bringing proofs of them to his masters. The sight of the indigenes, whom he had brought with him, increased the desire, so natural in Christian princes, of communicating the light of the gospel to those infidels. Ferdinand and Isabella resolved, in consequence, to have the young heathens educated to become apostles of their nation. They themselves, together with the hereditary prince, Juan, stood sponsors to them, and sent

---

[*] The former biographers of the cardinal have almost entirely omitted mentioning his activity in this respect.

them to Seville to receive the necessary instruction for their future office.* But, like Pope Gregory the great, who could not patiently await the moment when the Anglo-Saxon youths whom he had bought would become fit to be sent back to their native country as missionaries, so the Spanish monarchs could not wait, but at once organized a mission for the new Indies, the members of which set sail with Columbus for the New World in September of the same year.†

A Papal brief had placed Bernard Boil, abbot of the celebrated Benedictine monastery, Montserrat, in Catalonia,‡ at the head of the mission, and under his guidance, the Franciscan, Juan Perez of Marchera, is said to have built the first Christian chapel in Hispaniola.§ The assertion is false that Bartholomew Las Casas, then still a layman, and student of nineteen years of age, afterwards priest, and the warmest defender of the liberties of the Indians, accompanied Columbus and his own father to the New World.‖

* Herrera, " Historia de las Indias Occidentales," Madrid, 1730; decada i. lib. ii. c. v. p. 42.

† Benzon (" Historia Indiæ Occidentalis," 1586, p. 35) narrates that Columbus took four baptized Indians back with him to America. But as he arrived in Spain in March, 1493, and returned to the New World in September of the same year, these four can hardly have been sufficiently educated to act as missionaries, but only as interpreters for the missionaries.

‡ According to Raynaldi (" Contin. Annalium Baronii," ad. ann. 1493, n. 24) Boil was a Franciscan. But Herrera, who is the greatest authority for the early history of America, declares him to have been a Benedictine (decas i. lib. ii. c. v. p. 42). Nor does Wadding, the historian of the Franciscan order, claim him as a member of his fraternity ; he only refutes those who seek in Boil the first patriarch of India, and the real apostle of the new world. (Annales Minorum, tom. xv. p. 28 et seq.) Boil, indeed, effected but little. The papal brief for him and his companions is to be found in Raynaldus. § Wadding, tom. xv. p. 18, n. 2.

‖ Llorente, in his edition of Las Casas's works (p. ii.), asserts

The proofs of Ximenez' participation in this first mission to America are wanting, but we have the testimony of Gomez, that, eight years after, at his instigation, a new effort was made to christianize the transatlantic world, the mission of Boil and his companions having produced but little results.

Columbus was in the right path when he advised his priests to learn the language of the indigenes.[*] Several caciques, as, for instance, Guarinoer, showed inclination to embrace the Christian religion; but the firm rooting and propagation of the gospel was prevented, partly by the vices and the cruelty of the Spaniards, partly by the incapacity of the first missionaries.[†] We know nothing of the fruits of their exertions, except that Father Roman Pane, of the order of the Hermits of St. Jerome, together with John Borgoñon, a Franciscan, had for a short period won over the above cacique and his subjects. The cruelties of the Spaniards, however, as well as the representations of the other Indians, soon provoked this tribe to renounce the newly-adopted faith. This was the only glorious achievement of the whole mission. On the other hand, we know that Father Boil unjustly took part against Columbus, that he belonged to the party of the malcontents, complained bitterly of the hardships of his position, and especially of a famine which they had to endure, and returned in 1494, with several of his companions, to Spain, there to swell the number of the enemies of the great admiral.[‡]

that he accompanied Columbus only in his third voyage in the year 1498. Prescott has committed a double error with reference to him. In vol. i. he despatches him to America as early as 1493, and as an ecclesiastic; and in vol. ii. he places his first voyage in the year 1498 or 1502.

[*] Herrera, decas i. lib. iii. c. iv. p. 70.   [†] Ibid.

[‡] Idem, decas i. lib. ii. c. xii. p. 53; c. xvi. p. 59; c. xviii. p. 62.

In the year 1496, Columbus returned to Spain to defend himself against the accusations of his enemies. He was successful, but committed the grave fault of taking, for want of better colonists, a number of convicted criminals with him to America,[*] who soon turned the new world into a hell, and furnished the opponents of Columbus with numerous pretexts for complaints. Affairs grew worse through the opposition and rebellion of Francis Roldan, supreme judge of the New World. But the admiral himself completed the disorder, by the introduction of the *repartimientos* or distributions,[†] according to which the indigenes were portioned off to the Spaniards like so many cattle. The Indians were thereby exposed to numberless·tortures, and filled with the most intense hatred for their conquerors and oppressors. Ferdinand, and even Isabella, the great friend of Columbus, then conceived doubts, which may easily be excused, as to the fitness of the great mariner for the government and administration of their new possessions.[‡] This unfavourable opinion was nourished by Juan Rodriguez Fonseca, for several years president of the Council for India.[§] It increased, and reached its height, when, in June of the year 1500, two vessels arrived from America freighted with three hundred Indians, whom Columbus had given as slaves to ancient partisans of Roldan, who had before returned to Spain. "By what right," asked the indignant queen, "dares Columbus thus treat my subjects?"[‖]

In consequence of this injudicious act, the Spanish monarchs sent Francis de Bobadilla, a knight of the

---

[*] Herrera, decas i. lib. iii. c. ii. p. 66.
[†] Idem, decas i. lib. iii. c. xvi. p. 93 et seq.
[‡] Irving, Columbus, book xiii. c. i.
[§] Herrera, decas i. lib. iii. c. xv. p. 91.   Irving, book v. c. viii.
[‖] Herrera, decas i. lib. iv. c. xvii. p. 109.   Irving, book xiii. c. i.

order of Calatrava, as perquisidor to Hispaniola, with
full powers to inspect the administration of Columbus, and, in case of his being found guilty, to take
upon himself the reins of the government of the
colony. Documents left in blank, but signed by the
monarchs, were to enable him at once, there and
then, to execute under royal authority any and every
disposition he deemed necessary. Ferdinand and
Isabella had arrived at this decision as early as the
spring of 1499, but it was not carried into effect
until July of the following year, because more favourable news was still expected from Hispaniola.

Precisely about this period—that is, when this
resolution was first taken, and ultimately executed—
the monarchs resided in the southern provinces of
the kingdom, sometimes at Granada, sometimes at
Seville, for the purpose of organizing the administration of the newly-conquered kingdom, and suppressing
the rebellions which had broken out there. Ximenez
was also there, occupied with the conversion of the
Moors. He had an interview with the sovereigns
at Seville, in which, Gomez tells us, he proposed,
amongst other matters, another Christian mission
to the New World.* Gomez doubtless here alludes
to the journey of the archbishop to Seville, of which
we have before spoken at page 69, undertaken in
the beginning of the year 1500, to reassure Ferdinand and Isabella about the revolt in the Albaycim,
and justify himself and his proceedings. At the
instigation of Ximenez, Gomez continues, a number
of excellent monks from different monasteries of
Spain were then sent to Hispaniola, amongst them
also Francis Ruyz, the well-known friend and com-
mensal of the archbishop, John Tressiera, and John
Robled.† But although there can be no doubt about

* Gomez, p. 962, 27. † Idem, p. 962, 36.

2 K 2

a mission having, by the advice of Ximenez, been despatched to America in the commencement of the sixteenth century, his ancient biographer is not correct as to the date, and furnishes himself the proofs of his error. A few lines after telling the above facts, he informs us that, his health failing, Ruyz, at the end of six months, was compelled to return home, and made his voyage back in the same fleet which conveyed Bobadilla as prisoner.* This happened in the summer of the year 1502; therefore, if Ruyz had sailed with Bobadilla, he would in reality have stayed two years in the New World, and not a few months only.

The dates of Gomez are easily rectified if we consult the profane history of the New World of the next two or three years. Bobadilla landed on Hispaniola on the 23rd August, 1500,† and immediately treated Columbus as a criminal, sending him to Spain in irons, "for fear," as Columbus's son and biographer ironically observes, "he might by some miracle be enabled to swim back to Hispaniola."‡

Thus degraded, treated like a criminal, on the 25th November, 1500, the man whose monument is the discovery of a new world, arrived in Spain. Indignant at such ill-treatment, the monarchs released him without delay, decreeing shortly after the revocation of Bobadilla, who had so shamefully abused the authority confided to him. Nicolas Ovando, knight of the order of Calatrava, was in his stead appointed governor of the Indies, and sailed on the 13th February, 1502. In July of the same year he sent Bobadilla as prisoner back to Spain.§ But a violent storm

* Gomez, p. 962, 43.

† Herrera, decas i. lib. iv. c. viii. p. 110. Navarette, Relation des Quatre Voyages entrepris par Ch. Colomb (Paris, 1828), tom. iii. p. 57.

‡ Fernan Colon, Historia del Almirante, c. 86.

§ Herrera, decas i. lib. v. c. i. p. 123; c. ii. p. 126.

destroyed nearly the entire fleet : Bobadilla found his grave in the waves ; and a few vessels only, one of them bearing Ruyz, were fortunate enough to reach the Spanish coast.

Thus it is clear that the six months of which Gomez speaks are correct, if we assume Ruyz to have started with Ovando in February, 1502, and returned in the summer of the same year with the shipwrecked fleet. This assumption is strengthened by the account of Herrera, who records that ten Franciscan friars, under the guidance of Father Alonso del Espinar, embarked for the New World with Ovando.*

The sincerity of Ferdinand, and particularly that of Isabella, to christianize the New World, is beyond doubt, and best shown by their exhortations to Ovando : to proclaim the liberty of all the Indians, to rule them justly, and to be zealous in the propagation of the holy Catholic faith; but, above all, carefully to avoid ill-treating the Indians, so as not to retard or prevent their conversion.†

It is hardly necessary to add that Wadding, the great chronicler of the Franciscan order, correctly places the above mission in the year 1502.‡ It may, however, not be unimportant to investigate the cause which has given rise to the mistake committed by Gomez. He knew that the Franciscan, John Tressiera, accompanied Bobadilla to America;§ and this fact in all probability led him to assert that the other missionaries embarked at the same time, whilst in reality they followed him two years after.

---

* Herrera, decas i. lib. v. c. i. p. 123. Irving, book xvi. ch. iii. Together with Bobadilla, six other missionaries embarked for the New World.—Irving, book xiii. c. i.

† Herrera, decas i. lib. iv. c. ii. p. 117 ; c. xii. p. 118.

‡ Wadding, Annales, tom. xv. p. 247, n. 3.

§ Ibid. p. 229, n. 2 ; p. 248, n. 4. Herrera, decas i. lib. iv. c. ix. p. 113.

From the year 1502 to his nomination as regent, ancient chronicles are silent about any further participation of Ximenez in the christianizing of the New World.

True to the instructions received from Isabella, Ovando at first abolished the repartimientos, and declared the Indians free. But when he saw that their natural dislike to work could not even be overcome by money, that they remained equally averse to the Christian religion, and that the utter ruin of the Spanish colonies was thereby threatened,* Ovando introduced on his own responsibility another species of repartimientos, which he called "hirings." By these the Indians were for a specified time, and against a stipulated sum, forced to work the mines and till the soil for the Spaniards. Ovando succeeded in obtaining for his measure the consent of Isabella, this great patron of the Indians, not without receiving from her fresh and excellent instructions for the conversion of the savages.† The severity, however, by which his administration, in other respects wise and praiseworthy, is darkened, prevented the spreading of the gospel.

The cruelties perpetrated by Christians in the New World were carefully concealed from Isabella. When, shortly before her death, she heard of them, she gave in the last days of her life touching proofs of her solicitude for the unfortunate victims, and on her deathbed forced the promise from her husband to recall Ovando,—a promise which was but tardily executed by Ferdinand. She, moreover, introduced a clause in her testament, by which she admonishes her successors to hasten the baptism and civilization of the poor Indians, to treat them with the greatest

---

* Herrera, decas i. lib. iv. c. xi. p. 140.
† Idem, decas i. lib. v. c. xi. p. 140; c. xii. p. 143.

humanity, and repair the injustice done to their persons and property.*

In spite of these exhortations, the lot of the indigenes became worse after the death of the queen, under the administration of Diego, a son of Columbus, and more particularly that of Albuquerque. The avarice of the Spaniards rose to such a pitch that the cacique Hatuey believed, not without reason, that gold was the real god of the Christians. It was in vain, under these circumstances, to build Christian churches, and erect episcopal sees in America. The Indians conceived such a hatred against the religion of their oppressors, that the same cacique Hatuey declared he would rather not go to heaven if Spaniards were there.

In these calamitous times there arose Christian priests, foremost amongst them Las Casas† and the missionaries of the Dominican order, to defend the liberty and inalienable rights of the poor Indians. They preached from the pulpit, and spoke in the confessional in their favour. As early as 1511 Montesino, one of the most gifted preachers of the Dominicans in America, preached a sermon in the cathedral of St. Domingo, in the presence of the governor Diego Columbus, the principal public functionaries, and nobles of all kinds, in which he thundered against the ill-treatment of the Indians, in the most impassioned tones of popular eloquence. The auditors, fearing the dangers of a reform which would be prejudicial to their interests, demanded of his superiors the punishment of the audacious monk who had dared to speak against the royal ordinance. But the vicar of the Dominicans, a firm and enlightened man, rejected their unreasonable demands, declaring: " What the father

---

* Prescott, vol. ii.

† He had accompanied Ovando to America in the year 1502.

has said is unanimously embraced by the whole convent; he has in his sermon said nothing incompatible with the service of God or the king." The order being threatened with expulsion if Montesino did not retract, the latter appeared willing to do so. On the following Sunday the church was overflowed; but when the father, to the universal astonishment of his audience, not only repeated his assertions, but strengthened them by fresh proofs, the functionaries became enraged, and carried their complaints direct to the king. Nevertheless, the Dominicans persevered in their zeal, obstinately refusing absolution and the sacraments to every one who owned an Indian as a slave. The Franciscans, Father Espinosa at their head, pursued a less rigorous practice. Envoys were, by both parties, sent to Spain, to plead their cause with the king. Montesino, who was one of them, made a favourable impression upon the king. But, unwilling to decide without a previous thorough investigation of the affair, Ferdinand appointed a committee composed of a considerable number of statesmen and theologians, who, taking the last will of Isabella for their basis, declared the Indians free, and entitled to all the rights which nature has given to man.*

This declaration did not stop the repartimientos. The king contented himself with commanding, in the year 1512, a better treatment of the Indians, and restricting real slavery to the anthropophagous Caribs.† In the following year he favoured the Spaniards still more, by proclaiming that, according to the matured opinion of the learned, and in virtue of the bull of Alexander VI., which made him possessor of the New World, the repartimientos

---

* Herrara, decas i. lib. viii. c. xi. pp. 221, 222; c. xii. p. 123.
† Idem, decas i. lib. viii. c. xii. p. 124.

were quite in accordance with divine and human rights. Every one might therefore, without scruples of conscience, be owner of Indians, as the king and his council would bear all responsibility. The Dominicans he admonished to show in future more moderation.*

This edict induced Las Casas to return to Spain in the year 1515, where he pleaded the cause of the Indians with so much warmth that Ferdinand promised to remedy the evil. But death prevented the execution of his resolution. Las Casas prepared to go to Flanders, there to renew his exertions with the new king Charles, when Ximenez, now become regent of Castile, kept him back by promising to look personally into the matter.†

The cardinal gave several audiences to Las Casas, in presence of Hadrian, the dean of Louvain, of the minister and licentiate Zapata, the doctors Carvajal and Palacios Rubios, and of Francis Ruyz, who had been raised to the episcopal see of Avila.

After having made himself acquainted with the laws which the affair of Father Montesino had called into existence, he charged the zealous missionary, in conjunction with Dr. Palacios Rubios, to consider the best mode of governing the Indians. Their reports determined him to the following resolution, which struck the ministers of the late king with terror. According to his opinion, it was not in the province of statesmen to decide upon this question, but of priests, who, invested with full powers, could investigate the matter in Hispaniola. Neither the Franciscans nor the Dominicans appearing to him sufficiently unbiassed and unprejudiced for an impartial inquiry, he addressed himself to the General of the Jeronimites, requesting him to select

* Herrera, decas i. lib. ix. c. xiv. p. 255.
† Idem, decas ii. lib. i. c. xi. p. 16; lib. ii. c. iii. pp. 26, 27.

several members of his order, to send them with royal authority to America. The general, who resided in the monastery of St. Bartholomew of Lupina, immediately called together all the priors of the province of Castile to a private chapter, in which, agreeably to the desire of the cardinal, twelve of the most worthy members of the order were selected. Four priors were sent to Madrid to acquaint the cardinal of what had been done. Ximenez received them one Sunday afternoon, in the monastery of St. Jerome, in the presence of Hadrian, Zapata, Carvajal, Rubios, and the bishop of Avila. Las Casas, present on the occasion, was charged to repair to the general of the Jeronimites and invite him to select from the chosen twelve, three monks of his order whom he considered fittest for the mission. The choice fell on Father Bernardin of Manzanedo, on Ludwig of Figueroa, prior of La Mejorada at Olmedo, and on the prior of the Jeronimite monastery at Seville.*

Ximenez remained steadfast in his resolution, in spite of the insinuations of almost all the Spaniards who had returned from the New World and were then living at the court. They accused Las Casas of having grossly exaggerated his accounts of the condition of the New World, and of often having committed imprudent actions by his impetuous zeal. If his plans were adopted, the civilization and conversion of the Indians would become an impossibility; these could only be achieved by forcing the barbarous and indolent indigenes to work and associate with the Christians.†

Ximenez now ordered the instructions to be drawn up, which his monastic commissaries were to take with them to the New World. Immediately

---

* Herrera, decas ii. lib. ii. c. iii. p. 27. Gomez, 1085.
† Herrera, ibid.

after their arrival, and before proceeding to other matters, they should liberate all the Indians whose masters were not resident in America. They should assemble the Spanish colonists, and declare to them that evil reports of their conduct were the sole cause of their arrival in the New World ; and should, if necessary on oath, question them on the real state of the country. They should, at the same time, not neglect to obtain privately the fullest information, and think of the best means of remedying the abuses.

The fathers should call the principal caciques to a meeting, and declare to them, in the name of Queen Isabella and her son Charles, that they were free subjects of their majesties, that any injustice which had been done to them would be repaired, and that they should communicate this to the other caciques and to their own subjects to deliberate with them about the measures to be taken for the improvement of their condition, which was a matter of great concern to their majesties. In order that the Indians might believe them, these meetings should be attended by several monks who already possessed the confidence of the savages and spoke their language.*

The other chapters of the instructions charged the three fathers to send monks of the country to the different islands of the New World, to investigate their condition, and obtain the fullest information as to the treatment to which the Indians had hitherto been subjected. It would be advisable to build villages for the Indians in the four islands in which mines existed, as the work would be less irksome to them if they lived nearer the place of their occupation. Each of these villages should consist of three hundred families, as many houses, a church,

---

* Herrera, decas ii. lib. ii. c. iv. p. 28.

a larger habitation for the cacique, and an hospital; and the choice of the place be left to the cacique and his Indians.

Such tribes of the Indians as were too far removed from the mines should be collected in villages built on their native soil, be taught agriculture and the breeding of cattle, and in return pay a certain tribute to the king.

To each village sufficient territory should be allotted, and this divided in such a manner that each of the citizens received one portion, the cacique four, the remainder to serve as thrashing-place and pasture ground. No Indian could be forced to join the community. If the subjects of one cacique were insufficient to fill a village, several tribes were to be united, each cacique retaining his authority over his own subjects, the lesser caciques as heretofore being subordinate to the greater ones. Each village to be governed by the principal cacique in conjunction with the priest of the community and the royal administrator. The latter to have the superintendence of several villages and his post to be filled by none other but a Castilian. If a cacique had no male issue, and a Castilian married the hereditary daughter, the latter to be cacique after the death of his father-in-law. In concert with the priest, the caciques to be permitted to punish their subjects, but their power not to extend beyond the sentence of flogging. Graver cases to be brought before the ordinary royal courts, which punished also the caciques if they failed in doing their duty.*

The fathers should exhort the administrators of the districts to visit, from time to time, the villages of which the inspection was confided to them, to be watchful that the Indians lived orderly with

---

* Herrara, decas ii. lib. ii. c. iv. pp. 28, 29.

their families in their habitations, and were indus-
trious in the mines as well as in the field.
The Indians were, however, in no wise to be oppressed, and the administrators to be sworn not to
burden them with too much work. The latter
might, in the execution of their functions, be accompanied by three or four armed Castilians; but only
such weapons to be given to the Indians as were
required for hunting. The administrators and
priests of the villages of the Indians should endeavour to accustom the savages to wear dresses, to
sleep in beds, to retain their furniture and working
tools, to wean them from eating squatted on the
ground, &c., to exhort them to content themselves
with one wife and not to abandon her, also to recommend chastity to the women, or to threaten them
with flogging in case of adultery.

The administrators were to receive an adequate
remuneration for their services, one half of which
was defrayed by the king, the other half by the respective villages; they should be married, to prevent
abuses, and keep a book in which the names of the
caciques and their Indians were to be inscribed, as
also the greater or lesser industry with which they
performed their work.

One regular or secular priest to be appointed for
every village, whose duty would be to instruct the
Indians in the Christian faith, to teach each individual according to his faculties, to preach to them,
to administer the sacraments, to accustom them to
hear mass, and there to keep the women apart from
the men; to admonish them to pay their tithes, and
bring their firstlings as offerings for the Church and
her servants. These ecclesiastics were to say mass for
the Indians every Sunday and festival, as also several
times during the week. For this they were to
receive, in addition to casual offerings and presents,

a portion of the tithes, but nothing for confessions, marriages, interments, or the administration of the sacraments in general. On the evenings of the Sundays and festivals the Indians should be called together by the bell to receive instruction in the catechism, and light penances should be imposed on such as were absent. For the inferior service of the Church, a sacristan was to be appointed in every village, whose duty would be, besides, to teach the children to read, taking particular care gradually to accustom the Indians to the Spanish language. The hospital, which was to be erected in the centre of each village, to be supported by the inhabitants, and to admit the sick, the aged who could no longer work, and orphans. Every poor person to receive daily one pound of meat from the common slaughter-house.

All the male inhabitants of a village between the years of twenty and fifty should, one third at a time, work in turns at the mines, and be relieved every three months, according to the directions of the cacique. The women to be exempt from these occupations, unless they offered themselves of their own free will or by order of their husbands. The places of master-miners and inspectors could only be given to Indians. Until these had accustomed themselves to the breeding of cattle and poultry, a number of mares, cows, sows, hens, &c., should be kept for the benefit of the whole community, as also a common slaughter-house erected.

The gold ore should remain with the Indian master-miners until the time of melting, which was to take place every two months, in presence of the principal cacique and the administrator. The products to be divided into three equal portions—one for the king, and two for the Indians. From the latter were to be deducted the costs of the implements and cattle, as well as the expenses connected with the construction of the villages. The rest to be equally distributed amongst all the families, the caciques receiving six, the master-miners two portions. Each Indian to defray from his portion, the expense of his tools for mining operations.

Besides these Indians, twelve Castilian master-miners should be appointed to search for gold mines, which, if found, were to be given over to the Indians for working.

The Castilians should respect the liberty of the Indians in general, but be permitted to make slaves of the anthropophagous Caribs. Whoever, under this pretext, dared to oppress the peaceful Indians, was to be punished with death, and any one ill-treating them to be brought for punishment before the court, which admitted even the depositions of the Indians themselves.

These instructions were, however, in no way binding for the Jeronimite commissaries. Ximenez gave them full powers, in each individual case, to modify or otherwise alter them, according to their best judgment and circumstances. He did this the more readily, as he really had the civilization of the New World at heart.*

Foreseeing the possibility of the Jeronimites being, after due inquiry, compelled to sanction the continuance of the repartimientos, the cardinal provided them with the necessary instructions. They should, in this case, adopt the laws of the year 1512, but modify their rigour in the following points : the women and children should not be forced to work, the Indians not be burdened with heavy loads, nor exchanged; their time for work be diminished, and they allowed three hours' rest every day. They should receive daily rations of meat, and their pay be increased. Whoever treated an Indian as a slave

* Herrera, decas ii. lib. ii. c. v. pp. 29—31.

who was not given him by the repartimientos should
be punished. One-third only of the working population should be employed at a time, and the administrators take an oath not to overwork the Indians. It
should be the duty of the administrators during the
whole year to visit the villages, and their particular ·
endeavour to find out whether any Indians were fit to
be emancipated, and able to live without supervision
as free subjects of the king ; care should be taken to
promote this object as much as possible. Lastly,
a well-informed and conscientious man should be
appointed to defend the cause of the Indians at
court; and Spanish workmen sent to the island, to
hasten the construction of the buildings.*

The despatches for the Jeronimites completed,
Ximenez appointed Las Casas protector of all the
Indians, with a yearly salary of 100 pesos, and
directed him to join the three monks, in order to
assist them by his experience, and give them further
instructions. At the same time, he nominated the
licentiate Alonso Zuazo, a distinguished and very
honest jurist of Valladolid, criminal judge, to accompany the commission, and investigate the administration hitherto practised in the country. The
ministers Zapata and Carvajal refused at first to
sign the very extensive powers conceded to this
man; but Ximenez, in his quality of regent, ordering
them peremptorily to do so, they ultimately affixed
their signatures ; not, however, without reserving
the right of acquainting King Charles, at his arrival,
of their refusal, and the force employed by the cardinal. The commission then prepared to depart ;
but the prior of Seville being unable to join his
companions, Alphonso, the prior of St. John of
Ortega, at Burgos, was chosen in his stead; and

---

* Herrera, decas ii. lib. ii. c. vi. pp. 31, 32.

Father Ludwig of Figueroa, appointed the head of the commission.

Meanwhile, fourteen Franciscans, pious and learned men, had arrived in Spain from Picardy, to join the American mission. Amongst them was a brother of the king of Scotland, an old grey-headed man, who was greatly revered for his virtues; and at their head, Father Remigius, who had once been a missionary in the New World. Ximenez showed great kindness to these monks, members of the same Order to which he belonged, and provided for their passage to Hispaniola.

By the hands of his commissaries, Ximenez forwarded several despatches to the royal functionaries in America, by which he ordered a correct statement to be prepared of the revenues which the royal fiscus had derived from America, until the death of Ferdinand; as, according to the will of Isabella, one half of these belonged to Ferdinand, the other half to the crown of Castile. The cardinal also took occasion earnestly to remind the governors and judges of the necessity of treating the Indians with humanity, and of continuing the zeal for their conversion. At the same time, he forbade them to send out any ships for fresh discoveries, &c., without an ecclesiastic who could watch over the strict observance of his orders and regulations.

A third edict of still greater importance was at this period issued by the cardinal-regent. Negro slaves had repeatedly been sold to America, and been employed there in the colonies. They were in special demand, and well paid for, on account of their aptitude and strength for work, one negro being calculated to do the work of four Indians. Shortly before the departure of the Jeronimites, proposals were made to Ximenez to permit the trade

in negro slaves, particular stress being laid upon
the advantage which the royal exchequer could
derive from an impost laid upon this trade. It is
not known from whom these proposals emanated,
but there is nothing to justify our charging Las
Casas with them; although, it is a well-known fact
that this patron of the Indians in the interest of
his favourites ultimately carried this point with
Charles V.* Ximenez not only stanchly resisted
all insinuations, but published an edict forbidding
all and every importation of negro slaves.†

Everything having at last been arranged, the
Jeronimites and their companions set sail for the
New World on the 15th November, 1516. Zuazo,
who was not ready yet, and Las Casas, were left
behind; the latter on the alleged ground that the
ship was already too full to accommodate him properly. The real motive, however, was the desire
of the Jeronimites not to arrive in America in
company of a man who was, already, bitterly hated
by the colonists, as by appearing to share his
sentiments, they would, from the very beginning,
lose much of their influence. The Jeronimites
landed in Hispaniola on the 20th December, 1516,
and Las Casas, who had sailed in a second vessel,
thirteen days after them.‡ They fixed their residence in the monastery of the Franciscans, much
astonished, says Gomez, at perceiving ripe grapes
and figs in the gardens, and finding the air so hot
that they perspired, in the middle of the night, whilst

---

* Las Casas began only in the year 1517 to advocate the
introduction of negroes, after a great number of them had already
been imported there.

† Herrera, decas ii. lib. ii. c. viii. p. 34. It is doubtful whether
Ximenez refused the importation of negro slaves from humanity
or for political reasons. Irving is of opinion that his clear
political mind foresaw the future revolts of the negroes.

‡ Gomez, p. 1085.

singing their matins, as plentifully as during the dog days in Spain.*

The fathers, after having handed their powers to the astonished royal functionaries, began at once to inquire into the condition of the island, the treatment of the Indians, and all the other points indicated to them by Las Casas, showing much tact and prudence in their proceedings.† They interrogated the judges about the administrators, conversed with a great number of indigenes and ecclesiastics, consulted Las Casas at every step, and abolished the repartimientos of persons not living in America, those present being permitted to retain theirs under the condition of treating the Indians kindly. These concessions were intended to allay the excitement produced amongst the Spanish colonists by the zeal of Las Casas. They considered it necessary to proceed slowly and gradually with an affair so grave as the emancipation of the Indians. Their sudden and complete delivery threatened not only greatly to injure the interests of the colonists, but to endanger altogether the colonization and civilization of the New World, and to stop the propagation of Christianity.

Las Casas, for his part, was highly exasperated by these concessions, having imagined the Jeronimites would, on their arrival in Hispaniola, entirely suppress the repartimientos. He grew so passionate in his zeal, that he even threatened the fathers, and retired every night into a monastery of the Dominicans to place his life in security against the hatred of the Spaniards. The Jeronimites, knowing the purity of his intentions, did not resent his violence,

* Herrera, decas ii. lib. ii. c. xii. pp. 40, 41.

† The Indians showed so little understanding, that several ecclesiastics were of opinion that they were not real men, and objected, therefore, to the blessed sacrament being given to them. .

but used every effort to improve the condition of the Indians, to shield them from oppression, and convert them to the Christian faith.

Zuazo, arriving soon after from Spain, commenced at once an inquiry into the conduct of the royal functionaries, and decided a great number of suits, both civil and criminal, with great despatch and equity, to the complete satisfaction of the fathers. The latter verified the accounts, ordered the construction of buildings, and introduced numerous very praiseworthy arrangements and regulations.*

Hispaniola possessed already the two bishoprics of St. Domingo and Concepcion de la Vega in Hispaniola, which had recently been established. The former was confided to the learned Alessandro Geraldino, a Roman, who had before been tutor at the court of Castile. Ximenez, in his office of grand-inquisitor, appointed these two bishops inquisitors for these islands; thus introducing the Holy Office into the New World.

But the Inquisition became formidable to the Indians only under Charles V., who, however, in the year 1538, exempted them from the jurisdiction of this institution, and confined it to the heretical Europeans.†

The colonies were soon thrown again into violent agitation, by Las Casas accusing the royal judges of Hispaniola of being the authors and accomplices of the horrible massacres of the Indians, and of numerous barbarities committed towards them.

Desirous of leaving the decision to the king himself, and his ministers, the fathers tried to prevent these accusations from being inquired into in America. Las Casas, thereupon, and suspecting besides that his last letters to the cardinal had

* Herrera, decas ii. lib. ii. c. xv. p. 44.
† Ibid. c. xvi. p. 46.　Llorente, tom. ii. pp. 195, 196.

been intercepted at Seville, determined once more to return to Spain.* He sailed from America in May, 1517, and immediately on his arrival repaired to Aranda, where the court then resided; but the cardinal was too ill to communicate with him. Las Casas therefore departed to Valladolid, to await the arrival of Charles V. Meanwhile the Jeronimites had, on their part, despatched their colleague, Bernardin de Manzanado, to Spain, to give an account of their proceedings in India.†

Whilst Las Casas awaited the king at Valladolid, Ximenez died, on the 8th November, 1517. He had to negotiate now with the chancellor of Charles, Jean Sauvage, the Duke of Chièvres, his tutor, and La Chaux,‡ his grand chamberlain, who all three, from their jealousy of Ximenez, were well disposed to censure the former administration of America, and the commission of the Jeronimites. The latter were recalled, and Rodrigo de Figueroa appointed supreme judge in the place of Zuazo. But the new administration recognized the impossibility of suddenly emancipating the Indians from compulsory work. This became feasible only after they had adopted the proposal formerly rejected by Ximenez, and now made by Las Casas, of importing into America a sufficient number of negro slaves from Africa.§

As the history of the New World ceases here to touch the biography of our cardinal, we turn to another subject—the history of the last year of his life.

* Herrera, decas ii. lib. ii. c. xv. p. 45.
† Ibid. c. xvi. p. 46. ‡ Ibid. p. 47.
§ Gomez, p. 1086.

CHAPTER XXVI.

THE civil disturbances, of which we have spoken in a preceding chapter, continued during the last year of the cardinal's life, and even till the arrival of Charles in Spain. But after the sketch we have given of them in connection with other occurrences, it remains for us only to relate the events which took place in the year 1517.

The prolonged absence of Charles had caused great discontent in Spain, which, fanned by French misrepresentations, soon broke forth in loud complaints and reproaches. The king, it was said, had not the wish to come to Spain; would, if on board a vessel to convey him thither, disembark again under the pretext of being unable to endure the sea-sickness, &c.* Ximenez had great difficulty in quieting these false rumours. To appease them, Seigneur de la Chaux was sent to Spain, who, after having been a favourite of Philip, filled now the office of chamberlain to Charles, and was distinguished for his skill in political negotiations.† Peter Martyr has a less favourable opinion of him: he describes him indeed as a man of wit and ability, but fitter to enliven a company than to apply himself to serious work; one who could offer but little consolation to Spain.‡

Urged by the enemies of Ximenez, Hadrian had complained to the king that his authority was insufficient to counterbalance that of the cardinal, who

* Gomez, p. 1108.   † Ibid.   ‡ Petrus Martyr, ep. 581.

would admit no colleague into the regency. In order to support him, La Chaux was sent to Castile, and the grandees already rejoiced at the success of their intrigues against Ximenez. The latter, although well aware of the purport of the mission, prepared great festivities for the arrival of the royal envoy, and received him with all the honours usually accorded only to royalty. La Chaux had scarcely entered Madrid, and Ximenez paid his addresses to him in person, when the grandees began to incite him against the cardinal. Ximenez feigned ignorance of all these machinations, but consulted La Chaux rarely and only in very urgent cases on state affairs, and then he invariably consigned to him the place after Hadrian. One day Hadrian and La Chaux thought they had found a favourable opportunity for conquering for themselves the first places in the triumvirate. They hastened to affix their signatures first, to a number of newly-drawn-up decrees, leaving only sufficient room for the cardinal to sign his name after theirs. When the papers were brought to Ximenez, he, without saying a word, ordered fresh copies to be made out, signed these by himself only, and issued them. Henceforth neither Hadrian nor La Chaux was ever asked again to sign a decree: they ventured not to resist, but contented themselves with complaining to the king, and asking for further assistance. Charles sent a third ambassador, in the person of Baron Amerstorf, who remained, however, as much a cipher in matters of business as his colleagues. The complaints continued, and the king, annoyed by these constant accusations, at last reproved the opponents of Ximenez, and confirmed him in the exclusive administration of the regency.[*]

* Gomez, p. 1109. Robles, p. 186 et seq. Fléchier, liv. v. p. 414—418. Prescott, vol. ii.

This gave a moment's respite to the cardinal, but the intrigues soon revived. In order effectually to break his power, his Flemish and Spanish enemies advised Charles to appoint, as his colleague, a man of greater distinction, proposing as such, Count Ludwig of the Palatinate, a relative of the king. Ximenez energetically protested against such an arrangement. He declared to the king " That the nomination of a co-regent would inevitably be attended by quarrels and discord: the reins of the government should either be left exclusively to himself or taken altogether out of his hands; he would greatly prefer a successor to a colleague. The age of the king, he continued, rendered the regency unnecessary, the avarice and cupidity of his councillors paralyzed his actions, and the continual disturbances threatened destruction to Spain. He was weary of the struggle, and would much rather retire to his diocese, there to await, as in a secure haven, the tempest which threatened to break over the kingdom. If the king protracted his arrival much longer, he could see but one safeguard against the impending dangers,—that of investing him with the power of appointing all the judges and civil functionaries, whilst Charles retained the nominations of the bishops and military, the distribution of mercy and favours. Charles and his Flemish ministers were loth to accede to these demands. But fearing lest they should lose a man of whom they stood so much in need, they praised his conduct, and accepted his conditions, not without the secret hope of displacing him and indemnifying themselves, after their arrival in Spain. Ximenez thanked the king as if the powers given to him had been granted heartily and with the best will.*

---

* Gomez, p. 1110. Fléchier, liv. v. p. 418—420.

Meanwhile the Emperor Maximilian, who possessed great influence over his grandson Charles, and already strove to secure for him the German crown, had departed for Flanders. He held several conferences with Charles at Vilvorda, near Brussels, in which he urged him to accelerate his voyage to Spain. Ximenez being wrongly informed about the purport of these meetings, and supposing Maximilian opposed to the departure of Charles, with the intention of visiting Spain himself, wrote a letter to Chièvres, in which, with great ability, he demonstrated by numerous examples from history, the dangers of such a course.[*]

When, in spite of the representations of Maximilian, Charles still hesitated to go to Spain, but demanded fresh supplies of money from Ximenez, and Chièvres and Sauvage openly continued their shameful traffic in public offices, the discontent in Castile broke out afresh. Important towns, such as Burgos, Leon, Valladolid, and others, openly declared that the kingdom would go to ruin if prompt remedies were not applied. The movement of the towns was with difficulty kept within the limits of the law. But the citizens were ultimately prevailed upon to send a deputation to Ximenez and the royal council, in order to state to them the deplorable condition of the country, and demand the convocation of the general cortes. Their request was not unreasonable. Ximenez, however, dreading the effects of a violent agitation of the country in the absence of the king, replied that he could not accede to their demands until it had been established that the king had really postponed his voyage to Spain for a considerable period. At the same time he wrote to Charles, acquainting him with these occurrences, and

[*] Gomez, p. 1111. Petrus Martyr, ep. 582. Fléchier, liv. v. p. 421.

urging him so to arrange his departure, as to arrive in the country before the meeting of the states could take place. Gomez has preserved a Latin translation, made by him, of one of Ximenez' letters of this period, in which the cardinal strongly urges the king to appoint only men of ability and merit as councillors and other officials, and to hasten his departure for Spain.* Charles, who received the letter kindly,

* Gomez, pp. 1111, 1112. The editors of the "Documents Inédits" have reprinted this letter in the Latin translation of Gomez, in the collection of the "Papiers d'Etat du Cardinal de Granvelle" (tom. i. p. 85—88), as if it had never been published before. The letter runs as follows:—

"Ximenius gubernator et senatus regius Carolo regi salutem. Pro antiqua et fideli observantia, qua erga majores parentesquo tuos et nunc demum erga teipsum obnoxii sumus, ut fidos ministros, optimos cives et consiliarios incorruptos decet, tuis reipublicæ commodis, ad quam suscipiendam, tot regni hæredibus parvo temporis intervallo extinctis, Dei nutu vocatus es, necessario prospicere cogimur; teque ipsum continuo admonere ea, quæ reipublicæ convenire visa sunt. Ita nos enim culpa vacabimus et crimine neglectæ reipublicæ, aut potius proditæ, liberati erimus. Magni principes et suscipiendi reges tamdiu a Deo potestatem, et ab hominibus reverentiam consequi merentur, quamdiu justo et recto imperio populos eorum fidei commissos regunt. Id autem ab ipsis fieri nullo meliori argumento intelligi potest, quam si ad tantam molem sustinendam adjutores et socios quam spectatissimos et idoneos elegerint. Neque enim unus aliquis, quantumlibet præclaris dotibus et virtutibus excelluerit, rebus tam diversis abeundis par esse potest. Nam nihil aliud priscos illos centimanos esse existimamus, nisi reges consideratos et sapientes, qui per egregios et probos ministros, æque ac per seipsos regna sibi commissa tuerentur. Sed fabulosa ista relinquamus; majorum tuorum res gestas, cæteris exemplis prætermissis, intueamur. Enricus tertius, atavus tuus, qui propter assiduas in ætate florenti imbecillitates Valetudinarius cognominatus est, cum se viribus corporis destitutum regio muneri imparem videret, prudentissimo consilio usus, viros, literis et moribus et religione præstantes ad se accersitos, magno semper in pretio habuit, eisque comitibus et consiliorum participibus adeo rempublicam pacatam et optime institutam tenuit, ut magno ejus merito successoribus optimi principis exemplum sit habitus. Contra, Enrico quarto, tuo majori avunculo, omnia dura et infausta contigerunt, quoniam eos rerum gerendarum suasores per summam socordiam apud se

would certainly have yielded to the desire of the Spaniards, had not his egotistical and avaricious Flemish advisers exercised too great an influence over

retinuit, qui nullo hominum pudore, nulla Dei immortalis reverentia, omnia sursum ac deorsum miscentes, gravissima mala reipublicæ intulerunt. Sed quid in aliis commemorandis immoramur? Annon avi tui, Catholici reges, satis magno documento esse possunt? Quibus id unum ante omnia curæ fuit, muneribus publicis viros egregios, quicumque tandem ii essent, præficere. Unde, propriis ministris et aulæ familiaribus prætermissis, qui suo voluti jure hæc importune solent extorquere, ignotos homines nec sibi unquam visos, quod essent meritis suis commendati et publica opinione celebres, præter omnem expectationem ad res magnas vocarunt. Nemo, illis regnantibus, ambitus est convictus; nemo lege Julia de repetundis condemnatus; quod, proh dolor! miserrimo hoc tempore frequens esse magnopere dolemus. Fuit etiam illorum regum hoc præclarum institutum, raro cuiquam summa concedere, nisi per inferiores gradus devolutus, specimen suæ probitatis et virtutis exhibuisset; ut pro cujusque facultate et ingenio hæc aut illa munera deferrentur. Qua nimirum ratione factum est, ut omnia suis numeris quadrantia, concentum quemdam reipublicæ constituerent, qualem numquam ad id tempus videramus. His igitur artibus et consiliis, ut de cæteris taceamus, rempublicam aliorum principum negligentia collapsam, et sicariis hominibus atque tirannicis violentiis vehementer afflictam, suscipientes, tibi hisce difficultatibus liberam tradiderunt. Proinde cum Deus optimus maximus, sub cujus tutela reges estis, id tibi ingenium et judicium dederit, eam prudentiam in juvenilibus annis largitus sit, denique singularibus virtutibus majestem tuam exornaverit, quales homini principi necessariæ sunt, æquum est ut quæ diximus animadvertas, et quantum ponderis habent, consideres. Invenies enim gravissimam cladem et ingentem perniciem, si hæc contempseris, reipublicæ imminere; contra, si hæc egeris, maximam quandam felicitatem promitti. Res universæ a principiis suis pendent, et errores in principio solent minimo labore emendari, ut facile in viam rectam redire possimus. Sero remedium parari a sapientibus dicitur, dum mala vires diutinas sumpserunt. Quare tuis pedibus Hispania universa supplex provoluta, ut ejus commodis prospicias, ut hominum corruptorum cupiditates reprimas, ut gliscentia vitia cohibeas, ut tuorum regnorum tranquillitati consulas, te votis omnibus et precibus orat et obtestatur. Id autem facile fiet, si Hispaniam, amplissimam et nobilissimam regionem suorumque principum obsequio devotissimam, secundum leges patrias et antiqua majorum instituta gubernari et vivere concesseris. Vale.

him. The people, seeing themselves again deluded, broke forth in fresh murmurs, and pressed Ximenez and the royal council more earnestly than ever to convoke the cortes. To refuse would have been both unjust and impolitic. It was then the month of January, 1517. Ximenez fixed the meeting of the cortes for the following September, hoping Charles would by that time have arrived in Spain. The clamour of the nation was appeased. Ximenez now besieged the king with such pressing letters, begging him no longer to delay his voyage, that Charles at length determined, in the autumn of 1517, to embark on board of one of the vessels which Ximenez had despatched from Castile to convey him to Spain.*

In the interim the enemies of the cardinal had not been idle. Amongst other things, they had circulated the report that the energy employed by the cardinal in the suppression of the popular movements, had sprung only from his desire of showing to the king that there was no necessity for hurrying himself, and that he had acted in this in concert with Chièvres.† Others published pasquils against him, Chièvres, and Ruy Blaz, in which the latter was represented as the Davus of the whole comedy. Ximenez took little heed of these things; nevertheless, he saw himself forced to do so, on the protests of Hadrian and La Chaux. The culprits were prosecuted, but the inquiry against them conducted so carelessly that they came off unharmed.‡

A matter of greater importance, and much more harassing to Ximenez, was the constant opposition

---

* Gomez, p. 1113. Fléchier, liv. v. p. 424.

† How much Ximenez, on the contrary, desired the speedy arrival of Charles, we learn by Peter Martyr, letter 598, in which he says: "Regis adventum affectu avidissimo desiderare videtur. Sentit, sine rege non rite posse corda Hispanorum moderari ac regi."

‡ Gomez, p. 1113. Fléchier, liv. v. p. 426.

and persevering hatred of the dukes of Alba and
Infantado, and of the Count Giron of Ureña. The
Duke of Infantado, as we have seen before, was
already embittered against Ximenez, on account
of his having prevented a marriage of his nephew
with a niece of the cardinal. His irritation was
increased by the quarrel about the seigniory
over Veleña, near Guadalaxara. This little town
had formerly belonged to the elder brother of the
duke, but in due legal form, been sold to the count
of Coruña. Already, during the lifetime of Ferdinand, the duke had demanded the restitution of
this possession, on the ground that it was inalienable from the property of the family. But although
a favourite of Ferdinand, he had not been able to
accomplish his design. When Ximenez became
regent, the duke insisted upon the judgment in
this case being deferred until the arrival of Charles,
as the cardinal was related to the count of Coruña.
Charles granted him a privilege to this effect, but
revoked it on the representations of Ximenez. The
judgment of the court of Valladolid was averse to
the duke. Exasperated at this, he revenged himself on Ximenez in a manner equally mean and
illegal. The vicar-general of the archbishop of
Alcala, having sent a fiscal to Guadalaxara, in order
to institute an inquiry about a crime committed
there, the duke ordered the fiscal to be imprisoned,
under the pretext of his having infringed on the
rights of his brother Bernardin Mendoza, the archdeacon of Guadalaxara; and not content with this,
ordered him to be beaten, and threatened to hang
him if he dared to come again. Ximenez received
intelligence of this outrage at Madrid. Before resorting to forcible measures, he caused the report to
be circulated that the duke could, for this double
crime against the civil and ecclesiastical authorities,

be dispossessed of his duchy; hoping thereby to intimidate him. But instead of suing for peace, the duke sent his chaplain Peter to Madrid, to insult the cardinal. Having obtained an audience of Ximenez, the chaplain, after the usual ceremony of throwing himself at the feet of the cardinal, began to hurl against him a torrent of threats and invectives. Ximenez listened composedly until he had finished, then asked him if he had anything more to say. On receiving a negative reply, he advised him to return to his master, who no doubt repented already of this hasty step. His prediction proved true. The duke quarrelled already with his friends, for not having prevented his folly, and when the chaplain returned, reproached him bitterly. The grand-constable, on learning these events, endeavoured to bring about a reconciliation between the duke and the cardinal. A personal interview was arranged to take place in Fuencarral, a village near Madrid. The duke, accompanied by the grand-constable, had hardly entered the room in which the cardinal awaited them, when he flew into a passion. Ximenez calmly and earnestly represented to him that he could punish him in his double capacity of regent and grand-inquisitor, but that he bore him no ill-will, and had given before, special proofs of his esteem for him by nominating him patron of the university of Alcala. Such language could not fail to disarm the duke—the reconciliation was accomplished. Whilst still seated together in conversation, the clatter of arms was heard before the house. The two nobles feared they had been entrapped, and that the arrest of the duke was intended. It turned out, however, that John Spinosa, a captain of the guard, having heard of the cardinal's secret journey to Fuencarral, had considered it his duty to follow him with his company, as the usual escort of honour.

Ximenez rebuked him kindly for his over-zeal, and the two noblemen, re-assured for their safety, parted amicably from the cardinal, who returned at once to Madrid.*

The affairs of the proud and daring Count Giron of Ureña caused still greater convulsions in the kingdom. Ximenez, who had undertaken to arrange the disputes between the nobles, wished also to settle the celebrated case of the seigniory of Villadefredes, a town near Valladolid, which was in possession of Giron, but claimed by Gutierre Quijada. The court of Valladolid, having inquired into the matter, pronounced judgment in favour of Quijada. But when the commissaries arrived, to take possession of the estate, Giron and his younger son Roderick assailed and miserably beat them with sticks, and drove them away. Several young friends of Roderick, belonging to the first families of the kingdom, such as Bernardin, the son of the grand-constable, and Ferdinand, a son of the grand-admiral, had joined in the affray. The excitement and indignation at this violation of the royal authority was universal. The bishop of Malaga, president of the court of Valladolid, a man otherwise calm and moderate, at once assembled a considerable force to send to Villadefredes, and punish the offenders. Seeing the danger which threatened his son and his friends, the grand-constable hastened to Villadefredes, and persuaded the young nobles to quit the town, before the arrival of the royal troops. They followed his advice; on which the bishop of Malaga, praising the grand-constable for his intercession, dismissed his troops. When Ximenez was informed of these occurrences, he ordered a criminal inquiry for high treason to be instituted against Giron and his confederates; and

---

* Gomez, pp. 1115, 1116. Fléchier, liv. v. pp. 429—434.

sent the supreme judge, Sarmento, at the head of a detachment of soldiers, to Villadefredes, to punish the inhabitants for their participation in this act of violence. Reduced to this extremity, Giron and his friends roused the surrounding country to open rebellion against Ximenez. They forcibly took possession of the contested town, caring little for the proclamations of the cardinal, which declared them traitors; nor for the laws against rebels, which he had had posted up everywhere. The relatives of the parties implicated in the revolt were greatly frightened. A meeting of the grandees took place at Portillo, to consult about the best means to avert the impending danger. They resolved to have recourse to supplication, and accordingly drew up a very humble petition, in which they begged Ximenez for mercy for their children and kinsmen. Simultaneously with this they despatched a letter to King Charles, in which they complained that the excessive rigour of the cardinal had thrown the whole of Castile into disorder. Giron, in particular, accused the royal judges of partiality, trying to demonstrate, at the same time, that he had once before been treated unjustly in the quarrel about the duchy of Medina Sidonia. Having been informed of these intrigues by the bishop of Malaga, Ximenez hastened, in concert with the royal council, to send an exact and faithful account of the facts to Flanders. He assured Charles that he was not moved by any personal hatred towards Giron, and that it was folly to accuse a court of partiality, or rather conspiracy, against him, which had always enjoyed so high a reputation for its justice and equity. But it could not be wondered at that a man so turbulent and quarrelsome as the count hated those who kept a watchful eye on his unlawful deeds, and resisted them energetically. In conclusion, he begged Charles not to prevent the execution of the sentence of the court by an exemption of the count, but to respect the laws of the country, whose guardian and vindicator he had been appointed by Heaven.

In spite of the humble petition mentioned above, a considerable portion of the nobles persevered in their armed opposition to the cardinal. Several of them, foremost amongst them the restless bishop of Zamora, collected troops, and incited whole provinces to rebellion. The grand-constable played a double part by openly exhorting the people to order and obedience, but secretly aiding the revolt, and fanning the excitement. Ximenez intercepted one of his letters, which seriously incriminated him; he did, however, not make use of it for the destruction of his enemy. The duke of Alva too, otherwise a stanch adherent of the royal house, had already resolved to levy an army and place himself at the head of the armed insurgents, when he was deterred from this dangerous proceeding by the advice of his friend Cueva. The young friends of Giron, who were shut up in Villadefredes, pushed their defiance of the cardinal so far, as to drag an effigy of him, dressed up in pontifical attire, through the streets of the town. They were, however, soon compelled to surrender, fled, and left the town in the hands of Sarmento, who had conducted the siege. Sarmento, master of the place, sentenced the town, for its participation in the revolt and in the ill-treatment of the royal functionaries, according to ancient laws, to be rased to the ground, the land to be torn up with the plough, and strewn with salt, as a sign that the spot was condemned to eternal solitude. The sentence was executed; the town was given to the flames, and the most guilty of the inhabitants chastised with rods. Giron, his son Roderick, and his accomplices, were declared guilty of high treason. The severity and rigour of this measure was blamed by many, and even by such nobles as were on good terms with Ximenez. But the fate of the unfortunate town struck such terror into the hearts of the discontented,* that an attempt of Pedro Giron, the eldest son of the rebellious count, to raise troops against the cardinal in Andalusia, miscarried. And when King Charles approved of everything Ximenez had done, and, moreover, declared Giron guilty of high treason if he did not deliver himself up to justice by a certain time, the authority of the cardinal, as well as the respect for the law and the royal power, increased considerably. Villadefredes thus became the tomb of a great portion of the authority and independence of the Spanish aristocracy.

There remained only the submission of Giron, which was effected through the mediation of the duke of Escalona and Francis Ruyz. The proud count humbled himself before Ximenez, surrendered himself to the law, and begged for mercy, which the king, at the intercession of Ximenez, granted him. Nevertheless Giron continued to vent his sarcasms upon the cardinal whenever an opportunity offered. One day, when going to pay him a visit, he asked his servant if King Ximenez was at home. Every one will perceive in these words an allusion to the despotism of the cardinal, but for the Spaniard they had a deeper meaning. Tradition enumerates amongst the early kings of Spain a fabulous one of the name of Ximenez, and it had become customary to say of anything rough and uncouth, or contrary to the manners of the day, that "it belonged to the times of King Ximenez."†

Whilst these occurrences took place, Leo X.

---

* "Erigere cristas posthac nullus audebit," says Peter Martyr, ep. 591.

† Gomez, pp. 1117—1120. Petrus Martyr, epp. 584, 591. Fléchier, liv. v. pp. 434—441.

created thirty-one new cardinals; amongst them also Hadrian, who still took part in the administration of the kingdom, in conjunction with Ximenez. The latter thought this a propitious moment for the removal of Hadrian, and solicited Charles either to recall him to Flanders, or to send him to Rome as ambassador, or to his bishopric of Tortosa, pleading as ground that in his new dignity he was likely to become an obstacle to the unity of the government. But his representations were not listened to, and Hadrian remained at Madrid.*

The affair with Giron was hardly settled when Ximenez saw himself entangled in another quarrel with the ducal house of Alva, about the priorate of Consuegro, which belonged to the order of St. John of Jerusalem, and was one of the most lucrative places in Spain. The former possessor of this dignity had resigned in favour of his nephew, Antonio Zuñiga, who had been confirmed in it by King Philip and Pope Julius II. But when Ferdinand, after the death of Philip, ascended the throne, desirous of rewarding the duke of Alva for his services and fidelity to him, he installed his third son, Diego, in the priorate still held by Antonio Zuñiga. To save appearances, and justify this glaring violation of the law, the grand-master of the order declared that Zuñiga possessed the priory illegally, having received it only from the pope, and not from him, the head of the order. Zuñiga had to relinquish his post in favour of Diego Alva, whom the grand-master duly nominated prior of Consuegro in the year 1512. Antonio Zuñiga complained in vain to the pope:

* Gomez, p. 1120. Fléchier, liv. v. p. 441. The simultaneous creation of so many cardinals was severely censured. It was believed that the Pope had taken money for several of the hats. Petrus Martyr, ep. 596.

he could get no redress, and fled to Flanders for the purpose of inducing Charles to inforce the decision of his father as soon as he had the power of doing so. Immediately after the death of Ferdinand, Zuñiga renewed his suit about the priory. He brought it before the court of Rome, where young Alva also tried to defend his rights. The court decided in favour of Zuñiga, who returned to Spain, armed with the papal decree, and the following letter of Charles :—

"Charles, king of Spain, to Franciscus, cardinal of Toledo, our beloved friend : What you have reported to us concerning the priorate of St. John of Jerusalem has in every respect met with our approbation. But the importance of the case, as well as the high rank of the contending parties, demand first to exhaust all means for an amicable settlement of the dispute before we resort to more stringent measures. We have therefore, in our mildness, considered it best to take possession of the priory with all its castles, towns, and revenues, and to keep it in our own hands until we are enabled to give a final decision. You will endeavour to induce the rivals to obey. They are to select us as umpire, and send us, without delay, a legally-authenticated document to that purport. We, for our part, shall keep their interest as much as possible in view : if they obey, they will render us an agreeable service; but if they refuse, we give them fifteen days for consideration, after the lapse of which you will take possession of the priory in our name, and place faithful governors in the castles and towns. If Alva and Diego intend in no wise to yield, we exhort you and command the royal council to execute in virtue of our royal authority, and without regard to any one, the papal decree which Zuñiga has brought from Rome. Farewell.—Brussels, the 15th January, 1517."

Zuñiga and his brother, the duke of Bejar, brought this letter to the cardinal, and, together with several other grandees, assured him of their aid and assistance against Alva, if he should require it. Alva, for his part, declared that he would defend his rights to the last, not against the king, but against the cardinal, the enemy of his family. A violent fever, which confined Ximenez at this time to Madrid and to his bed, increased his boldness. He incited his numerous relatives and other members of the higher aristocracy to opposition. Both parties contending for the priory prepared for strife. Francis Ruyz, during the illness of the cardinal, added three hundred men to the body-guard of the latter, which he kept constantly under arms to prevent either of the parties from taking possession of Madrid. When Ximenez had somewhat recovered, he ordered the two chiefs, Zuñiga and Alva, to appear before him and exhorted them to peace, until, his health being re-established, he would be able to settle their quarrel. During this time public prayers were read in all the churches of Madrid, and the whole of Castile, for the recovery of the cardinal, on whose life the future tranquillity of the kingdom seemed to depend.

Alva now sought, by perverted representations of the facts of the case, to determine the young king to a different decision; but Ximenez solicited Charles by letter to adhere to his former resolution, as the word of a king should be firm and unalterable.

Meanwhile the royal senate had taken up the matter. Several members of it, amongst them even Hadrian and La Chaux, favoured the cause of Alva. They raised objections to the royal decree, and hesitated to execute it until Ximenez, having partly recovered his health, re-established unity in the senate, and induced the members forthwith to carry out the royal commands. Alva then addressed himself to the dowager queen, Germaine, with whom he was a great favourite. Through her inflüence even the kings of France and England interceded for him with Charles and the duke of Chièvres. Charles had begun to waver, when Ximenez, by a letter to Chièvres, strengthened him again in his first resolution. At the same time he endeavoured to persuade Alva to accept the king as arbiter: but all amicable representations and peaceful remonstrances proving unavailing, Ximenez ultimately ordered the general, Ferdinand d'Andrada, to take possession of the priory by force of arms, in the name of the king. Hadrian and La Chaux, frightened by the possibility of a civil war, begged the cardinal to postpone the settlement of the question until the arrival of Charles. Anton Fonseca too, one of the ablest nobles, but a friend of Alva, remonstrated with Ximenez, pointing out the probability of a great revolt and a universal rising of the discontented: but Ximenez remained stedfast. "Be composed, Fonseca," he said, "and not alarmed at the result. I will so arrange matters that everything shall end well." He forthwith ordered a thousand horse and five hundred foot to march to Consuegro, where Diego had intrenched himself, and besides levied a considerable number of soldiers in his own dominions to be able to strengthen his army in case of need. Before attacking Diego, and laying siege to the fortress, he summoned him once more to surrender it, as well as the other possessions of the priory, to Charles, and accept the king as arbiter: on his repeated refusal to do so, the place was invested. Alva sent a body of troops, consisting of a thousand foot and a detachment of horse, to the assistance of his son; but they were routed by the army of

Ximenez, and lost their treasure-chest and provisions. Hereupon Alva once more went to Madrid to settle the matter amicably through the intercession of Germaine and Hadrian. Ximenez' condition was, the unconditional surrender of the priory to the king, in return for which he promised pardon for his late acts. Diego Alva submitted, and Anton of Cordova was appointed temporary administrator of the disputed possessions. But after the death of Ximenez, Diego obtained again possession of the priory. The quarrel which ensued in consequence between him and Zuñiga was not even settled by the division of the property between them, and terminated only on the death of the latter.*

The dispute about the county of Ribadeo in Galicia, was of less importance, but equally disagreeable to Ximenez. The estates were not considerable in extent, but situate in a very fertile and pleasant country, and desirable on account of several privileges connected therewith. Count Villandrado, the former owner, had, by virtue of a papal dispensation, been divorced from two wives, both marriages having remained without issue. By his third marriage with Leonora, a lady belonging to a Moorish family of rank, he had a son, Roderick, who, as his sole descendant, inherited the possessions of his father. The collateral relations, however, declared Roderick a bastard; and the strong-minded and influential Doña Maria Ulloa, countess of Salinus, in particular, laid claim to the inheritance. Ximenez viewed the matter in a different light: his opinions were based on the canon law, according to which he declared Roderick the lawful heir to the disputed property. Ulloa, however, achieved what Alva could not accomplish in his quarrel with

* Gomez, pp. 1121—1124. Robles, pp. 189—193. Fléchier, liv. iv. pp. 442—448.

Zuñiga : she obtained a decree of Charles which
upset the decision of the cardinal and adjudicated
the county of Ribadeo to the son of Maria Ulloa.
Ximenez' remonstrances were unavailing, though he
pointed out to Charles the pernicious effect which
the perversion of justice, and injustice done to
orphans, would produce.   His representations were
not listened to.   As sole consolation, he received the
reply that the king had finally determined to repair
to Spain, and that the cardinal should make the
necessary arrangements.*   Ximenez sent in consequence a well-equipped fleet to Flanders to fetch
the king, garrisoned the best and healthiest har-
bours of the north of Spain, provided them with
everything requisite for a magnificent reception of
Charles and his suite, and fixed his own residence
farther north, at Aranda, to be nearer the king at
his landing.†   But before departing for Aranda he
settled another very important affair, that about
the ecclesiastical tithes.

After leaving Madrid, Ximenez first visited his
own cathedral, Toledo, to make fresh arrangements for the diocese, and inspect the monasteries
founded by him.   This opportunity was chosen by
the wily prefect of Toledo, Portocarrero, surnamed
the Fox, to obtain surreptitiously from the cardinal
a favourable decision in the dispute between Toledo
and Burgos about the precedence in the Cortes.
But Ximenez refused his artfully-veiled request,
and left him no hope of ultimately gaining his
point.‡

The question of ecclesiastical tithes caused the
cardinal considerable trouble.   With the consent of
the fifth Lateran council,§ Leo X. had imposed a

---

* Gomez, pp. 1124 et seq.
† Idem, 1125.   Fléchier, liv. iv. p. 448.
‡ Gomez, pp. 1113 et seq.   § Harduin, tom. ix. p. 1851.

tithe on ecclesiastical property to guard the coast of Italy against the irruptions of the Turkish emperor, Selim. When the news arrived that the Pope intended to introduce this measure in Spain, many of the clergy were highly exasperated. They contended that this tax was contrary to the ecclesiastical immunities and decisions granted by ancient synods, and the more unjust as the princes upon whom the protection of Christendom devolved had neither fitted out a fleet nor enlisted an army for the purpose. The clergy of Aragon, in a provincial synod presided over by the archbishop of Saragossa, who was at the same time regent of this kingdom, agreed to refuse the payment of the tithe. They solicited Ximenez to use his influence at Rome for the protection of the interests of the Spanish clergy.* The cardinal, equally unwilling to introduce the tithe in Castile, readily consented, but advised the Aragonians to dissolve the synod and abstain from further opposition to Rome, in order to facilitate his negotiations with the Pope and Charles. He forthwith communicated to the king his opinion that the clergy of Castile should likewise investigate the admissibility of the demands of the pope, but their meeting could, according to ancient custom, take place only at the residence of the royal court. On the other hand, Ximenez offered the pope, through his agent at Rome, Arteaga, not only the tithes of his own diocese, but all his revenues, the sacred vessels, and the treasure of the church, if the welfare of Christendom should require these sacrifices, and the Pope in reality be willing to institute a crusade against the Turks. He could, however, not lend his assistance to a taxation of the Spanish clergy for other than these purposes, and foresaw the

---

* His primacy extended over the whole of Spain.

impossibility of surmounting their aversion to such
an impost. Simultaneously, he ordered his agent
to give him an exact report of the decisions of the
Lateran council concerning the tithes. The cardinals, Lawrence Pucci and Julian of Medicis (afterwards Clement VII.), who possessed the greatest
confidence of the Pope, replied in the name of his
Holiness, that the Pope would, by virtue of the
Lateran decrees, impose a universal ecclesiastical
tithe only in the last extremity. He had, hitherto,
not done so, and if his nuncio in Spain had announced
such a tax, he had done so prematurely, without
instructions from Rome. On the arrival of this
communication, Ximenez dismissed the clergy who
had assembled at Madrid, and already decided on
supplicating the Pope for the suppression of the
tithe, or in case of denial to refuse payment. Peter
Martyr, who assisted this synod, informs us that
Ximenez had given in his adhesion to these decisions
and promised his assistance. But the fears of the
clergy were now allayed, as Leo levied the tithe, for
the present, only in the papal states. Fresh quarrels arose after the death of the cardinal, when Leo
granted the Spanish tithes to the emperor Charles,
to enable him to equip a fleet against the Turks.
The clergy of the country refused to pay; the pope
threatened excommunication and interdict, and laid
the whole country under the latter, but finding it
of no avail, he annulled it after four months, on the
solicitation of Charles himself. The tithe was not
paid.*

In August, 1517, Ximenez, accompanied by the
court and Prince Ferdinand, travelled to Aranda de
Duero, near Burgos; intending to fix his residence
in the Franciscan monastery, Aguilera, which was

---

* Gomez, p. 1114. Petrus Martyr, epp. 596, 606, 642. Miniana,
lib. i. c. v. p. 13.

situated in a pleasant and healthy neighbourhood. Hadrian and Amerstorff were also in his suite, but not La Chaux, who took a different road to meet the king. On his way Ximenez visited Torrelaguna, the place of his birth, which he left on the 11th August, 1517. On the following day he arrived at Bozeguillas, a place in a mountainous part of the country. Here an attempt is said to have been made to poison him. The suspicion is strengthened by the circumstance, that, on the same day, a masked rider called to the provincial of the Franciscans, Marquina, and several monks who were passing him on their way to Ximenez, "If you are going to the cardinal, hasten yourselves, and warn him not to eat of the large trout—it is poisoned. If you come too late, urge him to prepare for death, for he will not be able to overcome the poison." Marquina, immediately after his arrival, related to the cardinal what had happened, but the latter would not credit the warning. "If I really am poisoned," he said, "it is by a letter received from Flanders a few days ago, the sand of which has considerably affected my eyes; yet even this I do not believe." Moreover, Francis Carillo, who served Ximenez at Bozeguillas, and, as customary, tasted first of every meal, fell seriously ill. Some supposed the poison to have been sent from Flanders, others suspected Baracaldo, the secretary of the cardinal, but the friends of the cardinal declared him entirely innocent of the crime and he enjoyed the confidence and intimacy of Ximenez until the death of the latter. There are, besides, strong doubts on the subject. Even well-informed writers such as Peter Martyr and Cara-vajal, who were near the cardinal at the time, say not a word about it.*

* Gomez, p. 1125. Petrus Martyr, ep. 598. Fléchier, liv. v. p. 449.

Shortly after the arrival of Ximenez at Aranda, a revolutionary movement took place at Valladolid. It was rumoured that Charles was not coming, that Ximenez had spread the report of his departure only in order to be better able to send Prince Ferdinand to Flanders, and to govern Spain himself. Order was, however, soon restored by the publication of the real facts of the case.*

Ximenez had occasion to show at Aranda how little illness had impaired his courage and energy. We know that Prince Ferdinand, who was born and educated in Spain, enjoyed more popularity with the Spaniards than Charles, who was a thorough stranger to them. Incited by the courtiers surrounding him, Ferdinand constantly coveted the Spanish throne. His instructor, Pedro Nuñez de Guzman, grand-commander of the order of Calatrava, and his tutor Osorio, bishop of Astorga, in particular, exerted themselves in winning the favour of the people for the prince, to the detriment of Charles. Ximenez, who for this reason disliked them much, wished to remove them from the prince, and repeatedly urged on the king the necessity of this measure. Charles yielded at last: on the 7th September, 1517, shortly before his departure, he wrote a letter to the cardinal, in which he ordered him to pension off the two tutors of his brother, as well as his chamberlain, Gonsalvo Guzman, and gave him powers to proceed with the rest of the household of Ferdinand according as he thought proper. In a second letter to Ferdinand† himself, Charles acquainted his brother with these instructions. Both letters, together with

---

* Gomez, p. 1126.

† These two letters of Charles's are to be found, in the Spanish original, together with a French translation, in the collection of the "Documents Inédits," amongst the "Papiers d'Etat du Cardinal Granvelle," tom. i. pp. 89—105.

a third to Hadrian, were addressed under cover to Ximenez, and intended to be read first by him, that he might make the necessary arrangements before the delivery. Ximenez being then in the monastery, the packet was opened by Hadrian, who forthwith forwarded to the prince the letter destined for him. Thus Ferdinand received intelligence of the orders of the king before Ximenez, and the latter was prevented from carrying them into effect without *éclat*. Nuñez and Osorio incited the prince, advising him to oppose the cardinal. On the following day, Ferdinand, with a well-studied speech, went to the monastery Aguilera, reproached the cardinal bitterly, complained that his truest and most faithful friends should without reason be torn from his side, and begged Ximenez, by the memory of Ferdinand and Isabella, to spare him this disgrace. Deeply moved by the grief of the youthful prince, Ximenez spoke to him in the kindest terms, praised him for his attachment to his friends, but represented to him " that his own brother and king should occupy the first place in his heart, and be dearer to him than any of his friends, and that it would be neither wise nor just to disobey his commands. Such resistance would be pernicious, not only to himself, but also to the friends whom he wished to guard." The prince was deaf to these remonstrances; he replied, " Formerly you often gave me proofs of your affection, but now that I need it most, withdraw it from me; if you are resolved to ruin me and my friends, I will myself seek for means to save us." Irritated by this stubbornness, Ximenez answered, " You may do what you like, but I swear by the head of Charles, to-morrow by sunset his orders, which you should be the first to obey, shall be executed." Ferdinand left the cardinal with premature Spanish *grandezza*, and returned to Aranda. Ximenez, for his part, intrusted the

supervision of the town and the prince to the two
colonels of his body-guard, Canabillas and Spinosa,
who posted guards everywhere to prevent Ferdinand's escape.   The prince uttered violent threats
against the cardinal, and handed a document to
his friends and servants, who saw the necessity of
yielding, by which he pledged himself to recall
them as soon as he was free, and to reward them for
their fidelity towards him.   He summoned, besides
the papal nuncio, several bishops, and all the royal
councillors, to his presence, declaring to them that
he obeyed the commands of the king, but begged
them to acquaint his brother with the ill-treatment to
which he had been subjected; which they promised
to do.   Ximenez, on the other hand, requested
Hadrian to send Nuñez and Osorio to him, that he
might open to them his plans, and appease their
irritation.   They appeared before him: after a long
conference they promised to obey, and begged the
cardinal to intercede in their behalf for an indemnification.   Before sunset, as Ximenez had declared, the
orders of the king were carried out, and the marquis
of Aguilar appointed major-domo to Ferdinand, who
soon gained the sincere affection of the prince.   In
all, thirty-three servants of the prince were dismissed
and replaced by others.   The measure, though hard,
found universal approbation with the wisest and
most experienced men of the nation, who considered
it necessary for the future peace of the country.*

Meanwhile, Ximenez, confined to the monastery
of Aguilera, suffered severely from dysentery and
suppuration of the ears.   The rumour having spread
of his death being near, and of his having retired
from public affairs Pedro Giron again took up arms
to reconquer the duchy of Medina Sidonia, the Moors

* Gomez, pp. 1126—1129. Petrus Martyr, ep. 600. Fléchier,
liv. v. pp. 450—467.

returned to their ravages of the coast of Spain, and the Turks threatened to lay siege to Oran. But his usual spirit and energy had not deserted the cardinal. He immediately despatched Count Luna, prefect of Seville, with a large army against Giron, who, perceiving that Ximenez was still alive, hastened to disarm, while his father, mindful of the fall of Villadefredes, humbly petitioned the cardinal to pardon his son. If Charles had followed the advice of Ximenez, Giron would not have escaped this time, but been severely punished as an example to others. The inroads of the Moors were successfully repulsed, and the garrison of Oran, and in particular the governor of this town, Ferdinand Comario, were exhorted bravely to defend themselves behind the ramparts until the arrival of reinforcements. They were, however, not required; for the Numidians themselves drove back the Turks.*

While these events took place, Charles, after having concluded a treaty of peace with France at Noyon, at last embarked from Flanders on the 7th September, 1517, in spite of the warnings of his courtiers, who feared the dangers of navigation during this season. Towards the middle of the same month,† after a tempestuous voyage, Charles landed near Tazonas, in the province of Asturia, where he was not expected, and repaired at once to the neighbouring town of Villaviciosa, accompanied by his sister Eleonora, and numerous Spanish and Flemish nobles; Chièvres and Sauvage were of the number, and La Chaux, too, appeared again in the suite of the king.‡ The

* Gomez, pp. 1129 et seq. Fléchier, liv. v. p. 469.
† Gomez, p. 1130, gives the 27th September as the date of Charles's arrival. This is wrong, for he was then already several days at Villaviciosa, as is proved by a letter directed on that day to Ximenez, which is still preserved, and quoted by us in a subsequent page.
‡ Charles wrote to Ximenez, in his letter from Middleburg:

inhabitants of the coast were greatly alarmed at the
sight of an unknown fleet. Fearing a secret invasion
of the French, they sent their wives and children to
the mountains, and posted themselves, armed with
arrows and other weapons, on the hills near the sea,
to prevent, if possible, the landing of the supposed
enemy. On seeing this, Charles ordered the admiral
to exclaim, "Spain, Spain, the king is coming!"
and his arms, the lion of Leon and the castle of
Castile, to be hoisted. The Asturians, upon this,
evinced the greatest enthusiasm, saluted the king
on their knees, and accompanied him to Villaviciosa,
frantic with joy. The grand-constable, who owned
large property in this part of the country, upon being
apprised of the arrival of Charles distributed great
quantities of corn to the poor of the neighbourhood,
supplied the villages with all kinds of provisions,
and hastened himself, with a retinue of four hundred
of his kinsmen and retainers on horseback, to Villaviciosa to pay homage to the king. But he and his
followers soon retired, as the country was too poor
to provide all the necessaries for so large a court.
For this reason, also, the other grandees were forbidden to render their homage to the king during
his residence in this part of the country.*

The news of the arrival of the king appears to
have worked beneficially upon the health of Ximenez.
On the 4th of October, the feast of St Francis, he
celebrated mass in the monastery of Aguilera, and
dined in the refectory together with the monks.
Charles was highly delighted at this, and, to the
great disgust of his Flemish courtiers, frequently
expressed to them the great obligations he was

"La Chaux will bring me your despatches to the harbour where
I land."—Fléchier, liv. v. p. 461.

* Gomez, p. 1130. Petrus Martyr, epp. 597, 599, 601.
Fléchier, liv. v. pp. 469—471.

under to the illustrious man. They dreaded an interview between Charles and Ximenez, fearing lest the latter might gain too powerful an influence over the young prince, and therefore employed every possible artifice to prevent such an interview. Acting upon the intelligence which they daily received from two physicians, touching the condition of the cardinal, and the probable duration of his life, they retarded the king's progress to Castile, in the hope of the cardinal dying in the mean time. Ximenez, though weak and infirm, wrote several letters to the king containing advice as to how his majesty should deport himself in Spain, how receive this or the other grandee, what care he should take to retain the royal possessions in Africa, &c. Charles received these letters with much pleasure, apparently willing to be guided by the directions contained therein.* A letter of Charles addressed to Ximenez, from the Spanish coast, bearing date the 27th September, 1517, is still preserved, which clearly shows the solicitude which the cardinal retained for the weal of the state, even in this last stage of his life. The king acknowledges therein the receipt of his letter of the 23rd of the same month, and informs him that he has listened attentively to the communications he had intrusted to his agent, Don Lopez de Ayala. He expresses his regret at the bad state of his health, thanks him cordially for the zeal and prudence displayed in the affair with Prince Ferdinand, and acquaints him of his intention to proceed with his attendants to Santander, where the cardinal had made every arrangement for his reception, begging him at the same time to remain with Ferdinand and the royal council at his present residence, until he could appoint a place for an interview with him.

* Gomez, p. 1131. Robles, p. 198. Fléchier, liv. v. pp. 471, 472.

Charles concluded this letter with expressions of displeasure at the conduct of Giron, and of hopes that Ximenez would be able effectually to settle this matter, and continue to acquaint him of any future occurrence of importance.[*]

The Flemish ministers, in order to carry out safely their plans of frustrating an interview, persuaded the king to visit Aragon before entering Castile to receive the homage of the people. Ximenez opposed these designs, exhorting the king to send his brother to Germany to the Emperor Maximilian, but to arrange this in such a manner that it would be evident this was done in the prince's own interest. This could best be done by ceding to Ferdinand part, if not the whole, of his hereditary provinces there, since Providence had already given Charles such ample and vast dominions.[†] This advice, backed by Chièvres, was ultimately followed by Charles. He gave Austria, and afterwards Bohemia and Hungary to his brother, After the cardinal's death, when the revolt of the States broke out, Charles was principally indebted to this wise measure for the preservation of Spain.

Ximenez still continued to stay in the monastery of Aguilera. Convinced of the approach of his death, he was anxious to renew, and correct the will which he had previously made by the permission of the pope,[‡] and revised before his departure from Aranda.

The principal heir to his vast property was the university of Alcalá, founded by him. Large

---

[*] Documents Inédits, l. c. pp. 105—109.

[†] Gomez, p. 1131. Fléchier, liv. v. pp. 472, 473.

[‡] According to ancient canon law the Church inherited, after the death of a priest, everything he had acquired by his office. Whoever wished to dispose of his property obtained when a priest, required the permission of the pope to do so.

legacies were left besides to the monasteries, hospitals, and other establishments, which he had erected, and considerable sums destined for the endowment of poor young women, the ransom of prisoners, the embellishment of churches, and the foundation of anniversaries and masses for the dead. We have already seen how, by a special clause in the will, all those were indemnified who had suffered losses in the expedition against. Oran. Francis Ruyz, bishop of Avila, the faithful companion of his life, was named his chief executor, and also intrusted with the care of his interment, as well as the publication of the Complutensian Polyglot.*

During these preparations for death, the cardinal often repeated, that he was particularly grateful to God for enabling him to say, that he had never wilfully or knowingly wronged any one, but always administered justice without being biassed by friendship or hatred.†

Antonio de Rojas, archbishop of Granada, president of the royal council, and constant enemy of Ximenez, tried to take advantage of the debility of the cardinal to pay his respects to the king in conjunction with the senate, but without Ximenez. The latter, who anticipated his desire, had obtained from Charles two documents, which forbade the archbishop and the senate to leave the cardinal. The archbishop having, nevertheless, departed with several members of the senate, Ximenez induced Charles to despatch couriers to order them to return to the cardinal, and beg his pardon.‡

His treatment of the grandees was quite different.

---

* The will is reprinted in Quintanilla, "Archetypo," pp. 36—50 of the Appendix.
† Gomez, p. 1131.   Fléchier, liv. v. p. 473.
‡ Gomez, p. 1132.   Fléchier, liv. v. p. 474.

The grand-admiral had politely offered to accompany him, if it should be his intention to go and meet the king, asking, as a particular favour, to be allowed to form one of his suite. Ximenez thanked him for this honour, but recommended him to proceed to Charles, with a large retinue of his own, that the Flemish might see the difference between Flemish and Spanish noblemen. The same advice he gave to other grandees who had equally offered to accompany him.*

Winter being near at hand, Ximenez quitted the monastery of Aguilera on the 17th October. Carefully wrapped in furs, and accompanied by the prince and the senate, he departed for Roa, a place situated between Valladolid and Segovia, to enable him with greater facility to reach whichever of these towns the king should visit first. Ximenez had before advised Charles to repair to Valladolid; but a contagious malady having broken out there, he requested him now, on the 22nd October, to change it for Segovia. At the same time, he endeavoured to persuade him to postpone the convocation of the cortes for a while, as the agitation of the people had not entirely subsided, and might find vent in that assembly. This advice was unfortunately not attended to. Disturbances broke out in the kingdom which caused great annoyance and uneasiness to Charles, and convinced him too late of his imprudence.

A deputation from Toledo arrived at Roa with the object of inducing Ximenez to persuade the king to select that ancient capital of Spain for the first convocation of the Cortes. Ximenez supported their petition in vain. The influence of the Flemish ministers, who preferred a town less central

---

* Gomez, p. 1132. Fléchier, liv. v. p. 474.

than Toledo, prevailed, and Valladolid was chosen instead.*

Before departing for this town, Charles wished to pay a visit to his mother at Tordesillas. He publicly notified this resolution to Ferdinand, to Ximenez, and all the grandees, declaring that "he had come to Spain to comfort his mother and would in every way be guided by her in the government of the kingdom." Ximenez highly praised him for his filial love, but did not approve of this wordy and evidently hypocritical declaration, saying that "it showed less love for his mother than fear a certain party might gain influence over her, and thereby oppose him." "Kings," he added, "should do many things without talking about them."†

Preparations were now being made at Valladolid for the reception of the king and his suite, at the approaching meeting of the cortes. The care of finding suitable residences was intrusted by Charles to four Flemish officers. Ximenez intended to fix his with the lawyer Bernardin, whose house seemed to be situated in a particularly healthy neighbourhood. The four commissioners, however, refused to let him have it, and in order to baffle him more effectually, destined it for the Queen Germaine. Alba was the instigator of these intrigues. Ximenez ultimately gained his point, but his servants were quartered in a neighbouring village,—a slight which would never have been offered him by Ferdinand, Isabella, or Philip. Yet he was too proud to show his annoyance and pain at such ignoble treatment. Still greater insults were reserved for him. At the suggestion, it is said, of Motta, the bishop of Badajoz, a favourite of Chièvres, Charles had the ingratitude to write to Ximenez that as it was now

* Gomez, p. 1133.
† Ibid. Fléchier, liv. v. p. 477.

his intention to set out for Tordesillas * there to
pay his respects to his mother, he wished greatly to
meet the cardinal at Mojados, and receive his advice
on the government of the kingdom and the private
affairs of the royal house. This done, he would no
longer deprive him of the quietude so necessary to
him, and relieve him of his burdensome duties.
God alone could worthily recompense him for all
his labours for the good of Spain; he, for his part,
would, as long as he lived, retain for him the
respect and affection a son owed to his father.
These words contained in reality, not only the dismissal of the cardinal from the regency, but also from
all other participation in the conduct of public affairs.
Many writers assert that this cruel letter accelerated
his death. But Francis Ruyz assures us that this
testimony of the ingratitude of princes never reached
the cardinal. Too ill to bear the shock, it was only
communicated to the royal senate. Hadrian also
acquainted the king, that, considering the condition
of Ximenez, the letter could not be delivered to
him.†

At the approach of his death, Ximenez, with
Christian fortitude, spoke to his servants, who had
been summoned to his presence, of the instability of
all earthly things, and the infinite mercies of God.
Then embracing, with pious affection, a crucifix
which he held in his hands, he asked God for the
remission of his sins, and invoked the intercession
of all the saints, particularly that of the Blessed
Virgin, St. Michael, the Apostles Peter and Paul,
St. James, the patron of Spain, St. Francis of Assisi,
SS. Eugene and Ildephonse, the first two bishops

---

* Petrus Martyr, who relates this visit in his 602nd letter,
says "that the sight of her children, Charles and Eleanor, gave
great joy to Johanna."

† Gomez, p. 1133. Fléchier, liv. v. pp. 479, 480.

of Toledo. All those surrounding him burst into tears. He then received the holy Viaticum and extreme unction. A few hours before, he dictated a letter to Charles, in which he recommended to him his university of Alcalá, and the monasteries he had founded, but was unable to sign it. Petrus Lerma, Antonio Rodrigo, and Balbas recited the prayer for the dying, when he calmly expired, exclaiming the words of David, " In te, Domine, speravi," on the 8th November 1517, in the eighty-second year of his life, and the twenty-second of his episcopacy.*

His death occurred on a Sunday. A herald having proclaimed the sad news, all the inhabitants of Roa and the surrounding country hastened to kiss the cardinal's hands, whilst he was lying in state. The corpse was embalmed, and temporarily transferred to the church at Roa, until, according to the orders of the deceased, it could be removed to Alcalá. A few days after, it was conveyed thither. The journey was commenced under a deluge of rain, which rendered the removal as dangerous as that of the remains of Queen Isabella to Granada. On the second day the funeral procession arrived at Torrelaguna, the birthplace of Ximenez. Here the grief of the population was excessive. The body was conveyed, amidst the blaze of innumerable torches, to the monastery of St. Mary, founded by him, and a funeral service celebrated there. On the third day the procession reached Alcalá. In the gate leading towards Burgos the university had erected a mortuary chapel. All the students and professors of the university together with their rector Michael Cerrasco, all the religious of the city, the corporation, the bishops, the grandees, the abbot and chapter of the collegiate church of SS. Justus and

---

* Gomez, p. 1134. Fléchier, liv. v. p. 480. Robles, p. 201.

Pastor, and an immense concourse of people, met the body before the town. It was then placed in the mortuary chapel, where the matins for the dead were chanted.

A discussion arose between the university and the chapter of San Justo respecting the place of interment. The dispute was ultimately settled by the bishop of Avila declaring that Ximenez himself had expressly notified his wish to be buried in the college of San Ildefonso, upon which the canons withdrew their opposition.

Ximenez had ordered in his will that his funeral should be as simple and unostentatious as possible; but Francis Ruyz departed from these instructions, arranged a befitting ceremony, and permitted Sirvelo, a learned and eloquent doctor, to preach the panegyric of the deceased, in which allusions were not wanting to the dangers which threatened Spain. through the Flemish courtiers.

The remains of the illustrious deceased arrived at Alcalá on the 15th November, the feast of St. Eugene, who is considered to have been the first archbishop of Toledo.* In celebration of the event, the university decreed that a funeral service should annually be held on this day, and a panegyric of Ximenez be preached.

A monument of marble was erected over his tomb, on which, besides other ornaments by eminent artists, a portrait of the cardinal in his pontifical robes was sculptured. The front side was covered by the following hexastich by the young Vergara, selected

---

* This is Eugene the elder, a disciple of St. Denis of Paris, who lived in the third century. Spanish tradition asserts that he founded the bishopric of Toledo. His body was, under Philip II., conveyed from St. Denis to Spain. He is not to be confounded with the Archbishop Eugene, of Toledo, who died in the year 657. Gomez, p. 1155.

from a number of inscriptions sent in for that purpose.

> " Condideram musis Franciscus grande lyceum,
> Condor in exiguo nunc ego sarcophago.
> Prætextam junxi sacco, galeamque galero,
> Frater, Dux, Præsul, Cardineusque pater.
> Quin virtute mea junctum est diadema cucullo,
> Cum mihi regnanti paruit Hesperia."

Fifty-eight years after the foundation of the university, the then rector, Alphonse Mendoza, under whose auspices Gomez wrote his biography of our cardinal, ordered the monument to be surrounded by a magnificent enclosure of bronze, on which were represented the principal events of the life of Ximenez.*

Ximenez was tall and thin, but firmly and strongly built; his face long, his nose aquiline, his nostrils wide, his forehead high and wrinkled; his eyes of middle size, deep set, piercing, but frequently dimmed by moisture; his teeth closely set, the two eye-teeth somewhat prominent, which gained him the nickname of "the elephant;" his lips thick, but well formed; his voice firm and agreeable. On opening his tomb in 1545, his skull was found to be without seam, whence arose probably his violent headaches, which often bordered on melancholy. He always, even in anger, spoke to the point, but in as few words as possible, and never without previous reflection. He gave more than he promised, and jested but rarely with his friends. According to the custom of the times, he kept a dwarf, whose jokes he relished, and whom he recommended at his death to the college of St. Ildephonse at Alcalá. He devoted a great deal of his time to study, entered frequently into scientific discussions with learned men, and was fond of attending the disputations of the students.†

* Gomez, p. 1135.   † Ibid. p. 1136.   r

As regards his personal virtues and brilliant talents for government, they need not further be extolled. His zeal in prayer and all devotional exercises, his extraordinary charity, his severity towards himself, the unimpeachable purity and chastity of his manners, as well as his prudence, love of justice, undaunted courage, and, above all, his extreme firmness, have constantly come under notice in the preceding pages. Gomez observes justly : "The news of his death produced a deep sensation and sorrow in the minds of all good men and patriots. The discontented rejoiced to be rid of a man who was the terror of all miscreants and sinners.* Former political adversaries of the cardinal such as the duke of Alva, candidly acknowledged, now that passion was at an end, that Ximenez was one of the most remarkable men, a truly old Spanish, heroic character."†

His virtues were so well recognized by Spain, that efforts were made for his canonization. In the years 1650 and 1655, Philip IV. corresponded with the Holy See on the subject, while, at the same time, Quintanilla, a Franciscan friar, to prove the great virtues of the cardinal, composed his "Archetypo de Virtudes," a work which has been repeatedly quoted by us. The negotiations with Rome remained without result ; nevertheless, in many parts of the peninsula, Ximenez is honoured as a saint. His name occurs in seven martyrologies of the Spanish church, and on the celebration of the anniversaries founded by him, prayers were offered only for the dead in general. The special ones were left out, the cardinal being supposed already to be amongst the blessed in Heaven.‡

* Gomez, p. 1136. † Ibid.
‡ The documents relating to this are reprinted in "Quintanilla," in the Appendix.

The archbishop of Saragossa, Alphonse of Aragon, expected to succeed Ximenez in his dignity of primate of Spain. He had long coveted this dignity, and even before the actual death of the cardinal, taken steps to secure it for himself. But to the great scandal of the Spaniards, Chièvres procured it for his young nephew, William of Croy, who died, however, a few years afterwards, in 1521.[*]

We cannot part from Ximenez, without drawing a parallel between him and another great man with whom he has often been compared—the Cardinal Richelieu.

[*] Petrus Martyr, p. 602.

CHAPTER XXVII.

XIMENEZ AND RICHELIEU.

THE similarity between these great statesmen has repeatedly been pointed out by former historians, and in the beginning of the last century furnished the subject for a special work in a hundred chapters, by the Abbé Richard.* We confine ourselves here to the most important and remarkable points in the lives of the two cardinals, and will endeavour to show the similarity or difference of their destinies, political principles, and moral character.

Both, scions of noble but poor houses, attained high ecclesiastical and civil dignities, became bishops and cardinals of the Roman Church, and powerful ministers, who exercised an extraordinary influence on the destinies of their countries. The family of Ximenez, being obscure and unknown, entitled its son to no aspirations for a position in the world for dignities and offices ; whilst the descendant of the ancient and illustrious house of Richelieu, gifted by nature, could easily obtain them. Although François de Plessis, lord of Richelieu, and other domains in Poitou, knight of the Order of the Holy Ghost, &c., had died poor, the name of an illustrious family supported his sons. Alphonse, the elder, obtained the bishopric of Luçon, an appanage to the family. Armand Jean, the younger, born at Paris, on the 5th September, 1585, was destined for the army,

* " Parallèle du Cardinal Ximénez, Premier Ministre d'Espagne, et du Cardinal de Richelieu, Premier Ministre de France. Par M. l'Abbé Richard." Rotterdam, 1705. Several times reprinted.

and received in consequence a secular education and instruction in chivalrous exercises. Alphonse, having suddenly resolved to become a Carthusian, Jean Armand quitted the army, and, with all the energy of his character, studied theology to be able to replace his brother in the bishopric of Luçon. King Henry IV. nominated him to it, and Pope Paul V. confirmed the appointment, after Richelieu, by a well-sustained disputation, had gained the degree of Doctor of Theology. In 1606 or 1607, when 21 or 22 years old, he was consecrated at Rome.* Thus Richelieu sought and obtained in his youth a high ecclesiastical dignity, which Ximenez attained only in riper age. Richelieu owed his elevation to his pedigree, Ximenez solely to his merits. Both travelled to Rome when still young—the one, in spite of his youth, to receive a bishopric; the other, like a poor pilgrim, unable to win even the smallest benefice. Richelieu, in order to obtain the dispensation of the Holy Father, is said to have stated his age to be more than it really was, and confessed this *ruse* to the pope, and begged his forgiveness, only after having been confirmed in his dignity. If this be a fact, it is a spot on Richelieu's character, of which Ximenez would never have rendered himself guilty for all the riches of the world.[†]

The return of the two to their native countries, is marked by a strong contrast. The young, vigorous, talented, zealous, and undoubtedly very able Bishop Richelieu, was received with every possible mark of honour and solemnity; Ximenez was imprisoned by his bishop, for aspiring to the place of archpriest of Uzeda.[‡] And yet he was destined to become as great and powerful as Richelieu !

---

* Aubery, "Histoire du Cardinal Richelieu," pp. 5—9. Richard, pp. 1—6. Raumer, " Geschichte Europa's," vol. iv. p. 58.

† Richard, p. 6.   ‡ Ibid. pp. 7, 8.

After his liberation, Ximenez was appointed vicar-general of Siguenza, and began to make a name for himself. But he quitted his diocese to take leave of the world in a Franciscan monastery of very severe discipline. Richelieu, too, quitted his diocese after a few years, but for quite a different purpose, to enter the great theatre of the world, and play a distinguished part at court.*

Mary of Medici, the imperious widow of Henry IV., conducted at this time the reins of government for her son, who, although only fourteen years old, had been declared of age. The Bishop of Luçon, having gained the favour of the omnipotent Marshal d'Ancre, was nominated her almoner and shortly after, in November 1516, Secretary of War and Foreign affairs. Like Ximenez, who was recommended to Queen Isabella by the grand-cardinal Mendoza, Richelieu was proposed to the dowager Queen Mary by the Marshal d'Ancre. Isabella made Ximenez her confessor, and adviser even in political affairs; the Queen of France, Richelieu her almoner and influential member of the council of state.† But whilst Ximenez all his life long showed the greatest attachment and respect for Isabella, Richelieu and Mary became in later years the bitterest enemies, so much so, indeed, that Richelieu was the cause of her banishment and poverty, and gave her just reason for charging him with the foulest ingratitude.‡ To the justification of Richelieu be it said, that the blame of this enmity

* Richard, p. 9.

† Ibid. pp. 12—17. Aubery, pp. 10—12. Richelieu is generally considered to have been appointed almoner to the dowager-queen; but Daniel, in his "Histoire de France," quotes the document of his nomination, which proves that he held this post to the young wife of Louis XIII.

‡ Raumer, pp. 99, 109, 126.

rests not with him, but with the queen, who had nearly ruined the kingdom by her intrigues, and forced him to proceed against her in the manner in which he did. He remained faithful to her cause as long as possible, longer even than his own interests permitted, endeavouring in every possible way to bring her back to the right path.

Whilst Ximenez, from the moment of his nomination as confessor of Isabella until his death, never suffered a reverse in power or honours, the path of Richelieu was soon beset with dangers. Luynes, a favourite of the king, gradually undermined the influence which Mary and the Marshal d'Ancre possessed with the latter. He succeeded even in inducing the king to countenance the murder of the marshal (1617), and to proclaim the banishment of the queen from the court.* The king and Luynes wished to retain Richelieu in the council of state, but he preferred following Mary to Blois, where he exerted himself in making her relations to the court as smooth as possible. His intentions being suspected, he received orders to return to his diocese, the administration of which he conducted again with much zeal and success. He led a simple and exemplary life, introduced reforms in ecclesiastical affairs, converted many Huguenots, and wrote for this purpose several theological works which were much admired at the time. His influence being still considered too dangerous, even at Luçon,* he was, in the passion week of the year 1618, banished to Avignon; one year later, however, recalled to effect a reconciliation between Mary and the king, and sent to Angoulême, where the former resided. His mission succeeded. Mary returned to court, and

* Aubery, pp. 12—86. Richard, p. 20.

in return for this service procured him a cardinal's hat in the year 1622.* In the like manner, Ferdinand the Catholic showed his gratitude to Ximenez who had been the means of his return to Castile as regent.

Shortly after having been created cardinal, Richelieu endeavoured to get the reins of government into his hands. He showed in this so much eagerness, that the angry king exclaimed: "This man would like to be admitted to my council, but I cannot make up my mind to allow this, after what he has done against me." In spite of this reluctance, the cardinal succeeded, in the year 1624, in becoming minister in the place of Vieuville, and soon exercised by far the greatest influence in the cabinet of the king. In the year 1629 he became prime minister, which position he retained until his death.† In opposition to this striving after influence and this hunting after honours, Ximenez, as we know, rejected the dignity of archbishop and that of grand-chancellor, and could only be prevailed upon to accept them by the express commands of the king and the pope. Like Richelieu, he remained in the possession of his power to the end of his days. Both had great opposition to contend against. King Ferdinand endeavoured to induce Ximenez to resign in favour of the archbishop of Saragossa. He refused. The grandees exhausted every means to overthrow him after the death of Ferdinand, but in vain. Nevertheless, Ximenez, through the ascetic turn of his character, was willing at any time to return to the solitude of the Franciscan monastery. Richelieu had to fight much harder battles with his opponents. His fall was several times, and particularly in the year 1630, imminent. He repeatedly

* Aubery, pp. 16—21. Richard, p. 61.
† Aubery, pp. 24, 25. Raumer, p. 59.

solicited his dismissal, when the affairs of the state rendered the grant of his request impossible. Hence we have no hesitation in alleging that it was never seriously meant, and that the withdrawal from his power would have cost him a thousand times more self-restraint than it would to the cardinal of Spain. Ximenez pardoned those who endeavoured to overthrow him, and never revenged himself for personal injuries. Richelieu, on the other hand, ordered his enemies to be executed, and took the life of almost every one who had opposed, threatened, or plotted against him. Thus, Count Chalais, Marshal Marillac, Duke Montmorency, De Thou, Cinqmars, and others were executed by his orders.* He has been justly censured for this, and forms, indeed, in this respect, a strong contrast to Ximenez. But circumstances attenuate his proceedings. All these rebels were the instruments of members of the royal house : the dowager-queen Maria, the brother of the king, the Duke Gaston of Orleans, who exerted themselves not only to overthrow the minister Richelieu, but also the whole state, together with the king. Richelieu was, therefore, justified in identifying his interests with those of the kingdom. Leniency towards the rebels would probably have ruined both.

The latter days of the two cardinals show equally strong marks of resemblance. When Ximenez died, the power of Spain attained its greatest development under Charles V. Richelieu left France more powerful than she had ever been, full of confidence in the Dauphin (Louis XIV.), who was destined to raise her to the pinnacle of her greatness. In the like manner in which Ximenez was retained by Ferdinand and Charles, less from affection

* Raumer, pp. 81, 100, 111, 113, 132, 138. Richard, pp. 102 —104.

than from necessity, so Richelieu was retained by
Louis XIII., who had long become reserved in his
manner towards the cardinal, and even jealous of
his power.* The prudent, but feeble king saw too
well the impossibility of doing without him. The
treatment of the two by their respective sovereigns
was, however, widely different. Louis accorded to
his minister outwardly every mark of respect and
esteem, and visited him repeatedly during his last
illness; so that Richelieu may be said, almost literally, to have died in the arms of his sovereign.
Charles, on the contrary, carefully avoided every
interview with Ximenez, wounded his feelings, and,
even whilst he was lying on his deathbed, signed
the warrant for his dismissal, the reading of which
the cardinal, however, was spared.†

Ximenez and Richelieu both died like good
Christians, provided with the holy sacrament, resigned to the will of God, and forgiving their
enemies. "I have," said Richelieu, shortly before
his death, "never had other enemies than those of
the state and my master." These words may be
taken almost literally. His last prayer — "In
manus tuas, Domine, commendo spiritum meum."
—is similar to that of Ximenez: "In te, Domine,
speravi." Like Ximenez, who, in his last moments,
protested that he had never willingly wronged any
one, but treated all with justice, so Richelieu exclaimed: "I pray God, from the bottom of my
heart, to condemn me, if, during my administration,

---

* One evening the king, accompanied by Richelieu, was going
to another room in the castle. On arriving at the door, Richelieu
made room for the king, but the latter exclaimed, angrily, "Go
on, go on; you know you are master!" Whereupon the cardinal
took a wax candle from one of the pages in attendance, and carried
it before the king, saying, "Sire, I can only precede your majesty
when performing the duties of one of your humblest servants."

† Richard, pp. 156—158, 164—168.]

I have ever had any other object in view than the interest of religion and the state.*

The truth of Ximenez' words was fully recognized and publicly confirmed at his death by the universal grief of the whole nation, even his former political adversaries testifying to his virtues in the most eulogistic terms; only the enemies of Spain inwardly rejoiced at his decease. Not so Richelieu, whose death was sincerely mourned by but a few. The nation in general received the intelligence with loud acclamations of joy; bonfires were lighted, and balls were given.†

Ximenez was universally beloved; Richelieu feared by all. Hence the ingratitude of his contemporaries. Posterity only has awarded him more justice.

Richelieu died on the 4th December, 1642, in his fifty-eighth year, or at the age when Ximenez just started on his important career. Both were at the head of the government for nearly an equal length of time; Ximenez twenty-two, Richelieu eighteen years.‡

The similarity which marks their destinies is also observable in their political principles and sentiments.

Both were eminent in the conduct of affairs by the combination of two qualities rarely united in statesmen: talent and industry, and an activity as indefatigable as their genius was great. "Real statesmen," said Richelieu, very justly, "are not those who, chained to their desks, catch at the smallest flies. Such mass of writing serves only to

* Richard, p. 168. Joly, "Histoire du Ministère du Cardinal Richelieu" (1816, Paris), tom. ii. p. 217. Raumer, p. 139.
† Richard, p. 172.
‡ The cranium of Ximenez was found to be without suture, whence probably arose his frequent headaches; whilst that of Richelieu showed twelve small apertures, which led to the belief that he never suffered from headache. Richard, p. 169.

deaden genius, and to incapacitate the mind for the conception of great thoughts." To these two qualities both cardinals united a third, equally necessary and important: an unshakable firmness in the execution of their commands, which were only issued after mature reflection. Ximenez has given proofs of his firmness in the revolt of the Albaycim, and in many other instances, and shown that his courage was greatest in the time of danger. Richelieu is reported to have once said of himself: " I am timid by nature, and never venture upon an undertaking without previous repeated reflection; but my resolution taken, I act boldly, press onwards to my aim, overthrow every obstacle, mow everything down, and cover the whole with my cardinal's mantle."* In his famous political testament he declares courage and intrepidity to be two of the most essential qualities of a statesman.

Both cardinals exercised a most extraordinary influence on the affairs and history of their countries, with this difference, however, that Ximenez served sovereigns who were themselves masters of the art of governing, and ruled the state with a firm hand, whereas Richelieu, who served a virtuous and prudent, though weak king, could apply himself to the administration of the kingdom more independently than Ximenez.

Richelieu may be said, for eighteen years, to have been absolute ruler of France. He was minister only by name, similar to Charles Martel and the Pepins in the Merovingian era. Ximenez, on the contrary, was under Ferdinand and Isabella really only a minister, and his power, even during the year and a half of his regency, more restricted than that of his French colleague. Backed by the

* Raumer, p. 71.

royal name, Richelieu could act more independently than the regent of Castile, whose actions were paralysed by the intrigues at the court of Brussels. To prove this, it suffices to recall that Ximenez had never, even when regent, the power of appointing officials, and particularly bishops, whilst in France no place of importance, either ecclesiastical or civil, no bishopric or military command, was given away by any but Richelieu.* Besides, France, when Richelieu took the reins of government, was in a much less flourishing condition than Spain at the time of Ximenez' accession to power. Hence the reforms introduced by the former appear much more striking than those of the latter. Richelieu was the only great politician of his time.† The generation of Ximenez had to divide its admiration between several illustrious ministers and cardinals, for instance, in France the great cardinal and minister d' Amboise; in Spain the famous Grand-cardinal Mendoza; not to forget the able Cardinal Wolsey, and the acute Granvella; all men of the first rank, and his rivals on the field of glory.

But this difference belongs more to the times and to circumstances, than to the men. Both applied one and the same fundamental maxim to the internal administration of their countries : aggrandisement of the royal power, by the weakening of the nobles, and the suppression of their independence, to which Richelieu, more than Ximenez, added another—the humiliation of the Parliaments. Both ministers succeeded in raising

* Raumer, pp. 162, 194, 209. It must be owned that Richelieu gave the bishoprics to very efficient men.—Aubery, pp. 599—602.

† Even Olivarez, the prime minister of Spain, at the time of Richelieu, acknowledged this, saying: "The king of France has the ablest minister which Christendom has possessed for the last thousand years." His successor, Mazarin, rivalled him in sagacity, but not in elevation of thought.

the royal power to a height unknown before; both suppressed and punished every disturbance of the peace by the nobles, and shielded the people from their oppression and violence. But Ximenez was more a friend of the people; Richelieu, more a man of the court: Ximenez universally beloved; Richelieu hated by a great part of the nation. It was said of him, that he had done everything for the king, nothing for the people.*

At first sight, a striking contrast is to be found in their external politics. Ximenez strove to raise the Spanish Austrian power; Richelieu, on the contrary, endeavoured to weaken, and, if possible, to break it altogether. Yet this conflict in their actions emanated from a common principle: the wish to raise their country to the first rank amongst the powers of Europe. Both succeeded in this, only their measures for attaining it differed frequently. Both cared for the maintenance of justice, introduced reforms in the finances, lessened the number of the officials, and kept a sharp control over them, abolished unnecessary salaries, watched over the interests of the colonies, promoted those of trade and commerce, strengthened the navy, &c. But whilst Ximenez knew no other justice than that of the ordinary courts, Richelieu frequently appointed, for political offences, special commissions dependent from the court. Abuses as revolting and immoral as the traffic in places, which Ximenez would not have tolerated for one hour, were permitted by Richelieu if he considered them to the interest of the state. Scrupling little in the choice of his means, as long as they tended to further his object, he more than once subordinated his conscience to state reasons,

* Richard, p. 87. Raumer, pp. 60, 61, 63, 70, 71, 141.

and blamed statesmen who were more conscientious and had a greater regard for morals.* It is undeniable, and can be proved by numerous examples, that he·went too far in this, and often pursued dishonourable and antichristian politics, in the interest of France, the effects of which are still felt by Germany.

It was Richelieu· who, in order to humiliate Austria, and break the power of Germany, called the king of Sweden, Gustavus Adolphus, into the empire, and, after the death of the "Goth," continued to add fuel to the religious war ; it was he who excited and assisted the rebellious Puritans against the king of England, the Catalonians in their revolt against the king of Spain; who tried to detach Maximilian of Bavaria from the cause of religion and the country, and constantly sought his own selfish interest in the misfortunes of others. Ximenez knew nothing of such artifices; his honest, upright nature revolted against them.

The rigour used by Ximenez in the christianizing of the Moors, and his activity as grand-inquisitor, have frequently been compared to the measures adopted by Richelieu against the Huguenots. Richelieu, it is true, destroyed their political influence, "their state in the state," but left their religious freedom not only untouched, but protected and defended it. His co-religionists have, for this reason, reproached him with lukewarmness for his own Church. In his capacity of statesman he considered it advisable not to encroach upon the religious liberties of the Huguenots, but as bishop he converted many by peaceful missions.† After they had themselves violated the treaties, Richelieu had as much right to attack their

* Raumer, pp. 63, 64, 66, 72, 88, 130. Richard, pp. 124, 151, 208.

† Richard, p. 36. Aubery, pp. 37—40, 603—606.

liberties as Ximenez had in his proceedings against
the Moors; yet he reasoned differently from the
Spaniard, and did not vindicate for the state the right
of governing consciences. "As statesman I do not
attack the religious opinions of the Huguenots,"
said he, " but their disobedience."*   Nevertheless,
his conduct against them furnishes a parallel with
Ximenez.   Both placed themselves at the head of
an army; Ximenez to conquer Oran, Richelieu to
conduct the siege of Lá Rochelle, with marvellous
firmness and ability.   But whilst Ximenez led his
soldiers, mounted on a mule, and attired in pontifical
robes, Richelieu appeared on a war-horse, clad in
armour, with a sword at his side and pistols in his
belt.†   Like Isabella, he had the morality of his
soldiers at heart, and instituted a mission of the
Jesuits in the army.‡   The taking of La Rochelle
procured him the gratitude of his sovereign; Ximenez
obtained from Ferdinand but little thanks for his
conquest of Oran.§

Ximenez and Richelieu had each a friend, their
adviser and instrument in their private and political
affairs.   We have often spoken of Francis Ruyz in
the preceding pages.   Father Joseph, a Capuchin,
occupied a similar position with Richelieu, only his
influence was greater, as he had a greater aptitude
for politics, and often surpassed his master and
friend in prudence and courage.   Descended from
the illustrious family of the Le Clerc du Tremblai,
son of a president of the parliament of Paris, god-
child of the brother of the king (Henry III.), a man
of talent and erudition, he suddenly, already on the

---

* Raumer, pp. 80, 90.
  † Aubery, pp. 63—74, 81—84.   Richard, pp. 73, 74, 83.
Raumer, p. 94.
  ‡ Aubery, p. 597.   § Richard, p. 78.

high-road to honours, turned Capuchin and a zealous missionary amongst the Huguenots. He soon became provincial of his order, and, having gained the esteem of both the pope and the king, was intrusted by the latter with several important political missions. Through his exertions, Richelieu was called back to the court, from his exile at Avignon, and the two lived henceforth in the most intimate friendship, inhabiting the same palace, and seeming like two souls in one body. After Richelieu, Joseph was the most powerful man of his time in France, so that, in this respect, he far outstripped the friend of Ximenez. Ruyz was, by the intercession of Ximenez, nominated bishop. Joseph repeatedly rejected this dignity, and died, before Richelieu, in the year 1638, when he was about to receive the cardinal's hat.*

Convinced that no state could flourish without the cultivation of the sciences, Ximenez and Richelieu became powerful protectors of the same. Ximenez founded the university of Alcalá, Richelieu the French Academy, and, besides, reopened the Sorbonne. Like Ximenez, he ordered the publication of many excellent works, collected numerous very valuable manuscripts, particularly in the Oriental languages, and took a delight in conversing with learned men. But, unlike Ximenez, he also esteemed and patronized the *belles lettres* and the drama.† Whilst his own writings, theological and historical, secure for him the place above Ximenez, the latter surpassed him by the fame of having called into existence so stupendous and beneficial a work as the " Complutensian . Polyglot." Richelieu seems to have felt this, by the anxiety he showed to take part in the publication of the " Paris Polyglot,"

* See the article " Joseph," in Moreri Dictionnaire.
† Fléchier, liv. v. p. 525. Richard, pp. 15, 51, 131, 187.

then in course of progress. But the editor, Le Jay, jealous to secure the glory of this undertaking entirely for himself, rejected all his overtures.*

The preceding will doubtless have suggested already that, with reference to personal character, the comparison will not turn out to the advantage of Richelieu. The anti-christian politics which he pursued in the temporary interest of France, as well as his severity against his political adversaries, place him, in point of morality, much below Ximenez. But our political parallel has now reached a point in which few statesmen, nay, men in general, can vie with our cardinal—that of his extraordinary personal virtues.

In a comparison with other diplomatists, Richelieu would, even in this respect, carry off the palm over many. He was zealous in the performance of his devotional and pious duties; took the sacrament every Sunday; sang the holy mass himself—at least on festivals; recited the daily prayers, and begged the pope to dispense him from them, and prescribe him shorter ones, when his multifarious duties would no longer permit him to say them; conversed frequently on religious topics; showed always a sincere repentance of his sins; and often closeted a preacher with him, to listen to a discourse specially made for him only.† But with all this, Richelieu never attained the heroic piety of Ximenez, whose whole nature was more deeply pervaded by a real Christian spirit, and filled with a more ardent faith. Compared to Ximenez, he is, in this respect, like a respectable man of the world *vis-à-vis* a man who, by his ascetic exercises, has become almost a saint. As regards the allegations of his enemies, concerning

* Richard, p. 49. On the learning of Richelieu, and his patronage of the sciences, see Aubery, pp. 606—611.

† Aubery, pp. 595—598.

his questionable relations to his niece, the duchess of Aiguillon, they seem to us to be utterly unfounded.

Ximenez and Richelieu were both charitable, and spent, in particular, large sums for the ransoming of Christian prisoners.* The charity of the Spaniard, however, is at once on a more colossal scale, and nobler, by his renouncing and abstaining from all the enjoyments of life.

Both were faithful friends, and careful, indulgent masters. Yet the affection of Richelieu was more worldly. He procured offices and dignities for his favourites, with the view of increasing his friends, and through them his influence. Ximenez, on the contrary, procured his friends very few places; and never, like Richelieu, promoted them to the detriment of, or by doing injustice to others.†

Both showed zeal and attachment for their relations. But whilst the family of Ximenez was never more than well to do, his niece only marrying into a higher family, Richelieu obtained for his the ducal title, considerable property, and high offices, and married all his nieces to members of the first houses.‡

The difference between Ximenez and Richelieu is also shown in their wills.§ Ximenez bequeathed the bulk of his fortune to his beloved university; Richelieu left his to his relatives. The other heirs of Ximenez were the poor, the hospitals, and the monasteries; that of Richelieu, the man of the world, was the king, to whom he bequeathed his palace, afterwards the Palais Royal, his carriages, and his chapel. Ximenez made, in his will, numerous

---

* Aubery, pp. 611—612, 626. Richard, p. 52.
† Aubery, pp. 592—594. Richard, pp. 81, 87, 151, 183, 198.
‡ Richard, p. 88.
§ That of Richelieu is to be found in Aubery, pp. 619—626.

arrangements for the salvation of his soul, Richelieu
left his famous political testament, full of excellent
advice for the administration of the kingdom.

Both have been the object of many pasquils, and
of much blame and calumny from their adversaries.
Ximenez disdained such attacks, and proceeded
against the perpetrators only when compelled to do
so. by others, and then with great leniency. Richelieu never pardoned an injury or offence. The maxim
that the lion should not care for the barking of
little dogs, was recognized by him in theory, and
a painting, conveying this idea, hung up in his
castle of Richelieu; in practice, however, he could
never raise himself to this height, but persecuted
the pasquillants with the utmost rigour, even into
foreign countries.*

We seek also in vain in Richelieu for the straight-
forwardness, the truthfulness and honesty, which
distinguished Ximenez, and at times showed itself
in rather a rough and awkward manner. Richelieu
was always the polished courtier, who liked as much
to address pleasant words and flatteries to others
as he was pleased to hear them himself. After all
this, Ximenez undoubtedly carries the palm, in
reference to personal excellence. Abbé Richard,
in spite of his patriotism, justly acknowledges this
in his work; and Robertson, in his history of Charles,
observes rightly, that in the whole history of the
world Ximenez is the only prime minister who was
revered by his contemporaries as a saint, and to
whom the people he ruled ascribed the power of
working miracles.† The modern Spanish acade-

---

* Raumer, pp, 66, 140. Richard, pp. 15, 186.

† Leonce de Lavergne also draws a kind of comparison between
the two cardinals, and gives the palm to Richelieu. But his
comparison is very prejudiced and one-sided, as indeed is the
entire essay. Revue des Deux Mondes, tom. xxvi. p. 554.

mician Arnab, in adopting these words of the English historian, adds, "Ximenez knew how to unite in his person the virtues of the most pious monk, of the most zealous bishop, and the most accomplished statesman."* "Spain," he continues, "passed, under him, through the most prosperous and happy phase of her history : would that another Ximenez were born to her in the nineteenth century ! "† We heartily join in his wish, adding only, that not Spain alone, but other countries too, may after so many centuries of errors and disastrous experiments, recognize that true religion is the only sound basis for the real happiness of nations.

* Memorias, tom. iv. p. 2.   † Ibid. pp. 13, 23.

APPENDIX.

THE following interesting account of the translation of the remains of Cardinal Ximenez is taken from a pamphlet* on the subject, kindly sent to me from Madrid, by his excellency the Marqués de Morante.

The ceremony took place at Alcalá de Henares, on the 27th of April, 1857, with the greatest pomp, solemnity, and devotion. But before we describe the particulars of an event which does such honour to all those concerned in it, and especially to the queen and her ministers, it will be necessary to mention the different translations which were made of the cardinal's venerable remains.

Ximenez, in his will, expressed his desire to be interred in the chapel belonging to the college of San Ildefonso, at Alcalá. Accordingly, after his death in 1517, his remains were conveyed there from Roa, and interred in the said chapel with great solemnity. Here they remained for the space of eighty years,—viz. from 1517 to 1597. But as the vault was found to be very damp, the remains were taken up in 1597, by order of the king, and

* The following is the Spanish title of the pamphlet: "Relacion de la Solemne Ceremonia celebrada para la Inhumacion de los Restos Mortales del Cardenal, Don Fray Francisco Ximenez de Cisneros, en su sepulcro de la Iglesia Magistral de Alcalá de Henares, el dia 27 de Avril de 1857. Escrita por Don Roman Goicoerrotea." Madrid, 1857.

placed in a reliquary* on the gospel side, next to the high altar in the church of San Ildefonso, where the relics of the saints belonging to the college were usually preserved. In this reliquary the remains were kept for a period of forty-seven years, when, in 1664, they were removed to a niche on the gospel side, near the steps of the altar : the niche had an iron grating before it, which formed a part of the sepulchre of San Diego. There they continued for twenty-four years. But in the year 1668, as the veneration of the faithful towards the remains of the cardinal, whom all considered to be a saint, was daily becoming more intense, it was considered prudent to remove them to the original spot, where the body had first been interred. His translation was accordingly made. There they continued for nine years. But in 1677 the members of the university, fearful lest the bones of their illustrious founder might be injured, if not destroyed, by the dampness of the vault (in spite of every precaution which had been taken), resolved *privately* to remove them, and place them in a niche on the right of the high altar, in the church of San Ildefonso. This translation was effected under the direction of Padre Quintanilla. The bones, and part of the skull, were carefully wrapped in silk and cloth-of-gold. All the particulars of this private translation, together with an accurate account of the state and number of the bones, were inscribed in the archives of the university, signed by the rector, Dr. Canal, Padre Quintanilla, and his brother, Fray P. de Quintanilla. In the niche was also placed another shorter document, containing the principal particulars. The niche was then entirely closed up.

In this niche the remains continued till the year

* The Spanish word is "Alacena," or "Armario," which signifies a recess in the wall, with folding doors.

1778, when they were seen by el Señor Dr. Luque, Don Orozco y Rojas, and Don Juan José Barrios. They took a copy of the acts of the translation made in 1677. But from the year 1778 to 1850, it seems that all traces of the cardinal's remains had been lost: owing, no doubt, to the confusion of the times, and perhaps to the carelessness or indifference of those in authority, the documents had disappeared. But what was still more deplorable, the government had allowed the magnificent college of San Ildefonso to fall into decay, the university of Alcalá having been translated to Madrid. The chapel which contained the remains of Ximenez was daily becoming a complete ruin, the whole of the building having been sold to an individual named Quinto, who, heedless of the associations connected with the college, began to pull down the famous towers, in which were hung the bells cast from the cannon taken at the siege of Oran. This act of barbarism was too much for the inhabitants of Alcalá to endure. With a spirit and enthusiasm deserving of the greatest praise, they repurchased from Quinto their beloved college of San Ildefonso, at a cost of 90,000 reals.*

In the chapel of this college had been erected a magnificent monument to Ximenez, in the year 1520. But in 1845 the government, considering the damp situation in which the monument was placed, and that the chapel was falling into ruins, appeared inclined to remove the whole of the mausoleum to the monastery of St. Jerome (San Gerónimo) in Madrid. Workmen had actually begun to take down the grating which enclosed the monument,

* Amounting, in English money, to about 900 guineas. Quinto purchased the college from the government for 700 guineas! That *any* Spanish government could have allowed such a thing, seems incredible.

2 P

when the inhabitants of Alcalá, anxious to preserve amongst them such an interesting memorial of Ximenez, petitioned the government to allow them to remove the monument to the Iglesia Magistral,* which they promised to do at their own expense. Their request was fortunately granted, but not till the year 1850, when a royal decree was signed by her majesty to remove the said monument. The inhabitants were filled with joy, on beholding their ardent wishes at last realized. A commission was accordingly formed, to collect subscriptions for repairing the monument and placing it in the church. Everything succeeded so admirably, and such a spirit of enthusiasm and generosity prevailed, that the first stone was laid on the twenty-first of October, 1850, in presence of the archbishop of Toledo, his eminence Cardinal Bonel y Orbe, and a numerous assembly of the clergy and civil authorities belonging to Alcalá and the neighbourhood.

But when the tomb came to be examined, the remains of Ximenez could not be found, though the constant tradition in Alcalá was, that they were beneath the spot, or behind the high altar in the church of San Ildefonso. In vain, however, was a diligent search made for them. In the mean time, the restoration of the tomb continued with unabated activity. But of what use would it be without the remains of Ximenez? In this critical juncture, Providence unexpectedly came to the assistance of the searchers. A document was found amongst some old papers in the town, which proved to be a copy of the translation of the remains made in the year 1677. This document indicated the exact spot where they were to be found, in the church of San Ildefonso. The news of this important dis-

* Called also the Church de San Justo y Pastor. It formed a part of the university.

covery filled all the inhabitants with unbounded delight. The authorities hastened to the spot. The cavity was soon discovered, and the chest also, containing the bones of the illustrious cardinal, enclosed in which was a parchment, testifying that the chest contained the remains of Ximenez.* An examination of their authenticity having been made, all doubts were removed from the minds of the most sceptical. Nothing now remained to be done except the translation of the remains to the new mausoleum, which was completed in the beginning of June, 1851.

Through various causes, however, the solemn ceremony did not take place till April 27th, 1857. That day will ever be memorable in Alcalá. The minister of state at that time was Ramon Maria Narvaez, who proposed to the queen, that the translation of the remains of Ximenez should be made at the expense of the crown. Her majesty most willingly complied with the request of her prime minister, and, by a royal decree, ordered a sum of 60,000 reals† to be placed at the disposal of the commission engaged in restoring the tomb. Prefixed to the royal decree was an eloquent tribute to the worth and memory of Ximenez.

On the morning of the 27th of April, Alcalá was a scene of the greatest animation and enthusiasm. Nearly all the ministers of her majesty's government were to be seen in the palace of his excellency el Marqués de Morante, to whom too much praise cannot be given for his hospitality, and the lively

---

* The following is the inscription :—

✠

"Hæc sunt ossa S. N. Em. D. Fundatoris, ne amplius putrescerent, huc translata, postquam juridice ab Episcopis Arcadiæ et Cesaræ, p . . . . . pect : : : : sunt.

"Rre Lesaca Anno 1677."

† Amounting to 600 guineas.

interest he took in everything connected with the ceremony. The evening before they had arrived from Madrid, together with the canons belonging to the metropolitan cathedral of Toledo, and the chaplains of the Mozarabic rite, belonging to the said cathedral. A few days previous, came also the representatives of the chapter of Sigüenza, of the clergy and civil authorities of Torrelaguna, and of other places. An immense number of persons of distinction arrived on different days; consisting of dukes, marquises, rectors of colleges and universities, military men, professors in the universities of Madrid and Salamanca, senators, literary notabilities, &c. ; indeed, all classes and ranks were represented on this solemn occasion.

The procession, having been formed at the palace of the Marqués de Morante, passed through the principal streets of Alcalá, accompanied by a military band to the Iglesia Magistral, where the cardinal's remains were deposited some days before. Troops of soldiers and the civil guard lined the streets, to preserve order. On arriving at the gates of the church, the authorities were received by the civil governor of the province, and conducted to their appointed seats in the choir, while the rest of the procession occupied various places in the body of the church, which was beautifully adorned with tapestry and festoons. Over one of the principal doors of the presbytery hung the glorious standard of Ximenez, which was carried before him at the siege of Oran ; whilst in the choir were seen his breviary, pastoral staff, and the keys of Oran. The whole spectacle was most imposing and exciting; an immense multitude of people filled the naves of the beautiful Gothic church.

After a solemn pontifical mass, which was celebrated by his grace the patriarch of the Indies, a magnificent panegyric was pronounced on Ximenez by one of her majesty's chaplains, Doctor D. Bernardo Rodrigo. The usual prayers for the dead being chanted, the urn containing the remains of the cardinal was placed in a small hearse, and carried by four canons in procession round the church, attended by the clergy and civil authorities. Having arrived at the tomb, the urn, which was enclosed in a coffin of lead, and another one of wood, was deposited in the crypt prepared for it. And so ended a funeral ceremony in honour of Spain's most illustrious prelate, Cardinal Ximenez. Every one, throughout the country, was delighted on hearing that such a tribute was paid to the memory of one whose deeds will never be forgotten in the annals of the Spanish Church.

LAUS DEO SEMPER.

COX AND WYMAN, PRINTERS, GREAT QUEEN STREET, LONDON.

www.ingramcontent.com/pod-product-compliance
Lightning Source LLC
Chambersburg PA
CBHW021931110726
47901CB00003B/791